ON HEROES AND TOMBS

Ernesto Sabáto

ON HEROES AND TOMBS

---

translated by Helen R. Lane

DAVID R. GODINE
PUBLISHER · BOSTON

First published in English in 1981 by
DAVID R. GODINE, PUBLISHER, INC.
306 Dartmouth Street
Boston, Massachusetts 02116

Library of Congress Cataloging in Publication Data

Sábato, Ernesto R.
  On heroes and tombs.
  Translation of: Sobre héroes y tumbas.
  I. Title.
PQ7797.S214s613 1981   863   80-83957
ISBN 0-87923-381-8   AACR2

The author has made certain cuts and changes, which have been incorporated into the English edition and which will be used in any future editions of the book.

 Assistance in the translation of this volume was given by the Center for Inter-American Relations.

Printed in the United States of America

AUTHOR'S NOTE

THERE EXISTS a certain type of fictional narrative whereby the author endeavors to free himself of an obsession that is not clear even to himself. For good or ill, this is the only sort of fiction I am able to write. I have found myself forced to write countless numbers of stories, incomprehensible to me, since my adolescence. Fortunately, I made few efforts to see them into print, and in 1948 I decided to publish just one of them, "El Túnel" [The Tunnel]. In the thirteen years that followed I continued to explore that dark labyrinth that leads to the central secret of our life. I tried at one time or another to express in writing the outcome of my research, until I grew discouraged at the poor results and ended up destroying the majority of my manuscripts. Today a few friends who have read those that survived have urged me to publish them. I wish to express here my gratitude to all of them for that faith and confidence that unfortunately I have never had myself.

I dedicate this novel to the woman who has persistently encouraged me at moments when I lacked faith, which is most of the time. Without her I should never have had the fortitude to finish it. And despite the fact that she doubtless deserves something better, with all its imperfections, this belongs to her.

—ERNESTO SABATO

CONTENTS

ON HEROES AND TOMBS

FOREWORD

THE INITIAL investigations revealed that the old Mirador* that Alejandra used as a bedroom had been locked from the inside by Alejandra herself. Then (although the amount of time that elapsed cannot be precisely determined by logical deduction) she killed her father with four bullets from a .32-caliber pistol. And finally, she poured gasoline around and set the Mirador on fire.

The tragedy, which shocked Buenos Aires because this old Argentine family had been a prominent one, appeared in the beginning to have been the consequence of a sudden attack of insanity. But a new element that alters this earlier reconstruction of events has now entered the picture. A curious "Report on the Blind," which Fernando Vidal finished drafting on the very night of his death, was discovered in the Villa Devoto apartment that he had been living in under an assumed name. Those persons who have examined it agree that it is the manuscript of a paranoiac. Nonetheless it would appear that it lends itself to certain interpretations that throw light on the crime and make the hypothesis of an act of madness less plausible than another more sinister, more obscure explanation. If this line of reasoning is correct, it would explain why Alejandra did not commit suicide with one of the two bullets that remained in the pistol, choosing instead to burn herself alive.

[Excerpt from a police report published June 28, 1955, in *La Razón*, Buenos Aires.]

---

* A small tower or belvedere found on the grounds of old-fashioned country houses. [*Author's note*]

PART ONE

The Dragon and the Princess

ON A SATURDAY in May, 1953, two years before the events in Barracas, a tall, stoop-shouldered youngster was walking along one of the footpaths in the Parque Lezama.

He sat down on a bench, near the statue of Ceres, and remained there, doing nothing, lost in thought. "Like a boat drifting on a vast lake that is apparently calm yet agitated by currents far beneath the surface," Bruno thought when, after the death of Alejandra, Martín recounted to him, in a confused and fragmentary way, some of the episodes connected with that story. And he not only thought this but understood it—indeed he did!—since that seventeen-year-old Martín reminded him of his own forebear, the remote Bruno whom he glimpsed at times across a distance of thirty years, a nebulous territory enriched and devastated by love, disillusionment, and death. He had a melancholy image of him in that old park, with the dying afternoon light lingering on the modest statues, on the pensive bronze lions, on the paths covered with limp, dead leaves. At this hour when little murmurs begin to make themselves heard, when loud noises fade into the distance little by little, just as overloud conversations in the sickroom of a man fatally ill die away; and then the splash of the fountain, the footsteps of a man walking off, the chirping of birds endlessly stirring about trying to settle themselves comfortably in their nests, the distant shout of a child, become audible, bring with them a strange solemnity. A mysterious event takes place at this time: darkness falls. And everything is different: the trees, the benches, the pensioners lighting a little bonfire of dead leaves, a ship's siren at Dársena Sur, the far-off echo of the city. That hour when everything enters upon a more profound, more enigmatic existence. And a more fearful one as well for the solitary beings who at that hour continue to sit, silent and pensive, on the benches of the plazas and parks of Buenos Aires.

Martín picked up a piece of a newspaper someone had thrown away, a piece in the shape of a country: a nonexistent but possible country. Mechanically he read the words referring to Suez, to tradesmen being sent off to prison in Villa Devoto, to what was described as Gheorghiu's imminent arrival. On the other side, half spattered with mud, was a photograph: PERON VISITS THE TEATRO DISCEPOLO. Lower down was a news item reporting that a war veteran had hacked his wife and four other persons to death with an ax.

He threw the paper down: "Almost nothing ever happens," Bruno was to say to him years later, "even when the plague ravages an entire region of India." Once again he saw his mother's painted face saying: "You exist because I was careless." Courage, yes, courage—that was what she had lacked. Otherwise he would have ended up in the sewer. *Sewer-mother*.

"When all of a sudden," Martín said, "I had the sensation that somebody was standing behind me looking at me."

For a few seconds he sat there absolutely rigid: a tense, expectant rigidity, as when, in the darkness of one's bedroom, one thinks one hears a suspicious creak. For he had felt this sensation on the nape of his neck many times before, but usually it was simply annoying or disagreeable; since (he explained) he had always considered himself ugly and ridiculous-looking; and the mere idea that someone might be studying him or simply observing him from behind his back bothered him; this was the reason why he always sat in the seat farthest to the rear in streetcars and buses, or entered a movie house only when the house lights had already been lowered. Whereas at that moment what he felt was something different. Something—he hesitated as though searching for the right word—something *disquieting*, something similar to that suspicious creak we hear, or think we hear, in the dead of night.

He made an effort to keep his eyes trained on the statue, but in reality he could no longer see it: his eyes were turned inward, as when we think of past things and try to reconstruct dim memories that require total concentration.

"Someone is trying to communicate with me," he said he thought in agitation.

The sensation of feeling himself observed exacerbated, as always, his awareness of the things he was ashamed of: he saw himself as ugly, awkwardly proportioned, dull-witted. Even his seventeen years seemed grotesque to him.

"But what if all that isn't true?" the girl who was at that moment behind his back was to say to him two years later; an enormous span of time—Bruno thought—because it was not measured in months or even in years, but rather, as is peculiar to this class of beings, in spiritual catastrophes and days of utter loneliness and inexpressible sadness; days that lengthen and become distorted, like shadowy phantoms on the walls of time. "If it's in no way true," and she scrutinized him the way a painter observes his model, drawing nervously on her eternal cigarette.

"Wait," she said.

"You're something besides just a nice kid," she said.

"You're an interesting young man who has real depth, and besides that you're a physical type that's extremely rare."

"Yes, of course," Martín agreed, smiling bitterly, as he thought "you see, I'm right," because all that is the sort of thing people say when you're not a nice kid, and all the rest really doesn't matter.

"But wait, I tell you," she answered in an irritated tone of voice. "You're tall and have a very narrow build, like an El Greco figure."

Martín grunted.

"Be quiet, I tell you," she went on indignantly, like a learned scholar who is interrupted or distracted by trivialities at the very moment that he is just about to come up with the earnestly sought-for definitive formula. And again drawing greedily on her cigarette, as was her habit when she was concentrating, she added with a furious frown:

"But, you know: it's as though you'd suddenly changed your plan to be a Spanish ascetic, because your lips have gotten sensual. And what's more, there are those melting, liquid eyes of yours. Be quiet, I know that everything I'm saying isn't to your liking, but let me finish. I think women must find you attractive, despite what you imagine. Then too there's your expression. A mixture of purity, melancholy, and repressed sensuality. But besides that ... wait a minute ... An anxiety in your eyes, below that forehead of yours that looks like a balcony jutting out. But I'm not certain that all that is what pleases me about you. I think it's something else.... The fact that your spirit dominates your flesh, as though you were permanently standing at attention. Anyway, *pleases* may not be the right word; perhaps you surprise me, or astonish me, or irritate me, I don't know.... Your spirit ruling over your body like an austere dictator.

"As though Pius XII were obliged to keep order in a brothel. Come on, don't get angry—I know you're an angelical being. Besides, as I've already said, I don't know whether that's what pleases me about you or whether it's what I hate most."

He tried his best to keep his eyes fixed on the statue. He said that at that moment he felt fear and fascination—fear of turning around and a fascinating desire to do just that. He remembered that once, standing at the very edge of the Devil's Gorge in Humahuaca, contemplating the black abyss at his feet, an irresistible force had suddenly impelled him to leap to the other side. And at that moment something similar was happening to him: it was as though he felt impelled to leap across a dark abyss "to the other side of his existence." And then that unconscious yet irresistible force made him turn his head.

After having caught no more than a glimpse of her, he immediately averted his eyes, his gaze coming to rest on the statue again. He was terrified by human beings: they seemed to him not only unpredictable, but above all perverse and filthy. Statues on the other hand brought him a quiet happiness; they belonged to a beautiful, clean, ordered world.

But it was impossible for him to see the statue: his eyes continued to retain the fleeting image of the unknown girl, the blue patch of her skirt, the black of her long straight hair, the paleness of her face, riveted on him. These were simply patches shaded in, as in a painter's quick sketch, without a single detail that might indicate a specific age or a definite type. But he *knew*—he emphasized the word—that something extremely important had just happened in his life: not so much because of what he had seen, but because of the powerful message he had silently received.

"You've told me so many times, Bruno. That things don't always happen, that things almost never happen. Someone swims across the Dardanelles, a man assumes the presidency in Austria, the plague ravages an entire region in India, and none of all that has any importance to a person. You yourself have told me that that's horrible, but that's the way it is. On the other hand, at that moment I had the distinct feeling that something had just happened. Something that would change my life."

He could not say how long a time elapsed, but he remembered that after an interval that seemed extremely long to him he was aware that the girl was rising to her feet and going off. Then as she walked away he took a good look at her: she was tall, she was carrying a book in her left hand, and she was making her way along with a certain nervous energy. Without even being aware of what he was doing, Martín got up and began to walk in the same direction. But almost immediately, on realizing what was happening, and afraid that she might turn her head and see him behind her, following her, he halted. As he watched, he saw her walking uptown along the Calle Brasil toward Balcarce.

She soon disappeared from sight.

He slowly made his way back to his bench and sat down.

"But I was no longer the same person as before," he said to Bruno. "And I never would be again."

∾ 2 ∾

HE WAS EXCITED for days afterward. Because he *knew* he would see her again; he was certain she would return to the same spot.

During all that time he did nothing but think of the unknown girl, and each afternoon he went back and sat on that same bench, with the same mixed feelings of fear and hope.

Then one day, thinking that the whole thing had been utterly absurd, he decided to go to La Boca instead of hurrying yet again, like an idiot, to that bench in the Parque Lezama. And he had already gone as far as the Calle Almirante Brown when suddenly he began walking back toward the usual place; slowly at first, and as though hesitating out of timidity; and then faster and faster, finally breaking into a run, as though he were going to be late for a meeting at a time and place already agreed on.

Yes, she was there. He could see her in the distance walking toward him.

He halted, his heart pounding.

The girl walked toward him and when she reached his side she said to him:

"I've been waiting for you."

Martín felt weak in the knees all of a sudden.

"For me?" he asked, his face reddening.

He didn't dare look at her, but he was nonetheless aware that she was wearing a high-necked black sweater and a skirt that was also black, or perhaps very dark blue (he couldn't be certain which, and in fact it was not at all important). It seemed to him that her eyes were black.

"Black eyes?" Bruno commented.

No, of course not: that had been his first impression. But when he saw her for the second time he was surprised to note that her eyes were dark green. Perhaps that first impression had been due to the dim light, or to the timidity that had prevented him from looking directly at her, or probably to both things at once. He was also able to observe, on meeting her this second time, that the long straight hair that he had thought was coal black in fact had reddish glints in it. Later on he filled in her portrait little by little: full lips and a large mouth, too large perhaps, with lines running downward from the corners, suggesting bitterness and disdain.

"Imagine explaining to *me* what Alejandra looks like, what her face is like, how the lines around her mouth are!" Bruno said to himself. And the thought came to him that it was precisely those disdainful lines and a certain dark gleam in her eyes that particularly distinguished Alejandra's face from that of Georgina, whom he really loved. Because he now realized that it had been she whom he had loved, for when he had thought he was falling in love with Alejandra it was her mother that he had been seeking in her, like those medieval monks who endeavored to decipher the original text beneath the corrections and restorations and substitutions of one word for another. And this folly had been the cause of sad misunderstandings with Alejandra, since at times he had experienced the same sensation that one might feel on returning to one's childhood home after many years' absence, trying to open a door in the night, and finding oneself confronted by a wall. Alejandra's face was almost the exact replica of Georgina's of course: the same black hair with reddish glints framing it, the same gray-green eyes, the same large mouth, the same Mongolian cheekbones, the same pale matte skin. But that "almost" was unbearable, so subtle and so nearly imperceptible that it made the illusion all the more profound and all the more painful. For it is true that bones and flesh are not enough to constitute a face, he thought, and that is why it is infinitely less physical than the body: it is characterized by the look in the eyes, the expression of the mouth, the wrinkles, by all that conjunction of subtle attributes whereby the soul reveals itself by way of the flesh. This is the reason why, when somebody dies, his body is at that very instant suddenly transformed into something different, so different that we say "he doesn't seem like the same person," despite his having the same bones and the same envelope of flesh as a second before, a second before that mysterious moment when the soul abandons the body, which thereupon lies there as dead as a house when the beings who inhabit it, who above all suffered and loved each other in it, leave it forever. For it is not the walls, nor the roof, nor the floor that give a house its unique character, but rather those beings who bring it alive with their conversations, their laughter, their loves and hates; beings who impregnate the house with something immaterial yet profound, with something as far removed from the material as is the smile on a face, even though this something is expressed through the intermediary of physical objects such as carpets, books, or colors. For although the pictures we see on the walls, the colors in which the doors and windowframes have been painted, the figures in the carpets, the flowers in the rooms, the records and books are material objects (as lips and eyebrows are corporeal), they are nonetheless manifestations of the soul, since the soul is unable to manifest itself to our material eyes save by way of matter; and this is part of the soul's fragility but at the same time one of its curious subtleties.

"What's that you say?" Bruno asked.

"I came to see you," Martín said, repeating what Alejandra had said.

She sat down on the grass. And Martín must have had a look of utter astonishment on his face because she added:

"Don't you believe in telepathy? It would surprise me if you didn't— you look to be exactly the type that does. When I saw you on the bench those other days, I was certain you'd eventually turn around. And wasn't that what happened? Well, I was also sure you'd remember me this time."

Martín said nothing. How many times scenes of this sort were to repeat themselves later: her reading his thoughts and him listening to her in silence! He had a distinct feeling that he knew her, that feeling of having seen someone in a previous life that we sometimes experience, a sensation that resembles reality as dream events resemble those of waking life. And much time was to go by before he would understand why Alejandra seemed in some vague way to be someone he already knew, *and then Bruno smiled to himself again.*

Martín looked at her in a daze: her black hair against her pale, matte skin, her tall angular body; there was something about her that was reminiscent of models who appear in fashion magazines, but at the same time she had about her a harshness, a hint of hidden depths not found in such women. Only rarely, indeed almost never, was he to see signs of a gentle side of her, of a sweetness considered to be characteristic of women and above all of mothers. Her smile was cruel and sarcastic, her laughter violent, like her movements and her temperament in general: "It was a great effort for me to learn to laugh," she said to him one day, "but I never laugh inside."

"Nonetheless," Martín added, looking at Bruno with that sensual pleasure that lovers take in obliging others to recognize the attributes of the creature they love, "it's quite true, isn't it, that men—and even women—turn around to stare at her?"

And as Bruno nodded, smiling inwardly at this naive expression of pride, he reflected that indeed this was quite true, that everywhere and always Alejandra attracted men's attention, and women's too. For different reasons, however, because Alejandra could not bear women, she detested them, she maintained that they were a contemptible lot and insisted that she could be friends only with certain men; and women in turn detested her with the same intensity, though for reasons that were precisely the opposite of hers, a phenomenon that aroused in Alejandra little more than the most scornful indifference. Although surely they detested her without ceasing to admire in secret that face that Martín called *exotic* though, ironically, it was really quite typically Argentine, for this type of face is common in South American countries when the skin color and features of a white are conjoined with the high cheekbones and slanting eyes of the Indian. And those deep, troubled eyes, that large disdainful mouth, that mixture of feelings and contradictory passions that one sensed in Alejandra's features (a mixture of anxiety and ennui, of violence and a sort of remoteness, of almost fierce sensuality and a kind of vague, profound loathing of her most intimate self) all conspired to give her a face impossible to forget.

Martín also said that even if nothing had ever happened between the two of them, even if he had been with her or talked with her only once, apropos of some triviality or other, he still would have been unable to forget her face all the rest of his life. And Bruno was of the opinion that this was quite true, for it was more than just a pretty face. Or better put, one could not be certain that she was pretty. It was something else about her. One had only to walk along the street with her for it to be evident that she was vastly attractive to men. She had a certain air about her, at once distracted and intense, as though she were thinking of something that was making her anxious or gazing deep within herself, and he was certain that anyone who chanced to meet her must surely have asked himself: who is this woman, what is she searching for, what is she thinking?

That first meeting was decisive for Martín. Until that moment women to him were either the pure and heroic virgins of legend, or superficial, frivolous beings, malicious gossip-mongers, selfish hypocrites, grasping deceivers. ("Like his own mother," Bruno thought that Martín thought.) And then suddenly he found himself with a woman who fitted into neither of these two molds, molds that until that meeting he had believed were the only ones. For a long time he was deeply disturbed by this novelty, this unexpected type of woman who on the one hand seemed to possess some of the virtues of that heroic model that had so excited him in the books he read as an adolescent and on the other hand gave signs of that sensuality he believed to be characteristic of the sort of female he detested. And even after Alejandra was dead, even after having had such an intense relationship with her, he could not contrive to see into that great enigma with any degree of clarity; and he used to ask himself what he would have done at that second meeting had he been able to guess what she was like, what later events revealed her to be. Would he have fled?

Bruno looked at him in silence: "Yes, what would you have done?"

Martín stared intently at him in turn and then after a few seconds he said:

"I suffered so much on account of her that many times I was on the verge of suicide. Yet even if I had known beforehand everything that was to happen to me later, I would still have hastened to her side."

"Naturally," Bruno thought. Moreover, what other man, whether a mere youngster or a mature adult, foolish or wise, would not have done the same thing?

"She fascinated me like a dark abyss," Martín added, "and if I was in despair it was precisely because I loved her and needed her. How can something to which we are indifferent plunge us into despair?"

He remained lost in thought for a long time and then returned to his obsession: stubbornly remembering (trying to remember) the moments spent with her, as lovers reread the old love letter that they keep in their pocket, when the creature who penned it has long since departed forever; and like such a letter, memories gradually aged and fell apart, entire sentences got lost in the folds of his soul, the ink grew fainter and fainter, and with it the beautiful, bewitching words that had created the magic spell. And then it was necessary to strain his memory as one strains one's eyes and brings them closer to the folded and refolded paper that has turned yellow. Yes, yes, she had asked him where he lived, as she plucked a little weed and began to nibble on the stem (a fact he remembered clearly). And then she had asked him who he lived with. With his father, he answered. And after a moment's hesitation, he had added that he also lived with his mother. "And what does your father do?" Alejandra had asked him then, a question he did not answer immediately, and then finally he replied that he was a painter. But on uttering the word *painter* his voice quavered just a bit, as though it were fragile, and he feared that his tone had attracted her attention, as though he were cautiously making his way across a glass roof. And Alejandra had doubtless noted something strange about that word, for she leaned toward him and looked at him closely.

"You're blushing," she remarked.

"Who, me?" Martín said.

And as always happens in such circumstances, his face grew redder still.

"What's the matter?" she insisted, the little stem of the weed hanging from her lips.

"Nothing. Why do you ask?"

There was a moment's silence, and then Alejandra lay down on her back on the grass again, nibbling at the little stem once more. And as Martín watched a battle between cruisers made of cotton in the sky overhead, she reflected that there was no reason for him to feel ashamed of his father's failure.

A ship's siren blew down at Dársena, and Martín thought "Coral Sea," "Marquesas." But he said:

"Alejandra's an odd name."

"And what about your mother?" she asked.

Martín sat down and began to pull up little tufts of grass. He found a little pebble and seemed to be studying it, like a geologist.

"Didn't you hear me?"

"Yes."

"I asked about your mother."

"My mother is a sewer," Martín answered in a low voice.

Alejandra sat halfway up, leaning on one elbow and looking at him closely. Martín sat there in silence, still examining the little pebble, his jaws tightly clenched, thinking *sewer, sewermother*. And then he added:

"I've always been a bother to her. Ever since I was born."

He felt as though fetid poison gases had been injected into his soul at thousands of pounds of pressure. Swelling more dangerously each year, it could no longer be contained inside his body and threatened at any moment to pour out a flood of filth from between the cracks.

"She keeps screaming 'Why was I so careless!' "

As though all his mother's garbage had been continually accumulating in his soul, under pressure, he thought, as Alejandra lay there leaning on one elbow and looking at him. And words like *fetus, bath, creams, womb, abortion* floated in his mind, like sticky, stinking refuse on stagnant, polluted waters. And then, as though talking to himself, he added that for a long time he had believed that his mother hadn't nursed him for lack of milk, until one day she screamed at him that she hadn't done so in order not to ruin the shape of her breasts and explained to him that she had done everything possible to abort herself, short of getting her womb scraped, and that she hadn't done because she hated feeling pain as much as she adored eating caramels and chocolates, reading radio magazines, and listening to nice hummable tunes. Though she liked classical music and Viennese waltzes— and Prince Kalender* too, she said, who unfortunately wasn't around any more. So Martín could imagine how happily she had greeted his birth, after having fought against having him for months, jumping

---

* One of the many popular radio musicians who played the sort of syrupy versions of Strauss waltzes and Chopin pieces calculated to appeal to the ear of sentimental female listeners. [*Author's note*]

rope like a boxer and punching herself in the belly, the reason why (his mother screamed at him in explanation) he'd turned out to be more or less defective from birth. Only a miracle had kept him from ending up in the sewer, she added.

He fell silent, examined the little pebble once more, and then flung it far away.

"That's doubtless the reason why I always associate her with the word *sewer* when I think of her."

He laughed that laugh of his again.

Alejandra looked at him, amazed that he still had the courage to laugh. But on seeing his tears she doubtless understood that what she had been hearing was not a laugh but rather (as Bruno maintained) that extraordinary sound that in certain human beings is produced on very rare occasions and that, because of the uncertainties of language perhaps, we persist in classifying as laughter or as weeping; for it is the result of a monstrous combination of facts that are sufficiently painful to produce weeping (and even disconsolate weeping) and of events grotesque enough to make the person want to transform those tears into laughter. There thus results a sort of terrible hybrid manifestation, perhaps the most terrible one a human being is capable of, and perhaps the one most difficult to offer any consolation for, in view of the complex mixture of feelings that provokes it. So that as a consequence we often experience in the face of it the same contradictory feeling as when we are confronted with certain hunchbacks or cripples. Martín's sufferings had kept piling up one by one on his child's back like a growing, disproportionate, grotesque burden, so that he constantly felt that he must move carefully and cautiously, proceeding with every step like an acrobat obliged to traverse an abyss on a tightrope while carrying on his back a bulky, stinking burden, tremendous loads of garbage and excrement, along with a pack of howling monkeys, and little jouncing, jeering tumblers, who as he concentrated all his attention on traversing the abyss, the black abyss of his existence, without falling, screamed hurtful things at him, mocked him, and set up an infernal clamor of insults and abuse up there on top of the load of garbage and excrement. A spectacle that (in his opinion) ought to awaken in those witnessing it a mixture of pain and enormous, monstrous hilarity, seeing how tragicomic it was; the reason he did not consider himself to be possessed of the right to abandon himself to pure and simple weeping, even in the face of a being such as Alejandra, a being he seemed to have been waiting a century for; yet on the other hand he thought he had the right, the almost professional right of a clown who has had the greatest possible misfortune overtake him, to convert that weeping into a wry grin. Nonetheless, as he had gone on confessing those few key words to Alejandra, he felt a sort of liberation and for an instant he thought that his grinning grimace might finally turn into a great, convulsive, tender fit of weeping as he fell into her arms, having managed to cross the abyss at last. And that is what he would have done, that is what he would have liked to do, for heaven's sake, but he did not do so: all he did was bow his head very slightly and turn away to hide his tears.

∾ 3 ∾

BUT YEARS LATER when Martín spoke with Bruno of that meeting, scarcely anything remained of it save disjointed phrases, the memory of an expression, of a caress, the melancholy siren of that unknown ship: like fragments of columns. And if any one sentence lingered in his memory, perhaps because of the surprise it had aroused in him, it was one she had uttered at that time, looking at him intently:

"You and I have something in common, something very important."

Words that Martín heard with amazement, for what could he have in common with this prodigious creature?

Alejandra told him, finally, that she had to leave, but that some other time she would tell him many things, things—and this seemed even stranger to Martín—that she *needed* to tell him.

As they parted, she looked at him one more time, as though she were a doctor and he a patient, and added a few words that Martín was to remember forever after:

"Even though I think I shouldn't ever see you again. But I'll see you because I need you."

The mere idea, the mere possibility that this girl might never see him again plunged him into despair. What did the reasons that Alejandra might have for not wanting to see him matter? What *he* wanted with a passion was to see her.

"Always, always," he said fervently.

She smiled and answered:

"Yes, it's because that's the way you are that I need to see you."

And Bruno thought that it would take Martín many years more to arrive at the probable meaning of those enigmatic words. And he also thought that if Martín had been older and more experienced at the time, words such as that, uttered by a girl of eighteen, would have left him dumbfounded. But they would also very soon have seemed natural to him, because she had been born mature, or had matured in her early childhood, at least in a certain sense; even though in other ways she gave the impression that she would never grow up: as though a little girl who still plays with dolls were at the same time capable of giving signs of the frightful wisdom of an old man; as though terrible events had precipitated her toward maturity and then toward death without her having had time to abandon the traits of childhood and adolescence once and for all.

On going their separate ways, after he had walked on a few steps he suddenly remembered or became aware that they had made no plans for meeting again. And turning around, he ran to Alejandra to tell her so.

"Don't worry," she answered. "I'll always know how to find you."

Without thinking those incredible words through and without daring to press the point, Martín turned away and walked off once more.

∽ 4 ∽

FOLLOWING that meeting, he kept hoping day after day to see her again in the park. Then week after week. And finally, in despair now, month after month. What could have happened to her? Why didn't she come? Could she be ill? He didn't even know her name. The earth seemed to have swallowed her up. He reproached himself a thousand times for not even having asked her what her name was. He knew nothing about her. Such stupidity on his part was incomprehensible. He even reach the point of suspecting that the whole thing had been a hallucination or a dream. Hadn't he fallen asleep on that bench in the Parque Lezama more than once? His dream might have been so vivid that it would later seem to be a real, lived experience. Then he dismissed this idea because he remembered that there had been two meetings. But then he reflected that this didn't argue against the whole thing being a dream, since both meetings might have been episodes in a single dream. He had no material object belonging to her that would dispel his doubts, but in the end he convinced himself that all of it had indeed happened and that what was happening now was that he was merely being the idiot that he had always thought of himself as being.

In the beginning he was miserable, thinking of her night and day. He tried to draw her face, but it came out as no more than a hazy impression, since during the two meetings he had not dared look at her closely save at a few rare moments; hence his sketches were vague and lifeless, resembling many of his previous sketches in which he had drawn the ideal, legendary virgins who peopled his imaginary love-life. But though his drawings were vapid and ill-defined, his memory of the meeting was extremely vivid and he had the impression of having been with someone very strong, with very pronounced traits of character, someone as unhappy and as lonely as he himself was. Nevertheless the face was only a tenuous blur. And in the end the whole thing was more or less like a spiritualist séance, in which a dim, ghostly materialization suddenly gives clear, sharp taps on the table.

And when his hope was nearly exhausted, he remembered the two or three key phrases of their second meeting. "I think I shouldn't ever see you again. But I'll see you because I need you." And that other one: "Don't worry. I'll always know how to find you."

Phrases—Bruno thought—that Martín interpreted in the most favorable light possible, as a promise of certain happiness, without noticing, at the time at least, how self-centered they also were.

And it was true of course—Martín said he then thought—that she was a strange girl, and why should a creature of that sort see him a day or so later or the following week? Wasn't it quite possible that weeks and even months might go by without her feeling the need to meet him? These reflections raised his spirits again. But later, in moments of depression, he would say to himself: "I'll never see her again; she's dead; perhaps she's killed herself; she seemed desperate and anxious." He remembered his own thoughts of suicide then. Why shouldn't Alejandra not have experienced something similar? Hadn't she in fact said that they resembled each other, that there was something profound that they had in common and that thus made them alike? Couldn't an obsession with suicide be what she had been hinting at

when she spoke of this resemblance between them? But then he reflected that even if she had wanted to kill herself she would have come
looking for him before going through with it; not to have done so
would have been a sort of trick on her part that seemed inconceivable
to him.

How many desolate days he spent there on that park bench! The
entire autumn went by and winter came. Winter ended, spring began
(it appeared for a moment here and there, fleeting and frigid, like a
person peeking out to see how things are going, and then, little by
little, showing itself more forthrightly and for longer and longer
periods of time) and slowly the sap in the trees began to run more
warmly and energetically and leaves suddenly began to appear; and
finally in a few weeks the last tag ends of winter retreated from the
Parque Lezama toward other remote corners of the world.

The first hot spells of December came then. The jacaranda trees
turned violet and the tipa trees were covered with orange blossoms.
And then these flowers began to dry up and fall off, the leaves began
to turn gold and blow away in the first autumn winds. And then—
Martín said—he definitely lost all hope of ever seeing her again.

∽ 5 ∽

THE "HOPE" of seeing her again (Bruno reflected with melancholy
irony). And he also said to himself: aren't all men's hopes as grotesque as this one perhaps? For given the ways of the world, we place
our hopes in events which bring us nothing but frustration and bitterness once they materialize—the reason why pessimists are recruited
among former optimists, since in order to have a black picture of the
world it is necessary to have previously believed in that world and its
possibilities. And it is an even more curious and paradoxical fact that
pessimists, once they have been disillusioned, are not constantly and systematically filled with despair, but rather seem prepared, in a manner of
speaking, to renew their hope at each and every instant, although by
virtue of a sort of metaphysical modesty they conceal this fact beneath
their black envelope of men suffering from a universal bitterness—as
though pessimism, in order to keep itself strong and ever-vigorous,

needed from time to time the impetus provided by a new cruel disillusionment.

And hadn't Martín himself (Bruno thought, looking at him there in front of him), a budding pessimist, as is only fitting for every very pure soul prepared to hope for Great Things from men in particular and from Humanity in general, hadn't Martín himself already tried to commit suicide because of that sort of sewer his mother was? Didn't this in itself reveal that he had hoped for something different, something incontrovertibly marvelous from that woman? But (and this was even more surprising) after this disaster hadn't he again come to have faith in women on meeting Alejandra?

And now here he was, a little lost soul, one of many in this city of lost souls. For Buenos Aires was a city positively swarming with them, as was true of every gigantic, frightful latter-day Babylon.

What happens (he thought) is that one doesn't notice them at first glance, either because a goodly number of them don't appear to be lost souls, or because in many cases they go out of their way not to appear so. Then too, great numbers of beings who are merely pretending to be so further compound the problem, with the result that one ends up believing that there are no true lost souls.

Because if a man is missing both legs or both arms, we all know of course, or think we know, that such a man is helpless. And at that very instant such a man begins to be less so, because we have noticed him and pity him, we buy useless combs from him or colored photographs of Carlitos Gardel.* Whereupon this mutilated man missing two legs or two arms ceases to be, either partially or totally, the sort of totally lost soul that we are thinking of, to the point that we come to experience a vague feeling of resentment, perhaps on account of the infinite number of absolutely lost souls who at that very instant (because they do not have the nerve or the sense of security or the aggressiveness of the peddlers of combs and colored photos) are suffering in silence and with supreme dignity their lot as authentic wretched creatures.

Those silent and solitary men, for instance, who ask nothing of anyone and speak with no one, sitting brooding on the benches of the

---

* The great Argentine composer and singer of tangos. [*Translator's note*]

great plazas and parks of the city: some of them old men (the most obviously helpless ones, to the point that they ought to prey on our minds less, for the same reason as the peddlers of combs), those old men with pensioners' canes who watch the world pass by as though it were a memory, those old men who meditate and in their own way perhaps pose once again the great problems that powerful thinkers have posed regarding the overall meaning of existence, the whys and wherefores of everything: weddings, children, warships, political battles, money, kings, and horse or automobile races; those old men who stare into space or appear to watch the pigeons eating little grains of oats or corn, or the superactive sparrows, or the different types of birds in general that fly down onto the plaza or live in the trees of the great parks. By virtue of that notable attribute of independence and superimposition possessed by the universe, as a banker makes ready to bring off the most formidable operation involving strong currencies that has ever been carried out successfully in the Rio de la Plata (incidentally scuttling Consortium X or fearsome Corporation Y), a bird, a hundred paces away from the Powerful Office, hops across the grass of the Parque Colón, searching here for some little bit of straw for its nest, some stray grain of wheat or rye, some little worm of nutritional interest to it or to its young; while in another even more insignificant stratum, and one in a way even farther removed from everything (not from the Great Banker but from the slender cane of the pensioner), tinier, more anonymous, more secret beings live an independent, and on occasion an extremely active, existence: worms, ants (not only the big black ones, but also the little red ones and others even smaller that are practically invisible) and enormous numbers of other more insignificant tiny creatures, of different colors and very different habits. All these beings live in different worlds that are foreign to each other, except when Great Catastrophes occur, when Men, armed with Fumigators and Shovels, undertake the Fight against the Ants (an absolutely useless fight, let it be said in passing, since it always ends with the triumph of the ants), or when Bankers unleash their Petroleum Wars; so that the infinite number of tiny creatures that until that moment lived on the vast greenswards or in the peaceful subworlds of the parks are wiped out by bombs and gases; while others that are more fortunate, those belonging to those species of worms that are invariably victorious, make hay while the sun shines and prosper with astounding rapidity, as meanwhile, up above, the Purveyors and Manufacturers of Armaments thrive.

But outside of such times of interchange and confusion, it seems a miracle that so many species of beings can be born, develop, and die in the same regions of the universe without being acquainted with each other, without either hating or esteeming each other; like those multiple telephone messages which, we are told, can be transmitted by a single cable without ever getting mixed up with each other or interfering with each other, thanks to ingenious mechanisms.

So (Bruno thought) we have, firstly, the men sitting pensively in the plazas and parks. Some of them look at the ground and take advantage of the myriad anonymous activities of the small creatures already mentioned to distract themselves for entire minutes and even hours: examining the ants, considering their various species, calculating what loads they are capable of transporting, noting how two or three of them collaborate on work that is unusually difficult, and so on. At times, using a little bit of straw or a dry branch of the sort that can readily be found on the ground in parks, these men amuse themselves by turning the ants aside from their frantic trajectories, getting one or another of the most confused ones to climb up the straw and then run to the tip of it, where, after cautious little acrobatic tricks, the creature turns back and runs to the other end, continuing these useless goings and comings until the solitary man tires of the game and out of pity, or more generally out of boredom, leaves the little straw on the ground, whereupon the ant hurries off in search of its comrades, holds a brief and agitated conversation with the first one it meets so as to explain its delay or so as to inform itself as to the General Progress of the Work in its absence, and then immediately resumes its task, joining once again the long, industrious Indian file. Meanwhile the solitary, pensive man returns to his general and somewhat erratic meditation, which does not fix his attention overmuch on any one thing: looking now at a tree, now at a child playing round about and remembering, thanks to this child, long-gone and now incredible days in the Black Forest or a narrow street in Pontevedra that descends toward the south, as his eyes grow a bit more cloudy, thus accentuating that tearful gleam that the eyes of oldsters have; we will never know if it is due to purely physiological causes or if in some way it is the consequence of memory, nostalgia, a feeling of frustration, or the idea of death, or of that vague but irresistible melancholy that the words THE END always arouse in us mortals at the conclusion of a story that has touched us by its mystery and sadness. Which is the same as saying the story of any man, for what human being exists whose story in the final analysis is neither sad nor mysterious?

But the men sitting pensively on the benches are not always old men or pensioners.

Sometimes they are relatively young men, individuals thirty or forty years old. And—a curious thing, worth pondering (Bruno thought)—the younger they are the more pathetic and helpless they seem. For what can be more frightful than the sight of a youngster sitting brooding on a bench in a public square, overwhelmed by his thoughts, silent and estranged from the world round about him? Sometimes the man or the youngster is a sailor; at other times he is perhaps an emigré who would like to return to his country and is unable to; many times they are beings who have been abandoned by the woman they love; others, beings who are out of step with life, or who have left home forever, or are brooding about their loneliness and their future. Or it may be a youngster like Martín himself, who is beginning to realize, to his horror, that the absolute does not exist.

Or he may also be a man who has lost his son and on returning from the cemetery finds himself alone and feels that his existence lacks all meaning now, reflecting that meanwhile there are men round about him who are laughing or are happy (even though they are so only momentarily), children who are playing in the park, right there (he can see them), while his own son now lies beneath the ground in a little coffin befitting the smallness of his body, which perhaps has finally ceased waging a desperate battle against a horrible, disproportionately powerful enemy. And the man sitting there pensively again ponders, or ponders for the first time, the overall meaning of the world, for he cannot understand why his child has had to die in such a way, why he has had to pay for some remote sin of others with such immense suffering, why his little heart has been overcome by asphyxia or paralysis, as he struggled helplessly, not knowing why, against the black shadows beginning to descend upon him.

And this man is indeed a true lost soul. And, curiously, he may not be poor, he may possibly even be rich, and he may even be the Great Banker who was planning the formidable Operation involving strong currencies, of which disdainful and ironic mention was made earlier. Disdain and irony that (as he now found it easy to understand) turned out, as always, to be excessive, and in the last analysis unjust. For when all is said and done, no man deserves disdain and irony, since sooner or later, with strong currencies or without, misfortunes come his way: the deaths of his children or his brothers and sisters, his own old age, and his own solitude in the face of death. And in the end he turns out to be more helpless than anybody else; for the very same reason that the man at arms who is surprised without his coat of mail is more defenseless than the humble man of peace who, because he has never had a coat of mail, never feels its lack.

ન‌ 6 ન‌

I T WAS CERTAIN fact that since the age of eleven he had never entered any of the rooms in the house, much less that little one that was something like his mother's sanctuary: the place where, on climbing out of her bath, she spent her time listening to the soap operas on the radio and completing her toilette before going out. But what about his father? Martín had lost track of his habits in recent years and knew only that he spent his days shut up in his studio: in order to reach the bathroom it was not absolutely necessary to pass through his mother's little room, but it was not impossible to reach the bathroom that way either. Was she perhaps trying to make sure that her spouse would see her there in her intimate sanctuary? Was it her merciless hatred of him that had caused her to conceive the idea of humiliating him to such a point?

Anything was possible.

On not hearing the radio turned on, Martín presumed that she was not in there, because it was utterly inconceivable that she would stay there in her little room amid silence.

In the half-light, the double monster on the divan thrashed restlessly, furiously.

He wandered about the neighborhood like a sleepwalker for a little over an hour. Then he went back up to his room and threw himself on the bed. He lay there staring at the ceiling and then his eyes swept the walls until they stopped at the illustration from *Billiken* that had

been hanging there with thumbtacks in the corners since his childhood: Belgrano making his soldiers swear on the blue and white flag
at the crossing of the Salado River.

The immaculate flag, he thought.*

And key words of his existence also came to mind: *cold, cleanness,
snow, solitude, Patagonia.*

He thought of taking a boat, a train, but where would he get the
money? Then suddenly he remembered the big truck that always
parked in the garage near the Sola station; one day, magically, his eye
had been caught by the lettering on it: PATAGONIA TRUCKING. Might
they need a worker, a helper, anything?

"Sure, kid," Bucich said, a dead cigar butt dangling from his mouth.

"I've got eighty-three pesos," Martín said.

"Don't be silly," Bucich said, taking off his grease-spattered coveralls.

He looked like a circus giant, though a somewhat stoop-shouldered
one with gray hair. A giant with the innocent expression of a child.
Martín looked at the truck: on the side, in big letters, it said PATAGONIA
TRUCKING, and at the back, in gilt letters, it said: MAMA, LOOK AT ME
NOW.†

"Come on," Bucich said, his dead cigar butt still dangling from his
mouth.

On the wet, slippery pavement a milky, deliquescent red gleamed
for a moment. It was immediately followed by a violet flash, only to
be replaced once more by the milky red: CINZANO-AMERICANO GANCIA,
CINZANO-AMERICANO GANCIA.

"It's turning cold," Bucich remarked.

Was it drizzling? No, it was a fog of very fine, impalpable, floating
drops. The truck driver walked along in great strides at Martín's side.

---

* The Argentines won their independence from Spain in 1910. General Belgrano
was one of the first (impromptu) leaders of the forces of liberation. He created
the national flag, and was the first to require an oath of allegiance to it. *Billiken*
is a children's magazine. "The immaculate flag" is a phrase from a patriotic song
sung in classrooms. [*Author's note*]

† In Buenos Aires such inscriptions are common on delivery vans and trucks.
Often they are picturesquely philosophical—one on an ancient truck, for example,
that read: "I too was once the latest model." [*Author's note*]

He was straightforward and strong: the symbol, perhaps, of what Martín was looking for in that exodus to the south. He felt protected and abandoned himself to his thoughts. Here we are, Bucich said. CHICHÍN'S. PIZZA, BEER, WINE, AND SPIRITS. How you doin', fella? Bucich said to Chichín. How you doin' yourself? Chichín replied, picking up the bottle of Llave gin. Make it two. This kid's a pal of mine. Hiya, kid, the pleasure's all mine, Chichín said. He was wearing a cap and red suspenders over a sunflower-colored shirt. How's your mom doing? Bucich asked. So-so, Chichín said. Did they run the analysis on her? Yeah. And Chichín shrugged. You know how these things go. *Going far away, the cold, clear south.* Martín thought to himself. *Jumping rope, everything except getting her womb scraped, like boxers, she even punched me in the belly, that's why you turned out more or less defective of course, laughing rancorously and scornfully, I did everything, I wasn't going to get my body all out of shape for you she said to him, and he must have been eleven or so.* Where's Tito? Bucich asked. He'll be along any sec, Chichín said, and *he decided to go live up in the garret.* What's the scoop about what happened Sunday? Bucich asked. How the hell should I know? Chichín answered in fury, I swear I don't get upset any more *as she went on listening to boleros, plucking her eyebrows, eating caramels, leaving sticky papers around everywhere,* nothing gets me upset any more, Chichín was saying, absolutely nothing, I swear, *a dirty, sticky world* as he wiped a glass in silent fury and repeated absolutely nothing *fleeing to a cold, crystalline world* until finally he set the glass down, and looking Bucich straight in the eye he exclaimed losing on account of a lummox like that, as the truck driver blinked, considering the problem with all the attention due it and commenting No kidding: damn, *as Martín kept hearing those boleros, feeling that atmosphere heavy with steam from the tub and the smell of deodorant creams, air that was hot and turbid, a hot bath, a hot body, a hot bed, a hot mother, bed-mother, basketbed, milky legs raised up like in a horrible circus more or less in the same way he'd come out of the sewer and then into the sewer or almost,* as a skinny, nervous man came in who said how you doin'? and Chichín said here he is now, Humberto J. D'Arcángelo in person, hiya Puchito how you doin'?, the kid here's a pal of mine pleased to meet you the pleasure is mine, he said. *D'Arcángelo scrutinizing him with those little bird's eyes, with that anxious expression that Martín was always to see on Tito's face, as though he'd lost something very valuable and was looking everywhere for it, glancing all about quickly and worriedly, taking everything in.*

"Go on. *You* tell him what happened."

"That's right—you miss out on everything tooling along out there in your truck, don't you?"

"But I don't get upset any more," Chichín said yet again. "Nothing, not a single fuckin' thing upsets me any more, I swear to you on the memory of my mother. An all-time loser like that though. I ask you. But tell this guy, go on, tell him."

Humberto J. D'Arcángelo, commonly known as Tito, voiced his opinion on the subject frankly and forthrightly:

"Real garbage."

And then he sat down at a table near the window, took out *Crítica*, which he always carried about folded to the sports page, slapped it down indignantly on the little table, and picking at his pitted teeth with the toothpick that was forever in his mouth, he gazed gloomily out at the Calle Pinzón. A short man with narrow shoulders, dressed in a threadbare suit, he seemed to be pondering the general fate of the world.

After a time, he directed his gaze toward the bar counter and said:

"This Sunday was a disaster. Boca lost like a bunch of utter idiots, San Lorenzo won, and even Tigre won. Can you tell me where the hell we'll end up?"

He kept his eyes trained on his friends as though taking them as witnesses, and then he gazed out toward the street again and picking at his teeth he said:

"There's no hope for this country."

∽ 7 ∽

*I*t can't be, he thought, with his hand resting on the seabag, *it can't be.* But there had been the cough, the cough and those creaking noises.

And years afterward, he also thought, remembering that moment: *like solitary inhabitants of two islands that are close to each other, yet separated by unfathomable abysses.* Realizing, years later, when his father was rotting in his grave, that that poor devil had suffered at least as much as he had and that from that nearby but unreachable island on which his father lived (on which he survived) he had perhaps at some time made a silent but pathetic gesture asking for his aid, or at least his understanding and his affection. But this he realized only after painful experiences, when it was too late, as almost always is the case. So at that point, in that premature present (as though time amused itself by presenting itself before it should, so as to arouse impressions as grotesque and rudimentary as those left by certain amateur theatrical groups who lack experience: Othellos who have not yet loved), in that present that should have been a future, his father was entering off-cue, coming up those stairs that for so many years he had never set foot on. And with his back to the door, Martín was aware that he was approaching as though he were an intruder: he heard his panting tubercular breath, his hesitant pause. And with deliberate cruelty, Martín pretended not to have noticed him. *Of course, he's read my note, he wants to keep me from going.* But why? For years and years they had scarcely spoken to each other. He was torn between resentment and pity. His resentment impelled him not to look at his father, to ignore his entry into the room, and what was worse still, to make him understand that he was deliberately ignoring it. But he turned his head nonetheless. Yes, he turned it, and saw him as he had imagined him: clutching the banister with both hands, resting after his effort, with a lock of white hair fallen down over his forehead, his feverish, slightly bulging eyes, smiling feebly with that guilty expression that annoyed Martín so much, telling him "Twenty years ago, I had my studio up here," glancing all around the garret then, with perhaps the same feeling that a traveler, old now and disillusioned, experiences upon returning to the village of his youth, after having met persons and journeyed through distant countries that had awakened his imagination and his desires in younger days. He walked over to the bed and sat down on the edge of it, as though he did not feel he had the right to take up too much room or be too comfortable. And then he remained silent for quite some time, panting for breath, but as motionless as a lifeless statue. He said in a faint voice:

"There was a time when we were friends."

His pensive eyes lit up, gazing into the distance.

"I remember once in the Parque Retiro.... You must have been

... let's see ... four, perhaps five years old ... that's right ... you were five ... you wanted to go on the little electric cars by yourself, but I wouldn't let you, I was afraid it would scare you when they bumped together."

He laughed softly, nostalgically.

"Later, as we were returning home, you got onto a little merry-go-round in a vacant lot on the Calle Garay. I don't know why, but I always see you in my mind's eye from the back, just as you'd gone past me each time you circled round. The wind ruffled your little shirt, a little shirt with blue stripes. It was already dusk, the light was almost gone."

He stood there pensively and then repeated, as though it were an important fact:

"That's right, a little shirt with blue stripes. I remember it very well."

Martín said nothing.

"At that time I thought that with the years we'd come to be pals, that we'd be able to have ... a sort of friendship between us ..."

He smiled again, that guilty little smile, as though that hope had been ridiculous, a hope of something he had no right to. As though he had committed a petty theft, taking advantage of Martín's helplessness.

His son looked at him: he was sitting there with his elbows on his knees, all hunched over, gazing off into space.

"Yes ... everything is different now ..."

He picked up a pencil lying on the bed and examined it with a thoughtful expression.

"You mustn't think I don't understand you.... How could we be friends? You must forgive me, Martincito ..."

"I have nothing to forgive you for."

His harsh tone of voice contradicted the statement.

"You see? You hate me. And you mustn't think I don't understand you."

Martín would have liked to answer: "It's not true, I don't hate you," but the monstrously certain fact was that he did indeed hate him. And this hatred made him feel even more lonely and wretched. When he saw his mother paint her face and go out on the street humming some bolero, his hatred of her was extended to his father and finally came to be centered on him, as though he were the real object of it.

"I understand, of course, Martín, that you can't be proud of a painter who's a failure."

Martín's eyes filled with tears.

But they remained suspended in his enormous bitterness, like drops of oil in vinegar, without the two commingling. He shouted:

"Don't say that, papa!"

His father looked at him, touched and surprised by his reaction.

Almost without realizing what he was saying, Martín shouted in a voice full of rancor:

"This is a disgusting country! The only ones who get ahead here are bastards!"

His father stared at him in silence. Then, shaking his head, he said:

"No, Martín, you mustn't think that."

He contemplated the pencil he was holding and after a moment's pause, he concluded:

"We must be fair. I'm a miserable wretch, a real failure, and I deserve to be: I have neither talent nor the strength to keep going. That's the truth."

Martín began to retreat to his island again. The bathos of this scene made him feel ashamed and his father's resignation was beginning to bring all his bitterness toward him to the surface once again.

The silence became so intense and oppressive that his father got up to leave. He had doubtless realized that Martín's decision was irrevocable, that the abyss between them was too great, that absolutely nothing could be done to lessen that distance between them. He came over to Martín and clutched his arm with his right hand: he would have liked to embrace him, but how could he?

"Well, then ..." he murmured.

Would Martín have said something affectionate to him at this point had he known that these were literally the very last words he would ever hear from his father?

Would we be so hard on human beings—Bruno used to say—if we truly realized that some day they will die and that nothing of what we have said to them can be taken back then?

Martín saw his father turn around then and retreat toward the stairway. And he also saw that, before he disappeared from sight, he turned and looked back one last time, with a look in his eyes that years after his father's death, Martín would remember in despair.

And on hearing him cough as he was going down the stairs, Martín flung himself down on his bed and wept. It was hours later before he felt up to finishing packing his seabag. When he left the house at two that morning, he saw that there was a light still on in his father's studio.

"There he is," he thought. "Despite everything he's alive, he's still alive."

He headed for the parking garage and the thought came to him that he ought to be experiencing a feeling of great liberation, but that was not how it was: a dull heaviness of heart kept him from feeling any such thing. He walked on, more and more slowly, and finally he halted altogether. What was it he really wanted?

ᘐ 8 ᘐ

BEFORE I SAW her again many things happened ... at home.... I didn't want to live there any more, I thought of going off to Patagonia, I spoke with a truck driver named Bucich—haven't I ever told you about Bucich? But in the wee hours of the morning that day, to make a long story short ... well, in the end I didn't go south. But I didn't go back home either."

He fell silent, remembering.

"I saw her again in the same place in the park, but not until February of 1955. I had gone there every time I possibly could. Yet I didn't have the feeling that I would find her again just because I always waited there in that same place for her."

"And why is that?"

Martín looked at Bruno and said:

"Because *she* wanted to find *me*."

Bruno didn't seem to understand.

"If she finally turned up there it was because she wanted to find you, you mean."

"No, that's not what I mean at all. She would have found me in any other place just as easily. Do you understand what I'm getting at? She knew where and how to find me if she wanted to. That's what I mean. Waiting there for her, there on that bench, for so many months was one of my many naivetés."

He sat there lost in thought and then he added, looking at Bruno as though seeking an explanation from him:

"For that very reason, because I believe she went looking for me with all her strength of will, deliberately, for that very reason I find it all the more inexplicable that later on . . . in much the same way . . ."

His eyes did not leave Bruno, who sat there with his gaze riveted on that emaciated, suffering face.

"Do *you* understand it?"

"Human beings aren't logical," Bruno replied. "Moreover, it seems fairly certain that the very same reason that led her to search for you also impelled her to . . ."

He was about to say "abandon you" when he stopped and said instead "go away."

Martín stared at him for a moment more and then he again became lost in thought, saying nothing for quite some time. Then he explained how Alejandra had reappeared.

It was almost dark and there was no longer enough light to correct his proofs, so he had sat there leaning back against the bench looking at the trees. And all at once he had fallen fast asleep.

He dreamed that he was on an abandoned boat whose sails had been destroyed, heading up a great stream that appeared to be calm, though powerful and steeped in mystery. He was making his way upriver in the twilight. The countryside round about was dead still and deserted, but one was somehow aware that in the forest that rose up like a wall along the banks of the great river a secret life fraught with peril was pursuing its course. Then he was suddenly startled by a voice that appeared to be coming from the dense, dark jungle growth. He could not make out what it said, but he knew that it was addressing him, Martín. He tried to rise to his feet, but something prevented him from doing so. He struggled nonetheless to stand up because he could hear the remote, enigmatic voice calling to him more and more clearly, calling (as he now noticed) in anguished tones, as though it were the voice of someone in terrible danger and he, only he, were capable of coming to the rescue. He woke up trembling all over with anxiety and practically leaping off the bench.

It was she.

She had been shaking him and now she said to him, with her harsh laugh:

"Get up, you lazy bum."

Frightened, frightened and disconcerted by the contrast between the terrified, anguished voice of the dream and that carefree Alejandra who was now there before him, he could not manage to get a single word out.

He saw her pick up several of the proof sheets that had fallen off the bench as he slept.

"The boss of the company isn't Molinari, I'm certain of that," she commented, laughing.

"What company?"

"The one that gives you this work to do, silly."

"Its López and Company, the printers."

"Whatever you say, but it's certainly not Molinari."

He didn't understand a word of what she was saying. And as would happen many times with her, Alejandra didn't bother to explain. He had felt—Martín commented—like a bad pupil in front of a sarcastic teacher.

He put the proof sheets back in the right order, and this mechanical task gave him time to overcome to a certain degree the emotion of this meeting that he had so anxiously awaited. And then too, as on many later occasions, his silence and his inability to carry on a conversation were compensated for by Alejandra, who always, or almost always, divined his thoughts.

She ruffled his hair with one hand, as adults do to children.

"I told you I'd see you again, remember? But I didn't tell you when."

Martín looked at her.

"Did I tell you by any chance that I'd see you again soon?"

"No."

And so it was (Martín explained) that the whole terrible story began. Everything had been inexplicable. You never knew what would happen with her, and they met in places as absurd as the lobby of the Banco de Provincia or the Avellaneda bridge. And at any hour: at two in the morning sometimes. Everything was unexpected, nothing could be predicted or explained: neither her playful, joking moods nor her sudden rages nor those days when she never once opened her mouth from the time they met till she suddenly upped and left. Nor her prolonged disappearances. "And yet that was the most wonderful period of my life," he added. But he knew it couldn't last because the whole thing was hectic; it was—had he already said as much?—like a series of gas explosions on a stormy night. Although at times, very few times it is true, he did seem to have restful moments with her, as though she were someone suffering some illness and he a sanatorium or a place in the mountains to which she had betaken herself to lie in the sun in silence. At other times she gave the impression of being in torment, and it was as though he might be able to offer her water or some sort of remedy, something indispensable to her, so that she might return once again to that dark, wild realm in which she appeared to live her life.

"A realm I was never able to enter," he concluded, his eyes staring into Bruno's.

⚘ 9 ⚘

H ERE IT IS," she said.
        One could smell the intense perfume of jasmine in flower. The iron grating was very old and half-covered with wisteria. The rusty door swung reluctantly on its hinges, creaking.

Puddles from the recent rain gleamed in the darkness. There was a light on in one room, but the silence seemed more like that of a house with no one living in it. They skirted an abandoned garden, choked with weeds, by way of a little path running along a gallery, supported by cast-iron columns, on one side of the house. The house was very old; its windows looked out on the gallery and still had their colonial bars over them; the huge flagstones were surely from that era too, for they felt sunken, worn, and broken.

A clarinet could be heard: a phrase with no musical structure, languid, disjointed, obsessive.

"What's that?" Martín asked.

"Uncle Bebe, the madman," Alejandra explained.

They went along a narrow walkway between very old trees (Martín could now smell the heavy fragrance of magnolias) and continued along a brick path that ended at a winding staircase.

"Watch your step. Follow me slowly."

Martín stumbled over something: a garbage can or a wooden crate.

"Didn't I tell you to watch your step? Wait."

She stopped and lit a match, shielding it with one hand and bringing it over close to Martín.

"But Alejandra, isn't there a light around? I mean ... some sort of light in the patio?"

He heard her curt, nasty laugh.

"Lights? Come on, put your hands on my hips and follow me."

"That's fine for blind men."

He felt Alejandra halt dead in her tracks as though paralyzed by an electric shock.

"What in the world is wrong, Alejandra?" Martín asked in alarm.

"Nothing," she answered shortly, "but kindly do me the favor of never mentioning blind people to me again."

Martín put his hands on her hips once more and followed her through the darkness. As they made their way, slowly and cautiously, up the metal stairway, broken in many places and shaky in others where it had rusted nearly through, he felt Alejandra's body beneath his hands for the first time, so close and at the same time so remote and so mysterious. Something, a tremor, a hesitation betrayed that subtle sensation he was experiencing, whereupon she asked him what was wrong and he answered, sadly, "Nothing." When they reached the top of the stairs, Alejandra said as she tried to open a rebellious lock: "This is the old Mirador."

"Mirador?"

"Yes, at the beginning of the last century there were nothing but *quintas** hereabouts. The Olmoses, the Acevedos used to come here for weekends."

She laughed.

"In the days, that is, when the Olmoses weren't dying of hunger ... and hadn't gone mad."

"The Acevedos?" Martín asked. "Which Acevedos? The one who was vice-president?"

"Yes, that branch of the family."

Finally, after great effort, she managed to get the old door open. She reached up and turned on a light.

---

* Suburban, semirural properties belonging to old Argentine families. [*Author's note*]

"Well," Martín said, "there's electricity here anyway. I thought perhaps all there was to light the house was candles."

"Don't jump to conclusions. Grandfather Pancho uses nothing but kerosene lanterns. He claims electric light is bad for people's eyes."

Martín's gaze swept the room as though he were reconnoitering an area of Alejandra's unknown soul. The ceiling was not finished off and the great wooden roof beams were visible. There was a divan covered with a poncho and a motley assortment of furniture that looked as though it had come straight off the floor of an auction house: of different periods and styles, but all in a sorry state and about to fall apart.

"Come on, you'd better sit on the bed. The chairs around here are dangerous."

On one wall was an old-fashioned Venetian mirror, with a painting in the upper part. There were also a broken-down bureau and a chest of drawers. And there was an engraving or a lithograph pinned to the wall with thumbtacks at its four corners.

Alejandra hunted up an alcohol burner and started making coffee. As she waited for the water to heat she put a record on.

"Listen," she said absently, staring up at the ceiling as she puffed on her cigarette.

Pathetic, tumultuous music filled the room.

Then suddenly she took the record off.

"Ouf," she said, "I can't bear to listen to it now."

She went on preparing the coffee.

"When it was performed for the first time, Brahms himself was at the piano. Do you know what happened?"

"No."

"They booed him. Do you have any idea what humanity is really like?"

"Well, maybe..."

"What do you mean, maybe!" Alejandra exclaimed. "In your opinion then there's a possibility that humanity isn't pure pig-shit?"

"But Brahms was part of humanity too..."

"Look, Martín," she commented as she poured coffee into a cup, "men like that are the ones who suffer for the rest. And the rest are nothing but soccer fans, bastards, or idiots, see what I mean?"

She brought him the coffee.

He sat down on the edge of the bed, lost in thought. Then she put the record back on for a minute.

"Listen, just listen to that."

They heard the opening measures of the first movement again.

"Do you realize, Martín, the quantity of suffering that there had to be in the world so that there would be music like that?"

As she took the record off again, she commented:

"Terrific."

He remained lost in thought still, finishing his coffee. Then he put the cup down on the floor.

Suddenly amid the silence the sound of the clarinet came through the open window; it was as though a child were scribbling on paper.

"He's crazy you say?"

"Don't you realize? This is a family of crazy people. Do you know who lived up here in this garret for eighty years? Miss Escolástica. You know of course that once upon a time it was fashionable to have a member of the family who'd gone mad, shut up in some back room. Bebe is more a gentle madman, a sort of fuzzy-minded fool, and in any case nobody can do any harm with a clarinet. Escolástica was a gentle madwoman too. Do you know what happened to her? Come here." She got up and went over to the lithograph pinned to the wall with four thumbtacks. "Look: these are the remains of Lavalle's legion, in Humahuaca Valley.* On this dapple gray charger is the general's body. This is Colonel Pedernera. The one next to him is Pedro Echagüe. And this other man with a beard, on the right, is Colonel Acevedo. Bonifacio Acevedo, Grandpa Pancho's great-uncle. We call Pancho grandfather, but he's really my great-grandfather. This other

---

* Argentina took up arms against Spain in 1810 and won its independence. There then followed a long period of civil war between Unitarists and Federalists. The Federalist dictator Juan Manuel de Rosas ruled the country with an iron hand for twenty years with the aid of the Mazorca, a sort of terrorist political police. During this time Rosas's most stubborn enemies, among them the Unitarist general, Lavalle, a hero of the fight for Independence, lived in exile in Montevideo. In 1840 Lavalle, at the head of his celebrated Legion, began a campaign against Rosas. The struggle lasted nearly two years, and in the end nearly all the Unitarists were annihilated after a retreat of eight hundred leagues to the north of Buenos Aires, fleeing toward the Bolivian border. [*Author's note*]

one is Lieutenant Celedonio Olmos, Grandpa Pancho's father, or in other words my great-great-grandfather. Bonifacio had to flee for his life to Montevideo. He married a Uruguayan girl there, an easterner, as grandfather puts it, whose name was Encarnación Flores, and that was where Escolástica was born. Now there's a name for you! Before she was born, Bonifacio joined the Legion and never saw his daughter, because the campaign lasted two years and then, after Humahuaca, they crossed the border into Bolivia, where he stayed for several years; he was also in Chile for a time. In 1852, at the beginning of '52, after thirteen years without seeing his wife, who lived here in this house, Major Bonifacio Acevedo, who was in Chile with other exiles, had had all he could take of sadness and came to Buenos Aires, disguised as a muleteer: people were saying that Rosas was about to fall from power from one moment to the next, that Urquiza would enter Buenos Aires amid fire and blood. But Bonifacio didn't want to wait around for that to happen, so he took off from Chile by himself. Someone denounced him, of course, otherwise there's no explanation. He arrived in Buenos Aires and the Mazorca caught him. They beheaded him and came by the house here; they knocked on the window and when somebody opened it they threw the head into the parlor. Encarnación died of the shock and Escolástica went mad. And a few days later Urquiza entered Buenos Aires! You must bear in mind that Escolástica had grown up hearing about her father and gazing at his portrait."

She took a miniature, in color, out of a drawer of the commode.

"Here he is when he was a lieutenant of cuirassiers, during the Brazil campaign."

His bright uniform, his youth, his grace contrasted with the bearded, ravaged face in the old lithograph.

"The Mazorca had gone on the rampage at the news of Urquiza's uprising. Do you know what Escolástica did? Her mother fainted dead away, but Escolástica grabbed her father's head and ran up here. She stayed locked up in this room with her father's head from that year till her death in 1932."

"In 1932!"

"Yes, 1932. She lived up here for eighty years, locked in with the head. Meals had to be brought up here to her and all her garbage taken down. She never went out and never felt any desire to. Another thing: with that cleverness that mad people have, she'd hidden her father's head so no one would ever be able to find it and take it away. They could have found it, of course, if they'd really searched for it, but she would get frantic if they tried and there was no fooling her. 'I have to get something out of the chest of drawers,' they would say to her. But there was nothing doing. And nobody was ever able to get a thing out of the chest of drawers, or the bureau, or that leather trunk over there. And everything remained just the way it had been in 1852 till she died in 1932. Can you believe it?"

"It seems incredible."

"It's the absolute historical truth. I used to ask all sorts of questions myself: how did she eat? how did they clean the room? They brought her food up to her and managed to do at least a minimum of cleaning. Escolástica was a gentle madwoman and even talked normally about almost everything, with the exception of her father and the head. For the entire eighty years that she kept herself locked up here, for instance, she never spoke of her father as though he were dead. She spoke in the present. What I mean is, she spoke as if it were 1852 and she were twelve, and as if her father were in Chile and would be coming home any minute. She was a nice quiet old lady. But her life and even her turns of phrase had stopped in 1852; Rosas was still in power as far as she was concerned. When 'that man' falls from power, she would say, gesturing toward the outside world with her head, out there where there were electric streetcars and Yrigoyen was in office. It seems that her reality had vast gaps in it or perhaps it's as if they too were under lock and key and she were taking roundabout ways, like a child, to avoid speaking of these things, as though if she didn't speak of them they wouldn't exist and therefore her father's death wouldn't exist either. She had erased everything having to do with Bonifacio's beheading."

"And what happened to the head?"

"Escolástica died in 1932 and they were finally able to search the major's chest of drawers and the leather trunk. The head was wrapped in rags (apparently that old woman took it out every night and put it on the bureau and spent the hours looking at it or perhaps she slept with the head over there on top of it, like a flower vase). It was shrunken and mummified, of course. And that's the way it still is."

"What!"

"Of course—what do you expect happened to the head? What does one do with a head in a case like that?"

"Uh—I don't know. The whole story is so mind-boggling I don't have any idea."

"And above all remember what sort of family mine is—the Olmoses, I mean, not the Acevedos."

"What sort of family are they?"

"Do you still have to ask? Don't you hear Uncle Bebe playing the clarinet? Don't you see the sort of place we live in? Tell me, do you know anybody with a famous name in this country who lives in Barracas, smack in the middle of tenements and factories? That should tell you that nothing normal could happen to the head, apart from the fact that nothing that happens to a head that's not attached to its corresponding body can possibly be normal in any case."

"And so?"

"Well, it's very simple: the head's stayed here in the house."

Martín gave a start.

"Don't tell me that surprises you! What did you think could be done with it? Make a little coffin and hold a little funeral for it?"

Martín laughed nervously, but Alejandra's manner remained grave and thoughtful.

"And where do you keep it?"

"Grandpa Pancho keeps it downstairs in a hat box. Would you like to see it?"

"Heavens no!" Martín exclaimed.

"What's the matter with you? It's a nice head and I can assure you it does me good to see it from time to time when I see all the trash that's around these days. In those days at least men were real men, and they gambled their lives on what they believed in. I can tell you for a fact that almost all my family has been Unitarists, except Fernando and me."

"Fernando? Who's Fernando?"

Alejandra suddenly fell silent, as though she had said more than she should have.

Martín was surprised. He had the feeling that Alejandra had revealed something she hadn't meant to. She had risen to her feet, gone over to the little table where she'd set up the alcohol burner, put more water on to boil, and lit a cigarette. Then she peered out the window.

"Come on," she said, leaving the room.

Martín followed her. The night shadows were intense yet etched in bright moonlight. Alejandra walked over to the edge of the terrace and leaned over the balustrade.

"Once upon a time you could see ships arriving at Riachuelo from here," she said.

"And who lives here now?"

"Here? Well, there's practically nothing left of the house. In the old days it occupied a whole block. Then they began to sell parts of it off. The land where that factory and those sheds are all belonged to the *quinta* once upon a time. There are tenements here on this other side. All the back part of the house was also sold off. And this part that's left is all mortgaged and any day now it'll be going on the auction block."

"And that doesn't make you feel sad?"

Alejandra shrugged.

"I don't know. Maybe I feel sorry for grandfather. He lives in the past and he's going to die without realizing how this country's changed. Do you have any idea what it's like for that old man? What's happening is that he hasn't the slightest notion what shit is. And he has neither the time nor the ability to find out now. I don't know if that's better or worse for him. The other time they were about to sell the house off at auction I had to go see Molinari to get him to fix things."

"Molinari?"

"Yes, a sort of mythological animal. As though a hog were the director of a corporation."

Martín looked at Alejandra, who added with a smile:

"There's a certain sort of tie between us. As you can well imagine, it would kill the old man if the place were put up for auction."

"Your father you mean?"

"Of course not, silly: I mean my grandfather."

"And your father isn't worried about what might happen?"

Alejandra looked at him with an expression that could well have been the grimace of an explorer who is asked whether the automobile industry is very highly developed in the Amazon.

"Your father," Martín said, pressing the point, as usual out of sheer timidity, feeling he'd said something stupid (although he didn't know what) yet getting himself in deeper despite himself.

"My father never sets foot in this house," Alejandra confined herself to saying in reply, in a tone of voice that was no longer the same.

Like those who are learning to ride a bicycle and are obliged to keep pedaling if they are not to fall off, and, most mysteriously, inevitably end up crashing into a tree or some other obstacle, Martín stubbornly pursued the subject:

"Does he live somewhere else?"

"I've just told you he doesn't live here!"

Martín flushed.

Alejandra walked over to the other end of the terrace and remained there for a good while. Then she walked back and stood leaning over the balustrade alongside Martín.

"My mother died when I was five. And when I was eleven I found my father here with a woman. But I think now that he'd been sleeping with her for a long time before my mother died."

With a laugh that appeared to be a normal one to the same degree that a hunchbacked criminal resembles a man sound in mind and body she added:

"In the same bed that I sleep in now."

She lit a cigarette and in the flame of the lighter Martín could see on her face traces of her laugh of a moment before, the stinking corpse of the hunchback.

Then he saw, there in the darkness, the glow of Alejandra's cigarette each time she inhaled deeply on it: she was smoking, sucking on it with intense, anxious greed.

"Then I ran away from home," she said.

∝ 10 ∝

That freckle-faced little girl is Alejandra: she is eleven and her hair has reddish glints in it. She is a thin, pensive child, but a violently and cruelly pensive one, as though her thoughts were not abstract, but crazed, burning-hot serpents. It is that child who has remained intact in some obscure region of her self, and now the Alejandra who is *eighteen, silent and attentive, trying not to frighten the apparition away, draws aside and observes it cautiously and curiously. It is a game she often plays when she reflects on her fate. But it is a difficult game, as subtle and as frustrating as spiritualists say materializations are: one has to know how to wait, how to be patient, how to concentrate intensely, closing one's mind to all extraneous or frivolous thoughts. The shadow emerges little by little and one must encourage it by remaining absolutely silent and being very careful: the least little thing will cause it to withdraw, to disappear back into the region from which it was beginning to emerge. It is here now: it has come out and she can see herself with her reddish braids and her freckles, observing everything round about her with those mistrustful, hard-staring eyes, ready and waiting for fights and insults. Alejandra looks at her with those mixed feelings of tenderness and resentment we have toward younger brothers and sisters on whom we vent the wrath that we have for our own defects, screaming at them: "Stop biting your fingernails, you disgusting creature!"*

"On the Calle Isabel la Católica there is a house in ruins. Or rather, there used to be a house there, because it was torn down a short time ago to make way for a refrigerator factory. It had stood empty for many years on account of a lawsuit or a disputed inheritance. I believe it belonged to the Miguenses, a *quinta* that at one time must have been very pretty, like this one. I remember that it had pale green walls, sea green, all peeling, as though they had leprosy. I was very excited and the idea of running away from home and hiding out in an abandoned house gave me a feeling of power, perhaps resembling the one that soldiers must have as they launch an attack, despite their fear or because such a feeling is the other side of the coin of fear. I've read that somewhere, haven't you? I say this because I suffered from frightful night-terrors, so you can imagine what I thought might await me in an abandoned house. I used to go out of my head at night, I saw bandits entering my room with lanterns, or men from the Mazorca with bloody heads in their hands (Justina used to tell us tales about the Mazorca all the time), I fell into wells of blood. I'm not sure whether I was awake or asleep when I saw all those things; I think, though, that they were hallucinations, that I was awake when I saw them, because I remember them as clearly as though I were having them this minute. I would start screaming then, till Grandma Elena would come running and calm me little by little, because the bed would continue to shake for a long time as I shuddered from head to foot: they were anxiety attacks, really severe ones.

"So that planning what I was planning, to hide by night in a lonely house in ruins, was an act of madness. And I think now that I planned it so that my vengeance would be all the more terrible. I felt it was a beautiful act of revenge and would be all the more beautiful and terrible the more frightful the dangers I would be forced to confront, do you follow me? As though I thought, as perhaps I indeed did: 'Let them see how much I'm suffering, and it's all my father's fault!' It's curious, but after that night my terror was transformed, in one fell swoop, into the fearlessness of a madman. Doesn't that strike you as curious? What's the explanation for a thing like that? It was a sort of mad arrogance, as I've told you, in the face of any danger, real or imaginary. It's quite true that I'd always been bold, and on the vacations I spent at the country estate of the Carrascos, old maids who were friends of Grandma Elena's, I had trained myself to be brave. I would run across the fields and gallop over them on a little mare they'd given me. I'd chosen her name myself and I liked it a lot: *Scorn*. I had a .22-caliber rifle to hunt with and a little single-bullet pistol. I was a good swimmer and despite all the warnings and all my promises I would swim out into the open sea and more than once I had to fight against the tide (I forgot to tell you that the estate of those tottering old spinsters was on the coast, near Miramar). And yet, despite all this, I still shook with fear in the face of imaginary monsters at night. Anyway, as I was saying, I decided to run away and hide in the house on the Calle Isabel la Católica. I waited for nightfall so as to scale the fence without being seen (the gate had a padlock on it). But someone must have seen me going over the fence, and even though at first he may not have thought it was anything to get excited about, since, as you can imagaine, more than one boy must have already done the same thing out of curiosity, when the news that I was missing spread through the neighborhood and the police were called in, the man doubtless remembered what he'd seen and told them. But if that's what happened, it must have been many hours after I'd run away, because the police didn't show up at the big empty house till eleven. So I had plenty of time to confront terror. Once I'd climbed over the fence, I went around to the back of the house, along the old driveway for carriages, amid weeds and old garbage cans, refuse and stinking dead cats or dogs. I forgot to tell you that I'd also taken along my flashlight, my little hunting knife, and the single-shot pistol that Grandpa Pancho had given me for my tenth birthday. As I was saying, I made my way around to the back of the house along the driveway. There was a gallery, like the one we have here. The windows that looked out on this gallery or covered walkway had shutters over them, but the shutters were rotted and some of them had almost fallen off or were full of holes. It may well have been that bums or hobos had used the house to sleep in overnight and even longer. And what was to prevent one or another of them from turning up that night to sleep there? I trained the beam of my flashlight over the windows and the doors at the back of the house and finally spied a door with shutters that had one panel missing. I pushed on the door and finally managed to force it open. It creaked as though it had been a very long time since it had last been opened, and at that instant the terrifying thought came to me that this was a sign that even bums didn't dare take refuge in this ill-omened house. I hesitated for some time and finally decided it would be best not to enter the house; I made up my mind to spend the night in the gallery instead. But it was freezing cold, and after a while I realized that I was going to have to go inside and make a fire —I was sure I knew how to do that, because I'd seen it done in so many movies. I decided the kitchen would be the most suitable place because I could get a good bonfire going in there on the flagstone floor. I also hoped the fire would chase the rats away; the disgusting things have always turned my stomach. Like all the rest of the house, the kitchen was in ruins. I didn't feel up to sleeping on the floor, even if I piled up straw for a bed, because I had the idea that rats could get at me more easily if I did. It seemed a better idea to bed down on top of the cookstove. It was an old-fashioned kitchen, similar to the one we have and the ones that can still be seen on certain ranches, with coal ovens and burners for simmering things all day. As for the rest of the house, I would explore it the next day: at that hour of the night I didn't have the courage to go through all of it, and what was more there was no purpose in my doing so. My first task was to gather firewood in the garden, that is to say remains of wooden boxes, loose boards, straw, papers, fallen tree limbs and branches of a dead tree that

I found. I made a fire of all this near the kitchen door so the inside of the room wouldn't fill up with smoke. After a few trials the fire caught, and the moment I saw the flames in the midst of the darkness I felt warmed, both literally and figuratively. I immediately took my provisions out of my sack, sat myself down on a crate near the fire, and enjoyed every last bite of my meal of bread and butter and salami, followed by sweet-potato candy. When I finished it was just eight o'clock by my watch—was that all! I didn't want to think about what awaited me during the long hours of the night.

"The police arrived at eleven. I don't know, as I said, whether someone had seen a youngster climbing over the fence. It is just as likely that some neighbor had seen the light or the smoke from the bonfire I had made, or had noticed me moving back and forth there inside with my flashlight. In any event the police had arrived, and I must confess I was glad to see them. If I had had to spend the entire night there, when all the noises outside gradually fade away and you have the impression the whole city is sound asleep, I think I might have gone mad, what with the rats and the cats scurrying around, the wind howling, and the sounds that my imagination could easily lay to ghosts prowling about. So when the police arrived I was awake, huddled on top of the cookstove quaking with fear.

"I can't describe the scene at home when they brought me back. Grandpa Pancho, poor thing, had tears in his eyes and kept asking me why I'd done such an insane thing. Grandma Elena scolded me and hugged me, both at the same time, hysterically. As for Aunt Teresa, my great-aunt really, who spent most of her time at wakes and in the sacristy, she kept screaming that they ought to send me straight off to the boarding school on the Avenida Montes de Oca. The family deliberations must have gone on far into the night, for I could hear them arguing downstairs in the parlor. The next morning I found out that Grandma Elena had finally sided with Aunt Teresa, more than anything, I think today, because she thought I might repeat my scandalous exploit at any moment; and then too, she knew I was very fond of Sister Teodolina. I refused, of course, to say one word about the entire matter, and locked myself in my room. But at heart the idea of leaving that house did not displease me: I supposed that in this way my father would be even more keenly aware of my vengeance.

"I don't know whether it was my entering the school, my friendship with Sister Teodolina, or the crisis I was going through, or all of these things together, but in any event I threw myself into religion with the same passion with which I swam or rode horseback: as though I were gambling my life. From that moment till I was fifteen. It was a sort of madness..." *akin to the wild ardor with which she swam in the sea on stormy nights, as though she were swimming furiously in a great religious night, engulfed in dark shadows, fascinated by the great tempest raging within.*

Father Antonio is there: he speaks of Christ's Passion and fervently describes the suffering, the humiliation, and the bloody sacrifice of the Cross. Father Antonio is tall and bears an odd resemblance to her father. Alejandra weeps, silently at first and then her sobs grow violent and finally convulsive. She flees. The nuns run fearfully after her. She sees Sister Teodolina before her, consoling her, and then Father Antonio approaches and also tries to console her. The floor begins to move, as though she were on a boat. It heaves in waves like the sea, the room gets bigger and bigger, and then everything begins to turn round and round: slowly at first and then at dizzying speed. She is drenched with sweat. Father Antonio approaches, his hand is gigantic now, it draws closer to her cheek like a warm, loathsome bat. Then she collapses, felled by a great electrical discharge.

"What's the matter, Alejandra?" Martín cried, hurrying to her side.

She had fallen to the floor and was lying there rigid, not breathing, her face turning purple, and then suddenly she went into convulsions.

"Alejandra! Alejandra!"

But she did not hear him, did not feel his arms: she groaned and bit her lips.

Then finally, like a storm at sea that dies down little by little, her moans came farther and farther apart, grew softer and softer and more and more plaintive, her convulsions gradually ceased, and finally she lay there limply, as though dead. Martín picked her up in his arms then, carried her to her room, and laid her down on the bed. After an hour or more she opened her eyes and looked about her, as though drunk. Then she sat up, passed her hands across her face as though trying to erase the traces of something and remained silent for a long time. She looked utterly exhausted.

Then she got up, looked about for some pills, and took them.

Martín watched her in consternation.

"Don't make such a face. If you're going to be a friend of mine you'll have to get used to all this. It's nothing serious."

She searched about for a cigarette on the little night table and began to smoke. For a long time she rested quietly, saying nothing. Finally she asked:

"What was I talking about?"

Martín reminded her.

"I lose my memory, you know."

She sat smoking pensively, and then said:

"Let's go outdoors. I'd like to get a breath of air."

They leaned out over the balustrade of the terrace.

"So I was telling you about running away that time."

She dragged on her cigarette in silence.

"I would torture myself for days, analyzing my feelings, my reactions. After what had happened to me with Father Antonio I began a whole series of mortifications of the flesh: I knelt for hours on broken glass, I let burning wax from candles fall on my hands, I even cut my arm with a razor blade. And when Sister Teodolina, in tears, tried to get me to tell her why I had cut myself, I refused to explain. To tell the truth I didn't know myself, and it seems to me I still don't know. But Sister Teodolina told me I shouldn't do those things, that such excesses were displeasing to God, that such behavior was proof of enormous satanic pride. As though I hadn't known that all along! But all that was stronger, more incontrovertible than any logical argument. You can see where all that madness got me."

She remained lost in thought.

"How curious," she said after a time. "I try to remember what that year was like as it went by, and all I remember is separate, juxtaposed episodes. Does the same thing happen to you? Right now I can feel the passage of time, as though it were coursing through my veins, along with my blood, beating along with my pulse. But when I try to remember the past I don't feel the same thing. I see separate scenes, as fixed and frozen as photographs."

Her memory is made up of fragments of existence, ecstatic and eternal: time in fact does not flow between these fragments, and events that happened at very different times are related or connected to one another by strange sympathies and antipathies. Or at times they may rise

to the surface of consciousness linked by absurd but powerful associa-
tions: a song, a joke, a common hatred. The thread that unites things
for her now, that causes them to emerge one after another is a certain
fierce search for something absolute, a certain perplexity, one that joins
together words such as father, God, beach, sin, purity, sea, death.

"I see myself one summer day and hear Grandma Elena saying:
'Alejandra has to go to the country, she must get out of here, she must
be outdoors in the fresh air.' Curious: I remember that at that moment
Granny had a silver thimble on her finger."

She laughed.

"Why are you laughing?" Martín said, intrigued.

"It's not anything really, nothing of any importance. They sent me
to the country to stay with the Carrascos, old ladies who were distant
relations of Grandma Elena's. I don't know if I told you that she
wasn't an Olmos; her name was Lafitte. She was a very kind woman
and married my grandfather Patricio, Don Pancho's son. Some day
I'll tell you a bit about Grandfather Patricio, who's dead now. Anyway, as I was saying, the Carrascos were second cousins of Grandma
Elena's. They were hidebound old maids who'd never changed; even
their names were ridiculously old-fashioned: Ermelinda and Rosalinda.
They were saints, and to tell the truth they mattered as little to me
as a marble slab or a sewing table; I didn't even hear them when they
spoke. They were so innocent they'd have died of fright if they'd been
able to read a single one of my thoughts. So I liked going to their
country place: I had all the freedom I wanted and could gallop my
little mare to the beach, because the old ladies' estate went down to
the ocean, a little to the south of Miramar. What's more, I was eager
to be by myself, to swim, to have a good run with the mare, to feel
myself alone in the face of the immensity of nature, far from the
crowded beaches where all the filthy people I hated so were piled one
atop the other. I hadn't seen Marcos Molina for a year and meeting up
with him again was an intriguing prospect too. It had been such an
important year! I wanted to share my new ideas with him, tell him
about a marvelous plan I had, inspire in him the same ardent faith
I possessed. My entire body was bursting with vitality; even though
I'd always run half wild, that summer my energy was boundless,
though I now sought entirely different outlets for it. I put Marcos

through a lot that summer. He was fifteen, a year older than I was. He was a good sort, and very athletic. In fact I think he'll make an excellent family man some day and he's sure to end up president of a chapter of Acción Católica. You mustn't get the idea he was a sissy; he was, rather, the sort people call a 'nice boy,' the kind of wishy-washy Catholic who believed every word he'd ever heard in catechism class; decent, rather naive, quiet. Imagine this now: the moment I arrive in the country I get my hands on him and begin to try to convince him we should go to China or the Amazon as soon as we've turned eighteen. As missionaries, see? That first day we rode far out along the beach, toward the south, on horseback. Other times we rode bicycles or walked for hours. And with long, fervent speeches, I tried to get him to understand the grandeur of an act such as I was proposing. I told him about Father Damien and his work with the lepers in Polynesia, I told him stories of missionaries in China and Africa, and nuns massacred by Indians in Matto Grosso. To me, the greatest joy I could possibly conceive of was to die a martyr's death. I imagined the savages grabbing us, stripping me naked and tying me to a tree, aproaching with a sharp stone knife amid wild howls and dances, slitting my breast, and ripping out my bloody heart."

Alejandra fell silent, relit her cigarette, and went on:

"Marcos was Catholic, but he heard me out each time without a word. And then one day he finally confessed to me that the sacrifices of missionaries who died and suffered martyrdom for the faith were undoubtedly admirable, but that he didn't feel capable of following their example. It seemed to him, moreover, that one could serve God in a more modest way, by being a good person and not harming anybody. These words made me boil.

" 'You're a coward!' I shouted at him in fury.

"This scene, with slight variations, was repeated two or three times.

"He was mortified, humiliated. Whipping up my mare, I broke into a hard gallop and rode away, in a rage and full of scorn for that poor devil. But the next day I returned to the charge, more or less in the same vein. Even today I don't understand why I was so stubborn, for Marcos awakened no sort of feelings of admiration in me. But one thing is certain: I was obsessed and gave him no rest.

" 'Alejandra,' he said to me good-naturedly, putting one of his big paws on my shoulder, 'stop preaching now and let's go for a swim.'

" 'No! Wait a minute!' I cried, as though he were trying to go back on a promise he'd made. And I began harping on the same subject all over again.

"Sometimes I talked to him of marriage.

" 'I'm never going to get married,' I explained to him. 'Or if I do marry, I'll never have children.'

"He looked at me dumbfounded the first time I announced this to him.

" 'Do you know how you get babies?' I asked.

" 'More or less,' he answered, blushing.

" 'Well, if you know, you understand that it's a filthy business.'

"I said these words to him firmly, almost angrily, as if it were one more argument in favor of my theory regarding missions and self-sacrifice.

" 'I'll go but I have to have somebody to go with me, do you understand? I have to get married to someone, because otherwise they'll get the police to search for me and I won't be able to leave the country. That's why I thought of marrying you. Look: I'm fourteen now and you're fifteen. When I'm eighteen I'll have finished school and we'll get the permission of the juvenile court judge and get married. That way nobody can stop us from getting married. And if worse comes to worst, we'll run away and then they'll have to agree. And then we'll go to China or the Amazon. How about it? But it's understood: the only reason we get married is to be able to get out of the country without any fuss—not to have children, as I've already explained to you. We won't ever have children. We'll live together always, we'll visit countries full of savages together, but we won't ever touch each other. Isn't that a marvelous idea?'

"He looked at me in stupefaction.

" 'We mustn't flee from danger,' I went on. 'We must confront it and overcome it. I have temptations, naturally, but I'm strong and able to get the better of them. Can you imagine how nice it would be to live together for years and years, to sleep in the same bed, and maybe even see each other naked and rise above the temptation to touch each other and kiss each other?'

"Marcos looked at me in utter amazement.

" 'Everything you're saying seems to me to be sheer madness,' he said. 'Besides, isn't it God's command that a husband and wife have children?'

" 'I'll never have children, I tell you!" I cried. 'And I warn you that you'll never touch me, that nobody, nobody will ever touch me!'

"I felt a sudden explosion of hatred and began to strip naked.

" 'You'll see now!' I shouted, as though challenging him.

"I had read that the Chinese keep their women's feet from growing by placing them in iron molds and that the Syrians, I think it is, deform their children's heads by binding them tightly with bands of cloth. So when my breasts began to grow I cut a long strip from a sheet, a good three yards long: I wrapped it round and round my chest several times, cinching it cruelly tight. But my breasts kept on growing just the same, like those plants that spring up in the cracks of stones and finally split them apart. So once I'd taken off my blouse, my skirt, and my panties, I began to unwind the long strip of cloth. Marcos was horrified and couldn't take his eyes off my body. He had the look of a bird fascinated by a serpent.

"When I had stripped naked, I lay down on the sand and challenged him.

" 'Come on, you strip naked now. Prove you're a man!'

" 'Alejandra!' he stammered, 'What you're doing is madness and a sin.'

"He repeated the word *sin* like a stutterer, several times, without taking his eyes off me, and I for my part kept shouting 'you fairy' at him, more and more scornfully, until finally, with clenched teeth and in a rage, he began to strip naked. When he was all undressed, however, his energy seemed to have drained away altogether, because he stood there paralyzed, looking at me in terror.

" 'Lie down here,' I ordered.

" 'Alejandra, it's madness and a sin.'

" 'Come on, lie down here!' I repeated.

"He finally obeyed me.

"The two of us lay there on our backs on the hot sand next to each other, looking up at the sky. The silence was oppressive; you could hear the slap of the waves on the stones. Overhead, the gulls screamed and wheeled about us. I could hear Marcos's labored breathing, as though he had just run a long race.

" 'You see how simple it is?' I commented. 'We could be like this all the time.'

" 'Never! Never!' Marcos shouted, scrambling to his feet as though to flee from some terrible danger.

"He hurriedly dressed again, repeating: 'Never, never! You're mad, utterly mad!'

"I didn't say anything but smiled smugly to myself. I felt all-powerful.

"And as though his words scarcely deserved a reply, all I said was:

" 'If you'd touched me I'd have killed you with my knife.'

"He stood there frozen with horror. Then suddenly he took off at a run, heading toward Miramar.

"I lay on my side and watched him disappear in the distance. Then I got up and ran into the water. I swam for a long time, feeling the salt water envelop my naked body. Every particle of my flesh seemed to vibrate with the spirit of the world.

"Marcos vanished from Piedras Negras for several days. I thought he was frightened or had perhaps taken sick. But a week later he timidly reappeared. I acted as though nothing had happened and we went for a walk, as we had so often in the past. Then all of a sudden I said to him:

" 'Well, Marcos, did you think about what I said about getting married?'

"He halted, looked at me gravely, and said to me in a firm voice:

" 'I'll marry you, Alejandra. But it won't be the way you say.'

" 'What's that?' I exclaimed. 'What do you mean?'

" 'I'll get married so as to have children, like everybody else.'

"I felt my eyes getting red, or else saw red. Before I realized what I was doing, I flung myself on Marcos. We fell to the ground, struggling. Even though Marcos was strong and a year older than I was, we fought as equals in the beginning, no doubt because my fury gave me added strength. I remember that all of a sudden I even managed to get him underneath me and knee him in the belly. My nose was bleeding, and we were growling like two mortal enemies. Struggling hard, Marcos finally managed to turn over, and a moment later he was on top of me. I felt his hands gripping me and twisting my arms like tongs. He gradually got the better of me and I felt his face coming closer and closer to mine until finally he kissed me.

"I bit his lips and he drew away, crying out in pain. He let go of me then and took off at a run.

"I got to my feet, but strangely enough I didn't chase after him. I stood there petrified, watching him running off. I passed my hand across my mouth and rubbed my lips, as though trying to scrub dirt off them. And little by little I felt my fury rising in me again like water boiling in a pot. Then I took my clothes off and ran into the water. I swam for a long time, hours perhaps, leaving the beach far behind, venturing out into the open sea.

"I experienced a strange sensual pleasure as the waves lifted me. I felt at once powerful and alone, miserable and possessed by demons. I swam and swam till I felt my strength giving out, and then I began to stroke my way back to the beach.

"I lay resting on the beach for a long time, on my back in the burning sand, watching the seagulls soaring. Far overhead peaceful, motionless clouds made everything round about me seem absolutely calm as night fell, whereas my mind was a maelstrom agitated and rent by furious winds: looking inward, I seemed to see my consciousness as a little boat lashed by a storm.

"Night had fallen by the time I returned home, full of vague animosity toward everything, including myself. I felt possessed by criminal ideas. I hated one thing in particular: having felt pleasure during that fight and that kiss. Even after climbing into bed, lying on my back looking at the ceiling, I was still overcome by a vague sensation that left me trembling as though I had a fever. The curious thing is that I had almost no memory of Marcos as Marcos (in fact, as I've already told you, he seemed rather fatuous and dull to me and I had never felt any sort of admiration for him): what I felt, rather, was a confused sensation on my skin and in my blood, the memory of arms holding me tight, the memory of a weight pressing against my breasts and my thighs. I don't know how to explain it to you, but it was as if two opposing forces were struggling within me, and this struggle, which I was at a loss to understand, tormented me and filled me with hatred. And this hatred seemed to be nourished by the same fever that made my skin quiver and was concentrated in the tips of my breasts.

"I couldn't sleep. I looked at my watch: it was around midnight. Almost without being aware of what I was doing, I got dressed and climbed out the window of my room to the little garden below, as I had often done before. I don't remember if I've already told you that the Carrasco sisters also had a little house right in Miramar, where they sometimes stayed for several weeks or spent their weekends. We were at that house at the time.

"I went over to Marcos's house almost at a run (even though I had sworn to myself never to see him again).

"His room, on the upstairs floor, overlooked the street. I whistled, the way I usually did, and waited.

"He didn't answer. I searched around in the street for a pebble, threw it through his open window, and whistled again. Finally he poked his head out and asked me in an anxious voice what was going on.

" 'Come downstairs,' I said to him. 'I want to talk to you.'

"I think that at that moment I still hadn't realized I wanted to kill him, even though I had been foresighted enough to bring my little hunting knife along with me.

" 'I can't, Alejandra,' he answered. 'My father's angry enough as it is and if he hears me I'll be in even more trouble.'

" 'If you don't come down, you'll be in far worse trouble still, because I'll come up,' I answered with calm, calculated spite.

"He hesitated for a moment, perhaps weighing the possible consequences for him if I carried out my threat to come upstairs, then told me to wait.

"Shortly thereafter he came down through the back door.

"I walked off down the street ahead of him.

" 'Where are you going?' he asked in alarm. 'What are you up to?'

"I didn't answer and strode on till I reached a vacant lot half a block away from his house. He had followed along behind me as though I were dragging him along bodily.

"Then I suddenly turned around and said to him:

" 'Why did you kiss me today?'

"My voice, my attitude, something, I don't know what, must have had its effect on him, because he could hardly get a word out.

" 'Answer me,' I spat out at him.

" 'I apologize,' he stammered. 'I didn't mean to. . . .'

"Perhaps he had caught a glimpse of the gleaming blade, perhaps it was merely the instinct for self-preservation, but at almost that same instant he threw himself on me and grabbed my right arm with his two hands, pressing down hard so as to make me drop the knife. He finally managed to wrench it out of my hand and fling it far away among the weeds. Weeping with rage I ran off and began searching for it, but it was absurd to hope I'd find it in the dark amid that tangle of weeds. I then ran down to the beach, possessed by the idea of swimming far out to sea and drowning myself. Marcos ran after me, perhaps suspecting what I was up to. Suddenly I felt him strike me behind the ear, and I lost consciousness. I found out later that he picked me up and carried me to the Carrascos' house, leaving me on the doorstep and ringing the doorbell until he saw lights go on inside and heard someone coming to answer, at which point he fled. If you think about it, this may strike you at first as a cruel thing for Marcos to have done, since it was certain to cause an uproar. But what else could he have done? If he had stayed there, with me lying there passed out at his feet at twelve o'clock at night when the old ladies thought I was slumbering away, safe and sound, in my bed, can you imagine the fuss there would have been? Everything considered, he did the right thing. In any case you can imagine the scandal I created. When I came to, the two Carrasco sisters, the maid, and the cook were all there hovering over me, with cologne, with fans, and I don't know what-all. They wept and wailed as though confronted with a terrible tragedy. They plied me with questions, they screamed at the top of their lungs, they crossed themselves, they exclaimed 'God have mercy on us,' they gave orders, and so on and so forth.

"It was a disaster.

"And as you can well imagine, I refused to explain one single thing.

"Grandma Elena came out from the city, all upset, and did her best to get me to tell her what was behind the whole affair. I developed a fever that lingered on nearly all summer.

"Toward the end of February I began getting up and around again.

"I had become more or less of a mute and would say nothing to anyone. I refused to go to church, since the very idea of confessing the thoughts that I'd been having horrified me.

"When we went back to Buenos Aires, Aunt Teresa (I don't remember if I've already told you about this hysterical old woman who spent all her time going to wakes and masses and was forever talking about illnesses and treatments)—Aunt Teresa said, the minute she laid eyes on me:

" 'You're the very picture of your father. You'll be a fallen woman. I'm glad you're not my daughter.'

"I left the room boiling with rage at that crazy old woman. But oddly enough, my most violent rage was aimed not at her but at my father, as though those words of my great-aunt's had struck me first, then headed straight for my father and hit him like a boomerang, and then finally come back and hit me.

"I told Grandma Elena I wanted to go back to the boarding school, that I wouldn't sleep even one more night in that house. She promised to have a word with Sister Teodolina so that some way might be found to admit me before the school year started. I don't know what the two of them talked about, but in any event a way was found to take me in at the school then and there. That same night I knelt at my bedside and asked God to make my Aunt Teresa die. I asked this of Him with fierce fervor and repeated it every night for several months when I went to bed, and also during my long hours at prayer in the chapel. Meanwhile, despite all Sister Teodolina's urging, I refused to go to confession: my rather clever idea was to see to it that Auntie died and then go to confession, because (I thought) if I confessed before she died I'd have to admit what I was up to and would be obliged to stop praying for her death.

"But Aunt Teresa didn't kick off. On the contrary, when I came back home during vacations the old lady seemed to be in better shape than ever. I should explain that even though she spent her days complaining and downing pills of every color imaginable, she had an iron constitution. She talked continually of the sick and the dead. She would come into the dining room or the parlor and say triumphantly:

" 'Guess who died!'

"Or, commenting on the person's death with mingled self-pride and irony:

" 'Inflammation of the liver indeed.... When I told them it was cancer! A six-pound tumor, no less.'

"Then she would run to the telephone to pass on the news with that typical fervor of hers when it came to announcing catastrophes. She would dial the number and without wasting a moment's time she would blurt out the news, in telegraphic style so as to reach the maximum number of people in the shortest possible time (so that no one else would spread the word ahead of her). She would say 'Josefina?

Pipo cancer!' and then repeat the same thing to María Rosa, Beba, Nini, María Magdalena, María Santísima. Anyway, as I was saying, when I saw that she continued to be the picture of health despite all my praying, I began to take my hatred out on God. It seemed as though He had tricked me, and feeling Him to be in some way on the side of my Aunt Teresa, that old, ill-natured, hysterical woman, He suddenly assumed in my eyes qualities similar to hers, and my hatred of her caught Him on the rebound, so to speak. All my religious passion seemed suddenly to have changed poles, from positive to negative, though at the same time remaining as strong as ever. Aunt Teresa had said that I was going to be a fallen woman and therefore God thought so too, and He not only thought it but surely wished it to be so. And so I began to plan my vengeance, and as though Marcos Molina were God's representative on earth, I imagined what I would do with him the minute I got back to Miramar. Meanwhile I got a few minor tasks out of the way: I smashed the crucifix over my bed to smithereens, I threw religious prints down the john, and wiped my behind with my communion dress as though it were toilet paper and flung it in the trash can.

"I found out that the Molinas had already left for Miramar and persuaded Grandma Elena to telephone the old Carrasco sisters. I left the day after, arriving about dinner time, and was therefore obliged to go on out to the Carrasco sisters' estate in the car that was waiting for me at the station and didn't have a chance to see Marcos that day.

"I couldn't sleep that night."

The muggy heat is unbearable. The moon, nearly full, is surrounded by a yellowish halo like pus. The air is charged with electricity and not a leaf is stirring: everything presages a storm about to break. Alejandra tosses and turns in her bed, naked and suffocating, tense from the heat, the electricity in the air, and hatred. The moonlight is so bright that everything in the room is visible. Alejandra goes over to the window and looks at her watch to see what time it is: two in the morning. Then she looks outside: the countryside seems to be illuminated like a stage set showing a night scene; the silent, motionless woods seem to harbor great secrets, the air is saturated with an almost unbearable scent of jasmine and magnolias. The dogs are restless; they bark intermittently and their answers back and forth fade into the distance

and then return again, in wave after wave. There is something un-
healthy in that oppressive yellow light, something that seems radio-
active and malevolent. Alejandra is having difficulty breathing and has
the feeling that the room is stifling her. Then on a sudden irresistible
impulse, she climbs out the window. She walks across the lawn and
Milord the dog hears her and wags his tail. She feels the wet contact
of the grass, at once soft and rough, beneath her bare feet. She heads
toward the woods, and when she is far from the house she flings her-
self onto the grass, spread-eagling herself. The moon falls full on her
naked body and she feels her skin quiver where it touches the grass.
She lies there like that for a long time: it is as though she were drunk,
her mind focused on nothing in particular. She feels her body burn
and strokes her hips, her thighs, her belly. As her fingertips barely
brush her breasts she feels as though her skin were cat's fur, bristling
and quivering all over.

"Early the next day I saddled the little mare and galloped to Miramar. I don't know if I've told you that my meetings with Marcos were
always secret ones, because his family couldn't stand me and I felt the
same way about them. His sisters, above all, were two little feather-
brains whose highest aspiration was to marry polo players and appear
as often as possible in *Atlántida* or *El Hogar*. Both Monica and
Patricia detested me and ran and tattled on me the minute they saw
me with their younger brother. So when I wanted to get in touch with
him I would whistle under his window when I thought he might be
home, or else leave a message with Lomónaco, the bath-attendant
down at the beach. Marcos was out when I arrived at his house that
day because he didn't answer my whistles. So I went on down to the
beach and asked Lomónaco if he'd seen him: he told me Marcos had
gone to Dormy House and wouldn't be back till late that afternoon.
For a moment I thought of going in search of him, but I didn't because Lomónaco told me he'd gone off with his sisters and some girls
who were friends of his. There was nothing to do but wait for him,
so I left a message for him to meet me at Piedras Negras at six P.M.

"I went back to the Carrascos' in a foul mood.

"After taking a siesta I set out for Piedras Negras on the mare and
waited for Marcos there."

The storm that had been threatening since the day before had been building up all during the day: the air had turned into a heavy, sticky liquid, enormous clouds had gradually gathered toward the west throughout the morning and like a giant, silently boiling, had blanketed the entire sky during the afternoon. Lying in the shade of the pines, nervous and anxious, Alejandra feels the atmosphere becoming more and more charged by the minute with the electricity that precedes heavy storms.

"Impatient at Marcos's delay, I grew more and more annoyed and irritated as the afternoon wore on. Then he finally turned up as it was getting dark, earlier than usual because of the huge black clouds moving in from the west.

"He arrived almost at a run and I thought: he's afraid of the storm. I still wonder today why I vented all my hatred of God on that unfortunate wretch, when all the poor youngster really deserved was my contempt. I don't know whether it was because he was the sort of stuffy Catholic who had always seemed to me to be typical of that entire breed, or whether it was because he was such a good, decent person that the injustice of treating him badly seemed to me to be all the more heady for that very reason. It may also have been because he had something purely animal about him that attracted me, something strictly physical, of course, but nonetheless it set my blood on fire.

" 'Alejandra,' he said, 'the storm's about to break and I think we'd best get back to Miramar.'

"I turned over onto my side and looked up at him scornfully.

" 'You've just gotten here, you've just set eyes on me for the first time in ages, you haven't even asked why I wanted to see you right away, and already you're thinking about turning tail and running for home,' I said.

"I sat up so as to get undressed.

" 'I've lots of things to talk to you about, but we're going swimming first.'

" 'I've been in the water all day, Alejandra. Besides, look what's coming,' he said, pointing a finger toward the sky.

" 'It doesn't matter. We're going swimming anyway.'

" 'I don't have a swimsuit with me.'

" 'A swimsuit?' I said mockingly. 'I don't have one either.'

"I began to slip off my blue jeans.

"With a firmness I couldn't help but notice, Marcos said:

" 'No, Alejandra, I'm leaving. I don't have a suit and I won't swim naked with you.'

"I had my jeans off now. But I stopped there and said in an innocent tone of voice, as though I didn't understand:

" 'How come? Are you afraid to? What sort of Catholic are you if you have to keep your clothes on so you won't commit a sin? Are you a different person when you're naked?'

"And as I began taking off my panties, I added:

" 'I always thought you were a coward, a typical Catholic coward.'

"I knew that would turn the trick. Marcos, who had averted his eyes the moment I'd started taking off my panties, looked at me then, his face red with embarrassment and rage, and clenching his teeth, he began to undress.

"He'd grown a lot that year, his athlete's body had filled out, his voice was a man's voice now, having lost the ridiculous childish inflections it had still had the year before. He was only seventeen, but very strong and well-developed for his age. I for my part had given up my absurd habit of binding my breasts with the strip of sheet and they had had ample room to fill out; my hips had filled out too and I felt a powerful force in my body impelling me to do extraordinary things.

"Wanting to mortify him, I scrutinized every inch of his body once he was naked.

" 'Well, you aren't the little brat you were last year, are you?'

"He had turned away in embarrassment and was standing almost with his back to me.

" 'You even shave now.'

" 'I don't see anything wrong with shaving,' he snapped angrily.

" 'Nobody said there was anything wrong with it. I merely remarked that I see you shave now.'

"Without answering me, and perhaps so as not to be obliged to look at my naked body and let me see his own nakedness, he ran down to the water, just as a flash of lightning illuminated the entire sky, like an explosion. Then, as though this detonation had been a signal, flashes of lightning and claps of thunder began to follow one upon the other. The leaden gray water had grown darker as the sea became rougher and rougher. The sky, entirely covered with the huge black clouds, was suddenly illuminated again and again, as though by a series of flashbulbs mounted on some immense camera going off.

"The first drops of rain began to fall on my tense, vibrant body. As the waves lashed furiously against the shore, I ran down to the water's edge.

"We swam out to sea. The waves lifted me like a feather in a violent wind and I felt a marvelous sensation of strength—and of fragility at the same time. Marcos never left my side and I had no idea whether it was out of fear for himself or fear for me.

"Finally he shouted to me:

" 'Let's go back, Alejandra! In a minute we won't even be able to tell which way the beach is!'

" 'Always the prudent one, aren't you?' I shouted back at him.

" 'All right then, I'm going back by myself.'

"I didn't answer. But it scarcely mattered, since it was impossible now to hear each other anyway. I began to swim back toward the beach. The clouds were pitch black now and rent with flashes of lightning, and the continuous thunderclaps seemed to have come rolling in from far off so as to burst just above our heads.

"We reached the beach and ran to the place where we had left our clothes, just as the storm finally broke in all its fury: a savage, icy *pampero** swept the strand as the rain began to come down in nearly horizontal torrents.

"It was impressive: alone, in the middle of a deserted beach, naked, feeling on our bodies that rain swept by a furious, violent wind, in that landscape shaken by thunder and illuminated by blinding flashes of lightning.

"Badly frightened, Marcos was trying to struggle back into his clothes. I lunged at him and tore his pants from his body.

"And pressing against him as we stood there, feeling his palpitating, muscular body against my breasts and belly, I began to kiss him, to bite his lips, his ears, to dig my fingernails into his back.

"He resisted me and we fought to the death. Each time he managed to tear his mouth away from mine he stammered unintelligible yet obviously desperate words, till finally I heard him cry:

---

* A strong cold wind from the vast pampas to the Southwest. [*Author's note*]

" 'Let me go, Alejandra, let me go for the love of God! We'll both go to Hell!'

" 'You utter imbecile!' I shouted back. 'There's no such thing as Hell! It's a story made up by priests to take in idiots like you! God doesn't exist!'

"He struggled frantically and finally managed to push me away.

"A flash of lightning suddenly revealed the expression of sacred horror on his face. Staring wide-eyed with terror, as though he were living a nightmare, he shouted:

" 'You're mad, Alejandra! Utterly mad! You're possessed by the devil!'

" 'I don't give a damn about Hell, you imbecile! I laugh at eternal punishment!'

"A terrible energy possessed me; I was overwhelmed at the same time by mingled feelings of cosmic force, hatred, and unutterable sadness. Laughing and weeping, flinging my arms open wide, with adolescent theatricality, I cried out again and again unto the heavens, challenging God to destroy me on the spot with His lightning bolts if He existed."

Alejandra looks at Marcos's naked body as he flees as fast as his legs can carry him, momentarily illuminated by the flashes of lightning, a ridiculous and touching sight; the thought occurs to her that she will never see him again.

The roar of the sea and the storm seem to be bringing down obscure and awesome threats of the Divinity upon her head.

ꙮ I I ꙮ

THEY WENT BACK inside her room. Alejandra made her way over to her little night table with the lamp on it and took two red pills out of a tube. Then she sat down on the edge of the bed, and patting the place beside her with the palm of her left hand she said to Martín:

"Come sit down."

As he did so she downed the two pills, without water. Then she lay down on the bed, with her knees tucked up, close to Martin.

"I must rest for a minute," she explained, closing her eyes.

"Well, I'll be going then," Martín said.

"No, don't go yet," she murmured, as though she were about to drop off to sleep. "We'll talk some more later . . . in a minute . . ."

And she began to breathe deeply, already asleep.

She had let her shoes fall to the floor and her bare feet were tucked up next to Martín. He was puzzled by the story Alejandra had told out on the terrace, and his mind was still in a whirl: everything was absurd, everything followed some plot that made no sense to him, and no matter what he did or didn't do seemed all wrong.

What was he doing here? He felt stupid and clumsy, but for some reason that he could not contrive to understand, it would appear that she needed him. Hadn't she come looking for him? Hadn't she told him of her experiences with Marcos Molina? She had never told anyone else about them, he was certain of that, not a soul, a thought that made him feel both proud and perplexed. And she hadn't wanted him to leave and had allowed herself to fall asleep at his side, that supreme gesture of trust that going to sleep at someone else's side represents: like a warrior who has laid down his arms. There she was, defenseless yet mysterious and inaccessible. So close, yet separated from him by the weightless though dark and impenetrable wall of sleep.

Martín looked at her. She was lying on her back, breathing anxiously through her half-open mouth, her large, scornful, sensual mouth. Her long straight blue-black hair (with those reddish glints that indicated that this Alejandra was the same little red-headed girl she had been in her childhood, yet at the same time something so different, so different!) fanning out over the pillow set off her angular face, those features of hers that had the same clean, sharp edge, the same hardness as her spirit. He trembled, full of confused ideas that had never before crossed his mind. The lamp on the night table illuminated her relaxed body, her breasts clearly outlined beneath her clinging white blouse, and those long, beautiful, tucked-up legs that were touching him. He reached one of his hands out toward her, but before he could bring himself to place it on her body, he drew it back in fright. Then, after great hesitation, his hand went out toward her again and finally came to rest on her thigh. He allowed it to linger there for a long time, his heart pounding, as though he were committing a shameful theft, as though he were taking advantage of a warrior's rest to steal a little souvenir. But then she turned over and he withdrew his hand. She drew her legs up again, raising her knees and curling up in a ball as though returning to the fetal position.

The deep silence was broken only by Alejandra's restless breathing and a far-off ship's siren sounding somewhere down at the docks.

I'll never know her completely, he said to himself, as though the thought were a sudden, painful revelation.

She was there, within reach of his hand and his mouth. In a certain sense she was defenseless, yet how far away, how inaccessible she was! He sensed that vast abysses separated her from him (not only the abyss of sleep but others) and that in order to reach the center of her he would be forced to endure fearful trials, to make his way for many long days amid dark crevasses, through defiles fraught with peril, along the brink of erupting volcanoes, amid blinding flames and deep shadows. *Never*, he thought, *never*.

But she needs me, she's chosen me, he also thought. In some way or other she had sought him out and chosen him, for some purpose that as yet he failed to understand. And she had told him things that he was certain she had never told anyone else, and he had the presentiment that she would tell him many others, more terrible and more beautiful still than those that she had already confessed to him. But he also felt that there would be others that never, absolutely never, would be revealed to him. And weren't these mysterious, disquieting shadows the truest ones, the only really important ones? She had shuddered when he had mentioned the blind—why? The moment she had uttered the name Fernando she had regretted doing so—why?

The blind, he thought, almost fearfully. *The blind, the blind.*

Night, childhood, shadows, shadows, terror and blood, blood, flesh and blood, dreams, abysses, unfathomable abysses, loneliness, loneliness, loneliness, we touch yet remain immeasurable distances apart, we touch yet we are alone. He was a child, beneath an immense dome, in the center of the dome, amid a terrifying silence, alone in that immense, gigantic universe.

And all at once he heard Alejandra stir, raising up and seemingly pushing something away from her with her hands. From her lips came unintelligible, violent, panting murmurs, until, as though forced to make a superhuman effort to get a single word out, she shouted "No, no!" and sat up all of a sudden.

"Alejandra!" Martín cried out to her, shaking her by the shoulders, trying to wrench her away from that nightmare.

But eyes wide open, she continued to groan, violently fighting off her enemy.

"Alejandra! Alejandra!" Martín called out again, shaking her by the shoulders.

Finally she seemed to rouse herself from her sleep as though climbing out of a very deep well, a dark well full of spider webs and bats.

"Ah," she murmured in an exhausted voice.

She sat there in the bed for a long time, her head resting on her knees and her hands crossed over her drawn-up legs.

Then she climbed out of the bed, turned on the overhead light, lit a cigarette, and began to make coffee.

"I woke you because I realized you were having a nightmare," Martín said, looking at her anxiously.

"I always have nightmares when I sleep," she replied without turning round as she put the coffeepot on the alcohol burner.

When the coffee was ready she handed him a cupful, sat down on the edge of the bed, and drank hers, lost in thought.

Martín thought: *Fernando. The blind.*

"Except Fernando and me," she had said. And although he knew Alejandra well enough to know he shouldn't ask any questions about that name that she had immediately retreated from, an insane impulse kept taking him back again and again to that forbidden region, drawing him closer and closer to its perilous edge.

"And is your grandfather also a Unitarist?"

"I beg your pardon?" she said, her mind elsewhere.

"I asked if your grandfather is also a Unitarist."

Alejandra turned her eyes toward him, looking somewhat taken aback.

"My grandfather? My grandfather's dead."

"What's that? I thought you told me he was still alive."

"No, no! My grandfather Patricio is dead. The one who's still alive is my great-grandfather, Pancho—didn't I explain all that to you?"

"Well, yes, I meant to say your great-grandfather Pancho—is he a Unitarist too? It's amusing to me to think that there can still be Unitarists and Federalists here in this country."

"You don't realize that we lived all that here. In fact, just imagine:

Grandpa Pancho is still living it—he was born just after Rosas's down-fall. He's ninety-five years old—didn't I tell you that?"

"Ninety-five?"

"He was born in 1858. The rest of us can just talk about Unitarists and Federalists, but he lived all that, do you see what I mean? Rosas was still alive when he was a little boy."

"And does he remember things from those days?"

"He's got a memory like an elephant. And what's more he talks of nothing else, all day long, whenever he gets you within range. That's only natural: it's his only reality. All the rest doesn't even exist."

"I'd like to hear him some day."

"I'll show him to you right now."

"What! You can't mean it! It's three in the morning!"

"Don't be silly. You don't understand that for grandpa there's no such thing as three in the morning. He hardly ever sleeps. Or maybe he takes a little snooze at any and all hours of the day or night, for all I know. . . . But it's at night that he has the most trouble sleeping, and he spends all his time with the lamp lit, thinking."

"Thinking?"

"Well, who knows? . . . What can you know about what's going on in the head of an old man who's lying awake not able to sleep, an old man who's almost a hundred years old? Maybe all he does is re-member—how should I know? . . . They say that at that age all you do is remember . . ."

And then she added, with her dry laugh:

"I'm going to be very careful not to live that long."

And heading toward the door of the room quite naturally, as though it were simply a question of a normal visit to normal people at a sensible hour, she said:

"Come on, I'll show him to you now. Who knows—he may die tomorrow."

She halted.

"Get your eyes accustomed to the dark a little and you can see your way down better."

They leaned on the balustrade of the terrace for a time, looking at the sleeping city.

"Look at that light in the window in that little house," Alejandra commented, pointing with her hand. "Lights like that in the night always overawe me: can it be a woman who's about to give birth to a baby? Somebody who's dying? Or maybe a poor student reading Marx? How mysterious the world is! It's only superficial people who don't see that. You chat with the watchman on the corner, you make him feel confident, and in a little while you discover that he too is a mystery."

After a moment she said:

"Well then, let's be off."

∾ 12 ∾

THEY WENT downstairs and around the house along the gallery on the side until they reached a back door, under an arbor. Alejandra felt around with her hand and turned on a light. Martín saw an old kitchen that had all sorts of things piled up in it, as though it were moving day. This impression grew stronger as they went down a hallway. The thought occurred to him that in the successive divisions of this big old house no one had wanted to or known how to get rid of things: furniture with rickety legs, gilded armchairs without seats, a huge mirror leaning against a wall, a grandfather clock that had stopped running and had only one hand, console tables. As they entered the old man's room, Martín was reminded of one of the auction houses in the Calle Maipú. One of the former parlors had become part of the old man's bedroom, as though the rooms of the house had been shuffled together like a deck of cards. In the feeble light of a kerosene lantern, he saw an old man dozing in a wheelchair amid a jumble of furniture. The chair was placed in front of a window that looked out onto the street, as though to allow the grandfather to contemplate the world.

"He's asleep," Martín murmured in relief. "You'd best leave him be."

"I've already told you—you never know if he's really sleeping or not."

She went over to the old man, leaned over him, and shook him a little.

"What, what?" the grandfather muttered, half opening his little eyes.

They were little green eyes, crisscrossed with red and black streaks, as though they were cracked, buried deep in their sockets, surrounded by the parchmentlike folds of a mummified, immortal face.

"Were you asleep, grandfather?" Alejandra shouted in his ear.

"What, what? Asleep, you say? No, my girl, I was just resting."

"This is a friend of mine."

The old man nodded his head with a sudden decelerating motion, like a weighted doll set to bobbing. He offered Martín a bony hand in which huge veins seemed to be trying to work their way out of skin as dry and transparent as the head of an old drum.

"Grandfather," she shouted at him. "Tell him about Lieutenant Patrick."

The weighted doll moved again.

"Ah, yes," he muttered. "Patrick, that's right, Patrick."

"Don't worry, it's all the same story," Alejandra said to Martín. "It's the same every time, no matter what it is. He always ends up talking about the Legion, until he forgets and falls asleep."

"Ah, yes, Lieutenant Patrick, that's right."

His little eyes grew teary.

"Elmtrees, son, Elmtrees. Lieutenant Patrick Elmtrees, of the famous 71st. Who would ever have thought he'd die in the Legion?"

Martín looked at Alejandra.

"Explain to him, grandfather, explain to him," she shouted.

The old man cupped his enormous gnarled hand around his ear, leaning his head toward Alejandra. Underneath the mask of cracked parchment well on its way to death, what remained of a pensive, kindly human being seemed to be just barely surviving. The lower jaw hung down slightly, as though it no longer were strong enough to stay shut, revealing toothless gums.

"That's right, Patrick."

"Explain to him, grandfather."

He lost himself in thought, looking back toward far-distant times.

"Olmos is the Spanish for Elmtrees. Because grandfather got tired of being called Elemetri, Elemetrio, Lemetrio, and even Captain Demetrio."

He gave a sort of tremulous laugh, raising his hand to his mouth.

"That's right, even Captain Demetrio. He was sick and tired of it. And he had taken on so many of the ways of the country that he didn't like it when they called him the Englishman. And so he upped and changed his name to Olmos. The way the Islands took the name Isla and the Queenfaiths Reinafé. It rubbed him the wrong way—*a sort of little laugh*—. He was a man who got his dander up very easily, so that was a smart move, a very smart move, yessiree. And what's more, this was his real country. He'd taken himself a wife here and his children were born here. And seeing him sitting on his South American horse with his silver-studded riding gear, not a soul would have suspected he was a foreigner. And even if anyone had suspected—*again a little laugh*— he wouldn't have opened his trap because Don Patricio would have brought him low with one lash of his whip the minute the words were out—*little laugh*—Yessiree, Lieutenant Patrick Elmtrees. Who would ever have thought it? No, fate, is more complicated than a Turkish business deal. Who would ever have thought that his fate would be to die for the general?"

He suddenly appeared to be dozing, his breath wheezing slightly.

"General? What general?" Martín asked Alejandra.

"Lavalle."

Martín didn't understand at all: an English lieutenant serving under Lavalle? "When?"

"In the civil war, stupid."*

One hundred seventy-five men, ragged and desperate, pursued by Oribe's lancers, fleeing toward the north through the great valley, ever northward. Second Lieutenant Celedonio Olmos rode along thinking of his brother Panchito Olmos, dead in Quebracho Herrado. And with a growth of beard, miserable, ragged, and desperate, Colonel Bonifacio Acevedo too rode toward the north. And another hundred seventy-two

---

* Between 1806 and 1807, the English, then at war with Spain, twice invaded the Río de la Plata in order to take over these Spanish colonies. Among the English troops was the famous 71st, which had covered itself with glory in many battles. The Creoles successfully resisted both invasions; these victories made them aware of their strength and led them to take up arms against their Spanish oppressor. Many English officers found the country delightful and settled permanently in Argentina. They became so thoroughly integrated into the mainstream of Argentine life that they later took part in the country's civil wars. [*Author's note*]

now-unrecognizable men. And one woman. Fleeing night and day toward the north, toward the border.

The lower jaw hung down, quivering: "Uncle Panchito and grandfather, run through with lances in Quebracho Herrado," he murmured, as though in assent.

"I don't understand anything of all this," Martín said.

"On June 27, 1806," Alejandra told him, "the English were advancing through the streets of Buenos Aires. When I was this big—*she put her hand down near the floor*—grandfather told me the story a hundred and seventy-five times. The 9th Company brought up in the rear of the famous 71st." ("Why famous?") "I don't know, but that's what they always said. I think it had never been defeated, anywhere in the world. The 9th Company was advancing down the Calle de la Universidad." ("Calle de la Universidad?") "Of course, silly, the Calle Bolívar. I'm telling it to you the way grandfather does; I know it by heart. When they arrived at the corner of Nuestra Señora del Rosario, Venezuela for those who are backward, it happened." ("What happened?") "Keep your shirt on and I'll tell you. They threw everything. From the roof-terraces, I mean: boiling oil, plates, bottles, pots, even furniture. They also shot bullets. They were all shooting: women, blacks, kids. And that was how he got wounded." ("Who?") "Lieutenant Patrick. On that corner was the house of Bonifacio Acevedo, grandfather's grandfather, the brother of the man who was later General Cosme Acevedo." ("The one the street is named after?") "Yes, the one with the street named after him: that's all we have left, street names. This Bonifacio Acevedo married Trinidad Arias, from Salta," she went over to a wall and brought back a miniature, and in the light of the kerosene lantern, as the old man seemed to assent to something that had happened long ago and far away, with his jaw hanging down and his eyes closed, Martín saw the face of a pretty woman whose Mongolian features seemed to be the secret echo of Alejandra's, an echo amid conversations between Englishmen and Spaniards. "And this woman had a whole bunch of kids, among them María de los Dolores and Bonifacio, who later was to be Colonel Bonifacio Acevedo, the man with the head."

But Martín thought (and said) that he understood less and less as the story went on. What did Lieutenant Patrick have to do with this whole confused tale, and how had he died serving Lavalle?

"Wait, dummy, here comes the way it all fits together. Didn't you hear grandfather say that life is more complicated than a Turkish business deal? Fate this time took the form of a ferocious big black, one of my great-great-grandfather's slaves, a black named Benito. Because Fate doesn't manifest itself in the abstract—sometimes it's a slave's knife and other times it's the smile of an unmarried girl. Fate chooses its instruments, then it incarnates itself, and then the shit hits the fan. In this case it incarnated itself in Benito the black, who struck the lieutenant such an unlucky blow (from the point of view of the black) with a knife that Elmtrees was able to turn into Olmos and I was able to be born. My life, as they say, hung from just a thin thread and the situation was a very delicate one, because if the black hadn't heard María de los Dolores's shouts from the rooftop terrace, ordering him not to do the lieutenant in, the black would have liquidated him in due and proper form, as was his desire, but not that of Fate, because even though it had incarnated itself in Benito it didn't think exactly the way he did, it had its little differences with him. That's something that happens very often, because naturally Fate can't choose the exact means suited to the people who are going to serve it as an instrument. Just as when you're in a hurry to get to a certain place, when it's a matter of life or death, you aren't going to notice if the car has green upholstery or the horse has a tail you don't particularly like. That's why Fate is something that's confused and a little ambiguous: it knows very well what it really wants, but the people who are its agents don't know quite so much. Like those half-witted subalterns who never execute perfectly the orders given them. So Fate is obliged to act like President Sarmiento: doing things, even though they turn out badly, but nonetheless doing them. And lots of times it has to get its agents drunk or drive them out of their wits. And that's why people say that someone was as though he were beside himself, that he didn't know what he was doing, that he lost control. Naturally. Otherwise, instead of killing Desdemona or Caesar, heaven only knows what sort of silly clown act the person would pull. So, as I was explaining to you, at the moment that Benito was about to decree that I would never exist, María de los Dolores gave such a loud shout from up above on the terrace that the black stayed his hand. María de los Dolores. She was fourteen years old. She was pouring down boiling oil, but she shouted in time."

"I don't understand this part either; wasn't it necessary to keep the English from winning?"

"You're really mentally retarded: haven't you ever head of a *coup de foudre*? That was precisely what happened, amid all the chaos. So you can see how Fate works. Benito the black obeyed his mistress's orders reluctantly, but he dragged the young officer inside, as ordered by the grandmother of my great-grandfather Pancho. And then the women in the house gave him first aid while they waited for Dr. Argerich to come. They took off his uniform jacket. 'But he's just a child!' Mistress Trinidad said in horror. 'He can't be a day over seventeen!' she said. 'How dreadful,' they lamented as they washed him with clean water and cane alcohol and bandaged him with strips of sheets. Then they put him to bed. During the night he was delirious and kept saying words in English, as María de los Dolores, praying and weeping, changed his vinegar compresses. Because, as grandfather told me, the girl had fallen in love with the young foreigner and had already made up her mind to marry him. And you should know, grandfather said to me, that when a woman gets an idea like that in her head there's no power on earth or in heaven that can stop her. So while the poor lieutenant was delirious and no doubt dreaming of his country, María de los Dolores had decided that that country had ceased to exist, and that Patrick's descendants would be born in Argentina. Afterwards, when his mind became clearer, it turned out that he was none other than the nephew of General Beresford himself. And you can imagine the scene when Beresford came to the house and the moment when he kissed Mistress Trinidad's hand."

"One hundred seventy-five men," the old man mumbled, nodding.

"And what's that?"

"The Legion. He keeps thinking about the same things all the time: either his childhood or the Legion. I'll go on with the story. Beresford thanked them for what they'd done for the boy and it was decided that he would stay there in the house till he'd recovered completely. And so, as the English forces occupied Buenos Aires, Patrick came to be a friend of the family, which wasn't all that easy when you think of it, since everyone, including my family, hated the occupation. But the worst part began with the reconquest: there were great scenes with weeping and all the rest. Patrick naturally rejoined his army unit again and was obliged to fight against us. And when the English were forced to surrender, Patrick felt both great happiness and great sadness. Many of those who had been defeated asked to stay here and were interned. Patrick, of course, wanted to stay and they interned him at La Horqueta ranch, one of my family's estates, near Pergamino. That was in 1807. A year later he and María de los Dolores were married and lived happily ever after. Don Bonifacio gave him part of the family holdings as a present, and Patricio began the task of converting himself into Elemetri, Elemetrio, Don Demetrio, Lieutenant Demetrio, and then suddenly Olmos. And it was a thrashing for anyone who called him English or Demetrio."

"It would have been better if they'd killed him in Quebracho Herrado," the old man murmured.

Martín looked at Alejandra again.

"He means Colonel Acevedo, do you understand? If they'd killed him in Quebracho Herrado they wouldn't have beheaded him here, at the very moment that he was hoping to see his wife and daughter again."

"It would have been better if they'd killed me in Quebracho Herrado," Colonel Bonifacio Acevedo thinks as he flees northward, but for another reason, for reasons he thinks are horrible (the desperate march, the despair, the misery, the total defeat), though they are infinitely less horrible than those he was to have twelve years later, at the moment he felt the knife at his throat, there in front of his house.

Martín saw Alejandra go over to the glass case, and cried out in terror. But saying "don't be such a sissy," she took out the box, took the cover off, and showed him the colonel's head, as Martín hid his eyes. She laughed harshly and put it away again.

"In Quebracho Herrado," the old man murmured, nodding.

"So," Alejandra explained, "once again I owed my birth to a miracle."

Because if they had killed Second Lieutenant Celedonio Olmos in Quebracho Herrado, as they had killed his brother and his father, or if they had beheaded him in front of the house, as they had Colonel

Acevedo, she would not have been born, and at this moment she would not be there in that room, remembering that past. And shouting in her grandfather's ear, "tell him about the head," and announcing to Martín that she had to leave and disappearing before he could even try to follow her (perhaps because he felt utterly confused), she left him alone with the old man, who kept repeating "the head, that's right, the head," bobbing like a weighted doll. Then his lower jaw moved and hung there quivering for a few moments, as his lips mumbled something unintelligible (perhaps he was making a mental resumé, like children about to be called on to recite their lesson) and finally he said: "The Mazorca, that's right, they threw the head right inside the house, through the parlor window. They dismounted with great bursts of laughter and joyous shouts, they came over to the window and yelled 'watermelons, ma'am, nice fresh watermelons!' And then they opened the window and threw in Uncle Bonifacio's bloody head. It would have been better if they'd killed him in Quebracho Herrado too, the way they killed Panchito and grandfather Patricio, I do believe that." *Something that Colonel Acevedo also thought as he fled northward through the Humahuaca Valley, with one hundred seventy-four comrades (and one woman), pursued by the enemy, in tatters, defeated and overcome with sadness, not knowing that he was to live twelve long years more, in distant lands, waiting for the moment when he would see his wife and daughter again.*

"They shouted 'nice fresh watermelons!' and it was the head, young man. And poor Encarnación fell into a dead faint when she saw it, and in fact never came to and died a few hours later. And poor Escolástica, who was a little eleven-year-old girl, went clean out of her mind. That's right."

And nodding his head, he began to doze off, as Martín stood there paralyzed by a strange silent terror, in the middle of that nearly dark room, with that old man a hundred years old, with the head of Colonel Acevedo in the box, with the madman who might very well be prowling round about. The best thing to do is to leave, he thought. But the fear of meeting up with the madman paralyzed him. And then he told himself that it would be better to wait for Alejandra to come back, that she wouldn't be long, that she couldn't be long, since she knew that there was nothing he could do with that old man. He felt as though he had gradually entered a strangely calm nightmare in which everything was unreal and absurd. From the walls the gentleman painted by Prilidiano Pueyrredón and the lady with the big curved comb in her hair seemed to be watching him. The souls of warriors, of conquistadors, of madmen, of municipal councilors and priests seemed to fill the room with their invisible presence and murmur quietly among themselves: stories of conquest, battles, attacks with lances and beheadings.

"One hundred seventy-five men."

Martín looked at the old man: his lower jaw nodded, hanging down, quivering.

"One hundred seventy-five men, yessiree."

And one woman. But the old man does not know this, or does not want to know it. This is all that is left of the proud Legion, after eight hundred leagues of retreat and defeat, of two years of disillusionment and death. A column of one hundred seventy-five mute, miserable men (and one woman) galloping northward, ever northward. Will they never reach the border? Does Bolivia exist, there beyond this endless valley? The October sun beats down and rots the general's body. The cold of night freezes the pus, arrests the army of worms. And then it is daylight again, with the rear guard firing at their pursuers, with the threat of Oribe's lancers.

The smell, the frightful smell, of the general's rotten body.

The voice, singing now in the silence of the night:

> *Palomita blanca*
> *que cruzas el valle,*
> *vé a decir a todos,*
> *que ha muerto Lavalle.**

"Hornos abandoned them, confound him. He said 'I'm going to join Paz's army.' And he left them, and Major Ocampo did too. Confound him. And Lavalle saw them going off with their men, toward the east,

---

* White dove
   crossing the vale
   go tell one and all
   that death has come to Lavalle.

in a cloud of dust. And my father said the general seemed to have tears in his eyes as he watched the two squadrons going off. He had one hundred seventy-five men left."

The old man sat there pensively, still nodding his head.

"The blacks were fond of Hornos, very fond of him. And papa finally ended up receiving him. He came here to the *quinta* and they drank maté* together, and shared memories of what had happened during the campaign."

His head nodded, his jaw fell, and he murmured something about Major Hornos and Colonel Pedernera. Then he suddenly said no more. Was he perhaps sleeping? Perhaps there flowed through him that silent, latent life, close to eternity, that flows through lizards during the long winter months.

Pedernera thinks: twenty-five years of campaigns, of battles, of victories and defeats. But in those days we knew why we were fighting. We were fighting for the freedom of the continent, for the Great Fatherland. But now.... So much blood has been shed on American soil, we have seen so many desperate afternoons, we have heard so many battle cries between brothers.... And now Oribe is at our heels, ready to behead us, to run us through with lances, to exterminate us— didn't he fight with me in the Army of the Andes? Brave, tough General Oribe. Where is truth? How marvelous those days were! How dashing Lavalle was in his uniform of a major of grenadiers when we entered Lima! Everything was clearer then, everything was beautiful, like the uniform we wore ...

"I'm certain of one thing, young feller: there were many fights in our family because of Rosas, and the separation of the two branches, especially in the family of Juan Batista Acevedo, goes back to those days."

He coughed, appeared to be about to fall asleep, but suddenly spoke up again:

"Because people may say anything they like about Lavalle, son, but

---

* Maté is a typical Argentine infusion, drunk through a metal tube. [*Author's note*]

no man of good faith can deny his integrity, his honesty, his gentlemanliness, his unselfishness. Yessiree."

I have fought in one hundred five battles for the freedom of this continent. I fought in the fields of Chile under the command of General San Martín. I then fought against the imperial forces in Brazilian territory. And then later, in those two years of misfortune, through the length and breadth of our poor country. I may have committed great errors, the greatest of them all the execution of Dorrego by firing squad. But who is master of the truth? I know nothing, except that this cruel land is my land and that it was here that I was obliged to fight and die. My body is rotting on my cavalry charger, but that is all I know.

"Yessiree," the old man said, coughing and clearing his throat, as though lost in thought, with his teary eyes, repeating "yessiree" several times, moving his head as though nodding at an invisible conversational partner.

Lost in thought, with teary eyes. Looking toward reality, toward the only reality.

A reality organized in accordance with very strange laws.

"It was around '32, the way my father told it, yes, '32, that's right. Because I can tell you one thing for sure: the business of improving cattle had its pros and its cons. It was Miller the Englishman who began. The gringo Miller, an excellent sort. A hard worker and thrifty like all Scots, it's true. A tightwad, to put it more clearly (*a little laugh and repeated coughs*). Not like those of us who were born here in this country, who are too open-handed, and that's why we're where we are (*coughs*). Don Juan Miller had married Dolores Balbastro. A lady with lots of spunk—there was many a time that she took charge of the defense of the ranch against Indian bands, and she handled a rifle like a man. Like grandma, who was also mighty handy with firearms. They were tough women, my boy, and of course it was the hard life they had to lead that made them so, more or less. What was I talking about?"

"About Miller the Englishman."

"About Miller the Englishman, that's right. Everybody was talking about him and the famous Tarquino."

He began laughing again and coughing, and daubed clumsily at his teary eyes with a handkerchief.

"What was I talking to you about?"

"About pedigreed bulls, sir."

"Ah, yes, bulls."

He coughed and nodded his head for a moment. Then he said:

"Evaristo's family never forgave us. Never. Not even when the Mazorca beheaded my uncle. There's no getting around it, our family was divided on account of the tyrant Rosas. I could tell you about a thousand things that happened around that time, in '40 especially, when they beheaded a young man named Iranzuaga, the fiancé of one Isabelita Ortiz, who was a relative of ours on one side of her family. Nobody had a peaceful night's sleep in those days. And you can imagine all the worries in my parents' house, what with my mother being all alone after papa joined the Legion. And my grandfather, Don Patricio, had gone off too—did I tell you the story of Don Patricio?—and my great-uncle Bonifacio and Uncle Panchito. So the only one left on the *estancia** was Uncle Saturnino, who was the youngest one, just a lad. And all the rest were women. Every last one of them women."

He wiped his teary eyes with the handkerchief again, coughed, nodded his head, and seemed to drop off to sleep. But suddenly he said:

"Sixty leagues. And with Oribe's men close on their heels. And my father said the October sun was terribly hot. The general was rotting very fast, and nobody could stand the smell after two days' gallop. And they still had forty leagues to go before they reached the border. Five days and forty leagues more. Just to save Lavalle's bones and his head. For that one reason, son. Because they were doomed and there was nothing else left to do: no war against Rosas, nothing. They would cut the head off the corpse and send it to Rosas on the tip of a lance, in order to dishonor him. With a placard that said: 'This is the head of the savage, of the filthy, of the loathsome Unitarist dog Lavalle.' So they had to save the general's body at all costs, by crossing the

---

* *Estancia*: A large rural estate owned by the dominant old-line families of the Argentine oligarchy. [*Author's note*]

border into Bolivia, shooting their way out as they fled for seven days. Sixty leagues of frantic retreat, almost without stopping to rest."

I am Major Alejandro Danel, son of Major Danel, of the Napoleonic Army. I can still remember when he returned with the Grande Armée, in the garden of the Tuileries or on the Champs-Elysées, on horseback. I can still see him followed by his escort of Mamelukes, with their legendary curved sabers. And later, when France was finally no longer the land of Liberty and I dreamed of fighting for oppressed peoples, I embarked for these territories, along with Bruiz, Viel, Bardel, Brandsen, and Rauch, who had fought at Napoleon's side. Heaven preserve us—how much time has gone by, how many battles, how many victories and defeats, how many deaths, and how much bloodshed! That afternoon in 1825 when I met Lavalle and he seemed to me to be an imperial eagle, at the head of his regiment of cuirassiers. And then I marched off with him to the Brazilian war, and when he fell at Yerbal I picked him up and with my men brought him through eighty leagues of rivers and mountains, pursued by the enemy, as we are now ... and I never once left his side.... And now, after eight hundred leagues of sadness, I am marching alongside his rotted body, toward nothingness....

He seemed to wake up again and said:

"Some things I've seen myself, others I heard from papa, but above all from mama, because papa was a quiet man and seldom said much. So that when General Hornos or Colonel Ocampo came to drink maté and reminisce about the old days and the Legion, papa would just listen and say from time to time: 'That's something, isn't it?' or 'That's the way things are, old friend.'"

He nodded again and dozed off for a moment, but very soon awakened again and said:

"Some day I'll tell you the curious story of my grandfather, whose name wasn't Olmos but Elmtrees, who arrived in this country as a lieutenant in the English army at the time of the invasions. It's a curious story, believe me" (*laughing and coughing*).

He nodded and suddenly began to snore.

Martín looked toward the door again, but there was not a sound to be heard. Where was Alejandra? What was she doing in her room?

The thought also came to him that if he hadn't left already it was so as not to leave the old man alone, though the latter couldn't even hear him and perhaps didn't even see him: the old man was merely going on with his mysterious subterranean existence, paying no attention to him or to anyone living at present, isolated as he was by the years, by deafness and bad eyesight, but above all by the memory of the past that interposed itself like a dark wall of dreams, living in the bottom of a well, remembering blacks, cavalcades, beheadings, and happenings in the Legion. No, that wasn't true: he hadn't stayed out of consideration for the old man, but rather because he was as though paralyzed by a sort of terror at traversing those regions of reality in which the grandfather, the madman, and even Alejandra herself seemed to live. A mysterious, mad territory, as absurd and tenuous as dreams, as frightening as dreams. Nonetheless he got up from the chair to which he seemed to have been nailed and with cautious footsteps began to move away from the old man, amid the jumble of furniture mindful of an auction house, with the watchful eyes of the ancestors on the walls staring down at him, his own eyes never leaving the box in the glass case. He finally managed to make his way over to the door and stood there in front of it, not daring to open it. He moved closer and put his ear to the crack: he had the impression that the madman was on the other side, waiting, clarinet in hand, for him to come out. He thought he could even hear him breathing. Then in terror he slowly made his way back to his chair and sat down again.

"Just thirty-five leagues more," the old man suddenly muttered.

Yes, there are thirty-five leagues left to go. Three days' journey at full gallop through the great valley, with the swollen corpse that stinks for yards around, distilling the horrible liquids of putrefaction. On and on, with a few sharpshooters in the rear guard. From Jujuy to Huacalera, twenty-four leagues. Only thirty-five leagues more, they say, so as to keep up their courage. Only four, perhaps five days' journey more, if they are lucky.

In the silent night the hoofbeats of the phantom cavalry can be heard. Heading ever northward.

"Because in the valley the sun beats down, young feller, because this is very high country and the air is very pure. So that after two days' journey the body had swelled up and you could smell the stink for yards around, my father said, and on the third day they had to strip the flesh off it, that's what."

Colonel Pedernera orders them to halt and confers with his comrades: the body is decomposing, the stench is frightful. They will strip the flesh off it and keep the bones. And the heart too, someone says. But above all the head: Oribe will never have the head, he will never be able to dishonor the general.

Who is willing to do the deed? Who is able to do it?

Colonel Alejandro Danel will do it.

They then take the general's stinking body down from the horse. They place it on the bank of the Huacalera River, as the Colonel kneels alongside it and takes out his field knife. He contemplates the naked, deformed body of his leader through his tears. The battle-hardened men standing about in a circle also look at it, stolid and pensive, their eyes too dimmed by tears.

Then he slowly sinks the knife into the rotten flesh.

He nodded his head and said:

"Later on he was mayor, until the Federalists came to power. What was I talking to you about?"

"About his leaving the mayoralty, sir." (Who?)

"That's right, the mayoralty. He left it when the Federalists came to power, that's right. And he used to say to whoever would listen to him, perhaps so that his words would reach Don Juan Manuel, that what with cows and Indians he had more than enough trouble on his hands and didn't have time for politics (*a little laugh*). But the Restorer, who was no dummy—nosiree!—never believed that (*little laughs*). He wasn't fooled for a minute, because my grandfather found out that Don Juan Manuel was sending letters to the mayor of La Horqueta telling him not to take his eyes off the Englishman Olmos (*laughs and coughs*) because he'd had word that he was conspiring with other landowners of Salto and Pergamino. That crafty devil wasn't taken in one bit, how could he have been, a lynx like him! Because grandfather had in fact been going around palavering with the others, as everybody could plainly see when General Lavalle disembarked in San Pedro, in August of '40. Grandfather presented himself there with his cavalry and his two oldest sons: Celedonio, my father, who was eighteen then, and Uncle Panchito, who was a year older.

A disastrous campaign, that one in 'forty! Grandfather held out in Quebracho Herrado till they were down to the last cannon ball, covering Lavalle's retreat. He could have saved his skin and gotten out, but he didn't. And when all was lost, he shot the very last cannon ball he had left and surrendered to Oribe's troops. When he was told of the death of Panchito, the son he loved the best, all he said was: 'At least the general was saved.' And that was how my grandfather Don Patricio Olmos ended his life in this country."

The old man nodded, murmuring "Armistron, that's right, Armistron," and then suddenly fell into a deep sleep.

༄ I 3 ༄

MARTIN WAITED, time went by, and the old man did not wake up. He thought he'd really fallen asleep now, and so, little by little, trying not to make noise, he got up and began walking toward the door that Alejandra had left by. He was terrified, because dawn had broken already and the first light of day was already illuminating Don Pancho's room. He thought that he might run into Uncle Bebe, or that old Justina, the servant, might be up. And if so, what would he say to them?

"I came last night with Alejandra," he would tell them.

Then the thought occurred to him that in this house nothing could possibly attract people's attention, and that therefore he had no reason to fear that there would be some unpleasant scene. Except, perhaps, if he bumped into the madman, Uncle Bebe.

He heard, or thought he heard, a creaking noise, the sound of footsteps, in the hallway outside the door. With his hand on the doorknob and his heart pounding, he waited in silence. A train whistled far off in the distance. He put his ear to the door and listened anxiously: there wasn't a sound. He was about to open the door when again he heard a faint creaking noise, unmistakable this time: footsteps, cautious ones with pauses in between them, as though someone were slowly creeping closer and closer to that same door on the other side of it.

"The madman," Martín thought in a panic, and for a moment he withdrew his ear from the door, fearing that it might suddenly be jerked open from the other side and he'd be discovered in that compromising position.

He stood there a long time, unable to make up his mind what to do: on the one hand he was afraid to open the door since he might then find himself face to face with the madman; on the other hand, as he looked back across the room to where Don Pancho was sleeping, he feared the old man would wake up and seek him out.

But then he thought that perhaps it would be best if the old man were to wake up, because then if the madman came into the room the old man could explain. Or perhaps one didn't have to give the madman any sort of explanation.

He remembered that Alejandra had told him that he was a peaceable madman, who did nothing but play the clarinet: eternally repeating, rather, a sort of tootle. But did they let him wander about loose in the house? Or was he shut up in one of the rooms, the way Escolástica had been, this being the custom in these old family mansions?

He spent some time absorbed in these thoughts, still listening.

As he heard nothing more, he put his ear to the door again, calmer this time, listening intently so as to make out the slightest sound or the slightest suspicious creaking noise: but he couldn't hear a thing now.

He began to turn the doorknob very slowly: it was just above one of those huge old-fashioned locks with keys a good half a foot long. The doorknob seemed to make a terrible noise as it turned. And the thought came to him that if the madman were anywhere about he couldn't help but hear it and be on his guard. But what else was there to do at this point? Since opening the door was now practically a *fait accompli,* he screwed up his courage and flung it wide open.

He very nearly screamed.

Standing there, hieratically, in front of him was the madman: a man past forty, with a beard many days old and disheveled hair, dressed in threadbare clothes, without a tie. He was wearing a sports coat that at one time had been navy blue and gray flannel trousers. His shirt was unbuttoned and his whole attire was wrinkled and dirty. His right hand was hanging down along his side, and in it was the famous clarinet. His face was the self-absorbed, emaciated countenance with staring, hallucinated eyes so common in those who are mad; it was a pinched, angular face with the gray green eyes of the Olmoses and a pronounced aquiline nose, but his head was enormous and elongated like a dirigible.

Paralyzed with fear, Martín was unable to get a single word out.

The madman stood there staring at him for some time in silence and then turned around without a word, his body waggling slightly, in a way reminiscent of the slow contortions of youngsters in a street band, but barely perceptible, and walked off down the passageway toward the inside of the house, doubtless heading for his room.

Martín made off in the opposite direction almost at a run, toward the courtyard that was now flooded with the light of the dawning day.

An aged Indian woman was doing laundry in a stone basin. "Justina," Martín thought, giving another start.

"Good morning," he said, doing his best to appear cool and collected, as though his presence there at that hour were quite normal.

The old woman answered not a word. "Perhaps she's deaf, like Don Pancho," Martín thought.

Her mysterious, inscrutable Indian gaze nonetheless followed him for several seconds that seemed endless to Martín. Then she went on with her washing.

Martín, who had halted in his tracks in a moment of indecision, realized that he ought to act as though nothing were out of the ordinary, so he headed as casually as possible for the winding staircase leading up to the Mirador.

He reached the door at the top of the stairs and knocked.

After a few moments, not having received any answer, he knocked again. There was no response this time either. Then putting his mouth to the crack between the door and the doorframe, he called out "Alejandra!" in a loud voice. But time went by and there was no answer.

He decided then that the best thing to do would be to leave. But instead he found himself walking toward the window of the Mirador. When he reached it he saw that the curtains had not been drawn. He looked inside and tried to spy Alejandra in the semidarkness. But when his eyes had adjusted to the dim light there inside, he discovered, to his surprise, that she was not in the room.

For a moment he couldn't move or think a coherent thought. Then he headed for the stairway and began to make his way carefully down it, as he tried to set his thoughts in order.

He crossed the back patio, went around the old house by way of the abandoned side garden, and finally found himself out on the street.

He walked hesitantly down the sidewalk toward Montes de Oca, intending to take the bus there. But after walking along for a moment, he stopped and looked back toward the Olmoses' house. He was still all confused and unable to decide exactly what he should do.

He took a few steps back toward the house and then halted again. He looked toward the rusty iron gate as though he were expecting something. What? In the light of day the house looked even more ridiculous than by night, as a ghost is more absurd in broad daylight, for with its cracked and peeling walls, the weeds overrunning the garden, its rusted iron grille at the entrance and its front door practically falling off, it stood out in even more violent contrast to the factories and smokestacks looming up behind it.

Martín's eyes finally came to rest on the Mirador: towering above the house, it seemed to him to be as lonely and mysterious as Alejandra herself. Good heavens! he said to himself, what have I gotten myself into?

In the light of day, the night that he had spent in that house seemed like a dream to him now: the old man who appeared to be practically immortal; Major Acevedo's head inside the hatbox; the mad uncle with his clarinet and his wild eyes; the ancient Indian woman, deaf or indifferent to everything to the point that she had not even bothered to ask who he was and what a stranger like him was doing coming out of the bedrooms and then going up to the Mirador; the story of Captain Elmtrees; the incredible tale of Escolástica and her madness; and above all, Alejandra herself.

He began slowly to think things through: it was impossible to get on a bus at Montes de Oca; the transition would be too much of a shock. So he decided instead to walk down Isabel la Católica to Martín García; the old street would allow him to put all his conflicting thoughts in order little by little.

What most intrigued him and preoccupied him was Alejandra's absence. Where could she have spent the night? Had she taken him to see the grandfather in order to get rid of him? No, because if that had been her intention all she would have had to do was let him leave when he had wanted to after hearing her story about Marcos Molina, the scene on the beach, and missions to convert the Indians in the Amazon. Why hadn't she let him go home after that?

But it might be that everything was unpredictable even to her. Perhaps she had taken it into her head to go off somewhere while he was with Don Pancho. But in that case why hadn't she told him so? In the final analysis, her way of going about things mattered little. What did matter was that she had not spent the night in her Mirador. It was only natural, therefore, to presume that she had had somewhere else to spend it. And frequently stayed overnight there, wherever it was, since there was no reason to think that anything out of the ordinary had occurred the night before.

Or had she simply gone wandering about the streets?

Yes, yes, he thought, suddenly relieved: no doubt she had gone out walking around the neighborhood, so as to be able to think, so as to clear her head. That was how she was: unpredictable and tormented, strange, capable of wandering about lonely suburban streets in the middle of the night. Why not? Hadn't they met in a park? Didn't she often return to those park benches where they had met for the first time?

Yes, all this was quite possible.

He walked along for several blocks, his mind at ease now. Then suddenly he remembered two things that had attracted his attention at a certain point and that now began to prey on his mind once more: Fernando, that name that she had uttered just once, only to immediately regret having done so, it seemed to him; and the violent reaction that she had had when he had happened to refer to blind people. What was her connection with blind people? It was something important, he was certain, because it had been as though she were suddenly paralyzed with fear. Could the mysterious Fernando be blind? And in any event, who *was* this Fernando whose name she appeared to be unwilling to utter, overcome by that sort of awe which causes certain peoples to avoid uttering the name of their divinity?

He began to think once again, sadly, that he was separated from her by dark abysses and doubtless always would be.

But then, he thought with renewed hope, why had she come to him in the park? And hadn't she said that she needed him, that they had something very important in common?

He hesitantly walked on a few steps more, and then, halting and looking down at the pavement as though questioning himself, he said to himself: but why should she need me?

He felt a dizzying love for Alejandra. She on the other hand felt no such thing for him, he thought sadly. And even if she needed him, her feeling toward him was not the same as his toward her.

His mind was in a whirl.

        ⱷ 14 ⱷ

FOR MANY DAYS he had no news of her. He went prowling round the house in Barracas and several times kept watch from afar on the rusty gate in the iron fence.

His discouragement reached its low point the day he lost his job at the printing company: there wouldn't be any work available for a while, they had told him. But he knew very well that the real reason for letting him go was altogether different.

        ⱷ 15 ⱷ

HE HADN'T GONE there consciously: but there he was, standing outside the big window looking out on the Calle Pinzón, thinking he might faint at any moment from hunger. The word PIZZA seemed to bypass his brain; instead it was his stomach that reacted directly, as with Pavlov's dogs. If only Bucich were there inside. But still he didn't dare go in. Anyway, Bucich was bound to be in the south; heaven only knew when he'd be back. Chichín was there inside, with his cap and his colored suspenders, and Humberto J. D'Arcángelo, better known as Tito, with his toothpick stuck in his mouth like a cigarette and *Crítica* rolled up in his right hand, "distinguishing marks," so to speak, since only a vulgar fraud could pretend to be Humberto J. D'Arcángelo without the toothpick in his mouth and *Crítica* rolled up in his right hand. There was something birdlike about him, with his sharp hooked nose and his little eyes set wide apart on the two sides of a flat, bony face. As terribly nervous and restless as always: picking at his teeth, straightening his threadbare tie, his prominent Adam's apple continually bobbing up and down.

Martín looked at him in fascination until Tito caught sight of him and with his infallible memory recognized him immediately. And signaling to him with the rolled-up *Crítica,* like a traffic policeman, he motioned him to come in, sat him down, and ordered him a Cinzano with bitters. As he unfolded the paper, which was open to the sports page, he tapped on it with his skinny hand, and leaning over to Martín across the little marble table, with the toothpick shifting about on his lower lip, he said to him: *Do you know how much they paid for this guy?* At this question, a scared expression came over Martín's face, as though he were a pupil who didn't know his lesson, and although his lips moved he couldn't manage to get a single word out, as D'Arcángelo, his little eyes gleaming with indignation, with his Adam's apple stuck in the middle of his throat, awaited the reply: with a sarcastic smile, a bitter irony before the fact as he awaited the inevitable wrong guess not only on the part of the youngster but on the part of *anybody with five cents' worth of brains.* But luckily, as Tito's Adam's apple remained momentarily stuck, Chichín arrived with the bottles. Then turning his sharp face toward him, tapping the sports page with the back of his bony hand, Tito said to him: *Come on, Chichín, tell me, just take a guess, how much did they pay for that broken-down cripple of a Cincotta?,* and as Chichín served the Cinzanos he answered: *How should I know? five hundred, maybe?,* to which Tito replied *ha,* smiling a bitter twisted, yet happy smile (because it demonstrated that he, Humberto J. D'Arcángelo, was somebody really in the know). Then after folding *Crítica* up again, like a professor who puts the apparatus back in the case after the demonstration, he said *Eight hundred thou,* and after a silence befitting such an enormity, he added: *And now just try and tell me we're not all batty in this country.* He kept his eyes fixed on Chichín, as though searching for the slightest sign of disagreement and everything remained frozen in place for a few seconds: D'Arcángelo's Adam's apple, his ironic little eyes, Martín's attentive expression, and Chichín with his cap and his red suspenders, holding the bottle of vermouth in the air.

The strange snapshot lasted perhaps one or two seconds. Then Tito squirted soda water into the vermouth, took a few sips, and fell into a gloomy silence, staring out the window at the Calle Pinzón, as he usually did at such moments: an abstract gaze and in a manner of speaking an entirely symbolic one, since in no case would it condescend to take in external facts as they really were. Then he went back to his favorite subject of conversation: *There was no more soccer these days. What could you expect of players if they were bought and sold?* His gaze grew dreamy and he began to hark back, once more, to the Golden Age of the game, when he was a lad "this high." And as Martín, out of sheer timidity, drank the vermouth that after two days without eating he knew would have a terrible effect on him, Humberto J. D'Arcángelo said to him: *You've got to sock dough away, kid, take it from me. It's the one law of life: make yourself a pile, even if you have to raffle off your heart,* as he straightened his worn tie and pulled at the sleeves of his threadbare jacket, a suit and tie that were ample proof that he, Humberto J. D'Arcángelo, represented the categorical denial of his own philosophy. And as out of sheer kindness he urged the youngster to finish the vermouth, he talked to him of the old days, and it soon seemed to Martín as though the conversation were taking place on the high seas, for he was feeling queasier and queasier.

And D'Arcángelo sat there lost in thought, chewing on his toothpick and looking out at the Calle Pinzón.

"Those were the days," he murmured to himself.

He straightened his tie, tugged on the sleeves of his suitcoat, and turned toward Martín with a bitter look on his face, like someone coming back to hard reality, and tapping on the newspaper he said: *Eight hundred thou for a lousy no-good like that. That's how it is in this world.* With his little eyes gleaming with indignation, he straightened his worn tie. And then, pointing vertically with his index finger, as though he were referring to the table, he added: People in this country have got to wake up. And looking at the youngsters who had gathered round but addressing Martín symbolically (as Martín began to see Alejandra sleeping before his eyes, as in a vague poetic dream), brandishing the newspaper that he'd rolled up again, he added: *You read the paper and find about about a shady deal. And maybe you go on dreaming about the moon or reading those books of yours.* And then, straightening his tie, he looked with wrathful eyes at the Calle Pinzón. Turning around after a brief instant of (raging) philosophical meditation, he added: *You go ahead and study, make an Edison of yourself, invent the telegraph or be a Christian priest and take yourself off to Africa like that old German with the big handlebar moustache, sacri-*

fice yourself for humanity, sweat bullets, and you'll see how they crucify you and how others end up rolling in dough. Haven't you ever noticed that the real heroes of humanity always end up poor and forgotten? None of that for me, thanks, and directing his furious gaze toward the Calle Pinzón once again, he straightened his worn tie and tugged on the threadbare sleeves of his suit jacket and the youngsters laughed or said *Ah, come on, do we have to listen to bullshit from you too,* and Martín, in his lethargy, again saw Alejandra lying all curled up fast asleep before his eyes, breathing raggedly through her half-open mouth, her large, scornful, sensual mouth. And he could see her long straight hair, blue black with reddish glints, spread out on the pillow framing her angular face, the features that had the same harshness as her tormented spirit. And her body, her long, abandoned body, her breasts beneath the clinging white blouse, and those beautiful long legs curled up touching him. Yes, there she was, within reach of his hand and his mouth, in a certain way defenseless, but how far away, how inaccessible!

"Never," he said to himself bitterly and almost aloud, as somebody shouted *Perón's doing the right thing and all those oligarchs ought to be strung up together in the Plaza Mayo,* "never," yet she had chosen him, but what for, in heaven's name, what for? Because he would never know her most intimate secrets, he was quite certain, and once more the words *blind* and *Fernando* came to his mind as one of the youngsters put a coin in the Wurlitzer and they began to sing "Los Plateros." Then D'Arcángelo exploded, and grabbing Martín by one arm he said to him: *Let's clear out, my boy. A person can't stand it any more even here at Chichín's. What's this country coming to with all these clowns shattering your eardrums with their damned foxtrots?*

∾ 16 ∾

THE COOL WIND cleared Martín's head. D'Arcángelo went on muttering and it took some time for him to calm down. Then he asked Martín where he worked. Martín replied shamefacedly that he was out of work. D'Arcángelo looked at him.

"Have you been out of work long?"

"Yes, a fair time."

"Do you have a family?"

"No."

"Where do you live?"

Martín didn't answer immediately: his face was red, but luckily (he thought) it was dark. D'Arcángelo looked at him intently once again.

"To tell the truth . . ." Martín murmured.

"What's that?"

"Ah . . . I had to give up a furnished room I had . . ."

"And where are you sleeping now?"

Embarrassed, Martín stammered that he slept most anywhere he could find. And as though to make light of the fact, he added:

"Luckily the weather hasn't turned cold yet."

Tito halted in his tracks and looked at him in the light of a street lamp.

"Do you at least have money to eat on?"

Martín didn't answer. Then D'Arcángelo burst out:

"Why in the world didn't you say something? Me rambling on and on about great soccer players and you sitting there nibbling on the free appetizers. Damn!"

D'Arcángelo took him to a cheap restaurant and as they ate, he looked at Martín thoughtfully.

When they had finished they left the restaurant, and as D'Arcángelo straightened his tie he said to Martín:

"Don't worry, my boy. We're going to my place now. And we'll see what happens after that."

They entered an old building that in days gone by had been the coach-house of some splendid mansion.

"My old man was a coachman, you know, till some ten years or so ago. But he's got rheumatism now and can't get around any more. And who's going to hire a coach these days anyway? My old man's one of the many victims of urban progress. All he had left was his health, and now that's gone."

The coach-house was now partly a tenement and partly stables: one could hear cries, conversations, and several radios blaring at once, amid a strong odor of manure. One could hear the sound of horses' hoofs pawing. In the old coach-stalls were several delivery vans and a small truck.

They walked to the back of the place.

ᴖᴖ 17 ᴖᴖ

HE WAITED for several days in vain. But finally Chichín motioned to him to come in and handed him an envelope. He opened it with trembling fingers and unfolded the letter. All it said, in Alejandra's huge, uneven, shaky handwriting, was that she'd be waiting for him at six o'clock.

A few minutes before six he was sitting on the park bench, restless but happy, thinking that now he had someone to tell his troubles to. And someone like Alejandra—it was as incongruous as though a beggar were to discover Morgan's treasure trove.

He ran toward her like a child, and told her what had happened at the printer's.

"You mentioned somebody named Molinari to me," Martín said. "I think you said he was head of a big corporation."

Alejandra raised her eyes toward him, arching her eyebrows in surprise.

"Molinari? I spoke to you of Molinari?"

"Yes you did, right here, when you found me asleep on this very bench, remember? You said to me: 'You surely don't work for Molinari,' remember?"

"I may have."

"Is he a friend of yours?"

Alejandra looked at him with a sarcastic smile.

"Did I say he was a friend of mine?"

But Martín was too hopeful at that moment to attribute any hidden meaning to the expression on her face.

"What do you think?" he said, doggedly pursuing the subject. "Do you think there's a chance he might give me work?"

She looked at him the way doctors size up recruits reporting for military service.

"I know how to type, I can draft letters, correct proofs ..."

"One of tomorrow's winners, eh?"

Martín's face turned red.

"But do you have any idea what it's like to work in a big company? With a time clock and all that?"

Martín took out his white penknife, opened its smallest blade, and then closed it again, with his head bowed.

"I have no false pride. If I can't work in the office I can work in the shop, or as a day laborer."

Alejandra looked at his threadbare suit and his worn shoes.

When Martín finally raised his eyes, he saw that she had a very serious expression on her face and was frowning.

"What's the matter? Would it be hard for you to arrange?"

She shook her head, then said:

"Anyway, don't worry, we'll find some solution."

She got up from the bench.

"Come on. Let's walk around for a while, I have a terrible stomach ache."

"Stomach ache?"

"Yes, it hurts lots of times. It must be an ulcer."

They walked to the bar on the corner of Brasil and Balcarce. Alejandra asked for a glass of water at the counter, took a small bottle out of her handbag and poured a few drops out of it into the glass.

"What's that?"

"Laudanum."

They walked through the park again.

"Let's go down to Dársena for a while," Alejandra said.

They walked down Almirante Brown, turned down Arzobispo Espinosa and Pedro de Mendoza and finally came to a Swedish freighter that was taking on cargo.

Alejandra sat down on one of the tall crates that had come from Sweden, looking toward the river, and Martín sat down on a lower one, as though he felt himself to be merely a humble vassal in the presence of this princess. And both gazed at the great tawny river.

"Have you realized that we have lots of things in common?" she asked.

And Martín thought: *Can this be possible?* And though he was quite sure that both of them enjoyed looking out across the river, he thought that this was a mere detail compared to all the other differences that separated the two of them, a detail that no one could take seriously, least of all Alejandra herself. Any more than one could take seriously the form in which she had just smilingly phrased her question: like grown-ups suddenly having themselves democratically photographed in the street alongside a worker or a nursemaid, smiling condescendingly. Although it was also possible that that phrase was a key to the truth, and that the fact that both of them were eagerly looking out across the river was a secret formula making them allies for much more important endeavors. But how to know what she was really thinking? And looking at her sitting up there on the crate, he felt nervous, like a person watching a beloved tightrope walker performing at extremely dangerous heights at which no one can come to his aid. He looked at her, an ambiguous, disturbing figure, as the breeze ruffled her straight blue black hair, and outlined her pointed breasts set rather far apart. He watched her smoking a cigarette with a far-off look in her eyes. The wind-swept landscape seemed to be enveloped in a quiet melancholy now, as though the winds had died down and a dense fog lay over it.

"How nice it would be if one could go far away," she suddenly remarked. "If one could go far away from this filthy city."

It pained Martín to hear that impersonal verb form: *if one could go away*.

"Would *you* go away?" he asked in a choked voice.

Without looking at him, almost completely absorbed in her own thoughts, she answered:

"Yes, I'd like it a lot if I could go away. To some far-off place, a place where I didn't know anybody at all. To an island maybe, one of those islands that must still exist out there somewhere."

Martín lowered his head and began to scratch at the crate with his penknife as his eyes scanned the words THIS SIDE UP. Alejandra turned her gaze toward him, and after watching him for a moment, she asked if something was the matter, and as he continued to scratch the wood and look at the words THIS SIDE UP he answered that nothing was wrong, but Alejandra continued to look at him, not seeing him, lost in thought. Neither of them spoke for some time, as it grew darker and the dockside fell silent: the cranes had stopped working and the stevedores and porters were beginning to wend their way homeward or toward the bars along the dockside.

"Let's go to the Moscow," Alejandra said then.

"To the Moscow?"

"Yes, in the Calle Independencia."

"But isn't it terribly expensive?"

Alejandra laughed.

"It's a neighborhood bistro. Furthermore, Vanya's a friend of mine."

The door of the place was closed.

"There's nobody here," Martín remarked.

"Shaddup," was all Alejandra said, imitating American movies, and knocked on the door.

After a while a man in shirtsleeves came and let them in: he had straight white hair and a kind, refined face with a permanent melancholy smile. A nervous tic was making his cheek twitch, up near his eye.

"Ivan Petrovich," Alejandra said, holding out her hand to him.

The man raised it to his lips, bowing slightly.

They sat down next to a window looking out on the Paseo Colón. The place was dimly lighted, with just one feeble little lamp next to the cash register, where a short, plump butterball of a woman with a Slavic face was drinking maté.

"I have Polish vodka," Vanya said. "They delivered it to me yesterday—a boat from Poland came in."

As he went off to get them some, Alejandra commented:

"He's a great guy, but the fat woman—and she pointed toward the cash register—is a vicious bitch. She's trying to get Vanya put away in an asylum so the place will be all hers."

"Vanya? Didn't you call him Ivan Petrovich?"

"Vanya is the diminutive of Ivan, dummy. Everybody calls him Vanya, but I call him Ivan Petrovich—it makes him feel as though he's in Russia. And besides, I think it's a charming name."

"And why should he be put away in an asylum?"

"He's a morphine addict and has attacks when he can't get the stuff. And that's when the fat woman sees her chance to get what she can while the getting's good."

Vanya brought the vodka, and as he was serving it he said to them:

"Record player works fine. I have Brahms's violin concerto—shall I play it? It's Heifetz, no less."

When he left the table, Alejandra commented:

"You see? He's generosity itself. He used to be a violinist at the

Colón but it's pitiful to hear him play now. And yet he offers you a violin concerto, with Heifetz playing."

She pointed, calling his attention to the walls: Cossacks galloping into a village, Byzantine churches with golden domes, gypsies. The whole scene was clumsily painted and the effect was dismal.

"I sometimes think he'd like to go back. One day he said to me: 'Don't you think that, everything considered, Stalin is a great man?' And he added that in a certain way he was another Peter the Great and that when everything was said and done, what he was aiming at was the grandeur of Russia. But he said all this in a low murmur, casting continual glances in the fat woman's direction. I think she can read his lips."

From a distance, as though not wanting to bother the young couple, Vanya was going through an elaborate pantomime, pointing to the record player, as though praising Heifetz's performance. And as Alejandra nodded with a smile, she said to Martín:

"The world is nothing but filth."

Martín reacted violently.

"No, Alejandra! There are all sorts of nice things in the world!"

She looked at him, thinking perhaps of his poverty, his mother, his loneliness. And still he was capable of finding the world full of marvelous things! An ironic smile superimposed itself on her original expression of tenderness, causing the latter to contract, as though it were an acid applied to a very delicate skin.

"What are they?" she asked.

"There are so many of them, Alejandra!" Martín exclaimed, taking one of her hands and clasping it to his breast. "That music ... a man like Vanya ... and most of all you, Alejandra ... you ..."

"Really now, I can't help thinking you haven't ever got past childhood, you dimwit."

She sat there for a moment, her mind elsewhere, took a sip of vodka, and then went on:

"Yes, you're right of course. There are beautiful things in this world ... there's no doubt of that ..."

And then, turning toward him, she added in a bitter tone of voice:

"But I'm garbage, Martín, do you hear? You mustn't have any illusions about me."

Martín clasped one of Alejandra's hands in his, raised it to his lips and kept it there, kissing it fervently.

"No, Alejandra! Why do you say such a dreadful thing? I know that's not true. Everything you've said about Vanya and lots of other things I've heard you say prove that isn't true."

His eyes had filled with tears.

"All right, never mind, it's not worth getting upset about," Alejandra said.

Martín leaned his head on Alejandra's breast and nothing in the world mattered now. Looking out the window he could see night descending on Buenos Aires, enhancing his feeling that he was safe and sound here in this refuge, this hidden corner of the implacable city. A question he had never asked anyone (whom could he have asked?) welled up from within him, a question with the clean-cut, shiny edges of a coin that has never been circulated, that millions of anonymous dirty hands have not yet worn thin, deteriorated, and debased:

"Do you love me?"

She appeared to hesitate for an instant, but then she answered:

"Yes, I love you. I love you a lot."

Martín felt magically isolated from the cruel reality of the outside world, as happens in the theater (he thought years later) during the space of time that we are living the world shown onstage, while outside the painful sharp edges of the everyday universe await, the things that will inevitably strike us with brute force the moment the footlights go out and the spell is broken. And just as in the theater the outside world at certain moments manages to reach us there inside, though in an attenuated state, in the form of distant sounds (a car horn honking, a newsboy's shout, a traffic policeman's whistle), so too there reached his consciousness, like disturbing little whispers, small facts, certain phrases that clouded the magic and left cracks in it: those words that she had uttered down at the dockside, those words that left him feeling terribly excluded ("I'd like it a lot if I could go away from this filthy city"), and the phrase that she had just uttered ("I'm garbage; you mustn't have any illusions about me"), words that throbbed like a slight, dull pain in his mind, words that as he sat there with his head leaning on Alejandra's breast, giving himself over to the marvelous happiness of the instant, swarmed like ants in a deeper, more insidious region of his soul, exchanging whispers back and forth with other enigmatic words: the blind, Fernando, Molinari. *But it doesn't matter*, he said to himself obstinately—it doesn't matter, pressing his head against her warm breasts and caressing her hands, as though he would thus be able to ensure that the magic spell would last.

"But how much do you love me?" he asked childishly.

"A lot—I just told you that."

Nonetheless her tone of voice seemed distant, and raising his head he looked at her and could see that it was as though her mind were distracted, as though her attention were now focused on something that was not there with him but elsewhere, somewhere far off and unknown.

"What are you thinking about?"

She didn't answer, as though she hadn't heard.

Then Martín repeated the question, squeezing her arm as though to bring her back to reality.

And she said then that she wasn't thinking about anything: nothing in particular anyway.

Martín was to experience this sort of absence on her part many times: her eyes wide open and even going on doing this or that, yet at the same time a total stranger to herself, as though she were being manipulated by some remote force.

Suddenly, glancing over at Vanya, she said:

"I like people who are failures. Don't you?"

He sat there thinking that singular statement over.

"There's always something vulgar and horrible about success," she added.

After a moment's silence, she went on:

"Whatever would become of this country if everyone were a success! I don't even want to think about it. The fact that so many people are failures helps save us somewhat. Aren't you hungry?"

"Yes."

She got up from the table and went over to say goodbye to Vanya. When she returned, her face flushed, Martín confessed to her that he was flat broke. She burst out laughing, opened her purse, and took out two hundred pesos.

"Here, take this. When you need more, just tell me."

Embarrassed, Martín tried to refuse the money, whereupon Alejandra looked at him in amazement.

"Are you crazy? Or are you one of those petty bourgeois who think a man shouldn't take money from a woman?"

When they had finished dinner, they headed for Barracas. After crossing the Parque Lezama in silence, they started down Hernandarias.

"Do you know the story of the Enchanted City of Patagonia?" Alejandra asked.

"I've heard a little about it, not much."

"Some day I'll show you papers that are still in that leather trunk of Major Acevedo's. Papers about this guy."

"This guy? What guy?"

Alejandra pointed to the street sign.

"Hernandarias."

"Papers in your house? How does that happen?"

"Papers, names of streets. That's all we have left. Hernandarias was an ancestor of the Acevedos. In 1550 he headed the expedition in search of the Enchanted City."

They walked along for a time in silence and then Alejandra recited:

> *Ahí está Buenos Aires. El tiempo que a los hombres*
> *trae el amor o el oro, a mí apenas me deja*
> *esta rosa apagada, esta vana madeja*
> *de calles que repiten los pretéritos nombres*
> *de mi sangre: Laprida, Cabrera, Soler, Suárez...*
> *Nombres en que retumban ya secretas las dianas,*
> *las repúblicas, los caballos y las mañanas,*
> *las felices victorias, las muertes militares...* *

---

* Here is Buenos Aires. Time, that brings men love or gold
has left me just this faded rose, this vain skein
of streets repeating names of old
that are my blood: Laprida, Cabrera, Suárez, Soler...
Names full of secret echoes now
of reveilles and republics, chargers, combat in the cool dawn air
of glorious victories, and soldiers' solemn deaths...

Poem by Jorge Luis Borges, the famous contemporary Argentine writer. [*Author's note*]

She fell silent again for several blocks, and then suddenly she asked: "Do you hear bells ringing?"

Martín listened intently and answered no.

"What's all this about bells ringing?" he asked, intrigued.

"Nothing; it's just that I sometimes hear bells that are real and at other times I hear bells that aren't."

She laughed and added:

"Speaking of churches, I had a strange dream last night. I was in a cathedral, one in total darkness almost, and I was having to walk forward carefully so as not to push people in front of me aside. I couldn't see a thing, but I had the impression that the nave was jammed with people. With great difficulty I finally managed to work my way up close to the priest preaching in the pulpit. I wasn't able to hear what he was saying, even though I was very close now, and the worst thing about it was that I was certain that he was addressing me. I could hear a sort of vague murmur, as though he were speaking over a bad phone connection, and this made me more and more anxious. I opened my eyes wide, trying to see the expression on his face at least. And to my horror I saw that he didn't have a face, his face was just smooth skin, and there was no hair on his head. At that moment the bells began to ring, tolling slowly at first and then gradually they began to peal louder and louder, till finally they were clanging furiously and I woke up. And the curious thing is that right there in the dream, standing with my hands over my ears, I kept saying, as though the very thought horrified me: 'They're the bells of Santa Lucía, the church I went to when I was little.'"

There was a pensive look on her face.

"I wonder what that can possibly mean," she said then. "Don't you think dreams have a meaning?"

"A psychoanalytic interpretation, you mean?"

"No, no. Well, that too, why not? But dreams are mysterious, and mankind has been reading meaning into them for thousands of years."

Then she gave the same strange laugh that had come from her lips a moment before. It was not a healthy or calm laugh, but a nervous, anxious one.

"I always dream. Of fire, of birds, of swamps that I'm sinking into or panthers that are clawing me to bits, of snakes. But fire especially. In the end, there's always fire. Don't you think there's something uncanny, something sacred about fire?"

They were almost there. In the distance Martín could already see the big old house with its Mirador up above: the ghostly remains of a world that no longer existed.

They entered the gate, went through the garden, and walked around to the back of the house: the madman's absurd but tranquil tootling on the clarinet could be heard.

"Does he play all the time?" Martín asked.

"Just about. But after a while you don't even notice."

"Did you know that I saw him the other night as I was leaving? He was listening behind the door."

"Yes, he's in the habit of doing that."

They climbed up the winding staircase and Martín again felt the magic of that terrace in the summer night. Anything could happen in that atmosphere that seemed to be situated both outside of time and outside of space.

They went inside the Mirador and Alejandra said:

"Sit on the bed. The chairs here are dangerous, as you know."

As Martín sat down, she flung her purse down and put water on to boil. Then she put a record on: the dramatic chords of the concertina began to take on the configuration of a somber melody.

"Listen: The words are tremendous."

Yo quiero morir contigo,
sin confesión y sin Dios,
crucificado en mi pena,
*como abrazado a un rencor.**

After they had drunk the coffee they went out onto the terrace and leaned over the balustrade. The sound of the clarinet could be heard from below. The night was pitch black and stifling.

"Bruno always says that unfortunately our lives are lived in the

---

* I want to die with you,
  Without confession and without God,
  Crucified in my pain,
  As though pinned in rancor's embrace.

form of a rough draft. A writer can always revise something that's not perfect or simply toss the whole thing into the wastebasket. Not life: there's no way to correct or clean up or throw away what's already been lived. Do you realize how awful that is?"

"Who's Bruno?"

"A friend."

"What does he do?"

"Nothing; he's a contemplative sort, though he claims he's merely pathologically apathetic. I think he does write though. But he's never shown anybody what he's done and I don't imagine he'll ever publish anything."

"And what does he live on?"

"His father owns a flour mill in Capitán Olmos. That's how we came to know each other; he was a very good friend of my mother's. I think he was in love with her," she added with a laugh.

"What was your mother like?"

"They say she was like me—physically I mean. I hardly remember her. I was only five when she died, you see. Her name was Georgina."

"Why did you say she was like you physically?"

"I meant we looked like each other, that's all. Because in other ways I'm very different. According to what Bruno tells me, she was a gentle, feminine, sensitive, quiet person."

"So who is it you resemble? Your father?"

Alejandra was silent. Then, stepping away from Martín, she said in a tone of voice that was no longer the same, a harsh, choked voice:

"Who, me? I don't know. Maybe I'm the incarnation of one of those demons who are Satan's familiars."

She unbuttoned the two top buttons of her blouse and shook the little lapels of it with her two hands as though she were trying to give herself more air. Panting slightly, she went over to the window, took several deep breaths, and after a while seemed to calm down.

"I was just joking," she said as she sat down on the edge of the bed as usual, making room for Martín alongside her.

"Turn the light out," she said then. "It bothers me terribly sometimes; it makes my eyes burn."

"Would you like me to leave? Do you want to sleep?" Martín asked.

"No, I wouldn't be able to sleep. Stay, if it doesn't bore you to just sit here, not talking. I'll lie down for a while and you can stay right here."

"I think it would be better if I left and let you get some rest."

With an edge of irritation in her voice, Alejandra answered:

"Can't you see I want you to stay? Turn out the night light too."

Martín got up and turned out the night light and then sat down again alongside her, with his mind churning, completely puzzled and overcome with shyness and diffidence. Why did Alejandra need him? He for his part thought of himself as a useless, dull-witted sort who could do nothing but listen to her and admire her. It was she who was the strong one, the powerful one; what kind of help could he possibly be to her?

"What are you sitting there muttering?" Alejandra asked, shaking him by the arm as though to summon him back to reality.

"Muttering? Nothing."

"Well, thinking then. You're certainly thinking something, you idiot."

Martín was reluctant to share his thoughts with her, but he supposed that as usual she'd eventually guess what they were anyway.

"I was thinking...that...why in the world would you need me?"

"Why not?"

"I'm nobody.... You, on the other hand, are a strong person, you have very definite ideas, you're courageous.... You could defend yourself against a whole tribe of cannibals all by yourself."

He heard her laugh. Then she said:

"I don't know the answer myself. But I sought you out because I need you, because you...Anyway, what's the use of racking our brains?"

"And yet just today, down at the dockside, you said you'd gladly go to some far-off island—isn't that what you said?" Martín answered with a trace of bitterness in his voice.

"So what?"

"You said that *you'd* go, not that *we'd* go."

Alejandra laughed again.

Martín took one of her hands in his and asked her in an anxious voice:

"Would you take me with you?"

She appeared to be thinking it over: Martín could not make out her features.

"Yes . . . I think so. . . . But I don't see why you'd find such a prospect pleasing."

"Why not?" Martín asked in a hurt voice.

"Because I can't bear to have anybody with me all the time and because I'd hurt you a lot, a whole lot," she answered gravely.

"Don't you love me?"

"Oh, Martín . . . don't start bringing up questions like that again . . ."

"Well then, it's because you don't love me."

"Of course I do, silly. But I'd hurt you for the pure and simple reason that I love you, don't you understand? You don't hurt people you feel indifferent toward. But the word *love*, Martín, covers such a lot of territory. . . . You love a paramour, a dog, a friend . . ."

"And what about me?" Martín asked, trembling. "What am I to you? A paramour, a dog, a friend?"

"I've told you I needed you—isn't that enough for you?"

Martín fell silent: the derisive phantoms that had been prowling about in the distance drew closer: the name *Fernando*, the phrase *always remember that I'm garbage*, her absence from her room that first night. And he thought, sadly and bitterly: "Never, never." His eyes filled with tears and his head bent forward as though the weight of those thoughts had made it double over.

Alejandra raised her hand to his face and felt his eyes with the tips of her fingers.

"I thought as much. Come here."

She put one arm round him and held him close.

"Let's see if he's going to be a good boy now," she said, the way one speaks to a child. "I've already said that I need him and love him a lot, what else does he want?"

She put her lips to his cheek and gave him a kiss. Martín felt a shiver run through his whole body.

Embracing Alejandra violently, feeling her warm body next to his, he began, as though an invincible power had overcome him, to kiss her face, her eyes, her cheeks, her hair, finally seeking out that large, full-lipped mouth he could feel next to his. For a fleeting instant he was aware that Alejandra was trying to avoid his kiss: her whole body seemed to grow hard and rigid and her arms pushed him away for a moment. Then she suddenly melted and a frenzy seemed to take possession of her. And then something happened that terrified Martín: he felt her hands grip his arms as though they were claws and tear his flesh, as at the same time she pushed him away and sat up.

"No!" she shouted, getting to her feet and running to the window.

Martín was terrified and did not dare approach her. He could see her standing there, breathing in great gulps of night air as though she were suffocating, her hair in wild disorder, her breast heaving, her hands clutching the window recess, her arms taut. With a violent tug she ripped her blouse open with both hands, tearing the buttons off, fell to the floor, and lay there rigid. Her face slowly turned purple, and then suddenly her body began to heave convulsively. In a panic, Martín had no idea how to deal with her, what to do for her. When he saw that she was falling, he ran to her and took her in his arms and tried to quiet her. But Alejandra saw and heard nothing: she writhed and moaned, her eyes wide open and delirious. It occurred to Martín that all he could do was carry her over to the bed. He did so and little by little he saw to his relief that she was calming down and that her moans were gradually becoming softer and softer.

Sitting on the edge of the bed, in utter confusion and terror, Martín could see her naked breasts in the gaping neck of the blouse. The thought crossed his mind that in some way he, Martín, was indeed necessary to this tormented, suffering creature. Then he closed Alejandra's blouse and waited. Little by little her breathing grew quieter and more regular, her eyes had closed now, and she seemed to be asleep. More than an hour went by in this way, and then, opening her eyes and looking at him, she asked for a drink of water. He held her up with one arm and gave her some.

"Turn out that light," she said.

Martín obeyed and sat down alongside her again.

"Martín," Alejandra said in a faint voice, "I'm very, very tired, I'd like to sleep, but don't go away. You can sleep here, next to me."

He took off his shoes and lay down at her side.

"You're a saint," she said, curling up next to him.

Martín felt her suddenly drop off to sleep, as he tried to put his chaotic thoughts more or less in order. But his mind was in such turmoil and his thought processes so incoherent or contradictory that little by little he was overcome by an irresistible drowsiness and the very pleasant sensation (despite everything) of being at the side of the woman he loved.

But something kept him from dropping off to sleep, and gradually he grew more and more anxious.

It was as if the prince, he thought, journeying through vast, lonely regions, had at last found himself before the cavern where the beauty is sleeping, guarded by the dragon. And as if, moreover, he had become aware that the dragon was not a menacing creature there at her side watching over her, as we imagine him in the myths of our childhood, but instead, and much more frighteningly, a creature inside of her: as if she were a dragon-princess, an unfathomable monster, at once chaste and breathing fire, at once innocent and revolting: an absolutely pure-hearted child in a communion dress, possessed by the nightmares of a reptile or a bat.

And the mysterious winds that seemed to be blowing out of the dark cavern of the dragon-princess shook his soul and rent it apart; all his conceptions of things were shattered to bits and hopelessly jumbled together; his body shuddered from head to foot with complex sensations. His mother (he thought), his mother, flesh and filth, a hot moist bath, a dark mass of hair and odors, a repugnant manure of skin and warm lips. But (he was trying to impose order on his chaos) he had divided love into filthy flesh and purest sentiment; into purest sentiment and repugnant, sordid sex that he must reject, even though (or because) his instincts so often rebelled, recoiling from their very rebellion with the same horror with which he suddenly discovered his filthy bed-mother's features on his own face. As though his bed-mother, a treacherous, crawling thing, managed to cross the huge moats that he kept desperately digging each day in order to defend his tower; like an implacable viper, she returned each night, appearing in the tower like a fetid phantom as he defended himself with his clean, sharp-edged sword. And what in the name of heaven was happening with Alejandra? What ambiguous sentiment was now throwing all his defenses into confusion? The flesh was suddenly beginning to appear to him to be spirit, and his love for her was turning into flesh, into burning desire for her skin and her damp, dark dragon-princess cavern. But in heaven's name why did she appear to defend this cavern with fiery blasts and the furious cries of a wounded dragon? "I mustn't think," he said to himself, pressing hard on his temples, trying to keep from thinking as he might try to keep from breathing, doing his best to quiet the tumult in his head. And then, his mind clean and blank now, if only for an instant, he thought with painful clarity BUT THERE ON THE BEACH WITH MARCOS MOLINA, IT WASN'T LIKE THIS. FOR SHE LOVED HIM AND DESIRED HIM AND KISSED HIM WILDLY. So that it was he, Martín, whom she rejected. He gave in to his tension once again, and once again those winds swept through his mind, like a furious storm, as he felt her there at his side, writhing, moaning, murmuring unintelligible words. "I always have nightmares in my sleep," she had said.

Martín sat there on the edge of the bed and looked at her: in the moonlight he could scrutinize her face agitated by that other storm, the one within her, the one he never (absolutely never) would know. As though amid mud and excrement, amid shadows there grew a delicate white rose. And the strangest thing of all was that he loved this equivocal monster: dragonprincess, mudrose, childbat, that same chaste, warm, and perhaps corrupt being shuddering there at his side, next to his skin, tormented by heaven only knew what terrible nightmares. And what was most upsetting of all was that though he accepted her as being that, she seemed not to want to accept him: it was as though the little girl in white (amid the mud, surrounded by hordes of bats, filthy, slimy bats) had cried out to him for help, moaning, and at the same time had rejected him, pushing him away from that dark realm with violent gestures. Yes: the princess was writhing and moaning. From desolate regions in darkest shadow she was calling to him, Martín. But he, a poor, hopelessly confused youngster, separated from her by unbridgeable abysses, was unable to make his way to her.

There was nothing he could do, then, but gaze at her anxiously from this side of those abysses and wait.

"No, no!" Alejandra exclaimed, thrusting her hands out in front of her as though to push something away. Then finally she awoke and the scene that Martín had already gone through that first night was repeated: he calming her, calling her by name; and she, in some far-off place, emerging little by little from a deep abyss swarming with bats and covered with spiderwebs.

Sitting up in bed, hunched over her bent legs, her head resting on her knees, Alejandra came to little by little. After a time she looked at Martín and said to him:

"I hope you've gotten used to it by now."

In reply, Martín tried to stroke her face with his hand.

"Don't touch me!" she exclaimed, drawing away.

She got up out of bed and said:

"I'm going to take a bath. I'll be back."

"What took you so long?" he asked when she finally reappeared.

"I was terribly dirty."

She lit a cigarette and lay down alongside him.

Martín looked at her: he could never tell when she was joking.

"I'm not joking, silly; I mean it."

Martín said nothing: he simply sat there, as though paralyzed by his doubts, his confused thoughts and feelings. Frowning, he gazed up at the ceiling and tried to order his thoughts.

"What are you thinking about?"

He did not reply immediately.

"About everything and nothing, Alejandra. . . . To tell you the truth . . ."

"Don't you know what you're thinking about?"

"I don't know anything. . . . Ever since I met you I've been living in the midst of utter confusion. I have no idea what I think or feel. . . . I haven't the slightest notion what to do at any time. . . . Just now when you woke up and I tried to caress you . . . And before you went to sleep . . . When . . ."

He fell silent and Alejandra said nothing. Neither of them spoke for a long time. The only sound in the room was Alejandra's breath as she took deep, avid drags on her cigarette.

"You aren't saying a word," Martín commented bitterly.

"I already told you that I love you, that I love you a lot."

"What was it you dreamed just now?" Martín asked in a gloomy tone of voice.

"Why do you want to know? It's not even worth talking about."

"You see? You have a world of your own that's unknown to me—how can you say you love me?"

"But I do love you, Martín."

"Sure. You love me the way you would a little kid."

She did not answer.

"You see!" Martín said bitterly. "You see!"

"No, silly, that's not it at all.... I'm thinking.... Things aren't clear at all for me either.... But I love you, I need you, I'm absolutely certain of that..."

"You wouldn't let me kiss you. You wouldn't even let me touch you a minute ago."

"Good heavens! Can't you see I'm sick, that I'm suffering terribly? You can't imagine the nightmare I just had..."

"Was that why you went and took a bath?" Martin asked sarcastically.

"Yes: I took a bath on account of the nightmare."

"Can nightmares be washed away by water?"

"Yes, Martín, with water and a little detergent."

"It doesn't seem to me that what I'm saying is anything to be laughed at."

"I'm not laughing, my boy. Or maybe I'm laughing at myself, at my ridiculous notion that I can get my soul clean with soap and water. If you could only see how furiously I scrub myself!"

"That's a crazy idea."

"Naturally."

Alejandra sat up, stubbed out her cigarette in the ashtray on the night table and lay down again.

"I'm young and inexperienced, Alejandra. I've little doubt that you find me terribly stupid and backward. But I keep wondering nonetheless: if you don't like me to touch you and kiss you on the mouth, why is it you asked me to stay and sleep here in this bed with you? That seems to me a cruel thing for you to do. Or is it another experiment, like the one with Marcos Molina?"

"No, Martín, it's not an experiment at all. I didn't love Marcos Molina—I can see that clearly now. But with you it's different. And it's really strange—something I can't even explain to myself: suddenly I need to have you close, to have you next to me, to feel the warmth of your body beside me, the touch of your hand."

"But without my really kissing you."

Alejandra hesitated a moment before going on.

"Look, Martín, there are lots of things about me, about ... The thing is, I just don't know. . . . Maybe because I'm very fond of you ... do you understand?"

"No."

"No, of course you don't. . . . I can't even explain it to myself very well."

"Won't I ever be able to kiss you, won't I ever be able to touch your body?" Martín asked, with childish, almost comical bitterness.

He saw her raise her hands to her head and press it between them as though her temples ached. Then she lit a cigarette and without a word went over to the window, remaining there until she had finished it. Then she came back to the bed, sat down, gave Martín a long, searching look, and began to undress.

Almost in terror, like someone who is witness to an act that he has long awaited but that he realizes is also in some way vaguely horrifying once it is actually about to come to pass, Martín saw her body begin to emerge little by little from the darkness. On his feet now, he contemplated in the moonlight her slender waist that a single arm could easily encircle; her wide hips, her high, pointed breasts set far apart, quivering as she moved; her long straight hair fanning out over her shoulders now. Her face was grave, almost tragic, marked by a bitter, dry-eyed despair so intense it was almost electric.

Curiously, Martín's eyes had filled with tears and he was shivering, as though suffering an attack of fever. He saw her as an antique amphora, a tall, beautiful amphora of trembling flesh; flesh that at the same time appeared to him to be suffused by an ardent desire for communion, for as Bruno said, one of the tragic frailties of the spirit, yet one of its most profound subtleties, was that it was impossible for it to exist save through the intermediary of the flesh.

The outside world had ceased to exist for Martín, and now the magic circle isolated him, to the point of vertigo, from that terrible city, from its miseries and its ugliness, from the millions of men and women and children in it—talking, suffering, quarreling, hating, eating. Through the fantastic powers of love all that was abolished; nothing existed save that body of Alejandra's waiting at his side, a body that one day would die and be corrupted, but at this moment was immortal and incorruptible, as though the spirit that inhabited it were communicating to its flesh the attributes of its eternity. The pounding of his heart demonstrated to him, Martín, that he was ascending to a height never before attained, a summit where the air was completely pure but electric, a lofty mountain perhaps surrounded by a highly charged atmosphere, to immeasurable heights towering far above the dark and pestilential swamps in which he had previously heard grotesque, filthy beasts splashing.

And Bruno (not Martín, of course), Bruno thought that at that moment Alejandra uttered a silent but dramatic, perhaps tragic, prayer.

And he too—Bruno—would think immediately thereafter that that supplication had gone unheard.

❧ 18 ❧

W HEN MARTIN AWOKE, the first morning light was already entering the room.

Alejandra was not lying beside him. He sat up in bed anxiously and saw that she was leaning on the windowsill, pensively looking out.

"Alejandra," he said lovingly.

She turned around with an expression that seemed to reveal a brooding, anxious sadness, as though melancholy thoughts were preying on her mind.

She came over to the bed and sat down.

"Have you been up long?"

"Quite a while. But I often get up during the night."

"Last night too?" Martín asked in amazement.

"Of course."

"How come I didn't hear you?"

Alejandra bowed her head, looked away, and with a frown, as though to emphasize her preoccupation, was about to say something, but in the end said nothing.

Martín looked at her sadly, and although he did not exactly understand the reason for her melancholy, it seemed to him he could perceive the distant sound of it, a vague, mysterious sound.

"Alejandra ..." he said, looking at her fervently. "You ..."

She turned and looked at Martín then, with an ambiguous expression on her face, and said:

"I what?"

And without waiting for his pointless reply, she went over to the night table, searched about for her cigarettes, and walked back over to the window.

Martín's eyes followed her anxiously. He feared that, as in children's fairy tales, the palace that had magically arisen in the night would disappear without a sound in the light of dawn. Some vague presentiment told him that that harsh creature he was so afraid of was about to reappear. And when Alejandra turned toward him again after a moment, he realized that the enchanted palace had returned to the realm of nothingness.

"I told you I'm garbage, Martín. Don't forget that I warned you."

She turned away again and looked out the window, continuing to smoke in silence.

Martín felt ridiculous. He had pulled the sheet up over himself on noticing her cold, hard expression and he told himself he ought to get dressed before she looked at him again. Trying not to make noise, he sat down on the edge of the bed and began putting his clothes on, without taking his eyes off the window and dreading the moment when Alejandra would turn around. And once he was all dressed, he waited.

"Are you through dressing?" she asked, as though she had known all the time what Martín was doing.

"Yes."

"Well, leave me here alone then."

ᖰᕬ 19 ᖰᕬ

THAT NIGHT Martín had a dream: in the midst of a crowd, a beggar whose face it was impossible for him to see approached him, took his bundle off his shoulder, put it down on the ground, untied the knots, opened it, and laid its contents out before Martín. Then the beggar raised his eyes and murmured something unintelligible.

In and of itself, there was nothing terrible about the dream: the beggar was simply a beggar, and there was nothing out of the ordinary about his gestures. Martín nonetheless awoke in the grip of a terrible anxiety, as though everything in the dream were the tragic symbol of something beyond his understanding; as though he had been handed a letter of crucial importance, and on opening it he had found the words in it indecipherable, disfigured, and effaced by time, dampness, and the folds in the paper.

∽ 20 ∽

WHEN, YEARS LATER, Martín tried to discover the key to his relations with Alejandra, among the things he related to Bruno was the fact that, despite her violent changes of mood, he had been happy for several weeks. Bruno raised his eyebrows and horizontal furrows visibly crossed his forehead when he heard such an unexpected word uttered in connection with anything having to do with Alejandra, and since Martín understood that little tacit commentary of Bruno's, he added, a moment's reflection:

"Or rather: almost happy. But immensely so."

Because the word *happiness*, in fact, was not an appropriate one for anything in any way related to Alejandra; yet for all of that it had been something, a feeling, or a state of mind, that came closer to what is commonly called happiness than anything else, even though it never reached the point of being absolute and perfect happiness (and hence the "almost"), in view of the uncertainty and the insecurity of everything having to do with Alejandra. And it had been something that had attained what might be called the utmost heights (and hence that "immensely"), heights on which Martín had felt that majesty and that purity, that sensation of fervent silence and solitary ecstasy that mountain climbers experience on the loftiest peaks.

Bruno looked at him thoughtfully, leaning his chin on his fist.

"And what about Alejandra?" he asked. "Was she happy too?"

A question marked, even if involuntarily, by an almost imperceptible, affectionate note of irony, similar to that which might be attached to the question: "Everything going well at your house as usual?" addressed to a member of the family of one of those specialists from Texas who are experts at putting out oil field fires. A question whose subtly incredulous overtones Martín may not have noticed, but whose formulation in precisely those words gave him pause, as though he had not previously given any serious thought to the matter one way or another. So that after a moment's silence, he answered (already disturbed by Bruno's doubt, which had rapidly though wordlessly communicated itself to his own mind):

"Well ... maybe ... during that period ..."

And Martín sat there pondering what measure of happiness Alejandra might have felt, or at least manifested: in a smile, a song, a few words. Meanwhile Bruno said to himself: *Well, why not? What is happiness, after all? And why wouldn't she have felt happy with that youngster, at any rate at those moments when she had won a victory over herself, during that period when she was forcing her body and her mind to do fierce battle so as to free herself from demons?* With his head resting on one fist, he continued to look at Martín, trying to understand Alejandra a little better through Martín's sadness, his hopes even after everything was over, his fervor; with the same melancholy attentiveness (Bruno thought) thanks to which one more or less finds that a distant and mysterious country that one has once visited with passion is suddenly brought to life again through the accounts of other travelers, even though one's own journey through that country has been along other paths, in other times.

And the same thing happened as almost always occurs when opinions are exchanged and a certain common ground is arrived at in which neither party's opinion has the rigidity and the dogmatic quality displayed at the beginning of the discussion: while Bruno ended up conceding that Alejandra might well have felt some type or some measure of happiness, Martín, for his part, reexamining memories (an expression, a grimace, a sarcastic laugh) came to the conclusion that even during those few weeks Alejandra had not been happy. How otherwise to explain her frightful collapse later? Didn't that collapse mean that within her tormented spirit a terrible battle had continued to be waged between those demons that he knew existed, but that he more or less put out of his mind, as though in this purely magical way be were capable of doing away with them altogether? And not only did he recall words freighted with meaning that had attracted his attention from the very beginning (*the blind, Fernando*), but also gestures and sarcastic remarks about third parties such as Molinari, silences and moments of reticence, and above all that alienation in which she appeared to live for days on end, periods during which Martín was convinced that her mind was elsewhere, and during which her body remained as abandoned as those of savages when their soul has been torn out of them by witchcraft and wanders about in unknown regions. And he also recalled her abrupt changes of mood, her accesses of raging fury, and her dreams of which she had occasionally given him a vague and troubled account. Nonetheless he still believed that in that period Alejandra had loved him intensely and had had moments of tranquility or of peace if not of happiness; for he remembered beautiful, calm afternoons that they had spent together, the silly, affectionate phrases that couples exchange at such times, the little gestures of tenderness and the friendly jokes. And in any case she had been like one of those combatants who come back from the front, wounded and battered, bled white and nearly helpless, and who little by little come back to life, in quiet, serene days spent at the side of those who care for them and restore them to health.

He passed on some of these thoughts to Bruno, and Bruno sat there pondering the matter, not really persuaded that it had been that way either, or at least not that way entirely. And as Martín looked at him, waiting for a reply, Bruno growled something unintelligible, words as unclear as his thoughts.

Martín did not see things clearly either, and in truth he was never able to explain to himself why the progress that Alejandra had seemingly made had assumed the form or developed along the lines that it had, even though he felt more and more inclined to believe that Alejandra never emerged completely from the chaos in which she had been living before he met her, despite the fact that she had managed to have calm moments; but those dark forces at work within her had never abandoned her, and had again exploded in all their fury toward the end, as though once she had exhausted her capacity to fight back and once she had realized her failure, her desperation had reappeared with redoubled violence.

Martín opened his penknife and allowed his memory to wander back over that period that now seemed extremely remote to him. His memory was like an old, nearly blind man who, cane in hand, goes feeling his way along paths of yesteryear that are now overgrown with weeds. A landscape transformed by time, by calamities and tempests. Had he, Martín, been happy? No, what an absurdity to think so. There had been, rather, a succession of ecstatic moments and catastrophic ones. And he remembered once again that dawn in the Mirador, hearing as he was finishing getting dressed that terrible phrase of Alejandra's: "Well, leave me here alone then." And after that walking down the Calle Isabel la Católica like an automaton, completely bewildered and upset. And then the days that followed, days when he was out of work, lonely days waiting for some favorable sign from Alejandra, other moments of vast exhilaration, and then disillusionment and pain again. Yes, he was like a maidservant who each night was taken to the enchanted palace, only to awaken each morning in the palace pigsty.

PART TWO

The Invisible Faces

A CURIOUS FACT (curious when viewed from the perspective of later events): Martín had seldom been as happy as in the hours preceding the meeting with Bordenave. Alejandra was in an excellent mood and had wanted to go to the movies: but she did not even get out of sorts when Bordenave caused this plan of hers to come to nothing by telling Martín that he would meet with him at seven. And as Martín was on the point of stopping this or that person on the street to ask how to get to the American bar where Bordenave had said he would be, Alejandra kept dragging him away by one arm, as though she were familiar with the place. This was the first thing that marred the happiness of that afternoon.

A waiter pointed Bordenave out to him. He was with two other men, talking with them at a table with some sort of papers in front of them. Bordenave was a man of about forty, tall and elegantly dressed, bearing a rather marked resemblance to Anthony Eden. But eyes with an ironic little glint in them, and a certain crooked smile gave him a very Argentine air. "Ah, it's you," he said to Martín, and apologizing to the other two gentlemen for leaving them, he invited him to sit down with him at a nearby table. But as Martín stammered something and looked in Alejandra's direction, Bordenave, after allowing his eyes to linger on her for a few seconds, said: "Ah, very well, let's join her over there then."

The instant antipathy that this man aroused in Alejandra was obvious to Martín, for she drew birds on a paper napkin during the entire conversation between the two of them: one of the signs of her displeasure that Martín knew only too well. Upset by her sudden change of mood, Martín had to concentrate in order to follow what Bordenave had to say, which appeared to have little to do with the reasons for which Martín had come to meet him. In a word, Bordenave struck him as an unscrupulous adventurer but what was most important was that D'Arcángelo and his father would not be thrown out of their lodgings.

On leaving the bar, he and Alejandra crossed the street and sat down on a bench in the square. Martín, in an anxious mood, asked her what sort of person Bordenave had seemed to her to be.

"What sort do you suppose? An Argentine, of course."

In the light of the match struck for her cigarette, Martín noted that her face had taken on a hard, set expression. Then she just sat there, saying nothing. Martín for his part wondered what could have made her mood shift so suddenly and so drastically, but it was evident that Bordenave was the cause. Speaking at one point of the Italians who had been with him at the other table, Bordenave had spoken, unnecessarily, of certain things they had done that had rubbed him the wrong way. What could all that be about anyway? What was certain was that it was Bordenave's appearance on the scene that had disturbed the peace that had reigned before that, like a snake gliding into a well of crystal clear water from which we are drinking.

Alejandra said she had a headache and would rather go home now and go to bed. And as he was about to say goodbye to her on reaching the Calle Río Cuarto, she finally opened her mouth to say that she would have a word with Molinari about him, but not to get his hopes up.

"How shall I go about getting in to see him? Will you give me a letter to him?"

"We'll see. Maybe I'll just telephone him and then leave you a message."

Martín looked at her in astonishment. A message? Yes, she'd leave word for him as to what Molinari had said.

"But . . ." he stammered.

"But what?"

"What I mean is . . . Can't you tell me what he's had to say when we see each other tomorrow?"

Alejandra's face looked older all of a sudden.

"Look. Right now I can't tell you when we'll be seeing each other."

In consternation, Martín stammered something about the plans they had made that very afternoon for what they would do together the following day, whereupon Alejandra exclaimed:

"I don't feel well! Can't you see that?"

Martín turned around to leave as she was opening the front gate, and had already begun to walk off when he heard her calling after him.

"Wait."

In a less peremptory tone she said to him:

"I'll phone Molinari tomorrow morning, and leave you a message at noon."

She was already inside the gate when she added with a harsh, malicious laugh:

"Take a good look at the secretary he's got, the blonde."

Martín stood there staring at her in bewilderment.

"She's one of his mistresses."

Those were the things that happened that day. Some time was to pass before Martín thought again about that meeting with Bordenave, as after a crime a place or an object that no one had previously thought was important is examined carefully.

᮫ 2 ᮫

YEARS LATER, when Martín came back from the South, one of the subjects of his conversations with Bruno was the relationship between Alejandra and Molinari. Martín had begun speaking of Alejandra again—Bruno thought—like someone trying to restore a soul that has already started to decompose, a soul that he would have liked to be immortal but that he now was aware was cracking apart and falling to pieces little by little, as though accompanying the gradual putrefaction of the body, as though it were impossible for it to survive any longer without its physical support and could linger on only so long as the subtle emanation that had disengaged itself from that body at the instant of death lingered on: a sort of ectoplasm or radioactive gas that in turn will slowly fade away: an emanation that some people consider to be the ghost of the dead person, a ghost that for a time vaguely retains the form of the being who has disappeared, but then becomes more and more immaterial until it finally dissolves into the ultimate nothingness; it is at this moment, perhaps, that the soul vanishes forever, if one excepts those fragments of it, or echoes of fragments of it, that linger on—but for how long?—in the soul of others, of those who knew and hated or loved that being who has disappeared.

And so Martín tried to recover fragments; he wandered down certain streets once more, went back to certain places, had conversations with Bruno, madly gathered together little things, a word or two here and there, like those family members, crazed with grief, who go about doggedly collecting the mutilated bits and pieces of a loved one's body at the spot where the plane crashed; not immediately however, but a long time later, when those remains are not simply mutilated but decomposed as well.

In no other way could Bruno explain why Martín insisted on recalling and analyzing that business with Molinari. And as Bruno thus reflected upon the body and the disintegration of the soul, Martín, talking more or less to himself, said that in his opinion that absurd interview with Molinari was doubtless a key moment in his relationship with Alejandra; an interview that at the time seemed surprising to him, both because Alejandra had arranged it for him, knowing full well that Molinari would not give him work, and because an important, very busy man like Molinari had devoted such a lot of his time to an insignificant youngster like him.

If at that moment—Bruno thought—Martín had had the same perspicacity that he had now, he would have been able to see or would at least have suspected that something extremely disturbing was on the point of exploding in Alejandra's mind. And these signs could have told him that her love, or her affection, or whatever sentiment it was that she felt for him, was about to come to an end: catastrophically.

"We all have to work," Alejandra had said at the time. "Work gives man dignity. I've made up my mind to go to work too."

Despite the irony in her voice, these words made Martín happy, for he had always thought that any sort of concrete occupation would surely be good for her. And the look on Martín's face caused Alejandra to comment: "I see that that piece of news makes you happy," with an expression that had the same irony as before underlying it, though on top of it a few signs of tenderness appeared to be struggling to manifest themselves; just as in a field devastated by calamities (he thought later), amid the swollen, stinking bodies of dead animals, amid corpses ripped open and torn to pieces by vultures, a blade of grass or two struggles to grow despite everything, sucking up tiny invisible traces of water that by some miracle still exist far below the surface of the wasteland.

"But you shouldn't be that happy," she added.

And as Martín looked at her, she explained.

"I'm going to work with Wanda."

Whereupon his happiness vanished—Martín told Bruno—like crystal clear water running off into a sewer, where one knows that it will be mingled with loathsome detritus. Because Wanda belonged to that area of her life, that milieu that Alejandra appeared to have come from when he first met her (although it would be more exact to say "when she searched him out"), an area that she had kept away from in those weeks of relative serenity; although it would also be more exact to say that *he believed* that she had kept away from it, because now, dizzily, he remembered that in recent days Alejandra had begun drinking again, and that her disappearances and sudden absences were becoming not only more and more frequent but more and more inexplicable. But just as it is difficult even to imagine a crime on a bright, clear day, so it was not easy for him to imagine that she might have returned to that region in the midst of their unclouded relationship. Hence he remarked stupidly (an adverb he added to his story much later): "Women's dresses? Design women's dresses? You?" to which she replied by asking if he did not understand the pleasure one can get from earning money by doing something that one has nothing but contempt for. A phrase that at the time seemed to him one of Alejandra's typical clever rejoinders, but one that after her death he was to have other reasons to remember as its hideous overtones echoed in his mind.

"And what's more, it's like a boomerang, don't you see? The more I despise those painted parrots, the more I despise myself. Don't you see that I benefit no matter how you look at it?"

Phrases that kept him from sleeping that night as he analyzed them, until fatigue finally pushed him gently but firmly toward what Bruno called the provisory outskirts of death, premonitory regions wherein we work out our apprenticeship for the great sleep, awkward little stammerings of the dark ultimate adventure, confused rough drafts of the enigmatic final text, with the inferno of nightmares as transitional passages. Hence the next day we are and are not the same, for weighing over our heads are the night's abominable secret experiences. And for that very reason we possess something of that quality of those brought back from death to life and of ghosts (Bruno used to say). Heaven only knows what perverse metamorphosis of Wanda's soul pursued Martín during that night; in any event the next morning he felt for a long time that something heavy but indefinable was stirring in dark regions of his being, until he realized that what was moving about so confusedly deep within him was the image of Wanda. Worse still, he realized this at the very moment that he was entering that imposing waiting room, when it was impossible for him to turn back, if only out of timidity, and when the absurdity of what he was doing finally dawned on him; as in that story by Chekhov or Averchenko (he thought) in which a poor devil finally gets in to see the manager of a bank and declares that he wants to open an account by making a deposit of twenty rubles. What sort of madness was all this? And he was just on the point of summoning up all his courage and stealing out of the waiting room when he heard a Spanish flunky in a fancy doorman's outfit call out "Señor Castillo." In a sarcastic tone of voice, of course (he thought). Because nobody feels as much disdain for poor devils as poor devils in uniform. Very dignified men waiting in the huge leather armchairs, with shoes polished till they gleamed like mirrors, vests with the bottom button unbuttoned, and briefcases stuffed full of Decisive Papers, looked at him with puzzled, ironic expressions (he thought) as he walked toward the big door to the inner offices, as in another stratum of his consciousness he repeated "twenty rubles" to himself in bitter self-mockery, thinking of his shabby shoes with holes in the soles and his stained suit: highly respectable men, all of them, with gold watches on their wrists precisely marking off a time also made of gold, full of Important Financial Deals; a time that stood in sharp contrast to the great useless spaces of his own life, in which his one occupation was thinking on a park bench; crumbs of ragged time that stood in sharp contrast to that golden time as his miserable room in La Boca contrasted with the formidable IMPRA building. And at the very moment that he entered the holy of holies he thought "I have a fever," as he always did in moments of intense anxiety. At the same instant he caught sight of the man sitting behind the gigantic desk in his huge armchair, a corpulent man whose hulking proportions seemed made to order for that enormous building. And with a sort of mad nervous energy Martín repeated to himself: "I've come, sir, to deposit twenty rubles."

"Do sit down," the man said to him, pointing to one of the armchairs as he went on signing Documents being presented to him by a platinum blonde exuding a sensuality that did its share to overwhelm him even more, because (he supposed) she would be capable of stripping herself naked in front of him as though he were simply an artifact, an object with neither a consciousness nor senses; or as great favorites undress before their slaves. "Wanda," he thought then: Wanda drinking dry martinis, flirting with men, with him even, laughing her frivolous, sensual laugh, moistening her lips with her tongue, eating bonbons the way his mother did. At the same time he caught sight of a little chromed mast on the huge desk, flying a miniature Argentine flag; a leather desk cover; an enormous autographed portrait of Perón signed "To Señor Molinari"; various framed Diplomas; a photograph in a leather frame turned toward Señor Molinari; a plastic thermos bottle; and Rudyard Kipling's poem "If," in gothic script, framed on one of the walls. Endless numbers of clerks and functionaries kept parading in and out with papers, and the platinum blonde secretary as well; she had gone out and then come back in to show Molinari other Papers as he spoke to her in a low voice, without the slightest trace of familiarity however, so that no one, least of all the Employees of the Establishment, would possibly suspect that she was sleeping with the Boss.

And then turning to Martín, he said:

"So you're a friend of Drucha's."

And seeing the youngster's baffled look, he laughed and commented, as though it were terribly funny: "Ah, yes, of course, of course," as Martín, dumbfounded, rent with jealousy, said to himself Alejandra, Alejandrucha, Drucha, despite which, or precisely because of which, he took inventory of that tall, corpulent man, dressed in a dark cashmere suit with light-colored stripes, a blue tie with little red polka dots and a pearl stickpin, a silk shirt with gold cufflinks, a silk handkerchief peeking out of the top pocket of his suitcoat, and a Rotary pin in his lapel. A man gone nearly bald, but with what little hair he had left carefully brushed and combed. A man who smelled of cologne and who appeared to have shaved a tenth of a second before Martín had entered his office. And in terror Martín heard him say as he leaned back in his chair, prepared to entertain Martín's Important Proposition:

"What can I do for you?"

A curious desire to mortify himself, to humiliate himself, to confess to the world once and for all his frightful insignificance and his stupid naiveté (so Molinari called Alejandra Drucha, did he?), almost impelled Martín to say: "I've come to deposit twenty rubles." He man-

aged to repress this curious impulse, and with enormous difficulty, as
in a nightmare, he explained that he was out of work and that perhaps
... just possibly ... he had thought ... he had imagined that there
might be some sort of job for him at IMPRA. And as he spoke Señor
Molinari's frown grew deeper and deeper, until nothing remained of
his initial professional smile as he asked him where he had last worked.

"In the López Print Works."

"In what capacity?"

"Proofreader."

"How many hours a day?"

Martín remembered what Alejandra had said, and flushing, he confessed that he had had no fixed working hours, that he had taken
proofs home with him to correct. At this moment Señor Molinari's
frown grew even deeper as he listened to a message over the intercom.

"And why did you lose that job?"

Martín explained that in the printing business there are times when
there is a great deal of work and other times when there is less, and
that in the latter case free-lance proofreaders are let go.

The secretary came in again and said something in Molinari's ear.
He nodded, the secretary went out again, and he listened once more
to a message over the intercom, something about a representative in
Córdoba this time, to which his only reply was: "We'll see next week."
He jotted something down in a notebook, and then, turning back to
Martín, he said:

"So when work picks up they'll no doubt take you on again."

Martín's face turned red again, as the thought crossed his mind that
this man was altogether too shrewd and his last question intended to
make him confess to the truth, a truth that naturally was fatal:

"No, Señor Molinari, I don't believe so."

"And why is that?" he asked, drumming on the desk top with his
fingertips.

"I think, sir, that I had too many things on my mind and ..."

Molinari eyed him in silence, with a cold, penetrating look. Lowering his eyes, Martín found himself saying, without consciously intending to do so: "I need work, sir, I'm having a hard time of it, I'm
desperate for money," and when he raised his eyes, it seemed to him
that he noted an ironic gleam in Molinari's.

"Well, I'm terribly sorry, Señor del Castillo, but I can't help you.

In the first place our work here is very different from the sort you did at the print works. But there's another very important reason as well: you're a friend of Alejandra's and this creates a very delicate problem for me here in the organization. We prefer to have a more impersonal relationship with our employees. I don't know if you follow me."

"Yes, sir, I understand perfectly," Martín said, rising to his feet.

Perhaps Molinari noted something in Martín's attitude that displeased him.

"Nonetheless, when you're older...How old are you? Twenty?"

"Nineteen, sir."

"When you're older you'll see that I'm right. And you're even going to thank me for not taking you on. I'd be doing you no service, you see, if I were to give you a job simply because we have a mutual friend, especially if within a short time, as is not at all difficult to foresee, we'd be having difficulties."

He examined a Document that had been brought in to him, made a few observations in a low voice, and then went on:

"That would have unfortunate consequences for you, for our organization, and even for Alejandra.... I have the impression, moreover, that you're too proud to accept a job that's offered you merely because we have a mutual friend, isn't that so? Because if I were to make a place here for you merely to do Alejandra a favor you wouldn't accept my taking you on, isn't that true?"

"That's true, sir."

"I thought as much. And we'd all come out losers in the end: you, the Company, mutual friends, everybody. My motto is never to mix sentiments with figures."

At that moment a man with Papers came in, but he looked at Martín as though he were at a loss as to what to do with him sitting there. Martín again rose to his feet, but Molinari, taking the papers and starting to examine them without looking up, told him to stay because he hadn't finished what he had to say to him. And as Molinari went through the memorandum or whatever it was, Martín, terribly nervous and humiliated and bewildered, tried to figure the whole thing out: why Molinari was keeping him there, why he was wasting his time with a nobody like him. And to top it all off, the office Mechanism suddenly seemed to go berserk: calls on one or another of the four telephones, conversations over the intercom, the platinum blonde popping in and out, the signing of Papers. When Molinari was informed over the intercom that Señor Wilson wanted to know what had been decided about the Central Bank matter, Martín thought surely he loomed no larger in this entire picture than an insect. Then, on being asked a question by the secretary, Molinari, with unexpected vehemence, almost shouted:

"Let him wait!"

And just as she was about to go out the door, he added:

"And I don't want anybody bothering me till I call. Have you got that straight?"

There was a sudden silence: everyone appeared to have vanished, the telephone stopped ringing, and Señor Molinari, nervous and ill-humored, sat there thoughtfully for a moment, drumming on his desktop with his fingertips. And then, eyeing Martín intently, he asked:

"Where exactly did you meet Alejandra?"

"At a friend's house," Martín lied, turning beet red because he never told lies, but realizing that he would cover himself with ridicule if he told the truth.

Molinari appeared to be scrutinizing him very intently:

"Are you a close friend of hers?"

"I don't know ... what I mean to say is ..."

Molinari raised his right hand, as though there were no need for Martín to go into further detail. After a moment, still observing Martín attentively, he went on:

"You young people today think men of my generation are reactionaries. The fact is, however, and I know this will surprise you, I was a Socialist in my heyday."

At that moment an Important Man peeked in through the side door.

"Come in, come in," Molinari said to him.

The man came over to Molinari, put an arm around his shoulders, and murmured something in his ear, as Molinari nodded his head.

"All right, all right," he commented, "that's fine, let them do as they like."

And then, with what seemed to Martín to be a secretly mocking smile, he added, pointing to him with a little wave of his hand:

"This young man here is a friend of Alejandra's."

The unknown man, his arm still draped across the back of Moli-

nari's chair, smiled at Martín dubiously, and acknowledged the introduction with a slight nod.

"You've come at just the right moment, Héctor," Molinari said.
"You are aware, naturally, of how concerned I am about the problem
of Argentine young people."

The unknown man looked at Martín.

"I was just saying to him that young people always think that the
older generation isn't worth anything, that the way it goes about things
is all wrong, that we're all a bunch of reactionaries, and so on and so
forth."

The unknown man smiled benevolently, and Martín had the impression that he looked upon him as a representative of the New Generation. And the thought also crossed his mind that the Struggle between
Generations was such an uneven battle that his feeling that this entire
situation was absurd was suddenly even more overwhelming, though
he would have thought such a thing impossible at that point: the two
of them, behind that imposing desk, with the entire IMPRA corporation, the autographed photo of Perón, the Mast with the Flag, the
Rotary Club International, and the twelve-story building to back them
up; and confronting them there *he* was, with his threadbare suit and
his belly that had been empty for two whole days now. *More or less
like the Zulus defending themselves against the imperial British Army
with nothing but arrows and painted leather shields*, he thought.

"As I was telling you, I was a Socialist, even an anarchist in fact,
in my day too"—and at that both he and the man who had just come
in smiled broadly, as though remembering something amusing—"and
my friend Pérez Moretti here wouldn't let me lie to you on that score,
because the two of us have been through a lot together. What's more,
you mustn't get the idea we're ashamed of our past. I happen to be
one of those who think it's not a bad thing for young people to have
pure ideals like that in their salad days; there's plenty of time for them
to lose such illusions later on. Later on life proves to you that man
is not made for such utopian societies. In all this world there are not
even *two* men who are alike: one is ambitious, the other an idler; one
is active, the other indolent; one wants to make his way up in the
world, like my friend Pérez Moretti or myself, and the other couldn't
care less if he spends his whole life as a miserable second-rater. In a

word, why go on? Man is by nature unequal, and it is useless to try to found societies in which everyone is equal. Moreover, just think what a vast injustice that would be: why should a hard worker get as much as a loafer? And why should a genius, an Edison, a Henry Ford, be treated in the same way as an unfortunate wretch born to mop up the floor of this room? Doesn't it seem to you that that would be an enormous injustice? And how, in the name of justice, precisely in the name of justice, can a reign of injustices be instituted? This is one of this world's many paradoxes, and I've always been of the opinion that it ought to be spelled out in big capital letters and dealt with at length. I confess that I myself have often been tempted to write something along those lines," he said, looking at Pérez Moretti as though taking him as his witness. And as Martín noted how the latter stood there nodding his head in agreement, he asked himself: *Why in the world is this man wasting all this time with me?*, and arrived at the conclusion that there must be some vitally important connection between Molinari and Alejandra, something that for some mysterious reason meant a lot to this man; and the very idea that there could be important ties of any sort between Molinari and Alejandra tormented him more and more as the interview went on, for the length of the interview was no doubt a measure of the importance of those ties. And then he began to wonder again about Alejandra's reasons for sending him to Molinari, and without knowing why exactly, he concluded that she had done so in order to "prove something," at a time when their relationship was entering a dark period. He therefore began to review once more all the episodes, both important ones and trivial ones, surrounding the name "Molinari" in his memory, as a detective searches with his magnifying glass for any trace or sign, however insignificant it might appear to be at first glance, that could possibly lead to the truth. But his brain got all confused, for Molinari's voice, as he went on expatiating upon his General Conception of the World, was superimposed upon this anxious search for enlightenment. "The passing of the years, life, which is hard and pitiless, little by little convince one that such ideals, however noble they may be, because there is no question that they are extremely noble ideals, are not made for men such as they really are. They are ideals conjured up by dreamers, by poets, I am tempted to say. They are surpassingly beautiful, hence very conducive to the writing of books, to the delivering of speeches on the barricades, yet utterly impossible to put into practice. I'd like to see a Kropotkin or a Malatesta managing a corporation like this one and struggling day after day with the regulations imposed by the Central Bank (and at this point he laughed, with Señor Pérez Moretti joining in with a hearty laugh of his own) and having to engage in a thousand and one maneuvers to keep the labor unions or Perón, or both of them together, from tripping a person up. Or taking things from another point of view, it's all very well for a boy or a girl to have those ideals of unselfishness, or social justice and theoretical societies. But then you get married, you want to regularize your situation in the eyes of society, you must settle down and make a home, the natural aspiration of anyone with a decent background, and this brings about the gradual abandonment of these chimeras, if you follow me. It's very easy to uphold the anarchist doctrine when you're young and being supported by your parents. But it's another thing altogether to have to confront life, to find yourself obliged to support the household you've established, especially when children and other obligations that go with family life come along: clothes, school, textbooks, illnesses. Social theories are all well and good, but when it's necessary to bring home the bacon, as the vulgar saying goes, it's necessary then, my young friend, to bow to reality and realize that the world isn't made for idle dreamers, for Malatestas or Kropotkins. And please note that I'm talking only about anarchist theoreticians, because they at least don't preach the dictatorship of the proletariat the way the Communists do. Can you imagine anything as horrendous as a dictatorial government? Take Russia, for example. Millions of slaves laboring under the knout. Freedom, my friend, is sacred, it is one of the great values that we must preserve, at whatever cost. Freedom for all: freedom for the worker, to seek work wherever he chooses, and freedom for the employer, to give work to anyone he pleases. The law of supply and demand and the free play of the social mechanism. Take your own case: you come here, of your own free will, and offer me your labor; for x reasons it doesn't suit me and I don't accept it. But you are a free man and can leave here and offer your services to the company across the street. Just think how invaluable all that is: you, a humble young man, and I, the president of a great corporation, are nonetheless on an equal footing as we act in accordance with this law of supply and demand; those in favor of a controlled economy can say what they please, but this is the supreme law of any well-organized society and each time that this man (he pointed to the autographed photo of Perón), each time that this man interferes with the workings of free enterprise it only does us harm, and in the final analysis it harms the country. And that's why my motto, as my friend Pérez Moretti knows very well, is: neither dictatorships nor social utopias. And I won't say a word about the other problems, the ones we might call problems of an ethical and moral nature, inasmuch as man does not live by bread alone. I am talking about the need of the society in which we live for order, for a moral hierarchy, without which, believe me, everything collapses. Would you like it, for instance, if someone were to question your mother's decency? Please understand: that is a hypothetical case that I permit myself to put before you as an example. I note that you yourself frowned just now; that does you honor, for it reveals in and of itself precisely how sacred the concept of the mother is for you, as it is for me. Well then, how to reconcile this concept with a society in which free love exists, in which no one is responsible for the children swarming all over the place, in which marriage has been thrown overboard as a mere bourgeois institution? I don't know if you understand what I mean. If the foundations of the home are undermined . . . Is something wrong?"

Martín, deathly pale and about to faint, was passing his hand across his forehead, which was covered with an icy sweat.

"No, no," he answered.

"Well, as I was saying, if the foundations of the home, which are the very cornerstone of the society in which we live, are undermined, if you destroy the sacrosanct concept of marriage, what is left, I ask you? Chaos. What ideals, what examples can be held up to young people growing up today? All these are things that can't be played around with, young man. And I'll tell you something else, something that I rarely tell anybody but that I feel it my duty to tell you. I am referring to the problem of prostitution."

But at that instant the intercom buzzed, and as Molinari testily spoke into it and asked *What? What?*, Martín went on searching with his magnifying glass, reeling, more and more lost in that repellent fog and saying *Wanda, Wanda* to himself, repeating to himself those cynical words of Alejandra's about the necessity of working, and that phrase about her contempt for painted parrots and her consequent contempt for herself; so that, he said to himself, as though summing up his investigations, Wanda was one of the elements of that enigma, and Molinari was another, and what others might there be? And then he went over previous episodes in his mind again and found nothing that stood out, since all there had been was that meeting with that individual named Bordenave, a person unknown to Alejandra and moreover someone she had taken an instant dislike to, with the result that her mood had suddenly changed and she had become sullen and gloomy. Meanwhile he saw that the stern expression that Molinari had presented to the intercom was now beginning to transform itself into the affable expression that he had decided to present to him, Martín. With his eyes fixed on him, Señor Molinari seemed to be searching for the lost thread of what he had been saying, and then finally he went on:

"Ah yes, prostitution. Just consider for a moment what a paradox it represents. If I tell you that prostitution is necessary, I know perfectly well that you, at this moment, are going to be inclined to reject that conclusion, isn't that so? I am convinced, however, that once you have analyzed the problems carefully, you will be obliged to agree with me. Imagine what the world would in fact be like if it were not for this safety valve. Right now, and without going any farther afield, right here in our own country, a mistaken idea of what true morality is (and I'll tell you straight out that I'm a Catholic) led the Argentine clergy to press for the prohibition of prostitution. And so prostitution was made illegal in the year ..."

He hesitated for a moment and looked over at Señor Pérez Moretti, who was listening to him attentively.

"It was in '35, as I remember," Señor Pérez Moretti said.

"Right. And what happened as a result? What happened was that clandestine prostitution made its appearance. As was only logical. And to make matters worse, clandestine prostitution is more dangerous because there are no health inspections. And besides that it is expensive; it is out of the reach of the pocketbook of a worker or a salaried employee. Because there is not only the money one has to pay the woman;

there is also the money one has to spend to get a room somewhere. The result: Buenos Aires is undergoing a process of demoralization whose consequences we cannot predict."

Tilting his head to one side and addressing Señor Pérez Moretti, Molinari commented:

"As a matter of fact, at the last meeting of the Rotary Club I spoke about this very problem, which has come to be one of the serious vices of this city and perhaps of the entire country."

And addressing Martín again, he went on:

"It's like a boiler with all the valves closed in which the pressure is mounting. For that is what organized, legal prostitution is: a safety valve. Either there are women of easy virtue controlled by the State, or we end up with the situation we have now. Either we have good, solid, controlled prostitution or sooner or later society will run the extremely grave risk of seeing its basic institutions collapse. I am of the opinion that this dilemma is inescapable and I am one of those who think that the solution does not lie in behaving as the ostrich does in the face of danger, namely burying its head. I wonder if a nice girl from a decent family can have any peace of mind today, and above all if her parents can rest easy. I won't even mention the coarse and dirty things that the girl can't help hearing on the streets in the mouths of vulgar young lads or men who have no natural outlet for their instincts. I am leaving all this out of consideration, however unpleasant it may be. But what about the other danger? The danger that in the relationships between young people, between engaged couples, or even a boy and a girl who are simply good friends, things will go too far? What the devil, a boy's naturally hot-blooded; he's got instincts after all! You'll pardon me, I hope, for putting the matter so crudely, but there's no other way to look squarely at this problem. And to make things worse, this boy is constantly overexcited because of the lack of a form of prostitution within his means, because of films I pray God to rid us of, because of pornographic publications. In a word, what else can we expect? Moreover, young people no longer have the restraints that in other times were imposed on them by a home possessed of solid principles. Because to tell the truth, here in this country we're just Catholics from the skin out. But as for real Catholics, honest-to-goodness Catholics, believe me, they number probably no more than five percent, and I think that's a generous estimate at that. And the rest? Without that moral restraint, with parents who are more concerned about their personal affairs than they are about keeping an eye on what ought to be a real sanctuary . . . What's the matter?"

Señor Pérez Moretti and Señor Molinari hurried over to Martín.

"It's nothing, sir. It's nothing," he said, pulling himself together. "I beg your pardon, but it's best that I leave . . ."

He got up to go, but seemed to stagger. He was deathly pale and drenched with sweat.

"No, young man—wait and I'll have somebody bring you some coffee," Señor Molinari said.

"No, Señor Molinari. I'm all right now, thank you very much. The air outside will make me feel even better. Goodbye, and many thanks."

Molinari and Señor Pérez Moretti held him by the arm and accompanied him to the door. The moment he was out of their sight he ran with all the strength he could muster. When he reached the street he looked around for a café, but did not see one close by. Unable to hold back a moment longer, he rushed over to an empty space between two cars and vomited.

⁊ 3 ⁊

As HE WAITED in the Criterion, looking at photographs of Queen Elizabeth on one wall and engravings of naked women on the other, as though the Empire and Pornography (he thought) could honorably coexist, just as decent families and brothels coexist (and not despite this latter fact but rather precisely because of it), his thoughts returned to Alejandra, as he wondered how and with whom she had happened to discover this Victorian bar.

At the counter, beneath the petty-bourgeois smile of the queen ("there has never been a royal family who are such nonentities," Alejandra said immediately), British company managers and upper level executives were downing their gin or their whisky and laughing at each other's jokes. *The pearl of the Crown,* he thought, at almost the same moment he spied her coming in the door. She ordered a Gilbey's, and after listening to Martín's story she commented:

"Molinari is a respectable man, a Pillar of the Nation. In other words: a perfect pig, a first-class son of a bitch."

She called the waiter over as she said:

"By the way, you've asked me about Bruno lots of times. I'll introduce you to him now."

∽ 4 ∽

THEY WENT INTO La Helvética. It was a dark place, with its high wooden counter and its old *boiseries*. Clouded distorting mirrors enlarged and murkily repeated the mystery and the melancholy of this corner of Buenos Aires left over from another era.

A very fair-haired man with blue eyes and incredibly thick glasses rose to his feet. He had a sensual, pensive air about him and appeared to be about forty-five. Martín noticed that he was looking at him with a kindly expression, and thought, blushing: *She's told him about me.*

They talked together for a few moments, but Alejandra's mind was obviously elsewhere, and finally she got up, said goodbye to them, and left. Martín found himself sitting alone across the table from Bruno, feeling as ill at ease as though he were about to present himself for an oral examination and depressed by Alejandra's sudden disappearance, as inexplicable as ever. And suddenly he realized that Bruno was asking him a question, the beginning of which he had not heard. He was embarrassed and was about to ask him to repeat it when, fortunately, a redheaded man with freckles, an aquiline nose, and piercing eyes glinting from behind glasses arrived. He had a fleeting, nervous smile. Everything about him was intimidating and from time to time his manner had such a sarcastic abrasiveness about it that it would have prevented Martín, had he been alone with him, from so much as opening his mouth, even if the place caught on fire. Moreover, the man had a way of staring directly into a person's eyes, thus affording the timid no escape whatsoever. As he talked with Bruno, leaning toward him across the little table, he kept glancing furtively out of the corner of his eye, like someone who is a victim, or has been a victim in the past, of police persecution.

He laid a book down on the little table.

"I've just read the article by Pereira about it," Bruno remarked with a smile, referring to the book.

Méndez assumed one of his most successful diabolical expressions.

His red hair seemed to give off sparks, like those featherdusters charged with static electricity in classroom physics demonstrations. His eyes lit up with a sarcastic gleam.

"Ha! He starts in by attacking even the title. Imagine: *Latin America: One Country!*"

"Exactly. His thesis is that it was a whole made up of nationalities oppressed by Spain."

"Ha! That guy's head is stuffed full of Russian notions. A whole made up of nationalities! What he's thinking about all along is Kirgizes, Caucasians, Byelorussians." *The country (Martín thought), the country, the home, seeking the cave in the shadows, the home, the warmth of the fire, the tender and brightly lighted refuge amid the darkness,* and as Bruno raised his eyes, perhaps in doubt, *those eyes that had seen Alejandra as a child, those melancholy, gently ironic eyes, as he saw the figure of Wanda emerge along with the phrase "earn money by doing something that one has nothing but contempt for," not knowing at that moment, however, what monstrous import this phrase of Alejandra's would one day come to have, though already it had an import somber enough to fill him with anxiety, as he saw Wanda drinking dry martinis, talking about men, laughing her frivolous, sensual laugh, and that Janos creature, that inexplicable husband of hers* and Bruno listened to Méndez thoughtfully, stirring his cup of coffee *and then Martín looked at his slender nervous hands and wondered what sort of love this man could have had for Alejandra's mother, not yet knowing that that love had later been prolonged by being projected onto her very own daughter, so that the same Alejandra whom Martín was thinking about at that moment had also been the object of thoughtful reflections on the part of this man who was now before his eyes, as yet not suspecting that they had that in common, even though (as Bruno himself was to think many times and even hint as much) the Alejandra of his own thoughtful reflections was not the same Alejandra who was now tormenting Martín since (Bruno maintained) we are never the same person for different conversational partners, friends, or lovers; like those complex resonators in physics classes, one or another of whose strings responds to each sound that stimulates them, while the others remain silent, as though self-absorbed, estranged, reserved for a summons that may perhaps some day require their response; a summons that sometimes never*

comes, in which case those mute strings end their days as though for-
gotten by the world, alien and solitary, as meanwhile, carried away by
his ironic fury, Méndez exclaimed: "Somebody like him, talking about
an abstract internationalism! Bravo, Pereira, bravo! He's discovered
Argentina now. For years he lived Russian-style, eating borscht instead of soup, drinking tea instead of maté. Argentina was an exotic
island that we were condemned to live on, but our heart was in
Moscow, comrades! *and he could see Janos again, with that equivocal,*
anxious look in his eyes (why?), with that exaggerated, obsequious
politeness of his, kissing her hands, saying "oui, ma chère" or "comme
tu veux, ma chère" to her, and why had that repugnant man come to
mind now so insistently, seemingly forever in search of something,
seemingly keeping watch and on his guard at every moment, an
anxious watch, motivated no doubt by Wanda's wanton behavior, but
then he saw someone greet Bruno and sit down at another table with
a group talking together in low voices, as Méndez sarcastically noted
the greeting and said: "Those clerical nationalists, those arch-His-
panophiles who have now discovered the United States are busy
hatching one of their plots, naturally! They've had a scare thrown
into them by Peronism, of course, the only defense against Soviet
barbarism," *and once again he lost track of what the two of them were*
saying as he sat there thinking about Janos, until he seemed to hear
Bruno saying something about corruption, whereupon Méndez declared: "That's petty-bourgeois morality," *as Bruno gently shook his*
head and said: "That's not what I mean" *and Martín was very upset*
because he couldn't keep his mind on the discussion, thinking "I'm a
terrible egotist," because he found his thoughts returning again to
that dreadful obsequious figure and his attitude, his permanent watch-
fulness, something doubtless motivated by the presence or the absence
of Wanda, but what? and Wanda accepting him with a mixture of
condescension and sarcasm, as though the two of them, as though be-
tween the two of them, but then Bruno said "because he corrupts
everything he touches, because he's a cynic who believes in nothing,
who doesn't believe in the people or even in Peronism, because he's a
coward and a man without grandeur," *as Méndez shook his head*
ironically, doubtless thinking "an incurable petty bourgeois," *and as*
Martín thought how confused everything is, how hard it is to live and
understand: as though that equivocal Janos were something like the

symbol of the confusion that had taken possession of him, as though the very essence of human beings was ambiguity, Janos with his fawning and his affected politeness toward his wife and yet (and he had taken special note of this, like everything having to do with Alejandra) with that anxious, longing look of someone who fears or hopes for something, in this case something from Wanda, out of jealousy perhaps?, whereupon Alejandra had burst out laughing at him, commenting "What a child you still are!" adding those words that later, after the tragedy, he was to remember with terrifying clarity: "Janos is a sort of sticky monster," and at that moment Bruno got up from the table to make a phone call, so Martín was left there alone sitting across from Méndez, who scrutinized him with eyes full of curiosity as Martín, thoroughly intimidated, sipped at a glass of water, not daring to say a word.

Luckily Bruno reappeared.

"It's stifling in here," he said to Martín. "Shall we go outside?"

"It's a very stuffy café, but I like it. It's not going to be here much longer though—just think how many millions this corner is worth. It's bound to happen any day now: they'll tear it down and put up a skyscraper, and downstairs there'll be one of those interplanetary bars complete with all the garish colors and earsplitting noises the Yankees have invented."

Bruno loosened his tie.

When they arrived at the bridge on the Calle Belgrano, Bruno stopped and leaned over the railing, saying: "At least we can breathe now." Martín wondered whether Alejandra had gotten that habit of lingering on the bridge from Bruno; but then the thought came to him that it must have been the other way around, because Bruno struck him as a person who was essentially passive, following the wavering compass of this thoughts.

He noted his fine skin, his delicate hands, and compared them in his mind with Alejandra's hard, greedy hands, with her tense, angular face. Meanwhile Bruno thought: Only impressionism could render these landscapes, and impressionism was a thing of the past now, so that the artist who feels this and only this is plain out of luck. And looking at the overcast sky, the humid and rather heavy haze, the reflections of the boats in the still water, the thought came to him that the sky and air of Buenos Aires were very much like those of Venice, no doubt because of the vapor rising from the stagnant water, as on another level he continued to ponder Méndez's line of reasoning.

"Literature, for example. Méndez and others of his persuasion have opinions that are terribly cut and dried. Proust in their view is a degenerate artist because he belonged to a decadent class."

He laughed.

"If that theory were correct Marxism wouldn't exist, and hence Méndez wouldn't exist either. Marxism would have to have been invented by a worker, and more particularly by one with a job in heavy industry."

They strolled along the pedestrian walkway leading over the bridge and then Bruno suggested they sit on the parapet and watch the river.

Martín was amazed at this very young trait in Bruno, a trait that in his eyes was evidence of the cordial camaraderie that Bruno felt toward him; and all the time that the latter was willingly spending with him, his affectionate familiarity seemed like a guarantee of Alejandra's tender feelings toward him, Martín; for all this would not have been granted him by an important man if he, Martín, an unknown youngster, had not had Alejandra's esteem and perhaps even her love in his favor. Hence this conversation, this walk, their sitting together there on the parapet served as a sort of confirmation (albeit an indirect one, a tenuous one) of his love, a sort of guarantee (albeit a vague one, an ambiguous one) that she was not as remote and withdrawn as he had supposed.

And as Bruno breathed in the muggy breeze off the river, Martín remembered similar moments on that very same parapet with Alejandra. With his back leaning against the thick wall, with his head in her lap, he was (he had been) truly happy. In the silence of that late afternoon he could hear the quiet murmur of the river down below as he contemplated the endless metamorphoses of the clouds: heads of prophets, caravans in a pure white desert, sailboats, snow-covered bays. Everything was (had been) peace and serenity at that moment. And with tranquil sensual pleasure, as in the drowsy, fuzzy moments that follow waking, he had made his head comfortable on Alejandra's lap, as he thought how tender, how sweet it was to feel her flesh beneath the nape of his neck; that flesh that according to Bruno was something more than flesh, something more complex, more subtle, more mysterious than mere flesh made up of cells, tissues, nerves; for it was also (in Martín's eyes at this moment), it was already a *memory*, and therefore something that would resist death and corruption, something transparent, something tenuous, yet at the same time possessed of a certain eternal and immortal quality; it was Louis Armstrong playing his trumpet in the Mirador, the skies and clouds of Buenos Aires, the modest statues of the Parque Lezama in the late afternoon, a stranger strumming a zither, a night in the Zur Post restaurant, a rainy night when they had taken shelter beneath a marquee (laughing), streets in the southern section of the city, the rooftops of Buenos Aires seen from the bar on the twentieth floor of the Comega. And he had felt all of this by way of her flesh, her soft, palpitating flesh which, though destined to disintegrate amid worms and clods of damp earth (one of Bruno's typical thoughts), at that moment allowed him to glimpse that sort of eternity; for as Bruno would also one day tell him, we are constituted in such a way that the only means given us to catch a glimmer of eternity is by way of the fragile, perishable flesh. And he had sighed then and she had said: "What is it?" And he had answered "nothing," that word we answer when we are thinking "everything." And at that moment Martín said to Bruno, almost despite himself:

"Alejandra and I were here one afternoon."

And as though he were on a bicycle unable to stop, having lost control, he went on:

"How happy I was that afternoon!"

The moment he uttered these words he was overcome by regret and embarrassment: it was such an intimate, such a pathetic thing to have said. But Bruno neither laughed nor smiled (Martín was looking at him almost in terror), but instead sat there, grave and thoughtful, contemplating the river. And then, after a long silence that led Martín to think that he was not going to make any sort of comment, Bruno said:

"That's how happiness comes along."

What did he mean? Martín sat there listening intently, as he always did when it was something having to do with Alejandra.

"It comes in bits and pieces, at different times. When we're children we hope for great happiness, some enormous, total happiness. And as we wait for this phenomenon to take place we let the little happinesses, the only real ones, pass us by, or fail to appreciate them. It's as if..."

He fell silent at that point however. Then after a time he went on:

"Imagine a beggar who doesn't deign to accept alms as he makes his way from place to place, because people have told him about a fabulous treasure. A treasure that doesn't exist."

He sat there lost in thought once again.

"They seem to be mere trifles. A quiet conversation with a friend. Those seagulls wheeling about perhaps. This sky. The beer we drank a while ago."

He changed position.

"My leg's gone to sleep. It's as though somebody had squirted soda water into it."

He climbed down from the parapet and then added:

"Sometimes I think that these little happinesses exist precisely because they're little ones. Like those mere nobodies passing by that no one ever notices."

He fell silent, and then for no apparent reason he said:

"Yes, Alejandra is a complicated person. And so different from her mother. But then it's really absurd to expect children to be like their parents. Maybe the Buddhists are right, and if so how do we have any way of knowing who's going to be incarnated in the bodies of our children?"

As though he were telling a joke, he recited:

> Perhaps at our death the soul migrates:
> to an ant
> to a tree
> to a Bengal tiger
> as our body disintegrates
> amid worms
> and filters into the earth that has no memory
> thence to ascend through stem and leaf,
> and be transformed into a heliotrope or a blade of grass,
> and then into forage for cattle
> and thus into nameless animal blood,
> into a skeleton,
> into excrement.
> Perhaps a more hideous fate awaits it

in the body of a child
who will one day write poems or novels,
and in his mysterious fits of anguish
(without knowing it)
will purge his soul's past sins
as warrior or criminal,
or relive terrors,
the fear of a gazelle,
the loathsome ugliness of a weasel,
its dark condition as fetus, cyclops, lizard,
its fame as prostitute or pythoness,
its loneliness in remote places,
its forgotten acts of cowardice and betrayal.

Martín heard him out in bewilderment: on the one hand it seemed as though Bruno were reciting the whole thing as a joke, yet on the other hand he felt that in some way that poem was a serious expression of what he thought of life: his hesitations, his doubts. And knowing already how extremely modest and shy he was, he said to himself: *It's one of his own poems.*

He rose to his feet and said goodbye; he had to go see D'Arcángelo.

Bruno's eyes followed him affectionately, as he said to himself: *How many things he still has to suffer.* And then, stretching out on the parapet with his hands under the nape of his neck, he allowed his thoughts to wander.

The seagulls flew back and forth.

Everything was so fleeting, so transitory. He should write, if for no other reason than that: to immortalize something ephemeral. A love, perhaps. *Alejandra*, he thought. And also: *Georgina*. But what, exactly, of all that? How? How terribly difficult everything was, how fragile, like delicate glass.

Moreover, it was not only that, it was not simply a question of immortalizing, but of investigating, digging down into the human heart, examining the most secret recesses of our condition.

Nothing and everything, he almost said, with that habit of his of unexpectedly expressing his thoughts aloud, as he shifted to a more comfortable position on the parapet. He looked up at the stormy sky and heard the rhythmical lapping of the river against the shore, that river that (unlike the other rivers of the world) flows in no direction, stretching out almost motionless over an area a hundred kilometers wide, like a peaceful lake, or like a roaring sea on days when the wind is blowing from the southeast. But at that moment, on that hot summer day, on that humid and sultry afternoon, with the transparent haze of Buenos Aires blurring the silhouette of the skyscrapers standing out against the huge thunderheads in the west, it was only slightly rippled by a distracted breeze, its skin barely trembling, as though with the dim memory of great storms, those great storms that seas surely dream of when they doze, mere ghostly, incorporeal storms, dreams of storms, that can do no more than make the surface of their waters shudder slightly as great sleeping mastiffs dreaming of hunting or fights quiver and growl almost imperceptibly.

Nothing and everything.

He leaned over the parapet toward the city and contemplated the silhouette of the skyscrapers once again.

Six million people, he thought.

Suddenly everything seemed impossible to him. And useless.

Never, he said to himself. *Never.*

The truth, he said to himself, with an ironic smile. THE truth. Well, let us say A truth then—but wasn't a truth *the* truth? Couldn't "the" truth be reached by penetrating to the depths of a single heart? In the end, weren't all hearts identical?

A single heart, he said to himself.

A boy was kissing a girl. An eskimo-pie vendor pedaled by on a bicycle and he hailed him. And as he sat on the parapet eating the ice cream bar, he looked at the monster again, millions of men, women, children, workers, office clerks, pensioners. How to speak of all of them? How to represent that reality irreducible to numbers in a hundred pages, a thousand, a million pages? But—he thought—a work of art is an attempt, an absurd one perhaps, to represent an infinite reality within the limits of a single painting or a single book. A choice. But that choice turns out to be infinitely difficult, and in the majority of cases a disaster.

Six million Argentines, Spaniards, Italians, Basques, Germans, Hungarians, Russians, Poles, Yugoslavs, Czechs, Syrians, Lebanese, Lithuanians, Greeks, Ukrainians.

O Babylon!

The biggest Galician city in the world. The biggest Italian city in the world. Et cetera. More pizzerias than in Naples and Rome put together. "Typically Argentine." What in heaven's name did *that* mean?

O Babylon!

With the gaze of a little impotent god he contemplated the gigantic, chaotic conglomerate, tender and cruel, hated and loved, standing out like a fearsome leviathan against the great threatening storm clouds in the west.

Nothing and everything.

But it is also true—he reflected—that just one person is enough. Or perhaps two or three or four. If you probed deeply into their hearts.

Day laborers or rich men, day laborers or bankers, handsome devils or hunchbacks.

The sun was setting and the color of the clouds in the west kept changing by the second. Great gray violet tatters stood out against a background of clouds farther in the distance: gray, lilac, blackish. *That pink's an unfortunate touch*, he thought, as though he were at a painting exhibition. Then the pink started running more and more, cheapening the whole effect. But then it finally began to fade, and passing through purple and violet, it turned to gray and finally to the black that announces death, which is always solemn and always lends an air of dignity.

And the sun disappeared.

And one more day thus ended in Buenos Aires: something lost forever, something that inexorably took him one step closer to his own death. And so quickly now, so quickly. In the past the years had gone by more slowly and everything had seemed possible; time had stretched out before him like a highroad that was free and clear all the way to the horizon. But now the years were flying by faster and faster toward the west, and again and again he caught himself saying: "Twenty years ago, when I last saw him...," or some other thing as trivial yet as tragic as that; and then immediately thinking, as though on the brink of an abyss, how little, how miserably little remains of that march toward nothingness. And what was it all for?

And when he reached that point and it seemed that nothing had any meaning any more, he would perhaps come across one of those little mongrels that roam the streets, starving and longing for affection, with his little fate (as little as his body and his little heart that would courageously put up a struggle until the very end, defending that tiny, humble life as from a minuscule fortress), and then, gathering him up in his arms, taking him to an improvised doghouse where at least he wouldn't be cold, giving him something to eat, gradually becoming the very meaning of the poor creature's existence, something more enigmatic but more powerful than philosophy seemed to give meaning to his own existence again. Like two helpless waifs who in the midst of their loneliness sleep together to keep each other warm.

∾ 5 ∾

PERHAPS at our death the soul migrates," Martín repeated to himself as he walked along. Where had Alejandra's soul come from? It seemed ageless, it seemed to have come from the depths of time. "It's dark condition as fetus, its fame as prostitute or pythoness, its loneliness in remote places."

The old man was sitting at the door of the tenement building on his little straw chair. He was holding his knotty wooden cane in his hand, and his worn, greenish bowler looked entirely out of keeping with his coarse wool undershirt.

"Hello, papa," Tito said.

They made their way inside, clearing a path for themselves amid all the kids, cats, dogs, and chickens. Tito picked up two other little chairs in the room and handed them to Martín.

"Here, take these outside, and I'll be along with some maté right away," he said to him.

Martín took the chairs outside, set them down next to the old man, and sat down shyly and waited.

"*Sì, sì*," the old coachman murmured, "that's how it was..."

How what was? Martín wondered.

Sì, sì," the old man said again, nodding his head as though agreeing with an invisible conversational partner.

And suddenly he said:

"I was a little boy like that *bambino* over there with the ball and my *babbo* would sing:

Quando la tromba sonaba alarma
*co Garibaldi doviamo parti.**

He laughed, nodded his head several times, and repeated "Si, si ..."

The ball came their way and almost hit the old man. Don Francisco made a vague threatening gesture with his knotty cane as the kids came running after the ball, picked it up, and went off making faces.

After a moment the old man said:

"We were climbing up the *mondaña* with the *giovani* from Cafaredda and sat us down to look at the *mare*. Eating roasted *castagne,* we were. *Quiddo mare azule!*"

Tito came out with the maté gourds and the kettle.

"He's bending your ear about his village, that's for sure," he said to Martín. "Hey, papa, don't bore the kid to death with all those tall tales of yours"—winking an eye at Martín and smiling roguishly.

The old man shook his head, his eyes gazing toward that distant land now left behind forever.

Tito smiled with gentle irony as he prepared the maté. And then, as though his father didn't exist (and obviously he wasn't even listening), he explained to Martín:

"He spends his days thinking about the village he was born in, you see."

Tito turned to his father, shook his arm a little as though to wake him up, and asked him:

"Hey, pop! Would you like to see all that again? Before you die?"

The old man answered by nodding his head several times, still gazing off into the distance.

"If you had just a little pocketful of *soldi,* would you go back to Italy?"

The old man nodded again.

"If you could go back just for one minute, pop, just one little minute, even though you had to die the next minute, what would you say to that?"

The old man shook his head dejectedly, as though to say: Why even imagine such wondrous things?

---

* When the trumpet sounded the alarm
  We had to march off with Garibaldi.

And like someone who has demonstrated an important truth, Tito looked at Martín and remarked:

"Didn't I tell you, kid?"

"*Sì*," old Don Francisco murmured. "When *Natale* came round, they let 'em come down."

Tito winked at Martín.

"They let who come down, pop?"

"The *briganti.*"

"You see. It's always the same thing with him. Why did they let the bandits come down, pop?"

"*Per andare a la santa misa. Due hore.*"

He nodded his head, gazing off into the distance.

"*Sì*, they gave 'em two hours to go to Christmas mass. *La notte de Natale*. And *i fusilli* played the *zampogna.*"

"And what did the shepherds with the bagpipes sing, pop?"

"They sang:

> *La notte de Natale*
> *è una festa principale*
> *que nascio nostro Signore*
> *a una povera mangiatura.**

"And was there lots of snow, pop?"

"*Sì, sì* . . . lots."

And he sat there thinking his thoughts about that fabulous land. And Tito smiled at Martín with a look compounded of irony, sorrow, scepticism, and shyness.

"Didn't I tell you? It's always the same story."

∽ 6 ∽

MANY DAYS went by without any signs of life from Alejandra, and finally he decided to phone her. He managed to spend a few moments with her in the bar on the corner of Esmeralda and

---

* Christmas night
is a great feast
for Our Lord was born
in a lowly manger.

Charcas, a meeting that left him in a worse frame of mind than before for some reason; she had spent all of the brief time they were together doing nothing but tell him horrible things about the women who came to the boutique.

Then the endless days went by once again, and again Martín screwed up his courage and phoned. Wanda answered and told him Alejandra wasn't in just then, but she'd give her his message. But still there was no word from her.

Several times he was on the point of giving in to temptation and going round to the boutique. But he stopped himself from doing so in time, because he knew she would think he was interfering in her life and consequently (he thought) dropping by the boutique would drive her even farther away—just as (he told himself) the victim of shipwreck who is desperately thirsty as he drifts in his lifeboat must resist the temptation to drink salt water, because he knows that it will only make his thirst even more insatiable. No, of course he wouldn't call her. Perhaps what was happening was that he had already interfered with her freedom too much, been too much of a burden on her; because his loneliness had driven him to throw himself, to fling himself on her. And perhaps if he gave her all the freedom she could possibly want things would again be as they had been in the very first days.

But a more profound conviction (though it was one he could not have put into words) led him to believe that for human beings time never comes round again, that it is never again what it once was, and that when feelings change or deteriorate there is no miracle that can restore their initial quality: like a flag that gradually gets dirtier and dirtier and more and more worn (he had heard Bruno say). But his hope fought on, since (as Bruno thought) hope never gives up the struggle even though it is doomed to defeat, for the very reason that hope arises only in the midst of adversity and because of it. Could anyone else, later on, give her what he had given her? His affection, his understanding, his boundless love? But immediately the words "later on" made him feel even more downcast, for they brought to mind a future in which she would no longer be at his side, a future in which another—another!—would say words to her that resembled those that he had said to her, words that she had listened to with her eyes burning with fervor, at moments that now seemed unbelievable to him: eyes and moments that he had imagined would be his for all eternity, whose absolute, moving perfection would endure forever, like the beauty of a statue. And she and that Other whose face he could not even imagine would walk together through the same streets, visit the same places that she had gone to with Martín; while he would no longer exist for her, or would be little more than a fading memory, a figure vaguely evoking pity and affection, or perhaps annoyance or amusement. And then he forced himself to picture her in moments of passion, uttering the secret words that lovers say to each other in such moments, with the entire world and Martín too, Martín above all, terribly excluded, banished from that bedroom peopled only by their naked bodies and their moans. Then Martín would rush to a telephone, telling himself that all he need do to hear her voice was to dial six digits. But he would hang up before the call could go through, because he already had enough experience to realize that one can be at another's side, hear and touch that person, and yet be separated by impassable walls; just as once we are dead our spirit can be near the one we loved and yet tormentingly isolated from that being by this invisible but impassable wall that forever keeps the dead from communing with the world of the living.

Many long days went by then.

Then finally he made up his mind to go to the boutique, even though he knew that the only thing that would be accomplished thereby would be to goad the wild beast that existed within Alejandra, that wild beast that detested any sort of intrusion. And even as he was saying to himself "No, I won't go there," he found himself heading directly toward the Calle Cerrito; and at the very moment that he arrived at the door of the boutique he was still repeating to himself with stubborn but useless vehemence: "I absolutely must not see her."

A woman with malevolent-looking goggle-eyes, loaded with jewelry and wearing garish makeup, came out just then. Alejandra never seemed to be as far away from him as when she was with women like that: the wives or mistresses of corporation executives, prominent doctors, captains of industry. "And such conversations!" Alejandra often commented. "Conversations that can only be heard in fashionable boutiques like Wanda's or at a women's hairdresser's. Having dye jobs, sitting underneath Martian contraptions, with hair of every conceivable color dripping with liquid garbage, with mouths that look like sewer outlets, filthy holes in faces slathered with creams, out of which there inevitably come pouring out the same words and jokes; giving each other advice, letting all their rottenness show, telling what should and what should NOT be done with so-and-so. And all of it interlarded with talk of sicknesses, money, jewelry, clothes, tumors, cocktail parties, big bashes, abortions, company management, promotions, stocks, lovers who can or can't get it up, divorces, betrayals, secretaries, and who's cheating on whom." Martín listened to her in amazement and then she burst out laughing, a laugh as sardonic as the scene she had just described. "But how can you bear all that? How can you work in such a place?" Martín stammered, ingenuous questions that she answered with one of her sarcastic grins: "Because basically, mark my words, basically all women, each and every last one of us, have a body and a uterus. And we'd best not forget it, and take a good look at those caricatures, the way beautiful women in medieval engravings can be seen contemplating a skull. And because curiously enough, in their own way those monsters are really quite honest and true to themselves, since the garbage that they are is too evident for them to be able to fool anybody." No, Martín didn't understand, and he was certain that Alejandra also had other thoughts on the matter.

And then he opened the door and went into the boutique. Alejandra looked surprised to see him, but after greeting him with a wave of her hand, she went on with what she was doing and told him to have a seat.

At that moment a very odd creature entered the boutique.

"*Mesdames*," he said, bowing with grotesquely exaggerated politeness.

He kissed Wanda's hand, then Alejandra's, and added:

"As the divine Popesco put it in *L'habit vert:* 'I prostitute myself at your feet.'"

He then turned to Martín and inspected him as though he were a rare piece of furniture that he might be planning to acquire. Laughing, Alejandra introduced them from a distance.

"You look at me with astonishment and you have every reason in the world to do so, my young friend," he said candidly. "I shall explain. I represent a whole made up of unexpected parts. For instance, when I haven't yet opened my mouth, people who don't know me think I must have a deep bass voice like Chaliapin's, whereas in fact it's falsetto. When I am sitting down, they presume that I'm small in stature, because I have an extremely short torso, and then when I stand up I turn out to be a giant. Seen from the front, I look slender, but when seen in profile I'm very stout."

As he spoke, he demonstrated practically every one of his statements and to Martín's stupefaction he realized that all of them were true.

"I belong to the Gillette category, according to Professor Assole's famous classification. I have sharp features, a long nose that's also sharp, and above all an enormous belly with a sharp edge to it, like those idols on Easter Island. It's as though I'd grown up between two boards, do you realize*?"

Martín noticed that the two women were laughing, and they were to go on laughing the whole time that Bobby was in the shop, like background music in a film; imperceptibly at times, so as not to disturb his amusing flights of eloquence, and hilariously at other times, at certain high points, without this bothering him in the slightest. Martín looked at Alejandra with a pained expression. How he detested that face of hers, her boutique-face, the one that she seemed to put on deliberately in order to play her role in that frivolous world; a face that seemed to linger on once she found herself alone with him, its abominable features fading away only very slowly, as there gradually emerged one or another of the faces that belonged to him alone, a face he waited for as one awaits a beloved traveler amid a repulsive crowd. But as Bruno said, the word *person* means "mask," and each of us has many masks: that of father, professor, lover.... But which one is the real one? And is there in fact one that is the real one? At certain moments Martín thought that the Alejandra that he was now seeing there before him, laughing at Bobby's jokes, was not, *could not be* the same Alejandra that he knew, and above all could not be the more profound, the marvelous and fearsome Alejandra that he loved. But at other times (and as the weeks went by the more he began to be convinced of it), he was inclined to think, as Bruno did, that *all* these Alejandras were real and that that boutique-face was genuine too and in some way or other expressed a sort of reality inherent in Alejandra's soul: a reality—and heaven only knew how

---

* For "do you understand?" An Anglicism, frequent among the upper classes in Buenos Aires. [*Author's note*]

many others there were!—that was foreign to him, that did not belong to him and never would. And then, when she came to him still bearing the faint traces of those other personalities, as though she had not had the time (or the desire?) to transform herself, Martín discovered—in a certain sarcastic grin on her lips, in a certain way of moving her hands, in a certain glint in her eyes—the lingering signs of a strange existence: like someone who has been around a garbage dump and still retains something of its foul stench in our presence. That was the thought in his mind as he heard Wanda say, without so much as a pause between bonbons:

"Tell us more about last night."

A question that Bobby, laying a book that he had with him down on a table, answered in a few delicate, serene, well-chosen words:

"Pure shit, *ma chère*."

The two women laughed uproariously, and when Wanda could speak again she asked with her Slavic syntax:

"How much you make on paper?"

"Five thousand seven hundred twenty-three pesos and fifty-seven centavos, plus a bonus at the end of the year and the tips the boss gives me when I go out to buy him cigarettes or shine his shoes."

"Look, Bobby: why not leave paper and come here? We pay you thousand pesos more. Just to give us few laughs."

"Sorry, old girl. Professional ethics prevent my doing so—if I left the rag, you see, it'd be Roberto J. Martorell who'd take over the drama reviews. And that would be a national disaster, my pet."

"Be nice, Bobby. Tell about last night," Wanda wheedled.

"I've told you: pure shit. Unspeakably vulgar."

"Yes, of course, silly. But tell us details. About Cristina especially."

"Ah, *la femme!* Wanda, you're the perfect Weininger woman. Bonbons, prostitution, gossip-mongering. I adore you."

"Weininger?" Wanda asked. "Who's that?"

"Your delivery is perfect, absolutely perfect. Bravo!" Bobby said. "I adore you."

"Come on, be nice. Tell about Cristina."

"The poor dear. She kept wringing her hands like Francesca Bertini in one of those films the kids shown in their cine-clubs. But the chap who played the part of the writer came straight from his job at the Ministry of Commerce."

"Why, do you know him?"

"No, but I'm certain of it. A functionary who's worn to a nub, the poor bastard. It's plain to see he's frightfully concerned about some problem or other at work, getting himself pensioned off at half pay or something of the sort. A little short fat man who'd just left his paperwork on his desk and come to the theater *pour jouer l'écrivain*. I can't tell you how touching I found him: positively senile."

At that moment a woman entered the boutique. Martín, who felt as though he were in the midst of a grotesque dream, was vaguely aware that he was being introduced to her. When he realized that it was Cristina, the very same woman that Bobby had just been talking about, and when he saw how effusively Bobby greeted her, he flushed. Bobby bowed to her and said:

"You look positively *ravissante,* darling."

Feeling the material of her dress, he added:

"Absolutely divine. And that shade of lilac goes so well with your coiffure."

Cristina gave a shy, fearful smile: she never knew whether she should believe him or not. She didn't dare ask him his opinion of the play, but Bobby proceeded to offer it to her anyway:

"Stupendous, Cristina! And what a prodigious effort, you poor things, what with all that racket coming from next door.... By the way, what is all that next door anyway?"

"A dance hall," Cristina replied warily.

"Ah, of course.... How dreadful! Just as you got to the hardest parts, they kept breaking into a mambo. And to top it all off they apparently had a tuba. Unspeakably vulgar."

Martín saw Alejandra hurry into the other room, almost at a run. Wanda went on working, with her back turned to Bobby and Cristina, but her body shook all over in a silent fit of laughter. Bobby went on imperturbably:

"There ought to be a law against tubas, don't you think so, Cristina? What an utterly uncivilized instrument! And of course you had to shriek like savages, you poor dears, in order for people to hear you. Awfully hard for you, wasn't it? Especially that chap playing the part of the famous writer. What's his name? Tonazzi?"

"Tonelli."

"Ah, yes, Tonelli. The poor devil. Not somebody you'd think of as having the *physique du rôle*, would you say? And having to fight it out with the tuba all evening on top of everything else. What a prodigious effort! The public has no idea what that means, Wanda. And what's more, Cristina, it strikes me as a very good idea to have cast somebody like that in the role, somebody who doesn't look the least bit like a writer, who looks more like a functionary about to be pensioned off. When they put on O'Neill's *Rope* at Telón, for instance, the sailor looked exactly like a real sailor. Very clever: that way everybody knew right away that he was supposed to be a sailor. Though I must say that the minute the fellow began to talk, or to mumble rather (because nobody could understand a word he said), he was so indescribably awful that even though he looked just like a sailor he didn't seem like one at all: he might have been a street sweeper, a construction worker, a café waiter. But a sailor? *Jamais*! And why the devil do you suppose it is, Cristina, that amateur theatrical companies invariably go in for O'Neill? How awful for the poor man! But then O'Neill always did have the worst sort of luck; beginning with his father and his Oedipus complex. And then here in Buenos Aires, having to work as a stevedore down at the docks lugging huge sacks around. And now with all the amateur groups everywhere in the world putting his plays on." He spread his great long arms, as though to embrace this universal conglomerate, and with a look of genuine sadness on his face he added:

"Thousands, what am I saying, millions of amateur theatrical companies putting on *Rope, Mourning Becomes Electra, The Emperor Jones, Desire Under the Elms....* Poor chap! That's more than sufficient reason for taking to the bottle and not wanting to see a soul! Your group is different, of course, Cristina: in fact you're not really amateurs any more, since you charge as much as though you were professionals. And that's all to the good: it's just not possible for poor people to have to work during the day as sewer cleaners or bookkeepers and then have to play *King Lear* for nothing at night.... Especially since all those crimes are so exhausting.... Of course there's always another solution: putting on nice quiet works, with no crimes and no incest. Or one or two crimes at most. But amateur groups are only interested in works with lots of crimes, real mass slaughter, Shakespeare let's say. Not to mention the work on the side, sweeping out the hall, being responsible for the props, painting the walls, selling tickets at the box office, serving as ushers, scrubbing out the toilets. Just to keep up everybody's morale. A sort of phalanstery. Everybody taking his turn cleaning the john, with no exceptions. And so one day Señor Zanetta directs the company in *Hamlet,* and Norah Rolland cleans the loo. On another day the aforementioned Zanetta cleans the *double ve-ce* and Norah Rolland directs *Desire Under the Elms.* Not to mention the fact that for two years and a half they've all worked like crazy as bricklayers, carpenters, painters, and electricians, fixing up the place. Noble activities in the midst of which they've been photographed and interviewed by countless reporters, thus justifying the use of words such as *fervor, enthusiasm, noble aspirations, people's theater, authentic values,* and *vocation.* But naturally this sort of phalanstery sometimes comes a cropper. Dictatorship lurks eternally behind demagoguery. And so Señor Mastronicola, after having cleaned the john two or three times, invents the doctrine whereby Señorita Caca Spaghettini, known in theatrical circles by her *nom de guerre* Elizabeth Lynch, is altogether too high and mighty, having been corrupted by her rotten, decadent counterrevolutionarypettybourgeois tendencies and hence it is necessary, for the sake of her moral and dramatic education, for her to clean the crapper all during the year 1956, which to add insult to injury also happens to be a leap year. And all of this is complicated by the amorous *affaires* of Esther Abramovich, who joined the amateur theater group so as to sleep around with anything in pants, as the saying goes, since according to the director she has turned this noble bastion of pure art into a real bawdy house. And then there's the jealousy of Diana Ferrer, who wouldn't dream of letting the aforementioned Mastronicola escape her clutches. And then pent-up anger of the young character actor Ramsés Cuciaroni, whom they've stuck in the box office out of sheer spite ever since their revolving democracy began to break down. In short, a first-rate bordello. So the best thing, Cristina, is to turn professional the way all of you have. Even though that old gaffer works in some ministry in the daytime, doesn't he?"

"What old gaffer?"

"Tonazzi."

"Tonelli. . . . Tonelli isn't old. He's barely past forty."

"*Tiens!* I would have sworn he was over fifty at the very least. That just goes to show you what bad stage lighting can do. But he works in an office somewhere in the daytime, doesn't he? I seem to remember seeing him in the café across the street from the Ministry of Commerce."

"No, he has a little shop where he sells books and school supplies."

Wanda's shoulders were shaking as though she were having an attack of malaria.

"Ah, that's splendid! I can see now why they gave him the role of the writer. Of course. I must confess he looks more like a government functionary to me, but that's probably because I was terribly tired last night and what with that business with the electric company the lights are so dim, but that's not the group's fault naturally. Well, I'm glad to hear he's got a little shop anyway. That means he probably doesn't have to get up very early the days after a performance. Luckily, because his throat must be in a terrible state, the poor thing, what with that accursed mambo-playing next door and the tuba and all. Well, I must be running along, it's terribly late. Congratulations, Cristina. I bid you a fond farewell, dear girl!"

He kissed Wanda's cheek, filching a bonbon from her box at the same time.

"Ta-ta, Wanda. And watch your figure. Bye-bye, Cristina, and congratulations again. That *ensemble* is just darling on you."

He stretched out a hand to one side to shake Martín's, as the latter sat there as though turned to stone, and then from above the folding screen separating the boutique from the workroom in the back, he shouted to Alejandra on the other side:

"*Mes hommages,* darling!"

∞ 7 ∞

SITTING THERE petrified on the tall stool, Martín waited for some sign from Alejandra. As soon as Bobby had left, Alejandra motioned to him to come into the back room with her, where she was sketching.

"You see?" she said to him, as though to explain the reason why she hadn't gotten in touch with him. "I've got a tremendous amount of work to do."

As he mechanically opened and closed his white penknife, Martín watched Alejandra tracing lines on a blank sheet of paper. She went on sketching in silence and time seemed to be passing through blocks of cement.

"Well," Martín said, summoning all his strength of will, "I'll be off ..."

Alejandra came over to him, gave his arm a squeeze, and said they'd see each other soon. Martín bowed his head.

"We'll see each other soon, I said," she reiterated in an irritated tone of voice.

Martín raised his head.

"You know very well, Alejandra, that I don't want to interfere in your life, that your independence ..."

He didn't finish the sentence, but then he added:

"No, what I mean to say is ... at least ... I'd like to see you when you're not pressed for time ..."

"Yes, of course," she conceded, as though thinking it over. Martín's spirits rose.

"We'll try to be the way we were before, do you remember?"

Alejandra looked at him with eyes that seemed to betray sadness and disbelief.

"What, doesn't that seem possible to you?"

"Yes, Martín, yes," she replied, lowering her gaze and making little doodles on the paper with her pencil. "Yes, we'll spend a wonderful day together ... you'll see ..."

Feeling encouraged, Martín said:

"Lots of our misunderstandings lately have been due to your work, the pressures on your time, the appointments you've had to keep ..."

Alejandra's face had begun to change.

"I've already explained to you that I'll be very busy till the end of the month."

Martín made a great effort not to remonstrate with her, because he knew that recrimination would get him nowhere. But the words welled up from the depths of his mind with silent but uncontainable force.

"It hurts my feelings when I see you keep looking at your watch."

She raised her eyes and stared at him, frowning. In terror Martín said to himself: *not one more word of reproach,* yet he added:

"Last Tuesday, for instance, when I thought we were going to spend the whole afternoon together."

THE INVISIBLE FACES · 163

A severe look had already come over Alejandra's face; it made Martín draw up short as though on the brink of a precipice.

"You're right, Martín," she admitted nonetheless.

Martín dared to add then:

"That's why I'd rather have you be the one to say what day we can see each other."

Alejandra made some mental calculations and said:

"Friday. I think that by Friday I'll have finished the things that are most pressing."

She thought some more.

"But at the last minute there's always something to do over or something that's missing, things like that.... I wouldn't like to keep you waiting.... Don't you think it would be better to put the whole thing off till Monday?"

Monday! That was almost a week away.... But what could he do but make the best of it and agree?

He tried to dull his mind with work during that endless week, and he also whiled away the time reading, walking about the streets, going to the movies. He sought Bruno out, and even though he was eager to talk about Alejandra, he found himself incapable of even uttering her name. And since Bruno guessed what was going through his mind, he too avoided mentioning her and spoke of other things or dealt in generalities. Martín's spirits would then revive enough for him to say certain things that also appeared to have some general import, things seemingly pertaining to the abstract and disincarnated world of pure ideas, but in reality they were the barely impersonalized expression of his own hopes and anxieties. Thus when Bruno spoke to him of the absolute, Martín would ask, for example, whether true love were not precisely one of those absolutes; a question in which the word *love* had about as much to do with the word as employed by Kant or Hegel as the abstract word *catastrophe* has to do with a train derailment or an earthquake, with their dead and mutilated, with their screams and their bloodshed. Bruno replied that in his opinion the quality of love between two beings who are attached to each other changes from one instant to the next, becoming suddenly sublime, then descending to triviality, then later turning into something affectionate and comfortable, only to turn abruptly into a tragic or devastating hatred.

"Because there are times when lovers do not love each other, or when one of them does not love the other, or detests him, or has contempt for him."

Meanwhile Bruno thought about the phrase that Jeannette had once uttered to him: *L'amour c'est une personne qui souffre et une autre qui s'emmerde.* And he remembered, observer of unhappy people that he was, a couple he had seen one day in a deserted corner of a dark café; the man gaunt, unshaven, suffering, reading a letter for the hundredth time—surely one from the woman there with him—reproaching her, taking the absurd piece of paper as proof of heaven only knows what pledges or promises; and each time he concentrated furiously on some phrase or other in the letter, she looked at her watch and yawned.

Then as Martín asked him whether everything ought not to be completely clear and transparent and based on the truth between two beings who love each other, Bruno replied that in almost no instance can the truth be told when it is a question of human beings, since it can only bring pain, sadness, and destruction. He also remarked that he had always held high hopes for his plan to write a novel or a play on this very subject ("but that's all I am: a man who has plans," he added with a shy, self-deprecating smile): the story of a youngster who decides always to tell the truth, always, at whatever cost. And of course he sows destruction, horror, and death in his wake, until finally he ends up bringing about his own destruction, his own death.

"So it's necessary to lie," Martín concluded bitterly.

"I'm simply saying that it's not always possible to tell the truth. In fact, strictly speaking, it's almost never possible."

"So one lies by omission?"

"Something like that," Bruno replied, looking at him out of the corner of his eye, fearing he might be hurting his feelings.

"So you don't believe in the truth then."

"I believe that there is indeed truth in mathematics, in chemistry, in philosophy. But not in life. In life illusion, imagination, desire, hope count for more. Moreover, do we even know what the truth is? If I tell you that that bit of window over there is blue, I am voicing a truth. But it is only a partial truth, and therefore a sort of lie. Because that bit of window is not all by itself, it's in a house, in a city, in a physical setting. It's surrounded by the gray of that cement wall, the clear blue of the sky, those streaks of clouds, and countless other things.

And if I fail to mention everything, absolutely everything, I am lying. But saying *everything* is impossible, even in the case of this window, of a simple bit of physical reality, simple physical reality. Reality is infinite, and furthermore it has infinite shadings, and if I forget a single one of them I am lying. Now just imagine for a moment what the reality of human beings is like, what with their complications and their twists and turns and contradictions; and what is more, they are forever changing. Hence this reality changes with each passing moment, and we no longer are what we were a moment ago. Are we always the same person even? Do we always have the same feelings for instance? One can love someone and suddenly lose all respect for him and even detest him. And if on losing all respect for him we make the mistake of telling him so, this is a truth, but a momentary truth, one that will no longer be true within an hour or the next day or in other circumstances. And yet the person to whom we say that will believe that it *is* the truth, the truth from first to last, forever and always. And he will be overcome by despair."

ᴏᴡᴏ 8 ᴏᴡᴏ

Aɴᴅ ᴛʜᴇɴ it was Monday at last.

Seeing her walking toward the restaurant, Martín said to himself that the word *pretty* was not the right one for her, or even the word *lovely;* perhaps she could be said to be *beautiful,* but above all she was *regal.* Even in her simple white blouse, her black skirt, and her little flat-heeled slippers. A simplicity that brought out her exotic features even more, just as the beauty of a statue is more noticeable in a square that is not decorated in any way. Everything seemed to glow that afternoon. And even the calm weather that day, the lack of wind, the strong sun that seemed to be delaying the arrival of autumn (that autumn, he thought later, that had been lying in ambush somewhere, waiting till he was all alone before unleashing all its sadness), everything appeared to indicate that all the astral signs were favorable.

They walked down to Costanera.

A locomotive was pulling freight cars, a crane was hoisting a machine, a seaplane flew by low in the sky.

"The Progress of the Nation," Alejandra remarked.

They sat down on one of the benches overlooking the river.

They sat there for nearly an hour not saying a word, or at least not saying anything important, lost in thought, amid that silence that Martín always found so unnerving. Their sentences were as cryptic as a telegram in code and would have made no sense to an outsider: "that bird ...," "the yellow of that smokestack ...," "Montevideo...." But they did not make plans as they once had, and Martín was careful not to bring up things that risked ruining that afternoon, that afternoon he was treating like a beloved invalid, in whose presence one must speak in a low voice and who must be spared even the slightest momentary annoyance.

But that sentiment—Martín could not help thinking—was by its very essence contradictory, since if he wanted to preserve the happiness of that afternoon it was precisely for the sake of happiness, for what to him was the very definition of happiness: namely, being with her and not simply at her side. Better still: being *in* her, within each one of her interstices, her cells, her footsteps, her feelings, her ideas; within her skin, on top of her body and inside it, at one with that desired and admired flesh, *with* her *within* her: a communion and not a simple, silent, sad proximity. So that preserving the purity of that afternoon by not talking, by refraining from trying to be inside her, was easy, but at the same time as absurd and as pointless as not having any afternoon with her at all, as easy and as senseless as preserving the purity of crystal clear water by not drinking it even if one is dying of thirst.

"Let's go to your room, Alejandra," he said to her.

She looked at him gravely and then after a moment said she'd rather go to the movies.

Martín took out his penknife.

"Don't be like that, Martín. I'm not well, I really don't feel at all well."

"You're radiant," Martín answered, opening the little blade of the knife.

"I'm not feeling well again, I tell you."

"It's your own fault," he pointed out in a more or less spiteful tone of voice. "You don't take care of yourself. I saw you eating things just now that you shouldn't eat. And what's more you keep downing one martini after the other."

He sat there in silence and began to chip slivers of wood from the bench.

"Don't be that way."

But as he sat there stubbornly keeping his head down, she put her hand under his chin and raised it up.

"Listen, Martín, we promised each other we'd have a peaceful afternoon together."

Martín grunted.

"And naturally you think that if we aren't having a pleasant afternoon it's not your fault, isn't that so?" she went on.

Martín didn't answer; there was no point in doing so.

Alejandra fell silent. Then Martín heard her say all of a sudden:

"All right then. That's fine with me: let's go to my house."

But Martín didn't say a word. She had already gotten to her feet, and grabbing him by the arm she asked him:

"What's the matter now?"

"Nothing. You're acting as though it were a big sacrifice."

"Don't be silly. Let's go."

They began to walk uptown along the Calle Belgrano. Martín's spirits had revived and suddenly, as though the idea really appealed to him, he exclaimed:

"Let's go to the movies!"

"Stop talking nonsense."

"No, I don't want you to miss that film. You've been waiting to see it for such a long time."

"We'll go see it some other day."

"You really don't want to go see it?"

If she had said she did, he would have fallen into the blackest mood imaginable.

"No, no."

Martín felt happiness flow back into his soul, like a mountain river when it thaws. He strode along determinedly, with Alejandra's arm in his. As they passed the drawbridge they saw a taxi heading toward the river with passengers in it. They motioned to the driver to indicate that they were going back into the city, on the chance that he'd come back that way and pick them up. The driver nodded. The astral signs were definitely auspicious that day.

They stood there leaning on the parapet of the bridge. In the distance, to the south, the transshipping bridges of La Boca stood out amid the fog that had begun to settle.

The taxi came back and they climbed in.

Once in the Mirador, as Alejandra was making coffee, Martín searched about among the records and found one that she had just bought: "Trying." And when Ella Fitzgerald's raw, broken voice sang:

> *I'm trying to forget you, but try as I may,*
> *You're still my every thought every day ...*

he saw Alejandra stop dead still, with her cup in her hand, and heard her say:

"How great! *Knocking, knocking at your door ...*"

Martín looked at her in silence, saddened by the shadows that kept forever stirring behind certain of Alejandra's phrases.

But then those thoughts were swept away like leaves before a violent wind. And as they clutched each other in their arms like two beings trying to swallow each other (he remembered), that strange rite, each time more savage, more profound, more desperate, took place once again. Swept along by his body, amid the tumult and the consternation of the flesh, Martín's soul tried to make itself heard by that other on the far side of the abyss. But that attempt at communication that was to end eventually in cries almost without hope had begun some time before, in the moments leading up to the climax: not only by way of the words that were said but also by way of looks and gestures, caresses, and even the clawing of their hands and the rending of their mouths. And Martín tried to reach, to feel, to understand Alejandra by touching her face, stroking her hair, kissing her ears, her neck, her breasts, her belly; like a dog in search of a hidden treasure that sniffs at the mysterious surface concealing it, that surface full of signs, signs that remain obscure and imperceptible to those whose senses are not attuned to them. And as the dog, suddenly sensing that the mysterious thing that it is searching for is closer, begins to dig with febrile, almost maddened fervor (cut off altogether from the outside world now, crazed and demented, all thought and feeling centered on that unique and powerful secret thing so close now), so Martín attacked Alejandra's body, trying to enter her so deeply that he would reach the very bottom of the dark, painful enigma: digging, biting, frantically penetrating and seeking to perceive the faint sounds, closer and closer now, of the secret, hidden soul of this being so cruelly near and so hopelessly far away. And as Martín probed, Alejandra perhaps struggled there on her own island, shouting a message in code that for him, Martín, was unintelligible, and for her, Alejandra, most likely pointless, and for both desperate.

And then, as after a combat that has left the battlefield strewn with corpses and yet has settled nothing, both lay there in silence.

Martín tried to see the expression on her face, but could make out nothing in the almost total darkness that the room now lay in. They left then.

"I have to make a phone call," Alejandra said.

She went into a bar and made her call.

Martín watched her anxiously from the door. Whom could she possibly be calling? And what could she possibly be saying?

She came back looking depressed and said:

"Let's go."

Martín noted that she seemed distracted, that when he said something or other to her from time to time she kept answering only *Hmmm? What did you say?* And she kept looking at her watch every few minutes.

"What is it you have to do now?"

She looked at him as though she hadn't heard his question. Martín repeated it and she replied:

"I have to be somewhere at eight o'clock."

"Very far away?"

"No," she answered vaguely.

∽ 9 ∽

HE WATCHED HER walk off, feeling sad.

It was a day early in April, but autumn was already beginning to announce itself with premonitory signs, like those nostalgic trumpet echoes (he thought) that can be heard in a symphonic theme that is still dominant, though already they are warning us, with a certain hesitant, gentle, but growing insistence, that that theme is coming to an end, that these echoes of remote trumpets will draw closer and closer until finally they become the major theme. A few dead leaves, the sky that looked as though it were already preparing itself for the long cloudy days of May and June, announced that the most beautiful season in Buenos Aires was silently approaching. As though after the oppressive stridence of summer the sky and the trees were beginning to take on that air of withdrawal from the world round about of things readying themselves for a long period of lethargy.

〜 I O 〜

HIS FOOTSTEPS took him mechanically to Chichín's, but his mind continued to follow Alejandra. And with a sigh of relief, as though he were arriving at a known port after an anxious journey fraught with danger, he heard Tito saying: *This country's a hopeless mess,* pounding on his copy of *Crítica,* as though to prove something that they had just been discussing perhaps.

〜 I I 〜

BUT MARTIN soon left the bar and began to walk toward the park. He went up the stairs of the old *quinta,* smelled again the strong odor of stale urine that he could always smell when he passed that way, and sat down on the bench in front of the statue, the spot he returned to every time that his love seemed to be undergoing a crisis. He sat there a long time pondering his fate and torturing himself with the thought that at that very moment Alejandra was with someone else. He leaned back on the bench and abandoned himself to his thoughts.

〜 I 2 〜

THE NEXT DAY Martín telephoned the one person whom he could bear to see in Alejandra's stead: the one bridge leading to that unknown territory, an accessible bridge but one that ended in a hazy, dreary region, not to mention the fact that his reserve, and Bruno's, kept him from talking about the one thing that interested him.

He arranged to meet Bruno at La Helvética.

"I must go see Father Rinaldini, but we'll go there together," Bruno proposed.

He explained to Martín that Father Rinaldini was very ill and that he, Bruno, had just made representations to Monsignor Gentile in Rinaldini's behalf, hoping that the latter would be granted permission to return to Rioja. But the bishops detested Rinaldini and it was only fair to say that Rinaldini went out of his way to give them reason to do so.

"Some day, when he dies, people are going to talk a lot about him. It's the same as with Galli Mainini. Because in this country full of men burning with resentment one begins to be a great man only when one ceases to be resentful."

They were walking down the Calle Perú; grabbing Martín by the arm, Bruno pointed a man out to him who was walking in front of them, leaning on a cane.

"Borges."

When they drew closer, Bruno said hello to him. Martín found himself shaking a tiny hand, with scarcely any bones or strength in it. The features of the man's face seemed to have been sketched in and then to have been half rubbed out with an eraser. Borges mumbled something, acknowledging the introduction.

"Martín's a friend of Alejandra Vidal Olmos's," Bruno said.

"*Caramba, caramba* ... Alejandra ... that's fine."

He raised his eyebrows, observed Martín with watery blue eyes and an abstract cordiality addressed to no one in particular, his mind obviously elsewhere.

Bruno asked him what he was writing.

"Well, *caramba* ...," he mumbled, smiling a half-guilty, half-wicked smile, with that air that Argentine peasants assume, an air of modest irony, a mixture of secret arrogance and apparent diffidence, every time someone admires one of their horses or their ability to do fine leatherwork. "*Caramba* ... well, in a word ... trying to write a page or two that's something more than a scribble, eh, eh? ..."

And he mumbled something else, accompanied by a series of clownish facial tics.

And as they walked on toward Rinaldini's, Bruno imagined Méndez saying sarcastically: *A lecturer for snooty women's clubs!* But everything was much more complicated than Méndez thought.

"It's curious that fantastic literature is so important and of such high quality in this country," Bruno commented. "I wonder why that is?"

Martín timidly asked Bruno whether it might not be a way of escaping Argentine reality because it was so unpleasant.

"No. Reality is also unpleasant in North America. There must be some other explanation. And as for what Méndez thinks of Borges ..."

He smiled.

"They say he's not very Argentine," Martín ventured to remark.

"What else could he be but Argentine? He's a typical national product. Even his so-called Europeanism is national. A European is not Europeanist: he's simply European."

"Do you think he's a great writer?"

Bruno pondered the question for some time.

"I don't know. What I'm certain of is that his prose is the most remarkable of any being written in Spanish today. But his style is too precious for him to be a great writer. Can you imagine Tolstoy trying to dazzle his readers with an adverb when it's a question of the life or death of one of his characters? But not everything in Borges's works is Byzantine: far from it. There's something Argentine in his best things: a certain nostalgia, a certain metaphysical sadness ..."

He walked along in silence for a time.

"The fact is that people say all sorts of ridiculous things about what Argentine literature *ought* to be. The important thing is for it to be profound. All the rest is just an added fillip. And if it isn't profound it's useless to introduce gauchos or colorful picaresque rascals into the picture. The most representative writer in Elizabethan England was Shakespeare. Yet many of his works don't even have an English setting."

And then he added:

"... And what amuses me most is that Méndez denies the influence that Europe has had on our writers. And what does he base that opinion on? That's what's most amusing of all: on a philosophical doctrine that is the handiwork of a Jew, Marx; a German, Engels; and a Greek, Heraclitus. If we followed the strictures of such critics, we would be obliged to write about ostrich-hunting in Querandí. And all the rest would be imported frills and antinational. Our culture has its roots in Europe—how can we get around that? And for that matter, why even try to get around it? Somebody—I don't remember who—said he didn't read so as not to lose his originality. Can you imagine? If a person has been born to create or express original things, he's not going to lose anything by reading books.... Faulkner for one read Joyce and Huxley, Dostoevski and Proust. Moreover, and this is something new in history, we Latin Americans find ourselves on a different, violent continent; everything here takes a different turn altogether. So critics want total and absolute originality, do they? Such a thing doesn't exist. Neither in art nor in anything else. Everything is built on what has gone before. Nothing that is human is perfectly pure and pristine. The Greek gods too were hybrids and were infected (so to speak) with Oriental and Egyptian religions. There's a little passage in *The Mill on the Floss* in which a woman tries on a hat in front of a mirror: and it's Proust. What I mean to say is, it's the seed of Proust. All the rest is simply a process of development. One touched with genius, cancerous almost, but in the final analysis simply a process of development. The same thing is true of one of Melville's stories, called *Bertleby* or *Bartleby* or something like that. When I read it I was impressed by its Kafkaesque atmosphere. And that's the way it always is. We're Argentines, for example, even when we reject our country, as Borges frequently does. Especially when he repudiates it with real fury, the way Unamuno repudiates Spain; the way violent atheists put bombs in a church, that being their way of believing in God. The true atheists are those who are indifferent, those who are cynics. And what we might call an atheistic attitude toward this native land of ours is to be found among cosmopolitans, individuals who live no differently here than they would in Paris or London—they live in a country as though it were a hotel. But let's be fair: Borges is not one of them. I think that in a certain way his heart aches for his country, despite the fact that he doesn't have the sensitivity or the generosity, of course, for it to ache for his country the way the heart of a day laborer in the fields or a worker in a meat-freezing plant does. And that explains his lack of grandeur, his inability to understand and feel the whole of the country, including all its deep-rooted, complex rottenness. When we read Dickens or Faulkner or Tolstoy on the other hand we feel that total understanding of the human soul.

"And what about Güiraldes?"

"In what sense?"

"His supposed Europeanism, I mean."

"Well, yes, there is something of that about his work. In a certain sense a number of passages of *Don Segundo Sombra* could have been written by a Frenchman who had lived on the pampa. But please note, Martín, that I said 'in a certain sense' and 'a number of passages. ...' By that I mean that it is not a novel that could have been written by a Frenchman. The work as a whole strikes me as essentially Argentine, though Lynch's gauchos are truer to life than Güiraldes's. Don Segundo is a mythological peasant, but even so he has all the power of a myth. And the proof that it's a genuine myth is that it's taken hold in the very soul of our people. Not to mention the fact that Güiraldes's metaphysical preoccupation is Argentine. That is typical of our writers: just look at Hernández, Quiroga, Roberto Arlt ..."

"Roberto Arlt?"

"No question. Lots of fools think he's important for his local color. No, Martín, almost everything in his work that is picturesque local color is a defect. He's great *in spite of* that. He's great because of the awesome metaphysical and religious tension in Erdosain's monologues. *The Seven Madmen* is riddled with defects. I don't mean stylistic or grammatical ones; that would be of no importance. What I mean is that it's full of 'literature' in quotation marks, of pretentions or apocryphal characters, such as the Astrologer. But Arlt is a great writer despite all that."

He smiled.

"But ... on the whole the fate of great artists is quite sad: when they're admired, it's usually for their weaknesses and their shortcomings."

Rinaldini himself came to the door to let them in.

He was a tall man with very white hair and an austere, aquiline profile. In his expression there was an intricate combination of kindliness, irony, intelligence, modesty, and pride.

The apartment was very shabby, but full to overflowing with books. When Bruno and Martín walked in, there were remains of bread and cheese alongside his papers and a typewriter. Rinaldini shyly tried to whisk them away without their noticing.

"All I can offer you is a glass of Cafayate wine." He went and got a bottle of it.

"We've just seen Borges on the street, Father," Bruno said.

Rinaldini smiled as he set out glasses. Bruno explained to Martín that Rinaldini had written very important things about Borges.

"Well perhaps, but lots of water has gone under the bridge since then," Rinaldini commented.

"What, would you take back what you've written about him in the past?"

"No," Rinaldini replied with an ambiguous gesture. "But I'd say other things now. I find his stories less and less bearable as time goes by."

"But you liked his poems a lot, Father."

"Well, yes, some of them. But there's lots of high-flown rhetoric in them."

Bruno remarked that he was moved by the poems that recalled Borges's childhood, the Buenos Aires of another era, the old patios of bygone days, the passage of time.

"Yes," Rinaldini conceded. "But what I find intolerable are his philosophical entertainments, or better put, his pseudophilosophical ones. He's an ingenious writer, a cunning artificer. Or as the British say, a sophisticate."

"Nonetheless, Father, a French periodical has published a lengthy discussion on Borges's philosophical profundity."

Rinaldini offered them cigarettes as he smiled a Mephisthophelean smile.

"Do tell . . ."

He lit their cigarettes and said:

"Look, take any one of those entertainments of his. The Library of Babel, for instance. In it he plays sophisticated games with the concept of the infinite, which he confuses with the indefinite. An elementary distinction—one you can find dealt with in almost any little philosophical treatise of the last twenty-five centuries. And naturally one can deduce anything from an absurd premise. *Ex absurdo sequitur quod libet.* And as a consequence of this puerile confusion he comes up with a sort of impious parable that implies that the universe is incomprehensible. Any student knows, and even I would venture to conjecture (as Borges would say) that the actualization of all possibilities at one and the same time is impossible. I can be standing up and I can be sitting down, but not both things at once."

"And what about the story of Judas?"

"An Irish priest said to me one day: 'Borges is an English writer who goes out to the suburbs to blaspheme.' He should have added: the suburbs of Buenos Aires and of philosophy. The theological argument put forth by Señor Borges-Sörensen, that sort of centaur who's half Scandinavian and half a denizen of Buenos Aires, has scarcely even the appearance of a genuine argument. It's painted theology. If I were an abstractionist painter, I too could paint a chicken by setting a triangle and a few little dots down on canvas, but I wouldn't be able to make chicken soup out of it. Now the real question is: is the game deliberate on Borges's part, or is it simply something that comes to him naturally and spontaneously? What I mean is: is he a sophist or a sophisticate? The meaning behind this joke is not to be tolerated in any decent and honorable man, even though he tells himself it's art for art's sake."

"In Borges's case it's art for art's sake, pure literature. He himself would tell you so."

"So much the worse for him."

Rinaldini was angry now.

"Those charitable fantasies he weaves round about Judas betray a tendency toward softheadedness and cowardice. He retreats in the face of the supreme things, in the face of absolute goodness and absolute evil. As a result a liar today is not a liar: he's a politician. There's an elegant stratagem afoot here for saving the devil's soul: Come on, we're told, the devil isn't as black as he's painted."

He looked at them as though seeking their considered opinion.

"In reality it's the other way around: the devil is blacker than those people paint him. They're not bad philosophers; what's even worse for them is that they're bad writers. Because they aren't even aware of that capital psychological reality that Aristotle had already plainly seen. What Edgar Allan Poe called the imp of perversity. The great writers of the last century had already seen this with blinding clarity: from Blake to Dostoevski. But of course . . ."

He did not finish his sentence. He looked out the window for a moment and then finally said, with his subtle smile:

"So Judas is running around loose in Argentina. . . . The patron saint of the officials over at the Ministry of the Treasury, since he got money from sources that nobody else would ever have thought of. Nonetheless Judas, poor thing, never dreamed of governing. And it would appear that he's now about to obtain, or has already obtained, government posts in our country. Ah well, whether or not he's in the government, he still ends up hanging himself."

Bruno then explained to Rinaldini the representations that he had made to Monsignor Gentile in his behalf. Rinaldini gestured with his hand as he smiled with a certain resigned, good-natured irony.

"Don't let it upset you, Bassán. The bishops aren't going to let me out of their sight. And as for Monsignor Gentile, who unfortunately is a relative of yours, he'd be better off reading the Gospel from time to time instead of getting all mixed up in church politics."

They left.

And there he'll stay, all alone, penniless, in his worn cassock, Martín thought.

෨ 13 ෨

THERE WAS no sign of Alejandra, and Martín took refuge in his work and in Bruno's company. For him, these were times of thoughtful sadness: the days of chaotic, dark sadnesses had yet to arrive. It seemed the proper frame of mind for that Buenos Aires autumn, an autumn not only of dead leaves and gray skies and drizzling rain, but also of discomposure, of vague discontent. Everyone was mistrustful of everyone else, people spoke different languages, hearts did not beat as one (as happens during certain national wars, certain collective triumphs); there were two nations in the same country, and those nations were mortal enemies; they eyed each other grimly, there was rancor between them. And Martín, who felt lonely, asked himself questions about everything: about life and death, about love and the absolute, about his country, about man's fate in general. But this was in no way pure philosophical reflection, for inevitably his thoughts went back to words of Alejandra's and memories of her, memories revolving about her gray-green eyes, with her hostile and contradictory expression as a background. And suddenly it seemed as though it was Alejandra who was his native land, not that beautiful but conventional woman who serves as its symbolic representation. One's native land was childhood and a mother, a home and tenderness; and Martín had not had that. He doubtless hoped to find in Alejandra in some measure, in some way, warmth and a mother; but she was a dark and turbulent territory shaken by earthquakes, swept by hurricanes. Everything was all mixed up in his anxious mind, as though he were suffering from vertigo, with everything revolving dizzily around the figure of Alejandra, even when he thought about Perón and Rosas, since in this girl who was the descendant of Unitarists and nonetheless a partisan of the Federalists, in this living, contradictory end product of Argentine history there seemed to be synthesized in his eyes everything that was chaotic and contentious, perverse and dissolute, equivocal and opaque. And then he would see poor Lavalle again, venturing into the silent and hostile territory of the provinces, puzzled and resentful, reflecting perhaps on the mystery of the people on the long freezing nights, wrapped in his sky blue cape, wordlessly looking at the ever-changing flames of the campfire.

And Bruno too, to whom Martín clung, on whom he fixed anxiously questioning eyes, seemed to be consumed by doubts, perpetually pondering the meaning of existence in general and the being or nonbeing of this obscure region of the world in which so many lived and suffered: he, Martín, Alejandra, and the millions of inhabitants of Buenos Aires who seemed to wander through the city as though in the midst of chaos, with no one knowing where the truth was, with no one believing firmly in anything; the oldsters like Don Pancho (Bruno thought) living in a dream of the past, the adventurers lining their pockets without a thought in the world about anything or anybody, and the old immigrants (they too) dreaming of another reality, a fantastic, far-off reality, old Don Francisco D'Arcángelo for instance, gazing off toward that land that was now forever unreachable and murmuring:

> *Addio patre e matre*
> *Addio sorelli e fratelli.*

Words that some immigrant-poet might have said, standing at the old man's side as the ship drew away from the shores of Reggio or Paola, as those men and women, their eyes riveted on the mountains of what had once been Magna Graecia, looked back not so much with the eyes of their bodies (weak, uncertain, and in the end unable to see) as with the eyes of their souls, those eyes that continue to see those mountains and those chestnut trees across the seas and the years:

haggard eyes staring fixedly, unable to be defeated by poverty or misfortunes, distance or old age. Eyes with which old D'Arcángelo
(grotesquely decked out in his worn green bowler, like a caricatural
and comic symbol of time and Frustration, at once docile and un-
daunted) saw his far-distant Calabria as Tito, sipping maté, looked
at him with his sarcastic little eyes, thinking "Damn, if only I had
some money." So then (Martín thought, looking at Tito, who was
looking at his father), what is Argentina? Questions that Bruno would
often answer by telling him that Argentina was not only Rosas and
Lavalle, gauchos and the pampas, but also—and how tragically!—old
D'Arcángelo with his little green bowler and his far-off look, and his
son Humberto J. D'Arcángelo, with his mixture of scepticism and
tenderness, resentment against society and inexhaustible generosity,
spontaneous sentimentality and analytical intelligence, chronic despair
and anxious, undying hope of *something*. "We Argentines are pessimists (Bruno said) because we have great reserves of hopes and illusions, for in order to be a pessimist one has to have previously held out
hopes for something. We are not a cynical people, though the country
is full of cynics and fatcats; we are, rather, a tormented people, which
is the precise opposite, for the cynic reconciles himself to everything
and nothing matters to him. Everything matters to the Argentine
however; he frets and fumes, turns bitter, protests, is consumed by
rancor. The Argentine is unhappy with everything, including himself;
he holds grudges, he is full of resentment, he is dramatic and violent.
Yes, old D'Arcángelo's nostalgia...," Bruno said, as if to himself.
"But it's because everything here is nostalgic, because there must have
been few countries in the world where this feeling has been experienced so repeatedly: by the first Spaniards, because they were home-
sick for their far-off homeland; then by the Indians, because they
mourned for their lost freedom, the sense of life that had been theirs;
later by the gauchos, displaced by foreign civilization, exiles in their
own land, thinking back on the golden age of their wild and woolly
independence; by the old Creole patricians, like Don Pancho, because
they felt that the good old days of generosity and courtesy had turned
into an age of pettiness and lies; and by the immigrants, finally, because they missed their old homeland, their ancient customs, their
legends, their Christmases around the fire. How can one fail to understand old D'Arcángelo? For as we approach death we also grow closer
to the land, not to land in general, but to that little bit of land, that

tiny (but so beloved, so sorely missed) corner of this earth where we spent our childhood, where we played our games and had our magic, the irrecoverable magic of our childhood that is lost forever. And then we remember a tree, the face of a friend, a dog, a dusty path in the heat of a summer afternoon, with its chirring of cicadas, a little brook. Things like that. Not big things, little things, very modest things, which nonetheless take on an unimaginable importance in that moment that precedes death, especially when in this country of immigrants the man who is going to die can fight death only through the memory, so tormentingly imperfect, so transparent and so insubstantial, of that tree or that little brook of his childhood, from which he is separated not only by the abysses of time but also by the vastness of a whole ocean. And so it is that we see many old men like Don Francisco D'Arcángelo, who say hardly a word and seem constantly to be looking far off into the distance, when in reality they are looking inside themselves, into the very depths of their memory. For memory is what resists time and its powers of destruction; it is something like the form that eternity may assume in this endless passage. And even though we (our consciousness, our feelings, our cruel experience) keep changing down through the years, even though our skin and our wrinkles become proof of and testimony to this passage, there is something in us, deep within us, there in very dark regions, clinging tooth and nail to childhood and the past, to our people and our homeland, to tradition and dreams, that seems to resist this tragic process: memory, the mysterious memory of ourselves, of what we are and what we were. (How appalling everything would be without it! Bruno thought to himself.) Those men who have lost it, as though in a terrible explosion that has utterly destroyed those profound regions, are nothing but frail, uncertain, frighteningly light leaves swept away by the furious, senseless wind of time."

ᘓᕗ I 4 ᘓᕗ

A ND THEN SOMETHING that took him completely by surprise happened late one afternoon: as he was waiting for the trolley on the corner of Leandro Alem and Cangallo, when traffic stopped at the light he saw Alejandra with that man, in a Cadillac convertible.

The two of them spied him too and Alejandra paled.

Bordenave invited him to get in and Alejandra slid over to the middle of the seat.

"I found your friend waiting for the trolley too. What a coincidence! Where are you headed for?" Bordenave asked.

Martín explained that he was going home to his room in La Boca.

"Well, we'll leave you off first then."

Why? Martín wondered, his mind in a daze. That word "first" was to give rise to anxious questions in his mind.

"No," Alejandra said. "I'll get out first. Right here, on the Avenida de Mayo."

Bordenave looked at her in astonishment; or at least it seemed so to Martín when he thought about this meeting later, noting to himself that Bordenave's astonishment was in itself astonishing.

When Alejandra got out, Martín asked her if she would like him to see her home. She replied that she was in a tearing hurry and it would be best for them to see each other some other time. But just as she was about to walk away, she hesitated, turned around, and told him to meet her at the Jockey Club the following day, at 6 P.M.

Bordenave remained silent and almost sullen all during the rest of the drive to La Boca, as Martín tried to analyze this curious meeting. Yes, it was possible that this man had run into Alejandra by chance. Hadn't he himself met her by chance? Nor was it anything out of the ordinary if, on recognizing her standing there on the street, he had offered her a ride, given his urbane manners. None of this was really surprising. What was surprising was that Alejandra had accepted the ride. But on the other hand, why had Bordenave been surprised when she had said she'd get out at the Avenida de Mayo? That reaction on his part might indicate that they were together because they had arranged to meet, not because they had met accidentally, and she had decided to get out of the car first as though to prove to Martín that there was nothing between her and this individual save a chance meeting; a decision that had doubtless so surprised Bordenave that he had made that revealing gesture despite himself. Martín felt that something was crumbling to ruins in his mind, but he tried his best not to let his desperation get the better of him, and forcing himself to think clearly he went on analyzing the sequence of events that had taken place. With a certain relief, the thought crossed his mind then that

Bordenave's surprise might have another explanation: on getting into the car Alejandra had perhaps told him that she was on her way home, to the house in Barracas (and the fact that they had been heading south along Leandro Alem seemed to be proof that Bordenave had offered her a ride home), but thinking that Martín might suspect something if she remained with Bordenave after he, Martín, got out of the car in La Boca, Alejandra had decided to get out at the Avenida de Mayo; and Bordenave had been taken aback by that sudden contradictory resolve on her part. That was all well and good, but why had Bordenave been so sullen and out of sorts after that? No doubt because he had made up his mind to flirt with Alejandra once they were alone and his plans had been thwarted by her decision to get out at the Avenida de Mayo. One thing still preyed on Martín's mind however: why had Alejandra refused to allow him to see her home? Wouldn't she simply meet Bordenave later, at the place they had undoubtedly been headed for? There was one reassuring detail nonetheless: how could Alejandra have met Bordenave except by chance? She didn't know him, she didn't know where he lived, and Bordenave didn't even know what Alejandra's name was.

And yet a vague troubled feeling impelled him to go back and analyze that first meeting with Bordenave that had seemed so trivial but that now, in the light of this new meeting, suddenly took on extraordinary importance. Years after Alejandra's death he had become absolutely certain of what at this moment was scarcely more than an insidious spark of suspicion: Bordenave had had something to do with Alejandra's sudden impulse to send him to see Molinari after the meeting with Bordenave in the Plaza. The events that led to her suicide and his final conversation with Bordenave were one day to reveal to him the role that this man had played in that tragedy. And when, years later, he broached the subject in a conversation with Bruno, he couldn't help commenting ironically on the apparently trivial fact that it had been he, Martín, who had brought Bordenave into Alejandra's life. And he was to recall once again, in maniacally minute detail, everything that had happened at that first interview with Bordenave in the Plaza, that banal meeting that would have totally disappeared into the void of meaningless happenings if events at the end had not thrown an unexpected and appalling light on that forgotten manuscript, so to speak.

But for the moment Martín had no way of arriving at these ultimate implications of that episode. As he went over that meeting in the Plaza in his mind he remembered that at the moment that he had introduced Bordenave to Alejandra a fleeting gleam had appeared in her eyes, a gleam that had preceded the unbending attitude she had displayed all the rest of the afternoon. Although it was quite possible (Bruno thought) that this detail was a false memory, the fruit of that retrospective lucidity that catastrophes bring us, or that we believe that they bring, as when we say "I remember now that I heard a suspicious-sounding noise," when in reality that noise is a detail that our imagination adds to the bare concrete facts dredged up by our memory, a way in which the present habitually influences the past by modifying it, enriching it, and distorting it by virtue of supposed premonitory signs.

Martín tried to remember what Bordenave had said, word for word, at that meeting, but there was nothing important, as least as far as his own problem was concerned. Then Bordenave had said that those Italians—meaning the two men he had left sitting at a nearby table, whom he had pointed to with a rather cynical jerk of his head in their direction—were all alike: they all claimed they were engineers, lawyers, knight-commanders. But in fact they were such scoundrels one always ought to carry a gun around them. And Martín remembered that meanwhile, without so much as looking at Bordenave, Alejandra, in a foul mood all of a sudden, had occupied herself by making intricate sketches on a paper napkin. The first word they utter (Bordenave had gone on) is *corruzione*, and then you have to remind them that those wretches that the Italians had sent over to Africa to fight the English had had their tin cans of tanks fall apart on them on the roads. Wops like that didn't know which way was up. They could never do anything right: they greased the palms of people they shouldn't have, and didn't slip one lousy peso to people they should have, to make a long story short. So that when they came around to see him he couldn't help laughing right in their faces. What, they hadn't contacted Bevilacqua yet? To needle them he stressed the fact that that was an Italian name and that (despite its being translatable as "Drinkwater") the man in question in fact drank much stronger stuff. And he had added, he said: "Since you're Italian, you can appreciate the joke," but they didn't find it at all funny, just as he had expected. Little ways of getting back at them, what the hell. What business did they have coming on so strong with their holier-than-thou act here in this country? ... Furthermore, as he also had had to point out to them, if their moral sensibilities were all that delicate, how come they played along with the game? A person who accepted a bribe had as dirty hands as a person who offered one. Martín looked at him dumbfounded. After Alejandra's death, when he went over each one of the scenes at which she had been present, he concluded that at that moment Bordenave had been talking strictly for Alejandra's benefit, a fact that Martín found astonishing, since he was unable to understand how Bordenave could be trying to seduce her by coming out with things like that. Bordenave had started in on politicians then: they were all corrupt. He wasn't referring, of course, just to the Peronistas: he was talking about all of them in general, the councilors in '36, the Palomar affair, the shady business in the Coordination Department. In short, there was no end to their dirty deals. As for industrialists (Martín thought of Molinari), they bitched but they'd never made as much money as they were raking in these days, even though they spouted all sorts of nonsense about corruption, about not being able to import so much as a needle for a loom without slipping somebody a bribe, about workers who sometimes were willing to work and sometimes not. In short, the usual song and dance. But when, he kept asking himself, when had industry made such colossal fortunes as in the last few years? They'd put washing machines in tenements even. And there wasn't a single little Peronista housewife who didn't have her electric mixer. The military? From the rank of colonel on up, with a few honorable exceptions, a few madmen who still believed in the fatherland, all of them had been bought off with permissions to buy foreign cars and speculate in foreign currencies. Workers? The only thing that interested them was living high off the hog, getting their bonus at the end of the year, gambling on whether River or Boca Juniors would win the championship, collecting their fat unemployment checks when they were laid off—another national industry!—getting their paid vacations and a holiday on Saint Perón's Day. Laughing, Bordenave had commented: "The only thing they're lacking in order to be bourgeois is a little bit of capital." Then stirring the ice in his whisky with his index finger, he had added: "Belly-stuffers, nothing more nor less than belly-stuffers, every last one of them." Once bills were laid on the table, nothing was denied anybody in this country. If a person had a fortune, even though he was an out-and-out bandit, people fawned on him, he was automatically a gentleman of the old school. In a word: it was no use fretting and fuming in this country, everything was rotten to the core, and nothing could be done about anything. Foreigners had prostituted the country and this was no longer the nation that had brought freedom to Chile and Peru. Today it was a nation of the filthy rich, of cowards, of Neopolitan gamblers, of scoundrels, of international adventurers, like those two over there, of swindlers and soccer fans. And at that point Bordenave had risen to his feet and held out his hand, telling Martín not to worry, that D'Arcángelo wouldn't be put out on the street. When Martín and Alejandra had left the Plaza, they crossed the street and sat down on a bench overlooking the river. He could recall each one of Alejandra's gestures when he had asked her what sort of person she thought Bordenave was. She had lit a cigarette, and in the match flame he could see that her face was set in a hard, somber expression. "What sort do you suppose? An Argentine of course." And then she had fallen silent and everything about her attitude indicated that that was going to be her final word on the subject. At that moment the only thing that Martín was aware of was the fact that Bordenave's appearance on the scene had disturbed her inner peace, like a snake gliding into a well of crystal clear water from which one is about to drink. Then Alejandra had said that she had a headache and would rather go home and go to bed. And just as they were about to bid each other goodbye, in front of the iron gate on the Calle Río Cuarto, she had said to him, with a nasty edge in her voice, that she would have a word with Molinari, but that he shouldn't get his hopes up.

When he examined that old document stored in his memory, some of the things that she had said stood out with almost cruel clarity, words that after her death took on an unexpected meaning. Yes: between that peaceful afternoon when they had walked hand in hand and the grotesque interview with Molinari Bordenave had entered the picture. Something frightful had suddenly made its appearance.

ᐁ 15 ᐁ

THEN, without having headed there consciously, Martín found himself outside Chichín's place, and as he entered he heard Barragán the Madman, who as usual was drinking cane brandy and preaching the while, saying: *Times of blood and fire are coming, my boys,* waving his right index finger threateningly and prophetically at the older youngsters who were making fun of him, incapable of taking anything seriously except Perón or the Sunday soccer match with Ferrocarril Oeste. At that moment Martín's mind was occupied by the thought that Alejandra had paled when they had met, although it was also possible that this was merely the impression he had had, since it was not easy to establish that fact unequivocally inasmuch as she had been sitting in the shadow beneath the hood of the convertible; a fact that was enormously important, of course, inasmuch as it would indicate that she and Bordenave had not simply met by accident but had deliberately planned to do so, but how and when, for the love of heaven, how and when? *Times of vengeance, my boys*, and making gestures as though he were writing in the air with his right hand, in huge letters, Barragán added: *It is written*, whereupon the bunch of older boys laughed fit to kill, and Martín reflected that even if Alejandra had in fact paled this was not a fact whose meaning was unequivocal, since it might well have been a sign of the embarrassment she had felt at Martín's discovering her in the company of an individual for whom her contempt had been obvious. And furthermore, how could the two of them have expressly planned to meet if she didn't even know where Bordenave lived? Even in his most feverish imaginings it seemed inconceivable to Martín that she would have looked up his address or his telephone number in the phone book and called him. *Times of blood and fire, for this accursed city, this new Babylon must be purified by fire, inasmuch as we are all sinners* although there still remained the possibility, of course, that they had met in the bar of the Plaza, a bar that Alejandra obviously frequented or had at one time frequented, as was revealed by the fact that she had led him directly there on the day of that meeting with Bordenave, so that perhaps she had gone into the bar (but what for, in heaven's name, what for?) and on meeting Bordenave there the two of them might perhaps have struck up a conversation, most probably with Bordenave making the first overtures since it was evident that he was a skirt-chaser and a man of the world. *Yes, laugh, you bunch of ne'er-do-wells, but I tell you we must go through blood and fire*, and even though all of them laughed, and Barragán himself seemed to join in the laughter at his expense, being the good-natured sort he was, his eyes nonetheless took on a more feverish gleam as they lighted on Martín, a prophetic gleam perhaps, despite the fact that the eyes thus illuminated were those of a modest neighborhood prophet, and a dull-witted one in his cups at that (but, as Bruno might have reflected, what do we know of the instruments that fate elects in order to subtly further its dark designs? And perhaps, given the ambiguous and perverse ways in which it customarily proceeds, was it not possible that it might transmit its cunning messages through the intermediary of beings rarely taken seriously, such as madmen and children?), and as though it were another person speaking, not the one who was joking about with the kids in the bar, Barragán added: *But not you, my boy, not you, because you must save us all,* and everybody suddenly stopped talking and a silence surrounded the madman's unexpected words, though immediately thereafter the kids returned to the attack and asked: *Hey, madman, tell us what number's going to win tomorrow,* but Barragán, shaking his head, drinking his cane brandy, answered: *All right, go ahead and laugh, but you'll see that what I'm telling you is true, you'll see it with your very own eyes, because this whorish city must be punished and Someone must come, for the world can't go on this way,* whereupon Martín, impressed, staring at him intently, suddenly saw a connection between his words and Alejandra's concerning premonitory dreams and purification by fire.

"They've taken Christ away from us and what have they given us in return? Cars, airplanes, electric refrigerators. But you, Chichín, just to take you for an example, are you any happier now that you have an electric refrigerator than you were when Acuña with the gimpy leg came to deliver you blocks of ice? Let's suppose—and it's only a supposition—that tomorrow you, Loiácono, could go to the Moon"—a phrase that was greeted with roars of laughter—"listen, you idiots, I'm just supposing, I tell you—anyway, so what, would that make you any happier than you are now?"

"What kind of happiness you talking about, preacher, when I ain't ever been happy in my whole fuckin' life?" Loiácono answered in a surly tone of voice.

"Okay, okay, I'm just supposing, I tell you. But I'm asking you: would you be any happier if you could go to the Moon?"

"How the fuck should I know?" Loiácono answered bitterly.

But Barragán the Madman went on with his preaching, turning a deaf ear to Loiácono's answer since his question had been merely a rhetorical one.

"That's the reason why I tell you, boys, that the place to look for happiness is right in your own heart. But to do that Christ had to come again. We've forgotten him, we've forgotten his teachings, we've forgotten that he suffered martyrdom for our sins, for our salvation. We're a bunch of miserable wretches and bastards. And if he comes again, we may not even be able to recognize him and maybe we'd make mock of him."

"How much you want to bet you're Christ yourself and here we are making fun of you like fuck-all," Díaz commented.

They all laughed fit to kill at Díaz's joke, but Barragán, shaking his head with the kindly smile of a drunk, went on, sounding more and more thick-tongued:

"We're all sad" (at that a number of them protested, saying *hey look, not me, preacher,* and so on). "We're a sad bunch, all of us. Let's not fool ourselves. And why are we all sad? Because our hearts are unsatisfied, because we know we're miserable bastards. Because we're unjust, we're thieves, because our souls are full of hate. And we all keep running and running. And what for, I ask you? And where to? We're all struggling to save up a little pile of dough for ourselves, but what for? Aren't we all going to die, every last one of us? And what do we want to live for if we don't believe in God?"

"Hey, knock it off, that's enough of a sermon," Loiácono said. "You're a great one to talk, madman. Lots of God, lots of Christ, and lots of running off from here"—he pointed to his mouth—"but you make your old lady work like a dog to support you while you're hanging around in here making fancy speeches."

Mad Barragán looked him up and down with a kindly gaze. He took a swallow of his cane brandy and asked:

"And who told you I'm not a real swine?"

He pointed to his little glass of cane brandy and said in a sorrowful voice:

"I'm a souse and a madman, boys. They call me Barragán the Madman. I drink like a fish, I spend my days just bumming around and thinking, while my old lady slaves away from sunup to sundown. But what can I do? That's the way I was born to live and the way I'll die. I'm a bastard and I don't deny it. But that isn't what I'm trying to tell you, boys. Don't they say that little kids and madmen tell the truth? Well, I'm a madman, and lots of times, I swear by this cross I'm wearing, I don't even know why I keep talking."

They all laughed.

"Go ahead and laugh. But I tell you that Christ came to me one night and told me: 'Madman, the world must be purged by blood and fire, something tremendous has to happen, the fire will fall on all men alike, and I say unto you that not a stone will be left standing.' That's what Christ himself told me."

All the boys doubled over with laughter except Loiácono.

"All right, boys, go to it, laugh to your heart's content. Laugh and we'll see what happens. There's only one of you here that knows what I'm saying."

The laughter died away and a sudden silence followed these last words. But immediately thereafter they all went back to kidding around and arguing about who was going to win the Sunday soccer match.

But Martín looked intently at the Madman as he again remembered Alejandra's words having to do with fire.

ᖇ 16 ᖇ

ALEJANDRA didn't show up. But Wanda dropped by with a message from her: she wouldn't be able to see him that week.

"Much work," she added, contemplating her cigarette lighter that played a tune.

"Much work," Martín repeated, as the image of Bordenave insidiously came to his mind.

Wanda stood there lighting the lighter and extinguishing it several times.

"She'll call you."

"All right."

An enormous weight kept him from rising to his feet after Wanda had left, but finally he managed to get up and telephone Bruno. He was shy and reserved over the phone, and didn't tell Bruno he would like to see him, but Bruno nonetheless ended the conversation by urging him to come over.

He sat down in one corner and Bruno tried to distract him by talking about anything and everything under the sun.

He talked to Martín about the book that he was reading, one about time, and explained to him the difference between the time of astronomers and human time, meanwhile reflecting that none of all that could be very useful to Martín save as a simple distraction. No abstract consideration, even though it had a bearing on human problems, could ever serve to console a single human being, to alleviate any of the sadnesses and anxieties that might afflict a concrete flesh-and-blood creature, a poor creature with eyes that peer anxiously (toward what or toward whom?), a creature who survives only through hope. Because happily (he thought) man is not made only of desperation but of faith and hope; not only of death but of desire for life; not only of loneliness but of moments of communion and love. For if desperation were to prevail, we would all allow ourselves to die or kill ourselves and this is not at all what happens. Which in Bruno's opinion only served to prove the minimal importance of reason, since it is not reasonable to nourish hopes in this world in which we live. Our reason, our intelligence are constantly proving to us that this world is frightful; that is why reason is destructive and leads to scepticism, to cynicism, and in the end to annihilation. Fortunately, however, man is almost never a reasonable being, and therefore hope is reborn again and again amid calamities. And this very rebirth of something so absurd, so subtly and profoundly absurd, so baseless, is proof that man is not a rational being. And hence once earthquakes have leveled a vast region of Japan or Chile; once a gigantic flood has wiped out hundreds of thousands of Chinese in the Yangtze basin; once a cruel war, and a senseless one for the immense majority of its victims, such as the Thirty Year's War, has mutilated and tortured, brought on murder and rape, burned and destroyed women, children, and villages, the survivors, those who have witnessed, in helpless terror, these calamities visited upon them by nature or by men, those very beings who in those moments of desperation thought that they would never want to be alive again and never would, or never could begin their lives anew, those very same men and women (the women especially, because woman is life itself and mother earth, she who never loses a last small shred of hope), those same frail human beings nonetheless begin, like stupid but heroic little ants, to rebuild their little world of every day all over again: a small world, it is true, but for that very reason one that is all the more moving. So that it is not ideas that have saved the world, it is not intellect or reason, but their diametrical opposite: men's senseless hopes, their stubborn rage to survive, their ardent desire to breathe as long as possible, their petty, stubborn, grotesque heroism from day to day in the face of misfortune. And if anxiety is the experience of Nothingness, a sort of ontological proof of Nothingness, might not hope be the proof of a Hidden Meaning of Existence, something worth fighting for? And since hope is more powerful than anxiety (since it always triumphs over it, otherwise all of us would kill ourselves), might it not be that this Hidden Meaning is truer, so to speak, than the famous Nothingness?

Meanwhile, on a more superficial plane, Bruno said something to Martín that had no apparent connection with these profound reflections, though in reality it was connected to them by irrational but vital links.

"I've always thought I'd like to be something like a fireman."

Martín looked at him in surprise. And Bruno, thinking that perhaps reflections of this sort might be useful to Martín in his unhappy state, made a few further comments, accompanying them, however, with a smile that lessened their pretentiousness.

"Yes, a corporal in a fire brigade perhaps. Because then one would feel that he was devoting his life to something of benefit to the entire community, acting on behalf of others, and what is more, facing danger, risking death in the performance of this mission. And because if one were a corporal I suppose he would feel a responsibility for his little group. In their eyes he would be the law and hope. A little world in which one's soul would become one with a little collective soul. So that the sorrows of one would be the sorrows of all, and the joys too, and the danger of one the danger of all. Knowing, furthermore, that one can and must trust one's comrades, that in those extreme situations of life, in those ill-defined and dizzying realms in which death suddenly confronts us in all its fury, they, the comrades, will fight against it, will defend us and suffer and hope for us. And besides that, the petty and modest daily routine of keeping the equipment clean, polishing the bronze fittings, honing the axes, living in a simple way these everyday moments that nonetheless are a prelude to danger and death."

He took his glasses off and wiped them clean.

"I have often imagined Saint-Exupéry up there in his little plane, fighting a storm in the middle of the Atlantic, heroic and reserved, saying not a word, with his radio operator sitting behind him, united by the silence and by friendship, by the common danger but also by common hope; listening to the roar of the engine, anxiously checking the fuel gauges, looking at each other. Camaraderie in the face of death."

He put his glasses back on and smiled, with a far-away look in his eyes.

"Well, perhaps one admires most what one is not capable of doing oneself. I don't know if I'd be capable of going through with so much as the hundredth part of any one of Saint-Exupéry's exploits. That, of course, is heroism on a grand scale. But I meant that even on a small scale...corporal in a fire brigade...I, on the other hand...what am I? A solitary, contemplative sort, a useless person. I don't even know if I'll ever manage to write a novel or a play. And even if I did...I don't know if any of that can possibly be as valuable as belonging to a platoon and watching over one's comrades' sleep and their lives, rifle in hand.... It doesn't matter that war is the handiwork of bastards, of thieves in the world of finance or petroleum: that platoon, that sleep watched over, that faith between comrades will always be absolute values."

Martín looked at him, misty-eyed with admiration. And Bruno thought to himself: "Well, in the final analysis, aren't we all in the midst of a sort of war? And don't I belong to a little platoon? And in a certain way isn't Martín someone whose sleep I watch over and whose anxieties I try to calm and whose hopes I shield and shelter like a little flame in the midst of a raging storm?"

And immediately he felt abashed.

So he told a joke.

ᴐ∾ I 7 ᴐ∾

HE WAITED FOR Alejandra's call all day Monday, but none came. On Tuesday he impatiently phoned her at the boutique. It seemed to him that her voice sounded harsh, but it might have been because she was busy. When Martín pressed her, she said she'd meet him at the bar on the corner of Charcas and Esmeralda and have coffee with him.

Martín rushed to the bar and found her already there waiting for him, sitting smoking and looking out toward the street. Their conversation was brief because she had to go back to work right away. Martín told her he'd like to see her when she wasn't in a hurry, for a whole afternoon.

"That's impossible for me, Martín."

On seeing the look in his eyes, she began to tap on the table with her cigarette holder and appeared to be thinking things over and calculating, frowning and with a worried expression on her face.

"I'm really sick these days," she finally said.

"What's the matter?"

"What isn't the matter would be a better question."

Terrible dreams, headaches (the pain began in the back of her neck and then spread to her entire body), dazzling lights before her eyes.

"And as though that weren't enough, there are the church bells. The whole thing's part hospital and part church, as you can see."

"So that's the reason you can't spend time with me," Martín commented with a slight edge of sarcasm in his voice.

"No, I'm not saying that. But everything's connected, do you know what I mean?"

"Everything's connected," Martín repeated to himself, knowing that this "everything" included what was torturing her the most.

"So it's impossible for you to see me?"

Alejandra's gaze met his for a moment, but then she lowered her eyes and began tapping on the table with the cigarette holder again.

"Well, all right then," she finally said. "We'll see each other tomorrow afternoon."

"For how long?" Martín asked eagerly.

"All afternoon, if you like," Alejandra answered, without looking up, continuing to tap on the table with her cigarette holder.

Then raising her eyes and seeing that Martín's were shining, she added:

"But only on one condition, Martín."

The light in Martín's eyes suddenly went dead.

๛ 18 ๛

T HE NEXT DAY the sun was shining as it had that Monday, but
there was a strong wind blowing and there was a lot of dirt in
the air. So everything was similar yet nothing was the same, as though
the favorable conjunction of the stars that other day had already degenerated into a far less auspicious one, Martín feared. The agreement
they had made conferred a melancholy peace upon this next afternoon
together; they had a quiet conversation like two good friends. But for
that very reason this meeting seemed a sad one to Martín. And perhaps without being fully aware of the fact (Bruno thought), he
couldn't seem to find the right moment for going down to the river
and sitting down on the same bench again, as one tries to make an
event happen again by repeating the magic formulas that brought it
about the first time; moreover he had no way of knowing, of course,
to what degree that Monday, which had seemed perfect to him, had
been a time of silent anxiety for Alejandra; so that the same things that
for him would constitute a cause for happiness if they were repeated
would be a cause of uneasiness for her; not to mention the fact that it
is always a bit depressing to return to places that have been witnesses
of a perfect moment.

But finally they went down to the river and sat down on the same
bench as before.

For a long time they said nothing, amid a sort of serenity. A serenity
that for Martín, after his naive hope in the restaurant they had gone to,
became increasingly tinged with melancholy, since this peace existed
precisely by reason of the condition that Alejandra had imposed. And
as far as she was concerned (Bruno thought), that serenity was simply
a sort of parenthesis, as precarious, as insubstantial as the one that a
victim of cancer manages to secure for himself with an injection of
morphine.

They watched the ships, the clouds.

They also watched the ants, toiling away with their characteristic
hurried and persistent seriousness.

"Just look how busily they're producing," Alejandra commented.
"Second Five-Year Plan."

Her eyes followed one of them that was feeling its way along, stag-
gering beneath a load that in proportion to its size was as enormous
as an automobile would be for a man.

As she followed the little creature's progress, she asked:

"Do you know what Juancito Duarte said to Zubiza when Zubiza
arrived in Hell?"

Yes, he knew that one.

"And the one about Perón in Hell?"

No, he hadn't heard that one yet.

They also told each other the latest jokes about Aloé.

Then Alejandra returned to the subject of ants.

"Do you remember Mark Twain's story about ants?"

"No."

"Some ants take it upon themselves to transport a lobster claw all
the way back to their nest, thus proving they're the stupidest creatures
under the sun. It's quite a funny story: a sort of refreshing bath after
all the exaggerated sentimentality about insects we've had from
Maeterlinck and company. Doesn't that seem to you like the height
of stupidity?"

"I never thought about it."

"But chickens are worse. One afternoon at Juan Carlos's country
place I spent hours trying to train them to have a conditioned reflex,
using a stick and some feed. The Pavlov technique, see? But I got
absolutely nowhere. I would have liked to see Pavlov trying to work
with chickens. They're so dumb you end up being furious with them.
Doesn't stupidity make you furious?"

"I don't know, it depends. Maybe if it's a question both of stupidity
and of sheer boring persistence."

"No, no," she said heatedly. "I mean pure and simple, out-and-out
stupidity."

Martín looked at her in bewilderment.

"I don't think so. It would be like getting furious at a stone, it seems
to me."

"It's not the same! A chicken isn't a stone: it moves, it eats, it acts
purposefully."

"I don't know," Martín said, puzzled by her train of thought. "I
don't quite understand why that should make me furious."

They fell silent again, for different reasons perhaps—Martín with the impression that there would always be feelings and ideas of hers that he would never be able to understand; and she (Martín thought) with a certain contempt for his obtuseness. Or what was worse, with some feeling that he for his part could not even guess at.

Alejandra looked around for her purse, fished out an address book, and took a photograph out of it.

"Do you like it?" she asked.

It was a snapshot of her on the Barracas terrace, leaning over the balustrade. In it she had that unfathomable expression of profound, anxious desire, that hope of something escaping all definition that had so overwhelmed him when he had first met her.

"Do you like it?" she asked him again. "It's from *those* days."

Martín recognized the blouse and skirt. How long ago it all seemed! But why was she showing him this photograph now?

But she said again insistently:

"Do you like it or don't you?"

"Of course, why wouldn't I like it? Who took it?"

"Somebody you don't know."

A black cloud suddenly darkened the gloomy but calm sky.

He took the photo and examined it with mixed feelings, then asked timidly:

"May I keep it?"

"I brought it to give to you. If you liked it, that is."

Martín was touched, and at the same time he felt sad: it seemed to be some sort of farewell gesture on her part. He said something to that effect, but she didn't answer; she sat there watching the ants as Martín tried to read the expression on her face.

Disheartened, he bent his head and his eyes fell on Alejandra's hand lying on the bench alongside him, still holding the open address book: he could see a folded airmail envelope inside it. The addresses she noted down in that little book, the letters she received—for Martín all these things constituted a world from which he was painfully excluded.

And even though he always halted at the very edge of that world, sometimes an unfortunate question escaped him despite himself. This time too.

"It's a letter from Juan Carlos," Alejandra replied.

"And what does that bird-brain have to say?" Martín asked bitterly.

"The same nonsense as usual, as you can imagine."

"What for instance?"

"What do you suppose Juan Carlos talks about in a letter, whether or not it comes by airmail? You there, Del Castillo, answer teacher's question."

She smiled at him, but Martín, with a seriousness that (he was certain) must have seemed absurd to her, replied:

"The girls he's flirting with?"

"Very good, my boy. You get a grade of ninety. And the only reason I'm not going to give you a hundred is that you put it in the form of a question instead of stating it as a fact. Hundreds, thousands of very tall, very stupid Danish girls with soft blonde hair that he's been flirting with. In a word, the sort who have him falling at their feet every time. All of them with deep tans because they're fiends for open-air sports, for canoe trips millions of miles long, in fraternal camaraderie with boys who are as blond, as tan, and as tall as they are. And lots of practical jokes: he adores them."

"Show me the stamp," Martín said.

He still had the same passion for stamps from distant lands as in his childhood. As he reached for the letter, it seemed to him that Alejandra moved her hand, unconsciously perhaps, so as to keep the letter from him. Upset by this little gesture, Martín pretended to be examining the stamp.

As he handed the letter back to her, he looked at her intently and he had the impression that she was suddenly ill at ease.

"This isn't from Juan Carlos," he ventured.

"Of course it's from Juan Carlos. Can't you see the fourth-grade handwriting on the envelope?"

Martín fell silent, his usual reaction when such a situation arose and he was once again unable to get any farther inside that region of her soul that was dark and troubled.

He picked up a little stick and began to scratch in the dirt.

"Don't be silly, Martín. Don't ruin this day by talking nonsense."

"You tried to keep me from seeing the letter," Martín commented, continuing to scratch about in the dirt with the little stick.

There was a silence.

"You see? I was right," he said.

"Yes, you're right, Martín," she admitted. "It's because he says things about you in it that aren't complimentary."

"So what?" he replied, in a seemingly indifferent tone of voice. "I wasn't going to read it anyway."

"No, of course not. . . . But it seemed to me to be a tactless thing to do to just hand it to you when you had no idea what was in it. . . . Yes, now that I think of it, I realize that was the reason why I did that."

Martín raised his eyes and looked at her.

"And why does he say uncomplimentary things about me?"

"It's not even worth talking about. It would only hurt your feelings. Unnecessarily."

"And what does he think he knows about me anyway, the idiot? He's never even laid eyes on me!"

"Martín, it must surely have occurred to you that I've told him things about you now and again."

"You said things about me, about us, to that cretin?"

"But talking to Juan Carlos is like not talking to anybody at all, Martín. It's like talking to a blank wall. I haven't said a word to anybody, do you understand? Talking to him is like talking to a blank wall, I tell you."

"No, I don't understand, Alejandra. Why him? I'd like you to tell me or read me what he has to say about me."

"But if it's just some of Juan Carlos's typical blather, what's the point?"

She handed him the letter.

"I've warned you your feelings are going to be hurt," she said spitefully.

"It doesn't matter," Martín answered, snatching the letter eagerly, nervously, as she moved over closer to him, as one does when one is going to read something along with another person.

Martín surmised that she wanted to soften the impact of the letter, phrase by phrase, and said as much to Bruno. And Bruno thought that Alejandra's attitude was as absurd as the one that causes us to devote all our attention to the maneuvers of someone who is doing a bad job of driving the car in which we're passengers.

Martín was about to take the letter out of the envelope when he suddenly realized that by so doing he might well destroy the very few fragile remains of Alejandra's love. His hand fell dispiritedly, still holding the envelope, and remained in that position for a time, and then he finally handed it back to her and she put it away again.

"So you confide in a cretin like that," he commented, though with a certain vague awareness that he was doing her an injustice, for Alejandra would never be capable—and this he was certain of—of "confiding" in such an individual. Her feeling for him might be either something more or something less than that, but she would never confide in him.

He felt a need to hurt her, and knew, or sensed, that the words he had just uttered would hurt her.

"Don't say such absurd things! I told you: talking to him is like talking with a horse. Don't you understand? It's true, I admit: I shouldn't have said anything at all to him. You're right about that. But I was drunk at the time."

"Drunk with *him*" (Martín thought, more bitter still now).

"It's like showing a horse a photograph of a beautiful landscape," she added after a moment, her tone of voice already less severe.

Martín felt that a great happiness was doing its best to pierce dense storm clouds: in any event, the expression "beautiful landscape" reached his tormented soul like a message bathed in light. But this message had to force its way through those dense clouds, and above all through those words "I was drunk."

"Do you hear me?"

Martín nodded.

"Look, Martín," he heard her suddenly saying. "I'm going to leave you, but you must never allow yourself to have mistaken ideas about our relationship."

Martín looked at her in consternation.

"Yes. This can't go on, Martín, for lots of reasons. And it will be better for you this way, much better."

Martín could not manage to get a single word out. His eyes filled with tears and he began to look straight in front of him off into the distance so that she wouldn't notice: as in an impressionist painting, all he could see was the blurred image of a boat with a brown hull some way away, and some white seagulls wheeling about it.

"You're going to start thinking now that I don't love you, that I never loved you," Alejandra said.

Martín's eyes followed the boat, as though fascinated by its movement.

"And yet..." Alejandra added.

Martín bent his head and looked at the ants again: one of them was carrying a big triangular leaf that looked like the sail of a miniature boat: the wind was making it flutter and the slight movement back and forth accentuated the resemblance.

He felt Alejandra's hand cupping his chin.

"Come on," she said to him briskly. "Lift that face up."

But Martín stubbornly resisted the pressure of her hand.

"No, Alejandra, leave me alone now. I want you to go away and leave me alone."

"Don't be silly, Martín. I curse the moment you laid eyes on that stupid letter."

"And I curse the moment I first met you. It was the most unfortunate moment of my life."

He heard Alejandra's voice asking:

"Do you really believe that?"

"Yes."

She fell silent. After a time she got up from the bench and said:

"Let's at least walk for a while together."

Martín rose to his feet with an effort and started off after her. Alejandra waited for him to catch up with her, took him by the arm, and said:

"Martín, I've told you more than once that I love you, that I love you lots. Don't forget that. And I never tell you anything I don't really believe."

A gray peace slowly descended upon Martín's soul with these words. But how much better the storminess of the worst moments with her was than this calm, hopeless, dull gray!

They walked along, each lost in his own thoughts.

When they reached the confectioner's shop on the bathing beach, Alejandra said she had to make a phone call.

Everything in the place had that desolate air about it that pleasure spots always had for him on weekdays: the tables were piled one atop the other, and the chairs too; a waiter in shirtsleeves and with his pantlegs rolled up, was mopping the floor. As Alejandra made her call, Martín asked for a coffee at the counter, but was told that the machine wasn't turned on.

When Alejandra came back from phoning, Martín told her there was no coffee, and she suggested they go to the Moscow to have a drink.

But it was closed. They knocked and waited but no one came to the door.

They asked at the newspaper stand on the corner.

"What, you didn't know?"

Vanya had been locked up in the insane asylum at Vieytes.

It seemed symbolic: that bar was the first one in which he had been happy with Alejandra. At the most depressing moments in his relationship with her the memory of that evening always came back to Martín's mind, the peace he had felt as he sat there next to the window, watching night descend on the roofs of Buenos Aires. Never had he felt that far away from the city, from tumult and fury, lack of understanding and cruelty; never had he felt so far removed from his mother's filth, the obsession with money, the atmosphere of shady deals, cynicism, and the resentment of all against all. There in that tiny but powerful refuge, beneath the gaze of that man given over to alcohol and drugs, at once a failure and a generous man, it had seemed as though the vulgar reality of the world outside had vanished. The thought occurred to him later that perhaps it was inevitable that beings as sensitive as Vanya ended up addicted to alcohol or drugs. And those clumsy frescoes on the walls, those crude images of Vanya's far-off homeland also touched him. How moving all that was, precisely because it was so awkwardly done and so naive! It was not pretentious painting done by a bad artist who is convinced he has talent, but undoubtedly scenes executed by a painter who was as heavy a drinker and as great a failure as Vanya himself; as unhappy and as permanently exiled from his homeland as he; condemned to live here, in a country that for both of them was absurd and the very end of the world; until the day they died. And those images, even as awkwardly painted as they were, nonetheless served in some way to remind them of their far-off homeland, just as stage scenery, even though it may be made of paper, even though it may be crude and primitive, somehow contributes to making a drama or a tragedy real to us.

The man at the newspaper stand shook his head.

"He was a good man," he said.

And this verb in the past tense suddenly made the sinister meaning of the walls of the madhouse a grim reality.

They walked back to the Paseo Colón.

"In the end that filthy bitch got what she was after," Alejandra commented.

She had suddenly become very depressed and suggested going to La Boca.

When they reached the intersection of Pedro de Mendoza and Almirante Brown they went to the bar on the corner.

A fat, sweaty black was walking off a Brazilian freighter named *Recife*.

"Louis Armstrong," Alejandra remarked, pointing with her sandwich.

Afterwards they went walking along the docks. After strolling along for a fair distance, they sat down in an unsheltered spot along the edge of the wharfs, looking out at the signal lights.

"There are days of the week that are astrologically bad," Alejandra remarked.

Martín looked at her.

"Which day is bad for you?" he asked.

"Tuesday."

"And which color?"

"Black."

"Mine's violet."

"Violet?" Alejandra asked in a rather surprised tone of voice.

"I read that in *Maribel*."

"I see that you choose worthwhile reading material for yourself."

"It's one of my mother's favorite magazines, one of the great sources of her culture," Martín said. "It's her *Critique of Pure Reason*."

Alejandra shook her head.

"For astrology, there's nothing that can beat *Damas y Damitas*. It's terrific..."

They watched the ships going in and out. One with a gleaming white hull, long and slender, like a great seabird, was gliding over the Riachuelo, being towed toward the mouth of the river. The drawbridge slowly lifted and the ship passed through, sounding its siren repeatedly. And the contrast between the sleekness and elegance of the ship's lines, its silent slipping through the water, and the powerful, hooting tugboats was striking.

Doña Anita Segunda, Alejandra said, pointing to the name of the tugboat in front.

These names used to delight them and they would have contests and set up prizes for the one who discovered the prettiest: *Garibaldi Tercero, La Nueva Teresina. Doña Anita Segunda* wasn't bad, but Martín was no longer thinking of contests; he was thinking, rather, of how all that belonged to a time that was gone forever now.

The tugboat hooted, giving off a column of twisting black smoke. The cables were as taut as bowstrings.

"I always have the feeling that one of these days some tugboat is going to have a hernia come popping out," Alejandra remarked.

He thought disconsolately that all this, all of it, would now disappear from his life. Like that ship: departing silently but inexorably, heading for far-off unknown ports.

"What are you thinking about, Martín?"

"Things."

"Tell me."

"Just things, vague things I can't put into words."

"Don't be mean. Tell me."

"The times when we had contests. The times when we made plans to leave this city and go off somewhere."

"Yes," she nodded.

All of a sudden Martín informed her that he had managed to get hold of some ampoules that caused an immediate fatal cardiac arrest.

"You don't say," Alejandra commented, with no signs of any great interest.

He showed them to her. Then he said gloomily:

"Do you remember how we once talked of killing ourselves together?"

"Yes."

Martín looked at her and then put the ampoules back into his pocket.

It was already dark and Alejandra said they could go back now.

"Are you going downtown?" Martín asked, thinking sorrowfully that everything was almost over now.

"No, I'm going back to my place."

"Would you like me to see you home?"

He affected an indifferent tone, but it was an anxious question.

"All right, if you want to," she replied hesitantly.

When they arrived in front of the house, Martín felt he couldn't possibly say goodbye to her there, and begged her to let him come upstairs with her.

Again she hesitated but finally said yes.

And once in the Mirador, Martín seemed to collapse, as though all the world's misfortunes had fallen on his shoulders. He threw himself on the bed and wept.

Alejandra sat down beside him.

"It's better, Martín, it's better for you. I know what I'm talking about. We mustn't see each other any more."

Between sobs, he told her that in that case he was going to kill himself with the ampoules that he'd shown her.

She sat there thoughtfully, not knowing what to do.

Little by little Martín calmed down and then what ought not to have happened happened, and after it was all over he heard her say:

"I saw you again because you promised we wouldn't go this far. In a certain sense, Martín, you've committed a sort of ..."

But she did not finish the sentence.

"A sort of what?" Martín asked fearfully.

"Never mind, it's over and done with now."

She got up and began to get dressed.

They left the Mirador and Alejandra announced that she wanted to go have a drink somewhere. Her tone of voice was harsh and gloomy.

She walked along distractedly, concentrating on some obsessive, secret thought.

She had her first drink in one of the cheap bistros down at the port and then, as always when that vague restlessness, that sort of blankness of mind that made Martín so anxious began to take possession of her, she refused to remain very long in any one bar and it was necessary to leave and find another.

She was nervous and on edge, as though she had to catch a train and must keep close track of the time, drumming her fingers on the table, not listening to what he said to her or answering "Hmmm, what?" not taking in a single word.

Finally she went into a cheap bar in the windows of which were photographs of half-naked women and singers appearing in the floor show. The lighting inside the place was reddish. The proprietress was talking in German with a sailor who was drinking something in a very tall red glass. One could glimpse sailors and ships' officers sitting at the little tables with whores from the Parque Retiro. A woman of about fifty, with platinum blonde hair and her face plastered with garish makeup, came out onto the stage then. Her enormous breasts seemed about to burst beneath her satin dress like two overinflated balloons. Her wrists, her fingers, and her neck were loaded down with fake jewels that glittered in the reddish light of the stage. Her voice was raucous and vulgar, and hoarse from drinking.

Alejandra stared at her, fascinated.

"What's come over you?" Martín asked anxiously.

But she didn't answer, her eyes still riveted on the fat woman.

"Alejandra," he said again, touching her arm insistently. "Alejandra."

She finally looked at him.

"What's so fascinating?"

"She's such a wreck. She can't sing and she can't be much good in bed any more either, except to satisfy certain fantasies. Who would want to take on a monster like that?"

Her eyes turned back to the singer again and she murmured, as though talking to herself:

"What I wouldn't give to be like her!"

Martín looked at her in utter stupefaction.

Then his astonishment was followed by a feeling, habitual by now, of sadness and anxious loneliness in the face of the enigma of Alejandra, that enigma that condemned him to remain forever outside. And experience had already amply proved to him that when she reached that point her inexplicable rancor toward him would be unleashed, that burning, sarcastic resentment that he could find no explanation for and that in this last period of their relationship would suddenly come violently to the surface.

So when she turned her eyes toward him again, eyes glassy from alcohol, he knew already that cruel, vindictive words were about to come pouring out of her tense, scornful lips.

She looked at him for a few seconds that seemed an eternity to him, there from the height of her infernal pedestal: she resembled nothing so much as one of those ancient, bloodthirsty Aztec divinities who demand that the hearts torn from the breasts of the sacrificial victims be offered them still hot and palpitating. And then she said to him in a low, vehement voice:

"I don't want to see you here! Go away this instant and leave me alone!"

Martín tried to calm her, but succeeded only in making her more furious still. Rising to her feet she screamed at him to leave.

He got up from the table like an automaton and started for the door, amid the stares of the sailors and whores.

Once outside, the fresh air began to revive him. He walked to Retiro and finally sat down on one of the benches in the Plaza Británica: the clock in the tower said eleven-thirty.

His head was one vast chaos.

For a moment he tried to hold himself together, but then he broke down completely.

ოჳ 19 ოჳ

SEVERAL DAYS went by, and then in desperation Martín dialed the number of the boutique; but when he heard Wanda's voice on the other end he didn't have the heart to say anything and hung up. He waited three days and called again. This time it was Alejandra who answered.

"Why are you so surprised?" she said. "We agreed, I seem to recall, we wouldn't see each other any more."

A confused conversation ensued, with Martín stammering something more or less incomprehensible, and finally Alejandra promised to be at the bar on Charcas and Esmeralda the following day. But she didn't show up.

After waiting for more than an hour, Martín decided to go to the shop.

The door of the boutique was ajar, and there in the darkness, in the light of a dim lamp, he saw Bobby, in profile, sitting all alone. There was no one else in the room and Bobby was all hunched over, staring down at the floor, as though deep in thought. Martín stood there not knowing what to do next. It was obvious that neither Wanda nor Alejandra was in the back room, because if they were there would have been the sound of conversation and everything was silent. They were undoubtedly in the little fitting room that Wanda had upstairs in the rear of the apartment, which could be reached by climbing a little stairway; because otherwise Bobby's presence and the fact that the door of the boutique was open were inexplicable.

But Martín couldn't bring himself to go in: something about Bobby's lonely, self-absorbed air kept him from doing so. Perhaps it was just because he was sitting there like that, all hunched over, but he looked older somehow, and on his face was a grave expression that Martín had never seen before. Without quite knowing why, he suddenly felt sorry for that lonely man. For many years he was to remember him that way, and would ponder the question as to whether he had experienced that feeling of pity for him, that ambiguous sense of sadness for him at that very moment or years afterward. And he remembered something that Bruno had said to him: that it is always terrible to see a man who believes himself to be absolutely and unquestionably alone, for there is something tragic about him, something sacred almost, and at the same time something horrible and shameful. For we always wear a mask, Bruno said, a mask that is never the same but changes for each one of the roles that life assigns us: the mask of professor, of lover, of intellectual, of cuckolded husband, of hero, of affectionate brother. But what mask do we put on or what mask do we have left when we are all alone, when we believe that no one, absolutely no one is observing us, keeping tabs on us, listening to us, making demands of us, begging us, threatening us, attacking us? Perhaps the sacred nature of that instant is owed to the fact that man is then face to face with Divinity, or at least face to face with his own implacable conscience. And perhaps no one can forgive having been surprised with his face stripped down to this ultimate and essential nakedness, the most terrible and the most essential of nakednesses, because it reveals the soul in all its helplessness. And since this was all the more terrible and humiliating for a born actor like Bobby, it was logical (Martín thought) that he should awaken more compassion than an ingenuous or simple-hearted person. Hence when Martín finally made up his mind to go in, he silently retraced his steps and this time stamped his heels loudly as he came into the entryway leading to the boutique. And then, with the swiftness of the born actor, Bobby instantly put on for Martín's benefit the mask of perversity, of feigned candor, and of curiosity (what could be going on between this youngster and Alejandra?). And his cynical smile entirely swept away the inclination Martín had felt to be compassionate toward him.

Martín, who always felt ill at ease with strangers, couldn't even decide what position to sit in, because he was convinced that nothing about him escaped Bobby's notice and was immediately stored away in the latter's perverse memory: heaven only knew where and how he would poke fun at the way Martín had looked and the torments he was suffering. Bobby's theatrical gestures, his deliberate vulgarity, his hypocrisy, his brilliant phrases, all conspired to make Martín feel like an insect beneath the magnifying glass of an ironic, sadistic researcher.

"Did you know that you remind me of a figure straight out of El Greco?" he said to Martín the moment he caught sight of him.

Like all Bobby's phrases, this one could be interpreted either as a compliment or as a grotesque thumbnail portrait. He was famous for the double-edged compliments he handed out in his columns on the theater, for when one thought twice about them they were sly, venomous criticisms: "He never deigns to employ profound metaphors"; "At no time does he yield to the temptation to stand out from the others"; "He has no fear of squarely confronting the spectator's boredom."

Beating a silent retreat to one corner of the room, Martín had sat down on the tall sketching stool as he had on his previous visit, and as though on a battlefield he instinctively hunched over so as to expose the smallest visible surface possible. Luckily, Bobby began talking about Alejandra.

"She's in the dressing room, with Wanda and the Countess Téleki, *née* Iturrería, known as Kiki to the vulgar."

And scrutinizing Martín intently, he asked him:

"Have you known Alejandra long?"

"A few months," Martín answered, his face turning red.

Bobby drew his chair closer and said in a low voice:

"I don't mind telling you that I *adore* the Olmoses. The mere fact that they live in Barracas is sufficient reason to begin with for the *haut monde* to die laughing and for my cousin Zaza to have a *crise de foie* and fits of hysterics every time somebody discovers that our family and the Olmoses are distant relations. Because as Zaza said to me the last time, in absolute fury: Can you tell me who, WHO in the world lives in Barracas? And I of course calmed her down by answering that NOBODY lives there, outside of some four hundred thousand drudges and as many dogs, cats, canaries, and chickens. And I added that those people (the Olmos family) would never embarrass us in too spectacular a way, since old Don Pancho lives in a wheelchair, doesn't see or hear anything outside of Lavalle's Legion, so it's very hard to imagine his coming out some fine day to go calling in the Barrio Norte or making statements to the newspapers about Perón; old Escolástica was admittedly crazy, but she's dead now, thank God; Uncle Bebe, who's admittedly crazy, lives shut up in his rooms, a so-called recluse whose one interest is his clarinet studies; Aunt Teresa, who was admittedly crazy too, has also died, thank God; and anyway the poor dear spent all her time in church and at funerals, so she never had a moment to spare to come bother anybody in the respectable part of town, and moreover she was especially devoted to Santa Lucía and practically never overstepped the color line, not even to visit a parish priest to see how some other sick priest was getting on or inquire as to the real state of an archbishop's cancer. So the only two left (I said to Zaza) are Fernando and Alejandra. 'Two more lunatics!' my cousin shouted. And Manucho, who was there at the time, shook her head, raised her eyes heavenward, and exclaimed: 'As they say in *Phèdre, O déplorable race!*' But as a matter of fact Zaza is rather a calm person except when it comes to the Olmos family. Because as she sees it the world is the result of the struggle between things that are a Crashing Bore and things that are Real Class.

"Examples:

" 'What a Crashing Bore of a novel!'

" 'Look, I'm sorry, but what I have to tell you is going to be a Crashing Bore.'

" 'So-and-so's paintings are a Crashing Bore.'

" 'What a Crashing Bore that there's riff-raff (meaning Peronistas) even on the Calle Santa Fe these days.'

"Examples of Real Class:

" 'Monique's latest story in *La Nación* has Real Class.'

" 'That film with Michèle Morgan—now there's Real Class for you.'

"The world is divided between what's a Crashing Bore and what's Real Class. The Eternal and Never-Ending Struggle between these two powers is responsible for all the world's ups and downs. When Crashing Bores predominate, everything's unbearable: hideous fashions, complicated theological novels, lectures by Alberto Larreta* at Amigos del Libro that One simply has to go to because otherwise poor little Albertito's feelings will be hurt, visitors who arrive at impossible hours, rich relatives who refuse to kick the bucket ('What a Crashing Bore Marcelo is, he's going to live forever—and with all those acres and acres of land he's got!'). But when Real Class predominates, things get quite amusing (another word that's part of Zaza's basic vocabulary) or at least bearable: a youngster who's decided he wants to write, for instance, though for all that he hasn't given up playing polo; a colonel who has no intention of wooing the masses.† But things aren't always that clear-cut, because, as I said, there's a perennial struggle between the two forces, so that sometimes reality is more complicated and suddenly Larreta turns out to have actually told a joke during his latest lecture (thanks to the mysterious influence of Real Class), or else the opposite can happen, as with Wanda, who's got Real Class as a fashion designer, though when she takes it into her head to imitate Seventh-Avenue clown costumes straight from New York, it's a Crashing Bore. In a word, the world used to be rather amusing, but lately, what with the Peronistas and their street demonstrations, one has to admit that it's become more or less an absolutely Crashing Bore. That's my cousin Zaza's philosophy anyway. As you can see, it's a sort of cross between Anaximander, Schiaparelli, and Porfirio Rubirosa."

At that moment the voices of Wanda and the customer could be heard as they came down from the fitting room. They entered the boutique, followed by Alejandra a moment or so later. She seemed not at all surprised to see Martín there, but since he knew her so well,

---

* A pompous art-for-art's sake Argentine writer whom the younger generations make fun of. [*Author's note*]

† An allusion to Perón. [*Author's note*]

this very impassivity was a sure sign that she was taking great pains to conceal her enormous irritation. In that absurd milieu, answering his greeting with the same superficial cordiality with which she might have greeted a mere casual acquaintance, without bothering to step aside for a second to explain why she hadn't shown up at the bar as they'd arranged, with that frivolous air that she affected in the presence of Wanda and Bobby, Alejandra appeared to belong to a race that did not speak the same language as Martín and would perhaps not even be able to understand the other Alejandra.

The customer kept up a steady stream of conversation with Wanda on the subject of the *urgent* necessity of killing Perón and his followers.

"Those Peronistas are scum. All that riff-raff ought to be killed," she said. "It's getting so we decent people can't even walk down the streets any more."

A succession of confused and contradictory sentiments made Martín feel even more depressed.

"Communism is just around the corner, I tell you," the woman went on, after exchanging kisses on the cheek with Bobby. "But I've got everything all planned: if the country turns Communist, I'll simply go out to my *estancia* and that'll be the end of that."

And as she absent-mindedly acknowledged Martín's polite greeting when Alejandra introduced him to her, Bobby looked over her shoulder at Alejandra with a wicked grin, for as he said later: "How could anybody possibly invent a phrase like that?"

Martín looked at Alejandra, struggling to keep his expression as impassive as possible, but on his face, as though independent of his will, there gradually appeared the inevitable signs of reproach, pain, and questioning that always displeased her so.

∾ 20 ∾

MARTIN KEPT WAITING for a sign from Alejandra, for her to call him aside. Then, risking everything, he went over to her and asked her if they could leave the shop together for a moment. "All right," she answered. And turning to Wanda, she said to her:

"I'll be back in a few minutes."

"A few minutes," Martín thought.

They walked down Charcas to the bar on the corner of Esmeralda.

"I waited for you for an hour and a half," Martín said to her.

"A rush job came up that I couldn't leave and there was no way to get word to you."

Foreseeing catastrophe, Martín did his best to change at least the tone of his voice, to take things more calmly, to be indifferent. But that proved impossible.

"You seem altogether different when you're with those people. I can't understand why..." He fell silent and then went on: "I think you really are an entirely different person with them."

Alejandra didn't answer.

"Isn't that so?"

"Perhaps."

"Alejandra," Martín said. "When are you your real self, when?"

"I try to be my real self all the time, Martín."

"But how can you forget moments like the ones we've had together?"

She turned away indignantly:

"And who says I've forgotten them!"

Then after a moment's silence she said:

"It's for that very reason—because I don't want to drive you out of your mind—that I'd rather not see you any more."

She was grim-faced, silent, evasive. And then suddenly she said:

"I don't want us to have any more moments like that together."

And with biting sarcasm she added:

"Those famous perfect moments."

Martín looked at her in despair; not only because of what she was saying but because of her withering tone of voice.

"You're probably wondering why I'm saying such bitter things to you, why I'm making you suffer this way, isn't that so?"

Martín began to stare at a little brown spot on the dirty pink tablecloth.

"To tell you the truth, I don't know why," she went on. "And I don't know why I don't want to have even one more of those famous moments with you either. Listen, Martín: all this has to end once and for all. It's just not working out. And the most honest thing to do is not to see each other at all."

Martín's eyes had filled with tears.

"If you leave me, I'll kill myself," he said.

Alejandra looked at him gravely. And then, with an odd mixture of severity and melancholy in her voice, she said:

"I can't help that, Martín."

"Don't you care if I kill myself?"

"Of course. How can you possibly think I wouldn't care?"

"And yet you'd do nothing to prevent it."

"What could I do to prevent it?"

"In other words it would be all the same to you whether I killed myself or went on living."

"I didn't say that. No, it wouldn't be all the same to me. It would be awful for me if you killed yourself."

"Would it matter to you very much?"

"A whole lot."

"Well then?"

He looked at her anxiously and intently, as one looks at someone in imminent danger, searching for the slightest sign that that person will be saved. "This can't be," he thought. "Someone who has experienced the things she has with me, only a few weeks ago, can't really mean all that."

"So then?"

"So then, what?"

"I'm telling you I may very well kill myself straightway, by jumping under a train in Retiro station, or in the subway. Would you care at all?"

"I've already told you I'd care a lot. I'd suffer terribly."

"But you'd go on living."

She didn't answer: she stirred what was left of her coffee, staring at the bottom of the cup.

"So everything we've had together these last few months is nothing but garbage that ought to be thrown out into the street!"

"Nobody said that!" she almost shouted.

Martín fell silent, confused and heartsick. And then he said:

"I don't understand you, Alejandra. I've never understood you, really. These things you're saying, these things you're doing to me, change everything that's happened between us."

He tried desperately to think clearly.

Alejandra sat there glumly, not even listening perhaps. Her eyes were fixed on some point or other out in the street.

"Well then?" Martín said again insistently.

"It makes no difference," she replied drily. "We won't see each other any more. That's the most honest thing to do."

"Alejandra! I can't bear the idea of not seeing you any more. I want to see you, I don't care when or where or how, whatever way you like..."

She said nothing in reply and began to cry then, though her face was still set in the same rigid, seemingly vacant expression as before.

"Well, Alejandra?"

"No, Martín. I can't stand things that are neither one thing nor another. Either there'll be other scenes like this one, that hurt you so much, or we'll meet and things will end up the way they did last Monday. And I don't want to—do you hear me?—I don't want to go to bed with you again. Not for anything in this world."

"But why?" Martín exclaimed, taking her by the hand, feeling in an overwhelming rush of emotion that something, something very important, still existed between the two of them, despite everything.

"Because I don't!" she shouted, looking at him with hatred in her eyes and wrenching her hand away from his.

"I don't understand you...." Martín stammered. "I've never understood you..."

"Never mind. I don't understand myself either. I don't even know why I'm doing all this to you. I don't know why I'm making you suffer this way."

And burying her face in her hands, she exclaimed:

"How awful all this is!"

And covering her face with both hands she began to weep hysterically, repeating between sobs: "How awful, how awful!"

During their entire relationship, Martín had rarely seen her cry, and it had always affected him deeply. He found it almost terrifying, as though a mortally wounded dragon were shedding tears. But those tears were frightening (as he supposed a dragon's would be); they were not a sign of weakness nor of a need for tenderness: they seemed, rather, like bitter drops of liquid rancor, spilling over boiling hot and all-consuming.

Martín nonetheless dared to take her hands, trying to pull them away, tenderly but firmly, so that he could see her face.

"How you're suffering, Alejandra!"

"And despite everything you can still feel pity for me," she stammered from beneath her hands, in a tone of voice that as far as he could tell could be an expression of rage, scorn, sarcasm, or heartfelt sadness, or of all these feelings at once.

"Yes, Alejandra, of course I pity you. Don't you think I can see that you're suffering terribly? And I don't want you to suffer. I swear to you that this will never happen again."

She calmed down little by little and finally dried her tears with her handkerchief.

"No, Martín," she said. "It's better if we don't ever see each other again. Because sooner or later we would have to separate in a way that would be even more painful. I can't control the horrible things I have inside me."

She hid her face in her hands again and Martín tried once again to pull them away.

"No, Alejandra, we won't hurt each other any more. You'll see. It was all my fault, because I insisted on seeing you. Because I went looking for you."

Trying his best to laugh, he added:

"It's as though someone were to go looking for Dr. Jekyll and met up with Mr. Hyde. At night. In disguise. With Frederic March's long fingernails. Eh, Alejandra? We'll see each other only when you want to, when you call me. When you feel well."

Alejandra did not answer.

Long minutes passed and Martín desperately regretted all the time that was going by to no point or purpose, knowing that she should be getting back to the boutique, that she should be leaving, that she would go off from one moment to the next and leave him in this state of total disarray. And then would come the black days far away from her, completely outside her life.

And the inevitable finally happened: she looked at her watch and said:

"I have to go now."

"Let's not separate this way, Alejandra. It's awful. Let's decide first what we're going to do."

"I don't know, Martín. I just don't know."

"Let's at least plan to see each other some other day, when things are less pressing. Let's not make any final decisions when we're in this state of mind."

As they left the bar, Martín thought how little, how frightfully little time he still had left in the two blocks before they reached the boutique. They made their way along slowly, but even so, soon all that separated them from the boutique was fifty steps, twenty steps, ten steps, then none at all. In desperation Martín took her by the arm then and drawing her close to him he pleaded with her once again to at least see each other one more time.

Alejandra looked at him. Her gaze seemed to be coming from very far away, from a sadly inaccessible, alien region.

"Promise me that, Alejandra!" he begged with tears in his eyes.

Alejandra gave him a long, hard look.

"All right then. Tomorrow night at six, at the Adam."

ᔕ 21 ᔕ

THE HOURS WERE painfully long: as though he were climbing a mountain, the last stretches of which were well-nigh unconquerable. His feelings were complex ones, for on the one hand he felt a sort of nervous happiness at the idea of seeing her one more time, and on the other, he sensed that this meeting would be precisely that: one more time that he would be seeing her, perhaps the very last time.

Long before six o'clock, he was there in the Adam, keeping a watchful eye on the door.

Alejandra arrived sometime after six-thirty.

She was no longer the hostile Alejandra of the previous day, but on the other hand her face had that blank expression that always filled Martín with such despair.

Why had she come?

The waiter was obliged to ask her two or three times what she would like to drink. She finally ordered gin and immediately looked at her accursed watch.

"You mean you have to leave already? You've just gotten here," Martín remarked, at once sadly and sarcastically.

Alejandra glanced at him with a vague look in her eye, and without noticing the sarcastic edge in his voice said no, she could stay a little while longer. Martín bent his head and stirred his drink around in his glass.

"Why did you come?" he couldn't keep himself from asking.

Alejandra looked at him as though trying to gather her thoughts together and focus her attention on his question.

"Well, I promised I would, didn't I?"

The minute the waiter brought her gin she drank it down in one gulp. Then she said:

"Let's go. I'd like to get a little air."

Once outside, Alejandra headed for the square, walked up the grassy slope, and sat down on one of the benches facing the river.

They sat there for quite some time in a silence that she finally ended by saying:

"How restful it is to hate oneself!"

Martín contemplated the Torre de los Ingleses, with its clock marking off the time going by. The Cade wharf, with its great squat smokestacks, stood out behind it, and the Puerto Nuevo with its grain elevators and cranes: abstract antediluvian animals, with their steel beaks and their heads of giant birds bending down as though to peck at the ships.

Silent and depressed, he watched night descending over the city, the red lights at the top of the smokestacks and towers, the brightly lighted signs of the Parque Retiro, the streetlamps of the square beginning to gleam against the blue black sky. Meanwhile thousands of men and women streamed out of the maw of the subways and with the same daily despair entered the maw of the suburban trains. He contemplated the Kavanagh, where lights were beginning to go on in the windows. Perhaps up there too, on the thirtieth or thirty-fifth floor, a lonely man turned on a light to chase away the darkness of his little room. How many failures of two people to understand each other, as was happening to him and Alejandra, how many lonely lives there might be in that one skyscraper!

And then he heard what he had been fearing he would hear from one moment to the next:

"I have to go now."

"Already?"

"Yes."

They walked down the steep grassy slope together and once they had reached the bottom she said goodbye to him and began walking away. Martín followed her, keeping a few steps behind.

"Alejandra!" he shouted. (The voice was almost that of another person.)

She stopped and waited. The light from the display window of a gunsmith's shop fell full upon her: her face was set in hard lines, her expression impenetrable. What most pained him was that bitter resentment of hers. What had he done to her? Despite himself, driven to do so by his suffering, he asked her precisely that question. She clenched her jaws even more tightly and turned her eyes toward the window of the gunsmith's shop.

"I've never been anything but affectionate and understanding."

Her one reply was to say that she couldn't stay one minute more: she had to be somewhere at eight o'clock.

He watched her as she walked off.

And suddenly he decided to follow her. Could anything worse happen to him if she noticed that he was doing so?

Alejandra headed along Recova, turned off down Reconquista, and finally entered a little bar and restaurant called the Ukrania. Warily, Martín drew closer and stood there in the darkness peering inside. His heart contracted and turned hard, as though it had been torn from his body and left out on an iceberg, all by itself: Alejandra was sitting across from a man who seemed to Martín to be as sinister as the bar itself. His skin was dark, but his eyes were a pale color, gray perhaps. His straight white hair was combed straight back. His face was hard, with features that looked as though they had been carved out with an ax. A powerful man, possessed of a darkly mysterious beauty. Martín's pain was so great, he felt so insignificant alongside that unknown man, that nothing mattered any more. It was as though he had said to himself: *What worse thing could possibly happen to me now?* Fascinated and sad, he could follow the man's expression, his silences, his gestures. He spoke infrequently, and when he did so his phrases were brief and clipped. His thin, restless hands looked a bit like the talons of a falcon or an eagle. Yes, that was it: everything about that individual was reminiscent of a bird of prey; his thin but powerful aquiline nose; his bony, rapacious, pitiless hands. That man was cruel and capable of anything.

Martín had the vague feeling that the man looked like someone he knew, but he was unable to pin down who it was. At one point he thought that perhaps he had met him at some time or other, but it was a face that was impossible to forget, and if he had seen him even once he would surely recognize him now.

Alejandra was talking in a state of great agitation. It was strange: the two of them were cruel creatures and appeared to hate each other, yet that thought did not ease his mind. On the contrary, it made him feel all the more desperate the moment it occurred to him. Why? Suddenly he felt he knew the answer: those two creatures were united by a violent passion. As though two eagles loved each other, he thought. Two eagles that nonetheless could—and perhaps would—rip and claw each other to death with their beaks and talons. And when he saw Alejandra take one of the hands, one of the talons, of that man in one of her hands, Martín felt that from that moment on nothing mattered and the world lacked all meaning whatsoever.

∾ 22 ∾

H E WAS WALKING about at dawn when the revelation suddenly came to him: that man looked like Alejandra! He remembered instantly the scene in the Mirador, when she had uttered the name Fernando and then denied that she had done so the moment after, as though a name that ought to be kept a secret had escaped her.

"That was Fernando!" Martín thought.

The gray green eyes, the slightly slanting cheekbones, the dark complexion and the features of Trinidad Arias! Of course; that explained the feeling that he knew him. He looked a lot like Trinidad Arias, the woman in the portrait that Alejandra had shown him, and a lot like Alejandra. "Everyone except Fernando and me," Alejandra had said, like someone who has withdrawn from the world and lives a life apart with a man, a man, he now realized, whom she admired.

But who was Fernando? An older brother: a brother she didn't want to talk about? The idea that that man could be Alejandra's brother only halfway eased his mind however, when it should have calmed him altogether. Why (he asked himself) am I not happy at that thought? At that moment he could discover no answer to that question in his mind. He merely noted that despite the fact that he knew he should calm down he was unable to.

He found it impossible to put his mind at rest and drop off to sleep: it was as though he suspected that a vampire had gotten into the room. He lay there turning the scene that he had witnessed over and over in his mind, trying to discover the cause of his uneasiness. Then finally he thought he'd stumbled on it: the hand! Suddenly overcome with anxiety, he remembered how she had stroked the man's hand affectionately. That was not the way a sister acted with her brother! And she spent her days thinking of him: *him*, the hypnotizer! She kept fleeing from him, but sooner or later, like a woman driven out of her mind, she was always forced to return to him. He now believed he had found the explanation for many of her incomprehensible and contradictory actions.

But the moment he thought he had found the key, he was again confronted with the most puzzling enigma of all: the resemblance. There could be no doubt about it: that man was a relative of Alejandra's. A first cousin perhaps? Yes: he was her first cousin and his name was Fernando.

That had to be the answer, for it would explain everything: the striking resemblance between the two of them and her sudden reticence that night when the name Fernando had escaped her lips. That name (he thought) was a key name, a secret name. "Everyone except Fernando and me," she had said despite herself and then had abruptly fallen silent and not answered his question. Everything was clear to him now: out of lofty pride, the two of them kept altogether to themselves, lived in a world apart.

Moreover, she loved Fernando, and that was the reason why she had immediately regretted having uttered that revealing name in Martín's presence.

He became more and more distraught as the days went by, and finally, unable to bear it any longer, he phoned Alejandra and told her that there was something extremely urgent that he must speak with her about immediately: just one last thing, even though they would never see each other again afterward.

Yet when they met, he could scarcely get a word out.

∽ 23 ∽

"WHAT'S THE MATTER now?" Alejandra spat out violently, sensing that Martín felt aggrieved about something or other that had happened. And that made her temper flare up because, as she had already told him repeatedly, he had no special claim on her; she had promised him nothing and hence owed him no explanation of any sort. At this point especially, inasmuch as they had decided to end their relationship.

Martín shook his head to dispute her words, as his eyes filled with tears.

"Tell me what's troubling you," she said to him, shaking him by the arms. She waited a few moments, staring into his eyes the while.

"I want to know just one thing, Alejandra: I want to know who Fernando is."

Her face paled and her eyes flashed.

"Fernando? How did you come up with that name?" she asked.

"You mentioned it that night in your room, when you told me the story of your family."

"And why does such a silly thing as that matter to you?"

"It matters more than you can possibly imagine."

"Why?"

"Because it seemed to me you were immediately sorry you'd uttered that word, that name—isn't that how it was?"

"Let's suppose it was. But what makes you think you have the right to cross-question me?"

"I've no right at all; I know that. But I beg you, in the name of whatever is dearest to you: tell me who Fernando is. Is he your brother?"

"I don't have any brothers, or any sisters either."

"Well then, is he a cousin of yours?"

"What makes you think he's a cousin?"

"You said that everyone in the family except you and Fernando was a Unitarist. Well then, since you've said he's not your brother, he may well be a cousin. Isn't that right? Isn't he a cousin of yours?"

Alejandra finally let go of Martín's arms, which she had been gripping tightly in her hands, and simply stood there, silent and downcast.

She lit a cigarette then, and after a time she said:

"Martín, if you want me to remember you as a friend, don't ask me questions."

"I'm asking you just one question."

"But why?"

"Because it's very important to me."

"Why is it important?"

"Because I've come to the conclusion that you love that man."

A cruel expression came over Alejandra's face again and her eyes flashed with the anger she had always displayed at her worst moments in the past.

"And on what, pray tell, do you base this conclusion of yours?"

"On an intuition."

"You couldn't be more mistaken. I don't love Fernando."

"Well then, perhaps I put it badly. What I meant to say was that you're in love with him. You may not love him but you're in love with him."

His voice broke as he said these last words.

Alejandra seized his arms with her cruel, strong hands (like *his* hands, Martín thought with terrible anguish, like *his* hands!) and shook him, saying in a violent, bitterly resentful tone of voice:

"You followed me!"

"Yes!" he shouted. "I followed you to that bar on the Calle Reconquista and I saw you with a man who looks like you, a man you're in love with!"

"And how do you know that that man is Fernando?"

"Because he looks like you ... and because you said Fernando was a relative and because it seemed to me that there was some sort of secret between you and Fernando, because it was as though you and he formed something apart, something separated from everybody else, and because you deeply regretted having spoken his name and because of the way you took his hand."

Alejandra shook him as though she were striking him, and he let her do so, as though he were merely a limp, inert body. And then she let him go and put her two avid hands over her face, as though trying to scratch herself, and at the same time seemed to be sobbing, in her own way, without a sound and without a single tear. Then he heard her cry from between her half-open hands:

"You imbecile! You imbecile! That man is my father!"

And then she ran off.

Martín stood there rooted to the spot, unable to move, unable to speak.

❧ 24 ❧

As though a great drum roll had announced the dark shadows to come after those terrible words of Alejandra's, Martín felt as though he were in the midst of an immense black dream that weighed upon him as heavily as though he were sleeping at the bottom of an ocean of liquid lead. For many long days he drifted aimlessly about the streets of Buenos Aires, thinking that that portentous being had appeared out of the unknown and had now returned to the unknown. *Home and fireside*, he suddenly said to himself, *home and fireside*. Disjointed words that seemed meaningless, though perhaps they referred to the man who at the height of the storm, when the thunder and lightning become more and more violent amid the darkness, takes shelter in his warm, familiar, welcoming cave. Home and fireside, a brightly lighted, welcoming refuge. The reason why (Bruno said) one always feels more lonely in a foreign country, for one's native land too was like a home and fireside, like childhood, like a mother's sheltering arms; and being in a foreign country was as sad as living in a drab, anonymous hotel; without memories, without familiar trees, without a childhood, without ghostly presences: because one's fatherland was childhood and hence it was perhaps more appropriate to call it one's motherland, something that shelters and warms when one feels lonely and cold. But when had he, Martín, ever had a mother? Moreover, this fatherland of his seemed so inhospitable, so harsh, so unprotective. Because (as Bruno also used to say, though he did not so much remember this now as feel it physically, as though he were out of doors with no shelter in the midst of a furious storm) our misfortune as Argentines was that we had not yet finished building a nation when the world that had first given birth to it began to creak ominously and then collapse, so that here in this country we did not have even that simulacrum of eternity represented in Europe or in Mexico or in Cuzco by great stone structures centuries old. Because here (Bruno used to say) we are neither Europe nor America, but a region of faults and fractures, an unstable, tragic, turbulent area where everything cracks apart and is ripped asunder. So that here everything was more transitory and fragile, there was nothing solid to cling to, man seemed more mortal and his natural state more ephemeral. And he (Martín), who wanted something strong and absolute to cling to amid catastrophe and a warm cave in which to take refuge, had neither a home nor a homeland. Or what was worse, he had a home built on dung and disillusionment, and a tottering, enigmatic homeland. So that he felt *alone, alone, alone*: the only word he was able to feel and think clearly, yet one that no doubt expressed all of that. And like a shipwreck victim in the dark, he had flung himself on Alejandra. But that had been like seeking refuge in a cavern from whose depths voracious wild beasts had immediately rushed forth.

ᴐ∿ 25 ᴐ∿

AND SUDDENLY, on one of those days that had no meaning, he felt himself swept along by a crowd of people running, as overhead jet planes roared and the crowd shouted *Plaza Mayo*, amid trucks full of workers madly racing in that direction, amid confused shouts and the dizzying image of planes flying so low they nearly grazed the tops of the skyscrapers. And then the deafening din of bombs exploding, the rattling of machine guns and antiaircraft batteries. And people running still, shoving and pushing their way inside the buildings, but then coming out again the moment the planes had flown past, overcome with curiosity, talking nervously together, till the planes came back and they ran indoors again. Meanwhile other people, taking shelter by simply hugging the walls (as though all this were merely a passing shower), stood staring up at the sky, puzzled or curious, or vaguely waved their outstretched arms in one direction or another.

And then night fell. And a drizzling rain began to fall silently on a terrified city seething with rumors.*

---

* In June of 1955 there was an uprising of sailors against Perón, and navy planes bombed gatherings of his supporters. That same night, after the failure of this coup d'état, Peronist shock groups set fire to a number of churches since the Church had sided against Perón. [*Author's note*]

THE INVISIBLE FACES · 225

ᴏᴠ 26 ᴏᴠ

A DISMAL LONELINESS overtook people, and in the night fires
stood out with a sinister gleam against the leaden sky.

The roll of a big bass drum rallying Peronista supporters boomed
as for a carnival of madmen. Martín was in front of the church now,
swept along by a madly excited, confused crowd of people. Some of
them were carrying revolvers or pistols. "They're men from the Alliance," someone said. Soon the gasoline they had thrown around the
church doors burst into flame. They rushed inside, shouting. They
dragged benches over to the doors and the flames leapt higher. Others
carried prie-dieus, images, and benches out into the street. The drizzling rain kept falling, ice cold and indifferent. They poured gasoline
on everything and the wood burned furiously, amid the freezing gusts
of wind. There were shouts and reports of firearms close by; some
people ran and others took shelter in the doorways across the street,
hugging the walls, fascinated by the flames and the panic.

Someone grabbed up a statute of the Virgin and was about to throw
it into the fire. Someone else, a working-class youngster with Indian
features standing alongside Martín inside the church, shouted "Give
it to me! Don't burn it!"

"What?" the other one said, still holding the statue at arm's length
and looking at the youngster in fury.

"Don't burn it, I can make a little dough selling it," the boy said.

The man put the statue down, shook his head, and gave it to the
boy. Then he began heaving benches and paintings into the fire.

The youngster had his Virgin now, lying on the floor at his feet. He
looked around for someone to help him carry it away. He spied a
policeman standing watching the spectacle and asked him to give him
a hand.

"Don't get mixed up in this, kid," the policeman advised him.

Martín went over to him.

"I'll help you," he said.

"Okay, get hold of the feet," the working-class youngster said.

They went outside. It was still raining, but the bonfire in the street was getting bigger and the gasoline and the rain falling were making everything crackle. A tall blond woman with long disheveled hair, clutching a bronze cresset that she was wielding like a truncheon, was dragging along a sack and stuffing it full of religious images and objects.

"Bastards!" she said.

"Shut your trap, crazy woman," they shouted.

"Bastards!" she said. "You'll all go to Hell!"

She continued on with her big sack, defending herself with the cresset. A youngster fondled her obscenely, another shouted filthy words at her, but she continued on, lashing out with the cresset and repeating: "Bastards!"

"Clear out of here, you sanctimonious hypocrite!" some of those in the crowd yelled at her.

But she went on, repeating "bastards" in a hoarse croaking voice, more or less lost in a world of her own, stony-faced and fanatic.

"She's nuts, let her alone," others shouted.

A woman with Indian features was watching over the fire and poking it up with a big stick, as though a gigantic chunk of meat were being barbecued.

"She's a madwoman, let her go," they shouted again.

The blond woman continued on with the sack, elbowing her way through the youngsters who were shouting obscenities at her, throwing burning brands at her, and laughing as they tried to feel her up.

Great flames were now rising from the parish office: they were burning the records and the registers. A dark-haired man in a slouch hat was laughing hysterically and throwing rocks, cobblestones, chunks of pavement.

The blond woman had disappeared from the section of the street lighted by the fire.

A joyous carnival music was heard once again.

In the light of the flames the contortions of the boys in the street band seemed even more fantastic. They were using ciboria as cymbals: decked out in chasubles, they raised chalices and crosses on high, and pounded out the rhythm with gilded cressets. The bass drum boomed out regularly and the boys went on with their wild contortions amid the glow from the fire, still pounding out the rhythm with the gilded cressets.

Then shots were suddenly heard again, and a group of men came running down the street. No one knew who they were or where they were coming from. Panic ensued, and the cry "It's the Alliance" went up. Others tried to reassure the crowd, passing the word along to keep calm. Others ran about shouting "Here they come!" and others "Don't panic, fellows!"

The bonfire in the middle of the street was getting bigger and bigger. A bunch of young kids and women threw a confessional on it. People were still bringing statues and paintings to fling into the flames.

One man was dragging a Christ along, and a woman who had just appeared on the scene shouted in a fierce and determined voice:

"Give that to me!"

"The hell with you," the man said, giving her a withering look.

Someone said:

"She's from the Foundation."

"Who? Who?" the cry went up.

The woman followed the man and grabbed the Christ by the feet to keep him from dragging it off with him.

"Let go!" the man shouted.

"Give that to me!" the woman screamed.

And for a moment the Christ remained suspended in the air between the pair of them as they fought over it.

"Come here, señora," the boy who had brought the statue of the Virgin out of the church said.

"What?" the woman said, without letting go of the Christ's feet.

"Come over here, and leave the Christ there."

"What?" the woman said, still beside herself with excitement.

"Here, take this statue instead," he said to her.

The woman appeared to hesitate, still not letting go of the teetering Christ.

"Please come over here, señora," the boy said.

Again she appeared to hesitate, but the man tugged hard on the Christ and wrenched it out of her hands. As though she'd lost her wits entirely, the woman watched him walk off and then turned and looked at the Virgin lying on the ground alongside the boy.

"Come over here, señora," the boy repeated.

The woman came closer.

"It's the Virgin of the Helpless," the boy said.

The woman looked at him uncomprehendingly, in apparent disbelief: the boy was a Peronista. She may have thought that he and Martín intended to attack her.

"Yes, señora," Martín said. "We took the statue out of the church; this boy saved it from going into the fire."

She drew closer and looked at the boy.

"All right," she said, "we'll take it to my house."

Martín and the boy leaned down to pick up the Virgin.

"No, wait," she said.

She unbuttoned her coat, took it off, and put it over the statue. Then she tried to give them a hand.

"Let go," the boy said. "The two of us can carry it alone. Just tell us where we're to go."

They started walking, the woman preceding them. A man was following them. The rain was coming down harder now and the boy could feel the Virgin's star-studded crown digging into his face. He had no idea what was going on any more: everything was all confused.

"Somebody who's wounded," they said. "Let us past."

People stepped aside to let them by.

They walked down Santa Fe to Callao. The reddish glow grew fainter and little by little the gloomy, lonely, chill darkness enveloped them. The rain was falling silently and in the distance occasional shouts, a few shots, and police whistles could be heard.

They reached the woman's building and took the elevator to the seventh floor. They entered a luxurious apartment and Martín could see that the working-class boy was in a daze: he looked at the maid shyly and diffidently and moved uncertainly amid the dark antique furniture and the objets d'art.

They stood the statue in a corner and perhaps unwittingly the weary, dazed boy leaned his head against the Virgin, as though silently resting. Suddenly he realized that they were talking to him.

"Let's go," the woman said to him. "We have to go back now."

"All right," the boy answered mechanically.

He looked around, as though searching for something.

"What is it?" the woman asked.

"I'd like..."

"What is it you'd like, my boy? Tell me," the woman said.

"I'd like a glass of water."

Some water was brought to him and the boy drank as though he were dried out down to his very bones from the heat of the fire.

"All right, let's go now," the woman said.

The rain had let up a little, but the bonfire in front of the church was still burning, though the scene had turned into a silent one: the men and women were mute spectators now, watching in fascination from the sidewalk across the street.

One man had several chasubles under his arm.

"Can I have those chasubles?" the woman asked.

"What did you say?" the man replied.

"The chasubles. I asked you whether I could have them," the woman said.

The man stared into the fire without answering.

"The chasubles," the woman repeated calmly—the calm of a sleep-walker. "I want to keep them, for when they rebuild the church."

The man went on staring into the fire in silence.

"Aren't you a Catholic?" the woman said with hatred in her voice.

The man continued to stare into the fire.

"Aren't you baptized?" the woman asked.

The man went on gazing into the flames, but Martín could see that a hard glint had appeared in his eyes.

"Don't you have children? Don't you have a mother?"

The man exploded then:

"Why don't you get on back to the whore of a mother that bore you?"

"I'm a Catholic," the woman said, in the same impassive sleep-walker's voice. "I want the chasubles for when they rebuild the church."

The man looked at her and then, quite unexpectedly, he answered in a normal tone of voice:

"I'm taking them to keep the rain off me."

"Please give me the chasubles," the woman calmly repeated.

"I live a long way from here, in General Rodríguez," the man said. Someone standing behind the obstinate, insistent woman said:

"So you came from General Rodríguez, did you? You're one of those who set fire to the church a while ago then."

The obstinate woman turned her head: it was an old man with white hair who had spoken up.

A man in a slouch hat unbuttoned his raincoat and took out a pistol. He looked the old man up and down coldly and contemptuously:

"And who are you to ask questions?" he said.

The man with the chasubles also took out a pistol. A woman with a big kitchen knife in her hand went over to the other woman.

"How'd you like us to shove the chasubles up your ass?" she said to her.

The impassive, madly single-minded woman offered the man with the chasubles an exchange.

"This umbrella's got a solid gold handle," she said.

"What did you say?"

"I said I'll trade you this umbrella for the chasubles. It's got a gold handle. Look."

The man looked at the handle.

The woman with the knife held the tip of it against the rib cage of the woman who had proposed this exchange, and repeated the question she had just put to her.

"All right," the man said. "Give me the umbrella."

On hearing him agree to the trade, the woman with the knife screamed at him in fury:

"Scoundrel! Sellout!"

"What do you mean, sellout?" the man with the chasubles said with an irritated wave of his hand. "What the hell would I want chasubles for anyway?"

"You're a scoundrel and a sellout!" the woman with the knife shouted.

The man with the chasubles suddenly became enraged:

"Look, you'd better shut your trap if you don't want me to pump you full of lead."

The woman with the knife screamed more insults at him and waved her knife in his face, but he took the umbrella without deigning to answer her back.

The woman walked off with the chasubles, amid hoots and jeers.

Then the man in the slouch hat said:

"All right, boys, there's no need for us to hang around here any longer. Let's go."

The woman with the chasubles came back over to where Martín and the working-class boy were standing; they had apprehensively moved as far away from the scene as possible. They walked her home to the apartment on the Calle Esmeralda again. And again it seemed to Martín that the boy had an air of sadness about him as he stood at the door slowly looking around at the armchairs, the paintings, the porcelains.

"Come on in," the woman insisted.

"No, señora," the boy said. "I'll be going now. You don't need me any more."

"Wait," the woman said.

The boy obeyed, his manner respectful and dignified.

She looked at him.

"You're a worker," she said to him.

"Yes, señora. In a textile factory," the boy answered.

"And how old are you?"

"Twenty."

"And you're a Peronista?"

The boy hung his head in embarrassment and didn't answer.

The woman gave him a stern look.

"How can you possibly be a Peronista? Can't you see what atrocities they're committing?"

"The ones who burned the churches are armed thugs, señora," he replied.

"What do you mean? They're Peronistas."

"No, señora. They aren't real Peronistas. They aren't honest-to-goodness Peronistas."

"What!" the woman said in a fury. "What do you mean by that?"

"May I go now, señora?" the boy asked, raising his head.

"No, wait," she said, as though she were trying to puzzle something out. "Wait. . . . Why was it you saved the Virgin of the Helpless?"

"I really couldn't say, señora. I'm not somebody who likes burning down churches. And anyway, how is the Virgin to blame for all this?"

"For all what?"

"For the bombing in the Plaza Mayo, and I don't know what all."

"So bombing the Plaza Mayo strikes you as a bad thing to do?"

The boy stared at her in surprise.

"Don't you know that we have to get rid of Perón sooner or later? That shameful, wicked, depraved man?" she said.

The boy continued to stare at her.

"Eh? Don't you think so?" the woman insisted.

The boy bent his head.

"I was in the Plaza Mayo," he said. "Me and thousands of other comrades. A girl comrade in front of me had her leg blown off by a bomb. One of my friends got his head blown off, and another one got his belly ripped open. There were thousands of dead."

"Don't you see then that you're defending a man who's nothing but scum?" the woman said.

The boy was silent. Then after a moment he said:

"I'm from a poor family, señora. I grew up in just one room. That's the only roof over our heads we had—my folks and seven brothers and sisters besides me."

"Wait, wait!" the woman shouted.

Martín made a move to leave too.

"And what about you?" the woman said to him. "Are you a Peronista too?"

Martín didn't answer.

He went out into the night.

The dark, frigid sky was like a symbol of his soul. An impalpable drizzle was falling, driven before that wind from the southeast that (Bruno used to say) makes a person who lives in Buenos Aires even more melancholy, so that he looks out at the street through the rain-blurred window of a café and murmurs *what shitty weather*, while a more reflective sort thinks *what infinite sadness*.

And feeling the icy drizzle on his face, walking toward nowhere in particular, with a tense frown, his eyes staring fixedly in front of him, as though concentrating obsessively on a vast and enormously complicated enigma, Martín kept repeating three words to himself: Alejandra, Fernando, the blind.

ᦊ 27 ᦊ

HE WANDERED about the streets aimlessly for hours. Then suddenly he found himself in the Plaza de la Inmaculada Concepción, in Belgrano. He sat down on one of the benches. In front of him the circular church seemed to be still living the day's terror. A sinister silence, the dim light, the drizzle gave this corner of Buenos Aires an ominous air: it seemed as though some powerful and fearsome enigma were hidden in the old building standing at a tangent to the church, and a sort of inexplicable fascination kept Martín's eyes riveted on this spot that he was seeing for the first time in his life.

Then suddenly a shout almost escaped his lips: Alejandra was crossing the square, heading for that old building.

Sitting there in the darkness beneath the trees, Martín was hidden from her gaze. Moreover, she was moving across the square like a sleepwalker, with that automatism that he had noted many times in her, but that now struck him as even more powerful and impersonal. Alejandra was walking straight across the flowerbeds, like someone moving in a dream toward a fate determined by superior forces. It was evident that she saw nothing, heard nothing as she came across the square. She was walking straight on with the singlemindedness and at the same time the total indifference to her surroundings of a person in a deep hypnotic trance.

She soon reached the arcade of the old building, and heading unhesitatingly for one of the closed, silent doors, she opened it and went inside.

For a moment Martín thought that perhaps he was dreaming or suffering from a hallucination: he had never been in that little Buenos Aires square before, nothing that he was consciously aware of had guided his footsteps there on this gloomy night, nothing could have allowed him to foresee so portentous an encounter. There were too many chance factors involved, and therefore it was only natural that for a moment he should entertain the thought that this was a hallucination or a dream.

But the many long hours that he waited in front of that door left no room for doubt: it was indeed Alejandra who had gone into that building and was still inside, for no earthly reason that he could fathom.

Dawn came and Martín did not dare wait any longer, for he feared that Alejandra would spy him there now that it was daylight. And besides, what would he have learned that would be of any help to him if he did see her come out?

With a sadness that took the form of actual physical pain he left and walked to Cabildo.

A cloudy gray day, tedious and dreary, awoke from the depths of that phantasmagorical night.

PART THREE

Report on the Blind

O gods of night!
O gods of darkness, of incest and crime,
of melancholy and of suicide!
O gods of rats and caverns,
of cockroaches and bats!
O violent, inscrutable gods
Of dreams and death!

∽ I ∽

W HEN WAS THE beginning of all this that is about to end in my
murder? This fierce clearsightedness I now have is like a
searchlight, and I can watch an intense beam advance across vast
regions of my memory: I see faces, rats in a barn, streets of Buenos
Aires or Algiers, prostitutes and sailors: I move the beam and see
things farther away: a spring flowing at the *estancia*, a stifling-hot
afternoon, birds and eyes that I put out with a nail. It was then perhaps, but who knows? it may have been much farther back, in times
I don't remember now, ages and ages ago, in the days long past of my
earliest childhood. I don't know. And besides, what does it matter?

I remember perfectly, on the other hand, the beginnings of my
systematic investigation (as for the other one, the unconscious one,
perhaps the most profound one, how could I possibly know?). It was
a summer day in the year 1947, as I was passing by the Plaza Mayo,
along the Calle San Martín, on the sidewalk in front of the City Hall.
I was walking along absentmindedly, when suddenly I heard a little
bell ring, as though someone were trying to awaken me from a sleep
of thousands of years. I walked on, still aware of the little bell that was
endeavoring to penetrate to the farthest depths of my consciousness:
hearing it without listening to it. And then suddenly that faint but
piercing and obsessive sound seemed to reach some sensible zone of
my self, one or another of those places where the skin of the self is
extremely thin and delicate and abnormally sensitive: and I awoke
with a start, as though face to face with a sudden, insidious danger,

as though in the darkness my hands had touched the ice-cold skin of a reptile. Looming up in front of me, inscrutable and stony, observing me with her entire countenance, was the blind woman who sells trinkets there. She had stopped ringing her little bell; as though she had been shaking it back and forth only for me, to awaken me from my mad sleep, to warn me that my previous existence had come to an end, like a stupid preparatory stage, and that I must now confront reality. There we stood, she stock-still, blank face turned toward me, and I paralyzed as though by an infernal but icy apparition: we remained so for who knows how many of those moments that are not part of time yet open onto eternity. And then, as my consciousness reentered the river of time, I immediately fled.

And that was how the final stage of my existence began.

From that day forth, I knew that I could not lose a single moment, that I must begin, then and there, my exploration of that dark, mysterious universe.

Several months went by, and then one day in the autumn the second decisive encounter took place. I was already deeply involved in my investigation, but had fallen behind in my labors due to an inexplicable apathy, which I now believe was unquestionably a disguised form of fear of the unknown.

Nonetheless I closely observed and studied the blind.

The subject has always been of interest to me, and on a number of occasions I had entered into discussions as to their origin, hierarchical rank, manner of existence, and zoological condition. Despite the fact that at that time I had scarcely begun to lay down the rudiments of my cold-skin hypothesis, I had already been vilified, by letter and in person, by certain members of societies connected with the world of the blind. All this thanks to that most efficient, ultrarapid, and mysterious intelligence network that lodges and secret sects always have; those lodges and sects that are invisibly present everywhere among us men, and that, without our knowing or sometimes even suspecting it, continually spy on us, persecute us, determine our destiny, our downfall, and even our death. This is especially true of the Sect of the Blind, for to the even greater unhappiness and misfortune of the heedless, it has in its service normal men and women: some of them thoroughly gulled by the Organization; others taken in by demagogical, sensationalist propaganda; and finally, a great number of them motivated by the fear of the physical and metaphysical punishments that are rumored to be meted out to those who dare to probe its secrets. Punishments which, let it be said in passing, I had the impression at that time of having already had dealt out to me in part, and the conviction that I would continue to receive them in a more and more subtle and frightful form; the sole result of which, no doubt due to my pride, was to cause my indignation to wax all the hotter and make me all the more determined to pursue my investigations to the very end.

Were I a little more naive, I might perhaps boast of having verified through these investigations the hypotheses concerning the world of the blind that I had first conceived as a child, since it was the nightmares and fits of delirium of this early period of my life that brought me the first revelation. Then, as I grew older, I began to become more and more wary of these usurpers and began taking the proper precautionary measures against this species of moral blackmailers who, as is only natural, abound in subways, in view of that condition of theirs that makes them close kin to those cold-blooded, slippery-skinned creatures that inhabit cellars, caverns, basements, unused passageways, drains, blind ditches, sewers, deep underground fissures, abandoned mineshafts silently oozing water; and some of these beings, the most powerful of them, live in vast subterranean grottoes, sometimes hundreds of feet deep, as can be deduced from the ambiguous, reluctant, deliberately sketchy reports of speleologists and treasure hunters, reports that are nonetheless sufficiently clear to those who know the grave threats that hang over the heads of those who attempt to violate the great secret.

Before, when I was younger and less suspicious, even though I was convinced that my theory was correct, I was unwilling to test it or even to allow it to see the light of day, since those sentimental prejudices constituting the demagogy of the emotions prevented me from breaching the defenses erected by the Sect, defenses as impenetrable as they are subtle and invisible, consisting of watchwords learned in schools and newspapers that are respectfully observed by the government and the police, and passed on by charitable institutions, matrons, and schoolmasters. Defenses that prevent one from reaching those dark, mysterious suburban precincts where commonplaces begin to wear thin and one begins to suspect the truth.

Many years were to go by before I could get past these outer defenses. And then, by degrees, impelled by a power as great and as paradoxical as that which in nightmares makes us proceed straight toward horror, I gradually penetrated the forbidden regions where metaphysical darkness begins to reign, glimpsing here and there, indistinctly at first, like shadowy, fleeting phantoms, and then with greater and more terrifying clarity, an entire world of abominable beings.

I shall now relate how I came by this awesome privilege and how after years of searching and threats to my life I was able to enter the innermost circle where a multitude of monsters move restlessly about, ordinary blind men being merely the least fearsome form that these beings assume.

ↀ 2 ↀ

I remember that fourteenth of June very clearly: a rainy, freezing-cold day. I was carefully observing the behavior of a blind man operating on the Palermo subway line: a rather short, stocky, dark-skinned, extremely active, very ill-mannered man; one going through the subway cars with scarcely contained hostility, peddling collar stays, pushing and shoving his way through the dense throngs of passengers packed in the trains like sardines, holding out one hand for tribute that wretched office clerks were offering him with sacred terror; and keeping a tight grip on the symbolic collar stays with the other: for it is impossible for anyone to make a living by actually selling such trifling objects, inasmuch as a person may need one pair of collar stays per year, or at most one pair per month; but no one, not even a madman or a millionaire, is going to buy a dozen a day. So that, as is only logical, and as everyone knows full well, the collar stays are purely symbolical, a sort of emblem of the blind man, a kind of corsair's letters patent that, along with his famous white cane, distinguishes him from the ordinary run of mortals.

I was therefore observing the course of events, ready to follow this individual wherever he might lead me so as to confirm my theory once and for all. I made countless trips between the Plaza Mayo and Palermo, doing my best to escape his notice in the terminals at each end of the line, fearing I might arouse the suspicion of the sect and be denounced as a pickpocket or some other nonsense of that sort, at a time when my days were incalculably precious to me. Hence, taking certain precautions, I stayed as close as possible to the blind man, and at the end of the last trip at 1:30 A.M., I prepared to follow him to his lair.

The man got off the train at the Plaza Mayo terminal before it made its final run to Palermo, and left the station via the exit leading to the Calle San Martín.

We began to walk down this street toward Cangallo.

At the intersection he turned off in the direction of the port district.

I was obliged to redouble my precautions, since on this lonely winter night there was almost no one out on the streets except the blind man and me. I therefore followed him at a prudent distance, taking into account the acute sense of hearing that such individuals have and the instinct that warns them that their secrets are in danger of being discovered.

The silence and the loneliness were as overwhelming as always at night in the Banking District. A far more silent and lonely district at night than any other—by contrast, doubtless, with the violent commotion typical of these same streets during the day: the noise, the indescribable confusion, the frantic hustle and bustle, the immense multitude rushing back and forth during Business Hours. But also, almost certainly, on account of the sacred solitude that reigns in these places when Money is taking its rest, once the last employees and office managers have gone home and an end has come to the exhausting and absurd daily round of activities whereby poor devils who earn five thousand pesos a month handle five million, and whereby veritable multitudes deposit, with infinite precautions, pieces of paper with magic properties which other multitudes withdraw from other little windows with inverse precautions. A completely unreal, phantasmagorical process, for even though they, the believers, regard themselves as realistic and practical persons, they accept these dirty pieces of paper on which, if one looks at them very carefully, one can make out a sort of absurd promise, whereby a gentleman who does not even sign with his own hand pledges, in the name of the State, to give something or other to the believer in exchange for the aforesaid dirty bit of paper. And the curious thing is that this individual believes this promise, since so far as I know no one has ever demanded that this obligation be honored; and more surprising still, in exchange for these dirty bits of paper the person is generally handed another piece of paper that is cleaner but still more absurd, wherein another gentleman promises that in exchange for this paper the believer will be handed a certain quantity of the aforementioned dirty bits of paper: so that the whole thing is a sort of madness raised to the second power. And all this represents Something that no one has ever seen, something said to be deposited Somewhere, in the United States especially, in Steel caverns. And the fact that this entire process is of a religious nature is indicated first and foremost by words such as *credits* and *fiduciary*.

As I was saying, then, once such districts have been cleared of the frantic throngs of believers, they become more deserted than any other, since no one lives there at night and no one could live there, because of the absolute silence that reigns and the tremendous solitude of the gigantic lobbies of the temples of finance and the enormous underground caverns where the incredible treasures are kept, as meanwhile the powerful men who control this magic sleep uneasily, stuffed full of pills and drugs and haunted by nightmares of financial disasters. And also for the obvious reason that there is nothing to eat in these districts, nothing that would permit human beings, or even rats or cockroaches, to live there permanently; and finally, on account of the extreme cleanliness that exists in these redoubts of nothingness, where everything is symbolic or at most a mere piece of paper; and even these pieces of paper, which might conceivably provide nourishment for moths and other small insects, are kept in formidable steel safes, invulnerable to all living species.

Amid the total silence, then, that reigns in the Banking District, I followed the blind man down Cangallo toward the port district. His footsteps echoed with a dull, muffled sound, taking on a more and more secret and perverse aura with each passing moment.

We proceeded as far as Leandro Alem in this fashion, and after crossing the avenue headed toward the dock area.

I was extremely cautious: from time to time it seemed to me that the blind man could hear my footsteps and even my anxious breathing.

The man was now walking along with a self-assurance that seemed terrifying to me, for I rejected the banal notion that he was not really blind.

But what amazed me and frightened me even more was the fact that he suddenly turned to the left again, heading toward the amusement park. And I say that that frightened me because it was not logical, since if this had been his plan from the beginning, there was no reason for his having headed to the right after crossing the avenue. And since the supposition that the man had mistakenly turned in the wrong direction was totally unthinkable, in view of the self-assurance and the rapidity of his movements, there remained the (terrifying) hypothesis that he had realized that I was following him and was trying to throw me off the track. Or, what was infinitely worse, trying to lure me into a trap.

Nonetheless, the same tendency that causes us to draw closer and closer to the edge of an abyss made me more and more determined to follow the blind man. And so a hypothetical spectator would have seen an individual with a white cane and a pocketful of collar stays making his way along almost at a run (which would have been grotesque had it not been so sinister), silently but frantically pursued by another individual: heading north along Bouchard first, and then once past the amusement park, angling off toward the right, as though heading for the port district.

I lost sight of him at that moment, since, as was only natural, I was following him at a distance of about half a block.

In desperation I quickened my pace, fearing that I would lose track of him at the very moment (or so I thought at the time) that a good part of the secret was about to be revealed to me.

I arrived at the corner almost at a run and made an abrupt turn to the right, as the blind man had done.

What a shock! He was standing there against the wall, tense and nervous, obviously lying in wait for me. I could not help bumping into him, whereupon he grabbed me by the arm with superhuman strength, and I felt his breath on my face. The light was very dim and I could scarcely make out the expression on his face, but his entire bearing, his panting breath, his arm gripping mine like a pair of pincers, his voice, everything about him was evidence of his bitter resentment and indignation.

"You've been following me!" he exclaimed in a low voice, although it seemed as though he were shouting.

Suddenly sick to my stomach from the feel of his breath on my face and the smell of his moist skin, and frightened almost out of my wits,

I murmured a few mad monosyllables and stammered out a desperate denial: "You are mistaken, sir." I was close to fainting from nausea and repulsion.

How could he have realized that I was following him? At what moment? In what way? It was impossible to believe that he had been able to do so thanks to mere normal, human means. But how then? Accomplices perhaps? The invisible collaborators that the Sect has astutely placed everywhere, more or less, and in positions and posts where no one would suspect their secret mission: nursemaids, teachers in secondary schools, respectable matrons, librarians, streetcar conductors? Heaven only knows. But those early morning hours of that day brought confirmation of one of my intuitions about the Sect.

All this crossed my mind in a dizzying flash as I fought to free myself from the man's clutches.

I fled the scene the moment I managed to escape his grasp and for a long time afterward I did not dare go on with my research. Not only out of fear, though the terror I felt was so great that it was intolerable, but also out of deliberate calculation, since I imagined that that nocturnal episode could well have given rise to the strictest and most dangerous sort of surveillance of me. I would now be obliged to wait months, and perhaps years; I would be forced to throw them off the track; I would have to lull them into believing that my one motive for following the blind man had been to rob him.

Another event that took place more than three years later put me on precisely the right track once again, and I was finally able to enter the redoubt of the blind.

❧ 3 ❧

THERE IS A fundamental difference between men who have lost their sight through illness or accident and those blind from birth. It is to this difference that I owe having at last been able to penetrate their redoubts, though I have not entered the most secret dens from which unknown grand pontiffs rule the Sect, and therefore the World. In this sort of suburb, it was only with the greatest of difficulty that I contrived to garner information, the usual vague reports, furnished only with the greatest reluctance, of these monsters and the means they employ to dominate the entire universe. I did manage to discover in this way that this hegemony is achieved and maintained (apart from the trivial exploitation of the sort of vulgar sentimentality that is the common practice everywhere) through anonymous letters, intrigues, the spreading of contagious diseases, control of dreams and nightmares, somnambulism, and dealing in drugs. One need only call to mind the marijuana and cocaine operation that came to light in secondary schools in the United States, where from the age of eleven or twelve boys and girls were corrupted, so as to reduce them to a state of unconditional and absolute servitude. Naturally the investigation ended where it ought in reality to have begun: at the inviolable threshold. As for domination through dreams, nightmares, and black magic, it is doubtless not even worth demonstrating that the Sect has in its service for this purpose a whole army of seers and local witches, quacks, faith healers, fortune tellers, and spiritualists: many of them, the majority, are mere frauds; but others have genuine powers, and curiously, they are in the habit of concealing these powers beneath a certain apparent charlatanism, the better to hold the world around them in thrall.

If, as they say, God rules heaven, the Sect has dominion over the earth and the flesh. I do not know if, in the final reckoning, this organization must one day account for its actions to what might be called the Luminous Authority; but meanwhile, it is evident that the universe is in its absolute power, that of life and death, which it exercises through pestilence or revolution, sickness or torture, deceit or false compassion, mystification or anonymity, little instructresses or inquisitors.

I am not a theologian and am not qualified to state whether these infernal powers can be explained by way of some sort of contorted Theodicy. In any case, that would be merely a theory or a hope. The rest, what I have seen and suffered, is *fact*.

But let us go back to differences.

No, let us not: there still remains a great deal to be said on this subject of infernal powers, for some ingenuous soul may believe that it is a question of a simple metaphor, rather than a brute reality. The problem of evil has never ceased to preoccupy me, even since the days when as a child I would post myself alongside an anthill, armed with a hammer, and begin to kill the creatures without rhyme or reason. The survivors were panic-stricken and scattered every which way. I would then pour water down the anthill with a hose; a flood. I could imagine the scene inside, the emergency measures, the hectic running back and forth, the orders and counterorders concerning saving the stored-up food, eggs, the queens, and so on. Finally I would raise havoc with a shovel, opening up great tunnels, searching out the last remaining pockets, and frantically destroying everything: general catastrophe. Then I would begin to ponder the overall meaning of existence, and think of our own floods and earthquakes. And so it was that I gradually evolved a series of hypotheses, for the idea that we might be governed by an omnipotent, omniscient, and good God seemed so contradictory to me that I didn't believe it could be taken seriously. By the time I had reached the age when I became involved with the band of gangsters and armed holdup men, I had already conceived of the following possibilities:

1. God does not exist.

2. God exists and is a bastard.

3. God exists, but falls asleep from time to time: his nightmares are our existence.

4. God exists, but has fits of madness: these fits are our existence.

5. God is not omnipresent; he cannot be everywhere. At times he is absent: Off in some other world? In other things?

6. God is a poor bugger confronted with a problem that is too complicated for him. He struggles with matter as an artist struggles with his work. Sometimes, now and again, he manages to be Goya, but in general it is a disaster.

7. God was vanquished before the beginning of History by the Prince of Darkness. And vanquished, turned into a supposed devil, his prestige suffers twice over, since the creation of this wretched universe is attributed to him.

I did not invent all these possibilities, though at the time I thought I was the first to conceive of them; later, however, I learned that some of them had given rise to many a pertinacious believer's convictions, above all the hypothesis of the triumphant Demon. For more than a thousand years fearless, clearsighted men were forced to face torture and death for having bared the secret. They were annihilated and dispersed, since presumably the forces that dominate the world are not going to stop at trifles when they are capable of doing what they generally do. And so, poor buggers and geniuses alike, they were tortured, burned by the Inquisition, hanged, skinned alive; entire peoples were decimated and dispersed. From China to Spain, state religions (whether Christian or Mazdaist) ruthlessly suppressed any and every attempt at revelation. And it may be said that they more or less accomplished their objective. For even if certain of the sects could not be annihilated, they became in their turn a new source of falsehood, as happened with the Moslems, for example. Let us take a look at the mechanism: according to the Gnostics, the sensible world was created by a demon named Jehovah. For a long time the Supreme Deity allows him to operate freely in the world, but in the end he sends his Son into it to inhabit the body of Jesus temporarily, in order to free the world of the false teachings of Moses. So then: Mohammed thought, as did some of these Gnostics, that Jesus was a mere human being, that the Son of God had descended in him at baptism but abandoned him during the Passion, otherwise the famous cry: "My God, my God, why hast thou forsaken me?" would be inexplicable. And when the Romans and the Jews crucify Jesus, they are putting a sort of ghost to death. But the most serious consequence was that in this way (and the same thing happened, in a more or less similar fashion, in the case of other rebel sects) the mystification was not brought to light but, rather, was lent added strength. So it was with those Christian sects who maintained that Jehovah was the Demon and that the new era began with Jesus, and so it was with those Moslems who believed that the Prince of Darkness reigned until Jesus (or until Mohammed), but was then overcome and returned to his hells. As can be seen, this is a twofold mystification: as the great lie grew weaker, these poor devils came along and pumped new strength into it.

In my view the conclusion is obvious: the Prince of Darkness continues to rule with an iron hand. And the instrument of this rule is the Sacred Sect of the Blind. And all this is so clear that I would be tempted to burst out laughing were I not terror-stricken.

4

BUT LET US go back now, once and for all, to the differences. Most importantly, there is an essential disparity between those blind from birth and those who have lost their sight through illness or accident. The newcomers naturally acquire in time a good many of the attributes of the race, in part through the workings of the same process that causes Jews to mimic races in whose midst they live, in spite of the fact that these latter have only hatred or scorn for them. Because, and this is a most singular fact, the hatred of the blind for the sighted is far exceeded by their hatred of newcomers to the world of the blind.

To what ought we attribute this phenomenon? In the beginning I thought that it might be due to causes similar to those responsible for the tremendous hatred that often exists between neighboring countries or between citizens within a single country; it is a well-known fact that the cruelest wars are civil wars; we need only recall, for instance, the civil strife in Argentina during the last century or the Spanish Civil War. Norma Gladys Pugliese, a little elementary schoolteacher whom I used for several months in order to study certain reactions of people with intellectual pretensions, was naturally of the opinion that hatred and wars among humans were due to a mutual lack of understanding and general ignorance; I was obliged to explain to her that the one way of keeping peace among humans is in fact to prevent them from knowing and understanding each other, this being the sole condition in which this species of animal proves to be relatively kind and just, since all of us are fairly indifferent when it comes to things that are of no interest to us. With the aid of a couple of history books and the crime section of the evening papers in hand, I was obliged to explain the ABCs of the human condition to this poor girl whose mind had been formed by distinguished female educators and who was more or less convinced that teaching people to read and write would resolve mankind's principal problems: whereupon I had to remind her that it was the most literate nation in the world that had set up concentration camps for mass torture and the incineration of Jews and Catholics. Quite predictably, she leapt out of bed at that point, indignant not at the Germans but at me: for myths are always more powerful than the facts meant to destroy them, and the myth of elementary education in Argentina, however nonsensical and comical it may seem, has always resisted and will continue to resist any number of satires directed against it and any number of demonstrations of the facts.

But to return to the problem that interests us, I reflected later, when I had studied the Sect and come to know it better, that the prime cause of this hatred of newcomers is caste pride, and as a consequence resentment against those who attempt to enter it and to a certain degree succeed in doing so. This is not a phenomenon peculiar to the blind, of course, since it also occurs in the upper classes of society, where those who, thanks to their immense fortunes or their children's marriages, have gained access to them, are eventually reluctantly accepted; there is a subtle contempt for them which gradually becomes tinged with a growing resentment as well, perhaps because people who belong by birth to these circles sense, by the very fact of this slow but sure invasion of their world, that they are not as secure and as well-armored as they had imagined and hence begin to experience a paradoxical feeling of inferiority.

Another factor, finally, also enters into play inasmuch as beings who, the day before, were the unwitting victims of the Sect and the object of its most pitiless acts of aggression now have access to its secrets. They thus become troublesome witnesses who, despite the fact that they do not have the slightest possibility of returning to the world from which they originally came, are nonetheless stupefied to learn of the ideas and the sentiments of these beings that they had imagined as living in a state of utter wretchedness.

All of this is merely an analysis, however, and what is worse, an analysis by way of words or concepts that are valid only for us. Strictly speaking, we have about as much possibility of understanding the universe of the blind as we do that of cats or snakes. We say: Cats are independent, aristocratic, treacherous, insecure; but in reality all these concepts have only a relative validity, since we are applying concepts and human standards to beings with whom we have nothing whatsoever in common: just as it is impossible for men to imagine gods who do not possess certain human characteristics, no matter how grotesque this will make these divinities appear to be: we need only remember, for instance, that the Greek gods were very often cuckolds.

ᕀᔭ 5 ᕀᔭ

I AM NOW about to relate how the printer Celestino Iglesias entered the picture, and how I discovered that I was on the highroad leading to the truth. But first I want to tell who I am, what I do, et cetera.

My name is Fernando Vidal Olmos. I was born on June 24, 1911, in

Capitán Olmos, a little town in the province of Buenos Aires that bears the name of my great-great-grandfather. Height: five feet ten inches; Weight: approximately 155 pounds; Eyes: gray green; Hair: straight and gray; Identifying marks: none.

My reader may well ask why the devil I am offering this "official" description of myself. But nothing in the human world is mere happenstance.

When I was little I had the same dream again and again: I saw a child (and curiously enough that child was myself, and I saw and observed myself as though I were another) playing a silent game that try as I might, I was unable to understand. I watched him intently, doing my best to discover the meaning of his gestures, his glances, the words he was murmuring. And suddenly gazing at me with a grave expression, he would say to me: "I am watching the shadow of this wall on the ground, and if it moves I don't know what may happen." His words had an air of thoughtful expectancy and at the same time frightful anxiety. And then I too would begin to watch the shadow fearfully. I need hardly add that it was not simply a question of the banal shifting of the position of the shadow as a result of the movement of the sun; it was SOMETHING ELSE. And so I too would begin to peer anxiously at the shadow, until finally I would see it begin to move, slowly but perceptibly. And then I would wake up in a cold sweat, screaming. What did the dream mean? What sort of warning was it, what did it symbolize? I went to bed each night paralyzed by the fear that I would have the dream again. And each morning when I woke up I would breathe a huge sigh of relief when I realized that I had once again escaped that danger. On other nights, however, the dreaded moment would again arrive: I would see the little boy, the wall, and the shadow once again; he would again look at me with a grave expression, again utter the same strange words; and again, after watching the shadow of the wall in fearful expectation, I would finally see it begin to move and change shape. And at this point I would once again wake up in a cold sweat, screaming.

The dream obsessed me for years, for I realized that, like almost all dreams, it undoubtedly had a hidden meaning, and that in this case it unquestionably foreshadowed something that would one day happen to me. And yet I still am uncertain whether that dream was indeed the foreshadowing of what happened to me later on, or whether it was its symbolic beginning. The first revelation came to me many years ago, when I was not yet twenty and the leader of a gang of armed bandits and thugs (I shall decide later whether I want to tell about that experience). I suddenly realized that reality might begin to take on an entirely different form if I did not concentrate my entire will on keeping it stable. I feared that the world round about me might begin at any moment to move, to become deformed, slowly at first and then very abruptly, to fall apart, to be transformed, to lose all meaning. Like the little boy in the dream, I concentrated all my effort on watching that sort of shadow that the reality surrounding us is, the shadow of some structure or some wall not within our power to contemplate directly. And then suddenly one day (I was in my room in Avellaneda, all by myself, luckily, lying on my bed) I saw, to my horror, that the shadow was beginning to move and that that old dream of mine was becoming a reality. I felt a sort of vertigo, lost consciousness, and sank down and down into chaos, but finally I was able, by dint of enormous effort, to float back up to the surface and tie down the fragments of reality that appeared to be trying to drift away. A sort of anchor. That's it precisely: as though I found myself obliged to anchor reality, but also as though this boat were built of many separable parts and it was necessary to tie all of them down and then let out a huge anchor so that the whole would not go drifting away. Unfortunately, the entire episode was repeated on several occasions, and at times it was an even more overwhelming experience. Suddenly I would *feel* things begin to slip and slide away, soon followed by everything falling apart, but as I was now familiar with these symptoms, I didn't simply let go, as I had the first time; instead I immediately set to work with all the energy I could muster. People didn't understand what was happening to me, they saw me concentrating with my fixed, empty stare and concluded that I was going mad, not realizing that precisely the opposite was happening since this effort enabled me to keep reality in its usual place and state. But at times, however intense my efforts, reality would begin little by little to come apart, to change shape, as though it were made of rubber and enormous tensions were being exerted on it from different points (from Sirius, from the center of the Earth, from everywhere): a face would begin to swell up, like a balloon inflating lopsidedly, the eyes would gradually meet, the mouth would get bigger and bigger till it finally burst, as a hideous grimace pulled the face all out of shape.

In any event those moments terrified me, and I was tortured by the necessity of keeping my mind alert, attentive, vigilant, and active at all times. I suddenly wished I could be shut up in an insane asylum so as to get some rest, since in such a place no one is obliged to maintain a hold on reality such as it appears to others—as though in such a place one could say (as no doubt one can): all right then, let other people cope with reality as best they can.

But the worst was not what happened round about me but inside me, for my own self soon began to become deformed, to stretch out of shape, to be metamorphosed too. My name is Fernando Vidal Olmos, and those three words are like a seal, a guarantee that I am "Something," something well defined: not only by the color of my eyes, by my height and weight, by my age, by the date of my birth and the names of my parents (that is to say by those facts that appear on my identity card), but rather by something more profound, something of a spiritual nature: by a concatenation of memories, of sentiments, of ideas that underlie and support the structure of this "Something" that is Fernando Vidal and not the postman or the butcher. But what is there to prevent this body that has been assigned me from suddenly being inhabited, as a consequence of some cataclysm, by the soul of the janitor or the mind of the Marquis de Sade? Is there perchance some inviolable relation between my body and my soul? It has always seemed amazing to me that a person can grow up, have hopes and dreams, be the victim of disasters, go to war, suffer moral deterioration, change his opinions radically, come to have entirely different feelings, and nonetheless still be called by the same name: Fernando Vidal. Does that have any meaning? Or is it true that despite everything there exists a sort of thread that can be stretched endlessly and yet by some miracle always remain unbroken, that sustains the identity of the self through all these changes and catastrophes?

I do not know what may be the case with others. All I can say is that in my own case this identity is suddenly lost and this deformation of the self soon takes on enormous proportions: vast regions of my spirit begin to swell up (sometimes I can even feel the physical pressure in my body, in my head especially); they creep like silent pseudopods, blindly and stealthily, toward other regions of the species and in the end toward ancient, shadowy zoological regions; a memory begins to inflate and gradually ceases to be the strains of "The Dance of the

Dragonflies" that I heard being played on the piano one night in my childhood, and little by little becomes a stranger and stranger, wilder and wilder music that then turns into cries and groans and finally into terrible shrieks, and then into a tolling of bells that deafens my ears, and stranger still, these sounds begin to turn into an acid or intensely disagreeable taste in my mouth, as though passing from my ears into my throat, and my stomach contracts and I retch with nausea, as other sounds, other memories, other feelings undergo similar metamorphoses. And at such moments the thought sometimes occurs to me that perhaps reincarnation is a fact and that in the most hidden depths of our self memories of these beings that preceded us lie sleeping, just as our bodies preserve traces of fish or reptiles; dominated by the new self and the new body, yet ever ready to awaken and emerge the moment that the forces, the tensions, the screws and bits of wire that hold the present self together work loose and give way, for some reason unknown to us, and the wild beasts and prehistoric animals that inhabit us are unleashed. This is what happens every night as we sleep but suddenly the process becomes uncontrollable and we become subject to nightmares that now unfold in broad daylight.

But as my will continues to obey me, I feel a certain sense of security, because I know it will enable me to emerge from chaos and reorganize my world: my will is powerful when it is functioning properly. The worst is when I feel my self falling apart in the area of my will as well. Or as though my will still belonged to me, but not the system or the parts of my body that transmit it. Or as though my body were still mine, yet "something" interposes itself between it and my will. For example: I want to move my arm, but it does not obey me. I focus all my attention on this arm, but it does not obey me. I focus all my attention on this arm, I look at it, I make a concerted effort, but I note that it does not obey me. As though the lines of communication between my brain and this arm were cut off. This has happened to me very often, as though I were a region devastated by an earthquake, with great yawning fissures opening up and all the telephone wires down. And in such instances, anything may happen: there is no police force, no army. Any and every sort of calamity may occur, any and every sort of pillage and plundering, any and every sort of depredation. As though my body belonged to another, and I, mute and powerless, were observing the birth of suspect movements, of tremors presaging a new convulsion in this alien territory, until little by little catastrophe takes possession of my body and, finally, of my mind.

I set all this down so that my readers may understand me.

And also because many of the episodes that I shall recount would otherwise be incomprehensible and unbelievable. But it so happens that for the most part it was because of this catastrophic split in my personality that they came about; not despite it, but because of it.

∞ 6 ∞

AFTER MY DEATH, which is close at hand now, it is my wish that this Report be forwarded to any institute interested in pursuing an investigation of this world that to date has remained unexplored. Hence this Report is limited to FACTS, exactly as I experienced them. Its merit, in my opinion, lies in its absolute objectivity: I wish to tell of my experience as an explorer might tell of his expedition to the Amazon or Central Africa. And although passion and rancor may often tend to cloud my judgment, as is only natural, I am determined to be as accurate and precise as possible and not to allow myself to be carried away by sentiments of this sort. I have had frightful experiences, but for that very reason I wish to keep to the facts, even if these facts may at times shed an unflattering light on my own life. When I have finished, no sensible person can possibly maintain that the aim of this document is to arouse feelings of sympathy toward my person.

Here for instance is one of the unflattering facts about myself that I shall confess to, as proof of my sincerity: I do not have, and never have had, friends. I have, naturally, experienced passions; but I have never felt affection for anyone, nor do I believe anyone has ever felt affection for me.

I have nonetheless had relationships with many people. I have had "intimate acquaintances," as this equivocal expression goes.

And one of these acquaintances, who plays an important role in what is to follow, was a wizened, taciturn Spaniard named Celestino Iglesias.

I met him for the first time in an anarchist center in the Avellaneda district called Dawn. I frequented anarchist circles because I had vague plans for organizing a gang of armed bandits, which in fact I did organize later; although not all anarchists were holdup men, among their number one came across all sorts of adventurers, nihilists, and in a word that type of enemy of society that had always attracted me. One of these individuals was Osvaldo R. Podestá, who took part in the holdup of the Banco de San Martín and who during the Spanish Civil War was machine-gunned to death by the Reds, near the port of Tarragona, just as he was about to flee the country on an old tub loaded to the gunwales with money and jewels.

It was through Podestá that I met Iglesias: as though a wolf had introduced me to a lamb. For Iglesias was one of those tender-hearted anarchists who wouldn't have harmed a fly: he was a pacifist, a vegetarian (because he was repelled by the thought of living himself at the expense of the death of another living creature), and he cherished the utopian hope that the world would one day be an affectionate community built together by free and fraternal men of good will. This New World would speak a single language, and that language would be Esperanto. For that reason he eventually mastered, with enormous difficulty, the use of this sort of orthopedic device that not only is ugly (which is not an insuperable defect for a universal language) but also is spoken by practically no one (which is catastrophic for a universal language). And so it happened that in laborious letters penned with his tongue sticking out he communicated with one or another of the five hundred or so persons in the rest of the universe who thought as he did.

A curious fact, but a frequent phenomenon among anarchists: an angelic being such as Iglesias was nonetheless capable of devoting his time and effort to making counterfeit money. The second time I saw him, in fact, was in a basement in the Calle Boedo, where Podestá had all the equipment necessary for this type of work and where Iglesias carried out the secret projects assigned him.

He was about thirty-five at the time, a thin, very dark-skinned, short, wizened man, like so many Spaniards who appear to have lived on land burned to cinders, eating almost nothing, and dried up by the relentless summer sun and the pitiless cold of winter. He was extremely generous and never had a cent to his name (everything he earned, and the bills that he counterfeited, went to the anarchists or to finance Podestá's shady undertakings); he was always inviting one or another of the many parasites who hung about anarchist circles to share his one tiny room, and even though he couldn't have hurt a fly, he had nonetheless spent the greater part of his life behind bars in Spanish and Argentine jails. In somewhat the same way as Norma Pugliese, Iglesias imagined that all the ills of humanity would one day be remedied thanks to a combination of Science and Mutual Knowledge. It was necessary to combat the Dark Forces that for centuries had stood in the way of the ultimate victory of Truth. The March of Ideas, however, could lead only onward and upward, and sooner or later the Dawn was bound to come. Meanwhile it was imperative to combat the organized forces of the State, to denounce the Imposture of the Clergy, to keep a sharp eye on the Army, and to promote the Education of the Worker. Libraries were founded in which the reader could find not only the works of Bakunin or Kropotkin but also Zola's novels and volumes by Spencer and Darwin, for even the theory of evolution struck these anarchists as being usefully subversive, and a strange link existed between the history of Fish and Marsupials and the Triumph of the New Ideas. On the shelves there was also to be found, naturally, Ostwald's *Energetics*, that sort of thermodynamic bible in which God is replaced by a lay entity (though again an incomprehensible one) called Energy, which, like its predecessor, explained and did everything, and had the added advantage of being related to Progress and the Locomotive. The men and women who met each other in these libraries thereupon entered into "free unions" and produced offspring whom they named Light, Freedom, New Era, or Giordano Bruno, offspring who, in most cases, by virtue of that mechanism which sets child against parent, or in other cases thanks merely to the complicated and usually dialectical March of Time, eventually became vulgar bourgeois, strikebreakers, and even, in certain instances, fierce persecutors of the Movement, such as the renowned police commissioner Giordano Bruno Trenti.

I stopped seeing Iglesias when the Spanish Civil War broke out, for like many others he went to Spain to fight beneath the banner of the FAI, the Iberian Anarchist Federation. In 1938 he crossed the border into France as a refugee, and in that country he no doubt had the opportunity to appreciate the fraternal sentiments of its citizens and the advantages of Proximity and Knowledge over Remoteness and Mutual Ignorance. From France he was eventually able to make his way back to Argentina. And I met him again here in this country several years after the episode in the subway that I have already recounted. I was hand in glove at the time with a gang of counterfeiters, and since we needed an experienced man whom we could trust I thought of Iglesias. I went looking for him, making inquiries among old acquaintances and among the anarchist groups in La Plata and Avellaneda, and finally I located him, working as a typographer in the Kraft Print Works.

I found he'd changed considerably, above all on account of his limp: he had had his right leg amputated during the war. And he was more dried-up and reserved than ever.

He hesitated but finally accepted my proposal when I told him that the counterfeit money would be used to aid an anarchist group in Switzerland. It was not at all difficult to convince him of anything once it had to do with the Cause, however utopian the idea might appear to be at first glance; in fact, the more utopian it was the better. He was hopelessly naive: hadn't he worked for a crook like Podestá? I had hesitated a moment, unable to decide what nationality I should assign these imaginary anarchists, but I finally chose Switzerland since it was such a patent absurdity; to anyone in his right mind believing in Swiss anarchists would be like believing in the existence of rats in a strongbox. The first time I passed through that country I had the impression that it was swept down with a broom from one end to the other every morning by housewives (who of course dumped all the dirt on Italy). And this impression was so striking that I pondered once more the entire question of myths concerning different nationalities. Anecdotes are essentially true, because they are invented bit by bit so as to fit the individual exactly. Something similar happens in the case of national myths, which are made to order to describe the soul of a country, and in this particular instance it occurred to me that the legend of William Tell was a faithful description of the Swiss soul: when the archer's arrow hit the apple, no doubt square in the center, the Swiss missed their one and only historical opportunity to experience a great national tragedy. What can one expect such a country to produce? A race of watchmakers at best.

ᖇᔕ 7 ᖇᔕ

MY READER might well ponder the unbelievable number of hap-penstances that finally led me to enter the universe of the blind: if I had not been in contact with the anarchists, if among those anarchists I had not met a man such as Iglesias, if Iglesias had not been a counterfeiter, if he had not been a victim of that accident that blinded him, if...et cetera. Why go on? Events are fortuitous, or appear to be so, depending on the angle from which we observe reality. If seen from the opposite angle, what reason would there be not to suppose that everything that happens to us obeys final causes? Blind men had been an obsession with me since childhood, and as far back as I can recall I remember that I always had the vague but persistent aim of one day entering their universe. If I had not had Iglesias at my beck and call, I would have thought up some other way, for all my strength of spirit was aimed at achieving this objective. And when we pursue, energetically and systematically, an end that lies within the possibilities of the world in question, when not only the conscious forces of our personality but also the most powerful forces of our subconscious are mobilized, a telepathic field is eventually created round about us that imposes our will on others and even brings about events that to all appearances are fortuitous but in fact are determined by that invisible power of our spirit. On a number of occasions following the failure of my efforts involving the blind man in the subway, it occurred to me that it would be useful to have a sort of intermediary between the two domains, someone who, as a conse-quence of his having lost his eyesight in an accident, would still, if only for a time, be part of our universe of those able to see and at the same time would already have one foot in the other realm. And who knows? it may well be that that idea, which became more and more of an obsession with each passing day, took possession of my sub-conscious to the point that it eventually acted, as I have already said, as an invisible yet powerful magnetic field, causing one of the beings who entered it to become the victim of what I most desired at that moment in my life: accidental blindness. Thinking back on the sequence of events at the time that Iglesias was handling those acids,

I remember that the explosion was preceded by my entrance into the laboratory and by my being struck by the sudden, almost violent thought that if Iglesias went any closer to the Bunsen burner there would be an explosion. Was this a premonition? I am unable to say. Who knows whether that accident was not in some way the direct consequence of my desire, whether that event that at the time seemed a typical phenomenon of the indifferent material universe was not, on the contrary, a typical phenomenon of the universe in which our darkest obsessions are born and flourish? I myself have no clear idea of what really happened, since at the time I was going through one of those periods in which it required a great effort on my part simply to go on living, in which I felt like the captain of a ship in the eye of a tremendous storm, with the decks being lashed by gales of hurricane force and the hull creaking with the strain, trying my best to remain clearheaded so that everything would stay in its place, calling upon all my strength of will and devoting my entire attention to the harrowing task of keeping on course amid the crashing waves and the darkness. Afterwards I would collapse on my bunk, drained of all power of will and with great holes in my memory, as though my mind had been devastated by the violent storm. It was days before everything returned more or less to normal, and the people and events of my real life gradually appeared or reappeared, looking dreary and sad, battered and gray, as the waters slowly grew calm once again.

Following such periods, I would return to normal life with vague memories of my past existence. And thus, little by little Iglesias reappeared in my memory, and it was only with the greatest difficulty that I reconstructed the events leading up to the explosion.

ᧀ 8 ᧀ

A LONG PROCESS had to take place before I could even so much as glimpse the first results, for as can readily be imagined the intermediate region separating the two worlds is one full of dubious and equivocal facts, fumbling approximations, ambiguities: given the terrible, secret nature of the universe of the blind, it is only natural that no one can penetrate it without having first undergone a series of subtle transformations.

I studied this process closely and was away from Iglesias only when absolutely necessary: this was my best opportunity to infiltrate the forbidden world of the blind, and I was not about to miss it through some gross error. Hence I tried to spend as much time with him as possible, without at the same time arousing the slightest suspicion on his part. I took care of him, I read Kropotkin to him, I had long talks with him about Mutual Aid, but above all I watched and I waited. I hung a huge sign in my room that I could see from the head of my bed, with the words:

WATCH

WAIT

I said to myself: *They* are bound to appear sooner or later; there must surely be a moment in the life of a person who has recently gone blind when *they* come in search of him. But that moment (I also said to myself, in great anxiety) might give no sign of being a very special one; on the contrary, it was quite likely that it would appear to be a trivial or even an everyday occurrence. It was imperative to pay close attention to the least little detail, to keep a sharp eye on anyone and everyone who approached him, however harmless such persons might seem to be at first glance (indeed persons of this sort should be regarded as the most suspect of all), to intercept all letters and telephone calls, et cetera. As can readily be imagined, this program was extremely tiring and well-nigh labyrinthine. Only one detail need be mentioned to give some idea of the anxiety that consumed me in those days. Some other person in the rooming house might well be the intermediary of the sect, an entirely innocent one perhaps; and that individual might see Iglesias at moments when it was impossible for me to keep watch on him; he might even lie in wait for him in the bathroom. In the course of long nights spent pondering the problem in my room, I drew up such detailed plans for keeping Iglesias under constant surveillance that in order to carry them out I would have had to have at my disposal an espionage network as large as that required by an entire country in wartime; with the ever-present risk of counterespionage, since it is a well-known fact that any spy may be a double agent, a risk everyone necessarily runs. After lengthy analyses that nearly drove me mad, I ended up simplifying my plans and limiting myself to what was possible for me to carry out by myself. It was necessary to be thorough and patient, to have courage and at the same time use the slyest and most subtle of approaches: my disastrous experience with the blind peddler of collar stays had taught me that even though it might be easier and quicker, a frontal attack would get me nowhere in the end.

I have written the word *courage*; I might also have written *anxiety*. For I was tormented by the suspicion that the Sect might well have been keeping me under very close surveillance ever since that episode with the peddler. And it seemed to me that there was no such thing as being too cautious. I shall cite an example. As I sat in a café on the Calle Paso, ostensibly reading the newspaper, I raised my eyes all of a sudden, with the swiftness of a lightning bolt, so as to try to catch Juanito the waiter unawares and spy any sort of suspicious sign that might betray him, a certain indefinable gleam in his eye, a blush. Then I called him over with a wave of my hand. If he had *not* blushed, I said to him: "Juanito, how come you turned red in the face just now?" He denied, naturally, that he had. But this too was an excellent test: if he denied it without turning red in the face it was more or less proof of his innocence, but if he flushed as he denied it, he bore watching. According to the rules of logic, the fact that he did *not* turn red when I put my question to him did not constitute incontrovertible proof (and that is why I wrote "more or less proof") that he was not involved with the Sect or the plot in any way, since a good spy must be above such shortcomings.

All this may be taken as a typical symptom of my persecution mania, but subsequently events clearly *demonstrated* that my mistrust and my suspicions were unfortunately not as absurd as a person unaware of my situation might imagine if he were keeping me under observation. Why did I nonetheless dare to venture so dangerously close to the edge of the abyss? Because I counted on the inevitable imperfection of the real world, in which even the spy network and intelligence apparatus of the blind are bound to have their weak spots. I also counted on something that it was only logical to presume was the case: the existence of hatred and antipathies among the blind themselves, as among any other group of mortals. In short, I came to the conclusion that the difficulties that a person who can see might expect to encounter as he explored their universe were scarcely different in kind from those that a British spy might have encountered during the war while working inside the Hitler regime, an extremely well-organized system, certainly, yet for all that one full of weak spots and rancors.

The problem was nonetheless doubly complicated since, as was only to be expected, Iglesias's mentality had begun to change, though in fact it was more than (and less than) a question of mentality: it would be more apt to speak of a change of "species" or of "zoological condition." As though by virtue of a genetic experiment a human being were to change, slowly but inexorably, into a bat or a lizard, and what is even more horrible still, with practically no outward sign whatsoever that would betray such a profound inner change. Being alone in a dark, closed room at night, knowing that there is also a bat in it somewhere is always frightening, especially when we can hear this sort of winged rat flitting about and then suddenly experience an intolerable sensation: one of its wings has brushed against our face in its nasty silent flight. But how much more horrendous this sensation can be if the animal has a human form! Iglesias was the victim of such subtle changes that another person might not even have noticed them, but since I had been observing him very closely and systematically, they were quite perceptible to me.

He became more mistrustful with each passing day. This was only natural: he was not yet a real blind man, possessed of that power to move about in the dark and that acute sense of hearing and touch that the blind have; at the same time he was no longer a man possessed of normal eyesight. I had the impression that he felt lost: he had no real sense of distance, his kinesthetic reactions were impaired, he stumbled about, he would feel clumsily about for a glass in front of him and knock it over. This irritated him, though out of pride he did his best to conceal that fact.

"Never mind; it doesn't matter at all, Iglesias," I would comment, instead of pretending I hadn't noticed and saying nothing. This made him even more irritated and his movements would thereupon become clumsier still, which was precisely the reaction I had intended to provoke.

Then I would sit there not saying a word all of a sudden, allowing a total silence to envelop him, so to speak. For a blind man total silence round about him is like what a shadowy abyss separating us from the rest of the world would be for us. He does not know what to expect; all his links with the outside world have been cut off in the darkness that absolute silence is for the blind. He must listen for the slightest sound; danger awaits him on every hand.

At such times he is all alone and helpless. The mere ticking of a watch can be like a tiny light in the distance, the sort of tiny light that the terror-stricken hero in children's stories spies when he thinks he is hopelessly lost in the heart of a vast forest.

Then I would tap lightly on the table or chair, as though by accident, and would note how Iglesias, with morbid anxiety, would focus his entire awareness in that direction. In the midst of his solitude, he was perhaps wondering: What is Vidal up to? Why has he been sitting there in silence?

As a matter of fact, he greatly mistrusted me. He became more and more wary of me as the days went by, and after three weeks, when his metamorphosis was very nearly complete, he had ceased to trust me altogether. If my theories were correct, there was a certain sign that would mark Iglesias's definite entry into the new realm, his total transformation: the feeling of repulsion that real blind men always arouse in me. Nor does that repulsion or apprehension or phobia appear all at once: my experience had proved to me that this too comes about gradually, until one day we find ourselves confronted with the hair-raising *fait accompli:* that bat or the reptile is there before our very eyes. I remember that day: as I approached the room in the pension in which Iglesias had been living since his accident, I experienced an odd sensation of malaise, a vague apprehension that grew stronger and stronger as I drew closer to his room, becoming so intense that I hesitated a moment before knocking on his door. Then, almost trembling, I called out: "Iglesias" and *something* answered: "Come in." I opened the door and there in the darkness (for naturally there was no need for him to have a light on when he was alone) I heard the breathing of the new monster.

ᓂ 9 ᓂ

B UT BEFORE THAT crucial moment arrived, other things happened that I must recount, for they were the ones that allowed me to enter the universe of the blind before Iglesias's metamorphosis was complete. I was like those desperate wartime messengers on motorcycles who must cross a bridge that they know is about to be blown

up at any moment. Since I could see the fateful moment approaching
when the metamorphosis would be total, I tried to race along even
faster. There were times when I thought I wouldn't make it; the
bridge would be blown up by the enemy before my mad race could
get me safely across to the other side of the chasm.

I watched the days go by with growing anxiety. Iglesias's inner
transformation seemed to me to be following its inexorable course,
and yet I saw no sign that *they* had appeared. I had dismissed (on
the grounds that it was too absurd to believe) the hypothesis that the
blind might not be aware of the fact that a person had lost his eyesight and that therefore the time had come to seek that person out
and put him in contact with the Sect. The uneventful round of the
days and my growing anxiety nonetheless made me seriously consider
this hypothesis once again, along with others that were even more
preposterous, as though my emotions were clouding my ability to
reason and, moreover, causing me to forget everything I already knew
about the Sect. It is quite probable that emotions favors the writing
of a poem or the composition of music, but it is disastrous to the workings of pure reason.

I blush at the memory of the wild ideas that came to me when I
began to fear that I would not succeed in crossing the bridge. I even
went so far as to conjecture that a man who had gone blind might
possibly go on living as though he were a little island in the middle
of an immense, indifferent ocean. By that I mean to say: what would
become of a man who, as in Iglesias's case, became blind by accident
and because of his particular quirks of personality neither desires nor
actively seeks any sort of contact with other blind people? One who,
out of misanthropy, despair, or timidity does not care to have anything
to do with those societies that are the visible (and superficial) manifestations of the forbidden world: the Library for the Blind, Choral
Societies, and so on? On first reflection, what could prevent a man
such as Iglesias from keeping entirely to himself and not only failing
to seek out, but even actually fleeing the company of his fellows? Such
an idiotic notion made my head swim the moment it occurred to me
(for even idiotic notions can thoroughly upset us). I tried immediately
to reassure myself. Iglesias is poor, I said to myself, he is obliged to
work for a living, he cannot sit around doing nothing. How does a
blind man work for a living? He must go out on the streets and en-

gage in one or another of those activities traditionally reserved for the blind: selling combs and trinkets, photos of popular singers and renowned jockeys, the famous collar stays: something, in a word, that makes him easily visible, and likely sooner or later to be co-opted by the Sect. I did my best to hurry the process along by urging Iglesias to set himself up in one or another of these little businesses. I spoke enthusiastically of collar stays and how much money he could take in just one subway station. I painted a rosy picture of the future that lay before him, but Iglesias just sat there, silent and mistrustful.

"I still have a few pesos left. We'll see later on."

Later on! The very words filled me with despair. I suggested a newspaper stand, but this prospect did not arouse his enthusiasm either.

There was nothing I could do but watch and wait, until such time as necessity forced him to go out into the streets.

I repeat that I blush for shame today at having been reduced to such a state of utter imbecility out of sheer terror. Had I been in my right mind, how could I have supposed that the Sect would need an event such as Iglesias's setting himself up in business at a newspaper stand in order to learn of his existence? What about all the people who had seen Iglesias being carried out on a stretcher after the accident? And the doctors and nurses at the hospital? Not to mention the powers that the Sect possesses and the immensely complex intelligence and espionage network that covers the entire world like an awesome invisible spider web. I must say, however, that after several nights of ridiculous uneasiness, I concluded that these theories were utter nonsense and that there was not the slightest possibility that Iglesias had been abandoned or overlooked by the Sect. The one thing to be feared was that their getting in touch with him would come too late for me. But there was nothing I could do about that.

As it was no longer possible for me to be with him every moment, I looked for a way of keeping him under surveillance without actually being in his company myself. I took the following steps:

1. I gave a considerable sum of money to the woman who ran the pension, a certain Señora Etchepareborda who, fortunately, appeared to be more or less mentally retarded. I asked her to take care of Iglesias and to notify me of the least little thing out of the ordinary that hap-

pened to him, using, naturally, his blindness as the reason for my particular concern about him.

2. I asked Iglesias not to do anything without advising me beforehand, since I was eager to be of help to him in any way possible. I did not expect very much to come of this variation of my basic plan, since I imagined (and rightly so, as it turned out) that he would want to see less and less of me as time went by and come to mistrust me more and more.

3. Insofar as was possible, I tried to set up a system of surveillance that would allow me to keep track of his every move if he went out, as well as to keep close watch of the movements of those individuals who presumably would try to get in touch with him. The pension was in the Calle Paso. Luckily for me, there happened to be a café only a few steps away, where like so many idlers I could spend long hours, pretending to be reading the newspaper or chatting with the waiters whom I made it my business to become friendly with. It was summer, and as I sat at a table next to the open window I could keep an eye on the entrance to the pension.

4. I used Norma Gladys Pugliese, my purpose in so doing being twofold: to avoid arousing the suspicions that a lone man keeping watch for long hours was certain to arouse, and to alternate talk of football and Argentine politics with the mild pleasure of corrupting this little schoolteacher's mind and morals.

∽ 10 ∽

THE FIVE DAYS that followed plunged me into despair. What could I do except cogitate and chat with the waiter and leaf through newspapers and magazines? I seized upon the opportunity and read two things that had always fascinated me: the advertisements and the crime page. The only things I've read after reaching the age of twenty, the only things that shed light on human nature and great metaphysical problems. In the sixth edition: MAN SUDDENLY LOSES MIND, MURDERS WIFE AND FOUR CHILDREN WITH AX. Nothing is known about this man, except that his name is Domingo Salerno, that he is honest and hardworking, that he has a little shop in Villa Lugano, and adored his wife and children. And then out of the blue he hacks them to bits with an ax. A profound mystery! What is more, what a vivid ring of truth the crime page has after one reads the declarations of politicians! All of the latter seem to be charlatans and international confidence men, peddlers hawking hair tonic. How can one compare one of these frauds with a pure soul such as Salerno? I find the advertisements exciting reading too: TOMORROW'S WINNERS STUDY AT PITMAN SCHOOLS. Two glorious, glowing adolescents, a boy and a girl, smiling and proud, head arm in arm toward the Future. Another ad shows a desk with two telephones and an intercom; the empty chair is all ready to be occupied and bright little rays of light seem to be coming out of the telephone; the caption says: THIS PLACE IS WAITING FOR YOU. Another ad whose demagogic tone appeals to me is the one for Podestá Optical Company: YOUR EYES DESERVE THE BEST. Those for shaving cream take the form of little stories with a moral; in the first box, Pedro, who clearly needs a shave, invites María Cristina to dance; in the second box, in the foreground, one sees Pedro's doleful countenance and María Cristina's expression of profound distaste as she dances with him, trying to keep her face as far away from his as possible; in the third box, she comments to a girlfriend: "How repulsive Pedro is with that five-o'clock shadow!" and her friend replies: "Why don't you come right out and tell him so?"; in the next box, María Cristina answers that she doesn't dare, but that perhaps she, her girlfriend, could tell her boyfriend so that he in turn could drop a hint to Pedro; in the next-to-last frame, one can see the boyfriend whispering something in Pedro's ear; in the last frame, Pedro and María Cristina are shown dancing together, happy and smiling now that every last whisker is gone, thanks to the famous close shave provided by Palmolive; the caption says: THROUGH INEXCUSABLE CARELESSNESS HE MIGHT HAVE LOST HIS SWEETHEART.

Variants: in one, Pedro loses a splendid opportunity for employment; in another, he never gets promoted; at the back of a large room full of desks and employees, among whom it is easy to spot Pedro with his five-o'clock shadow; the boss is looking at him from across the room with an expression of loathing and disgust. Deodorant creams: engagements, marvelous positions in wonderful companies, invitations to parties, all foolishly missed out on because of not having used Odorono.

Ads with men who look like the type who go in for sports, carefully groomed and smiling, but at the same time vigorous and determined, with huge square jaws like Superman, pounding on their desks with their fists, amid numerous telephones, thrusting their torsos forward toward their invisible, hesitant conversational partner, exclaiming: SUCCESS IS WITHIN REACH OF YOUR HAND. In other ads, the Superman does not pound on the desk but instead points his finger straight at the reader of the newspaper, a lazy, spineless sort, in the habit of wasting his Time and his Remarkable Talents in stupid ways, and says to him: EARN FIVE THOUSAND PESOS A MONTH IN YOUR SPARE TIME, urging him to write his name and address inside the dotted lines of a little square coupon.

Stripped of skin, showing his powerful, ropelike muscles, Mister Atlas summons the weaklings of the world: in just seven days there will be Progress, anyone can have a splendid physique if he makes up his mind to, in no time one can have the build of Mister Atlas himself. The ad says: EVERYONE ADMIRES YOUR BROAD SHOULDERS. YOU'LL GET THE PRETTIEST GIRL AND THE BEST JOB!

But there's nothing like the *Reader's Digest* to promote Optimism and Good Feeling. An article by Mr. Frank I. Andrews, entitled "When Hotel-Keepers Get Together," begins: "Getting to know the distinguished hotel-keepers who arrived in the United States to represent their colleagues in Hispano-American countries was one of the most moving moments of my life." And hundreds of other articles destined to raise the morale of the poor, the leprous, the lame, the oedipal, the blind, the deaf and dumb, the epileptic, the consumptive, the victims of cancer, the crippled, the macrocephalic, the microcephalic, the neurotic, the sons or grandsons of raving madmen, the flatfooted, the asthmatic, the backward, the stutterers and stammerers, those with bad breath, the unhappily married, the rheumatic, painters who have lost their sight, sculptors who have had both hands amputated, musicians who have gone deaf (remember Beethoven!), athletes paralyzed by war injuries, victims of poison gas attacks in the Great War, women so ugly they frighten people, hare-lipped children, men with twanging voices, timid salespersons, people too tall, people too short (practically dwarfs), men who weigh over four hundred pounds, and so on. The titles: THEY KICKED ME OUT OF MY FIRST JOB; OUR ROMANCE BEGAN IN THE LEPROSARIUM; LEARNING TO LIVE WITH YOUR CANCER; I LOST MY EYESIGHT BUT WON A FORTUNE; YOUR DEAFNESS CAN BE AN ASSET, etc.

On leaving the bar, and after making my nightly visit to the pension to see Iglesias, I found myself absorbed in rapt contemplation of the big billboard for Saint Catherine vermicelli on the Plaza del Once, and although I didn't remember exactly who Saint Catherine had been, it seemed to me quite likely that she had suffered martyrdom, since martyrdom is the usual end of the professional careers, so to speak, of saints; and at that point I couldn't help but ponder that characteristic facet of human existence whereby someone who is crucified or skinned alive is in time converted into a brand of vermicelli or canned goods.

∽ I I ∽

I BELIEVE IT WAS her resentment toward me that led Norma to appear in the café one day in the company of an epicene creature named Inés González Iturrat. She was huge, with bulging muscles, a visible moustache, and gray hair, and was dressed in a severe tailored suit and wearing men's shoes. At a quick glance, if it hadn't been for her prominent full breasts, I might have made the mistake of addressing her as "sir." She was very energetic and decisive, and had Norma completely under her thumb.

"I've met you before," I said.

"Who, me?" she commented, surprised and annoyed, as though she found such a possibility offensive, since Norma had naturally told her a great deal about me.

I did in fact have the vague impression that I had seen her somewhere before, but it was not until the very end of this meeting in the café, throughout which I was very ill at ease (I was obliged to look past her enormous bulk in order to keep an eye on number 57) that I managed to solve this little enigma.

Norma was giving signs of an eager desire to see the two of us cross swords: Norma's repeated defeats at my hand made her anticipate with vengeful pleasure the idea of a lively debate between this atomic physicist and me, in which I would be ingloriously vanquished. But my mind was elsewhere, since I had necessarily to concentrate all my attention on number 57, and hence I did not give evidence of the slightest interest in arguing with this creature. It was unfortunately impossible for me simply to get up and leave, as I surely would have done in any other circumstances.

Norma's breast was heaving like a bellows.

"Inés was my history teacher, as I've told you."

"Ah, yes, so you did," I commented politely.

"We girls who studied with her are still very close. We've formed a study group and Inés is our mentor."

"An excellent idea," I said, in the same polite tone of voice.

"We discuss books and visit art galleries and attend lectures."

"Very good."

"We go on field trips."

"Magnificent."

She was becoming more and more irritated and added, almost indignantly:

"We've been going on guided tours of painting exhibitions, led by Inés and Professor Romero Brest."

She looked at me with blazing eyes, waiting to see what I would say to that.

"That's splendid," I said in my most urbane manner.

"You think women ought to do nothing but stay home and scrub floors, wash dishes, and do the housework," she replied, almost shouting now.

A man carrying a ladder had stopped outside number 57, and seemed to be on the point of going inside, but after having taken a good look at the number he went on to the house next door. Once this anxious moment was past and I felt a bit calmer, I asked her please to repeat her last remark, because I hadn't heard her very well. This made her even more furious.

"Of course you didn't hear!" she exclaimed. "You don't even listen to what I say. That's how much my opinions interest you."

"They interest me a great deal."

"Liar! You've told me a thousand times that women are different from men!"

"That's all the more reason for me to be interested in their opinions. People are always interested in what's different or unknown."

"Ah, so you admit then that you take a woman to be something entirely different from a man!"

"There's no point in getting all excited about anything as obvious as that, Norma."

The history professor, who had followed this exchange with an ironic, hostile expression on her face, having no doubt been fore-warned that I was an obscurantist, spoke up then:

"Do you really think so?" she asked.

"Do I think *what?*" I asked ingenuously.

"That the difference between a man and a woman is *obvious*," she replied, sarcastically emphasizing the word.

"Everyone agrees that there are certain appreciable differences be-tween a woman and a man," I explained calmly.

"*That's* not what we're talking about, and you know it!" Norma's mentor replied in icy fury.

"*That?* What exactly do you mean by 'that'?"

"I mean sex, as you know very well," she replied cuttingly. Her tone was like a very sharp, disinfected knife.

"Do you think sex is something of very little importance?" I asked her.

I was beginning to be in a good mood, and furthermore the two of them were helping to make the time go faster as I watched and waited. The only thing that was still bothering me was the vague feeling that I had seen this professor before, though I couldn't remember precisely where.

"It's not the most important thing certainly! Were talking about something else, about spiritual values. And the differences that you men insist on seeing between activities suitable for a man and those suitable for a woman are typical of a backward society."

"Ah, I understand now," I commented with a show of perfect serenity. "For you women the difference between the uterus and the phallus is a carryover from the Dark Ages. It will disappear one day, along with gas lighting and illiteracy."

Norma's mentor blushed: what I had said not only made her indig-nant but embarrassed her as well, not because the words *uterus* and *phallus* had been uttered (being scientific terms, they would no more disturb her than the words *neutrino* or *chain reaction*), but by virtue of the same mechanism whereby Professor Einstein would feel embarrassed if one were to ask him how his bowels were working.

"Those are mere words," she declared. "What is fact is that there are all sorts of activities in which women are competing with men today. And that's what absolutely unhinges you men. Take, for instance, the delegation of women that has just arrived here from the United States. Among them are three directors of heavy industry."

Norma, that very feminine creature, shot a glance at me, her eyes gleaming triumphantly. Resentment is a very powerful force. In some way or other these female monsters from America avenged her for her servility in bed. The development of the metallurgical industry in the U.S. more or less blotted out the shame of the cries she gave at the moment of climax, the frenzy of her unconditional surrender. A humiliating position was compensated for by Yankee petrochemistry.

It was true: now that I was obliged to leaf through the daily papers, I remembered having seen a story about the arrival of this group from the U.S.

"There are also women who box," I remarked. "If such a monstrosity appeals to you, well then ..."

"Is it monstrous, in your opinion, if a woman becomes a member of the board of directors of a major industry?"

Again I was obliged to look past the athletic shoulders of Señorita González Iturrat in order to keep an eye on a suspect passerby. This perfectly explainable bit of behavior on my part made that eminent harpy more furious still.

"And does it also seem monstrous to you that a genius such as Madame Curie distinguished herself in the realm of science?" she went on, her little eyes narrowing insidiously.

It was inevitable that Madame Curie's name should come up.

"A genius is someone who discovers similarities between seemingly contradictory facts," I explained calmly and didactically. "Relations between facts that to all appearances are totally unrelated. Someone who brings to light similarity amid diversity, reality beneath appearances. Someone who discovers that the stone that falls and the Moon that does not fall obey one and the same law."

Norma's menetor followed my argument with a sarcastic gleam in her little eyes, like a schoolteacher listening to a youngster who consistently tells whoppers.

"And is what Madame Curie discovered of trifling importance?"

"Madame Curie, señorita, did not discover the law of the evolution of species. She went out with a rifle to hunt tigers, and happened to meet up with a dinosaur. If we were to use this as a criterion, the first sailor who spied Cape Horn would also be a genius."

"You can say what you will, but Madame Curie's discovery revolutionized science."

"If you go out to hunt tigers and met up with a centaur, you will also revolutionize zoology. But this is not the sort of revolution brought about by geniuses."

"In your opinion, is science a preserve closed to women?"

"No, did I ever claim that it was? In point of fact, chemistry is pretty much like cooking."

"And what about philosophy? I am certain you would forbid girls entry to the faculty of philosophy and letters."

"No I wouldn't, why should I? They don't do any harm to anyone. What's more, they can catch themselves a man there and get married."

"And what about philosophy?"

"Let them study it if that's their heart's desire. It's not going to do them any harm. Nor any good either, for that matter. It won't do anything to them. And besides, there's no danger of their becoming philosophers."

"That's because this absurd society doesn't offer them the same possibilities as men!" Señorita González Iturrat shouted.

"How can that be? We've just agreed that nothing prevents them from enrolling in the faculty of philosophy. In fact, I'm told that this section of the university is full of women. Nothing is keeping them from engaging in philosophical pursuits. They have never been forbidden to think, either at home or outside the home. How can anyone forbid thinking? And all that philosophy requires is a head and the desire to think. This is true today, it was true in the time of the Greeks, and it will still be true in the thirtieth century. It's entirely possible that a society might keep a woman from publishing a philosophical work: by making fun of her, by boycotting the book, or something like that. But forbid her to think? How can any society put obstacles in the way of the idea of the Platonic universe inside a woman's head?"

"If everybody were like you, the world would never have made any progress," Señorita González Iturrat exploded.

"And what makes you think that it *has* made progress?"

She smiled scornfully.

"According to you, naturally, getting to New York in twenty hours isn't progress."

"I don't see the advantage of being able to get to New York in a big hurry. The more time it takes the better. And besides, I thought you were referring to spiritual progress."

"To progress of every sort, sir. It was not simply by chance that I spoke of the airplane: it is the symbol of progress in general. Including moral values. I hope you're not going to try to tell me that mankind's morals today are not superior to those of societies in the days when slavery was practiced."

"Ah, so you would prefer to see a society where there are wage slaves."

"It's easy to be cynical. But any person who is fair-minded will concede that the world today is acquainted with moral values that were unknown in antiquity."

"Yes, I see what you mean. Landru, the modern Bluebeard, traveling by rail is superior to Diogenes traveling by trireme."

"You're deliberately choosing ridiculous examples, but the evidence is there before you."

"A camp commander at Buchenwald is superior to the commander of a slave ship. It is better to kill human beings with napalm bombs than with bows and arrows. The bomb dropped on Hiroshima is more humane than the battle of Poitiers. It is a sign of progress to torture with an electric prod rather than with rats, the way the Chinese did."

"Those are mere sophisms, all of them, because they are isolated facts. Mankind will do away with these atrocities too one day. And in the end ignorance will necessarily give way, all along the line, to science and knowledge."

"The religious spirit is stronger today than in the nineteenth century," I remarked with calm perverseness.

"Obscurantism of every sort will eventually give way. But the march of progress necessarily involves minor retreats and detours. A moment ago you mentioned the theory of evolution: this is a good example of what science can accomplish in the fight against every sort of religious myth."

"I can't see that this theory has destroyed much of anything. Haven't we just agreed that the religious spirit today is on the rise again?"

"For other reasons. But the theory of evolution definitely did away with many patent falsehoods, the one concerning the Creation in six days, for instance."

"Señorita: if God is omnipotent, is it any trouble at all for him to create the world in six days and leave a few skeletons of giant sloths scattered about here and there so as to test men's faith—or their stupidity?"

"Oh, come now! Don't tell me you're asking me to take such a sophism seriously! Besides, a moment ago you were singing the praises of the genius who discovered the theory of evolution and now you're poking fun at it."

"I'm not poking fun at it. I'm simply saying that it doesn't prove the nonexistence of God, nor does it refute the Creation of the world in six days."

"If it were up to you, there wouldn't even be schools. If I'm not mistaken, you're in favor of illiteracy."

"In 1933 Germany was one of the most literate nations in the world. If people didn't know how to read, they at least wouldn't be turned into idiots day after day by newspapers and magazines. Unfortunately, even if they were illiterate, other marvels of progress would still exist: radio, television. It would be necessary to pierce children's eardrums and pluck their eyes out. But this would naturally be a more difficult program to carry out."

"Despite your sophisms, light will always prevail over darkness, and good over evil. Evil is ignorance."

"Thus far, señorita, evil has always prevailed over good."

"Another sophism. Whatever made you dream up such an absurd notion?"

"I haven't dreamed up anything, señorita: history itself proves my point. Open any history textbook you care to, Onckens for example, to any page you like and you'll find nothing but wars, beheadings, conspiracies, tortures, coups d'état, inquisitions. And besides, if good always prevails what's the point in preaching it? If man were not inclined to do evil by his very nature, why is he expressly forbidden to do evil, why is evil anathematized, and so on? Just look how even the most highly developed religions *preach* good, yet at the same time hand down *commandments* against adultery, murder, theft, and so on that *must* be obeyed. People must be *commanded* not to commit adultery, not to kill, not to steal. And the power of evil is so great and so perverse that it is even used as an argument in favor of good: if we do not do such and such a thing we are *threatened* with Hell."

"Well, according to you then, it's necessary to preach evil," Señorita González Iturrat shouted.

"I didn't say that, señorita. You've gotten all worked up and aren't even listening to what I'm saying. There's no need to preach evil: it turns up soon enough all by itself."

"What in the world are you trying to prove?"

"Don't get upset, señorita. You're the one, don't forget, who's defending the superiority of good, and yet I note that you'd gladly hack me to bits. All I wanted to say is that spiritual progress doesn't exist. And we would have to take a closer look at your famous material progress as well."

An ironic grimace twisted the lady educator's moustache out of shape.

"Ah, now you're going to prove to me that life is harder for contemporary man than for a Roman."

"That depends. I don't believe, for instance, that a poor devil who works eight hours a day in an electrically controlled foundry is happier than a Greek shepherd. In the U.S., that paradise of mechanization, two-thirds of the population is neurotic."

"I'd like to know if you would really prefer to travel by horse-drawn coach rather than by train."

"Of course I would. Travel by coach was a wonderful experience, and far more restful. And it was better still when people went about from place to place on horseback: they got out in the fresh air and enjoyed the sun and had all the time in the world to contemplate the landscape. The apostles of the machine promised us that each day would bring man more leisure time. The truth of the matter, however, is that man has less and less time to call his own each day, and is growing madder and madder. Even war was beautiful once upon a time; it was something amusing and manly, and a fine spectacle in the bar-

gain, what with all those fancy bright-colored uniforms. It even promoted good health. Take our war of independence and our civil wars
for instance: if a man wasn't run through with a lance or beheaded
he might well live to be a hundred, like my great-great-grandfather
Olmos. Quite understandable: all that outdoor life, lots of exercise,
great long gallops on horseback! When a youngster was frail, they
sent him off to war to make him stronger."

Señorita González Iturrat got up from the table in a rage. Turning
to her disciple, she said:

"I'm leaving, Normita. You of course can do as you like."

And she marched off.

With blazing eyes, Norma got up too. And as she walked off, she
said:

"You're a boor and a hopeless cynic!"

I folded my newspaper and settled down to continue watching
number 57, with an unobstructed view now that the considerable bulk
of Norma's mentor was no longer blocking it.

That night, as I was sitting on the toilet, in the condition that lies
somewhere between pathological physiology and metaphysics, trying
to move my bowels and at the same time meditating on the overall
meaning of life, as is frequently my habit in this one place in the entire house conducive to philosophy, I finally hit upon the reason behind
that lapse of memory that had troubled me so at the beginning of our
encounter in the café: no, I had never laid eyes on Señorita González
Iturrat before, but she bore an almost perfect resemblance to the disagreeable, rabid creature who throws suffragette leaflets from a balloon
in *Kind Hearts and Coronets*.

∾ 12 ∾

THAT NIGHT, as I weighed and reviewed the events of the day, as
was my habit, I was suddenly alarmed: why had Norma brought
Señorita González Iturrat to the café to meet me? The discussion
concerning the existence of evil that the two of them had forced me
to engage in couldn't be a mere coincidence either. On sober reflection,
I concluded that this lady professor possessed all the characteristic
traits of an associate member of the Library for the Blind. And I

immediately began to be suspicious of Norma Pugliese herself then, for I had originally become interested in her mainly because her father was a Socialist who volunteered two hours of his time each day to transcribing books into Braille.

I frequently create a mistaken impression of myself and my habits, and it is more than likely that readers of this Report will find certain dalliances on my part surprising. The truth is that despite my determination to be systematic, I am capable of acts that are entirely unexpected, and therefore dangerous, given the sort of activity in which I am engaged. And my most egregious errors have been due to women. I shall try to explain why this is the case, because it is not as utterly mad as it might appear to be at first glance: I have always regarded women as a suburb of the world of the blind, and therefore my dealings with them are neither as absurd nor as pointless as a mere superficial observer might imagine. That is not what I am reproaching myself for at the moment; what I blame myself for, rather, is the almost inconceivable failure to take precautions to which I am altogether too prone, as in the case of Norma Pugliese; a perfectly logical fact from the point of view of fate, since fate blinds those whom it seeks to destroy, while from my own point of view it is one that ranges from absurd to unpardonable. But this is because my periods of brilliant lucidity are followed by periods during which my acts seem to be commanded and carried out by some other person, and I suddenly find myself in extremely perilous situations beyond my control, as might happen to a solitary navigator in dangerous waters who, overcome by fatigue, grows drowsy and dozes off for a few moments from time to time.

It is not easy. I would like to see any of my critics in a situation such as mine, surrounded by countless clever and malevolent enemies, amid an invisible network of spies and observers, and being obliged to keep close watch, day and night, on each and every one of the persons round about him and on each and every event that occurs in his immediate vicinity. I wager that that critic of my behavior would thereupon become far less self-important and sure of himself and would understand that errors of this sort are not only possible, but virtually inevitable.

During the entire period that preceded my meeting Celestino Iglesias, for instance, there was a terrible confusion in my mind; during such periods it is as if the darkness were literally swallowing me up by way of alcohol and women: for that is how one enters the labyrinths of Hell, or rather, the universe of the Blind. So that it was not that I forgot my great objective during these dark periods, but rather that my lucid, systematic, scientific search was succeeded by a sudden chaotic interval, in which there predominated what naive observers would call mere coincidences, but which in reality represented the workings of blind chance. And in the midst of this disorder, with my head swimming and all my senses dulled, drunk and miserable, I suddenly found myself stammering: "It doesn't matter. In any event this is the universe that I must explore," and I abandoned myself to the heady, mad pleasure of vertigo, that sensual pleasure that heroes in combat experience at the most dangerous moments, when the promptings of reason avail us nothing and our will moves in the turbid domain of the blood and instincts. And then I would abruptly awaken from these long dark periods, and as license follows asceticism, so my mania for organization took the place of chaos, a mania that comes over me not despite my tendency toward chaotic disorder, but precisely because of it. My brain then begins to work at top speed, and with a rapidity and a clarity that are simply astonishing. I make clearcut, precise decisions, everything is as luminous and brilliantly evident as a theorem; not a single one of my actions is prompted by my instincts alone, for at such times I scrutinize them closely and have perfect control over them. But strangely enough, the steps that I resolve to take, or the people I meet during this period of heightened consciousness, soon lead me, yet again, to a period in which I lose all control. I meet the wife, let us say, of the president of the Board of Patrons of the Choir of the Sightless; I am well aware of the valuable information that I can procure through her, I go to work on her, and finally, for purely scientific purposes, I take her to bed; but it immediately turns out that the woman makes me sick to my stomach, she is oversexed or perverted, and all my plans come to nothing or are postponed or are seriously endangered.

This was not the case with Norma Pugliese, naturally. But even in her case I committed errors that I ought not to have made.

Señor Américo Pugliese is a long-standing member of the Socialist

Party, and he brought up his daughter in conformity with the principles that Juan B. Justo* insisted upon from the beginning: Truth, Science, Collectivism, the Fight against Nicotine, Anti-Alcoholism. A very decent person who detested Perón and was greatly respected by his adversaries as a holder of political office. As can readily be imagined, his espousal of such causes made me all the more eager to sleep with his daughter.

She was engaged to an ensign in the Navy, a fact perfectly compatible with the antimilitarist mentality of Señor Pugliese by virtue of that psychological mechanism which causes antimilitarists to be great admirers of sailors: the latter are not all that crude and brutish, they have traveled, and all in all they are very much like civilians. Even though this latter defect is scarcely a reason to sing their praises, for as I explained to Norma (who was furious), praising a Navy man because he does not appear to be one is like boasting of the merits of a submarine that has trouble submerging.

By setting forth arguments of this sort I sapped the bases of the Navy and was eventually able to lure Norma into my bed, all of which merely demonstrates that the road to bed can pass by way of the most unexpected institutions, and that the sole arguments of any importance to a woman are those that lead her to assume a horizontal position. The precise opposite of what happens, in short, in the case of the man, and the reason why it is difficult to get a man and a woman in the same geometrical position by virtue of a faultless logical argument: one must have recourse to paralogisms or to petting and pawing.

Once I had arrived at horizontality with Norma, it took me some time to educate her, to get her used to a New Conception of the World, to convert her from Juan B. Justo to the Marquis de Sade. It was not at all easy. It was necessary to begin with language itself, in view of the fact that as a devotee of science and an avid reader of works such as *Ideal Marriage*, she was in the habit of using expressions as unsuitable for sessions in bed as "the law of chromatic refractions" is to describe a twilight. Using this prime truth as a basis (and the truth was sacred to her), I gradually led her, step by step, to accept even the worst perversions. So many years of patient labor by deputies, munic-

---

* Founder of the Argentine Socialist Party. [*Author's note*]

ipal councilors, and Socialist lecturers reduced to nothing in the space of just a few weeks; so many neighborhood libraries, so many cooperatives, so many admirable free public institutions gone for naught, since Norma ended up actively engaging in such depravities. How can one be expected to have any faith in collectivism after that!

Yes, fine, let us have a good laugh at Norma Pugliese's expense, as I so often did in moments when I felt superior to her. One fact is certain. I began to be assailed by doubts and had the sudden feeling that she was one of the enemy's subtle spies. Moreover, this was only to be expected, since only a stupid or vulgar enemy resorts to using obviously suspect individuals as spies. Wasn't the very fact that Norma was so naive, so candid, so vehemently opposed to any sort of falsehood or mystification the most telling argument for being extremely wary of her?

I began to be extremely concerned when I analyzed our relations in detail.

I thought I had Norma Pugliese nicely pigeonholed, and in view of her upbringing in accordance with the principles of Socialism and Sarmiento,* it did not seem to me that it would be difficult to get to know her very well. A grave error. I was surprised more than once by some totally unexpected reaction on her part. Then too, in the end her utter depravity was irreconcilable with the wholesome, decent education that her father had given her. But if logic plays so little part in a man's life, what can we expect of a woman?

I therefore spent a sleepless night recalling and analyzing each and every one of her reactions toward me. And though I found many reasons for alarm, I also found a reason to be pleased with myself: the fact that I had become aware of the dangers of her company in time.

---

* Domingo Faustino Sarmiento was one of the young intellectuals who fought Rosas's tyranny from exile, writing in Chile his famous *Facundo*, one of Argentina's most important literary works. After Rosas's downfall, Sarmiento was one of the major figures in the movement for national reconstruction. On becoming president of Argentina (1868–74), his influence and his office enabled him to put many of his ideals into practice. Thanks in large part to his campaign for public education, combined with a wave of European immigration, Argentina under his presidency became a model of social progress far ahead of its time. [*Author's note*]

❧ 13 ❧

IT OCCURS TO ME that on reading the story of Norma Pugliese some of you may think me a bastard. I shall tell you straight away that you are absolutely correct. I consider myself a bastard and haven't the slightest respect for myself. I am a person who has probed his conscience, and how can anyone who has really explored all the hidden nooks and crannies of his conscience still respect himself?

I at least consider myself to be honest, for I do not deceive myself as to my true nature nor do I attempt to deceive others. You may perhaps ask me how it happens then that I have deceived, without ever feeling the slightest scruples, so many unfortunate wretches and so many women who have crossed my path. The fact is that there are many different degrees of deception, my dear sirs. And deceptions of this sort are mere trifles, of no importance whatsoever. Just as one cannot call a general who orders a retreat as a preliminary to a definite advance a coward. Mine are—and were—tactical, circumstantial, transitory deceptions aimed at furthering a basic truth, a pitiless investigation. I am an investigator of Evil, and how can Evil be investigated without plunging into filth up to one's neck? You will tell me that I seem to have taken keen pleasure in so doing, rather than feeling the indignation or the repugnance that a true investigator would feel on finding himself confronted with such an unpleasant duty. This is quite true also, and I proudly admit it. See how honorable I am? At no time have I said that I am a good person; I have said that I am an investigator of Evil, and that is something altogether different. I have admitted, moreover, that I am a bastard. What more do you want from me? A remarkable bastard, certainly. And proud of not belonging to that class of pharisees who are as base as I am, yet pretend to be respectable individuals, pillars of society, perfect gentlemen, eminent citizens whose funerals are attended by hordes of people and whose life stories then appear in serious newpapers. No, if my name is ever mentioned in such publications, it will doubtless be on the crime page. But I think I have already explained what I think of the serious press and the crime page, so I am far from feeling ashamed of myself.

I detest the universal comedy of noble sentiments. A system of conventions that also manifests itself, of course, in language: the supreme falsifier of Truth with a capital T. Conventions whereby the expression "little old man" is inevitably preceded by the epithet "poor," as though all of us didn't know that a scoundrel who grows old does not cease to be a scoundrel thereby; on the contrary his sentiments become all the more vicious due to the selfishness and the resentments that have cropped up or grown worse with age. A monstrous auto-da-fé ought to be made of all these apocryphal expressions that have been invented by popular sentimentality, hallowed by the hypocrites who govern society, and defended by the schools and the police: "venerable senior citizens" (the majority of whom deserve only to be spit on), "distinguished patronesses" (almost all of whom are motivated by vanity and the basest sort of selfishness), et cetera. Not to mention the "pitiful little blind men" who are the object of this Report. And I must say that if these pitiful little blind men fear me it is precisely because I am a bastard, because they know that I am one of them, a merciless individual who is not going to allow himself to be taken in by stupid prattle and vulgar commonplaces. How could they fear one of those miserable wretches who help them cross the street with tearful solicitude straight out of a Walt Disney film, complete with little birdies and Christmas ribbons in technicolor?

If all the bastards that exist on this planet were lined up, what a formidable army they would constitute, and what unexpected specimens! From little kiddies in white communion costumes ("the perfect innocence of childhood") to upright municipal employees who nonetheless steal paper and pencils from the office to take home with them. Ministers, governors, doctors, and lawyers, almost without exception, the already mentioned poor little old men (in enormous numbers), the also already mentioned distinguished patronesses who now direct aid societies for lepers and cardiac cases (after having had a good gallop in a great many different beds and having thus made a concrete contribution to the ever-increasing number of heart ailments), directors of large companies, young girls of delicate mien with gazelle eyes (but quite capable of plucking clean any fool who believes in feminine romanticism or in the weakness and helplessness of womankind), city inspectors, colonial civil servants, ambassadors loaded with decorations, et cetera, et cetera. BASTARDS, FORWARD MARCH! Good lord, what an army! Advance, you sons of bitches! No halting along the way, no whining, now that what I have in store for you awaits you!

BASTARDS! TO THE RIGHT!

A marvelous, edifying spectacle.

On arriving at the stable, each one of the troops will be fed on his own filth, converted into real (not metaphorical) excrement, with no sort of special considerations or favors to be expected. None of that business of allowing the pampered son of His Excellency the Minister to eat a crust of dry bread instead of his own turds. No sir: one does things as they ought to be done, or they are not worth doing at all. Let him eat his shit. Better yet: Let him eat *all* his shit. He would prefer, naturally, to be allowed to eat only a symbolic quantity. But no symbols: each one must eat his own filth, down to the last mouthful, no more and no less. That is only fair, you see: one cannot treat a poor wretch who has merely looked forward with great joy to the death of his parents so as to inherit a little dough in the same fashion as one deals with Minneapolis Anabaptists who expect to go to heaven even though they exploit blacks in Guatemala. No sir! JUSTICE AND MORE JUSTICE: To each one the shit that belongs to him, or nothing. There's no use counting on me for any special deals.

And let it be noted that my position is not unassailable but also disinterested, since in conformity with my own status as a perfect bastard, to which I have readily admitted, I myself would be in the ranks of this coprophagous army. The one thing I claim in my favor is the fact that I haven't tried to pull the wool over anybody's eyes.

And this makes me think of the need to invent beforehand some system that will allow the filth produced by respectable persons to be detected and precisely measured so that each individual may be apportioned the exact quantity that he deserves. A sort of filthometer with a gauge to indicate the quantity of shit produced by Señor X in his life up to the time of this Last Judgment, the quantity to be deducted on account of his sincerity or his good intentions, and the net quantity that he must swallow once the necessary calculations have been made.

And after the exact measure has been established for each individual, the immense army must march off toward its stables, where each one of the troops will consume his own rightful share of filth. An infinite operation, as can be readily seen (and this is the real joke of the whole thing), because on defecating, by virtue of the principle of the conservation of excrement, each one will expel the same quantity that he has ingested. A quantity that will once more be placed in front of each bastard's snout, thanks to a collective 180-degree turn on command, and will once again have to be ingested.

And so on, *ad infinitum*.

ᴄᴠ 14 ᴄᴠ

I STILL HAD two more days to wait. During this time I received one of those chain letters that normally one immediately tosses into the wastebasket. In my case the letter made me even more nervous and anxious, since my experience had demonstrated to me that nothing, and I mean

NOTHING

could be overlooked in a plot as fantastic as the one that I was involved in. So I read it through carefully, trying to find some possible relationship between the remote happenings having to do with lawyers and generals mentioned in the letter and my investigation of the blind. It said: "This chain letter comes from Venezuela. It was written by Señor Baldomero Mendoza and must go around the world. Make twenty-four copies of it and send them on to your friends, but do not send them for any reason to relatives, however distant. Even though you are not superstitious the facts will demonstrate how effective this letter is. For example, Señor Ezequiel Goiticoa made the copies, sent them to his friends, and in nine days' time received 150,000 *bolívares*. A man named Barquilla took this chain letter as a joke: his house burned down, several members of his family died in the fire, and as a consequence he went mad. In 1904 General Joaquín Díaz received a severe wound that made an invalid of him. Later on he came across this chain letter and ordered his secretary to make copies of it and send them out. He was soon cured of his infirmity and his health is excellent now. An office clerk at Garette made copies of the letter but forgot to send them out; nine days later he had a run-in with his superiors and lost his job; he made some more copies and sent them out, got his job back, and was even given back pay. Alfonso Mejía Reyes, an attorney in Mexico City, received a copy of this chain letter, and carelessly lost it; in nine days' time a cornice fell on his head and he died a tragic death. Delgado, an engineer, broke the chain and shortly thereafter it was discovered that he had been embezzling company funds. Do not break this chain for any reason. Make the copies and send them on. December, 1954."

◌◌ 15 ◌◌

AND THEN one day I spied a blind man slowly feeling his way along the Calle Paso, from Rivadavia to Bartolomé Mitre. My heart began to pound.

My instinct told me that this tall, blond man had something to do with the Iglesias problem, since he was not making his way along with that indifference with which a person proceeds along a street when his objective still lies far in the distance.

He did not halt in front of number 57, but instead went very slowly past the entrance, seemingly using his white cane to reconnoiter a sector in which decisive operations are later to take place. I concluded that he was some sort of advance scout and from that instant on I was doubly on the alert.

Nonetheless nothing else happened that day to attract my attention. A few minutes before 9 P.M. I went up to the seventh floor, but as far as I could tell nothing out of the ordinary had happened there either: delivery men, grocery boys, door-to-door salesmen, the usual lot, in a word, were the only ones who had come up there.

I couldn't sleep that night: I kept tossing and turning in bed. I got up before it was light and hurried to the Calle Paso, fearing that some important visitor might go up to the apartment once the street door down below was unlocked.

But nobody who seemed suspect to me went in and I noticed no sign of any interest all that day. Could the appearance of that tall blond blind man be a mere coincidence?

I have already remarked that I believe that very few things happen by pure chance, particularly if they have to do with blind men. And hence that very same night, when what I might call my day watch was over, I decided to go upstairs to the pension and subject Señora Etchepareborda to close interrogation.

In my anxiety I had descended to the basest sort of flattery. I detest fat women, and the owner of the pension was vastly overweight; wearing a dress that would have fit a normal-sized woman, with her double chin and her enormous dead white bosom showing, she reminded me of a giant, quivering custard: but a custard with intestines.

I complimented her on her complexion and told her no one would ever guess she was forty-five. I also studied the little sitting room where she lived; every table, every occasional piece, every horizontal surface in general was hidden beneath a macramé doily. A sort of *horror vacui* made it impossible for her to leave any empty space uncovered or unfilled: porcelain pierrots, bronze elephants, glass swans, chromed Don Quixotes, and a large, nearly life-size Bambi. On a piano that she hadn't touched, she explained, since the death of her late husband, were two large macramé runners: one draped over the keyboard and another over the top. On this latter, amid a number of gauchos and peasant girls in homespun shawls, was a portrait photograph of Señor Etchepareborda, in three-quarter profile, his serious gaze fixed on an enormous bronze elephant: he appeared to be presiding over this collection of monstrosities.

I said complimentary things about the hideous chromed frame around the photo, and as she contemplated the portrait with a sad, dreamy look in her eyes, she explained that he had died two years before, shortly after his forty-eighth birthday, in the prime of life, just as he was on the point, she told me, of seeing his fond hopes of a pension at half-salary realized.

"He was second in charge of domestic shipments at Los Gobelinos."

Doing my best to conceal my inner rage and impatience at the fact that thus far in our conversation it had been impossible for me to begin my interrogation, I commented:

"An important house, I must say."

"It certainly is," she agreed smugly.

"A position of trust," I added.

"I should say so," she said. "I wouldn't like to make unfair comparisons with others, but it's quite true that the company had complete confidence in my late spouse."

"He did his name honor," I commented.

"Quite true, Señor Vidal."

The Probity of Basques, British Phlegm, the French Spirit of Moderation in All Things: myths that like all myths are powerless in the face of mere facts. What does it matter that in the end these myths do not account for men on the take like the minister Etcheverry, energumens like the pirate Morgan, or freaks of nature like Rabelais? I resigned myself to contemplating the photos in a family album that the fat woman began showing me. In one of them the spouses were together on vacation at Mar del Plata in the year 1948, wading in the ocean.

"It was that very summer, in fact, that he gave me that lighthouse," she said, pointing to one made of little shells standing on a doily.

She rose from her chair and brought the lighthouse over to me to show me the inscription: "Souvenir of Mar del Plata," and underneath, added in ink, the date: 1948.

Then she went back to the album, as I sat there consumed with anxiety.

In another photograph Señor Etchepareborda appeared at his spouse's side in the Palermo gardens. In another one I believe he was surrounded by his nephews and his brother-in-law, a certain Señor Rabufetti or something like that. In yet another, celebrating an intimate occasion with the personnel of Los Gobelinos, as Señora Etchepareborda put it, in the El Pescadito restaurant, in La Boca. Et cetera.

There paraded by a series of children lying naked staring at the camera, wedding pictures, other vacations, brothers-in-law, cousins, little lady friends of Señora Etchepareborda's (the designation she employed for hulking creatures that weighed as much as she did).

I was happy to see her finally close the album and go over to a cabinet to put it back in its drawer. Above this piece of furniture, along with various little statues, was a little motto in a rustic frame that said:

OFFER YOUR HOUSE WITH ALL YOUR HEART

"So there's nothing new then as far as poor Iglesias is concerned?" I asked.

"No, Señor Vidal. He's shut up there in his room, poor thing, and doesn't want to see anybody. I'll be frank with you, Señor Vidal: it breaks my heart."

"Yes, naturally. Nobody's come round to ask about him? Nobody's taken an interest in his situation?

"Not a soul, Señor Vidal. Not so far, anyway."

"Curious, most curious," I muttered, as though to myself.

I had told her that I had contacted the proper agencies. Thanks to this lie I accomplished two ends, both of inestimable value: it put a stop to any personal initiative on her part (an initiative which, as can readily be understood, presented the danger of escaping my control); and at the same time it enabled me to keep track of any possible developments. It must be borne in mind that my plan was not only to use Iglesias to penetrate the secret circle, but also to conduct a prior investigation and confirm certain of my suspicions about the organization: if, without my informing anyone of the printer's situation, he was located, the very worst of my theory would be verified and I would be obliged to redouble my precautions. But on the other hand, waiting like this was becoming dangerous for me, and out of fear of not being on hand at the right moment, I was growing more and more anxious.

Meanwhile I continued waiting around in utter misery, keeping careful track of the progress of the transformation by examining all the signs and portents. It was at night, in particular, after the street door downstairs had been locked and hence there was no danger of the arrival at the pension of the simultaneously feared and desired messenger (for nothing in this world would I have wanted the Sect to find me there with the printer), that I went up to his room and tried to keep up a conversation, or at least tried to keep him company by listening to the radio with him. Iglesias, as I have said, was becoming more taciturn by the day, and along with his increasing mistrust there was now an almost visible appearance of that icy rancor characteristic of those of his breed. I also watched closely for the purely physical symptoms to develop, and when I shook hands with him I took careful notice of whether his skin had now commenced to secrete that almost imperceptible cold sweat that is one of the attributes revealing the kinship of his breed with toads and saurians and other creatures of that kind.

I would enter, then, after knocking at the door and hearing his *Come in*, turning on the light switch to the left of the door jamb.

Sitting there in a corner, next to the radio, more solemn and self-absorbed by the day, Iglesias would look at me as blind men do, with a blank, empty expression, a trait that in my experience is the very first one they take on in the course of their slow metamorphosis. His dark glasses, the only purpose of which was to conceal his burned-out eye sockets, made his expression all the more striking. I knew very well that behind those lenses there was nothing, but it was precisely that *nothing* that in the final analysis most overawed me. And I felt that other eyes, eyes located behind his forehead, invisible but more and more implacable and cunning eyes, were riveted on me, scrutinizing my innermost being.

An ungracious word never crossed Iglesias's lips: on the contrary, he exhibited a more and more pronounced courtesy, of that sort that is typical of natives of certain regions of Spain, that distant courtesy that causes simple peasants of the harsh plateaus of Castille to resemble great nobles of the most aristocratic lineage. But as the days went by one by one, in that oft-repeated scene wherein we sat contemplating each other in frozen silence, like two Egyptian statues, I felt Iglesias's resentment slowly take possession of every last nook and cranny of his being.

He would sit there smoking without a word. And suddenly, in order to break the intolerable silence, I would say something or other that in the past might have been of interest to the printer.

"The Workers' Federation has declared a longshoreman's strike."

Iglesias would mutter something in a monosyllable, take a deep puff of his cigarette of cheap black tobacco, and then to think to himself: *I know your kind, you bastard.*

When the situation became unbearable, I would leave. In any event however, these meetings, awkward and uncomfortable as they were, served my purpose: they allowed me to keep my eye on his transformation.

And once out on the street again, I would set out on a night patrol: pretending I was simply out for a breath of fresh air, walking aimlessly along, whistling in the dark, but in reality on the lookout for any and every possible sign of the presence of the enemy.

But in the two days following the appearance on the scene of the tall blond blind man I noticed nothing of any special import.

༄ 16 ༄

ON DROPPING BY the pension for my customary visit with Iglesias on that second night, however, I discovered a new and disturbing sign.

Before going to Iglesias's room, I was in the habit of paying a call on Señora Etchepareborda in order to do a little investigating. That night she invited me, as usual, to sit down and have a cup of coffee. At the time I thought that Señora Etchepareborda had taken it into her head that I was really dropping round the pension every night to see her, and that Iglesias's blindness was simply a pretext for my doing so. And as the saying goes in her milieu, I buttered her up: one night I complimented her on her dress, another night I went into ecstasies over some new chrome-plated knickknack she'd added to her collection, and another night I asked her to share with me some of Señor Etchepareborda's thoughts about life.

That night, as she was fixing the ritual cup of coffee for me, I put my usual questions about Iglesias's day to her. And as usual, she replied that not a soul had been round to see how the printer was doing.

"I can't believe it, Señor Vidal. It's enough to make a person lose their faith in humanity."

"One should never give up hope," I answered, borrowing one of Señor Etchepareborda's lofty phrases. (There were others, such as: "We must have Faith in the Country"; "That's the Way Life Goes"; "We must have Confidence in the Nation's Reserves," all of which were evidence of the precise place that the erstwhile second-in-charge of domestic shipments at Los Gobelinos occupied in the hierarchy, and all of which, now that he was dead, his widow found very moving.

"That's exactly what my late husband always used to say," she remarked as she handed me the sugar bowl.

She then brought up the subject of the high cost of living these days. It was all the fault of that bastard Perón. She'd never liked the man— did I know why? Because of the way he rubbed his hands together and smiled: he looked like a priest. And she'd never liked priests, though she respected all religions, she really did (she and her late husband were members of the Escuelas del Hermano Basilio*). And finally she commented on how scandalous the recent increase in electricity rates was.

"Those people do exactly as they please," she remarked. "Just imagine: only today a man from the electric company came and inspected the entire house to see if all the electrical appliances, the irons, the heaters, and all the rest were in good working order. I ask you, Señor Vidal, do they have the right to go poking their noses all over the house like that?"

Just as horses stop dead in their tracks and rear up when they notice some suspect object on the ground in front of them, tossing their heads and pricking up their ears, I was badly jolted by her words.

"An employee from the electric company?" I said in alarm, practically leaping out of my chair.

"That's right, a man from the electric company," she answered, taken aback by my violent reaction.

"What time was all that?"

She thought a moment and then said:

"Around three o'clock this afternoon."

"A fat man? A man in a light-colored suit?

"Yes, that's right, a fat man," she answered, more and more puzzled, looking at me as though I were ill.

"But did he have a light-colored suit on or didn't he?" I insisted, almost rudely.

"Yes...a light-colored suit...yes, a poplin suit, doubtless, lots of men are wearing them in this weather, one of those lightweight suits."

She was looking at me in such astonishment that I was going to be obliged to give her some reasonable explanation: otherwise my behavior might strike even that poor stupid creature as suspicious. But what explanation could I give her? I tried to invent something plausible: I spoke of some money that the person in question owed me, then hastily muttered a whole string of words, because I realized that there was no possibility of my saying anything that would really suffice to explain my alarm. I couldn't tell her, naturally, that my alarm stemmed from the fact that that very afternoon, around three, a fat

---

* A famous Buenos Aires spiritualist organization. [*Author's note*]

man dressed in a light-colored poplin suit, carrying a little suitcase and loitering about in the vicinity of number 57, Calle Paso, had attracted my attention. The fact was that this individual had aroused my suspicions at the time, and now that the proprietress of the pension had informed me that he had inspected the place, thus confirming my suspicions, I was frantic.

Later, when I went over all the events that had taken place in the course of my investigation, I decided that allowing my stuperfaction to show when I heard about the man from the electric company and offering Señora Etchepareborda a supposed explanation of my odd behavior had been most imprudent of me. If she had been at all intelligent these two things would have been enough to arouse her suspicions.

But it was not this crack that was to cause the entire edifice that I had so laboriously constructed to come tumbling down. My head was in a whirl that night; I had the feeling that the crucial moment was approaching. The next day I took my place at my observation post at a very early hour, as was my habit, although I was far more nervous than usual that morning. I drank my coffee, unfolded the newspaper, and pretended to be reading it, though in reality my eyes never left number 57. I had become remarkably adept at this bit of playacting. And as Juanito was telling me some bit of news or other about the metalworkers' strike, I saw, with an almost unbearable rush of emotion, that the man from the electric company had reappeared in the Calle Paso, carrying the same little suitcase and wearing the same light-colored suit as the day before, accompanied this time however by a little short, thin man whose face reminded me of Pierre Fresnay's. The two of them were walking along talking to each other, and when the fat man murmured something in his companion's ear, being obliged to bend down in order to do so, the latter nodded his head. When they reached number 57, the little short man entered the building and the man from the electric company walked on toward the Calle Mitre and finally stopped at the corner to wait for his companion, taking out a package of cigarettes and lighting up.

Would Iglesias come downstairs with the other man?

It didn't seem likely to me, because Iglesias was not the sort to accept an offer or an invitation on the spur of the moment.

I tried to imagine the scene upstairs. What would the man say to

Iglesias? How would he introduce himself? In all probability he would pass himself off as a member of the Library for the Blind or the Choral Society or some other such institution; he would tell Iglesias that he had heard about his unfortunate accident, that the organization he belonged to was set up to help the blind, and so on and so forth. But as I say, it seemed unlikely to me that Iglesias would agree to go anywhere with him the moment he met him: he had become too mistrustful. Moreover, there was his pride; as is so often true of Spaniards it had always been touchy, but it had become even more so now that he was blind.

When the emissary came downstairs alone and went off to join the man from the electric company, I was pleased that my suppositions had turned out to be true, for this was proof that my idea of the course that events would take was absolutely correct.

The man from the electric company appeared to listen with great interest to what the little short man had to report, and then, still carrying on an animated conversation, the two of them headed toward the Avenida Pueyrredón.

I ran upstairs to the pension: it was imperative for me to find out immediately what had gone on, but without arousing Iglesias's suspicions.

Señora Etchepareborda was all aglow as she received me.

"Those people from the society have finally come round!" she exclaimed excitedly, taking my right hand in both of hers.

I tried to calm her down.

"Whatever you do, señora," I said to her, "don't let on to Iglesias that I was the one who alerted those people."

She assured me she had remembered all my instructions.

"That's perfect," I replied. "And what are those people going to do for Iglesias?"

"They've offered him work."

"What sort of work?"

"I don't know. He didn't say."

"And what answer did he give them?"

"That he wanted to think it over."

"Till when?"

"Till this afternoon, because the man's coming back then. He wants to take him somewhere and introduce him."

"Introduce him? Where?"

"I don't know, Señor Vidal."

I decided I was satisfied with the results of this interrogation and took my leave of Señora Etchepareborda. As I was about to go out the door, I asked:

"Ah, I forgot. What time will that man be back?"

"At three."

"Perfect."

Things were beginning to go like clockwork.

⁓ 17 ⁓

A S ON OTHER occasions, my nervousness brought on a sudden call of nature. I went into the Antigua Perla del Once and headed for the toilet. It is curious that in this country the one place where the terms Damas and Caballeros are still used is the place where they invariably cease to be precisely that: Ladies and Gentlemen. I sometimes think this is merely one of Argentina's many forms of ironic scepticism. As I settled myself in the noxious little stall, I found it confirmed my long-held theory that the bathroom is the last true *locus philosophicus* we have left, and I began deciphering the palimpsests on the walls. On top of the inevitable, basic LONG LIVE PERON were XXXs violently obliterating the words LONG LIVE, for which someone had substituted DEATH TO, which in turn had been crossed out and superseded by another LONG LIVE, a grandchild of its primogenitor, and so on, alternately, in the form of a pagoda, or rather, a shaky building under construction. To the right and to the left, above and below, with pointing arrows and exclamation points or suggestive drawings, that original expression had been embellished, enriched, interpreted (as though by a race of rabid, pornographic exegetes) by various glosses having to do with Perón's mother, the social and anatomical characteristics of his wife Eva; and what the unknown defecating scholiast would do were he to have the great good fortune of finding himself in bed with her, or on a chair, or even right there in the toilet of the Antigua Perla del Once. Phrases and expressions of desire that in turn had been partially or totally expunged, distorted, or enhanced by the insertion of a derogatory or laudatory adverb, intensified or attenuated by the intervention of an adjective; with pencils and pieces of chalk of various colors; with illustrative drawings that seemed to have been executed by a drunken, drooling professor of anatomy. And in various blank spots, below or to one side, some of them enclosed in boxes with fancy borders (as in important newspaper ads), in different types of handwriting (anxious or languid, hopeful or cynical, persistent or frivolous, calligraphic or grotesque), were telephone numbers, supplied or wanted, by men possessed of this or that attribute, eager to realize such and such a feat or fantasy, to carry out such and such a combination or scheme, to be a partner in such and such a sadistic or masochistic abomination. Offers and requests that in turn were modified by ironic or insulting, hostile or humorous commentaries by third persons who for some reason were not inclined to participate in the precise arrangement suggested, but who at the same time in some sense (as their addenda proved) desired to share, and were in fact sharing, in that lascivious, delirious magic. And in the midst of that chaos, with pointing arrows, the anxious, hopeful reply of a person indicating where and when he would be waiting for the Cacographic Anal Prince, with a tender little note appended below that would seem to be an inappropriate or incongruous contribution to this lavatory bulletin board: I WILL HAVE A FLOWER IN MY HAND.

"The world hind side to," I thought.

As on the crime page of the paper, the ultimate truth of the species seemed to be revealed there.

"Love and excrement," I thought.

And as I buttoned my pants, I also thought: "Damas y Caballeros."

ᴄᴡ 18 ᴄᴡ

AT TWO P.M. I was already at my observation post in the café, so as to be sure to be there in time. But the little short man who looked like Pierre Fresnay didn't appear until three. He was making his way down the street without the slightest hesitation this time. As he approached the building he raised his eyes to make sure it was number 57 (because he had been walking with his head down, as though mulling something over in his mind) and then went inside.

I waited for him to come out, my nerves all on edge: the most dangerous part of my adventure was at hand, but even though for a moment I considered the possibility that they might have come round simply to take Iglesias to some mutual aid society or charitable organization, my intuition immediately told me that this would not be the way things would happen at all: they would do this later on. The first step was bound to be something much less banal, such as taking him to some blind man who was more or less of an important figure, one of the liaison men for the leaders of the Sect, for example. What reason did I have to presume that? My thought was that before putting a new blind man in circulation, if I may use such an expression, the hierarchs would want to be thoroughly familiar with his traits of character, his aptitudes, his capabilities, his cleverness or stupidity: a good head of a spy network does not assign one of his agents a mission without having first studied his good and bad points. And it is obvious that it does not require the same talents to take up a collection in the subway as it does to keep a place as important as the Naval Center under constant surveillance (the task assigned a tall blind man of about sixty, wearing a broad-brimmed hat, who sits outside the Center, eternally silent, with his pencils in his hand, somehow reminiscent of an English gentleman who has fallen on bad days because of some frightful turn of fortune). As I have had occasion to say before, there are blind men and blind men, and although they all possess the same essential characteristic, that minimum of physical infirmity that causes them to constitute a particular breed, we must not oversimplify the problem to the point of believing that all of them are equally sly and perspicacious. There are blind men who serve only as shock troops; among their number are the equivalent of stevedores or gendarmes; and then there are the Kierkegaards and the Prousts. Moreover, there is no way of knowing where a human being who enters the sacred sect as a result of an illness or an accident will end up, since, as in wars, there are unbelievable surprises; just as no one would ever have been able to predict that a timid little bank teller from Boston would turn out to be a hero at Guadalcanal, so one is unable to predict the surprising ways in which blindness may promote a concierge or a printer to the very top of the hierarchy: it is said that one of the four top world leaders of the Sect (who live somewhere in the Pyrenees, in one of those enormously deep caves that a group of speleologists tried to explore in 1950, an expedition that ended in a fatal accident) is not a person blind from birth and that, even more amazingly, before going blind he was a humble jockey who raced in the hippodrome of Milan, where he lost his sight in a fall. This is a piece of information I came by through the vaguest of hearsay, as can well be imagined, and although I believe it highly unlikely that a man not blind from birth is a hierarch, I repeat the story simply to give some idea of how a person is able to better himself by losing his sight. The system of promotion in rank is so esoteric that I seriously doubt that anyone will ever know precisely who the Tetrarchs are. The fact is that the world of the blind seethes with rumors and information that is not always correct circulates; in part perhaps because the blind have the same penchant for slander and gossip as all human beings do, though in the case of their breed this propensity reaches pathological proportions; and in part (this is my own theory) because the hierarchs use false information as one of the means of perpetuating the Sect's aura of mystery and ambiguity, two powerful weapons in any organization of this sort. Be that as it may, if a piece of information is to be believable it must at least be possible in principle, and this supposed case of the ex-jockey suffices to prove to what point blindness can enhance the personality of a quite ordinary individual.

To return to our problem, I surmised that on this first trip outside Iglesias would not be taken to one of the Sect's exoteric societies, that is to say one of those institutions where the blind exploit poor wretches who can see, or ladies with kind hearts and the brains of a fly, by resorting to the cheapest and most vulgar sort of sentimental demagoguery. I felt, therefore, that this first trip that Iglesias was about to be taken on might very well lead me directly inside one of the secret redoubts of the Sect, with all the dangers that that implied, naturally, but also all the marvelous possibilities. And so when I sat down in the café that afternoon, I had already taken all the measures that seemed reasonable if I were going to go along on such a trip. My reader might reply that it is easy to make reasonable plans for a trip to the Córdoba mountains, but not very understandable how, unless one is mad, one can make reasonable preparations for an exploration of the universe of the blind. Well: the truth is that these famous preparations consisted of hunting up two or three relatively logical things: a flashlight, some concentrated food, and a couple of similar articles. I decided that, as for long-distance swimmers, the best concentrated food for me to take with me would be chocolate.

Equipped with my pocket flashlight, my chocolate, and a white cane that at the last moment it occurred to me might be useful (as an enemy uniform would be for scouts on reconnaissance missions), I waited, so tense and nervous I could scarcely bear it, for Iglesias to come out of number 57 with the little short man. The possibility remained, of course, that Iglesias, being a typical Spaniard, would refuse to accompany the little short man and decide not to abandon his proud solitude, in which case the entire edifice that I had erected would collapse like a house of cards; and my chocolate, flashlight, and white cane would automatically become the grotesque equipment of a madman.

But Iglesias came downstairs!

The little short man was engaged in a lively conversation with him, and the printer was listening to him with his dignity of a wretched Spanish hidalgo who has never humbled himself before anyone and never will. He was walking along clumsily, using in a very gingerly way the white cane that the other man had brought him, suddenly raising it up in the air for several steps as though he were carrying a taper.

How much he still had to learn before his apprenticeship would be over! This observation revived my spirits and I began following along behind them with a certain feeling of self-assurance.

At no time did the little short man give any sign that he suspected I was tailing the two of them, and this too made me feel more sure of myself, to the point in fact of awakening in me a sort of pride that things were turning out exactly as I had calculated in my preliminary studies and my many long years of waiting. For I don't know if I have mentioned this before, but ever since my abortive attempt to penetrate the world of the blind through the intermediary of the collar-stay peddler in the Palermo subway, I had devoted very nearly all my time to the careful, systematic observation of the visible activity of any blind man I chanced to meet in the streets of Buenos Aires; during this three-year period I bought hundreds of magazines that did not interest me in the slightest; I purchased and threw away dozens and dozens of collar stays; I acquired thousands of pencils and notebooks of every size and description; I attended concerts by blind musicians; I learned Braille and spent endless days in the Library for the Blind. As is readily understandable, this activity involved great risks, since if I aroused the least suspicion, all my plans would go for naught, not to mention the fact that my life itself would be in danger.

But this was unavoidable, and paradoxically, it was my one chance to save myself from these same dangers that threatened my life: more or less like the apprenticeship that, at the risk of death, soldiers being trained to detect mines undergo, since at the most crucial point in their training they must confront the same dangers that they are being taught to avoid.

I had nonetheless not been so stupid as to confront those risks without having first taken certain basic precautions: I dressed in different clothes each time; I used false moustaches or beards; I wore dark glasses; I disguised my voice.

I thus investigated many things in the course of those three years. And thanks to this monotonous preliminary labor I was able to enter the secret domain.

And that was how it all ended for me...

Because in these days preceding my death I no longer have the slightest doubt that my fate was foreordained, perhaps from the very beginning of my investigation, from that accursed day on which I shuttled back and forth on the subway between Plaza Mayo and Palermo spying on the blind man. And I sometimes think that the more clever I believed myself to be and the more fatuously I congratulated myself on what I imagined to be my supreme cunning, the more closely I was watched and the more inexorably I brought about my own perdition. I even came to suspect Señora Etchepareborda. How grimly comical I now find the idea that all that *mise-en-scène*, complete with knickknacks and giant Bambis, with fake photos of a petty-bourgeois couple on vacation, with cute little mottoes in rustic frames, that whole setting in short, which I had superciliously allowed myself to secretly smile at, was in fact nothing but that: nothing but a vulgar, grimly comical *mise-en-scène*!

These are no more than conjectures, however, although they would appear to be quite close to the truth. And it is my firm intention to speak only of *facts*. Let us go back, then, to a precise description of events, exactly as they happened.

In the days that preceded Iglesias's first trip outside the confines of his room, I had studied, as though it were a chess problem, all the variations that this trip might involve, inasmuch as I would have to be prepared for any one of them. It might very well happen, for instance, that those people would come to get him in a taxi or a private car. As I had no intention of missing the most splendid opportunity of my life by not having taken into account such an easily predictable eventuality, I had borrowed a car from R., one of my partners in the money-counterfeiting operation, and kept it permanently parked in the vicinity of number 57. But when I saw the emissary who looked like Pierre Fresnay arriving on foot that day, I realized that this had been a useless precaution. There remained, of course, the variation whereby he would immediately climb into a taxi with Iglesias, and even though finding a taxi in Buenos Aires is as difficult these days as finding a mammoth would be, I kept this possibility in mind when I saw Iglesias come out to the street. But the two of them didn't stop and stand in front of the doorway of number 57 as though waiting for a taxi to cruise by; on the contrary, without looking either to the right or to the left, the little short man took the printer by the arm and led him off toward Bartolomé Mitre; it was obvious that wherever they were going, they would be using some means of public transportation to get there.

There remained, naturally, the variation whereby the other man, the fat man from the electric company, would be waiting for them somewhere with a car, but this possibility did not strike me as a logical one, since I could see no reason for him not to wait with the car right there in the Calle Paso. On the other hand it seemed reasonable that they would use public transportation such as a city bus or a public minibus, since in all probability they would not want to give the new blind man the immediate impression that they were representatives of a sect that is all-powerful: the modest means they employed, the downright poverty of the resources apparently at their disposal constitute an effective weapon in the midst of a society that is cruel and selfish but inclined toward sentimentality. Although this "but" should by all rights be replaced by the simple conjunction "and."

I followed them at a prudent distance.

When they reached the corner they turned right and walked on to Pueyrredón, halting at the bus stop. There was a fairly long line of people waiting, both men and women; but at the insistence of a man with a briefcase and glasses, who looked respectable enough but whom

I immediately sized up as a real scoundrel, everyone allowed the "poor little blind man" and his guide to go to the head of the line, which then immediately closed up again behind my two men.

There were three numbers painted on the sign at the bus stop, and for me they were the first key to a great enigma: they were not the numbers of the buses that went to Retiro and the Law School, to the Hospital-Clinic complex, or to Belgrano; they went, rather, to the portals of the Unknown.

The two of them boarded the Belgrano bus and I climbed in behind them, after letting a couple of people in ahead of me so as to screen me from their view.

When the bus got to Cabildo, I began to wonder what street in Belgrano they would get off at. The bus continued on without the little short man giving any sign of wanting to get off. Finally, when the bus arrived at Virrey del Pino he began to move to the front of the bus and the two of them stood waiting near the exit door. They got off at Calle Sucre. They walked down Sucre to Obligado, and then straight north along this street to Juramento, and from there to Cuba, again heading north; but when they reached Monroe they went back to Obligado and returned via this street to the little public square that they had already gone past once before, the one on the corner of Echeverría and Obligado.

It was plain to see that they were trying to throw somebody off their track. But who? Me? Any individual such as myself who might be tailing them? This hypothesis was not to be rejected, since I had surely not been the first to have ever tried to enter the secret world. It is more than likely that there have been a great many such persons in the course of human history; in any case, I suspect at least two: one, Strindberg, who paid the price for so doing by going mad; and the other, Rimbaud, whom they had begun to persecute even before his trip to Africa, as the poet hinted in a letter sent to his sister that the critic Jacques Rivière misinterpreted.

There was also reason to suppose that this was an attempt to disorient Iglesias, who now doubtless possessed that extremely acute sense of direction that a man acquires the moment he loses his eyesight. But why?

Whatever the reason, after retracing their steps a number of times, they finally returned to the little square where the Church of the

Immaculate Conception stands. For a moment it seemed as though they might go inside, and I thought dizzyingly of crypts and of some secret pact between the two organizations. But instead they headed for that odd corner of Buenos Aires formed by a row of old two-story houses, tangent to the circle formed by the church.

They entered one of the houses through a door leading to the upper floor and began climbing the dirty old wooden staircase.

ᐇ 19 ᐇ

THE MOST ARDUOUS and hazardous stage of my investigation now began.

I stopped in the square to reflect on the next steps that I could and should take.

Obviously, I could not follow them immediately, given the dangerous nature of the Sect. Two possibilities therefore remained: either I could wait for them to come out and then once they had gone away go upstairs myself to see what I could discover; or else I could proceed upstairs without waiting for them to come out after prudently biding my time for a while.

Although this second variation was more risky, it also offered more chances of turning up something, for if I didn't discover anything definite when I went upstairs, there still remained the other possibility of coming back downstairs again and waiting on a bench in the square till they came out. I waited some ten minutes and then began to creep cautiously up the stairs. There was every reason to believe that dealing with Iglesias's case, or presenting him to the others, or whatever it was that was involved, was not going to be a matter of minutes but of hours; if not, I had a totally mistaken idea of what this organization was like. The stairway was filthy, for it was part of one of those old houses that at one time had had pretensions but nowadays are dirty and run down and have for the most part been broken up into rented apartments since these old houses are too large for a single poor family and too dilapidated for a family that has more or less made its way up in the world and attained a certain social position. And the thought then crossed my mind that if the house were one of those that had been divided up into apartments, this made my problem vastly more complicated, indeed almost labyrinthine: whom could Iglesias and the other man be going to see, and in which one of the apartments? Moreover, it seemed to me very unlikely that the hierarch, or his liaison man, lived in such humble and indeed downright wretched quarters.

As I went up the stairs, I was overcome with uncertainty and bitterness, for it was discouraging to think that after so many long years of waiting I had quite possibly ended up at the entrance to a labyrinth.

Luckily I am always inclined to imagine the worst. I say "luckily" because this being true, my preparations are always more than adequate for the solution of the problems with which reality subsequently confronts me; since I am thus prepared for the worst, this reality turns out to be less fraught with difficulties than I had foreseen.

And such was the case now, at least insofar as the immediate problem of that house was concerned. As for the rest, for the first time in my life things were worse than what I had expected.

When I reached the second-floor landing, I noted that there was only one door opening onto it and that the stairway ended right there at that floor; hence there was no attic nor were there two apartments; all in all, the problem was as simple as it could be.

I stood outside that closed door for some time, listening intently for the slightest sound of footsteps and all set to run quickly back downstairs. Risking everything, I put my ear to the door and tried to detect any sound that there might be inside, but heard nothing. It gave every sign of being an empty apartment.

There was nothing left for me to do but wait in the square.

I went back downstairs, sat down on a bench, and decided to use the time to make a careful study of everything about the place.

I have already said that this complex of buildings is odd, for it occupies the entire length of one block and thus forms a tangent to the circular church. The center section, which touches the church itself, is no doubt the property of the latter, and I presume that it houses the sacristy and other ecclesiastical buildings. But the remainder of the complex, to the left and to the right, has families living in it, as the presence of flowerpots on the balconies, clothes hanging on the lines, cages of canaries, and so on proves. Nontheless the fact that the windows corresponding to the blind people's apartment had certain things about them that were different did not escape my careful scrutiny: these windows possessed no signs or objects that would indicate that there were people living there, and moreover the shutters over these windows were closed. It might be argued that the blind do not need light. But what about air? Furthermore, these signs bore out the impression I had received when I listened through the door up there on the second floor. As I kept an eye on the door leading out of the building I pondered this curious fact, and after turning it over and over in my mind I reached a conclusion that struck me as surprising but irrefutable: *There was no one living in that apartment.*

And I say that this conclusion was surprising because if no one lived there why had Iglesias gone inside it with the little short man who looked like Pierre Fresnay? The inference to be drawn from this was also irrefutable: *The apartment served solely as an entrance to something else.* And I said to myself "something else" because though that "something" might well be another apartment, the apartment next door perhaps, with an inside door connecting the two, it was also possible that it was "something" less easily imaginable, since it had to do with the blind. A secret inside passageway leading to the cellar? This was not unlikely.

I finally decided that it was pointless to continue racking my brains just then, since the moment that the two men came out of the building I would have the opportunity to examine the problem more closely.

I had foreseen that introducing Iglesias into that secret world was going to be a complicated business and therefore take a long time; but it must have been more complicated than I had supposed, for the two of them did not come out of the building again until two o'clock that morning. Around midnight, after eight hours of watching intently and waiting, an hour when the darkness made that strange corner of Buenos Aires more mysterious still, my heart shrank as though it were beginning to suspect that some sort of abominable initiation were taking place in some subterranean place, some damp underground cellar, under the direction of some fearsome blind mystagogue; and as though these ominous ceremonies were a forewarning of the trials that awaited me.

Two o'clock in the morning!

As he came out of the building, Iglesias seemed to be walking much more shakily and uncertainly than when he entered, and I had the feeling that something horrendous was weighing heavily upon him. But perhaps all that was merely the impression I received due to a lugubrious concatenation of circumstances: my ideas concerning the sect, the dim lighting in the square, the immense cupola of the church, and above all the feeble light shed on the stairway by the one dirty bulb hanging above the entryway.

I waited for them to leave, and noted that they headed toward Cabildo. When I was certain they would not be back, I ran to the building.

In the silence of that wee hour of the morning, the sound of my footsteps seemed deafening and each creak of the rickety stairs made me look back over my shoulder.

When I reached the second-floor landing the greatest surprise I had had thus far awaited me: the door of the apartment had a padlock on it! This was something I had utterly failed to foresee.

This discovery filled me with such despair that I was obliged to sit down on the top step of that accursed stairway. I sat there for some time, completely crushed. But soon my brain began to function again and my powers of imagination presented me with a series of hypotheses:

The two men had just left and no one had left after them, hence the padlock had been removed from the door when they entered the apartment and been put back on it again when they left by the man who looked like Pierre Fresnay. Therefore if there were people of some sort living in the place, or if it had a secret passageway to "something" that was lived in, these creatures nonetheless did not enter or leave by way of the door that was there before my eyes. This "something," then, this apartment or house or cellar or whatever it was, had another exit or various other exits, perhaps leading to other areas in the neighborhood or in the city. Was the door with the padlock reserved for the little short messenger or intermediary then? Yes: for him or for other individuals entrusted with similar missions, each one of whom was to be presumed to be supplied with an identical key. These initial steps in my reasoning process bore out the impression that I had had when I observed the house from the little square: there was nobody living in that apartment. From this I could already safely draw a conclusion of great importance for my future operations: that apartment was merely a passageway TO SOMEWHERE ELSE.

What could that "somewhere else" be? I couldn't imagine, and the only thing that would solve the question was a daring attempt on my part to force that padlock, enter the mysterious apartment, and once inside it see what it could possibly lead to. For this I would need a picklock, or else I could simply break it open with a pair of pliers or employ some other similar drastic means.

I was so impatient now that I could not wait till the next day. I gave up the idea of breaking the padlock on account of the noise that this would make, and decided that the best thing to do was to ask one of my acquaintances to help me. I went downstairs, walked over to Cabildo, and waited for a taxi to come by, since there was no lack of them at this hour of the morning. Luck seemed to be with me: in a few minutes I flagged one down and ordered the driver to take me to the Calle Paso. I got into the car that I had left parked there and drove to F.'s house in Floresta. I roused him by shouting at the top of my lungs (he's famous for being an incredibly sound sleeper) and explained that I needed to get a padlock open that very night. Once he was fully awake and realized what sort of lock I wanted him to help me open, he was so indignant that he very nearly went back to bed: waking him up to open a simple padlock was like asking Stavisky for advice on how to swindle someone of a mere thousand francs. I shook him, I threatened him, and finally I dragged him out to the car; racing along as though the organization were about to collapse that very night, I arrived in just over half an hour at the little square in Belgrano. I parked on the Calle Echeverría, and after making sure that no one was around, F. and I got out of the car and walked to the house.

F. got the padlock open in a matter of half a minute, whereupon I told him that he would have to get back to Floresta by himself because I was going to be staying behind in that house for a good long while. This made him more furious still, but I convinced him that I was up to something that was very important to me and anyway it was easy to catch a cab on Cabildo. He haughtily refused the money I tried to give him for taxi fare and went off without even saying goodbye to me.

I must admit that on the way to the Calle Paso there was one question that had plagued me: Why hadn't there been a padlock on the door when I went upstairs the first time? Well, it was logical that it hadn't been on the door since the two men had already entered the apartment and had no way to put it back on from the inside. But if that entry to the apartment was so important, as everything seemed to indicate, why was it that they had left the door unlocked like that so that anyone could have gotten in? I told myself that all this was explainable if the little short man had locked the door with a bolt or a crossbar from the inside.

As was only to be expected, inside the apartment it was completely dark and dead silent. The door had opened with a series of creaks that seemed deafeningly loud to me. I shone my flashlight on the inside of the door and noted with satisfaction that it had a bolt, a copper bolt that was not rusted, thus proving that it was used frequently.

My supposition that the door had been locked from the inside was thus confirmed and along with it the (alarming) hypothesis that that door at no time remained open.

Reflecting on these facts much later, I asked myself why, if this were such an important entry, the door was closed with a padlock that F. had been able to force open in just a shade more than half a minute. This rather striking fact could have only one explanation: it made the place appear to be an ordinary dwelling, a dwelling that for some reason or other was unoccupied.

Though I was quite convinced that no one at all lived there, I entered cautiously and began to shine my flashlight on the walls of the first room. I am not a coward, but anyone in my situation would have felt the same fear I did as I slowly and carefully went through that empty, abandoned apartment engulfed in shadows. And significantly enough, bumping into the walls with my white cane, like a real blind man! I have not given any thought to this disturbing sign until just now, even though I have always been of the opinion that one cannot fight against a powerful enemy for years without coming in the end to resemble him; if the enemy invents the machine gun, sooner or later we too must invent it and use it if we do not wish to disappear from the face of the earth, and what holds good for a gross physical object such as a weapon of war holds good, for more profound and subtle reasons, for psychological and spiritual weapons: pouts, smiles, ways of moving one's body and betraying others, typical turns of phrase, characteristic feelings, and manner of living; the reason why husbands and wives so often end up being exactly like each other.

Yes: little by little I had acquired many of the faults and virtues of the accursed race. And as is almost always the case, the exploration of their universe had been, as I am just now beginning to see, the exploration of my own dark world.

The beam of my flashlight soon proved to me that there was nothing in this first room: not a stick of furniture, not even a bit of junk left behind; nothing but dust, wooden floors with holes in the planks, and peeling walls from which hung shreds of a wallpaper that had once been luxurious. This examination reassured me somewhat, for it confirmed what I had already suspected as I sat in the little square downstairs: that there was no one living in that apartment. I then went through the rest of the rooms more rapidly and confidently, and they too confirmed that first impression that I had had. And then I realized why it was unnecessary to take excessive precautions with regard to the door leading into the apartment; if a thief chanced to force the padlock he would soon leave, feeling disappointed.

Things were different for me, because I *knew* that this ghostly house was not an end but a means.

Otherwise one would have to suppose that the insignificant little man who had gone in search of Iglesias was some sort of madman who had brought the Spaniard to a place like this, where, in complete darkness and not even anything to sit on, he had talked to him for ten hours about something that, however terrible it might be, he could just as well have told the printer back in his own room in the pension.

I would have to search for the exit that led somewhere else. The first and simplest thing to look for was a door, either one in plain sight or a hidden one, leading to the place next door; the second and less simple thing (though not thereby less probable, since why should one expect anything connected with such monstrous creatures to be simple?) was to presume that this visible or secret door opened onto a passageway leading to the cellar or to more distant dangerous places. In any case my task now was to search for the secret door.

I first examined all the doors in plain sight: without exception they were doors connecting the various rooms of the apartment. Hence, as was quite predictable, the door I was searching for was one that was invisible, or at least invisible at first glance.

I recalled similar situations that I had seen in movies or come across in adventure novels: a wall panel or a picture frame could well be a secret door. But as there was not a single picture in this abandoned apartment there was no need for me to explore that avenue.

I went through room after room, examining the peeling walls to see if some corner or cornice or plinth concealed an electric button or some other similar mechanism.

I found nothing.

I examined with particular care the two rooms, the bathroom and the kitchen, that had permanent fixtures. Although they were bare of furniture too and in a sorry state, they nonetheless presented greater possibilities than the other rooms. The toilet, which had no seat, offered no major possibilities; nevertheless I tried to move the old hinges of the missing toilet seat, I pulled the chain, took the cover off the toilet tank, tried to press or turn all sorts of stopcocks and faucets, attempted to lift the ancient bathtub off the floor, and so on. I then proceeded to investigate the kitchen in a similar fashion, but turned up nothing.

My examination was so thorough and each step repeated so many times that if I hadn't known for certain that those two men had been there in that apartment that same afternoon I would have abandoned the entire search.

Discouraged, I sat down on the old gas stove. Previous experience had taught me that once a certain point has been reached, there is no use going over the same ground in one's mind again and again, for this merely creates a mental rut that prevents one from taking some other approach to the problem at hand.

I began suddenly to munch on my chocolate bars, thinking how comical that would appear to be to an invisible spectator hidden somewhere in the apartment. I was more or less laughing to myself as I pictured how this scene would look to an imaginary observer when a thought suddenly occurred to me that almost gave me heart failure: what proof did I in fact have that there wasn't SOMEONE watching me from some hidden spot? There were ceilings with cracks in them, there were peeling walls that might well conceal peepholes through which someone might be watching from the apartment next door. I was again overcome with terror and turned off my flashlight for a few moments, as though such a precaution, even after all this time, might be of some use. As I sat there in the dark, trying to detect the significance of the least little creak, I nonetheless had enough good sense to realize that my precaution was idiotic, not only because it was so useless, but also because it might produce precisely the opposite result from what I had intended, for without light I was even more helpless than with it. So I turned on my providential flashlight again, and although I was now even more tense and nervous than before, I did my best to concentrate my thoughts on the mystery that I was going to be obliged to solve.

Obsessed by the thought of peepholes, I began to shine the beam of my flashlight on the various ceilings in the rooms of the deserted apartment and examine them carefully: they were smooth ceilings made of plaster applied over wooden lattices, and in fact great chunks of plaster had fallen off them; there were also many broken moldings. It was therefore possible, of course, for one or several persons to keep watch on the apartment through these holes, but at the same time the ceilings of the various rooms showed no signs of anything resembling an entrance or an exit. Moreover, a ladder would have been necessary in order to reach such an opening, and there wasn't one anywhere in the apartment. Unless of course the ladder was one of those little rope ladders that could be pulled back up from above after it had been used.

I was looking at the ceilings and thinking about this variation when the solution finally dawned on me: the floors! That was the simplest solution, and as often happens the last one to occur to me.

∽ 20 ∽

WITH MY NERVOUS tension mounting by the minute, I began to shine my flashlight along the floor, bit by bit, until I found what I was bound to find eventually: an almost imperceptible crack forming a square that was undoubtedly a trap door leading to the cellar. Who would ever have thought however that a second-floor apartment would have an entrance to the cellar? This was more or less confirmation of my original theory that the apartment was connected to a neighboring one by an invisible door, but who would ever have imagined that that apartment would be the one below? At that moment I was so excited that I didn't even give a thought to something that might otherwise have caused me to flee in terror:

the sound of my footsteps. How could the blind especially, the blind who lived in the apartment below, have failed to notice it? This heedlessness on my part, this careless mistake allowed me to go on with my search, for it is not always the truth that leads to great discoveries. I say this, moreover, in order to put before my readers a typical example of the many errors and omissions that I was guilty of in the course of my investigation, despite the fact that I had kept my brain working feverishly at all times. I now believe that in this type of search there is something more powerful that guides us, an obscure but infallible intuition that is as inexplicable, but at the same time as reliable, as the clairvoyance that enables sleepwalkers to head straight for their objective, their *inexplicable* objective.

The trap door was closed so tightly that there was no use even thinking of trying to pry it open without the aid of a strong instrument with a thin blade; it was obvious that it opened from below, at an hour agreed on with the emissary. I became desperate at the thought that I would be obliged to carry out this operation that very night, since the following day someone would be sure to notice that the padlock had been forced open and everything would be more difficult, if not impossible. What to do? I had no tools with me. I reviewed in my mind the few things there were in the empty apartment: only in the kitchen and the bathroom was there likely to be anything that would serve my purpose. I hurried to the kitchen and found nothing I could use. I then went into the bathroom and finally decided that the arm of the flotation ball in the toilet might more or less do as a tool. I removed the flotation ball, pulled on the arm of it till it broke off, and ran back to the room where I had discovered the opening in the floor. After working for more than an hour I managed to make a little opening on one side of the trap door by taking advantage of the rough edges of solder left on the metal arm of the flotation ball. I finally slid the arm down into this opening, and using it as a lever, began to pry the trap door open very carefully. After several unsuccessful attempts, I finally managed to raise the trap door up far enough to be able to put my fingers in the opening and complete the operation with my hands. I carefully removed the trap door, laid it to one side, and directed the beam of my flashlight down into the opening. It did not lead, as I had thought, to the apartment downstairs but to a wide spiral staircase enclosed in a metal tube.

I went down this staircase and thus reached an old cellar located underneath the downstairs apartment. It must have been the cellar of this apartment on the ground floor that through some agreement between the original owners of the two apartments had become the cellar of the second-floor apartment, reached by means of that odd and unexpected stairway.

The cellar was typical of those in many houses in Buenos Aires, but it was completely empty and as deserted as the apartment to which it belonged. Could I have been wrong? Could I have labored so hard only to arrive at an impasse? Even if this were the case, it was imperative that I inspect the cellar carefully, as carefully as I had gone over the entire apartment upstairs.

There was not much to inspect however: its cement walls were smooth and offered few interesting possibilities. As is frequent in this type of building, the cellar had a small grated opening that looked out on the street: through it one could see the dimly lighted little square. Farther on, the cellar made a right-angle turn, thus forming an L, and when I shone the beam of my flashlight into that corner that I hadn't noticed at first, I saw another opening with a grate, but this one was larger, and looked out on ... On what? The cellar of the building next door? Since there was no other exit and that was the only possible answer, the thought occurred to me that the grate might perhaps be removable and thus be the exit that I had been searching for. I grabbed the two bars at each end of the grate and saw that I could easily push it out: my heart began to pound once again.

I laid the false grate to one side and shone my flashlight through the opening. It was not the cellar of the building next door but a passageway, the end of which I could not see, but I naturally attributed this to the fact that the beam of my flashlight was not very powerful.

After I had gone some two hundred yards down the passageway, it made a sharp turn to the right, and in this angle was a stairway with twelve steps (I counted them as I went up so as to calculate how far above the passageway I had gone), and was absorbed in this calculation when to my surprise I saw that the landing where this stairway ended had only one door opening onto it, a very small, low door that I would be able to pass through only by stooping over.

I was not only surprised; I was also annoyed at the thought that this door was about to keep me from entering the key redoubt that night, and "that night" might well mean "forever," since after all the things that I had done in the fake apartment, the blind would surely take precautions the next day that would make it impossible for me to return. I cursed myself for being so impatient and for having sent F. home too soon, for even though I could not have persuaded him to participate in my great undertaking (which he would undoubtedly have dismissed as the scheme of a madman), I could nonetheless have asked him to accompany me until it became clear that I would no longer need his help. At this moment, for example, how the devil was I going to open this door?

I stood there on the landing, silently reflecting: could it be the entrance to the house or the apartment that I had imagined I would find when I'd been sitting there in the little square? Twelve steps, each of which was some twenty centimeters high, added up to a height of approximately two and a half meters. The apartment was thus located at street level, and it would almost certainly have a normal-sized door on one of the neighboring streets. It might be some sort of shop. I don't know why the thought came to me that it could be a dressmaker's or a fashion boutique.

Who would ever have suspected a dressmaker's shop of being the entrance to the great labyrinth? The fact that the little short man who looked like Pierre Fresnay had not gone in by way of this normal entry was logical however: what could two men, one of whom was blind, be doing at a dressmaker's? Perhaps one such visit could be made without attracting attention. But if they had come there several times, people would have begun to attach more importance to their visits, and I do not believe that the Lodge would have overlooked the possibility that such "people" might well include an individual such as myself. It was logical, therefore, for them to keep an empty apartment to use as an entry.

All of this went through my mind as I stood there in front of the mysterious little low door. There was not a sound, since at that hour the dressmaker was surely fast asleep: it was now four-thirty in the morning.

My entire effort had gotten me nowhere. And just as when a coup d'état fails the insurgents are called bandits and held up to ridicule, so I now found myself a ridiculous figure: I looked at my white cane and thought to myself: "What a hopeless, picturesque idiot I am!" A grown man, a person who has read Hegel and been an accomplice in a bank holdup, was now in a cellar in Buenos Aires, at four-thirty in the morning, standing in front of a little door that presumably led to the lodgings of a pseudo-dressmaker in the service of a secret society. Wasn't that absurd? And as I contemplated the white cane, shining the beam of my flashlight on it, with that sort of painful pleasure we feel when we press down on certain spots that are aching, it made my situation seem even more grotesque.

"Well then," I said to myself, "it's all over."

And I was about to grope and fumble my way back along the same labyrinthine path that had led me there when the thought came to me that the little door might not be locked. The very idea excited me and renewed my hopes, for at that moment I failed to draw the conclusion that such a propitious circumstance should have suggested to me: the terrifying conclusion *that they were waiting for me.*

I went back to the little door, and as I shone my flashlight on it, I had a moment's doubt. "No, it's not possible," I said to myself. "This door is doubtless open only when they are expecting one of the blind and the emissary."

A presentiment nonetheless guided my trembling hand toward the door handle. I turned it and pushed.

The door wasn't locked: it had no keyhole!

⁓ 2 1 ⁓

I STOOPED far enough over to get through the little low door and entered the room. Then I stood up again and raised my flashlight to see where I was.

An ice-cold electric shock ran through me: a face had loomed up before me in the beam of my flashlight.

A blind woman was looking straight at me. It was like an infernal apparition, though the hell it had come from was frigid and black.

It was plain to see that she had not hastened to that little secret door because she had been alerted by the faint noises that I had perhaps made as I entered. No: she was fully dressed and it was obvious that she had been WAITING for me.

I have no idea how long a time I remained petrified by the awesome, icy gaze of that Medusa before I fainted.

I had never fainted before in my life, and later I asked myself whether this phenomenon was brought on by terror or by the magic powers of the blind woman, since, as now seems evident to me, that hierophant had the ability to unleash or to convoke demoniacal forces.

Strictly speaking, I did not faint dead away, that is to say lose consciousness altogether; rather, when I fell to the floor (though it would be more apt to say "When I collapsed"), a drowsiness began to steal over me, a fatigue that rapidly affected my every muscle, as when one suffers a violent attack of the grippe.

I remember the pounding sensation in my temples, growing increasingly intense until at one point I had the feeling that my head might explode like a boiler under thousands of atmospheres of pressure. A sort of fever mounted in my body like a seething liquid in a vessel, as a phosphorescent gleam made the Blind Woman more and more visible amid the darkness.

And then an explosion seemed to rupture my eardrums and I fell, or as I have already said, I collapsed on the floor of that room.

☙ 22 ☙

I SAW NOTHING more, but I seemed to waken to a reality that appeared to me, or appears to me now, to be more intense than the other one, a reality possessed of the same powerful yet anxious quality as deliriums brought on by fever.

I was in a boat, and the boat was gliding over a vast lake with still, black, bottomless waters. The silence was oppressive and disturbing, for I suspected that I was not alone, and in that half-light (it was not light from the sun, but rather a weird, ghostly luminosity coming from a nocturnal sun) was being closely watched and observed by beings whom I could not see, but who surely dwelt somewhere beyond reach of my dim vision. What did they expect of me, and above all what awaited me in this desolate, gloomy stretch of stagnant water?

I was no longer able to think, though I still possessed a sort of vague consciousness and memories of my childhood that weighed heavily on me. Birds whose eyes I had plucked out in those bloody years seemed to be flying overhead, gliding above me as though keeping watch over my journey; because without consciously thinking about it, since it was as though I were incapable of thought now, I was rowing in a direction that appeared to be that in which that nocturnal sun would set hours or centuries later. It seemed to me that I could hear the slow, heavy beating of these creatures' huge wings, as though those birds of my childhood had now turned into immense pterodactyls or giant bats. Above me and behind my back, that is to say to what must have been the east of that vast black stretch of water, I was aware of the presence of an old man, bristling with resentment, also keeping watch over my journey: he had a single enormous eye in his forehead like a cyclops, and he was so huge that his head was more or less at the zenith and his body descended to the horizon. His presence, which *I felt* with an intensity that was well-nigh intolerable (to the point that I could even have described the horrible expression on his face) was preventing me from turning around, forcing me to keep not only my body but even my face turned in the opposite direction.

"Everything will depend on my being able to reach the shore before the sun sets," I found myself thinking or saying to myself. I rowed in that direction, but my progress was as slow as in nightmares. As the oars dipped in those black and muddy waters, I could hear their dull splash. Great floating leaves and flowers similar to giant water lilies, but lugubrious, rotten ones, parted with each stroke of the oars. I tried to concentrate on my laborious task, not wanting even to imagine what sort of horrible monsters peopled, I was certain, those foul, fathomless waters: with my eyes fixed on the west, or on what I took to be the west, I confined myself to rowing in that direction, obstinately and fearfully, bending my every effort toward reaching the shore before that sun set.

My progress across the waters was painfully slow and difficult. The sun descended just as slowly toward the west and the fury with which I pushed on those heavy oars that moved so ponderously was motivated by a single anxious thought: to reach the other side before that sun set.

That heavenly body was already nearing the horizon when I felt my boat touch bottom. I dropped the oars and rushed to the prow.

I leapt out of the boat and waded through muddy water that came up to my knees, heading toward the shore, which I could already dimly make out amid that semidarkness. I soon felt myself on what might be called terra firma, but was really a swamp, where my progress was as slow and difficult as in the boat: I was obliged to make an enormous effort to pull one foot after another out of the mire so as to be able to take one more step. I was nonetheless so desperate that I struggled on, slowly but steadily. And just as I had previously been possessed by the thought that I had to reach terra firma, I was now obsessed by the idea that I had to reach a mountain, also to the west, that was just barely visible in the distance. "The cavern is there," I remember thinking. What cavern? And why was it absolutely imperative that I reach it? I did not ask myself any of these questions at the moment, and even today I would be unable to answer them. All I knew was that I had to reach the cavern and enter it, at whatever cost. I must also mention that I could still feel the colossal presence of the unknown man at my back. With his single unblinking eye that gleamed with hatred, he appeared to be watching over and even guiding my journey toward the west, like a treacherous traffic director. His arms, opened wide, spanned the entire sky at my back, with his hands leaning on the north and the south, thus occupying the entire half of the heavenly vault that lay behind me. My situation was such that there was nothing else for me to do but walk westward, and in the midst of that insane reality this struck me as logical and reasonable. My idea was to flee his gaze and take refuge inside the cavern, where I knew that his gaze would at last be powerless. I struggled along in this fashion for what seemed to me to be a year. The nocturnal sun was still going down, and although the mountain was closer now, it was still a frighteningly long distance away. I covered this last stretch fighting against fatigue, fear, and despair. I could feel the Man's sinister smile at my back. Above me I could feel pterodactyls silently circling, gliding down and sometimes touching me with their great heavy wings. I was terrified not only by this frigid, gelatinous contact but by the possibility that in the end they would pounce upon me with their toothed beaks and pluck out my eyes. I suspected that they were allowing me to wear myself out in a futile effort, to continue my stupid, exhausting journey for years and years and then, when I believed that my goal lay close at hand at last, they would tear my eyes out and thus deprive me of this insane hope.

I began to have this feeling toward the very end of my journey, as though everything had been planned so that it would be as painful for me as possible. "Because if they had plucked my eyes out at the very beginning I would have had no hope at all and would never have attempted this arduous journey across unknown seas and filthy swamps," I concluded, quite rationally and lucidly.

I could feel the Old Man's face radiate a sort of fierce joy as I thought all this through. I understood that I had arrived at the truth and that the worst trial of the entire journey now awaited me. I nonetheless felt no desire to look upward, and in any case there was no need to do so: my ears told me that the birds, with their enormous sharp beaks, were beginning to glide closer and closer to my head; I could hear the beating of their heavy wings, wings that must have been several meters long, and from time to time I felt them momentarily brush against my cheeks and skin, lightly but sickeningly.

I had only a short way, a very short way, to go before reaching the cavern that I could already glimpse in the phosphorescent darkness. My body was covered with sticky mire and I was crawling on all fours now. My hands touched snakes and immediately drew away in repugnance: there were countless numbers of them writhing about in the vast swamp, but I was so terrified by what I knew now lay in store for me that they were almost unworthy of my notice.

My exhaustion finally became greater than my desperation and I fell.

I struggled to keep my head out of the mire, raising my forehead in the direction of the cavern, as the rest of my body began sinking into those nauseating waters.

"I have to be able to breathe," I thought.

But I also thought: "By keeping my head up I am enabling them to get at my eyes."

The thought came to me that it was as though there were a curse upon me and I was condemned to this horrible operation, and yet at the same time I was freely consenting to this hideous and apparently inescapable rite.

Buried up to my neck in the mud, with my heart beating frantically amid that filth that was holding me fast, with my eyes looking forward and upward, I saw the great birds circling slowly about my head. I saw one of them come gliding downward from behind me; I could see its gigantic silhouette close by, outlined against the setting sun, turning now and gliding back toward me, then landing with a hollow splash on the muddy surface of the swampwater, right in front of my head. Its beak was as sharp-pointed as a stiletto and its expression was as blank as that of blind men, for it had no eyes: I could now see its empty eye sockets. It resembled an age-old divinity at the moment of sacrifice.

I felt that beak enter my left eye, and for an instant I could feel the rubbery resistance of my eyeball, and then I felt the beak penetrate it, cruelly and painfully, and the liquid begin to run down my cheek. By virtue of a mechanism that I still am unable to understand since it seems completely illogical, I kept my head in the same position, as though I were endeavoring to make the great bird's evil task easier, just as we keep our mouth open and our head still in the dentist's chair, even though we are suffering intense pain.

And as I felt the liquid of my eye and the blood run down my left cheek, I thought: "Now I am going to have to endure having the same thing done to my other eye." Calmly, apparently without any sort of hatred (as I remember, this astonished me), the great bird finished its work on my left eye and then, drawing back a little, it repeated the same operation on my right eye. And again I perceived that slight, momentary rubbery resistance of my eyeball, followed immediately by the cruel and painful penetration of the bird's beak, and once again the gliding of the crystalline liquid and blood down my cheek: liquids that were perfectly distinguishable since the crystalline one was thin and ice cold and the other, the blood, warm and sticky.

Then the great bird took flight and its companions followed after it; I could hear the beating of their heavy wings as they took off and then they flew away. "The worst is over," I thought.

I could see nothing now, but even with the immense pain and the curious repugnance that I now felt toward myself, I was still determined to drag myself to the cavern.

And I did so, slowly and painfully.

Little by little my effort was rewarded: the swamp gradually disappeared beneath my feet and hands and soon a sort of strange silence, a sensation of being closed in but at the same time safe, made me realize that I had finally entered the great cavern. And I fell into a deep sleep.

ᕙ 23 ᕙ

WHEN I CAME to my senses again, my whole body was utterly exhausted, as though in my dreams I had performed colossal labors.

I was lying on the floor, unable to make out where I was. Feeling as though my head weighed a ton, I looked at the floor round about me and tried to remember: I supposed that, as sometimes happened, I had come back to my room drunk and fallen into a stupor. A feeble early morning light was filtering into the room from somewhere. I tried to lift my head up and then slowly and clumsily inspected the space round about me.

I almost leapt to my feet despite my exhaustion: the Blind Woman!

I dizzily recalled the incidents: Iglesias, the man who looked like Pierre Fresnay, the little square in Belgrano, the secret passageway. Sitting halfway up and making superhuman efforts to get to my feet, I reviewed the situation at a fantastic speed and tried to think of some way out of it. I finally managed to stand up.

The Blind Woman was still frozen in the same hieratic pose as when I had first seen her on raising the beam of my flashlight in the dark. Had I suffered from a mere fleeting illusion? Had my nightmare begun when I fell into a faint?

In the dim light of dawn I tried to make a rapid mental inventory of everything around me. It was an ordinary room with a bed, a table (a work table?), a few chairs, a sofa, a combination radio-phonograph. I noted that there were no paintings or photographs, which bore out my conviction that the people who lived there were blind. The door that was letting the dawn light in almost certainly led to a room at street level, which might be the dressmaker's shop that I had thought of when making my previous calculations. There was another door off to one side that might lead to a bathroom. I looked behind me: yes, the little low door was there. I almost wished it wasn't, for that absurdly small entry terrified me.

This entire visual inspection of the room had taken only a few seconds.

The Blind Woman before me remained utterly silent.

Two things contributed to my growing anxiety: the fact, first of all, as I now remembered with terrifying clarity, that she had been *waiting for me* just inside the little closed door through which I had entered: and secondly, her incredible, enigmatic, menacing immobility.

I pondered what I could possibly do and what I should say, what words would seem the least ridiculous and the most believable.

"Excuse me," I stammered, "I came in intending to rob the place, and fainted when I saw you ..."

I realized as I spoke how absurd these words were. They might perhaps have sounded convincing to a normal person living in a normal house, but how could I have expected the Blind Woman to be taken in by such nonsense? A blind woman who had obviously been WAITING FOR ME.

A sarcastic expression seemed to cross her face. Then she disappeared through the open door.

She closed it behind her and I heard the key turn in the lock.

I was in the dark now. Feeling my way along, in desperation, I rushed to the door and turned the handle, to no avail. Then, groping my way along the walls, I reached the other door, the one on the right, but that too was of no avail, for as was only to be expected, it too was locked.

I stood there leaning against the wall, overcome with dismay and fear and uncertainty. Thoughts rushed chaotically through my mind:

I had fallen into an inescapable trap.

The Blind Woman had gone in search of the Others: they would now decide my fate.

The Blind Woman had been waiting for me: therefore they knew that I had arrived. How long exactly had they known?

They had known since the day before: an electric eye permitted them to keep watch at a distance on any sort of activity at the door with the padlock on it.

They had known ever since Iglesias had acquired the supernatural powers of the Lodge, and consequently ever since he had managed to read my mind and discover my secret designs.

They had known immediately: I suddenly became aware of an enormous crack in the vast edifice I had constructed, since through an inexplicable oversight (oversight?) on my part, I had not remembered that when Iglesias was let out of the hospital, he had been taken to a pension that a Spanish male nurse had recommended to him, telling him that they would take good care of him there.

At this very moment that the light dawned on me, I was suddenly overwhelmed by the certainty, at once awful and grotesque, that the very times when I had congratulated myself on my cleverness most fatuously were the times when I was being kept under the closest surveillance by the Sect—and through the intermediary of that ridiculous figure, Señora Etchepareborda, at that!

I was struck then by how ludicrous a stage setting all those cheap bibelots, those little mottoes in rustic frames, those fake photographs of the Etcheparebordas had been! I was ashamed to think that they hadn't even thought it worth the trouble to invent something more subtle in order to pull the wool over my eyes. Or perhaps, besides pulling the wool over my eyes, they had also incidentally wanted to wound my pride, to fool me in such a way that later I myself would be struck by the irony of it all.

∾ 24 ∾

I DON'T KNOW how many hours I remained trapped there in the dark, a prey to my uncertainties and apprehensions. The worst of it was that I began to have the feeling that I was suffocating, a natural reaction inasmuch as that accursed room had no other ventilation except the tiny bit of air coming through various cracks; I could feel a very feeble current of air coming in from around the door leading to the room in the front at least. Would this be enough however to renew the oxygen in the room where I was? It didn't seem like it, for I felt more and more as though I were suffocating, though the thought did occur to me that there might be psychological reasons for this.

But what if the Sect intended to bury me alive in that locked room? I suddenly remembered one of the stories that I had turned up in the course of my long investigation. In the days when old man Echagüe was still alive, the family had a housemaid in their mansion on the Calle Guido who was being exploited by a blind pimp who sent her out hustling in the Parque Retiro. In the year 1935 a hot-tempered young Spaniard was taken on by the Echagües as a concierge. He fell in love with the girl and finally got her away from the pimp. The girl lived in terror for months, until little by little, as the concierge patiently explained to her, she understood that the punishments that the blind man who had been exploiting her threatened to inflict on her were purely theoretical. Two years went by. On January 1, 1937, the Echagüe family left for their *estancia*, where it was their habit to spend the winter months. Everyone had already gone, except the house-maid and the concierge, who lived on one of the upstairs floors; but old Juan, who was acting as the head servant, believing that the couple had already left with the family, shut off the electricity and then left himself, locking the big downstairs door behind him. But as it happened, at the very moment that Juan turned off the electricity the concierge and his wife were on their way downstairs in the elevator. When the Echagüe family came back three months later, they found in the elevator the skeletons of the concierge and the housemaid, with whom the family had made arrangements to stay in the house in Buenos Aires while the rest of the household was off in the country on vacation.

At the time I first heard this story from Echagüe, I hadn't the least idea as yet that I would one day be beginning this investigation of the blind. Years later, on reviewing all the information having to do in one way or another with the Sect, I remembered the blind pimp and was suddenly convinced that the elevator episode, due apparently to sheer chance, was in reality a deliberate plot mounted by the Sect. But how could this ever be proven? I spoke with Echagüe and informed him of my suspicions. He looked at me in stupefaction, and, it seemed to me, with a certain sarcastic gleam in his little slanty eyes. He none-theless admitted that there was a possibility that what I suspected was true.

"And how do you think we could prove anything?" he asked me.

"Do you know where Juan lives?"

"I can find out through González. It seems to me he's kept in touch with him."

"All right. And don't forget what I've told you: that man played an important part in what happened. *He knew* that the other two were upstairs. And what was more: he waited for the moment that they started the elevator from upstairs, and when he calculated that they were between two floors (everything had been carefully planned in advance, watch in hand, and trial runs made beforehand), he turned off the electricity, or gave a shout or gestured to the other one who doubtless already had his hand on the switch."

"The other one? What other one?"

"How should I know? Some other member of the gang perhaps, not necessarily one of your servants. Though it might even have been that González."

"So you think Juan was a member of a gang, a gang connected with or run by the blind?"

"I don't have the slightest doubt of it. Make a few inquiries about him and you'll see."

He looked at me again with scarcely concealed irony, but said nothing more except that he was going to look into the whole thing.

A little while later I telephoned him and asked him if he'd turned up anything. He told me he'd like to see me, and we met in a bar. When I walked in, the expression on his face was not the same one as before: there was utter amazement in his eyes now.

"What about that famous Juan?" I asked.

"González had kept in touch with him, it turned out. I explained to him that I wanted to see Juan. His answer struck me as being a bit fishy: he said he hadn't seen Juan for a long time, but would try to contact him at the place where he was living, though he thought Juan was about to move. He asked me if I wanted to talk to him about something important or urgent. I had the impression that he was nervous or anxious when he asked me that. I wasn't consciously aware of it at the moment, but realized it afterward, when I went over the whole scene in my mind. I didn't go about things as I should have, because I said straight out that I had always wanted to know the precise circumstances in which the incident with the elevator had happened and that perhaps Juan might be able to tell me more than I'd already found out about the accident. González listened to me with an impassive face—how can I describe it?—a poker face, more or less. That is to say, it struck me that his face was too impassive. This too didn't occur to me until later. Unfortunately. Because if I'd thought of it at the moment, I'd have taken him off into some corner, grabbed him by the lapels, and with two or three well-aimed punches I'd have gotten the whole story out of him. Anyway, there's no point in telling you how it all ended."

"How did it end?"

Echagüe stirred the remains of the coffee in his cup and replied:

"It didn't have an end, because I never set eyes on González again. He disappeared from the confectioner's shop where he worked. Of course, if you're interested in pursuing the matter, we can ask the police to step in and try to locate the pair of them."

"Don't give it another thought. That was all I wanted to know. I can imagine the rest."

This entire story was coming back to me now. And because of my habitual tendency to imagine terrible things, I could see every last detail in my mind's eye. First of all, the concierge's mild surprise when the elevator stops between floors. He presses the button to start it up again, several times; he opens and closes the folding door inside the elevator. Then he shouts downstairs to Juan to close the door down there in case he's opened it. Nobody answers. He shouts louder (he knows that Juan is there downstairs, waiting till everybody has left) and nobody answers. He shouts some more, louder and louder, and finally he begins to be alarmed. Time goes by, he and his wife look at each other, wondering what has happened. Then he begins shouting again, and then she shouts, and then both of them together. They wait a while longer, trying to guess what is going on downstairs. "He's gone to the toilet, he's outside chatting with Dombrowski (the Polish concierge from the house next door), he's gone to check the whole house to see that nothing's been left behind," they tell each other. Fifteen minutes go by and they start shouting again: there is no answer. They shout for five or ten minutes: still no answer. They wait a while longer, more and more upset now, looking at each other with greater and greater anxiety and fear. Neither of them wants to come right out and tell the other how desperate the situation appears to be, but they are both beginning to suspect that everyone is gone and that the electricity has been shut off. Then they begin to shout again, in turn and together: as loudly as they can at first, then screaming in terror, and finally howling like maddened animals cornered by wild beasts. These howls go on for hours, little by little growing weaker;

their voices are hoarse now, the physical efforts they have made and their terror have left them exhausted: they are moaning now, their voices growing fainter and fainter; they weep and pound on the walls, more and more feebly. From this point on one can imagine different variations: there may have been a period of absolute stupor, in which both simply huddle together there in the dark, silent and stunned. Then they may have started talking to each other, exchanging ideas and sharing slight hopes: Juan will surely be back, he's just gone to the corner bar to have a little nip; he's forgotten something in the house and will come back to get it; when he pushes the button for the elevator to go upstairs, he discovers they're trapped in it; they greet him in tears and tell him: "Oh, Juan, if you only knew what a scare we've had." And then the three of them, discussing what a nightmare the whole thing was, leave the house together and laugh at some silly little thing that happens in the street because they're so happy. But Juan doesn't come back, nor has he gone off to the bar on the corner, nor has he been whiling away the time with the Polish concierge next door; the one thing that is certain is that hour after hour is going by and nothing at all is happening in that silent, deserted mansion. Meanwhile they have gotten a bit of their strength back and the shouts begin again, and then the screams, followed by the howls, and finally, one supposes, moans that grow more and more feeble. It is probable that by this time they are lying exhausted on the floor of the elevator and thinking how impossible it is for such an appalling thing to happen: this is a quite typical reaction of human beings when something terrible happens. They say to themselves: "This can't be, this simply can't be!" But terror slowly creeps over the again, and it is probable that a new series of shouts and howls then begins. But to what avail? Juan is at this moment on his way to the *estancia*, since he is going there with his employers: the train has left at 10 P.M. Their shouts are useless, yet people always have a certain absurd confidence that shouts and screams will change things, as is evident from any number of catastrophes. And so with their last remaining strength they begin shouting and screaming again, and again their howls of terror die away to moans as before. This, naturally, cannot go on: a moment comes in which all hope is abandoned and then, though this may seem grotesque, they think of eating. But why eat? To prolong the torture? Lying on the floor, there in the dark in that tiny cubicle, hearing each other, touching each other, the two of them ponder the same awful thought: what will they eat when their hunger becomes unbearable? Time passes and they also think of their death, which is bound to occur in a few days. What will it be like? What is it like to die of hunger? They think of things that have happened in the past; memories of happy times come to mind. She now finds that period when she worked the Parque Retiro as a whore was a good time in her life: there was sun, the young sailors or army recruits were sometimes kind and affectionate; all those little things in life, in short, which always seem so wonderful when death is close at hand, even though they have been sordid. He is probably remembering things from his childhood, at the mouth of a river in Galicia; he is doubtless recalling the songs and dances of his village. Again the same thought occurs to him or to her or to both of them: "But this just can't be!" Things like this just don't happen. How could this happen? It is probable that this thought brings on a new series of shouts, but they are less energetic and of shorter duration than those of the previous series. Then again there come to mind thoughts and memories, of Galicia and the happy days of prostitution. But why go on with this minutely detailed description? Any person with the least little bit of imagination is capable of reconstructing what happens next: growing hunger, mutual suspicions, quarrels, recriminations having to do with various things that happened in the past. Perhaps the concierge wants to eat the housemaid and in order to have a clear conscience about it he begins to reproach her for having allowed herself to become a whore. Isn't she ashamed of herself? Didn't she realize that that was a filthy thing to do? Et cetera.

Then (after a day or two of hunger pangs) he thinks that even without killing her outright, he could at least eat some part of her body; he might just pull off a couple of her fingers and eat them, or an ear. Anyone who wishes to reconstruct this episode should not forget that these two human beings must also tend to their intimate needs there in the elevator as well, so that everything becomes more and more filthy, more and more sordid and abominable. But above all there is the couple's increasing hunger and thirst. Their thirst can be quenched by catching their own urine in their hands and then drinking it; there have been factual accounts of such a thing. But what about their hunger? Factual accounts also demonstrate that no one eats his own limbs if there is another human being with him. One has only to recall Dante's Count Ugolino, imprisoned in a dungeon with his own sons. In a word, it is probable—what am I saying?—it is certain that at the end of four days, or perhaps even less, of being trapped together in that stinking cubicle, with their resentment of each other growing more and more violent, the stronger one will eat the weaker. In this particular case, the concierge eats the housemaid, perhaps only bits and pieces of her in the beginning, starting with her fingers, and then, after hitting her over the head or knocking her senseless against the walls of the elevator, he devours all the rest of her.

Two details corroborate my reconstruction: her clothing had been ripped off her and was found scattered all over the floor of the elevator amid the filth; many of her bones also lay scattered about, as though they had been torn from her body one by one by the cannibal concierge. On the other hand, his own putrefied body, partially reduced to a skeleton, lay on its side, all in one piece.

In my desperation, my thoughts ranged even farther and I conjectured that my fate had perhaps been sealed from the moment that I had had my adventure with the blind peddler of collar stays, and that for more than three years I had believed that I had been following the blind when in reality it had been they who had been dogging my footsteps. The thought came to me that the search that I had carried out had not been a product of my will or of my famous freedom but the work of fate, that I was *destined* to pursue the men belonging to the Sect so as thus to pursue my own death, or something worse than my death. What certain knowledge did I have of the fate that now lay in store for me? Might the nightmare that I had just endured be merely a presentiment of things to come? Might they not pluck my eyes out? Might those huge birds not be symbols of the cruelly successful operation that now awaited me? And finally, hadn't I remembered in the nightmare how as a youngster I had mercilessly plucked out the eyes of cats and birds? Might I not thus have been condemned to this fate from my childhood?

ↄ‍ↄ 25 ↄ‍ↄ

THESE CONJECTURES, along with other memories having to do with my research on the blind, occupied that day. Every once in a while I would think again of the Blind Woman, her disappearance, and my subsequent imprisonment in this room. As I pondered the tragedy in the elevator it occurred to me that my punishment might be to die of hunger in this strange room; but I immediately realized that such punishment would be an extremely merciful one by comparison with that dealt out to those two unfortunate creatures. Dying of hunger in the dark? My naive hope of a fate as kind as that almost made me laugh.

As I was reflecting there in the dead silence of that room, I thought I heard the sound of muffled voices coming through one of the doors. I stood up without making any noise and walked in my bare feet over to that door, the one presumably leading to the room at the front of the building. I cautiously put my ear to the crack: complete silence. Then, feeling my way along the walls, I went over to the other door and repeated the operation: I had the impression that the persons talking in the next room fell silent the moment I put my ear to the door.

I had moved as quietly as I could but they had doubtless heard me. Nonetheless I stood with my ear to the door for a long time, listening intently. But I could not make out the slightest sound of voices or the slightest movement. I presumed that the Council of the Blind was assembled there on the other side of the door, not one of them moving a muscle as they waited for me to stop behaving so stupidly. Realizing that the only thing I would gain by my spying would be to cause all of them to become even more annoyed, I retraced my steps, being less cautious this time since I presumed that they had already discovered what I had been up to. I flung myself down on the bed and decided to have a cigarette. What else was there for me to do? Moreover, I was certain that that council would soon announce what they had decided to do with me.

Until that moment I had not given in to my desire to smoke, so as not to consume the little oxygen that according to my calculations was reaching me from the feeble currents of air coming through the cracks. But, I said to myself, at this point what kindlier fate could possibly await me than suffocating to death from cigarette smoke? From then on I began to smoke like a chimney, with the result that there was even less breathable air in the room than before. Thoughts and memories kept coming to my mind, in particular those having to do with acts of vengeance perpetrated by the Society. And I began to analyze the Castel affair again, a crime that had been the talk of Buenos Aires not only because of the people involved but because of the report sent by the murderer to a publishing house from the insane asylum to which he had been committed. It interested me enormously for two reasons: I had known María Iribarne, the murder victim, and knew that her husband was blind. It can readily be imagined then why I was so eager to meet Castel, and also why my terror kept me from doing so, inasmuch as it was more or less like thrusting my head directly into the lion's mouth. What else could I do then except read and study his report in minute detail? "I have always been prejudiced against blind people," he confessed. When I read that document for the first time, I was literally stupefied, for in it Castel spoke of the cold skin, the moist hands, and other characteristics of the race that I too had observed and been obsessed by, such as the tendency to live in caves or dark places. Even the title of his report made me shudder, for it struck me as highly significant: he had called it "The Tunnel."

My first impulse was to rush to the insane asylum and see the painter to find out how far he had gotten in his investigations. But I immediately realized that this was as dangerous as exploring a gunpowder factory in the dark by striking a match to light one's way.

Unquestionably Castel's crime was the inexorable result of an act of vengeance on the part of the Sect. But what, exactly, was the mechanism employed? For years I tried to take it apart and analyze it, but I was never able to get to the bottom of the sort of ambiguity that is typical of every operation planned and executed by the blind. I will set forth my conclusions here, conclusions that soon ramify like the paths of a labyrinth:

Castel was a well-known figure in intellectual circles in Buenos Aires, and therefore his opinions on any subject were doubtless also well known. It is scarcely possible that he could have managed to conceal an obsession as thoroughgoing as his about the blind. Through Allende, María Iribarne's husband, the Sect decided to wreak its vengeance on Castel.

Allende ordered his wife to go to the art gallery where Castel's latest paintings were being shown. She was to give signs of great interest in one of them, stationing herself before it as though contemplating it ecstatically, for a long enough time for Castel to notice her and study her, and then she was to disappear. Disappear, that is, in a manner of speaking. As invariably happens with the Sect, the pursuer becomes the person pursued, but in such a way that sooner or later his intended victim falls into his hands. Castel finally meets María again, falls hopelessly in love with her, and like a madman (and a fool) "pursues" her from one end of the city to the other and even goes to her house, where María's husband himself shows him a love letter addressed to her. This is a key fact: how to explain such a move on the husband's part unless it was intended to further the Sect's sinister purposes? Castel was tormented by this inexplicable fact, and what happened thereafter is not worth repeating here: I need only mention that Castel became madly jealous, eventually murdered María, and was committed to an asylum for the criminally insane; thus the plan of the Sect came off perfectly and there was not the least danger of the details of it ever coming to light. Who is going to believe arguments put forth by a madman? All this is as clear as day thus far. The ambiguity and the labyrinth begin at this point, for the following possibilities present themselves:

1. María's death had been decided upon as a way of ensuring that Castel would be punished by being shut up in the insane asylum, but Allende, who really loved and needed his wife, was not let in on this plan. Hence what seemed to Allende a "senseless" crime, and his desperation in the final scene.

2. María's death had been decided upon and Allende was aware of this decision. Here two subpossibilities present themselves:

A. The decision was accepted by Allende with resignation, because he loved his wife but at the same time was obliged to pay for some misdeed that he had committed before he went blind, a misdeed that we have no knowledge of and that he had already partially paid for by being blinded by the Sect.

B. The decision was received by Allende with satisfaction, for he not only did not love his wife but in fact hated her violently and thus hoped to avenge himself for her numerous betrayals of him. How to reconcile this variation with Allende's desperation at the end? Very simple: it was mere playacting for the gallery, and also playacting forced upon him by the Sect in order to make any clues to this complicated act of vengeance impossible to follow.

There remain variations of the variations that are not worth my going to the trouble to describe since each one of you can easily try your hand at inventing them as an exercise, and a very useful one, since one never knows when and how one may be caught up in one of the Sect's darkly ambiguous machinations.

As for myself, that affair, which happened shortly after my adventure with the blind man peddling collar stays, threw me into a panic. I was terrified and decided to cover up my tracks by putting not only time but space between me and him. I fled the country. For many readers of these memoirs, this step that I took may appear to be an exaggerated reaction on my part. The lack of imagination of those persons who believe that in order to discover a truth it is necessary to keep one's "proper sense of proportion" in the face of the facts has always made me laugh. These midgets imagine (for they too have an imagination, of course, albeit a dwarf-sized one) that reality is no bigger than they themselves are, and that it is no more complex than their fly's brains. Those individuals who call themselves "realists" because they are incapable of seeing beyond their own noses confuse Reality with a Circle-Two-Meters-in-Diameter centered on their own simple brains. Hicks from the provinces who laugh at what they are unable to understand and refuse to believe anything that lies outside their famous circle. With typical peasant cunning, they invariably turn a deaf ear to madmen who come to them with plans to discover America, but can easily be conned into buying a public mailbox on the corner the minute they come down to the city. And they tend to find logical (another of their favorite words!) things that are merely psychological. What is familiar thus becomes what is reasonable, through the workings of the same mechanism whereby the Laplander finds it reasonable to offer his wife to the passing traveler, whereas this strikes a European as madness. This sort of mistrustful troublemaker has successively refused to believe in the existence of the antipodes, the machine gun, microbes, and hertzian waves: realists whose particular distinguishing characteristic is their rejection of future realities, generally by way of mocking laughter, violent resistance, and sometimes even prison sentences or commitment to an insane asylum for those who do believe in such realities.

Not to mention that other supreme aphorism: "a proper sense of proportion." As though there had ever been anything important in the history of mankind that was not a gross exaggeration, from the Roman Empire to Dostoevski!

But enough talk of stupidities; let us return to *the one subject that ought to be of interest to mankind.*

I decided to leave the country, and though my first thought was to do so by crossing the Delta in one of the boats belonging to smugglers who were friends of F.'s, it then occurred to me that this would get me no farther than Uruguay. The only possible solution, then, was to get myself a fake passport. I hunted up a certain Nassif the Turk, who provided me with one in the name of Federico Ferrari Hardoy, one which, among many others stolen by Nassif's gang, had not yet been used. I chose this particular one because at one time I had had a little run-in with Ferrari Hardoy and this gave me a chance to commit a few misdeeds in his name.

But even though I had this document in hand, I decided it would be wiser to board a smuggler's boat and cross the Delta to Montevideo. So I went to El Carmelo, and from there I took a bus to Colonia, and then another bus to Montevideo.

I got a visa stamped in my passport at the Argentine consulate and bought a ticket on an Air France plane leaving two days later. What to do during this two-day wait? I was tense and nervous. I walked down the Avenida del 18 de Julio, visited a bookstore, drank quantities of coffee and cognac to combat the intense cold. But the day went by so slowly I was in despair: I couldn't wait for the moment to put an ocean between me and the blind man peddling the collar stays.

I naturally didn't want to run into anybody I knew. But unfortunately (and not by chance, but by a stroke of bad luck, and through carelessness on my part, since I ought to have spent those two days in some section of Montevideo where there would have been no possibility at all of running into people I knew), Bayce and a blonde girl, a painter whom I had met previously in Montevideo, spied me in the Tupi-Nambá Café. There was a third person with them, wearing blue jeans and odd shoes: a skinny young man, a typical highbrow intellectual, whom I was quite sure I had met somewhere before.

There was no way out: Bayce came over to where I was sitting and took me back to his table, where I said hello to Lily and struck up a conversation with the man in the strange-looking shoes. I told him I thought we'd met before. Hadn't he been in Valparaíso at one time? Wasn't he an architect? Yes, he was an architect, but he'd never been in Valparaíso.

This intrigued me. As is understandable, I found his denial suspicious. It seemed too much of a coincidence: not only did I have the impression that I had met him before, but I had correctly surmised that he was an architect. Could he be denying that he had ever been in Valparaíso in order to keep me from coming to dangerous conclusions?

I was so upset and anxious (my reader must bear in mind that the episode with the blind collar-stay peddler had taken place just a few days before) that it was impossible for me to make much sense of the conversation between these three people. They spoke (naturally) of Perón, of architecture, of some theory or other, of modern art. The architect had a copy of *Domus* with him. They lavished praise on a sort of ceramic rooster, which I was obliged to have a look at despite my uneasiness: it was by an Italian named Durelli or Fratelli (what did the name matter?), who had surely stolen the idea for it from a German named Staudt, who in turn had stolen it from Picasso, who in turn had stolen it from some black in darkest Africa, who was the only one who had not pocketed a single dollar from his rooster.

The architect was still very much on my mind: the more I looked at him the more certain I was that I had met him somewhere before. His name was Capurro, he said. But was that his real name? Of course; my suspicions were absurd: he was from Montevideo, Bayce and Lily were friends of his; how could he have given me a false name? Well, it wasn't important: the name he gave could be, and surely was, his real one, but had he lied when he said he'd never been in Valparaíso? If so, what was he hiding? With my mind in a whirl, I tried my best to remember whether there was anyone in that group in Valparaíso that I had known there who had ever mentioned anything having to do with the blind, either directly or indirectly. It seemed significant to me, for example, that this person appeared to be particularly interested in roosters, since the inevitable fate of fighting cocks is to be blinded in combat. No, I could remember no previous conversations among that group having to do with blindness. And suddenly it occurred to me that perhaps it was not in Valparaíso that I had seen this man before, but in Tucumán.

"Have you ever been in Tucumán?" I asked him point-blank.

"In Tucumán? No, I've never been there either. I've been to Buenos Aires lots of times, of course, but I've never been in Tucumán. Why do you ask?"

"It's just an idle question really. It's simply that I have the feeling I've met you before and I've been wondering where it could have been."

"Well, old pal, most likely you saw him right here in Montevideo at one time or another," Bayce said, laughing at my persistence in pursuing the subject.

I shook my head and sat there lost in thought again as they went on talking about the rooster in *Domus*.

I invented some excuse or other to leave, said goodbye to them, and went off to another café, still pondering the question as to where I'd run into the architect before.

I tried to reconstruct my past contacts with the Tucumán group, people who, as always, I had used to camouflage my real activities. That was only natural: I had had no intention of hanging out with local counterfeiters or of allowing myself to be seen in the company of petty hoodlums from the provinces. To aid me in my reconstruction I telephoned a girl I knew, an architect I'd slept with in the past.

I went to her place to see her. She had made her way up in the world, and was now teaching at the university and collaborating with a group of young architects who were designing some sort of building or other in Tucumán that she showed me later on: a factory or a school or a sanitarium. I have no idea what it was, because as everyone knows buildings these days are all alike: they can as readily house a machine shop as a kindergarten. This is what they call functionalism.

As I have said, my friend had prospered. She no longer lived, as she had in Buenos Aires, in a shabby little student's room. She now lived in a modern apartment that reflected her personality. When the maid let me in I very nearly left then and there, thinking that nobody lived there. But on lowering my eyes, I spied the furniture, all of it just a few inches off the floor, as though for the use of crocodiles. A foot and a half higher up the apartment was entirely empty. Nonetheless, once I was inside, I saw that one enormous stretch of blank wall was hung with just one painting, the work of one of Gabriela's friends doubtless: on a steel gray monochrome background was a single vertical line, drawn with a ruler, and some ten inches to the right of it a tiny little ocher circle.

We stretched out on the floor, in very uncomfortable positions: Gabriela crawled to a little table no more than ten inches high to serve coffee in little ceramic cups without handles. As I burned my fingers the thought came to me that unless I could down half a dozen whiskies I'd never get my body temperature up high enough in that refrigerator of an apartment to sleep with Gabriela again. I had already resigned myself to my fate when her friends arrived. As they came across the room I realized that one of them was a woman, though she was wearing blue jeans. The other two were architects, one of them the husband of the woman in pants and the other apparently a friend of Gabriela's or a lover. They were all dressed in blue jeans and odd boots of the sort that army recruits used to wear but that nowadays must be made to measure for the School of Architecture.

They talked shop for quite a while, in a jargon that at times seemed to have crossbred with that of psychoanalysis, so that they appeared to be as ecstatic about a logarithmic spiral by Max Bill as about the ano-buccal sadism of a friend who had just gone into analysis.

And then, in the midst of my reconstruction of events, the light dawned. It was surely my obsession alone that had led me to think that I had seen Capurro before, in Valparaíso or Tucumán. It was just that all those people looked alike, and it was very hard to see the differences between them, especially if one saw them from a distance or in the dark or, as in my case, in moments of violent emotion.

Having thus reassured myself about Capurro, I found the rest of my stay more pleasant: I went to a movie, stopped by at a suburban bar, and finally went back to my hotel. And the next day when the Air France plane took off from Carrasco I began to breathe more easily.

I arrived at Orly in the middle of a depressing heat wave (it was the month of August). I was panting and sweating. One of the functionaries who examined my passport, one of those Frenchmen who gesticulate with that exuberance that they find typical of Latin Americans, said to me, with a mixture of sarcasm and condescension:

"But you Argentines must be used to weather lots hotter than this, right?"

Everyone knows that the French are a very logical people and the reasoning process of that Descartes in the Bureau of Customs was unassailable: Marseilles was in the south and it's hot there; Buenos Aires is much farther south and therefore the heat there must be infernal. All of which merely proves the sort of absurdities that logic leads to: a well-reasoned argument can do away with the South Pole.

I reassured him (and flattered him) by confirming the correctness of his opinions on the subject. I told him that in Buenos Aires our usual attire was loincloths, and that when we had to get dressed up we suffered if the weather was at all hot, whereupon he cheerfully stamped my passport, handed it back to me with a smile, and said: "*Allez-y*. Go get civilized!"

I didn't have any definite plans on arriving in Paris, but it seemed prudent to do two things: first off, to contact F.'s friends, just in case I began to run out of money; and secondly, to cover my trail, as usual, by hanging out with my friends (?) in Montparnasse and the Latin Quarter: that collection of Catalans, Italians, Polish and Rumanian Jews who constitute the School of Paris.

I found myself lodging in a rooming house on the Rue du Sommerand, where I had lived before the war. But Madame Pinard no longer ran the place. Another fat woman had taken over in the concierge's lodge, to keep an eye on the comings and goings of students, unsuccessful artists, and pimps who constituted not only the population of the rooming house but also the endless subject of Gossip and inexhaustible material for the concierge's Philosophy of Life.

I rented a tiny room on the fourth floor, and then went out to hunt up my acquaintances.

I stopped by the Dôme first, and didn't see a soul I knew. I was told that everyone had immigrated to other cafés. I also found out where Domínguez was and dropped round at his studio, which was now in the Grand Chaumière, to see him.

But it is evidently my fate to be able to do nothing that does not eventually lead me to the Forbidden Realm; in fact it would seem that an infallible flair inevitably takes me in that direction. "This," Domínguez said to me, showing me a canvas, "is the portrait of a blind model." He laughed. He had always had a penchant for certain perversities.

I was so taken aback I was obliged to sit down.

"What's the matter?" he asked. "You've turned deathly pale."

He brought me some cognac.

"I've got stomach trouble," I explained.

I left, vowing to myself never to go back to Domínguez's studio. But the next day I realized that that was the worst thing I could possibly do, as the following series of probable events demonstrated:

1. Domínguez would be surprised at my disappearance.

2. He would search his memory for some fact that might explain it. He would recall only one such thing: my having nearly fainted when he had shown me the portrait of the blind woman.

3. This fact would stand out so clearly in his mind that he would end up saying something about it, to the blind woman in particular. This was well within the realm of possibility. Frighteningly so, since Domínguez's comments would have the following consequences:

4. The blind woman would ask questions as to who I was.

5. My first and last names, my background and so on would come to light.

6. This information would immediately be passed on to the Sect.

The rest was as plain as day: my life would be in danger once again and I would be forced to flee Paris, perhaps to Africa or Greenland.

My readers can well imagine what decision I came to, the only one that would occur to any intelligent person: there was just one way of keeping up appearances and that was to go back to Domínguez's studio as though nothing had happened and risk the possibility of meeting the blind woman in person.

After a long and expensive journey, I had again come face to face with my Destiny.

∽ 26 ∽

HOW ASTONISHINGLY lucid I am in these moments preceding my death!

I am hastily noting down points that I would like to analyze, if *they* leave me enough time to do so:

Blind lepers.

The Clichy affair, espionage in the bookstore.

The tunnel between the crypt of Saint-Julien-le-Pauvre and Père Lachaise cemetery, Jean-Pierre, be very careful.

∽ 27 ∽

Pᴇʀsᴇᴄᴜᴛɪᴏɴ mania. Those realists again, those famous individuals who believe in "the proper sense of proportion." When my adversaries have finally burned me to death, then and only then will they be convinced: as though it were necessary to measure the diameter of the sun with a ruler in order to believe what astrophysicists assert.

These documents will testify to the truth.

Posthumous vanity? Perhaps: vanity is such a fantastic thing, so far from being "realistic" that it even leads us to worry about what others will think of us after we're dead and buried.

Could this be a sort of proof of the immortality of the soul?

∽ 28 ∽

Rᴇᴀʟʟʏ, what a bunch of bastards! In order to believe you, they must see you burned to death.

∽ 29 ∽

Sᴏ I ᴡᴇɴᴛ back to Domínguez's studio. Now that I had made up my mind to do so, a sort of tremendous anxiety drove me there. The moment I arrived, I asked him to tell me more about the blind woman. But Domínguez was drunk and began to heap abuse on me, as was his wont when he drank too much and lost control. A fierce, enormous hulk with his shoulders hunched over, he turned into a terrifying monster when under the influence of alcohol.

The next day I found him calmly painting away with his usual bovine air.

I asked him about the blind woman again and told him I would like very much to watch her without her knowing that I was doing so. I was thus resuming my investigation, long before I had expected to however, even though a distance of fifteen thousand kilometers is more or less the equivalent of a couple of years' time. This at least was the idiotic thought that came to me at the moment. I need not add that I said nothing to Domínguez about these secret thoughts of mine, and used simple curiosity, morbid curiosity, as my pretext for asking to observe the blind woman without being seen myself.

He told me I could post myself up above and look and listen to my heart's content. I suppose that my readers are familiar with the way painters' studios are laid out: they are usually one big room with a high ceiling, in the lower part of which the artist has his easel, cupboards for his painting equipment, a divan for the model, chairs and tables to sit at or eat at, and so on; and to one side, about six feet above the floor, a loft with a bed to sleep in. This loft was to be my observatory: it could not have been better suited for the task that I had set myself if it had been made to order.

Excited by the prospect before me, I chatted with Domínguez about old friends as we waited for the blind woman to arrive. We recalled Matta, who was in New York, Esteban Francés, Breton, Tristan Tzara, Péret. And what was Marcelle Ferry up to? (I remember perfectly that at the time I didn't inquire about Víctor Brauner. Fate indeed makes us blind!) Finally a knock at the door announced the arrival of the model. I hurriedly climbed up to the loft where Domínguez slept, in a bed as messy and filthy as ever. From my post up there, I readied myself to be a silent witness to bizarre things, for Domínguez had already forewarned me that the blind woman was so lustful that sometimes "there was nothing else he could do" but make love to her.

A shiver ran down my spine and my skin crawled the moment I saw the woman standing there in the doorway. I never have been able to see a blind person appear without feeling that icy shiver.

She was of medium height, and rather slender, but there was something about the way she moved that was reminiscent of a cat in heat. She made her way over to the couch without help and disrobed. She had a soft, attractive body, but it was above all her feline movements that made her seductive.

As Domínguez painted she poured out a stream of bitter invective against her husband. I did not find this of any particular interest till it suddenly dawned on me that her husband was blind too. The sort of weak spot I had always been looking for! Seen from a distance, an enemy nation always appears to be a solid, compact block with no cracks or fissures, giving us the impression that we will never be able

to penetrate it. But inside it are hatreds, resentments, desires for revenge: if this were not so espionage would be very nearly impossible
and collaboration in occupied countries scarcely feasible.

I naturally did not fling myself into this fissure with great rejoicing.
It was first necessary to determine:

a) Whether this woman was really unaware of my existence and of
my presence;

b) Whether she really detested her husband (this could be mere
bait to catch spies);

c) Whether her husband was really blind too.

The wild rush of thoughts that the revelation of the woman's hatred
for her spouse unleashed in my head was mingled with the excitement
of my senses brought on by the scene that followed. Perverse and
sadistic as he was, Domínguez did countless filthy things to the
woman, taking advantage of her blindness, rousing her to such a point
that she went groping all about with her hands trying to find him.
Domínguez motioned to me to come join the two of them, but as it
was imperative that I profit from this precious opportunity, I was not
about to throw it away in return for mere sexual satisfaction. The
game went on but soon degenerated into a somber and almost terrifying sexual battle between a man and a woman possessed who screamed,
bit, and scratched.

No, I had no doubt now that the woman was sincere, a fact that was
of importance to my future investigation. And although I know that
a woman is capable of lying coldly even in the most passionate moments, I was nonetheless inclined to believe that what she had said
about her blind husband was true. But I would have to verify this.

When the two of them finally calmed down, the studio had been
turned upside down (for they had not only shouted and howled:
Domínguez had also gotten the blind woman so excited with his
teasing taunts and filthy suggestions that she had chased him all
around the studio, stumbling over all the furniture). They remained
silent for a long time and then she got dressed again and said: "See
you tomorrow," like an office girl leaving work at the end of the day.
Domínguez didn't even answer; he simply lay there bare naked on
the divan, practically falling asleep. Feeling a bit ridiculous, I stayed
up there in my observatory for a while and then finally decided to
come down.

I asked Domínguez if it was true that the woman's husband was blind, if he had ever seen him. I also asked him if she really detested the man as much as she seemed to.

Domínguez's only reply was to explain to me that one of the tortures that that woman had thought up was to take her lovers to the room where she lived with the blind man and allow them to possess her in front of him. As I couldn't believe that such a thing was possible, he explained that indeed it was, for the man was not only blind but paralyzed, and was thus forced to witness from his wheelchair the scenes she staged to torment him.

"But how can that be?" I persisted. "Can't he at least move his wheelchair around? Doesn't he chase them around the room?"

Yawning like a rhinoceros, Domínguez shook his head. No: the blind man was completely paralyzed; all he could do was move a couple of the fingers of his right hand and moan. When the scene before him was about to reach its climax, the blind man, in a fit of insane fury, would succeed in moving his fingers a little and giving a few thick-tongued moans.

Why did she hate him so? Domínguez did not know.

⌘ 30 ⌘

BUT LET US go back to the model. Even today I still shudder when I recall the brief liaison I had with that blind woman, for I have never been closer to the edge of the abyss than at that moment. How stupid and how lacking in foresight I still was! To think that I took myself to be as cunning as a lynx, that I believed I never took a single step without having previously examined every inch of the terrain, that I regarded myself as someone whose powers of reason were exceptional and well-nigh infallible. Alas for me, poor simpleton that I was!

It was not difficult for me to come to be on intimate terms with the blind woman (exactly the way an idiot would say "It was not difficult for me to become the victim of a confidence game"). I met her the next day at Domínguez's studio, we left together, we talked about the weather, about Argentina, about Domínguez. She did not know, of course, that I had watched the two of them from my observation post up in the loft the day before.

"He's a great guy," she said to me. "I love him like a brother."

To me this was proof of two things: first of all, that she had been unaware of my presence up in the loft; and secondly, that she was a liar. This conclusion put me on my guard: when she made other confessions in the future, everything she said would have to be examined and the truth carefully sifted from the lies. A certain period of time, whose duration was brief but whose importance was considerable, was to go by before I realized or suspected that the first conclusion I had arrived at was highly questionable at best. Had she been intuitively aware that I was up there in the loft, thanks to that sixth sense which tells a blind person that there is someone else present in the room? Had Domínguez let her in on the secret out of complicity with her? I shall return to this subject. For the moment allow me to go on with my description of the facts as they occurred.

I judge myself as pitilessly as I judge the rest of humanity. Even today I ask myself whether it was merely my obsession regarding the Sect that led me to have that affair with Louise. I ask myself, for example, if I would ever have been able to go to bed with a blind woman who was hideous-looking. Now that would have been an investigation conducted in the true scientific spirit! Like that of those astronomers who spend long winter nights stretched out on wooden benches, shivering with cold beneath the domes of the observatory as they note the positions of the stars, for they would fall asleep if they were comfortable and the object that they are pursuing is not sleep but truth. Whereas I on the other hand, an imperfect and lustful creature, allowed myself to become involved in situations in which danger awaited me at every moment and I neglected the great transcendent objectives that I had set myself for so many long years.

It is impossible for me, however, to decide to what point my activities were motivated by a genuine spirit of investigation and to what point by sick self-indulgence. Because I also tell myself that this self-indulgence was equally useful as a means of penetrating the mystery of the Sect. For if the Sect in fact rules the world by virtue of the forces of darkness, if I was to study the limits, the boundaries, the scope and range of these forces, what better means could there be than plunging into the horrors of the flesh and the spirit? I am not stating a fact that I am absolutely certain of at this moment, I am merely thinking things over in my mind, and without allowing myself the slightest complacency toward my weaknesses endeavoring to discover the precise degree to which I yielded to these weaknesses in those days, and the precise degree to which I had the fearlessness and the courage to approach and even to plunge straight into the abyss of truth.

It would serve no useful purpose to describe in detail the loathsome congress that I had with the blind woman, inasmuch as such details would add nothing of importance to the Report that I wish to leave behind for future researchers. A Report that I wish to bear the same relationship to this sort of detailed description that a sociological geography of Central Africa bears to the description of an act of cannibalism. I shall merely say that even if I were to live five thousand years, it would be impossible for me to forget, to my dying day, those summer afternoon siestas with that nameless female as multiple as an octopus, as slow and minute in her movements as a slug, as flexible and perverse as a giant viper, as electric and hypnotic as a female cat in the night. As meanwhile in his paralytic's wheelchair, the other, impotent and pathetic, moved two fingers of his right hand and with his toad's tongue muttered heaven knows what blasphemies, what dark (and useless) threats. Until the moment when that vampire, having sucked all my blood, abandoned me, reduced to the state of an amorphous, repulsive mollusk.

Let us therefore pass over this aspect of the question and examine those facts that will constitute a useful contribution to this Report: the glimpses I had of the forbidden universe.

My first task, obviously, was to ascertain the precise nature and the degree of sincerity of the hatred that the blind woman professed for her husband, since such a crack in the solid structure of the Sect was one of the possibilities that I had always eagerly sought. I must make it clear however that I did not conduct this inquiry by asking Louise direct questions, since such an interrogation would have attracted her attention and aroused her suspicions; my information was obtained, rather, in the course of long conversations about life in general, and the subsequent analysis, in the quiet of my room, of her replies, her comments, and her silences or her reluctance to answer my questions. I thus arrived at the conclusion, based on what I considered to be reliable evidence, that the blind paralytic was really her husband and that her hatred of him was as profound as her perverse idea of having me possess her in his presence seemed to prove beyond doubt.

And I have said "seemed to prove beyond doubt" because naturally

I immediately suspected that such scenes were deliberately staged in order to trap me, in accordance with the following schema:

a) she hates her husband;
b) she hates the blind in general;
c) I bare my heart to her!

My experience put me on my guard against such an ingenious trap, and the one and only way of getting at the truth was to investigate the genuineness of this resentment of hers. The fact that I considered most convincing was Louise's particular type of blindness: the man had lost his eyesight as an adult, whereas Louise had been blind from birth; and I have already explained that those blind from birth have an implacable hatred of newcomers.

The story of the couple's relations was this: they had met in the Library for the Blind, had fallen in love, and had decided to live together; a series of quarrels then ensued because of his violent jealousy of her, ending in mutual recriminations and terrible fights.

According to Louise, the blind man, Gaston, had no reason to be jealous, for she was truly in love with him: he was a good sort, and had a good head on his shoulders. But gradually he became so madly jealous of her that one day he decided to take his vengeance by tying her to her bed, bringing a woman in, and possessing her in Louise's presence. In the midst of her torment, Louise swore she would get even, and a few days later, as they were leaving their lodgings together (they lived on the fifth floor of a cheap hotel, and in Paris hotels of this sort the elevator is to be used only for going up), when they reached the stairway, she pushed him. Gaston took a terrible tumble all the way down the stairs to the floor below, and as a result of this fall was permanently paralyzed. The one thing that remained intact afterwards was his extraordinarily acute sense of hearing.

Since he was now incapable of communicating with others, being unable either to speak or to write, no one ever suspected what had really happened and everyone believed Louise's version of how Gaston had come to fall down the stairs, a story that seemed entirely plausible given the fact that he was blind. Totally powerless to explain what had really happened, and tortured by the scenes that Louise staged with her lovers as her way of avenging herself, Gaston was like a man imprisoned within a rigid carapace with an army of carnivorous ants devouring his living flesh each time the blind woman moaned in passion there in bed with her lovers in his presence.

Once I was satisfied as to the genuineness of Louise's hatred of Gaston, I tried to find out something more about him, since one night as I was going over the events of the day in my mind, I was overcome by a sudden suspicion: what if this man, before he went blind, had been one of those nameless, audacious, clearsighted, implacable individuals who for thousands of years have been endeavoring to penetrate the forbidden world of the blind? Wasn't it possible that having been blinded by the Sect as the first stage of his punishment, he had then been handed over to the terrible perpetual vengeance of that blind woman once she had succeeded, by order of the Sect, in making him fall in love with her?

I imagined myself for a moment trapped alive inside that carapace, my intelligence unimpaired, my desires perhaps exacerbated, my sense of hearing incredibly acute, listening to that woman who at one time had driven me mad with passion, moaning and howling with her successive lovers. Only the blind could have invented such a torture.

I got up out of bed in a terrible state of agitation. I couldn't sleep all night, and for hours I paced back and forth in my room, smoking and thinking. It was absolutely necessary for me to verify this hypothesis in some way or other. But such an investigation of the Sect would be the most dangerous one that I had thus far undertaken. What I would be trying to discover was to what extent Gaston's martyrdom prefigured my own fate!

When dawn broke, my head was swimming. I took a bath in order to clear my brain and put these wild imaginings in better focus. Once I had calmed down, I said to myself: if that individual was being punished by the Sect, why had the blind woman provided me with this information calculated to arouse precisely this sort of suspicion on my part? Why had she explained to me that she was *punishing* him? She could have, and should have, concealed this fact from me if she wanted to trap me. I would never have tumbled to the real significance of the situation had it not been for this information, for I would not have known otherwise that the man could hear what was going on and hence was tormented by it. Even more important, if the aim of the Sect was to cause me to fall into the blind woman's trap, what need was there to let me see the blind man in that bizarre situation that was bound to arouse my suspicions? On the other hand, I reflected, Domínguez had also gone to bed with that woman in the same circumstances, thus proving that it had nothing to do with my own investigation. This reassured me, but I decided nonetheless to be even more cautious than before.

That very same day, I had recourse to a stratagem that I had already thought of but that until that moment I had refrained from employing: listening at the door. If the blind woman's hatred was genuine, it was likely that when the two of them were alone she would also heap abuse on him.

I went up to the sixth floor in the elevator and then cautiously walked down the stairs to the fifth floor, remaining on each step for five minutes. I eventually reached the door of their room and put my ear to it. I heard Louise's voice and a man's. This immediately struck me as significant, since I knew Louise was expecting me, though admittedly not until an hour later. Would she be capable of being with another man until almost the very moment she expected me to arrive? All I could do was wait and see.

I tiptoed down the hall and waited in a corner, thinking that if anyone passed by that way I would head downstairs and no one would suspect anything. Fortunately there was no one coming in or going out at that hour and I was thus able to wait there till the time Louise had set for me to come, but I did not see a man leave her room. I then thought that some other friend or acquaintance was perhaps chatting with her while she was waiting for me to arrive. In any case, the appointed hour had come, so I went to her door and knocked. Louise came to the door and I went in.

I very nearly fainted!

There was not a soul in the room except the blind woman and the paralytic in his wheelchair.

With my head spinning, it dawned on me what a sinister comedy had been staged for my benefit: a blind man, who was supposedly mute and totally paralyzed, stationed there by the Sect to pose as that bitch's husband so that I would fall into the trap: her hatred of him, the famous crack, the inevitable confession.

I ran out of the room, and then, in a rare moment when my mind was lucid and my memory accurate, I recalled that I had been clever enough not to give my address to anyone; not even Domínguez knew where I was living. And I also suddenly remembered that whether or not he was a real paralytic, the fact that that sinister playactor was undoubtedly blind would prevent him from pursuing me down the stairs.

I rushed across the boulevard with the speed of the wind, entered the Jardin du Luxembourg, ran the entire length of it, and left it at the other end, still running. I caught a taxi there, intending to go by my hotel to pick up my suitcase and flee the country without losing a moment's time. But as I hurriedly made plans for the trip, it occurred to me that even though I had not told a soul where I was living, it was very likely (what am I saying?—it was certain) that the Sect had had someone tailing me from the moment I left Louise's, having foreseen that I would immediately attempt to light out for some other country. What the devil did it matter if I didn't pick up my suitcase? I always carried my passport and my money with me. Even more important: not knowing exactly what might happen to me, my long experience in the course of this investigation had led me to take a precaution that now seemed to me to be a veritable stroke of genius: I had valid visas in my passport for two or three countries. Because, as can readily be imagined, the moment the news of what had happened at the place on the Rue Gay-Lussac got out, the Sect would immediately post a guard at the Argentine consulate so as to follow my trail. Once again, in the midst of all my agitation, I experienced an extraordinary feeling of power, thanks to my foresightedness and my cleverness.

I instructed the taxi driver to take me down the *grands boulevards* and leave me off at the first travel agency we came to. I went in and bought a ticket on the next plane. It occurred to me that I might be followed to the airport, but then I decided that the Sect would be thrown off the trail because they would be expecting me to show up at the consulate first.

And that was how I got out of Paris and flew to Rome.

ↄ৶ 3 1 ৶ↄ

How many stupid mistakes we make when it seems to us that we are applying the most rigorous logic to the situation in which we find ourselves: Our logic is indeed faultless, we reason magnificently well, given premises A, B, and C. The only thing is that we have not taken premise D into account, not to mention E and F and all the rest of the Latin alphabet and the Cyrillic as well. The same mechanism that allows those clever inquisitors, psychoanalysts, to have untroubled minds after having drawn perfectly valid conclusions from the sketchiest of facts.

How many bitter thoughts occupied my mind during that flight to Rome! I tried to see the logic that lay behind my ideas, my theories, the events I had lived through, since we can be certain of the future only if we endeavor to discover the laws of the past.

How many gaps there were in that past! How many careless mistakes! How many naivetés, even yet! It was at that moment that I remembered the Víctor Brauner incident and realized what an equivocal role Domínguez had played in my search. Now, years later, my hypothesis had been confirmed: Domínguez ended up in an insane asylum and committed suicide.

During the flight I recalled the strange story of Víctor Brauner and I also recalled that when I had first met Domínguez again I had asked him about everyone: Breton, Péret, Esteban Francés, Matta, Marcelle Ferry. Everyone except Víctor Brauner. What a revealing "omission"!

I shall recount the story of Brauner, in case my readers are not familiar with it. This painter was obsessed by blindness and in a number of his canvases there are likenesses of men with an eye that has been put out or torn from its socket. There is even a self-portrait in which one of Brauner's eye sockets appears to be empty. And lo and behold, shortly before the war, during an orgy in the studio of one of the Surrealist painters, Domínguez, who'd been drinking heavily, threw a glass at someone; the person he was aiming at stepped aside and it missed him, but it put one of Víctor Brauner's eyes out.

Ask yourselves now whether there is any point in talking about sheer chance, whether sheer chance has any meaning at all in the affairs of men. On the contrary, men move like sleepwalkers toward ends that very often they are aware of only in the form of the vaguest of intuitions, but at the same time they are attracted to them as the moth is drawn to the flame. It was thus that Brauner was drawn to the glass hurled by Domínguez that put one of his eyes out; and it was thus that I was drawn to Domínguez in 1953, not knowing that once again it was my fate that was leading me to him. Of all the persons I might have contacted in that summer of 1953, my one thought had been to look up the man who in some way or other was in the service of the Sect. The rest is obvious: the painting that caught my eye and filled me with terror, the blind model (a model on this one occasion only), the farcical scene that took place as the two of them had intercourse and I watched them from my observation post up in the loft, my coming to be on intimate terms with the blind woman, the drama staged before the paralyzed man in the wheelchair, et cetera.

A word of caution to the naive:

NOTHING HAPPENS BY CHANCE!

And above all a word of caution to those who will read this Report after I am dead and decide to pursue my research and go even further than I was able to. I have had many a hapless precursor: Maupassant (who paid the price for his audacity by going mad), Rimbaud (who despite his fleeing to Africa also ended up a victim of wild delirium —and of gangrene), and so many other nameless heroes we have never heard of whose fate it was to end their days, unknown to anyone in this world, between the four walls of a madhouse, in the torture chambers of political police, asphyxiated in wells, swallowed up by swamp waters, eaten alive by giant ants in Africa, devoured by sharks, castrated and sold to Oriental sultans, or, like myself, destined to die by fire.

From Rome I fled to Egypt, and from there traveled by boat to India. As though Destiny had preceded me and were waiting for me there, I soon found myself in a bordello of blind women! In terror I fled to China and from there I went to San Francisco.

I spent a few quiet months in the pension of an Italian woman named Giovanna and then finally decided to return to Argentina when to all appearances nothing suspect had happened in some time.

Once back in Argentina, having learned my lesson, I kept on the alert, hoping to enter the secret universe by latching on to an acquaintance or a relative who had been blinded by accident.

My readers already know what happened after that: the printer Celestino Iglesias, waiting, the accident, waiting once again, the apartment in Belgrano, and at last the hermetically sealed room where I believed I would meet the end that my destiny had in store for me.

ᖄ 32 ᖄ

I DO NOT KNOW whether it was due to my fatigue, to the long, nerve-racking hours of waiting, or to the stuffy air in the room, but I began little by little to be overcome by drowsiness and finally I fell into a troubled half-sleep, or so it seems to me today, haunted by nightmares that appeared to be endless, mingled with or elaborating upon memories such as the story of the elevator or the Louise episode.

I remember that at a certain moment I thought I was smothering to death, and in desperation I got to my feet, ran to the doors, and began pounding furiously on them. Then I took off my suit coat and finally my shirt as well, because everything seemed like an enormous weight pressing down on me and suffocating me.

Up to this point, I remember everything very clearly.

I do not know, on the other hand, whether it was my pounding on the doors and my shouts that caused them to open the door, revealing the Blind Woman standing there.

I can still see her, a hieratic form outlined in the doorframe, surrounded by a light that seemed vaguely phosphorescent. There was a sort of majesty about her, and from her bearing and above all her face there emanated an irresistible fascination, as though in the doorframe, erect and silent, a serpent had appeared, with its eyes riveted upon me.

I struggled to break this spell that held me paralyzed: it was my intention (an absurd one, doubtless, yet more or less logical if one takes into account the fact that it was my last and only hope) to fling myself upon her, knock her over if necessary, and then find an exit leading to the street and make a run for it. But the fact of the matter was that I could scarcely remain on my feet: a torpor, an enormous exhaustion was gradually overtaking every last one of my muscles, the exhaustion of a sick man suffering an acute attack of fever. And in fact my temples were pounding harder and harder, to the point that at one moment it seemed as though my head were about to explode like a gas storage tank.

I was still just conscious enough, however, to tell myself that if I did not take advantage of this opportunity to make my escape, I would never have another one.

With an immense effort of will I marshaled all my remaining strength and flung myself on the Blind Woman. I shoved her violently aside and rushed into the next room.

∾ 33 ∾

STUMBLING ABOUT in the darkness of this room, I searched for a way out. I opened a door and found myself in another room, even darker than the one I had just been in, where I again knocked over tables and chairs in my desperation. Feeling my way along the walls, I searched for another door, found one, opened it, and again found myself in a dark room, even more pitch black than the one before.

I remember that in the midst of my total mental disarray I thought: "I'm lost." And as though I had used up every last bit of my strength, I sank to the floor, all hope gone: I was surely trapped in a labyrinth that I would never get out of. I must have lain there for several minutes, panting and sweating. "I must not lose my presence of mind," I told myself. I tried to collect my thoughts and suddenly remembered that I had a cigarette lighter with me. I lit it and saw that the room was empty and that it had another door. I went over to it and opened it: it led to a corridor, the end of which I could not see. But what other possibility was there except to venture down it? Moreover, a little reflection sufficed to prove to me that my previous conclusion that I was lost in a labyrinth was obviously a mistaken one, since the Sect would surely not condemn me to such an easy death.

So I made my way down the corridor, slowly and anxiously, since my lighter provided only a very feeble light; moreover I flicked it on for only a few moments at a time in order not to use up the fuel in it too fast.

After some thirty steps, the corridor ended at a stairway leading downward, like the one that I had taken from the very first apartment to the cellar, that is to say a stairway enclosed in metal tubing. It doubtless passed through the apartments or houses and led to the cellars and underground sewers of Buenos Aires. After some thirty feet or so, the stairway was no longer enclosed and passed through vast open spaces that were nonetheless pitch black. They might have been basements or storage rooms, though in the tiny flickering flame of my lighter it was impossible for me to see very far.

∾ 34 ∾

As I DESCENDED I heard the unmistakable sound of running water, thus leading me to believe that I was approaching one of those underground sewers that form an immense, labyrinthine network stretching for thousands and thousands of kilometers beneath the city. In fact I soon ended up in one of those fetid tunnels, at the bottom of which was a rushing torrent of foul-smelling liquid. A light far off in the distance probably indicated the location of a storm drain or a manhole leading up to the street or perhaps the place where this tunnel that I was in joined one of the main sewers. I decided to head in that direction. I had to pick my way along the narrow walkway that runs along the edge of these tunnels, for losing my footing in such a place could be not only indescribably sickening but fatal as well.

Everything was sticky and disgusting. The walls of the tunnel were damp, with little trickles of water running down them, doubtless infiltrations from strata above.

My thoughts had dwelt on this subterranean network more than once in my life, no doubt on account of my tendency to ponder such things as cellars, wells, tunnels, caves, caverns, and everything that in one way or another is related to that enigmatic subterranean reality: lizards, snakes, rats, cockroaches, weasels, and the blind.

The abominable sewers of Buenos Aires! A hideous inferior world, the fatherland of filth! I imagined splendid salons up above, full of beautiful, refined women, of prudent, dignified bank directors, of schoolteachers saying that one mustn't write bad words on walls; I imagined starched white aprons, diaphanous evening dresses of tulle or delicate chiffon, poetic phrases whispered to one's beloved, stirring discourses on civic virtues. Meanwhile here below, in obscene and pestilential tumult, there rushed along, mingled in a single stream, the menstrual blood of those romantic, beloved women, the excrement of those ethereal young girls dressed in tulle and chiffon, the condoms used by dignified bankers, aborted fetuses by the thousands, the remains of meals of millions of homes and restaurants, the immense, the immeasurable Refuse of Buenos Aires.

And everything was heading toward the Nothingness of the ocean by way of secret subterranean conduits, as though Those Up Above wanted to forget, to refuse to recognize the existence of this side of their reality. As though heroes in reverse, such as myself, were condemned by fate to the infernal and accursed labor of bringing this reality to light.

Explorers of Filth, witnesses to Refuse and Bad Thoughts.

Yes, I suddenly felt myself to be a sort of hero, a hero in reverse, a black and repugnant hero, but a hero nonetheless. A sort of Siegfried of darkness, advancing in the shadows and the stink with my black banner whipping in the hurricane blasts of Hell. But advancing toward what? That was what I was unable to discern then, and what, even today, in these moments just before my death, I still am unable to understand.

I finally arrived at what I had thought would be a storm drain, since the feeble light that had helped me make my way along the tunnel was coming from there. But in fact it was the place where the conduit in my tunnel emptied into another much larger one whose waters almost roared as they rushed along. At that spot, far overhead and to one side, was a little opening that I calculated to be about three feet long and approximately ten inches wide. It was impossible even to think of trying to get out through it since it was so narrow and above all so inaccessible. Disappointed, I headed to my right then, so as to follow the much larger sewer that I had now come upon, my thought being that by so doing I would be bound sooner or later to reach the place where it emptied, providing that the stifling, mephitic air didn't cause me to lose consciousness and fall into the filthy current before I got there.

But I could not have walked more than a hundred steps when, to my great joy, I spied a little stone or cement stairway leading up from the narrow walkway that I was so cautiously picking my way along. It was doubtless one of those manholes used by workers when they are obliged to enter these caverns from time to time.

My spirits revived by the very sight of this little stairway, I began climbing up it. After some six or seven steps it turned to the right. I continued on up the stairs for about the same distance and reached a landing leading to a new passageway. I began to walk along it, and finally arrived at another little stairway like the others. But to my vast surprise, it led down instead of up.

I was puzzled and stood there for some time hesitating as to what to do. Should I go back the way I had come till I reached the vast sewer and continue walking along the edge of it till I found a stairway leading up? I was surprised that this new stairway led down, when logically it should have led up. I decided, however, that the previous little stairway going up, the passageway that I had just come through, and this new little stairway going down no doubt formed a sort of bridge passing over a transverse sewer, as in subway stations where there is a transfer point for another line. I thought that in any event if I continued on in the direction I was going, I was bound to come out on the surface some way or other. So I walked on: I went down the new stairway and then followed the passageway that it had led to.

ᨆ 35 ᨆ

THE FARTHER I went along this passageway, the more it resembled a tunnel in a coal mine.

I began to feel a damp cold and then I noticed that I had been walking for some time on ground that was wet, doubtless because of the trickles of water silently flowing down the walls that had become more and more rough and cracked. They were no longer the cement walls of a passageway built by engineers but rather, it appeared, the walls of a tunnel carved out of the very subsoil of the city of Buenos Aires.

There was less and less oxygen in the air, or perhaps this was a subjective impression due to the darkness and the narrowness of the walls hemming me in inside this tunnel that seemed to be endless.

I also noted that the floor of the tunnel was no longer horizontal but rather slanted slowly downward, though not on an even slope, as though the tunnel had been excavated by following the irregularities of the terrain. In other words, it was no longer something planned and constructed by engineers with the aid of suitable machinery; one had the impression, rather, of being in a crude subterranean tunnel dug by men or prehistoric animals who had taken advantage of, or perhaps widened, natural fissures and the beds of underground streams. This impression was borne out by the amount of water in the tunnel; there was more and more of it now, making my progress more and more difficult. At times I waded through mud and mire and then reached sections that were firmer and rockier underfoot. The water was now filtering through the walls in heavier and heavier streams. The tunnel gradually widened out, until I suddenly realized that it was leading to a cavern that must have been immense, for my footsteps echoed as though I were inside a gigantic vault. Unfortunately, with only the feeble light of my cigarette lighter, it was impossible for me to make out precisely how large it was. I also noted a sort of fog, formed not by water vapor but due rather, as a very strong odor seemed to indicate, to the slow spontaneous combustion of some sort of rotten wood.

I had stopped dead in my tracks, intimidated I think by the sheer size of this vast, vague grotto or vault. I could feel the water covering the surface underfoot; not stagnant water however, for it was flowing in a direction that I presumed would lead to one of those underground lakes such as speleologists explore.

The absolute solitude, the impossibility of making out the precise size of this monstrous cavern in which I found myself and the extent of those waters that seemed to me to be immense, the vapor or smoke that was making me dizzy and sick to my stomach all contributed to my anxiety, to the point that it became unbearable. I felt utterly alone in the world and like a sudden flash of lightning the idea crossed my mind that I had descended to its very origins. I felt at once enormously important and utterly insignificant.

I feared that those vapors would sooner or later so intoxicate me that I would fall into the water and drown, at the very moment that I was about to discover the central mystery of existence.

From that moment on I am unable to distinguish between what actually happened to me and what I dreamed or what they made me dream, to the point that I am no longer certain of anything, not even of what I think happened in the years and even the days immediately preceding this, so that today I would even doubt that the entire Iglesias episode ever took place, except that I know for certain that he lost his eyesight in an accident that I myself witnessed. But everything else that happened after this accident I remember with that feverish clarity and intensity that events have in a long and horrendous nightmare: the pension on the Calle Paso, Señora Etchepareborda, the man from the electric company, the emissary who looked like Pierre Fresnay, entering the apartment in Belgrano, the Blind Woman, being trapped in that room waiting for the verdict.

My head began reeling, and being certain that sooner or later I would lose consciousness, I somehow had the good sense to go back to a spot where the water was not as deep, and once there I collapsed in utter exhaustion.

I then heard, in a dream I suppose, the sound of the waters of the little stream called Dead Indian Brook lapping on the stones as it empties into the Arrecifes River, back on our land in Capitán Olmos. I was lying on my back in the meadow, on a summer afternoon, hearing in the distance, far in the distance, the voice of my mother, who as usual was softly humming a song as she bathed in the little stream. This song that I could now hear seemed to be a happy one at first, but then it began to make me more and more anxious: I wanted to understand what she was singing and though I tried desperately to do so I was unable to, and my anxiety became more and more unbearable as the thought possessed me that the words of the song were crucial, a matter of life or death. I woke up shouting: "I can't understand!"

As often happens to us when we awaken from a nightmare, I tried to figure out where I was exactly, what my real situation was. There were many times, even after I was grown up, when I used to think that I was waking up in the room I slept in as a child there in Capitán Olmos, and it would take me long, frightening minutes to come back to reality, to the room where I in fact was, to the present: struggling like a person who is drowning, someone who fears that he will again be swept up by the dark and tumultuous river from which he has just begun to emerge, after painful effort, by clinging to the edges of reality.

And at that moment, when the anxiety brought on by that song or moan had become so severe that it was intolerable, I felt that strange sensation again and tried desperately to hang on to the edges of the reality to which I was awakening. Except that now this reality was even worse: as though I were awakening to a nightmare, so to speak. And my cries, which came back to me in the form of muffled echoes bouncing off the giant vault of the cavern, finally roused me to my true situation. Amid the empty silence and the darkness (my lighter had disappeared in the water when I collapsed on the ground) the words I had cried out on awakening resounded again and again until they died out at last in the distance and the darkness.

When the last echo of my cries had faded away in the silence, I sat there for a long while, completely overwhelmed: it was as though for the first time I was suddenly fully aware of my utter solitude, of the pitch black darkness round about me. Until this moment, or rather until the moment immediately preceding the dream of my childhood, I had been caught up in the vertigo of my investigation, as though irresistibly impelled by mad, unconscious forces; and the fears and even the terror that I had experienced up to that point had been incapable of holding me back; my entire being seemed to have been swept up in a mad dash to the abyss that nothing could stop.

As though it were an illusion, I now remembered the tumult in the world above, the other world, the chaotic Buenos Aires peopled by frenetic windup dolls: all that seemed to me to be a childish phantasmagoria, insubstantial and unreal. Reality was this other one here where I was. And all by myself there, at the very apex of the universe, as I have already explained, I felt at once immensely important and utterly insignificant. I have no idea how long I remained in this sort of stupor.

But the silence was not an unbroken, abstract block; rather, little by little it began to take on that complexity that it acquires when one is surrounded by it for long, anxious stretches of time. And then one notices that it is peopled with little irregularities, with sounds that are imperceptible at first, with indistinct echoes, with odd creaking noises. And as when one gazes patiently at the damp spots on a wall and gradually begins to be able to make out the outlines of faces, of animals, of mythological monsters, so in the vast silence of that cavern my attentive ear little by little discovered meaningful structures and forms: the characteristic murmur of a distant waterfall; the muffled voices of men speaking together cautiously; the whisperings of creatures who were perhaps very close by; mysterious faltering prayers; the cries of night birds. An infinity of sounds and signs, in short, arousing new terrors or absurd hopes. Because just as Leonardo did not invent faces and monsters in damp spots but rather *discovered* them in those labyrinthine redoubts that he frequented, so there was every reason to believe that it was not my anxiety and my terror that made me imagine that I could hear the meaningful sounds of muffled voices, of prayers, of the beating of wings or the cries of giant birds. No, my anxiety, my imagination, my long and terrifying apprenticeship as an investigator of the Sect, the increasing refinement of my senses and the acuteness of my intelligence during my long years of research allowed me to discover voices and malevolent forms that an ordinary person would never have noticed. I had already had my first premonitions of that perverse world in the nightmares and deliriums of my earliest childhood. Everything I did or saw later in the course of my life was related in some way or other to the secret designs of that universe, and facts that meant nothing to ordinary people leapt to my eye, in clear and precise outline, as in those drawings for children where one is supposed to find the dragon hidden among the trees and brooks. And thus, while the other children hurried through the pages of Homer, finding them a bore and reading them only because they were assigned them by their teachers, I felt my first shudder of terror when the poet describes, with frightening power and almost mechanical precision, with the perversity of a connoisseur and violent, vengeful sadism, the moment when Ulysses and his companions run a red-hot stake through the great eye of the Cyclops and make it boil in its socket. Wasn't Homer himself blind? And another day, on opening my mother's big mythology book, my eye chanced to fall on the passage that read: "And I, Tiresias, as punishment for having seen and desired Athena as she was bathing, was struck blind; but the Goddess, taking pity on me, gave me the gift of understanding the speech of birds that prophesy; and that is why I say to you, Oedipus, that you are that man who unwittingly killed his father and married his mother, and for so doing you are to be punished." And as I have never believed in sheer chance, even as a small child, that game, for I believed that Tiresias was merely playing a sort of game, struck me as a prophetic sign. And from that moment on I could not banish Oedipus's terrible end from my mind: putting his own eyes out with a pin after hearing those fateful words that Tiresias had uttered and being present when his mother hanged herself. Nor could I banish from my mind my intimate conviction, that with time became stronger and stronger and more and more well founded, that the blind rule the world, by way of nightmares and fits of delirium, hallucinations, plagues and witches, soothsayers and birds, serpents, and in general, all the monsters of darkness and caverns. It was thus that I was little by little able to make out the abominable world that lay behind appearances. And it was thus that I began to train my senses, exacerbating them through passion and anxiety, hope and fear, so as to be able in the end to see the great forces of darkness as the mystics are able one day to see the god of light and goodness. And I, a mystic of Refuse and Hell, can and must say: BELIEVE IN ME!

Thus, in that vast cavern I spied at last the outskirts of the forbidden world, a world to which few mortals save the blind appear to have had access. They have paid for their discovery with terrible punishments and until today no testimony of theirs concerning this world has ever incontestably reached the hands of men who in the world above continue to live their naive dream, scornfully dismissing any sort of account of this forbidden world or shrugging their shoulders when confronted with signs that ought to have awakened them: a dream, a fleeting vision, a tale told by a child or a madman. And only as a mere pastime have they read the truncated reports of those few who may have succeeded in entering the forbidden world, writers who also ended their lives as madmen or suicides (Artaud, Lautréamont, Rimbaud, to name three) and who therefore have earned only that condescending mixture of admiration and disdain that grownups display toward children.

I could hear, then, invisible beings moving about in the darkness, hordes of huge reptiles, snakes writhing one atop the other in the mud like worms in the decayed dead body of a giant animal; enormous bats, a sort of pterodactyl whose immense heavy wings I could now hear beating, sometimes lightly brushing my body and even my face in a most repulsive way; and men that had ceased to be really human, for either because of their perpetual contact with these subterranean monsters, or because of the necessity of moving continually over swampy terrain, they no longer walked upright but instead crawled along on their bellies through the mud and the filth that accumulated in these caverns. Things that I cannot claim to have seen with my very own eyes (given the eternal darkness that reigns in this world). but I have nonetheless been able to intuit them, thanks to unmistakable signs: a panting, a sort of grunting, a kind of splashing about.

I remained there for a long time, not moving a muscle, divining the repellent life in death that these creatures led.

When I rose to my feet, I felt as though the convolutions of my brain were full of dirt and covered with spider webs.

I stood there for a long time on unsteady legs, not knowing what to do. Finally I realized that I ought to make my way toward the part of this great cavern where it seemed to me I could glimpse a sort of very dim, diffuse light. I understood then how closely linked the words *light* and *hope* must have been in the language of primitive man.

The terrain I crossed to reach this light was uneven: in certain places the water came up to my knees and in others it had made the soil underfoot soggy. Thus it seemed to me to be exactly like the bottom of the lagoons of the pampas that I was familiar with as a child: a slimy, spongy mire. I detoured round the places where the level of the water rose and then continued walking in the direction of that faint far-off light.

ᘀᕀ 36 ᘀᕀ

THE LIGHT GREW brighter as I walked on, and finally I realized that the cavern that I thought I had been in was really an immense amphitheater opening out on a vast plain bathed in a very pale reddish violet light.

When I had come far enough out of the amphitheater for my eyes to be able to take in the whole of that unknown sky, I saw that the faint light was coming from a heavenly body perhaps a hundred times larger than our sun, but whose fading gleam indicated that it was one of those stars close to death which with their last remaining energy bathe the frigid and abandoned planets of their universe with a dim glow similar to the one produced in the darkness of a great silent room by a fireplace in which all the logs have been consumed by the flames and all that is left are a few embers about to go out beneath the ashes; a mysterious reddish glow that in the silence of the night always causes us to lose ourselves in nostalgic and puzzling thoughts: thus transported to the most profound depths of our being, we ponder the past, age-old legends, distant lands, the meaning of life and death, until, almost fast asleep now, we seem to be floating on a lake of vague reveries, drifting on a raft that takes us out onto a deep sea on which crepuscular shadows are descending and whose waters are very nearly stagnant.

A gloomy realm!

Overwhelmed by the desolation and the silence, I stood there motionless for a long time, contemplating that vast expanse.

Toward what seemed to me to be the west, in the deep violet twilight of a stormy but motionless sky, as though a great tempest had been frozen in place by a magic sign, against clouds that looked like tattered strips of cotton soaked with blood, there loomed up strange towers of colossal height, ruined by the ages and perhaps too by the same catastrophe that had devastated that dismal realm. Skeletons of huge beeches, whose spectral ash-colored contours stood out in sharp outline against the blood red clouds, appeared to indicate that a fire sweeping the planet had marked the beginning or the end of this cataclysm.

Amid the towers stood a statue as tall as they. And in its center, at the level of the navel, a phosphorescent beacon sent forth a brilliant beam that I would have sworn blinked on and off, had the death that reigned in that desolate country not been an indication that this blinking light was merely an illusion of my senses.

I was certain that my long pilgrimage would come to an end there, and that perhaps in those forbidden precincts I would finally discover the meaning of my existence.

To the north, this melancholy wasteland was bounded by a lunar mountain range that was at least sixty to ninety thousand feet high. This great *cordillera* was like the spine of a monstrous petrified dragon.

Toward the southern limits of the plain volcanic craters that resembled lunar cirques were clearly visible. Extinct and apparently ice cold now, they extended across the mineral plain all the way to the unknown territory lying to the south. Were these extinct volcanoes the ones whose streams of molten lava had set this country on fire and burned it to a cinder once upon a time?

From where I was standing, rooted to the spot in an utter daze, it was impossible to tell whether the colossal towers (perhaps sacred towers used for unknown rites) were standing all by themselves on the plain or whether, on the contrary, they were standing in the middle of the low-lying dead cities, though from that distance there was no sign of such cities.

The Phosphorescent Eye appeared to be summoning me, and the thought came to me that I was doomed by fate to walk toward the great statue in whose belly the Eye was embedded.

But my heart seemed to have entered a sort of dormant state, like that of reptiles during the long winter months: it was scarcely beating. And I was aware of a dull pain, as though it had shrunk and turned hard at the very sight of that funereal landscape. There was no sound, no voice, no cracking or creaking noise to be heard in that dismal realm, and an indescribable melancholy rose like a fog from that mysterious, desolate country that lay before me.

Could those enormously tall towers really be deserted? For an instant I imagined that in another age they might have been the redoubt of fierce, man-hating giants.

But the Phosphorescent Eye continued to draw me toward it, and little by little that attraction proved stronger than my feelings of utter exhaustion, and at last I began to walk in the direction of the towers.

For a period of time whose duration it is impossible for me to estimate, for the dying star remained in the same position in the stormy firmament, I slowly made my way across the vast silvery plain.

And as I walked on, I could see that there was not a single living thing anywhere, that everything had been burned to cinders by the lava or petrified by the burning ashes that that cosmic cataclysm had rained down aeons ago.

And the closer I came to the towers, the greater their majesty and mystery became. There were twenty-one of them, laid out in a polygon whose perimeter must have been comparable in size to that of Buenos Aires. The stone that they were built of was black, basalt perhaps, and hence they stood out in solemn grandeur above that ashen plain and against that violet sky rent by the ragged purple clouds. And though they were ruined by the ages and the cataclysm, their height was still awesome.

In the center of them I could now make out clearly the statue of a naked goddess in whose belly the Phosphorescent Eye gleamed.

The twenty-one towers seemed to be standing guard round about her.

The statue of the goddess was carved out of ocher-colored stone. Her body was that of a woman, but she had the wings and the head of a vampire, in gleaming black basalt. Her hands and feet ended in powerful talons. The goddess had no face, but where her navel would have been there shone the gigantic eye that had guided and attracted me: this eye might have been an enormous precious stone, a ruby perhaps, but it seemed to me more like the ever-changing reflection of a perpetual inner fire, for its bright glow seemed to be a living thing that in the midst of this gloomy desolation sent a shiver of terror and fascination down my spine.

This was a terrible nocturnal divinity, a demoniacal specter that surely held supreme power over life and death.

As I drew closer to the great polygon enclosing the goddess, the mineral plain began to be strewn with mortal remains: a charred museum of horrors. I saw hydras that had once been alive and were now petrified, idols with yellow eyes in silent abandoned dwellings, goddesses with striped skin like zebras, images of a mute idolatry with indecipherable inscriptions.

It was a country where the one rite celebrated was a petrified Death Ceremony. I suddenly felt so hideously lonely that I cried out in anguish. And in that mineral silence outside of history my cry echoed and reechoed, seemingly down through entire centuries and generations long since gone.

Then silence reigned once again.

I realized then that I must go on to the very end. The eye of the goddess gleamed, unmistakably beckoning me, with sinister majesty.

The twenty-one towers formed the vertices of a polygonal wall, which I approached in stages that became more and more exhausting. And as the distance separating me from this wall diminished, its height became more awesome. When I reached the foot of it and looked upward, I calculated that that apparently impenetrable wall was as tall as a Gothic cathedral. But the towers were probably a hundred times taller.

I *knew* that somewhere in this gigantic perimeter there must be an entrance that would enable me to enter this enclosure. *And perhaps it existed for this sole purpose.* My mind was now as though possessed by the absolute certainty that everything (the towers, the desolate landscape, the enclosure surrounding the goddess, the dying star) had been awaiting my arrival and that it had not been reduced to nothingness only because it had thus been awaiting me. Hence once I succeeded in entering the Eye, everything would vanish, like an age-old simulacrum.

This conviction gave me the strength to go on searching for the entrance until I found it.

And thus, after walking for many exhausting days round and round that colossal perimeter, I finally came upon the door leading inside.

Just inside this door was a narrow stone stairway ascending to the Phosphorescent Eye. I would be obliged to climb thousands of steps. I feared that vertigo and fatigue might get the better of me. But impelled by a fanatic will and sheer desperation, I began my ascent.

For a period of time whose duration I was once again incapable of determining precisely (since the star remained in exactly the same position, illuminating that country outside of time), I mounted the endless steps of that stairway, though my lacerated feet and my pounding heart were a measure of that inhuman effort I made amid the silence of the plain reduced to ashes and strewn with idols and petrified trees, with the great Northern Range of mountains looming up behind me.

No one, absolutely no one, aided me with his prayers or spurred me on by his hatred.

It was a titanic struggle that I *alone* was obliged to wage, amid the stony indifference of nothingness.

The Phosphorescent Eye grew larger and larger as I scaled the endless stairway. And when I stood before it at last, exhaustion and terror forced me to my knees.

I remained in this position for some time.

Then a cavernous, imperious voice that appeared to be coming forth from that Eye said:

Enter now, this is your beginning and your end.

I rose to my feet, and blinded by the brilliant red glow, I entered.

An intense but deceptive brightness, characteristic of phosphorescent light, which blurs the contours of things and causes them to vibrate, illuminated a long, very narrow tunnel leading upward, that I was forced to ascend by crawling on my belly. And that bright glow was coming from the end of this tunnel, as from a mysterious underwater grotto. A glow perhaps being emitted by algae, a luminosity at once phantasmagorical and powerful, resembling the one that on nights in the tropics, sailing over the Sargasso Sea, I had seen as I gazed intently down into the ocean depths. A fluorescent combustion of algae which in that silence of the bottom of the sea illuminate regions peopled by monsters: monsters that come to the surface only in most unusual and terrifying circumstances, thus sowing panic among the crews of ships unfortunate enough to find themselves in their midst, to the point that these seamen sometimes go mad and plunge into the water, so that their abandoned vessels, left to their fate, drift helplessly, mute witnesses to catastrophe, for years, for decades, enigmatic ghost-ships, driven hither and thither by the ocean currents and the winds; until the rains, the typhoons of Oriental waters, the powerful sun of the tropics, the monsoons of the Indian Ocean, and time (simply Time) rot and rend their hulls and their masts, until the entire vessel is eaten away by salt and iodine, by marine funguses and fish; and its last remains finally disappear into the ocean depths, often very close to the same monster that brought on the catastrophe and that for years and years, attentively, malevolently, inexorably, has been contemplating the absurd, senseless peregrinations of the doomed vessel.

Something hideous happened to me as I ascended that slippery, increasingly hot and suffocating tunnel: my body gradually turned into the body of a fish. My limbs slowly metamorphosed into fins and I *felt* my skin gradually become covered over with hard scales.

My fish-body could glide through that opening only with the greatest of difficulty now and I was no longer making my way upward by dint of my own effort, since it was impossible for me even to move my fins: powerful contractions of that narrow tunnel that now seemed made of rubber squeezed me tightly but at the same time carried me upward by virtue of their incredibly strong, irresistible suction, toward the end of the tunnel, bathed in a dazzling light. And then I suddenly lost my fish-consciousness. Vast planetary regions and enormous spans of time were devoured in fury. But in the few seconds that it took to ascend to this Center, there passed before my consciousness a dizzying multitude of faces, catastrophes, countries. I saw beings that appeared to be contemplating each other in terror, I saw clearly scenes of my childhood, mountains of Asia and Africa that I had traversed in the course of my life as a world-wanderer, vengeful birds and animals mocking me, afternoons in the tropics, rats in a barn in Capitán Olmos, dark brothels, madmen shouting fateful words that unfortunately were incomprehensible, women lustfully displaying their gaping vulvas, vultures on the pampas feeding on bloated corpses, windmills on my family's *estancia*, drunkards pawing through a garbage can, and huge black birds diving down with their sharp beaks aimed at my terrified eyes.

I imagine that all this took place in the space of just a few seconds. I then lost consciousness and felt that I was suffocating to death. But then my consciousness seemed to be replaced by a sensation, at once vague and extremely powerful, of having at last entered the great cavern and been swallowed up in its warm, gelatinous, phosphorescent waters.

❧ 37 ❧

I DON'T KNOW how long I remained unconscious. All I know is that when I came to, I had the impression that I had traversed entire zoological eras and descended into the abysses of some fathomless, archaic, unknown ocean.

At first I had no notion of where I was, nor did I remember the long pilgrimage to the Deity or the events that had preceded it. I was lying on my back in a bed; my head felt as heavy as though it were stuffed full of iron, and my clouded eyes could scarcely see: the only thing I could make out was a strange phosphorescence that little by little I realized was the same as that in the Blind Woman's room before I had made my escape. But an invincible torpor prevented me from moving so much as a muscle or even from turning my head from side to side to try to discover where I was. But little by little my memory seemed to reorganize itself, like a communications center after an earthquake, and recollections of my long journey began to come back to me in bits and pieces. Celestino Iglesias, entering the apartment in Belgrano, the passageways, the appearance of the Blind Woman, being trapped in the room, escaping, and finally, the descent to the Deity. I then realized that the phosphorescent light that appeared to bathe the room I was now in was the same as that in the grotto or the belly of the great statue and the same as that seemingly produced in the Blind Woman's room when she had reappeared.

Then that memory, as well as what my eyes little by little discerned on the ceiling and the walls, made me suspect that I was once again in the room of the Blind Woman that I had escaped from, or thought I had escaped from, before. My senses seemed gradually to become as acute as they had been before, and although I did not dare turn my head in the direction of the door, I now had the sensation that the Blind Woman was there in the doorway once again. Since I didn't dare turn my head, I tried to confirm this impression by looking out of the corner of my eye, and even though I was not able to make out any individual details, I glimpsed a woman's hieratic form.

I was in the Blind Woman's room again. And the whole of my pilgrimage through subterranean passages and sewers, my progress through the great cavern, and my final ascent to the Deity had thus been a phantasmagoria conjured up by the magic powers of the Blind Woman or of the entire Sect. Nonetheless, I was reluctant to admit that this was so, for the great devastated plain and those age-old towers and that formidable statue seemed more like a nightmare, whereas my descent into the sewers of Buenos Aires and my journey through the subterranean mire inhabited by monsters had, by contrast, the concreteness and the vividness of detail of something that I had actually experienced. And this led me to believe that the rest too, the journey to the Deity, had not been a dream but a reality. At that moment I had neither sufficient lucidity nor the necessary calm to analyze this impression, but I now think that I really and truly did live all that, and that even if by chance I had never left the Blind Woman's room, her powers had nonetheless caused me to experience everything that I had without moving, as commonly occurs in the magic practiced by primitive cultures; the body sleeps, or appears to sleep, as the soul journeys through distant realms. Hasn't the soul been conceived of as a bird that can fly to far-distant lands? Once it has escaped its prison of flesh and time, it can wing its way upward to a timeless heaven, where there is no *before* or *after* and where the things that are to happen, or will appear to happen, to its own body are already there, for all time, become eternal like statues of Calamity or Misfortune. Hence if every dream is a wandering of the soul through these realms of eternity, every dream, for the person who knows how to interpret it, is a prophecy or a report on what is yet to come. And so it was that on that journey I learned, as Oedipus learned from the lips of Tiresias, the inevitable end that was assigned me.

I felt the woman approach my bed. More than her footsteps, which could barely be heard in that silence, as though she were barefoot, it was my exacerbated senses that told me that this was so. Lying there motionless, as though petrified, staring up at the ceiling, I nonetheless perceived that she was treacherously creeping closer and closer. And closing my eyes, as if to avert the act that was fated to take place, I said to mself: "She is now only three steps from my bed," "she is now only two steps away," "she is right here beside me." I could feel the presence of that creature at the foot of my bed. I didn't want to open my eyes, but I *knew* that she was there waiting, watching me so intently that the suspense was unbearable.

I had the strange sensation that that woman had come to me in response to a mysterious but persistent summons of my own being. I am at a loss even now to explain it: it seemed certain that I was a prisoner of the Sect and that that woman who was now at my side and with whom I would have the darkest and most infernal of copulations was part of, or the beginning of, the Punishment that the Sect had in store for me, but it also seemed certain that it was the end of a long quest that *by my own will* I had slowly, patiently, and deliberately pursued, to the very end, over the space of many years.

It was as though a curious double magnetic attraction had been operating. I had been translated like a sleepwalker to the secret realms of the Sect, yet at the same time it seemed as though for years and years I had projected my most obscure and most intimate powers in order to convoke at last, there in that room in Belgrano, the woman that in a certain sense I had most desired in my life.

A complex sensation, then, at once paralyzed me and intoxicated me: an amalgam of fear and anxiety, of nausea and sensuality. And when I was able at last to open my eyes, I saw that she was standing there naked before me, and from her body there seemed to radiate an electric fluid flowing toward mine and awakening my lust.

How and by what means could that woman be the Punishment that since time immemorial the Sacred Sect had conceived, sadistically prepared, and was now visiting upon me? In terror, and at the same time with a hope that I ought rightly to call black (the hope that must exist in Hell), I saw how that serpent was preparing to lie with me. In the darkness of tropical nights I had seen the ghostly electricity of Saint Elmo's fire sparking forth from the masts of ships; and I could now see that that magnetic fluorescence illuminating the room was emanating in like manner from the tips of her fingers, from her hair, from her eyelashes, from the vibrant tips of her breasts straining like compass needles of burning flesh in the field of the powerful magnet that had drawn them through dark and delirious domains.

A Black Serpent possessed by demons, and yet endowed with a sacred wisdom!

Motionless, as still as a bird beneath the gaze that hypnotizes it, I saw her draw closer, slowly, voluptuously. And when her fingers touched my skin at last, it was like the electric discharge of the Great Black Ray that haunts the ocean depths.

A powerful flash of lightning blinded me, and for an instant I had the dizzying, now-certain revelation: IT WAS SHE! In that fleeting instant my mind was a whirlwind, but now, as I await death, I meditate on the mystery of that incarnation, perhaps similar to the one which, convoked by an imperious desire, takes possession of the body of a medium, with the one difference that it was not only the spirit, but the body as well that took on the traits invoked. And I also wonder whether it was my secret and involuntary will that had patiently called forth that incarnation that the Blind Woman so perversely offered me or whether the Blind Woman and all that Universe of the Blind to which she belonged was, on the contrary, a formidable organization in my service, for my voluptuous pleasure, my passion, and in the end my punishment.

But that instant of lucidity was no more than a lightning flash illuminating the abyss. I then lost all sense of everyday life, all precise memory of my real existence and the consciousness that determines the great and decisive categories within which man must live: Heaven and Hell, good and evil, flesh and the spirit. And time and eternity as well: for I do not know, and shall never know, how long that diabolical carnal union lasted, since in that cavern there was neither light nor dark and everything was a single, infernal long day's journey into night.

I do not doubt now that that being could command the inferior powers; powers that, if they do not create reality, are in any event capable of producing terrible simulacra outside of time and space, or even within them, transforming them, inverting them, deforming them. I witnessed catastrophes and tortures, saw my past and my future (my death), felt my time stop, thus conferring on me a vision of eternity, lived whole geological eras and evolved through entire species: I was man and fish, I was an amphibian, I was a great prehistoric bird. But all this is confused now and it is impossible for me to recall the precise metamorphoses I went through. Nor is there any need to do so, for the same union kept repeating itself again and again, obsessive, monstrous, fascinating, lewd.

I believe I remember a turbulent and torrid landscape of the sort that we imagine covered our planet in archaic periods, with giant ferns everywhere: a cloud-enshrouded, radioactive moon cast its light on a sea of blood licking yellowish shores. Beyond them lay vast stretches of swamp in which there floated the same huge lotuslike flowers as I had seen in my other dream. Like a centaur in heat I galloped across those burning sands, toward a woman with black skin and violet eyes who was waiting for me, howling at the moon. I can still see the mouth and the sex yawning open, blood red, in her coal black sweating body. I entered that idol furiously and had the sensation that it was a volcano of flesh, whose maw was devouring me and whose flaming entrails reached to the center of the earth.

The maw was still dripping with my blood, awaiting the next attack. Like a lustful unicorn I ran through the burning sands toward the black woman, who waited for me, howling at the moon. I crossed lagoons and stinking swamps, black crows took wing, screaming as I passed, and finally I entered the Deity. I again felt that it was a volcano of flesh that was devouring me, and the maw was still dripping blood as it awaited, howling, the next attack.

Then I was a serpent crossing hissing, electric sands. Again wild beasts and birds fled in terror as I passed, and I entered the cavity with savage fury. Once more I felt the volcano of flesh, reaching down to the center of the earth. Then I was a swordfish.

Then an octopus, with eight tentacles that entered the Deity, one by one, and one after the other were devoured by the flesh-volcano.

The Deity howled once more and again awaited my attacks.

I was then a vampire. Thirsting for vengeance and blood, I flung myself in fury on the woman with black skin and violet eyes. I felt the volcano of flesh opening its maw to devour me and felt its entrails reaching down to the center of the earth. And its maw was still dripping with blood as I flung myself upon her once again.

I was then a giant satyr, then a crazed tarantula, then a lewd salamander. And each time I was swallowed up by the furious volcano of seething flesh. Then suddenly a terrible storm broke. Amid flashes of lightning, amid a rain of blood, the Deity with black skin and violet eyes was a sacred prostitute, a cavern and a well, a pythoness and a sacrificial virgin. The hurricane-swept, electric air was filled with screams. On the burning sands, amid a tempest of blood, I was made to satisfy her lust like a magus, like a starving dog, like a minotaur. Only to be devoured yet again. Then I was in turn a fire-bird, a human serpent, a phallic rat. And then I was made to change into a ship with masts of flesh, into a lubricous bell-tower. Only to be devoured yet again. The tempest then became an immense chaos: beasts and gods cohabited with the Deity along with me. The volcano of flesh was then rent to pieces by the horns of minotaurs, voraciously eaten away by giants rats, cruelly devoured by dragons.

Struck by the lightning bolts, that entire archaic realm shuddered, set aflame by the electric flashes, swept by the hurricane of blood. Then the deadly radioactive moon exploded like fireworks: bits and pieces, like cosmic sparks, hurtled through black space, setting forests afire; a great conflagration broke out, and as it raged in fury it brought on the reign of utter destruction and death. Amid dark screams and cries, bloody tatters of flesh crackled and were borne upward. Whole vast domains turned into yawning chasms or great swamps, by which men and beasts alike were swallowed up or eaten alive. Mutilated beings ran about among the ruins. Severed hands, eyes that rolled and bounced like balls, heads without eyes that groped about blindly, legs that ran about separated from their trunks, intestines that twisted round each other like great vines of flesh and filth, moaning uteruses, fetuses abandoned and trampled underfoot by the host of monsters and abominations. The entire Universe collapsed on top of me.

∽ 38 ∽

I HAVE NO WAY of discovering now how long that day lasted. When I woke up (to describe what happened in some way or other) I felt that impassable abysses separated me forever from that nocturnal universe: abysses of space and of time. As blind and deaf as a man rising from the depths of the sea, I emerged into everyday reality once again. I ask myself whether this reality is at last the true one. For as my daytime consciousness recovered its strength and my eyes little by little were able to make out the contours of the world round about me, thus bringing the realization that I was in my room in Villa Devoto, in my one room in Villa Devoto that was so familiar to me, I thought in terror that perhaps another, even more incomprehensible, nightmare was just beginning.

A nightmare that will inevitably end with my death, for I remember the future of blood and fire that it was given me to contemplate in the course of that frenetic magic spell. Strangely enough, no one seems to be pursuing me now. The nightmare of the apartment in Belgrano has ended. I do not know how it is that I am free, here in my own room; no one (it would seem) is keeping watch on me. The Sect must be immeasurably far away.

How did I arrive back home again? How did the blind let me out of that room in the center of a labyrinth? I do not know. But I do know that all of that happened, exactly as I have recounted it. Including—most importantly—that last dark day.

I also know that my days are numbered and that death awaits me. And one thing seems strange and incomprehensible to me: the fact that this death that awaits me will come about because in a certain sense I myself have so willed it, for no one will come looking for me here and I myself will be the one who goes, who *must go*, to the place where the prophecy will be fulfilled.

Cunning, the will to live, desperation have caused me to imagine a thousand ways of fleeing, a thousand ways of escaping my fate. But how can one escape one's own destiny?

I therefore end my Report here, and shall hide it in a place where the Sect cannot find it.

It is midnight. I am going there now.

I know that it will be waiting for me.

PART FOUR

An Unknown God

O<small>N THE NIGHT</small> of June 24, 1955, Martín was unable to sleep. He saw Alejandra again, just as she had looked that first time, approaching him in the park; then suddenly there came back to him, in a chaotic rush, memories of tender or terrible moments he had spent with her; and then, once again, he saw her walking toward him at that first meeting; the fabulous, original image of her. Then at last a heavy, lethargic sleep gradually came over him and his imagination began to wander in the ambiguous realm of dreams. It seemed to him he could hear distant, melancholy bells tolling, and a vague moan, perhaps a cry, whose meaning he could not make out. Gradually it turned into a disconsolate, barely perceptible voice calling his name over and over, as the bells tolled more loudly still, until finally they rang out with real fury. The sky, the sky in the dream, seemed to be lighted now by the blood red glow of a fire. And then he saw Alejandra coming toward him in the red shadows, with her face contorted and her arms reaching out toward him, moving her lips as though in anguish and mutely repeating that call. *Alejandra!*, Martín shouted, his cry waking him from his sleep. When he turned the light on, trembling, he found himself alone in his room.

It was three o'clock in the morning.

He lay there for some time not knowing what to think, what to do. Finally he began getting dressed, and as he did so he became more and more anxious, to the point that he suddenly rushed down into the street and hurried to the Olmoses' house.

And the moment he spied the bright glow of a distant fire against the cloudy sky, not the slightest doubt remained in his mind. Breaking into a desperate run, he managed to reach the house and immediately fainted amid the crowd of onlookers. When he came to again in a neighbor's house, he ran back to the Olmoses', but the police had already removed the dead bodies, and the firemen were now struggling desperately to confine the fire to the Mirador.

Of that night, Martín remembered isolated incidents that bore no connection to each other: the idea that an idiot might have of a catastrophe. But events appeared to have unfolded thus:

Around two in the morning (as he stated later), a man who had been walking down the Calle Patricios to Riachuelo saw smoke. Then it turned out that as usual several people had seen smoke or fire or suspected that something was wrong. An old woman who lived in an adjoining tenement declared: "I don't sleep much, so I smelled the smoke and tried to rouse my son who works at Tamet and sleeps in the same room with me and tell him there was a fire, but he's a sound sleeper and he told me to let him alone"; "and I was right, you see," she added with that pride—Bruno thought—that the majority of human beings, and elderly people in particular, take in having correctly prophesied serious illnesses or fatal catastrophes.

As efforts were being made to put out the fire in the Mirador after the dead bodies of Alejandra and her father had been removed from it, the police carried old Don Pancho out of the house, wrapped in a blanket, sitting there in his wheelchair as always. *And what about the madman? And Justina?* the neighbors watching the fire wondered. But then they saw a man with gray hair and an elongated head in the shape of a dirigible being led out; he had a clarinet in his hand and appeared to be in rather a happy mood. As for the old Indian maidservant, her face was as impassive as always.

There were shouts to clear the street. Some of the neighbors gave the firemen and the police a helping hand, salvaging pieces of furniture and clothing. There was lots of running around, and signs of that euphoria with which people witness catastrophes that momentarily free them from a gray and altogether ordinary existence.

Bruno was unable to ascertain any other fact worthy of mention regarding the events that took place that night.

∾ 2 ∾

THE FOLLOWING afternoon, Esther Milberg telephoned Bruno to tell him that she had just read the police report in *La Razón* (the morning papers had doubtless not had time to include it in their editions). This was the first news that Bruno had had of what had happened: Martín was wandering about the streets of Buenos Aires in a stupor and had not turned up at Bruno's yet.

In the first few moments Bruno had no idea what to do. Then, although there was really no point in it, he hurried to Barracas to see what remained of the fire. A policeman kept him from getting any closer to the house. Bruno asked what had become of old Olmos, the maidservant, the madman. On the basis of what the policeman could tell him and the information he obtained later, he arrived at the conclusion that the Acevedos had hastily taken a number of steps, being indignant at and frightened by the news stories that appeared in the afternoon papers (though not as upset by the events themselves, due to the fact, he supposed, that nothing that that family of madmen and degenerates was responsible for could possibly have surprised them), news stories that made the entire family the object of a wave of scandal and gossip, even though the Acevedos and the Olmoses were only distantly related. As a result the Acevedos, the rich and sensible branch that had always tried to keep the Olmoses, that unsavory branch of the family, out of the limelight (and had succeeded to the point that very few of those who belonged to the best circles of Buenos Aires society were aware that there were still Olmoses around, and above all that they were related to the Acevedos), suddenly found their names linked to scandalous events, thanks to the police reports in the papers specifically mentioning the relationship between the two branches of the family. Hence (so Bruno's thoughts ran) the Acevedos would no doubt have hurriedly taken Don Pancho, Bebe, and even Justina off somewhere, for the express purpose of throwing people off the trail and keeping reporters from exploiting those irresponsible creatures for their own ends. For it was necessary to reject the possibility that the Acevedos had done so out of affection or compassion, knowing as Bruno did the hatred they professed toward these miserable figures who were all that was left of a brilliant past.

That same night when he returned home, he learned from his housekeeper that "that skinny youngster" had come round looking for him, a boy who, according to Pepa's reproachful expression (for she always seemed to hold Bruno responsible for the shortcomings of his friends) was "a lost soul now as well." And that "as well" made him smile amid his horror at what had happened, since it indicated a series of failings that his housekeeper had apparently discovered little by little in poor Martín, which had finally reduced him to that ultimate and wretched state that she summed up in the words "a lost soul," an expression that as it happened was an exact description of the state of mind that Martín was indeed in at the moment: like a child who discovers, in fear and trembling, that he has lost his way in a forest by night. Bruno did not find it at all surprising that Martín had come looking for him. Even though he was a youngster who was extremely reserved, to the point that Bruno had never heard him utter a complete sentence about anything, much less Alejandra, why wouldn't he have come to him, the only person with whom he could unburden himself of some of his anxiety and perhaps find some sort of explanation, consolation, or support? Bruno, of course, had some idea of the relationship that had existed between Martín and Alejandra, not because Alejandra had told him (she was not the kind of person to share confidences of this sort), but rather because of the sort of silent refuge that that youngster had sought with him, because of the few stammered words he had said about Alejandra from time to time, and above all because of that insatiable thirst that lovers have to hear anything at all that might in any way refer to their beloved (though Martín had not been aware that he was questioning or listening to a man who had also felt a sort of love for Alejandra, even though it was the echo or the false and momentary projection of another love, his real love, for Georgina). But despite the fact that Bruno knew or sensed that Martín had been having a certain type of relation with Alejandra (and the expression "a certain type" was inevitable when it was a question of relations with her), he did not know the details of that love-friendship that he had watched develop with amazement, for even though Martín was an exceptional boy in a number of ways, he was really very young still, almost an adolescent, whereas Alejandra, though only a year older than Martín as measured by the calendar, was possessed of experience that was frightening, and seemingly age-old. An amazement that revealed (Bruno told himself) a persistent and apparently inextinguishable naiveté in his own soul, since he knew very well (though he knew it with his intellect, not with his heart) that nothing pertaining to human beings should ever be cause for astonishment, above all because, as Proust said, the "even thoughs" are almost always unknown "whys," and no doubt it was precisely that abyss between their spiritual ages and their experience of the world that explained why a woman like Alejandra should have been drawn to a boy like Martín. This intuition of Bruno's was gradually confirmed after Alejandra's death and the fire, as he heard those confused but maniacal and at times minute details of Martín's relationship with her. Details that were maniacal and minute not because Martín was abnormal or a sort of madman, but because the hallucinatory, hopelessly intricate ways in which Alejandra's mind had always worked forced him to engage in that sort of almost paranoiac analysis: for the pain born of a passion constantly confronted with obstacles, especially mysterious and inexplicable obstacles, is always more than sufficient reason (Bruno thought) to cause the most sensible man to think, feel, and act like someone out of his mind. Naturally Martín did not recount all this when he turned up that first night after Alejandra's death and the fire after wandering all about the streets of Buenos Aires, still stunned by the tragedy and reduced more or less to the mental state of an idiot; but later, in those few days and nights that followed, until the unfortunate idea of turning to Bordenave occurred to him; those days and nights in which he spent hours at Bruno's side, sometimes not saying a word and sometimes talking on and on like a person who has been given an injection of some truth serum; or perhaps, to be more precise, one of those drugs that cause tumultuous and delirious images to come suddenly to the surface from the most profound and most secret regions of the human psyche. And years later too, when Martín would return to Buenos Aires from that remote region in the South and come to see him, out of that eager desire (Bruno thought) that causes men to cling to the last remaining traces of a person whom they have loved a great deal, those last traces of body and soul that the beloved has left behind in the world: in the vague, fragmentary immortality of photographs, of words spoken to others at one time or another, of a certain expression that someone remembers, or says he remembers, and even of those small objects that take on an inordinate symbolic value (a little box of matches, a ticket to a movie theater); objects or words that then bring about the miracle of giving that spirit a fleeting, intangible, though despairingly real presence, just as a fond memory is brought back by a breath of perfume or a snatch of music, a fragment that need not be important or profound and may indeed even be an unpretentious and even banal melody that made us laugh in those magic days because it was so vulgar, but that now, ennobled by death and eternal separation, seems moving and profound to us.

"Because"—Martín had said to him on his return from the South, raising his head for an instant as he stubbornly looked down at the floor, that typical pose of his that went back to his youth and no doubt his childhood and would never change, one of those poses that, like our fingerprints, are with us till we die—"because you loved her too, didn't you?"

A conclusion that—at long last!—he appeared to have arrived at there in the South, during endless nights of silent meditation. And Bruno had merely shrugged his shoulders and said nothing. What could he have said? And how could he have explained to him about Georgina and that sort of mirage of his childhood? Moreover, he wasn't even certain that it was true, true in the sense at least that Martín might imgine. He had therefore said nothing in reply and merely looked at Martín equivocally, thinking that after several years of silence and remoteness from civilization, years of reflection in those lonely expanses, that stoic youngster still needed to tell his story to someone; and because he still—still!—hoped perhaps to find the key to that tragic and marvelous lack of understanding between him and Alejandra, out of that anxious but ingenuous need that human beings have to find that presumed key, even though in all probability, if such a key in fact exists, it is as vague and mysterious as the very events that it is meant to explain. But on that first night following the fire, Martín seemed like a shipwreck victim who had lost his memory. He had wandered aimlessly about the streets of Buenos Aires and even when he finally found himself in Bruno's presence he had no idea what to say to him. He saw Bruno there in front of him, smoking, waiting, looking at him, understanding him, but what could he say? Alejandra was dead, dead beyond question, having suffered a horrible death by fire, and everything was pointless and more or less unreal. And when he eventually decided to leave, Bruno took him by the arm and said something to him that he did not altogether understand or that in any case he found it impossible to remember later. Then once he was out on the street again, he began wandering about like a sleepwalker once more, returning to those places where it seemed to him that Alejandra might suddenly appear at any moment.

But little by little Bruno began learning things, in bits and pieces, in the course of other meetings with Martín, absurd visits that at times were unbearable. Martín would suddenly begin talking like an automaton, babbling disjointed phrases, seemingly searching for some sort of precious trace left in the sands of a beach that have been swept

clean by a violent wind blowing off the sea. Fragile footprints of
phantoms. He was searching for the key, the hidden meaning. And
Bruno might know, he *had* to know: Hadn't he known the Olmoses
since his childhood? Hadn't he practically seen Alejandra come into
the world? Hadn't he been a friend of Fernando's or something of
the sort? Because he, Martín, was at a loss to understand any of it:
Alejandra's absences, those peculiar friends of hers, Fernando—what
did they all mean? And all Bruno did was look at him, understand
him, and doubtless pity him. Bruno learned the most crucial facts
when Martín returned from that remote region where he had buried
himself, when time seemed to have caused that pain to settle in the
very bottom of his soul, a pain that seemed to begin to disturb and
agitate him and cloud his mind from the moment he was once again
confronted with people and things that were indissolubly connected
with the tragedy. And even though by this time Alejandra's flesh
had rotted and turned to dust, that youngster, who had reached full
manhood now, nonetheless continued to be obsessed by his love, and
there was no way of knowing how many years (until his death, most
likely) he would continue to be thus obsessed; this, in Bruno's opinion,
constituted a sort of proof of the immortality of the soul.

Martín "had" to know, Bruno said to himself with melancholy
irony. Of course he "knew." But how much did he know? And what
sort of knowledge was it? For what do we really know about the
ultimate mystery of human beings, even those who have been closest
to us? He remembered Martín on that first night there at his place;
he was reminded of one of those youngsters whose photographs appear in the papers after earthquakes or train derailments in the night,
sitting on a bundle of clothes or a pile of debris, with dim, dull eyes,
grown suddenly old by virtue of that power that catastrophes have
to wreak upon a human being's body and soul, in a few hours, the
devastation that ordinarily is brought on slowly by the years, illnesses,
disappointments, and deaths. Then Bruno superimposed upon that
desolate image other later ones, in which Martín resembled those
wounded veterans who with time rise from their own ruins, with
the aid of crutches, far away now from the war in which they nearly
lost their lives, but no longer what they once were, since the experience
of horror and death now weighs heavily upon them forevermore.
Bruno would see Martín there before him, his arms hanging limply

at his sides, his eyes riveted on a point usually located behind and to the right of Bruno's head, seemingly probing his memory with silent, painful cruelty, like a man mortally wounded trying to remove, with infinite care, the poisoned arrow from his torn flesh. "How lonely he is," Bruno would think then.

"I don't know anything. I don't understand anything," Martín burst out all of a sudden. "What I had with Alejandra was..."

And he left the sentence unfinished, as he raised his bowed head and finally looked at Bruno with eyes that seemed not to see him.

"And yet...," he stammered, stubbornly and anxiously searching for words, though fearing that he would be unable to communicate the precise nature of "what I had with Alejandra"; a phrase that Bruno, being twenty-five years older, could easily complete: "What I had with Alejandra was at once marvelous and disastrous."

"You know...," Martín murmured, clenching his fingers painfully, "my relations with her were not at all clear.... I never understood..."

He took out his famous white penknife, examined it, opened the blade.

"Lots of times I thought it was like a series of powder flashes, of..."

He searched for an exact comparison.

"Like explosions of gasoline, that's it... like gasoline explosions on a dark night, a stormy night..."

His eyes stared at Bruno again, but undoubtedly they were gazing toward his own inner world, obsessed by that vision.

It was at this point during his visit that he added, after a thoughtful pause:

"Even though at times... very few times, it's true... it seemed to me that she found a sort of respite when she was with me."

A respite (Bruno thought) like the one soldiers find in a foxhole or an improvised refuge as they advance across a dark, unknown no-man's-land amid an inferno of machine gun fire.

"Yet I wouldn't be able to say exactly what sort of feelings..."

Martín raised his eyes again, but really looking at him this time, as though asking him for a key, but as Bruno said nothing, he lowered his gaze once again, examining the white penknife.

"Of course," he murmured, "it couldn't have lasted. It was like in wartime, when one lives from moment to moment...I suppose... because the future is never certain, and always awful."

Then he explained to Bruno that the signs of impending catastrophe had already begun to appear in the very midst of that frenzy, just as it is possible to imagine what is about to happen when one is on a train in which the engineer has gone mad. It made him uneasy, but at the same time it attracted him. He looked at Bruno again.

And then Bruno, simply to be saying something, to break the silence, said:

"Yes, I understand."

But what did he understand? What?

∾ 3 ∾

FERNANDO'S DEATH (Bruno said to me) has made me ponder not only his life but my own, thereby revealing in what way and to what degree my own existence, like that of Georgina, like that of many men and women, was thrown into upheaval by Fernando's.

People keep asking me, pressing me for details: "You who knew him intimately...," they say. But the words *knew* and *intimately* are little short of ridiculous when applied to Vidal. It is quite true that I was close at hand at three or four decisive periods in his life and that I knew one side of his personality: that side which, like one face of the moon, was turned toward us. It is also quite true that I have certain theories about his death, theories that I nonetheless do not feel inclined to reveal to others, for it is more than likely that any theory one has about him is totally mistaken.

I was (physically) close to Fernando at several periods in his life, as I have already said: during our childhood in Capitán Olmos, till 1923; two years later, in the Barracas house, after his mother had died and his grandfather had brought him there; then again in 1930, when we were adolescents, in the anarchist movement; and finally, in the fleeting encounters we had in recent years. But in this last period he was already someone completely outside my life, and in a certain sense completely outside everyone's life (though not Alejandra's, of course). He was already what is rightly called an alienated man, or one that could be so called, a stranger to everything that we consider, perhaps naively, to be "the world." And I still remember that day not long ago that I spied him making his way down the Calle Reconquista like a sleepwalker. He seemed not to see me, or pretended not to see me (these two possibilities being equally likely in his case), even though we had not laid eyes on each other for more than twenty years at the time and a normal person would have had any number of reasons to stop and talk with me. And if he did see me, as is possible, why did he pretend not to see me? Since it's Vidal we're talking about, it's impossible for me to give you any clearcut answer. One of the possibilities is that he was going through one of his periods of persecution mania, so that he might well have done his best to avoid me—not despite the fact that I was an old acquaintance, but indeed for that very reason.

But vast stretches of his life are a closed book to me. I know, of course, that he visited many countries, although if one is talking about Fernando, it would be closer to the truth to say that he "fled" through many countries. There are traces of these travels, these explorations. There are bits and pieces of information about his passage here or there, that came to light through people who saw him or heard stories about him: Lea Lublin met him once in the Dôme in Paris; Castagnino saw him eating in a trattoria near the Piazza di Spagna in Rome, though the moment Vidal realized that he had been recognized he ducked behind a newspaper and pretended to be reading it with all the concentration of someone who is very nearsighted. Bayce confirmed a paragraph in Vidal's "Report on the Blind": he had indeed met him in the Tupi-Nambá Café in Montevideo. And that is all. Because we have no sort of detailed or coherent picture of his travels in general, not to mention those far-ranging expeditions of his to the islands in the South Pacific or Tibet. Gonzalo Rojas informed me that he was once told about an Argentine "of such and such a description" who had been going around Valparaíso making inquiries as to the possibility of taking passage on a schooner that periodically called at Juan Fernández Island; by putting together this bit of information and what I knew about his life, the two of us arrived at the conclusion that the Argentine in question was Fernando Vidal. But why would he have wanted to go to Juan Fernández? We know that he had connections with spiritualists and people who dabble in black magic, but the testimony of individuals of this sort must be regarded as dubious at best. Of all these mysterious episodes, the only one that may perhaps be taken to be fact was his meeting with Gurdjieff in Paris, and this we are fairly certain of because of the fistfight he had with him that led to a run-in with the police which went on record. You may point out to me that we have his memoirs, the famous Report. In my opinion we cannot take it to be an objective document, a series of photographs of events that actually happened, so to speak, though there is good reason to regard it as being authentic in a more profound sense. This Report would seem to be an account of his moments of hallucination and delirium, moments which strictly speaking comprised almost the whole of the final period of his life, those moments in which he sequestered himself somewhere or disappeared from sight. On reading these pages I have the sudden impression that Vidal was someone sinking into the depths of Hell, waving his handkerchief to bid us goodbye, and delivering himself of delirious, mocking words of farewell, or desperate appeals for help perhaps, disguised and concealed by his arrogance and his hauteur.

I am endeavoring to recount this whole story to you from the beginning, but I find myself impelled again and again to speak only in generalities. Indeed, it is impossible for me to entertain a single important thought about my own life that does not in some way have something to do with Fernando's tumultuous existence. His spirit continues to dominate mine, even after his death. To me this is of no moment: it is not my intention to shield myself from his ideas, those ideas that made and unmade my life, though not his: like those experts who know everything there is to know about explosives and can both arm a bomb and defuse one with no risk whatsoever to themselves. I shall thus forbear henceforth from pondering whatever scruples I may have on the subject, and from engaging in reflections of this sort that are quite beside the point. Moreover, I consider myself to be fair-minded enough to concede that he was superior to me. My respect for him was only natural, to the point that I feel relief and a certain pleasure in recognizing that fact. Nonetheless I was never fond of him, though frequently I admired him. I detested him, yet I was never indifferent to him. He was not one of those beings whom we can watch pass our way with indifference: he instantly attracted us or repelled us, and usually both things at once. He possessed a sort of magnetic power, which could be either one of attraction or of repulsion, and when contemplative or hesitant persons such as myself entered his field, they were driven this way and that, like little compass needles entering regions disturbed by magnetic storms. And in addition to all this, he was an individual whose moods were constantly shifting, ranging unpredictably from the heights of enthusiasm to the depths of depression. This was but one of his hundred contradictions. He was capable of reasoning with an iron logic one minute, and the next he would turn into a madman who, though still seemingly arguing with the greatest rigor, would arrive at the most incredible absurdities, which nonetheless struck him as normal and valid conclusions. One minute he would take great pleasure in conversing brilliantly, and then suddenly he would turn into a haughty loner off in a corner whom no one would have dared say a word to. I have mentioned, I believe, the word *lustful* as being one of those that might characterize his nature; yet at certain moments of his life he would suddenly give himself over entirely to an extremely rigorous asceticism. At times he was quiet and con- templative; at others he would be caught up in frantic activity. I have seen him, as a child in Capitán Olmos, visit acts of hideous cruelty on defenseless animals and then display a totally incompatible tenderness toward them. Was he putting on some sort of show for my benefit, moved to do so by the irony, the cynicism that was also part of his nature? I have no idea. There were moments in which he appeared to admire himself with a narcissism that was absolutely dis- gusting, and the next moment he would be delivering himself of the most scornful opinions concerning himself. He would defend Latin America and then laugh at those scholars who have set great value on our way of life in the New World. Yet when someone, swept along by Fernando's epigrams or sarcasms aimed at one or another of our notables, added some minuscule contribution of his own, he was immediately annihilated by a withering irony aimed in his direction. Fernando was the precise opposite, in short, of what we take a well- balanced person to be, or simply what we consider a person to be, if what differentiates a person from a mere individual like countless others is a certain consistency, a certain constancy and coherency of ideas and feelings. There was no sort of coherency in him, save that of his obsessions, which were thoroughgoing and permanent. He was the diametrical opposite of a philosopher, of one of those men who think and develop a system as a harmonious construct; he was a sort of terrorist of ideas, an antiphilosopher. Nor did his face always appear to be the same face. The truth is that I always thought that several different persons dwelt within him. And despite the fact that he was no doubt a scoundrel, I would venture to say that he nonetheless possessed a certain sort of purity, though it may well have been an infernal sort. He was a kind of saint of Hell. I once heard him say in fact that in Hell, as in Heaven, there are many hierarchies, ranging from mere average sinners (the petty bourgeois of Hell, he said) to the enormously wicked and desperate, the black monsters privileged to sit at the right hand of Satan; and it is possible that without saying so explicitly he was at that moment expressing an opinion as to his own true condition.

Madmen, like geniuses, rise up in revolt against the limitations of their native land or their time, with results that are frequently catastrophic as they enter that absurd and magic, delirious and tumultuous no-man's-land that upright citizens contemplate with mixed feelings, ranging from fear to hatred, from apparent scorn to a sort of awed admiration. And yet these exceptional individuals, these men who live outside the law and outside their fatherland still retain, in my opinion, many of the attributes of the country in which they were born and of the men who until yesterday were their fellows, although these attributes are as though deformed by the distorting lenses and badly focused enlargers of a monstrous system of projection. What other sort of madman could Don Quixote possibly have been save a Spanish madman? And though his extraordinary stature and his madness universalize him and somehow make him comprehensible and admirable in the eyes of everyone in the world, he possesses certain traits that could only come into being in that country at once as cruelly realistic and magically absurd as Spain is. And despite everything there was a great deal that was typically Argentine in Fernando Vidal. A large part of his contradictions were, of course, a consequence of his own particular nature, of his sick heredity, and might have manifested themselves in any corner of the globe. But I am convinced that others were a product of his being Argentine, a certain type of Argentine. And though he belonged, on his mother's side, to an old family, he nonetheless was not, as might be supposed, the pure and simple expression of what is nowadays called the national oligarchy, or at least he did not have those peculiarities that the man in the street expects to find in such persons, in the same way, and with the same superficiality, that he invariably imagines all British to be phlegmatic and is comically disconcerted when he is reminded of the existence of individuals such as Churchill. It is true that those variations that made Vidal depart from the norm could have stemmed on the one hand from his heredity on his father's side and on the other hand from the fact that the Olmos family was a bit eccentric and empty-headed (although this too is a genuine national characteristic in many old families). This family on the decline gave the impression of being made up of ghosts or absentminded sleepwalkers, amid a cruel reality that they neither felt nor heard nor understood; curiously, and even comically, this immediately gave them the paradoxical advantage of being able to pass through the extremely solid wall of reality as though it did not exist. But Fernando did not resemble this family at all, since he possessed, if only in spurts, in furious bursts, a frenetic energy, though this energy was invariably used to negate or to destroy, this being a trait he had no doubt inherited from his father, a lesser spirit yet one possessed of a dark and violent streak that he had passed on to his son; Fernando, it must be said, hated his father and refused to recognize him because of the very fact that he discovered within himself the attributes of this man whom he hated so passionately and whom he had tried to poison when he, Fernando, was a child. This infusion of the Vidal blood in the old Olmos family produced a violent reaction in Fernando's case, and later in Alejandra's, as happens, I believe, with certain sick or weak plants when harmful external stimuli cause cancers to develop that eventually take over and finally kill the entire plant thanks to their monstrous vitality. That is what happened with that old-line Olmos stock, so generous and so pitifully ridiculous in their absolute lack of realism—to the incredible point of going on living in the old house, in what remained of Barracas, where their forebears had had their *quinta* and where, shut up in the last miserable bits and pieces of that *quinta*, they now lived out their lives surrounded by factories and tenements, and where the great-grandfather dozed, dreaming nostalgically of the old virtues, swept away forever by the hard days of our era, just as a chaotic din swallows up a soft, innocent ballad of another time.

I too, in my own way, had been in love with Alejandra, until I realized that it was her mother, Georgina, whom I loved, and who, on rejecting me, threw me into her daughter's arms. Time made me realize my mistake, and I then returned to my first (and futile) passion; a passion that I imagine will linger on till Georgina dies, as long as I have the least hope of having her at my side. Because, though this may surprise you, she is still alive, not dead as Alejandra believed ... or pretended to believe. Alejandra had many reasons to hate her mother, given Georgina's temperament and her conception of the world, and many reasons for wishing she were dead. But I hasten to assure you that, despite what you might suppose after all this, Georgina is a profoundly good and kind woman, incapable of hurting anyone, especially her daughter. Why then did Alejandra hate her so and why had she mentally killed her off ever since her childhood? And why did Georgina live far away from her and far away from all the Olmoses in general? I don't know if I can give you any satisfactory answers to these questions and others that may well continue to arise with respect to this family that has weighed so heavily in the balance of my life, and now the life of that youngster. I confess that I had intended to say nothing to you about my love for Georgina, because ... well ... let us say because I am not one to talk of my personal trials and tribulations. But I now realize that it would be impossible to shed light on certain aspects of Fernando's personality without telling you something about Georgina, if only a few brief details. Have I already mentioned that she was Fernando's cousin? Yes, she was the daughter of Patricio Olmos, and the sister of Bebe, the madman with the clarinet. And Ana María, Fernando's mother, was Patricio Olmos's sister, do you follow me? So Fernando and Georgina were first cousins. Moreover—and this is something that is highly significant—Georgina bore an amazing resemblance to Ana María: they not only had the same physical features, as was the case with Alejandra too, but also and even more importantly, the same traits of character: she was something like the quintessence of the Olmos family, without the taint of the violent and evil Vidal blood, refined, kindhearted, timid, and a bit dreamy, with a delicate and profoundly feminine sensibility. And as for her relations with Fernando...

Let us imagine ourselves in a theater, seeing a beautiful woman on the stage whose serious expression, discreet charm, and self-composure attract us. But she is serving as a medium or a subject for an experiment in hypnotism or thought transference being carried out by a powerful, evil-looking man. We have all attended such a spectacle at one time or another and we have all observed how the woman automatically obeys the orders or even the merest glance of the hypnotizer. We have all noted the empty gaze, a bit like a blind man's, of those subjected to such an experiment. Let us imagine that we feel an irresistible attraction for this woman and that during the intervals when she is awake or fully conscious she gives signs of being favorably inclined toward us. But what can we do when she is in the power of the hypnotizer? We can only feel sadness and despair.

That was what happened to me with Georgina. And only at a few exceptional moments did that evil force appear to loosen its hold on her, and then (O marvelous, fragile, fleeting moments!) she would lean her head on my breast, weeping. But how precarious those instants of happiness were! She would soon fall under that baneful spell once again and then there was nothing to be done. I could wave my hands in front of her eyes, talk to her, take her by the arm, but she did not see me or hear me or feel my touch in any way.

And did Fernando love her? And if so, in what way? I could not say for certain. In the first place, I believe he never really loved anyone. Moreover, he was so aware of his superiority that he was never jealous; at most, when he saw a man hovering about her, he would merely make some almost imperceptible sarcastic or scornful gesture. He was well aware that a very slight movement on his part was quite enough to put an end then and there to the least inclination she might be beginning to feel for the man, as a mere flick of a finger is sufficient to cause the sudden collapse of a house of cards that one has been laboriously constructing with bated breath. And she appeared to eagerly await this gesture on Fernando's part, as though it were his greatest expression of love.

He was invulnerable. I remember, for example, when he married. Ah, of course: you naturally didn't know that. And that too will no doubt surprise you. Not only the fact that he married but the fact that he did not marry his cousin. In reality, when one thinks about it, it would have been almost inconceivable for him to have done so, and if he had it would have been a real surprise. No: he had intimate relations with Georgina in secret, since at the time he was not allowed to set foot in the Olmoses' house, and I have no doubt that despite his extremely kindhearted nature Don Patricio would have killed him. And when Georgina had her baby girl...well, it would take me a long time to explain everything, and moreover there would be no point in it, so perhaps I need merely say that she left home; more than anything out of timidity and shame, since neither Don Patricio nor his wife María Elena was capable of dealing with her fall from virtue in a crude or crass way; but she left nonetheless, disappearing shortly before Alejandra was born, and I might almost be tempted to say that the earth swallowed her up, as the expression goes. In any event Georgina abandoned Alejandra when the little girl was ten years old. Alejandra then went to live with her grandparents in the Barracas house, and Georgina never went back there, but all of this would take me too far afield if I were to tell you the whole story in detail, but perhaps you can understand it in part if you recall what I have already told you about the hatred, the deadly, mounting hatred that Alejandra felt toward her mother as she grew up. So I'll go back to what I was telling you about before: Fernando's marriage. It might come as a surprise to anyone that a nihilist like Fernando, that moral terrorist who felt nothing but scorn for any sort of bourgeois ideas or feelings, could go so far as to actually get married. But he would be much more surprised if he knew how Fernando came to do so, and who his bride was...a sixteen-year-old girl, a very pretty one, and one with a large fortune. Fernando had a penchant for beautiful, sensual women, while at the same time he felt enormous contempt for them; but he was even more attracted to them if they were still of very tender years. I don't know the details because I never used to see him in those days; and even if I had spent time in his company, I would not have known much more, for he was a man capable of living quite comfortably on two or more entirely different planes at once. But I heard talk here and there, bits of gossip that must have had some truth behind them, an unsavory truth of course, as was invariably the case with all of Fernando's ideas and actions. People told me, naturally, that Fernando had his eye on the girl's fortune, that she was a young thing who was completely dazzled by that consummate actor. They added that he had had an affair (some said it had been before the marriage and others that he had gone on with it both during and after the marriage) with her mother, a Polish Jew around forty with intellectual pretentions, who did not get on well with her husband, a certain Szenfeld who was the owner of several textile mills. Rumor had it that while Fernando was having this affair with the mother, the daughter got pregnant and so "he had to marry the girl," a phrase that really made me laugh when I heard it, since it is utterly absurd to think of Fernando of all people feeling any such moral obligation. Certain informants, who considered themselves more reliable sources than others because they played canasta in the house in San Isidro, maintained that there had been stormy scenes between the actors in that grotesque comedy, scenes full of raging jealousy and violent threats, and that—and this too struck me as particularly amusing—Fernando then maintained that he could not marry Señora Szenfeld, even if she got a divorce, because he belonged to an old Catholic family, and that he was duty-bound, on the other hand, to marry the daughter with whom he had had intimate relations.

As you may suppose, to anyone who knew Fernando, as I did, these stories that were being whispered about were merely the source of a sort of regretful amusement, though of course there was a certain amount of truth to them, as is always the case with even the most fantastic tales. There were some things however that were demonstrable facts: Fernando did indeed marry a Jewish girl sixteen years old; for a couple of years he lived in a splendid house in Martínez that had been bought and given him as a gift by Señor Szenfeld; he soon squandered the money that he doubtless came into by marrying the girl, and finally the house too went down the drain, whereupon he abandoned her.

These are facts.

As for interpretations of these facts and rumors that made the rounds, they would require close analysis. Perhaps it would not be out of place for me to tell you what *I* think, since these episodes shed some light on Fernando's personality, though admittedly it is not much more than the light that can be shed on the essence of the devil by learning of some of his tragicomic treacheries. Curious: this is the first time the word *tragicomic* has come to my mind in connection with Fernando's personality, but I think it corresponds to the truth. Fernando was basically a tragic figure, but there are moments in his life that border on the humorous, though it is a black humor. In the course of those turbulent events surrounding his marriage he must surely have given vent to one of his fits of black humor and put on one of those infernal comic spectacles in which he took such delight. That phrase reported by the lady canasta players, for example, that phrase about his family's Catholicism and the impossibility of his marrying a divorcée. A doubly grotesque phrase, because in addition to coming out with it in order to poke fun at the Catholicism of his family and Catholicism in general, and everyone and everybody and any and every moral principle or basic foundation of society, he uttered it to the mother of the girl with whom he was also having intimate relations at the time. This way of mixing the "respectable" and the indecent was one of Fernando's specialties. The words, for instance, that he is rumored to have uttered so as to be able to keep the splendid house in Martínez for himself: "She has abandoned her home and fireside," when in actual fact his young wife must have fled it in terror, or what is even more likely, was forced out of it thanks to some diabolical trick of Fernando's. One of his favorite pastimes was to bring women who were obviously his mistresses home with him, persuading his young bride (his powers of persuasion were very nearly unlimited) to receive them and entertain them; but no doubt he gradually stepped up the experiment so that she would get more and more tired of the whole thing and finally flee the house, which was what Fernando was hoping for. How the property happened to remain in his hands I do not know; but I suppose he must have been clever enough to arrange things with the mother (who still loved him and hence was jealous of her daughter) and with Señor Szenfeld. How the latter could have become friends with someone rumored to be his wife's lover, how that friendship or the weakness of a man as sharp as a lynx in business could have reached such a point that he gave a luxurious house as an outright gift to an individual who was not only his wife's lover but was also making his daughter miserable will always be one of the mysteries surrounding Vidal's enigmatic personality. But I am convinced that in order to achieve such ends Fernando must have brought off some very subtle scheme, not unlike those successfully perpetrated by Machiavellian heads of government against opposition parties that have fallen out with each other. What I think happened is this: Szenfeld hated his wife, who not only cuckolded him with Fernando but also with a partner of her husband's named Shapiro before Fernando appeared on the scene. Szenfeld must have felt great satisfaction on discovering that at last someone had humiliated and wounded that self-important woman who so often showed nothing but contempt for him; and it was doubtless only a short step from that heartfelt satisfaction to admiration and even affection for Fernando, helped along by the latter's talent for utterly charming a person when he set his mind to it, a talent that was furthered by his total lack of sincerity and honesty. For sincere and honest persons, by allowing themselves to show in their friendships frank signs of displeasure at the thousand and one minor annoyances that inevitably create momentary resentment between human beings, even the best of them, never manage to produce those miracles of unfailing charm that lie within the powers of cynics and liars; through the same mechanism, in a word, by virtue of which a lie is always more pleasing to people than the truth, since the truth concerning even those beings closest to perfection whom we would most like to please and satisfy inevitably has its ugly side inasmuch as even they have their imperfections. Moreover, Señor Szenfeld's satisfaction was no doubt all the greater on seeing that his wife's sufferings stemmed from feelings of hurt pride having to do with her age, since Fernando was being unfaithful to her by sleeping with a beautiful girl much younger than herself. And finally (a factor that may also have entered the picture), Szenfeld may perhaps have felt great satisfaction because in this entire affair it was not he, Szenfeld, who came out the loser, since in any case his status as a cuckolded husband had been established previously, but rather Señor Shapiro, who, being the cuckolder, probably had a sense of pride that was much keener, but at the same time more vulnerable, than Señor Szenfeld's. And Shapiro's defeat in this area, which was the only one in which he was superior to his partner (for Szenfeld, whatever his shortcomings as a husband might have been, was by common consensus as cunning as a lynx when it came to business), placed him in such a humiliating position that by contrast Szenfeld's strengths were enhanced and his energies renewed. And this was surely how matters had gone, for not only did the textile firms suddenly embark on new and daring ventures, but following Fernando's marriage, Szenfeld's almost protective solicitude toward his partner in the presence of third parties was evident.

As for Georgina, I will tell you something about her that is quite typical of her. Fernando's marriage took place in '51. At about that time I met Georgina in the Calle Maipú, near the Avenida; something quite unexpected since she very rarely came downtown. At forty, her beauty had faded and she looked much older; she had an air of sadness about her and was quieter than ever; though she had always been reserved and not at all talkative, I found her silence at that moment almost unbearable. As always, I was overcome with emotion. Where had she been hiding herself all these years? In what absurd places was she secretly living out the drama of her life? What had she been doing all this time, what had she been thinking and suffering? I would have liked to ask her all this, but I knew that it was useless; while it was extremely difficult to drag any sort of conversation out of her, it was completely impossible to get her to answer any questions having to do with her personal life. Georgina always seemed to me to resemble those houses that one comes across in remote sections of the city, silent houses whose doors and windows are almost always closed, houses inhabited by enigmatic adults: two brothers who have never married, a recluse who has been the victim of some tragedy, a frustrated, or unknown, misanthropic artist with a cat and a canary; houses that we know nothing of, that are opened up only at a set hour so that foodstuffs can be unobtrusively brought in; opened not to peddlers or delivery boys but simply to the things that they are bringing, that, from behind a door opened scarcely more than a crack, are gathered in by one arm of the solitary inhabitant. Houses in which just a single light burns at night, corresponding perhaps to a sort of kitchen where the solitary occupant both eats his meals and spends his time; the light later on moving to another room, where presumably he sleeps or reads or devotes himself to some absurd labor such as putting a sailboat together inside a bottle. A single light that invariably has moved me to ask myself, as a curious person and one who lives on conjectures, who can that man, or that woman, or that pair of old maids be? And what does he or she live on? A pension, an inheritance? Why doesn't he or she ever go out? And why does that light stay on till the wee hours of the morning? Is he or she reading perhaps? Or writing? Or can the occupant be one of those lonely and at the same time fearful beings who can face his or her loneliness only with the aid of that great enemy of ghosts, be they real or imaginary, that light represents?

I had to take Georgina by the arm, and almost shake her before she recognized me. She seemed to be walking along half asleep, carrying a package. And it was still a surprise to see her alive there amid the chaotic hustle and bustle of Buenos Aires.

A smile stole over her weary face, like the soft glow of a candle being lighted in a dark, silent, dreary room.

"Come," I said, taking her to the London.

We sat down and I put my hand over one of hers. How old and worn out I found her! I had no idea, however, what to say to her or what questions to put to her, since the things that really interested me I could not ask her about, and why even inquire about the others? I confined myself to looking at her, like someone who silently visits scenes from bygone days, gazing tenderly and sadly at the work of the years that her face had undergone: fallen trees, houses that were ruins now, rusted moldings, unrecognizable plants in the former garden, a tangle of weeds and dust on the remains of pieces of furniture.

But unable to contain myself, with mingled irony and sadness, I commented:

"So Fernando married."

It was something I needn't have said, though I did so unthinkingly, moved by that abominable combination of emotions, and I immediately regretted having done so. Two barely perceptible tears began to fall from Georgina's eyes, as though one last small confession, murmured in the faintest of voices, as a consequence of one last brutal blow, had been able to be extracted from someone on the brink of death from starvation and torture.

It is strange, and not at all to my credit, that at that moment, instead of finding some way of making light of my unfortunate comment, I said testily:

"And you're weeping still!"

For a second her eyes blazed, with an intensity that resembled that of the old days as a memory resembles present reality.

"I forbid you to pass judgment on Fernando!" she replied.

I drew my hand away.

We said no more. We finished our coffee in silence, and then she said:

"I must go now."

The same pain as in the past overcame me, that pain that had lain dormant all those long years since I had given up all claim to her love. Heaven only knew when I would see her again.

We parted without a word. But after walking a few steps away, she halted for an instant, turned halfway around, almost shyly, and it seemed to me that I caught a glimpse of pain, tenderness, and desperation in her eyes. I thought of running to her and kissing her wrinkled face, her sad eyes, her embittered mouth, and of asking her, begging her to let us see each other again, to allow me to be close at hand. But I refrained from doing so. I knew very well that this was a dream that could never be, that each of us would be obliged to follow our own destiny, without ever meeting, till our death.

Shortly after that chance meeting, Fernando and his wife separated. I also learned that the house in Martínez, Señor Szenfeld's famous gift, had been auctioned off and that Fernando had gone to live in a little house in Villa Devoto.

It is probable that many things had happened in that period and that this sequence of events had been the result of terrible vicissitudes in Fernando's life: I happen to know, for instance, that at that particular time he had been frequenting the roulette table at Mar del Plata and losing enormous sums. I also heard that he had participated in a real estate deal or some sort of illegal transaction having to do with land out by the Ezeiza airport, although this may well have been an apocryphal story circulated by friends of the Szenfeld family. But it is quite true that he ended up in the very modest little house in Villa Devoto where, as it happened, the "Report on the Blind" was found hidden.

I have already mentioned the fact that Szenfeld gave Fernando a helping hand. I think now that it would be more apt to say that he "handsomely rewarded him" on the occasion of his incredible marriage. Like many others Szenfeld became entangled in Fernando's net, to the point that he helped him later on in his real estate speculations and got him out of financial difficulties in the period when he was gambling heavily. Nonetheless, for reasons unknown to me, the old friendship with Señor Szenfeld eventually came to an end—or probably came to an end, otherwise the fact that Fernando spent his last days in such miserable straits is inexplicable.

The last time I met Fernando on the street (not counting that time I ran into him in the Constitución district, when he pretended he didn't know me, or perhaps didn't even see me, since he had already entered that final period when his mind was totally absorbed by his mad obsession with the blind), he was with a very tall, fair-haired individual with a strikingly hard, cruel face. As I had practically knocked Fernando down, he was unable to make his escape and exchanged a few words with me, while the other man stepped a few paces away and looked toward the street after Fernando had introduced him to me: he had a German name that I don't remember now. A few months later I came across his photograph on the crime page of *La Razón*; his cruel face with its thin, tight lips was impossible to forget. He was shown alongside other individuals being sought by the police as the bandits suspected of holding up the Flores branch of the Banco de Galicia. A perfect holdup, which the police thought had been the work of wartime commandos. The individual in question was Polish and had been a commando in the Anders resistance group. But his name as given in the paper was not the one that Fernando had introduced him to me by.

The business of the two different names made me quite certain that the theory the police were going on was the right one. That individual had been planning a big job of some sort at the time I had chanced to run into Fernando. Was Fernando mixed up in some way with this big job? Most probably. As a young man he had been the leader of a gang of thugs and armed bandits from Avellaneda, and moreover, in view of his straitened financial situation it was more than likely that he had returned to his old passion: holding up banks. This was a method that had always seemed to him an ideal one for suddenly getting his hands on a large sum of money, while at the same time it had a symbolic value for him. "The Bank," he had said to me more than once when we were kids, "the Bank (it always seemed to have a capital letter when he said it) is the temple of the bourgeois spirit." Yet his name was not one of the ones on the list of suspects being sought by the police.

After that chance meeting, I had not seen him again during these last two years, during which, to judge by the bizarre writings he left behind, he would appear to have plunged into his mad exploration of the subterranean world.

He had been obsessed by the blind and blindness for as long as I can remember.

Shortly before the death of his mother, when we were still living in Capitán Olmos, I remember something that happened that was quite typical of him in this regard. He had caught a sparrow and taken it up to the room he had in the attic under the eaves (the room that he called his little fort), where he had put its eyes out with a needle. Then he let it go, and the bird, maddened with pain and fear, dashed frantically against the walls, unable to find the window and fly out. I had tried to prevent him from mutilating the bird, and felt sick to my stomach. I thought I would collapse as I went down the stairs and was obliged to cling to the banister for some time until I felt all right again, and meanwhile I heard Fernando, there upstairs in the attic, laughing at me.

Though he had often told me that he put out the eyes of birds and other animals, this was the first time that I had ever actually seen him do so. And also the last. I shall never forget the hideous sensation I experienced that morning.

Because of this episode I never went back to his house or to the *estancia*, thereby depriving myself of what for me was the most important thing when I went there: seeing his mother and hearing her talk. But, I now think, I did not return for that very reason, because I could not bear the thought that she was the mother of a boy like Fernando. And the wife of a man like Juan Carlos Vidal, a man I remember with loathing even today.

Fernando hated his father. He was twelve years old at the time, with the same dark hair and cruel face. And although he detested him, he had many similar traits, not only physical ones but personality traits as well. His face had some of the features typical of the Olmoses: green eyes, prominent cheekbones. All the rest came from his father's side of the family. As the years went by he denied, more and more vehemently, that he and his father were alike in any way, and I think that this resemblance between them was one of the principal causes of the sudden self-hatred he began to display. His violence, his cruel sensuality—all that came from his father.

I was afraid of Fernando. He said very little and then all of a sudden he would fly into a blind rage. He had a bitter, mocking laugh. As a reaction, perhaps, against his father, who was a heavy drinker and a woman-chaser, Fernando did not touch a drop of alcohol for many years in his youth and many times I saw him give himself over to a surprising asceticism, as though he were trying to mortify the flesh. Then these ascetic periods would suddenly come to an end and he would devote himself entirely to a sort of sadistic lust, using women only for his own demoniacal satisfaction, while at the same time feeling utter scorn for them and rejecting them immediately afterward with cold, violent irony, blaming them perhaps for his own failings. Despite all his pretenses and all his silly clowning and cutting up, he was at heart a lonely, stoic sort; he had no friends, he wanted none, and was able to make none. I am persuaded that the only person he was fond of was his mother, although I find it very difficult to imagine that youngster being able to be fond of anyone, if by that word we mean expressing some sort of affection, tenderness, or love. It may well be that the only thing he felt for his mother was a sick, hysterical passion. I remember one incident in particular: one day I had painted a watercolor of a sorrel horse named Fritz that Ana María often rode and was very attached to; she was delighted by my portrait of Fritz and gave me a warm, affectionate kiss, whereupon Fernando flung himself on me and began to pommel me; she separated us and scolded Fernando, who then disappeared; when I finally found him, on the bank of the little stream where he usually went to take a dip, I tried to make my peace with him; he listened to me without a word, biting his fingernails as he habitually did when he was upset, and suddenly he leapt upon me with an open penknife in his hand. I fought back desperately, not understanding his fury. I was able to get the penknife away from him and fling it far away, whereupon he let go of me, walked over and picked up his weapon, and to my vast surprise, since I thought he was going to come back over to me and attack me again, he plunged the knife into his own hand. It took me many years to realize what sort of fierce pride lay behind this act.

Shortly thereafter the incident with the sparrow took place, and I did not see him again; I never returned to his house or to the *estancia*. We were twelve years old at the time, and a few months later, during the following winter, Ana María died; of a broken heart, some said, and others that she had committed suicide by taking an overdose of sleeping pills.

Three years went by before I met Fernando again. I was living in a pension in Buenos Aires, and on those Sundays that seemed endless, all alone with my feeling that fifteen was a ridiculous age to be, my thoughts would insistently return to Capitán Olmos. I believe I've already told you that I hardly knew my mother, who died when I was only two. Is it any wonder, then, that for me Capitán Olmos was for the most part the memory of Ana María? I could still see her on those summer afternoons at the *estancia*, reciting those verses in French that I did not understand but that nonetheless brought me a subtle sensual pleasure, thanks to Ana María's grave voice. "They are there," I would think, "they are there." And in that plural, in an innocent attempt at self-deception by way of the conjugation of a verb in the plural, in the depths of my soul and my will I included her: as though in that old house in Barracas that I knew almost as well as though I had seen it with my own eyes (because Ana María had told me about it so often), her soul in some way lived on; as though in her son, in her loathsome son, in Georgina, in the father and in the sisters, the trace of Ana María, prefigured or disfigured, might be rediscovered. And I would walk round and round the big ramshackle house in Barracas without ever screwing up the courage to knock at the door. Then finally I saw Fernando coming to the house one day and I did not or could not make my escape.

"Is that you?" he asked with a disdainful smile.

I was again assailed by that incomprehensible feeling of guilt that I had always had in his presence.

What was I doing there? His piercing, hate-filled eyes kept me from lying. Moreover, it was pointless: he had already surmised, quite correctly, that I had been prowling round the house. And I felt like a dull-witted delinquent clumsily committing his very first crime, as incapable of telling him of my feelings, my nostalgia, as of writing a romantic love poem amid the cadavers in an autopsy room. Abashed and at a loss for words, I allowed Fernando to take me to the house with him, as though it was clear that this was simply an act of charity on his part, for this would at least give me a chance to see it. And as we crossed the grounds in the dying late afternoon light, I was over-

whelmed by the heavy fragrance of the jasmine, a word always pronounced in my mind with an aristocratic *a*, and a fragrance that would
forever mean to me: *far away, mother, tenderness, nevermore.* In the
Mirador I thought I glimpsed the face of an old woman, a sort of
ghost in the half-light, who silently withdrew. The main part of the
house was connected to the smaller wing with the Mirador by a covered gallery, so that the latter thus formed a sort of peninsula. This
smaller wing of the house consisted of two rooms on the ground floor,
where in earlier days some of the servants were doubtless housed; the
back part of the ground floor of the Mirador (which as I saw afterward, in the test to which Fernando subjected me, was used as a
storage room, with a wooden stairway leading to the upper floor); and
a winding metal staircase running up the outside wall to the terrace
of the Mirador. This terrace spanned the two large rooms I have just
mentioned and was surrounded, as was usual in many buildings of
that period, by a balustrade that had now fallen partially to ruins.
Without saying a word, Fernando walked along that covered gallery
and entered one of the two rooms. He turned the light on and I realized that it must be his own room: in it was a bed, an old dining room
table that he used as a desk, a chest of drawers, and a number of rickety
and apparently useless pieces of furniture kept there only because there
was nowhere else to put them, since the house had undergone a series
of reductions in size. The moment we entered the room a boy appeared
through a door that led to the second room. Without greeting me,
without any sort of explanation, he asked: "Did you bring it?" "No,"
Fernando brusquely replied. I stared at the boy in amazement: he was
about fourteen, with an enormous elongated head like a rugby ball,
a skin like ivory, fine straight hair, a prognathous jaw, a thin, pointed
nose, and feverish eyes that gave rise to an instinctive feeling of repulsion on my part: the repulsion that we might perhaps feel on being
confronted by a creature from another planet who is almost identical
to us, but with certain differences in appearance that for some obscure
reason are frightening. "But I asked you to bring it," the boy said.

Fernando did not answer, as the youngster, staring at him with his
feverish eyes, put the embouchure of a flute or a clarinet to his mouth
and began to play a sort of vague musical phrase. Fernando rummaged
around in a dusty pile of magazines lying on the floor in one corner,
apparently looking for something special, as heedless of my presence

as though I were one of the people who lived in the house. Finally he removed from the pile an issue with the hero of "Winged Justice" on the cover. When I saw that he was about to leave, as though he'd forgotten altogether that I was there, I felt extremely uncomfortable: I couldn't leave with him, as though I were a friend of his, since he hadn't invited me into the house as his guest in the first place nor was he inviting me to leave with him now. Nor could I remain there in that room, especially in the company of that strange boy with the clarinet. For a moment I felt like the most wretched and ridiculous person in the world. Moreover, I realize today that at that moment Fernando was doing all this deliberately, out of sheer perversity.

Hence when a red-headed girl appeared and smiled at me, I felt enormously relieved. Fernando left, with the magazine in his hand, smiling ironically, and I stood there looking at Georgina. She had changed a good deal; she was no longer the skinny kid I had known in Capitán Olmos at the time of Ana María's death; she was fourteen or fifteen years old now and beginning to take on the appearance of the woman she would become, as the first quick, rough sketch of a painter gives hints of the final portrait of his subject. Perhaps because I couldn't help noticing that her breasts were beginning to show underneath her sweater, I blushed and lowered my eyes.

"He didn't bring it," Bebe said, clarinet in hand.

"All right then, I'll bring it," she answered, in the tone of voice of a mother making a promise to her child that she has no intention of keeping.

"When?" Bebe said, stubbornly pursuing the subject.

"Soon."

"All right, but when exactly?"

"Soon, I said, you'll see. And now we're going to go sit quietly and play our clarinet, all right?"

She took him gently by the arm and led him into the next room, as she said to me: "You come too, Bruno," I followed the two of them into the next room: it was no doubt the one where Bebe and Georgina slept, and was altogether different from Fernando's room; though the furniture in it was just as old and broken down, there was something else there too, a delicate, feminine atmosphere.

She led her brother over to a chair, sat him down in it, and said to him:

"Now we're going to stay here and play, aren't we?"

Then, like the mistress of a house who is ready to turn her attention to her visitors after having taken care of certain domestic details, she showed me her treasures: a hoop on which she was embroidering a handkerchief for her father, a big black doll she called Elvira, who slept with her at night, and a collection of photographs of movie actors and actresses, pinned to the wall with thumbtacks; Valentino in a sheik's costume, Pola Negri, Gloria Swanson in *The Ten Commandments*, William Duncan, Pearl White. We discussed the good and bad points of each one of them and of the movies in which they had appeared, as Bebe repeated the same phrase as before on his clarinet. Valentino was by far her favorite, whereas I for my part preferred William Hart, though I conceded that Valentino was stupendous. As for the movies we liked best, I argued passionately in favor of *The Sign of the Octopus*, but Georgina said, and I admitted that she was right, that it was too terrifying; at the scariest moments she had had to look away.

Bebe stopped playing and looked at us with his feverish eyes.

"Play, Bebe," she said mechanically, as she began stitching away at the handkerchief on the embroidery hoop.

But Bebe continued to stare at me, not saying a word.

"All right then, show Bruno your collection of soccer player cards," she said.

Bebe's face lighted up and, laying the clarinet aside, he enthusiastically dragged a shoebox out from under his bed.

"Show him your collection, Bebe," she repeated gravely, without looking up from her embroidery hoop, in that mechanical way that mothers have of ordering their children about while absorbed in important household tasks.

Bebe sat down beside me and showed me his treasure-trove.

That was my first meeting with Georgina at her house: the two or three times I met her later were to surprise me, for in the presence of Fernando she turned into a defenseless creature. The odd thing is that I never got beyond those two rooms, that sort of suburb of the house (except for the terrifying experience in the Mirador, that I shall tell about later) and that my only contact with the people who lived in the house was with those three youngsters, those three creatures who were so dissimilar and so strange: an exquisite young girl, very sensitive and feminine, but dominated by an infernal being; a mentally retarded boy, or something of the sort, and a demon. As for the other people who lived in that house, I had heard occasional vague rumors about them, but the few times I was there it was not possible for me to see anything of what went on inside the four walls of the main wing, and my shyness of those days kept me from questioning Georgina (the only person I might have asked) as to what her parents, her aunt María Teresa, and her grandfather Pancho were like and what sort of life they lived. Apparently those three young people lived a life entirely apart in those two rooms, with Fernando in command.

Years later, around 1930, I met the others who lived in that house and today I realize that with such persons about anything that happened, or on the contrary did not happen, in the house on the Calle Río Cuarto was only to be expected. I believe I've already told you that all the Olmoses (with the exception, of course, of Fernando and his daughter, for reasons that I have already mentioned) suffered from a sort of total lack of a sense of reality, leaving one with the impression they in no way participated in the brute reality of the world around them. Becoming poorer and poorer, yet hitting on no sensible way of making money or at least of holding on to what remained of their patrimony, with no sense of proportion or of politics, living in a place that was the object of sarcastic and malicious comments on the part of their distant relations, more and more alienated from their own class, the Olmoses struck one as constituting the tag-end of an old family living amid the frenetic chaos of a cosmopolitan, commercial-minded, cruel, and implacable city. They still practiced, without even being aware of it naturally, the old Creole virtues that other families had thrown overboard like ballast so as not to go under: they were hospitable, generous, ingenuously patriarchal, unassumingly aristocratic. And perhaps the resentment their distant rich relatives felt toward them stemmed in part from the fact that these latter, by contrast, had not been wise enough to keep these virtues intact and had been caught up in the process of mercantilization and materialism that the country had begun to undergo at the turn of the century. And just as certain people suffering from guilt feelings conceive a hatred for those who are innocent, so the poor Olmoses, having naively and perhaps even absurdly isolated themselves in the old *quinta* in Barracas, were the target of their relatives' resentment; because they stubbornly continued to live in a district of the city that was now plebeian rather than move on to Barrio Norte or San Isidro; because they continued to drink maté instead of tea; because they were poor as church mice, and because they had friendly relations with modest people who had no distinguished family background. If we add that none of all that was done as a deliberate affront by the Olmoses, and that all those virtues, which struck the other relatives as being shocking defects, were practiced simply and spontaneously without the slightest affectation, it is not at all difficult to understand why that family represented to me, as it did to others, a sad and touching symbol of a tradition that was disappearing forever in our country.

I don't know why, but on leaving the house that night, as I was about to shut the gate of the iron fence behind me, I looked back toward the Mirador. The window was dimly lighted, and I thought I caught a glimpse of a woman peering out.

I was of two minds about going back to the house again. Fernando's presence put me off, but Georgina's set me to dreaming and I was eager to see her again. I seemed to be torn between these two opposing forces and I couldn't decide whether to go back or not. Then finally my desire to see Georgina again won out. During all this time I had been mulling things over in my mind, and when I went back I was determined to ask questions and if possible meet her parents. "Perhaps Fernando won't be home," I said to myself to help me screw up my courage. I supposed he must have friends or acquaintances, since I remembered his searching around for that copy of *Tid-Bits* and then leaving the house, which could only mean that he was going out to meet other youngsters; and although I already knew Fernando well enough to sense, even at my tender age, that he was not the sort to be able to keep friends, it was not impossible, on the other hand, that he had some other sort of relationship with boys his age. This conjecture of mine proved to be correct, for Georgina later reluctantly confessed to me that her cousin was the leader of a gang of boys inspired by movie serials such as *The Mysteries of New York* and *The Clutching Hand*, a gang that had its secret oaths, its brass knuckles, and suspect aims. As I look back on it today, that gang strikes me as more or less the dress rehearsal for the gang of thugs and armed bandits that he organized later, around 1930.

I posted myself on the corner of Río Cuarto and Isabel la Católica at midday. I said to myself: "He may or may not go out of the house after lunch; if he does go out, even though it's late, I'll go in."

You can imagine how eager I was to see Georgina again when I tell you I waited there on that corner from one o'clock till seven that night. At that hour I finally saw Fernando leave the house, whereupon I ran down Isabel la Católica almost to the next corner, far enough away so that I could slip away in case he turned down that street, or go back to the house if I saw that he went directly up Río Cuarto. And that is what happened: he went straight up Río Cuarto. I then rushed back to the house.

I am certain that Georgina was happy to see me. What was more, when I had been there before she had urged me to come back.

I questioned her about her family. She told me things about her mother and her father, about her aunt María Teresa, who spent her days predicting illnesses and catastrophes, and about her grandfather Pancho.

"The one who lives up above," I said, because I had sensed that there was some sort of secret hidden "up above."

Georgina looked at me in surprise.

"Up above?"

"Yes, up in the Mirador."

"No, grandfather doesn't live there," she replied evasively.

"But somebody lives there," I said to her.

I had the impression she didn't want to answer me.

"I thought I saw someone up there the other night."

"Escolástica lives up there," she finally answered reluctantly.

"Escolástica?" I said in surprise.

"Yes. In the old days they used to give people names like that."

"But she never comes downstairs?"

"No."

"Why is that?"

She shrugged.

I looked at her intently.

"I seem to remember Fernando saying something," I commented.

"Saying something? What about? When?"

"Something about a madwoman. When we were kids back in Capitán Olmos."

She blushed and bowed her head.

"He told you that? He told you Escolástica was mad?"

"No, he just mentioned something about a madwoman. Was she the one he meant?"

"I don't know if she's mad. I've never spoken to her."

"You've never spoken to her?" I said, dumbfounded.

"No, never."

"And why is that?"

"I just told you: she never comes downstairs."

"But haven't you ever gone up there?"

"No. Never."

I continued to stare at her in amazement.

"How old is she?"

"Eighty-four."

"Is she your grandmother?"

"No."

"Your great-grandmother?"

"No."

"Well, who is she then?"

"She's my grandfather's great-aunt. Major Acevedo's daughter."

"And how long has she been living up there?"

Georgina looked at me, knowing I wasn't going to believe her.

"Since 1853."

"Without ever coming downstairs?"

"That's right."

"Why?"

She shrugged again.

"I think it's on account of the head."

"The head? What head?"

"Her father's head. Major Acevedo's. They tossed it through the window."

"Through the window? Who did?"

"The Mazorca. Then she grabbed up the head and ran."

"Grabbed the head and ran? Ran where?"

"Up there, to the Mirador. And she never came down again."

"And that's why she's mad?"

"I don't know. I don't know if she's mad. I've never been up there."

"And Fernando has never been up there either?"

"No, Fernando's been up there."

At that moment I saw, with fear and dismay, that Fernando was back. Whatever he had gone out to do had evidently taken him hardly any time at all.

"Ah, you've come back," was all he said to me as he looked me up and down with his piercing eyes, as though trying to discover what possible motives there might be behind this second visit of mine.

From the moment that her cousin had entered the room, Georgina was a different person altogether. It may be that on my previous visit I had been too nervous to notice the change that came over her when Fernando was present. She suddenly turned very shy, stopped talking, and moved more awkwardly; and when she found herself obliged to answer a question of mine, she did so with a sidelong glance in her cousin's direction. What was more, Fernando had stretched out on the bed and lay there watching us intently and biting his fingernails furiously. The situation was beginning to be very uncomfortable, when suddenly he suggested that now that he was there we should invent some sort of game because, he said, he was terribly bored. The look in his eyes, however, was not one of boredom, but rather something that I found myself unable to put a name to.

Georgina looked at him fearfully, but then she bowed her head as though awaiting his verdict.

Fernando sat up and appeared to be thinking hard about something, still watching us intently and biting his fingernails.

"Where's Bebe?" he finally asked.

"He's with mama."

"Go get him."

Obeying this peremptory command, Georgina went off to fetch him. The two of us remained there in the room without a word until she came back with Bebe, clutching his clarinet in his hand.

Fernando explained the rules of the game: the three of them were to hide in different places in the two rooms or in the woodshed or in the garden (it was already dark out). I was to hunt for them and when I found one of them, recognize who it was without saying anything or asking any questions, just by touching the person's face.

"What for?" I asked, completely taken aback.

"I'll explain to you later. If you guess right, you'll get a prize," he said with a sarcastic little laugh.

I was afraid he was making fun of me, as he used to do back in

Capitán Olmos. But I was also afraid to refuse to go along with the game, because as always he would claim I was refusing out of sheer cowardice; he knew very well that invariably there was something about his games that was terrifying. But, I asked myself, how could there be anything terrifying about this particular game? It seemed more like a stupid joke, something calculated to make me end up looking utterly ridiculous. I glanced at Georgina as though searching her face for some sign, some helpful hint. But Georgina was not the same person as before: her deathly pale face and her wide-eyed stare were evidence of a sort of fascination or fear or of both things at once.

Fernando turned out the lights, the three of them hid, and I began fumbling about in the dark searching for them. I soon recognized Bebe, who had simply sat down on his bed. But Fernando had made it a rule of the game that I was to find and recognize at least two of the three of them.

There was no one else in that room. There remained the other room and the woodshed to explore. Stumbling now and again in the dark, I carefully went all round Fernando's room, till I thought I heard the sound of someone breathing amid the silence. I prayed it wasn't Fernando, since for some reason coming upon him this way in the dark struck me as a hideous prospect. Listening intently, I cautiously continued to move in the direction from which that muffled sound seemed to be coming. I bumped into a chair. Still feeling about to the right and to the left with my arms stretched out in front of me, I reached one of the walls: it was damp and dusty, with wallpaper that had come unstuck. Running one hand along the wall, I moved to my right, the direction the muffled echo of breathing seemed to me to be coming from. My hands touched a standing wardrobe first, and then my knees bumped into Fernando's bed. I bent over and felt around to check whether one of the two of them was sitting or lying on it, but there was no one there. Following the edge of the bed now, still heading toward my right, I came across the little night table with the lamp on it first and then the peeling wall again. I was certain now: the sound of breathing was becoming more distinct, turning into a very slight but increasingly nervous panting, doubtless because I was getting closer and closer. An absurd emotion made my heart pound, as though I were on the verge of discovering some terrible secret. I was now moving ahead very slowly, almost imperceptibly. And then suddenly my right hand brushed against a body. I drew it back as though I had touched a red-hot branding iron, for I realized instantly that it was Georgina's body.

"Fernando," I said in a low voice, lying out of a sort of shy embarrassment.

But she did not answer me.

My hand reached out toward her again, fearfully but eagerly, though this time I raised it to the level of her face. I found her cheek and then her mouth, tense and trembling beneath my fingertips.

"Fernando," I lied again, feeling my face turn red, as though the two of them could see me.

Again she did not answer me, and even today I wonder why. But at that moment I took it that she was thereby giving me permission to proceed with my investigation, since if she had been following the rules laid down by Fernando, she should already have announced that I had guessed wrong. It was as though I were committing a robbery, but a robbery to which the victim readily assents, and even today this still amazes me.

My hand lingered, trembling and hesitant, on her cheek, brushed across her lips and eyes, as though the gesture were a sign of recognition, a shy caress (have I already told you that in these two years Georgina had grown by leaps and bounds and changed enormously, that that adolescent girl was beginning to resemble Ana María?). She was breathing in intense, agitated gasps, as though she were making some sort of tremendous physical effort. For an instant I came close to shouting "Georgina!" and then running out of the room in desperation. But I contained myself and continued exploring her face with my hand, without her making any sort of move to draw away, an attitude on her part that perhaps was responsible for arousing my absurd hope that has lingered for so many long years, to this very day.

"Georgina," I finally said, in a hoarse, barely intelligible voice.

And then, about to burst into tears, she exclaimed in a low voice: "That's enough! Leave me alone!"

And she ran to the door.

I slowly followed her out of the room, in a dull stupor, feeling that something very confused and contradictory had happened, though I had no idea what it meant. My legs were shaky, as though I had been in some sort of great danger. When I went into the other room, where the light was on now, only Bebe was in there: Georgina had disappeared. Fernando turned up almost immediately thereafter, scrutinizing me with a somber look in his eyes, as though that perverse fire burning within him was now blazing amid shadows.

"You won," he commented in a dry, overbearing voice. "As a prize, you have earned the privilege of being subjected to a more important test tomorrow."

I realized this meant that I should leave and that Georgina would not appear again. Clarinet in hand, his mouth gaping open, Bebe stared at me with his mad, gleaming eyes.

"Very well," I said, heading for the door.

"Tomorrow night, after dinner, at eleven," Fernando called after me.

All that night I pondered what had happened to me and what might happen the following day. The thought that Fernando might go even farther along the same path terrified me, though I had no clear notion why. Yet somehow I realized that Georgina had been the central figure in his strange game. Why hadn't she said that it was not Fernando the moment I uttered his name? Why had she gone along with the whole thing in silence, as though expressly permitting my hand to touch her as it had?

The next night, on the stroke of eleven, I appeared in Fernando's room. He and Georgina were already there waiting for me. I noted in Georgina's eyes an expression of fearful expectancy, accentuated by the dead-white pallor of her face. With the cold preciseness of a leader of a patrol going out on scout duty, Fernando gave me my instructions:

"Old Escolástica lives up there in the Mirador. At this time of night she's already asleep. You are to take this flashlight and go in, walk over to a chest of drawers that is on the side of the room opposite the bed, open the second drawer from the top, find a hatbox that's inside it, and bring it back down here."

In a ghostly whisper, her eyes riveted on the floor, Georgina said:

"No, not the head, Fernando! Anything else, but not the head!"

"What else would be of any importance?" Fernando sneered, with a scornful gesture. "The head, I said."

I was about to faint, for I remembered the story Georgina had told me. It wasn't possible; such things simply didn't happen in real life. Moreover, what reason was there for me to do such a thing? Who was forcing me to?

"Why do I have to do it? Who's forcing me?" I said in a quavering voice.

"What do you mean why? Why does anyone climb the Aconcagua? There's no point whatsoever in climbing the Aconcagua, Bruno. Can it be that you're yellow?"

I realized that there was no way out: I had to go through with it.

"All right then, give me the flashlight and tell me how you get up there."

Fernando handed me the flashlight and was on the point of telling me how to get up to the Mirador when I said:

"Wait a minute! What if the old lady wakes up? She may wake up and start screaming. What should I do then?"

"The old lady can hardly see or hear or even move any more. Don't worry. The worst thing that can happen is that you might have to come back down without the head, but I hope you'll have the guts to bring it back with you."

I have already explained that underneath the Mirador there was a storage room with an old wooden stairway leading to the floor above. Fernando led me to this storage room, which didn't even have an electric light, and said to me:

"When you get upstairs you're going to come to a door that doesn't have a lock. Open it and go inside the Mirador. We'll be downstairs in my room waiting for you."

He left and I stood with the flashlight in the middle of that dark storage room, listening to my heart pounding with anxiety. After a few moments during which I asked myself again what sort of madness all this was and who or what was forcing me to go upstairs if not my own stupid pride, I put my foot on the first step. I went up the stairs, so slowly that I was ashamed of myself—but I did go up them.

And at the top of the stairs I found the little landing with the door leading to the aged madwoman's room. I knew that she was very nearly a helpless cripple, but I was nonetheless so terrified that I was dripping with sweat and afraid I was going to vomit. And to top it all off, I noticed that my body or my sweat stank unbearably. But I could not turn back now, and this being the case the best thing to do was to get the whole business over with as quickly as possible.

I turned the doorknob very carefully, trying not to make the slightest sound, since naturally the whole affair would be less hideous if the madwoman didn't wake up. The door swung open with a creak that seemed tremendously loud to me. The room was pitch dark. For a moment I hesitated between shining the flashlight on the old woman's bed to see if she was asleep and the fear of waking her up by doing precisely that. But how could I go into that strange room with a mad-woman shut up inside it without at least seeing whether she was asleep or sitting up in bed watching me? With a feeling of both repugnance and fear, I aimed the beam of the flashlight around the room in a circular sweep, trying to locate the bed.

I nearly fainted. The old woman wasn't asleep at all; she was stand-ing alongside her bed looking at me, wide-eyed with terror. She was so old she looked mummified, and was very tiny and terribly thin: a sort of living skeleton. From lips dry as parchment there came out something apparently having to do with the Mazorca, but I couldn't swear to that, for the moment I spied her standing there in the dark-ness I ran out the door and down the stairs. On reaching Fernando's room I fainted dead away.

When I came to, Georgina was holding my head in her arms and great tears were falling from her eyes. It took me some time to re-member what had happened just before I fainted and when I did I felt endlessly ashamed of myself. I was alone with Georgina. Fernando had doubtless gone off to his room after delivering himself of some sort of venomous, sarcastic comment on my utter lack of courage: I was certain of it.

"She was still up," I stammered.

Georgina did not say anything: she simply sat there silently weep-ing.

Those two cousins began to be an indecipherable enigma to me, an enigma that at once attracted me and frightened me. They were like two officiants celebrating a strange rite, one whose meaning I was un-able to comprehend and one which threatened to involve horrendous things. At one moment I was convinced that Fernando was making fun of me and the next I feared that he was setting some sort of sinister trap for me. Those two cousins lived apart from the rest of the house-hold, all by themselves, like a king with a single subject, although it would be more apt to describe them as a high priest with a single be-liever; and it was as though by appearing on the scene I had become the single victim of that dark and mysterious cult. Fernando had noth-ing but scorn for the rest of the world, or else haughtily ignored it, whereas he demanded of me *something* that I could not clearly discern, something, I think, that was related to deeply disturbed feelings, to dark emotions and secret sensual pleasures such as Aztec priests must have felt as they stood atop their sacred pyramids tearing the warm, palpitating heart out of the breasts of their sacrificial victims. And what I now find even more inexplicable, I too submitted with a certain dark sensuality to that sacrifice at which Georgina officiated like a terror-stricken hierophant.

For these episodes were only the beginning. Many strange, perverse rituals followed one upon the other until the day I fled, until I realized, in fear and anguish, that that poor creature was blindly carrying out Fernando's orders, as though in a hypnotic trance.

Today, thirty years later, I am still trying to understand the precise relationship that existed between the two of them, and I still find it impossible to do so. They were like two opposed universes, and yet they were intimately united by an incomprehensible but powerful bond. Fernando dominated Georgina, but I could not say for certain that a sacred terror was all that bound her to her cousin: it sometimes seems to me that she was also moved by a sort of compassion. Compassion for a monster like Fernando? Yes. She would suddenly flee in the face of his demoniacal acts and I have seen her weeping in horror in some dark corner of the house in Barracas. But I also remember her stoutly defending him in a most maternal way when I attacked him. "You can't imagine how much he suffers," she would say to me. To-day, when I can look back calmly at his personality and many of his acts, I readily grant that Fernando did not have that sort of cold indifference said to be typical of the born criminal; as I told you before, one had the impression, rather, that he was caught up in a chaotic, desperate inner struggle. But I must also confess that I do not possess sufficient nobility of soul to feel compassion for beings such as Fernando. Georgina, on the other hand, possessed such loftiness of soul.

What manner of sufferings? you may ask me. Many, and of every conceivable sort: physical, mental, even spiritual. Those that were physical and mental manifested themselves clearly. He was the victim of hallucinations; he had dreams that nearly drove him mad; he would suddenly faint dead away. And even when he did not lose conscious-ness altogether, I have seen him blank out, so to speak, struck dumb, neither seeing nor hearing those round about him. "He'll be over it in a few minutes," Georgina would say to me then, hovering anxiously about him. At other times (Georgina told me) he would say to her: "I can see you, I know I'm here beside you, yet I also know that I am somewhere else, somewhere very far away, locked up in a dark room. They're coming after me to pluck my eyes out and kill me." He would sometimes be in a state of violent euphoria and then suddenly lapse into a state of absolute passivity and melancholy: at such times, according to Georgina, he would turn into the most defenseless and helpless creature in the world, and like a little child he would come and curl up on her lap.

I naturally never saw him in any of the humiliating states, and I think that if I had Fernando would have been capable of murdering me. But it was Georgina who told me about them and she was a person who never lied. Nor do I believe that Fernando ever feigned any of these things that happened in her presence, despite the fact that he was a past master at playacting.

The side I did see of him was always his most disagreeable one. He considered himself, for instance, above social conventions and above the law. "The law applies only to unlucky bastards," he maintained. For some reason that I fail to understand, he was passionately interested in money, but I think he saw in it something over and above what it represents to ordinary people. He saw it as something magic and demoniacal, and a favorite word of his for it was "Gold." Perhaps his passion for alchemy and magic stemmed from this strange attraction. But his sick nature was even more evident when it came to anything having to do, either directly or indirectly, with the blind. The first time that I personally saw this manifest itself was back in the early days when we were still in Capitán Olmos. We were walking down the Calle Mitre toward his house when suddenly we spied the blind man who played the drums in the village band coming toward us. Fernando almost fainted and had to cling to my arm to stay on his feet, and I noticed then that he was shaking all over like someone suffering from an attack of malaria and that his face had turned as ashen and rigid as a dead man's. It took him a long time to pull himself together; he was obliged to sit down on the curb, whereupon he fell into a rage at me, insulting me hysterically because I had held him up by the arm to keep him from falling.

That hallucinatory period of my life came to a sudden end one day

in the winter of 1925. When I arrived at the Barracas house, I found
Georgina in bed in her room, weeping. I hastened to caress her, to ask
her why she was in tears, but the only words she could get out were:
"I want you to leave, Bruno, and not come back. Go now and don't
ever come back, I beg you!" I had known two Georginas: one who
was sweet and feminine like her mother; and another totally under
the sway of Fernando's demoniacal powers. And I now saw yet
another Georgina, her spirit broken, defenseless and terror-stricken,
who was asking me to go away and never come back. Why? What
terrible truth was she trying to hide from me? She never told me,
although later, with the passage of the years and what I had learned
from life, I suspected what it was and my suspicions were confirmed.
But what was most distressing about all this was neither Georgina's
terror nor the destruction of a delicate and tender soul thanks to Fernando's diabolical turn of mind; what was most distressing was that
she loved him.

I stupidly pressed for an explanation that day, but finally I realized
that there was nothing I could do or should do in that little corner of
the world that seemed to conceal an ominous secret.

I did not see Fernando again until 1930.

It is always easy to prophesy about the past, Fernando used to say
sarcastically. Today, thirty years later, the meaning of little things that
happened back in those days, seemingly fortuitous incidents of no importance, has now become clear; just as for the reader who has just
finished the last page of a long novel and the characters' destinies are
sealed forever, as death seals them forever in real life, phrases as seemingly prosaic as "Alexey Fyoderovitch Karamazov was the third son of
Fyodor Pavlovitch Karamazov, a landowner well known in our district" take on in retrospect a profound meaning, and very often a
tragic one. We never know, until the end, if what happens to us on
an ordinary day like any other is history or mere happenstance, if it
is everything (however trivial it may appear) or nothing (however
painful it may be). Events insignificant in themselves caused Fernando's path and mine to cross again, after many years of carefully
keeping my distance from him, as though he were inevitably destined
to play a role in my fate and as though my efforts to avoid him had all
been in vain.

As I think back now on those long-ago days, what comes to my mind are words such as *chess, Capablanca and Alekhine, Al Jolson, Singing in the Rain, Sacco and Vanzetti, Sandino and Nicaragua.* A strange, melancholy mixture! But is there any series of words put together from memories of the days when we were young that is not strange and melancholy? Everything that these words suggest was to culminate in that difficult but fascinating era in which national life and our own personal lives were to undergo radical change. A moment closely linked in fact to Fernando's very presence, as though he were an obscure symbol of that period in my life and at the same time the chief cause of the changes I underwent. For that year, 1930, was one of the crucial moments in my life, that is to say, a moment when I pondered the whole of it and passed judgment on it, and everything began to become shaky beneath my feet: the meaning of my existence, the meaning of my country, and the meaning of humanity in general, for when we pass judgment on our own existence we inevitably judge all mankind, though it might also be said that when we begin to judge all mankind it is because in reality we are examining the depths of our own consciousness.

These were dramatic and tumultuous years.

I think for example of Carlos, whose real name I never knew. I can still see him in my mind today—an image that still moves me deeply —bending with furious concentration over cheap editions of books costing a mere thirty or forty centavos, moving his lips with enormous effort, pressing his clenched fists against his temples, like a desperate lad, straining and sweating, digging deeper and deeper and finally unearthing a coffer which he has been told contains the key to his miserable existence, the central meaning of his sufferings as a working-class youngster. The Fatherland! Whose fatherland? They had arrived by the millions from caves in Spain, from wretched, poverty-stricken villages in Italy, from the Pyrenees. Pariahs from every corner of the world, crowded into the holds of ships but dreaming: freedom awaits them, they will no longer be beasts of burden. America! The mythical land where people throw money away on the streets. And then came the grinding toil, the miserable wages, the work days twelve and fourteen hours long. In the end that had proved to be the real America for the immense majority: poverty and tears, humiliation and pain, homesickness and nostalgia. Like children taken in by fairy tales and led off into slavery. And then they, or their children, turned their gaze toward other utopias, toward lands of the future described in violent books that at the same time were full of tenderness for their sort, the wretched of the earth, books that spoke to them of land and freedom and drove them to rise up in rebellion. And then great rivers of blood ran in the streets of Buenos Aires, and many men and women, and even the children of these unfortunates, died in 1905, in 1908, in 1910. The Centennial of the Fatherland! Whose fatherland? Carlos asked himself with a sarcastic, sorrowful grimace. There was no fatherland, didn't I know that? There was the world of the masters and the world of the slaves. "Bread and freedom!" workers who had come from all over shouted, as the lords and masters, terrified and furious, sent the police and the army in against that mob. And so there was more bloodshed and then more strikes and demonstrations and then more attacks against authority and more bombs. And as the son of the lord and master studied in some fancy school in Switzerland or England or France, the son of the nameless worker toiled in the cold storage plants for fifty centavos a day, caught tuberculosis in the ice-cold freezing rooms, and finally died an agonizing death in filthy, anonymous hospitals. And as the rich man's son in Europe read Keats and Baudelaire, the poor man's son painfully deciphered, letter by letter, some text by Malatesta or Bakunin, as Carlos was doing at that moment; and a youngster named Roberto Arlt* learned in the streets the general meaning of human existence. And then the Great Revolution broke out. The Golden Age was about to dawn! Arise ye wretched of the earth! The Apocalypse of the Powerful. And new generations of poor boys and restless or rebellious students read Marx and Lenin, Gorki and Kropotkin. And one of them was that same Carlos, whom I now see once again, as though he were here before me, as though thirty years had not gone by since, plowing through those books, letter by letter, stubbornly and eagerly. He strikes me now as a symbol of the crash of '29, when, with the collapse of its temples on Wall Street, the religion of Limitless Progress approached its end. Entire chains of

---

* Roberto Arlt was one of the great writers of this period. A populist writer with strong metaphysical overtones, he might best be described as a sort of existentialist *avant la lettre*, a writer-philosopher whose origins were the city streets, not the university. [*Author's note*]

imposing banks went under in '30, great industries collapsed, tens of millions committed suicide. And the crisis in the world capital of that arrogant lay religion spread in violent tidal waves to the most remote regions of the planet.

Poverty and cynical disbelief took bitter possession of the vast Babylon. Thugs, lone holdup men, saloons with mirrors handy for target practice, drunks and vagrants, bums, beggars, two-peso whores. And like resplendent emissaries of Punishment and Hope, men and boys who met in miserable little rooms to plan Social Revolution.

Carlos among them.

He was one of the links in the chain that brought me back to Fernando, although he immediately kept his distance from him as a saint avoids keeping the Devil company. Perhaps you yourself met him at some time, for he had connections with the anarchist group in La Plata, and it seems to me I even remember his mentioning you at one time or another. I think his bitter experience with Fernando was what turned him away from anarchism and brought him into the Communist movement, although, as you can well imagine, that simple shift of loyalties was not enough to change his basic personality, which remained the same as ever; a personality that explains his expulsion from the Communist movement on the grounds that he was a terrorist. I heard no more of him until 1938, that winter of 1938 when men and women who had managed to cross the Pyrenees after the crushing defeat of the Republicans in Spain began to turn up in Paris as illegal immigrants. Paulina (poor Paulina), whom I hid on several occasions in my room on the Rue des Ecoles, told me how Carlos had died in Spain, in the same tank in which Etchebehere, another Argentine, had met his death. Had Carlos become a Trotskyite then? Paulina didn't know: she had seen him only once: as much a loner as ever, glum and stoic and impenetrable. Carlos was a religious spirit, a simon-pure one, whose ideals admitted of no compromise. How then could he accept and understand Communists such as Crámer? How could he accept and understand men in general? The Incarnation, Original Sin, the Fall—how could this absolutely pure soul accept this contaminated human condition? But it is an exceedingly curious fact that beings who in a certain way are not human are capable of exercising tremendous influence on those who are merely human. I myself was brought to Communism by the sheer

force of Carlos's presence and his purity, and when he was forced
out of the Party, I too left it, perhaps because I was an adolescent who
had not yet fully accepted cold, hard reality. I doubt that today I
would judge militants such as Crámer, their struggles for personal
power, their petty, hypocritical, shabby maneuvers as harshly as I did
then. How many men would have the right to do so? And where
in heaven's name would it be possible to find human beings free of
such filth save in those realms, almost alien to the human condition,
constituted by adolescence, sanctity, or madness?

Like a messenger who has no knowledge of the contents of the
letter that he is bearing, that unknown youngster was the one who
was to put me back on Fernando's path once again.

In the last days of January, 1930, after spending my vacation in
Capitán Olmos, I went back to Buenos Aires, dropped my things off
at the pension in the Calle Cangallo, and headed for La Academia
almost automatically, out of sheer force of habit. Why was I going
to this café? To see Castellanos and Alonso, to follow the moves in
the eternal chess games, to see the same things as usual. Because the
moment in my life had not yet arrived when I would come to understand that habit is deceptive, that steps we take mechanically do not
always lead us to the same reality; because I did not yet know that
reality is surprising and, given the nature of men, in the long run
tragic.

Alonso's chess partner that day was a newcomer who looked like
Emil Ludwig. His name was Max Steinberg. It may seem astonishing
that unknown persons whom I had apparently run into by sheer
chance should lead me to someone who had been born in my very
own town, who belonged to a family with such close ties to mine.
Here we are obliged to acknowledge the truth of one of Fernando's
eccentric axioms: there is no such thing as mere happenstance, only
acts of fate. One finds only what one is searching for, and what one
searches for is what is in some way hidden in the deepest and darkest
depths of our heart. Because if not, why is it that when two people
meet the same person the consequences are not the same for both?
Why does meeting a revolutionary lead one of them to revolution
and leave the other one indifferent? It would seem, then, that we
end up meeting the persons whom we are fated to meet, and thus
sheer chance counts for very little. Hence those meetings which in

each of our lives seem to us to be utterly surprising, my meeting Fernando again for instance, are simply the result of the workings of those unknown forces that draw us to each other in the midst of an indifferent crowd, as iron filings are attracted at a distance toward the poles of a powerful magnet; movements that would not fail to surprise the filings if they were possessed of the slightest conscious awareness of their acts, without yet having attained full and total knowledge of reality thereby. Thus we make our way along, a little like sleepwalkers, but at the same time with the unfaltering sureness of step of sleepwalkers, toward beings who in some way have been those to whom we were destined to address ourselves from the very beginning. And I have lapsed into such thoughts because a moment ago I was about to tell you that until my meeting with Carlos my life had been that of almost any student, with his typical problems and illusions, with his jokes in his classrooms or in his boarding house, with his first affairs of the heart and his boldness and his timidity. And even before beginning to set those words down on paper, I realized that all that was not at all certain, that I was about to give a false idea of this period in my life prior to my meeting Carlos, and that this false idea would in turn cause my account of what my meeting Fernando again was really like to come as a surprise. The element of surprise is lessened and generally disappears altogether when we take a closer look at the circumstances that surrounded the happening that is apparently so amazing. And by so doing, we find this happening in the final analysis to belong to the mere world of appearances, being simply the product of shortsightedness, lethargy, and distraction. In those five years, in fact, my life had been one long obsession with that family, and I found myself able to banish from my memory neither Ana María nor Georgina nor Fernando: they were presences palpitating in the very depths of my being and they appeared frequently in my dreams. I also think today that as early as those meetings in 1925 I had repeatedly heard Fernando rehearse his plan of some day forming a gang of armed bandits, thugs, and terrorists. And I now believe that that idea of his, which at the time struck me as patently absurd, nonetheless remained deeply engraved in my subconscious, and perhaps my initial attraction to anarchist groups, without my being aware of the fact, as was the case with so many other inclinations of my spirit, stemmed from Fernando's ideas and obsessions.

I have already explained to you that this man exerted an irresistible and frequently pernicious influence on a great many youngsters, both boys and girls, since his ideas and even his manias were taken up by considerable numbers of people who thus became something like vulgar, confused caricatures of that demon. Hence you can readily understand that, as I explained to you before, my meeting him again was not all that surprising, since of all the persons I met I unconsciously kept my distance from those who did not bring me closer to Fernando, and when I discovered that Max and Carlos belonged to anarchist groups, I immediately joined them too; and since such groups, here as everywhere else in the world, represent very small minorities and those on the margins of society who belong to them always have very close ties among themselves (even though, as in this case, these ties stem, paradoxically, from mutual incompatibility or disapproval), I was fated to meet Fernando again. You may ask me why, if this was my ultimate goal, I did not simply go out to see Fernando at the house in Barracas; I will then be obliged to answer you that meeting Fernando again was in no way a conscious aim of mine, but, rather, an almost unavowable obsession. Neither my reason nor my conscious mind had ever approved of, much less recommended, my going in search of that malicious individual who could only cause me—and did in fact cause me—pain and perturbation.

There were other factors, however, that worked in favor of that unconscious movement back into Fernando's orbit. I believe I have already told you that I lost my mother when I was a very small child, and that on top of this misfortune, I was sent for my schooling to a huge city far from home. I was alone, I was shy, and unfortunately I was much too sensitive a youngster. How could the world have helped but appear to me to be a chaos full of evil, injustice, and suffering? How could I have failed to withdraw into my own lonely self and those far-off worlds that fantasy and the novel represent? I scarcely need tell you that I adored Schiller and his robbers, Chateaubriand and his American heroes, Goethe's Goetz von Berlichingen. I was ripe for reading the Russians and perhaps I would have read them at that point if instead of being the son of a bourgeois family as I was, I had been, like so many other youngsters that I met later on, the son of workers or from a poor family; for to those youngsters the Russian Revolution was the great event of our time, the great hope, and it was far easier to meet young people who were reading Gorki than it was to meet ones who were reading Masilla or Cané. This is one of the vast ironies of our education and upbringing and one of the facts that for so long a time created yawning abysses between us and our own country; by coming into contact with one reality we were alienated from another. But what is our country really, save a series of alienations? Be that as it may, these were the circumstances as I finished my secondary studies and got my diploma in 1929. I still remember how, a few days after the exams were over, the school was suddenly plunged into that total, melancholy solitude so characteristic of educational institutions when all the students have left for the long summer vacation. I felt the need then to see for one last time the place in which five years that would never return had gone by. I went out to the gardens and sat down on the edge of one of the stone flower beds and remained there lost in thought for a long time. Then I got up and walked over to the tree on which I had engraved my initials several years before, when I was still a child: BB, 1924. How lonely I had been in those days! How helpless and sad, a little boy from a small town, in a strange, monstrous city!

A few days later I went off to Capitán Olmos. This was to be my last vacation in my town. My father was old now, but he was still a cold, harsh man. I felt far removed from him and from my brothers, vague impulses churned within me, but all my desires were uncertain and confused. I sensed that something was about to take place soon, though I could not understand what, even though my dreams and my obsessive prowling about the Vidals' house might have told me. In any event I spent that vacation looking at my town without seeing it. Many years were to go by, I was to suffer many blows, lose great illusions, and come to know a great many people before my father and my native town were restored to me, so to speak; for the path that one takes back to the most intimate part of oneself always involves a long journey that passes by way of other people and other universes. That was how I was to get my father back. But, as almost always happens, it was too late by then. If I had foreseen back then that that would be the last time I would see him in good health, if I had guessed that twenty-five years later I would find him turned into a filthy heap of rotting bones and entrails, looking at me sadly from the depths of eyes that already scarcely seemed to belong to this world, I would have tried at the time to understand that harsh but good-hearted, strong-willed but candid, violent but incorruptible man. But we always understand the persons who are closest to us when it is too late, and just as we are beginning to master this difficult *métier* of living it is time for us to die, and more important still, those who would have benefited most from our applying our wisdom to them are already dead and buried.

When I returned to Buenos Aires I still had no idea what I would study. I liked everything, or perhaps I liked nothing. I liked painting, I liked writing stories and poems. But were these professions? Could you really announce to people in all seriousness that you would like to devote your life to painting or writing? Weren't they merely hobbies for idle, irresponsible people? All the other young people enrolled at the university seemed so stable, having settled down in medical school or the school of engineering, studying the way to cure a case of scarlet fever or erect a bridge, that I couldn't help but laugh at myself. It was out of a sort of diffidence, thus, that I entered law school, though in my heart of hearts I was certain that I would never be capable of practicing law.

I am straying from the subject that interests you, but the fact is that I find it impossible to speak of the persons who have had the greatest importance in my life without saying something about my feelings at the time as well. For how could those persons have been so important to me if not precisely on account of my own anxieties and my own feelings?

I return, therefore, to Max.

As he and Alonso were ending their game of chess I took a good look at him, for I was curious. He was a mild-mannered, easygoing Jew with a tendency to put on weight. He had a big aquiline nose, but on the whole his face, with its high forehead, had a serene nobility about it. And a certain contemplative, reflective composure made it a face that would have seemed more natural in a much older, fully mature man who has experienced many things. He was carelessly dressed, with buttons missing and a clumsily knotted tie; he seemed to have thrown all his clothes on haphazardly, as though out of the simple necessity of not going about the streets naked. I learned later that he did not have the slightest sense of practicalities, or any idea at all of how to handle his money: a few days after receiving his monthly allowance, which he spent as his fancy struck him, he was obliged to pawn his books, his clothes, and a ring that had been a present from his mother and invariably ended up in the pawn shop each month. When I eventually met his family, I discovered that his father was as serene and calm, but also as mad as he was. And thus both father and son turned out to be examples which in no way confirmed the notions of those who have a stereotyped image of the typical Jew. Both were utterly devoid of practical common sense, they were out of their minds (gently, serenely out of their minds), they were peace-loving persons who made good friends, they were much given to reflection and lazy, unselfish and utterly incapable of earning money, lyrically effusive and absurd. Later, when I began seeing Max at his rooming house, I could see with my own eyes the disorderly sort of life he led: he slept at any and all hours and munched on this or that in bed, keeping enormous salami or cheese sandwiches in the drawer of his night table for this purpose. On top of it, close at hand, was an alcohol burner for making maté, of which he drank endless quantities, alternating with cigarettes, without ever getting out of bed. It was there in that wretched, indescribably filthy bed, half dressed, that he did his studying and replayed famous chess matches on his pocket set, constantly consulting manuals and magazines devoted exclusively to chess.

It was through Max that I met Carlos: as though by crossing a fragile rubber bridge that threatened to collapse at any moment, I had reached an incredibly hard and resistant, mineral terrain, a continent of basalt studded with awesome volcanos about to erupt. Over the years I have often noticed how many times there are individuals who serve merely as a temporary bridge between two persons who are destined thereafter to be linked by a profound and permanent bond: like those frail bridges that armies improvise to span an abyss, taking them down again once the troops have gotten across.

I met Carlos one night in Max's room. The moment I arrived, the two of them fell silent. Max introduced Carlos to me, but all I caught was his first name. It seems to me that his surname was Italian. He was a very skinny youngster, with bulging eyes. There was something cruel and harsh about his face and his hands, and he impressed me as being extremely reserved and self-absorbed. He appeared to have suffered a great deal, and in addition to his obvious poverty there were, I was certain, other things causing him inner anguish and suffering. Thinking about him later, after he had aroused my intense interest because of his contact with Fernando, it seemed to me that he was pure spirit, as though his flesh had been turned to ashes by fever; as though his tortured, burned-out body had been reduced to a minimum of skin and bones and a very few, but very hard, muscles that enabled him to move and bear the tension of his existence. He did not speak, and his eyes suddenly blazed with indignation, as his lips, seemingly carved into his rigid face with a knife blade, clamped shut to lock in great, anguished secrets.

The relation between Max and Carlos amazed me at the time: as though a brick of butter were being sliced through with a sharp steel knife. I had not yet arrived at that point in my life when one knows that nothing about human beings ought to surprise us. Today I realize that Max possessed qualities that were precisely the right ones for that friendship that seemed so curious on the surface: his great kindheartedness, which no doubt relieved Carlos's spiritual tension as water quenches the thirst of a man who has crossed vast desert expanses; and his easygoing, gentle nature, which allowed him to bring together beings as different and as hard as Carlos and Fernando without too violent a clash resulting, as though he served them as a sort of shock absorber. Moreover, what police force anywhere in this world would ever have suspected that a person like Max was on intimate terms with anarchists and gangsters?

Max first met Fernando one Saturday night in the year 1928, at an anarchist study club in Avellaneda called Dawn, where González Pacheco was giving a lecture on the subject of "Anarchism and Violence." In those days this problem gave rise to heated debates, in large part as a consequence of Di Giovanni's terrorist attacks and holdups. These debates were extremely dangerous, for a fair number of those who attended them were armed and the anarchist movement had split up into factions that mortally despised each other. For it is an error to imagine, as those who come to a revolutionary movement from afar or from outside frequently suppose, that all its members are representative of a single well-defined type: this is an error of perspective similar to the one we commit when we attribute very definite characteristic traits to what could be called The Englishman, in capital letters, naively placing persons as unlike as Beau Brummel and a Liverpool docker in the same pigeonhole; or when we insist that all Japanese are alike, ignoring their individual differences or else not even noticing them, by virtue of that psychological mechanism that causes us to perceive mainly the traits common to a group when we observe it from the outside (since they are what is superficially the most noticeable and hence are what first leaps to our eye), though the workings of this mechanism are reversed once we are inside that group, so that what we notice most are the differences (inasmuch as what is important then are the traits that distinguish one member from another).

But the range of types among anarchists was limitless. There were the Tolstoyans who refused to eat meat because they were against any sort of violent death, and who were frequently theosophists and students of Esperanto as well; and on the other hand there were the proponents of violence even in its most extreme forms, either because they maintained that the only means of combatting the State was through the use of force, or because, as in the case of Podestá, anarchist violence served as an outlet for their sadistic instincts. Then there were the intellectuals or students who had come to the movement through having read Stirner and Nietzsche, as Fernando had, most of whom were extremely stubborn asocial individualists who often ended up supporting Fascism; and alongside them were the nearly illiterate workers who had been drawn to anarchism in their search for some sort of instinctive hope. There were the perennially resentful, who thus vented their hatred of their bosses or society and who frequently turned out to be pitiless bosses themselves once they came into a bit of money, or ended up on the police force; and pure souls full of goodness and nobility, who despite their being good and pure were capable of going so far as to commit violent crimes and even murder (as in the case of Simon Radovitsky, one of those noble souls who, moved by a certain rigorous sense of justice, was led to destroy a man he judged to be guilty of the death of women and innocent children). There was also the sponger, who managed to live very well off anarchism, eating and sleeping for nothing at the houses of comrades, and occasionally ending up stealing this or that from them or taking their wives away from them, and when his host would timidly chide the parasite for such excesses the latter would scornfully answer: "What kind of an anarchist are you anyway, comrade?" And then there was the hobo, the proponent of life lived free as a bird, of contact with the sun and the open air, who went wandering about the countryside with his bundle slung over his shoulder, preaching the good news, finding work harvesting one crop or another, repairing a mill or a plow here and there, and at night, in the farmhands' quarters, teaching the illiterate ones to read and write or explaining to them in simple but fervent words how a new society was coming, in which there would be neither humiliation nor suffering nor misery for the poor, or reading to them out of some book he carried about with him in his bundle: pages of Malatesta to Italian farm laborers, or Bakunin; as his listeners, not saying a word, squatting on their heels or sitting on an oil drum drinking maté, exhausted from the long day's work from sunup to sundown, perhaps remembering some far-off Italian or Polish village, would allow themselves to be taken halfway in by that marvelous dream, wanting to believe it but (prompted by the hard reality of every day) imagining it to be impossible, much as those who are overwhelmed by misfortunes nonetheless dream at times of the paradise that awaits them in the end; and perhaps among those peons there might be a native son who thought that God had made the countryside and the sky with its stars for everyone's benefit alike, that sort of Creole nostalgic for the old, proud, free life of the pampas with no barbed-wire fences, the stoic, rugged individualist from the wide open spaces who in the end was won over to the gospel preached by those remote apostles with peculiar names and embraced, fervently and forever, the doctrine of hope.

And when on that night in 1928 a Tolstoyan cobbler maintained that no one has the right to kill anyone, much less in the name of anarchism, that even the life of animals was sacred and that was why he was a vegetarian, a young man whom no one remembered having seen before, perhaps eighteen or so, tall and dark-haired, with greenish eyes and a hard, sneering expression on his face, answered:

"It's quite likely that by eating lettuce you make your bowels work better, but it seems to me you'll find it very difficult to overthrow bourgeois society that way."

Everyone stared at that young stranger.

And another Tolstoyan leaped to the defense of the cobbler, recalling the legend of how the Buddha allowed himself to be devoured by a tiger in order to appease the creature's hunger. But a partisan of justified violence asked what the Buddha would have done if he had seen that the tiger was about to leap not on him, but on a defenseless child. At this point the discussion grew stormy, sarcastic, lyrical, vituperative, stupid, ingenuous, or ferocious, depending on the temperament of the speaker, thus demonstrating once again that a society without classes and without social problems may well prove to be as violent and inharmonious as the present one. They trotted out the same old arguments and the same memories again: wasn't Radovitsky justified in having killed the chief of police guilty of the May Day massacre of 1909? Didn't the eight workers killed and the forty wounded cry out for vengeance? Were there not women among the victims? Yes, perhaps. The Bourgeois State, armed to the teeth, implacably defended its privileges, it spared neither people's lives nor their freedom, justice and honor did not exist for those despots whose one goal was the perpetuation of their privileges. But what about the innocent victims sometimes killed by anarchist bombs? Furthermore, was it possible to arrive at a better society through violence and vengeance? Weren't anarchists the true repositories of the greatest human values: justice and freedom, brotherhood and respect for every living being? And hence was it admissible that in the name of these lofty principles mere bank tellers or little cashiers in commercial establishments should be blown to bits if in the final analysis they were innocent and were massacred so as to obtain money that to top everything off was being used for dubious purposes? At this moment the debate ended amid a tumult of insults, shouts, and finally shots from firearms. A tumult that González Pacheco was barely able to quiet by calling upon all his talents as an orator and reminding the anarchists present that such behavior merely justified the worst accusations leveled against them by the bourgeoisie.

It was in those circumstances, Max told me, that he had first met Fernando. The latter's epigrammatic phrase and striking face had attracted his attention. They left together, with another young man named Podestá, whom I met later. Thus it was that the first step was taken toward the formation of the gang that Podestá undoubtedly wanted to organize and be the head of, though naturally it was Fernando who eventually came to be the leader of it. Osvaldo R. Podestá was an individual I loathed from the very first moment I met him: there was something vaguely suspect and shifty about him. He was mild-mannered, almost effeminate, and relatively cultivated, since he had been in the fourth year of his studies for his bachelor's diploma when he joined Di Giovanni's gang. He had a habit of half-closing his eyes and casting sidewise glances at a person that was most unpleasant. Time confirmed that first impression I had had of him, when I discovered the path that his life had taken. After Di Giovanni was shot down and the authorities began to stamp out the movement with all the force of martial law behind them, and after the holdup of the cashier of the Braceras company that he participated in as a member of Fernando's gang, Podestá fled to Uruguay in a motor launch belonging to smugglers of contraband goods, and from there he went to Spain. In Spain he began to take part in the campaign of armed violence organized by the labor unions in their fight to the death with management (there were three hundred people killed in those years preceding the Civil War), but for some reason unknown to me, he came to be suspected of working hand in glove with the police. As a proof of his loyalty, he offered to kill anybody the anarchists chose. The victim they pointed out to him was the chief of police of Barcelona, and Podestá gunned him down in cold blood, thus apparently getting back in the good graces of the anarchists. But when the Civil War came along, he and his gang committed such atrocities that the Federation of Spanish Anarchists put a price on his head. On learning of this decision, Podestá and two of his friends tried to escape by way of the port of Tarragona, in a motorboat loaded with money and valuables, but they were mowed down with machine guns before they could get away.

The fact that someone like Fernando should have an individual such as Podestá in his gang is explainable. What beggars belief is that a youngster such as Carlos was capable of participating in the activities of such a group, and the only possible explanation is the absolute purity of his motives and ideals. You must not forget, moreover, that Fernando's powers of persuasion were unlimited, and it must not have been very difficult for him to prove to Carlos that that was the only possible way of fighting against bourgeois society. Eventually however Carlos left the gang in utter disgust, having realized that the money they obtained in their holdups was not being used to fill the war-chest of any labor union or to aid the families or the helpless children of comrades who had been thrown in prison or deported. In fact he left the group the day he found out that Gatti had not received the funds that Fernando had promised to give him to help him escape from the penitentiary in Montevideo, so that his escape, which could not be postponed, had to be financed with money obtained elsewhere at the last possible moment. Carlos had great respect for Gatti (I myself saw that this was so) and that particular incident finally opened his eyes. You may recall the famous escape from the Montevideo penitentiary, in which fourteen prisoners got out by way of a tunnel more than thirty meters long that had been dug under Gatti's supervision (his nickname was "The Engineer"), starting from a fake coal yard that coplotters on the outside had set up opposite the prison. Gatti worked scientifically, using a compass and maps, a small electric drill, and a little flatcar on rails, dragged along with ropes so it wouldn't make any noise, to carry away the dirt that was excavated; this dirt was then put into sacks supposedly containing coal, whereupon trucks came and hauled these fake coal sacks away. This long and complicated operation took a great of money, most of which came from holdups. But as you can see, and as Fernando used to say scornfully, in the end it all turned out to be a sort of autophagy: holdups were committed to finance prison breaks by anarchists who'd been put away for previous holdups.

The anarchists had two major sources for obtaining funds: holdups and counterfeiting. And both activities had their philosophical justifications; since according to certain anarchist theoreticians property is theft, holdups restored to the community something that one individual had illegitimately appropriated, and putting bogus paper money into circulation represented not only an attempt to obtain money to finance prison breaks and strikes but also, especially when engaged in on a grand scale, an attempt to bankrupt the national treasury and cause the state to collapse. Following the historical example of England when it tried to sabotage the Revolutionary government in France by flooding that country with the famous false *assignats* that it smuggled in on fishing boats, the anarchists often carried off counterfeiting schemes of vast proportions. It was a clandestine task that became one of their chief concerns, and moreover it was not a difficult one for them, given the fact that many militants had a natural bent toward the graphic arts. Di Giovanni set up a large engraving workshop where ten-peso bills were turned out; and a Spanish printer named Celestino Iglesias worked in that shop, a generous and incorruptible man, whom Fernando met at that time and in the years just before his death sought out again to do a counterfeiting job for him, before the accident that cost Iglesias his eyesight.

But let us go back to our meeting each other again.

It was in January of 1930. I had gone with Max to see *High Treason*, and afterward we dropped in at a bar, still in the midst of a discussion we were having about Emil Jannings and the advantages and disadvantages of talkies (like René Clair and Chaplin, Max was horrified by the very thought of sound films). The moment we arrived, we spied Fernando, sitting waiting for Max at the table where Max's chess board was permanently set up. I recognized him immediately, though he was now a full-grown man; his features had become more pronounced but had not changed, for he belonged to that type of human being who from a very early age already has strong features which the years do not change but merely accentuate. I could have recognized him in the midst of a vast milling crowd; that was how striking and unforgettable the features of that face were.

I do not know if he really did not recognize me or was simply pretending he didn't. I held out my hand to him.

"Ah, Bruno, it's you," he commented, shaking hands with me distractedly.

The two of them stepped away from the table then and Fernando said a few words to Max in a low voice. I looked at him, still overcome with astonishment, an astonishment that had left me almost speechless. Because even though I later came up with a whole series of explanations as to why I had met up with him again, as I have told you before, at that moment his sudden reappearance on the scene struck me as a sort of miracle. A miracle brought about by black magic.

As Fernando left, he turned part way round in my direction and gave a vague wave of his hand to bid me goodbye. When Max came back to the table, I asked if Fernando had said anything to him about me, if he had told him how we happened to know each other.

"No," he didn't say anything to me about you," Max replied.

To him, of course, our meeting again did not seem all that surprising: there are so many people who know each other in a big city.

So that was how I came back within Fernando's orbit, and although I saw him only on very rare occasions, his turns of phrase, his theories, and his sarcasms had an enormous importance for me in that critical period of my life. I never in fact took part in any of the secret activities of his gang, but through Max or Carlos I anxiously followed from afar the outward signs of that stormy existence of his. To what degree and in what way a youngster such as Max could have participated in that organization remains an unfathomable secret to me even today. I think it probable that he played only a peripheral role of some kind in it, or merely acted as a liaison man, for neither his temperament nor his ideas really suited him for action, much less action of that particular sort. And even today I ponder the reason why Max associated himself with that gang. Out of curiosity? Out of a certain atavism or through the influence, however remote, of his family history? Even today I still smile to myself sometimes at how incongruous it was that Max of all people hung out with that gang. He was so accommodating that he would even have found reasons to become friends with the chief of police of Buenos Aires, and there is no doubt that he would have had a good game of chess with him if the opportunity had arisen. It was as wildly irrational to find him in that milieu as it would be to come across someone sitting in an easy chair calmly reading the daily paper in the midst of an earthquake. Surrounded by gangsters and terrorists discussing counterfeiting money, planting dynamite, and digging tunnels Max would offer me his comments on *King David*, which Honegger was directing at the Colón at the time, or on Taïroff, who was at the Teatro Odeón, or give me a detailed analysis of Capablanca's best game against Alekhine. Or he would suddenly come out with one of his gently humorous little remarks, as inappropriate in that context as a genteel little glass of port would be at a drinking bout of inveterate gin guzzlers.

Beginning on September 2, events followed one upon the other in rapid succession: student demonstrations, shooting in the streets, then the death of a student, Aguilar, strikes, and finally the revolution of September 6 and the fall of President Yrigoyen. And that turn of events (as we now know) marked the end of an entire era in the country's history. From then on we would never again be what we had been before.

With the military junta and the declaration of a state of siege the entire movement suffered a terrible blow; premises occupied by workers and students were broken into, foreign workers were deported, the insurgents were tortured and the ranks of the revolutionary movement decimated.

In the midst of all the chaos, I lost sight of Carlos, but I suspected that he was involved in something extremely dangerous. And when on December 1 I read in the papers about the holdup of the Braceras cashier, in the Calle Catamarca, I instantly recalled a long and highly suspect stroll that Carlos had taken in my company in that neighborhood, for the ostensible purpose of looking for a good place to set up a clandestine printing plant. I had no doubt that that holdup had been the work of Fernando's gang, and my suspicions were later confirmed. That operation was in fact the last one in which Carlos participated, for around about that time he had finally become convinced that the objectives that Fernando was pursuing had nothing in common with his own. And even though Fernando had taken it upon himself to undermine Carlos's sympathies for Communism by cynical but devastating arguments, Carlos joined a Communist party cell in Avellaneda. On a number of occasions I had heard those arguments of Fernando's, sarcastic arguments that Carlos would listen to with his gaze fixed on the floor and his jaws tightly clenched. This was at a time when Carlos was already being worked on by Communist youngsters and he was beginning to discover considerable advantages in this other movement: Communists seemed to be fighting for something solid and definite, they were demonstrating that terrorism on an individual basis was either useless or actually detrimental to the cause of revolution, they were criticizing, with serious and well-founded arguments, a movement that had sanctioned the rise of gangs such as the one led by Di Giovanni, and, finally, they were putting forward convincing proof that the only effective weapon against the organized power of the bourgeois state was the organized power of the proletariat. But unlike other anarchists, Fernando did not criticize the Communist movement for advocating the formation of a new régime that threatened to be even more oppressive than the one preceding it, or for militating in favor of the setting up of a dictatorship that would suppress individual freedom for the good of the future community as a whole: no, what he reproached the Communist movement for was its mediocrity and its hopes of solving man's ultimate problems by way of steel mills, hydroelectric dams, shoes, and a decent diet.

What horrified me was not that Fernando should try to destroy Carlos's new-found faith with sophistical arguments, but the fact, rather, that Communism and anarchism alike meant absolutely nothing to him, and that his sole aim in letting loose with his dialectical weapons was to destroy a person as helpless as Carlos.

But, as I say, this was before the Braceras holdup. After that I did not see Carlos again until 1934. As for Fernando, I lost sight of him for the next twenty years.

My having met Fernando again and the crisis I was going through, one that made me feel even more lonely than during the last years of my secondary studies, made me more eager than ever to return "to the Vidals," to a degree that became almost intolerable.

I had always been a quiet, reflective sort, and suddenly I had found myself amid a raging torrent, just as a mountain river in flood sweeps along with it many things that moments before had been placidly contemplating the world. For that very reason, that entire period now seems to me, with the passage of the years, as unreal as a dream, as seductive (but also as remote) as the world of a novel.

With my world suddenly complicated by the activities of the police and by my relation with Carlos, with my pension having been broken into by the forces of law and order, I was obliged to take refuge with Ortega, an engineering student who in those days had been trying to woo me over to Communism. He lived near Constitución, on the Calle Brasil, in a pension run by a Spanish widow who adored him. It was not hard for him, therefore, to come up with a temporary solution to my problems: he simply removed various odds and ends from a little room overlooking the Calle Lima and brought in a mattress for me to sleep on.

I slept very fitfully that night. When I woke up at dawn, I found myself almost in a state of terror; I did not remember immediately what had happened the preceding day and before I was fully awake I looked about in vast surprise at the puzzling reality that surrounded me. For we do not wake up all at once, but rather it is a gradual, complex process whereby little by little we recognize the world that we belong to, as though we were a traveler returning from a very long journey through dim and distant continents, in the course of which, after centuries of obscure existence, we have lost all memory of our previous existence, remembering of it only incoherent fragments. And after a span of time impossible to measure, the light of day begins to feebly illuminate the exits leading out of those labyrinths so full of anguish, whereupon we anxiously break into a run and head toward the everyday world. And we arrive at the edge of sleep like exhausted shipwreck victims who finally reach the shore after a long battle with the storm. And there, still partially unconscious, but feeling our fear gradually draining away, we begin to recognize with gratitude some of the attributes of the everyday world, the tranquil and comfortable universe of civilization. Antoine de Saint-Exupéry tells how after an anxious battle with the elements, lost somewhere out over the Atlantic, when he and his mechanic had lost almost all hope of ever reaching land, they finally spied a faint little light on the African coast, and touched down safely on their very last gallon of fuel; and how the cup of café au lait that they then drank in a little shack was the humble but transcendental symbol of contact with the whole of life, the trivial but miraculous reunion with existence itself. In the same way, when we return from that universe of sleep, an ordinary night table, a pair of worn shoes, a familiar lamp, are deeply moving lights shining on the coast that we are eager to reach: safety. That is why we are overcome with apprehensions when one of the fragments of reality that we begin to be able to make out is not the one that we were expecting: that little night table we know so well, our pair of worn shoes, the familiar lamp. Which is what usually happens to us when we wake up all of a sudden in a strange place, in a bare, cold, anonymous hotel room, or in the bedroom to which chance circumstances have unexpectedly taken us the night before.

Little by little I realized that that room was not mine and at the same time began gradually to remember the previous day with people's lodgings being broken into and police swarming all over. Now, in the dawn light, that entire day struck me as absurd and totally alien to my spirit. It was borne in upon me once more that the irrational violence of the events that were taking place was beginning to touch even the lives of people who weren't at all the violent sort. Through a curious chain of circumstances I, who am persuaded that I was born for contemplation and passive reflection, had found myself in the midst of confusion and even extremely dangerous events.

I got up, opened the window, and looked down at the indifferent city.

I felt lonely and distraught. Life seemed a complicated and hostile business.

Ortega appeared, cracking jokes about the anarchists with his usual healthy optimism. And before going off to his classes at the university he left me one of Lenin's works that he recommended that I read, for in it Lenin sets forth a definitive critique of terrorism. Having read, at a friend's suggestion, the memoirs of Vera Figner, who had been buried alive in the Czar's prisons as a consequence of the anarchists' terrorist attacks, I was unable to read that pitilessly sarcastic analysis of Lenin's with any sort of sympathy. "Petty-bourgeois desperation." How grotesque those romantics appeared to be in the implacable light of Marxist theory! As the years have gone by, I have gradually come to realize that reality was closer to Lenin's view of it than to Vera Figner's, but my heart has always remained faithful to those pure-hearted, slightly mad heroes.

Time suddenly seemed to have stopped for me. Ortega had urged me not to go out of the pension for a few days, and wait and see what course events would take. But after three days I could bear being cooped up no longer and began to go out, thinking it would be impossible for the police to recognize a youngster who had no criminal record.

At noon I went into one of the cafeterias on Constitución and had lunch. I found it strange to come across so many unconcerned people, seemingly without a care in the world, in the streets and cafés. Up there in my little room I was reading revolutionary works and had the feeling that the whole world might explode at any moment; then when I went out, I found life going on as usual, peacefully and calmly: office workers were going off to their jobs, tradesmen were selling their wares in their shops, and one could even see people lazing on the benches in the squares, just sitting there watching the hours go by: all of them equally dull and monotonous. Once again, and this would not be the last time, I felt more or less as though I were a stranger in the world, as though I had awakened in it all of a sudden and had no notion of its laws and its meaning. I wandered aimlessly about the streets of Buenos Aires, I watched its people, I sat down on a bench in the Plaza Constitución and meditated. Then I would return to my little room, feeling lonelier than ever. And it was only when I buried myself in books that I seemed to be in touch with reality again, as though that existence out in the streets were, by contrast, a sort of vast dream unfolding in the minds of hypnotized people. It took me many years to realize that in those streets, in those public squares, and even in those business establishments and offices of Buenos Aires there were thousands who thought or felt more or less as I did at that moment: lonely, anguished people, people pondering the sense and nonsense of life, people who had the feeling that they were seeing a world that had gone to sleep round about them, a world made up of men and women who had been hypnotized or turned into robots.

And in that solitary redoubt I began to write stories. I now realize that I would write whenever I was unhappy, whenever I felt alone or not properly attuned to the world in which it had been my fate to be born. And I think it likely that that is always the case, that the art of our time, that tense art that tears itself into bits and fragments, is invariably created out of our maladjustment, our anxiety, and our discontent—a sort of attempt at reconciliation with the universe on the part of that race of vulnerable, restless, covetous creatures that human beings are. For animals do not need art: they are content simply to live, since their existence slips peacefully by, in harmony with their instinctual needs. A bird needs only a few little seeds or worms, a tree to build its nest in, great open spaces to spread its wings in; and its life goes by from its birth to its death in a felicitous rhythm that is never violently shattered either by metaphysical despair or by madness. Whereas man, on raising himself up on his two hind legs and fashioning the first ax from a sharp-edged stone, laid down thereby the foundations of his grandeur but also created the sources of his anguish: for with his hands and with the tools made by his hands he was to erect that very strange and very powerful construct that is called culture and by so doing initiate the great rent in his very being, since he ceased thenceforth to be a mere animal yet at the same time had not reached the point of being the god that his mind prompted him to think he was. He will thenceforth be that miserable dual being who moves and lives between the earth of the animals and the heaven of his gods, that being who has lost the earthly paradise of his innocence and not yet reached the heavenly paradise of his redemption. That pain-racked, sick-spirited being who will ponder, for the first time, the reason for his existence. And thus his hands, and then that ax, that fire, and then science and technology will each day deepen the abyss separating him from his primordial race and his animal felicity. And the city will eventually be the last stage in his mad career, the supreme expression of his self-pride, and the ultimate form of his alienation. And then discontented beings, more or less blind and more or less mad, will fumble about trying to recover that lost harmony through mystery and blood, creating through painting or writing a reality different from the wretched one that surrounds them, a reality that often seems fantastic and demented but that, curiously, turns out in the end to be more profound and more real than everyday reality. And thus, in a sense dreaming for everyone, these vulnerable beings contrive to rise above their individual unhappiness and become interpreters and even (suffering) redeemers of the collective destiny.

But my unhappiness has always been a twofold one, for my weakness, my contemplative turn of mind, my indecision, my apathy have always kept me from attaining that new order, from creating that new cosmos that the work of art represents; and I have always ended up falling from the scaffoldings of that passionately desired construction that would save me. And having once fallen, badly battered and doubly saddened, I have hastened to seek out mere humble human beings.

And so it was that time too: my constructions were all nothing but dull experiments that miscarried, and again and again, with each failure, as has happened every time that I have felt lonely and confused, in the midst of my loneliness I could hear, there in the depths of my mind, mingled with the dimly remembered murmurs of a ghostly mother I had scarcely known, the gentle, quiet voice of Ana María, the only approximation to a flesh-and-blood mother I had ever known. It was like the echo of those bells of the engulfed cathedral of legend, set to ringing by wind and storm. And as always when my life grew dark, that remote tolling began to ring in my ears more and more loudly, like a summons, as though it were saying: "Don't forget that I am always here, that you can always hasten to my side." And suddenly, on one of those days, the summons grew so insistent that it was irresistible. I immediately leapt out of bed, where I was in the habit of spending long hours lost in fruitless reflection, and hurried off, with the sudden anxious thought that I ought to have done so long before, to recover what remained of that childhood, that river, those long-ago afternoons at Ana María's *estancia*. The house of Ana María.

I was mistaken, for our anxieties do not always lead us to the truth. Meeting Georgina again was not a meeting of our minds or hearts, but rather the beginning of a new sort of unhappiness that in a certain sense has lasted to this very day and that will surely linger on until the day I die. But this story is not the one that interests you.

I saw her a number of times, it is true; I often walked about those streets of other days with her; she was kind to me. But who has ever maintained that it is only those who are wicked who can make us suffer?

She not only said very little, but what few words she did utter were spoken reluctantly, as though she were living in constant fear. It was not Georgina's words that made me understand what she was at that time in her life or explained the sufferings she was undergoing. It was her paintings. Have I already told you that she had been painting ever since she was a little girl? I don't mean to say that her paintings were in any way direct self-revelations, since there were not even any human figures in them, let alone any sort of "story." They were still lifes: a chair alongside a window, a vase of flowers. But what a miracle: we say "chair" or "window" or "clock," words that designate mere objects in that cold and indifferent world that surrounds us, and yet we thereby communicate something mysterious and indefinable, something that is like a key, like a pathetic message from the innermost depths of our being. We say "chair," yet we do not mean "chair," and we are understood. Or at least we are understood by those to whom this cryptic message is secretly addressed, and it passes intact above the heads of the indifferent and hostile crowd. Thus that pair of wooden shoes, that candle, that chair are not saying something about those wooden shoes, that pale candle, or that chair with a woven straw seat; what they are "about" is Van Gogh, Vincent (above all Vincent): his anxiety, his anguish, his loneliness; so that what they really are is his self-portrait, the description of his most profound and most painful anxieties. Using those indifferent external objects, those objects of that cold, rigid world that is outside of us, that perhaps existed before us and that very probably will continue to exist, icy and indifferent, when we are dead and gone, as though these objects were no more than shaky, temporary bridges (as words are for the poet) thrown up to enable us to traverse the abyss that forever opens up between the universe and ourselves; as though they were symbols of that profound secret that it reflects; indifferent, objective, gray objects for those incapable of understanding the key to them, but warm and vibrant and full of secret intentions for those who possess that key. For in reality these painted objects are not objects belonging to that indifferent universe but objects created by this solitary, desperate being, anxious to communicate, who does with objects what the soul does with the body: impregnating it with its desires and its feelings, manifesting itself in the wrinkles of its flesh, the gleam in its eyes, the smiles and the corners of its mouth: like a spirit seeking desperately to manifest itself through the alien body, the sometimes grossly alien body, of a hysteric or a cold professional medium.

Thus I too was able to learn something of what was going on in the most hidden part, and for me the most nostalgically longed-for part, of Georgina's soul.

To what end, in the name of heaven? To what end?

↬ 4 ↫

FOR DAYS ON END he prowled round and round the house, hoping that the guard that had been posted there would be withdrawn. He confined himself to gazing from a distance at what remained of that room in which he had known utter happiness and utter despair: a skeleton blackened by the flames that the twisted spiral staircase seemed to be pathetically straining to rejoin. And when night fell, on the walls dimly lighted by the street lamp on the corner the empty frames of the door and the window formed hollows resembling the eye sockets of a charred skull.

What was he looking for? Why did he want to get inside? He would not have been able to answer. But he waited patiently for the now-pointless guard to be withdrawn, and once it was, he scaled the iron gate and entered the grounds that very night. Flashlight in hand, he retraced the same path that he had followed with her that first time, a thousand years ago, on a summer night, walking around the side of the main wing of the house and heading for the Mirador. The entire gallery, as well as the two rooms underneath the Mirador and the storage room to the back, was now nothing but black walls covered with ashes.

It was a cold, cloudy night, and the pre-dawn silence was profound. Martín heard the distant echo of a ship's siren, and then again there was not a single sound. He stood there for some time, not moving, in great agitation. And then (although it could not possibly be anything but his overworked imagination) he heard Alejandra's voice, faintly but clearly, uttering just one word: "Martín." Utterly devastated, he leaned against the wall, unable to move, for a long, long time.

He was able at last to overcome his deep depression and head toward the house. He felt a need to go inside, to see once again that sitting room of the grandfather's in which the spirit of the Olmoses seemed somehow to be crystallized, where eyes foreshadowing Alejandra's stared down forever from old portraits.

The entryway was locked. He retraced his steps and noticed that one of the doors of the house was barred with a chain and a padlock. He searched around in the ruins left by the fire and found a stout iron bar with which he pried loose one of the iron rings to which the chain was attached: it was not a difficult task, for the old wood was rotten. He entered the house through the corridor inside, and in the beam cast by his flashlight everything seemed even more bizarre, even more like an auction house full of odd bits and pieces of furniture.

In the old man's room everything was the same, except for the wheelchair, which was missing: the antique kerosene lamp, the portraits in oil of ladies with big ornamental combs in their hair and the gentlemen who had sat for Pueyrredón, the console table, the Venetian mirror.

He looked around then for the miniature of Trinidad Arias and contemplated once again the face of that pretty woman whose Indian features seemed to be the secret murmur of Alejandra's, a soft murmur amid conversations of Englishmen and Spanish conquistadors.

He had the impression that he was stepping into a dream, as on that night when he had entered this same room with Alejandra: a dream that fire and death had made even deeper still. That gentleman and that lady with the ornamental comb in her hair seemed to be watching him from the walls. The souls of warriors, of madmen, of municipal councilors and priests appeared to be stealing invisibly into the sitting room and telling stories of conquests and battles.

And above all the spirit of Celedonio Olmos, Alejandra's great-great-grandfather. Right there, perhaps in that very armchair, he had gone over in his mind in his old age his memories of that last retreat, that ending following the disaster at Famaillá that made no sense to reasonable men, with the forces of the Legion scattered by Oribe's army, divided by defeat and betrayal, dazed by despair.

They are marching toward Salta now along unknown paths, paths that only their guide knows. The defeated number a bare six hundred. Yet he, Lavalle, still believes in something, for he always seems to believe in something, even though—as Iriarte thinks, as Major Ocampo and Major Hornos mutter—it is only chimeras and illusions. With whom is he going to do battle with these tattered remnants of his troops, I ask you? And yet there he is, riding at the head of their ragged band, with his straw hat and the sky blue* cockade (which is no longer sky blue or any other color) and his sky blue cape (which is no longer sky blue either, which little by little has taken on the color of the earth itself), dreaming of who knows what mad undertakings. Although in all likelihood he too is trying not to allow himself to give in to despair and death.

As he rides along, Lieutenant Celedonio Olmos is struggling to hold on to his eighteen years, for he feels that this age that he has contrived to reach is at the very edge of an abyss and may fall at any moment into vast depths, into ages without end. Yet as he sits astride his horse, exhausted, wounded in the arm, he looks at his leader up there ahead of him and at Colonel Pedernera riding there at his side, pensive and gloomy; and he fights to defend those towers, those bright, lofty towers of his adolescence, those glowing words, proud guardians of the absolute whose great capital letters mark off the boundaries between good and evil. Within those towers he is still defending himself. For after eight hundred leagues of defeats and disloyalties, of betrayals and dissension, everything has become confused. With the enemy in close

---

* The symbolic color of the Unitarists; that of the Federalists was red. [*Author's note*] *pursuit, saber in hand, bleeding and desperate, he has mounted one by one the stairs of those towers that once were resplendent but now are defiled by blood and lies, by defeat and doubt. And as he stubbornly defends each step of those stairs, he looks around at his comrades, silently asking for the aid of those who are waging similar battles: Frías, Lacasa perhaps. He hears Frías say to Billinghurst as he eyes the commanders of the cavalry squadrons from Corrientes: "They'll abandon us, I'm certain of it."*

"They have made up their minds to betray us," those from the Buenos Aires squadron think.

Yes, Hornos and Ocampo, who are riding along side by side. And the others watch them and suspect them of plotting to betray or abandon them. And so when Hornos leaves his comrade's side and rides over to the general, one and the same thought occurs to all of them. Lavalle orders a halt then, and these officers talk together. What are they talking about, what are they discussing? And then, as they begin moving on again, terrible, contradictory rumors spread: they have given him fair warning, they have tried to persuade him, they have announced that they are abandoning him. And the story also makes the rounds that Lavalle has said: "If there were no hope left I would not try to go on fighting, but the governors of Salta and Jujuy will help us, they will provide us with men and equipment, we will retreat to the mountains, dig in, and become a force to be reckoned with; Oribe will be obliged to divert a goodly number of his troops in order to deal with us, and Lamadrid will hold out in Cuyo."

And then, when someone mutters: "Lavalle has gone utterly mad now," Lieutenant Celedonio Olmos unsheathes his saber to defend that last remaining part of the tower and flings himself upon the man, but his hand is stayed by his friends, and the other man is forced to hold his tongue and is vituperated, because above all else (they say), above all else, we must stick together and not let the general see or hear anything. "As though (Frías thinks) the general were sleeping and it were necessary to keep watch over him as he sleeps and dreams his dreams full of chimeras. As though the general were a mad but innocent and beloved child and we were his older brothers, his father and his mother, keeping watch over him as he sleeps."

And Frías and Lacasa and Olmos look at their leader, fearing that he may have awakened, but happily he goes on sleeping and dreaming, watched over by his sergeant Sosa, the eternal sergeant, ever the same, beyond the reach of all the powers of earth and man, stoic and silent.

Until that dream of aid, of resistance, of equipment, of horses and men is brutally shattered in Salta: the townspeople have fled, panic reigns in the streets, Oribe is only nine leagues away, and nothing is possible now.

"Do you see now, sir?" Hornos asks the general.

And Ocampo says to him: "Those of us who are all that is left of the Corrientes division have decided to cross the Chaco and offer our support to General Paz."

Night descends on the city caught up in disorder and confusion.

Lavalle has bowed his head and makes no answer.

What, is he still dreaming? Major Hornos and Major Ocampo exchange glances. But finally Lavalle replies:

"Our duty is to defend our friends in these provinces. And if our friends withdraw to Bolivia, we must be the last to do so; we must cover their retreat. We must be the very last to leave the soil of the fatherland."

Major Hornos and Major Ocampo exchange glances once again, and one and the same thought crosses both their minds: "He is mad." How could he cover a retreat, with what forces?

Hearing nothing, his eyes staring fixedly at the horizon, Lavalle repeats:

"The very last."

Major Hornos and Major Ocampo think: "He is moved by pride, his accursed pride, and perhaps also by his feelings of resentment toward Paz." They say:

"We are sorry, sir, but our squadron will join General Paz's forces."

Lavalle looks at them, then bows his head. His wrinkles grow deeper from moment to moment, years of life and death are coming crashing down upon him. When he raises his head and looks at them again, he is already an old man:

"Very well, major. I wish you luck. May General Paz carry on this fight to the very end. It is one that has no further use for me, it would appear."

The remaining troops from the Corrientes division gallop off, as the eyes of the two hundred men who are remaining at their general's side follow them in silence. Their hearts shrink and in their minds is

*a single thought: "Everything is lost now." The one thing left for
them is to die at their leader's side. And when Lavalle says to them:
"We will hold out, they'll see, we'll wage guerrilla warfare in the
mountains," they remain silent, staring at the ground. "We will march
to Jujuy for the moment." And these men, who know that going to
Jujuy is mad, who are not unaware that the only way of saving at
least their skins is to head for Bolivia along unknown paths, to dis-
perse, to flee, reply: "Yes, sir." For what man among them would be
capable of depriving this child-general of his last dreams?*

*They ride off now. There are not even two hundred of them. They
are marching along the highway to the city of Jujuy. The main highway!*

ᖇᖇ 5 ᖇᖇ

"DEL CASTILLO," he said to him, "Alejandra," he said to him. "Eh,
what's that?" They were disconnected, incoherent words, but
finally "death," "fire" aroused the man's amazement. And even though
Martín felt that talking with him about Alejandra was like trying to
extricate a precious stone from a mixture of clay and excrement, he
told him. "All right, I see," he replied. And when Bordenave arrived,
he scrutinized Martín with a look that betrayed his confusion and fear:
a Bordenave very different from the one that first time. Martín
couldn't get a single word out. "Here, drink this," he advised him. His
throat was parched and he felt terribly weak. "I wanted to talk to you
about . . ." But he sat there not knowing how to go on, looking at the
empty glass. "Here, drink this." But suddenly the thought occurred
to him that this was useless and stupid: what could they possibly talk
about? His head was getting fuzzier and fuzzier from the alcohol and
the world more and more chaotic. "Alejandra," another person said.
Yes, everything was turning into chaos. That person was different too:
he seemed to be someone bending over toward him solicitously, almost affectionately. For many years he analyzed that ambiguous moment, and later, when he returned from the South, he told Bruno
about it. And Bruno was of the opinion that by mistreating Alejandra,
Bordenave was taking vengeance upon her not only for his own sake
but for Martín's as well, like those Calabrian bandits who robbed the

rich to give to the poor. But, wait a moment, all that still wasn't clear at all. Why, to begin with, was Bordenave taking vengeance on Alejandra? For what affronts, what insults or humiliations? A certain word that Martín recalled amid all his confusion was very significant: Bordenave had spoken of contempt. But Bruno was of the opinion that it was not that so much as it was hatred and resentment toward her; no one has contempt for someone he hates, whereas one feels contempt for someone who is in some way inferior and one feels resentment toward persons who are superior. Hence he had once treated her badly or habitually treated her badly (it was difficult to determine which with so few facts to go on) in order to satisfy an obscure feeling of rancor. Rancor or a sentiment very typical of a certain sort of Argentine male who looks upon the woman as an enemy and never forgives her for a rebuff or a humiliation; a rebuff or a humiliation very easy to imagine, knowing the two persons in question, since it was almost certain that Bordenave possessed sufficient intelligence or intuition to realize that Alejandra was superior to him, and he was sufficiently Argentine to be humiliated by the feeling that he was able to dominate only her body, while in her mind she looked down upon him, mocked him, and scorned him, and her mind was a dimension of herself that was inaccessible to him. And he was humiliated too by the even more exasperating feeling that she was using him, as she undoubtedly used many others, as a simple instrument: the instrument, it would appear, of an extremely complex and perverse sort of vengeance that he never was able to understand. For all these reasons he would feel inclined to look upon Martín as a kindred soul, not only because he did not look upon him as a rival, not only out of a sense of fraternity in the face of their common enemy, but because by hurting a youngster as helpless as Martín Alejandra herself became a more vulnerable being, to the point that she could be attacked by Bordenave himself—as though someone who hated a rich man because he has a fortune, realizing that this sentiment is base and dishonorable, instead seized upon one or another of his more vulgar shortcomings (his niggardliness for example) so as to be able to detest him without feeling any sort of scruples. But Martín was unable to think any of this through at that moment; it was only much later that he was able to do so. It was as though they had removed his heart and were pounding it to pieces on the ground with a stone; or as though they had cut it out of him with a jagged knife and were now tearing it to bits with their fingernails. His confused emotions, his feeling of total insignificance, his dizziness, the immediate confirmation that that man had been Alejandra's lover all conspired to prevent him from saying a single word. Bordenave was staring at him in bewilderment. What was the point of all this anyway? "She's dead now," he commented. Martín continued to sit there with his head bowed. Yes, what indeed was the point in this need to know, this absurd desire to pursue the whole thing to the very end? Martín didn't know, and although he had a certain vague intuition as to the reason, he would not have been able to express it in words. But something was forcing him to go on in this absolutely senseless way. Bordenave eyed him thoughtfully; he appeared to be weighing something in his mind, to be pondering the proper dose of a tremendously powerful drug.

"Here," he said to him, handing him a glass of brandy. "You aren't feeling well. Drink this."

And as though he had had a sudden inspiration, Martín said to himself: "Yes, I want to get blind drunk, I want to die," as he heard Bordenave say something to him like: "Yes, on the next floor, upstairs, you know," looking at him attentively as he downed this glass too. All at once everything in the room began to turn round and round, he was nauseated, and his legs felt wobbly. His stomach, empty since the night of the fire, seemed all of a sudden to be full of something burning-hot and repugnant. Struggling upstairs to that infamous place, he spied, as in a dream, the river through the large bay window. And with a feeling of self-pity, along with the feeling that he was being ridiculous, he thought: "Our river." He had a mental picture of himself, as small as a young child, and felt sad, as though he were looking at himself standing there in front of him. And in the oppressive darkness of that place he could see nothing. An overpowering perfume made him feel even more like vomiting amid all those big cushions on the floor as Bordenave opened a cupboard that turned out to be a combination record player and tape recorder and said, "very practical," adding something about its being a secret and commenting, "Thieves . . . you can imagine . . . with all these documents": it was apparently some sort of trap. And it seemed to Martín that he heard something being said about business; the other individual was somebody enormously important who interested him, Bordenave, a whole lot on account of that little matter having to do with the aluminum factory (and incidentally, Bruno was thinking, who knows what sort of vengeance Bordenave was thus planning to take on Alejandra, a tortuous, masochistic vengeance, but vengeance all the same), and since Martín simply had to know, since he was so insistent, he might as well be let in on the fact that Alejandra had taken enormous pleasure in sleeping around for money. As he said this he turned the recording apparatus on, and he, Martín, finding himself unable to ask Bordenave to stop the abominable machine, was thus forced to hear words and cries and moans of pleasure as well, intermingled in a terrifying, horrid, unspeakable way. But then a superhuman force allowed him to react and run downstairs like one pursued, stumbling, falling, getting to his feet again and finally reaching the street, where the icy air and the drizzle finally awoke him from that obscene hell only to plunge him into a frigid death. And he began to make his way slowly along, like a body with neither soul nor skin, walking on shards of glass, pushed along from behind by an implacable multitude.

There are not even two hundred of them, and they are not even soldiers any more: they are defeated, filthy beings, and many of them no longer know why they are fighting. Lieutenant Celedonio Olmos, like all the others, rides along in grim silence, remembering his father, Captain Olmos, and his brother, lying dead in Quebracho Herrado.

Eight hundred leagues of defeats. He understands nothing now, and keeps hearing Iriarte's malicious words echoing in his mind: the mad general, the man who doesn't know what he wants. And hadn't Solana Sotomayor forsaken Brizuela for Lavalle? He can see Brizuela now in his mind's eye: drunk and disheveled, surrounded by dogs. Let no envoy of Lavalle's dare approach! And isn't that girl from Salta riding at his side this very moment? He doesn't understand anything any more. And everything was so clear two years ago: Freedom or Death. But now ...

The world has turned into chaos. And he thinks of his mother, of his childhood. But the figure of Brigadier General Brizuela appears before him once again: a vociferous puppet in filthy rags, surrounded by ferocious mastiffs, baring their teeth in fury. And then the lieutenant tries once again to remember that childhood.

He was walking along, unaware of his surroundings, as what few thoughts remaining in his mind were again fragmented by violent emotions, like buildings destroyed by an earthquake that are shaken by new tremors.

He climbed on a bus and the feeling that the world was meaningless came over him even more forcefully: a bus hurtling along so resolutely and so powerfully toward some destination that he didn't care at all about, a precise, technically efficient mechanism, transporting a person who had no objective and no longer believed in anything and hoped for nothing and had no need to go anywhere at all; a chaos borne from one place to another thanks to exact schedules, fares, corps of inspectors, traffic laws. And like an idiot he had thrown away the ampoules that would arrest his heart, and looking Pablo up again in order to get some more was like going to a ball in order to meet God or the Devil. But there was still the train, the grade crossing on the Calle Dorrego, maybe there . . . one second and it would all be over. He remembered the crowd that had gathered that time, what's happening? what's happening? impossible to elbow his way to the center of the crowd, he heard people saying how horrible, he wasn't watching and it hit him, what a terrible way to die, what do you mean? he threw himself in front of it deliberately, he wanted to kill himself, and another person shouting there's a shoe over here with a foot in it. Or perhaps water, the La Boca bridge, but the water down below was oily and then too there was the possibility of not being able to go through with it or repenting having jumped in those seconds during the fall, fragments of time that, who knows? may be entire existences, as endless and as monstrous as the seconds of a nightmare. Or shutting himself up in a room and turning on the gas after swallowing lots of pills the way Juan Pedro had, but Nené had left the window open just a crack. Poor Nené, he thought with affectionate irony. And his smile in the midst of tragedy was like a little sun appearing fleetingly on a stormy, freezing day of huge floods and tidal waves, as the conductor shouted "end of the line!" and the last passengers got off. What? what? where was he? let's see, yes, Avenida General Paz, that was where, a big tower; a little kid came running out of the entryway of one of the houses and from inside a woman, surely his mother, shouted after him: "I'm going to beat you black and blue, you thief," and the little kid ran down the street and around the corner in terror; he had on a pair of short brown pants and a red pullover that stood out against the rainy gray sky like an ephemeral little touch of beauty; a girl appeared, walking along the same sidewalk in a yellow raincoat, and he thought: she's being sent out to buy groceries or sweet biscuits to eat with maté, her mother or her pensioner father doubtless said to her: "It's a good afternoon for drinking maté with biscuits, go buy us some," or perhaps one of those boys that girls call "a special friend" had a day off work and was dropping by the neighborhood to chat with her for a little while, or perhaps she was being sent on some errand by her brother who had a little workshop nearby because now he could see a little garage where a young man who could well be the brother was standing, dressed in a pair of grease-stained blue overalls and hold- ing a wrench in his hand, and saying to the apprentice mechanic: "Get a move on, Perico, and go ask him for the battery charger," and the apprentice hurried out, but everything was like a dream and what was the point of any of it: battery chargers, wrenches, mechanics, and he felt sorry for the terrified little boy because, he thought, all of us are dreaming and so why punish kids and why fix cars and have crushes on nice boys and then get married and have children who also dream that they're alive, who have to suffer, go off to war or fight or give up hope all on account of mere dreams. He was simply drifting along now, like a boat without a crew swept along by shifting currents, and moving mechanically like those invalids who have lost almost all will and consciousness and yet allow themselves to be moved by the nurses and obey the instructions they are given with the obscure re- mains of that will and that consciousness without knowing why. The 493, he thought, I go as far as Chacarita and then I take the subway to Florida and then I walk from there to the hotel. So he got on the 493 and mechanically asked for a ticket, and for half an hour continued to see ghosts dreaming of things that kept them very busy; at the Florida stop he went out the exit on the Calle San Martín, walked along Corrientes to Reconquista and from there headed for the Warszawa rooming house, Accommodations for Gentlemen, went up the dirty, dilapidated stairs to the fourth floor, and threw himself on the wretched bed as though he had been wandering through labyrinths for centuries.

Pedernera looks at Lavalle, who is riding along just a little way ahead, with his gaucho trousers, his torn shirt with the sleeves rolled up, his straw hat. He is ill, thin, subdued: he seems like the ghost, in rags and tatters, of that Lavalle of the Army of the Andes.... How many years have gone by! Twenty-five years of battles, of victories, and defeat. But at least in those days they knew what they were fighting for: they wanted to free the Continent, they were doing battle for the Great Fatherland. But now ... So much blood has run in the rivers of America, they have seen so many desperate afternoons, they have heard so many battle cries ring out between brothers. Right here, with no need to look any farther, Oribe is at their heels: didn't he fight at their side in the Army of the Andes? And Dorrego?

Pedernera gazes soberly at the towering mountain peaks, his eyes slowly survey the desolate valley, he seems to be asking war what the secret of time is ...

The twilight darkness silently invaded the corners of the room, causing colors and objects to fade away to nothingness. The mirror on the standing wardrobe, cheap and ordinary as it was, began to take on the mysterious importance that all mirrors (cheap or not) take on at night, just as in the face of death all men take on the same profound, mysterious importance, be they beggars or kings.

Yet he still wanted to see her, one last time.

He turned on the little night lamp and sat down on the edge of his bed. He took the worn photograph out of one of his inside pockets, and moving a little closer to the night lamp, looked at it intently, as though he were examining a scarcely legible document, on whose correct interpretation events of great importance depended. Of the many faces that (like all human beings) Alejandra had, this was the one that belonged most intimately to Martín; or at least the one that had once belonged to him most intimately: a face with the profound and slightly sad expression of someone longing for something that he or she knows, beforehand, to be unattainable, a face full of desire but also already full of despair, as though it were possible for desire (that is to say hope) and despair to manifest themselves at one and the same time. And moreover, a face with that almost imperceptible yet violent expression of hers of scorn for something: for God perhaps or for all of humanity, or more probably, for herself. Or for all of these things together. And not simply scorn but also contempt and even loathing. And yet he had kissed and caressed that terrible mask during a period that now seemed to him to lie far in the past, although it had lasted until very recently: just as once we have awakened, the imprecise images that moved us in our dreams or terrified us in our nightmares seem infinitely far away. And very soon now that face would be disappearing forever, along with the room, with Buenos Aires, with the entire universe, with his own memory, as though everything had been nothing more than a gigantic phantasmagoria conjured up by an ironic, malevolent sorcerer. And as he further studied that static image, that sort of symbol of impossibility, amid the chaotic thoughts running through his mind he seemed to glimpse, albeit in a very vague, confused way, the idea that he was not killing himself for her, for Alejandra, but for something more profound and more permanent that he was unable to define: as though Alejandra had been nothing more than one of those mirages of an oasis that cause the traveler in the desert to go desperately onward across the burning sands, and whose vanishing can bring on his death: and yet the ultimate cause of his despair (and hence of his death) is not the false oasis but the implacable, endless desert.

His head was a maelstrom, but a slow-moving, ponderous one, made up not of transparent (though raging) waters but of a sticky mixture of refuse, grease, and decomposed corpses, along with beautiful abandoned photographs and the remains of beloved objects, as in great floods. He could see himself, all alone in the afternoon heat, walking along the bank of the Riachuelo, "like a little orphan" (he had once heard a neighbor say), sad and lonely, when after the death of his grandmother he had transferred all his affection to Bonito, who was running along ahead of him, leaping about chasing a sparrow and barking joyously. "What a happy thing it is to be a dog," he had thought then and had said as much to Don Bachicha, who had listened to him thoughtfully, puffing on his pipe. And suddenly, in the midst of that confusion of ideas and feelings, he also remembered a verse: not one from Dante or Homer, but from a poet who was as fond of wandering about the streets and as humble as Bonito. "Where was God when you went away?" that poor wretch had asked himself when he lost his beloved. Yes, where was God when his mother had jumped rope to kill him? And where was He when Bonito had been run over by the Anglo truck: Bonito, one of this world's poor insignificant creatures, with blood pouring out of his mouth, with his whole little hind end mashed to a repulsive pulp, and with his eyes looking sadly at him in his terrible agony, as though asking him a mute and humble question: a creature who had no sin to pay for, neither his own nor anyone else's, so little and so unimportant that he would seem to have deserved at least the grace of a peaceful death in his sleep in his old age, remembering some little pond in summer, some long walk along the banks of the Riachuelo in long-ago happy days. And where was God when Alejandra was with that bastard? And suddenly he also saw that scene from the documentary film that Alvarez kept at his house and would project over and over, out of a sort of masochism: and he could see once more, forever, that seven- or eight-year-old boy, during the exodus across the Pyrenees in the snow, amid the tens of thousands of men and women fleeing toward France, a little cripple, alone and helpless, hurrying along with awkward little hops on his one leg and his little improvised crutch, amid the terrifying anonymous fleeing multitude, as though the nightmare of the bombings in Barcelona would never end and as though he had left not only his leg behind there, on an infernal, nameless night, but also, for days now, days that seemed like centuries, he had also been leaving behind pieces of his soul that he had been dragging along with him out of loneliness and fear.

And suddenly Martín was jolted by an idea. It burst from his excited soul like a great electrical discharge amid huge black storm clouds. If the universe had any reason for being, if human life had any meaning, if God existed, in short, let Him present himself here in this room, this dirty room of his in a cheap rooming house. Why not? Why should He refuse to accept this challenge? If He existed, He was supremely strong, the Almighty. And the strong, the powerful can allow themselves the luxury of being somewhat condescending. Why not? Whom would He profit by not presenting Himself? What sort of pride would He thus satisfy? I'll give Him till dawn, Martín said to himself with a sort of vindictive pleasure: assigning Him this definite time limit made him suddenly feel possessed of a terrible power and enhanced his feeling of spiteful satisfaction, as though he had said to himself: "We'll see now, once and for all." And if He didn't appear, he would kill himself.

He got up from the bed in great agitation, as though a sudden, monstrous vitality had brought him to life again.

He began to pace back and forth nervously, biting his fingernails and thinking, thinking, as though he were in an airplane plunging toward the earth in a dizzying tailspin which thanks to a superhuman effort he had managed to put on a precarious straight and level course again. And suddenly an indescribable terror rooted him to the spot, tense and rigid.

The thing was, if God did appear, how would He do so? And what would He be like? An infinite, awesome presence, a face, a vast silence, a voice, a sort of gentle, reassuring caress? And what if He appeared and he, Martín, had no way of knowing that He had? He would then have killed himself for no good reason, and by mistake.

There was a deep silence in the room: the sounds of the city down below could scarcely be heard.

He thought that any one of those sounds might well be significant. It was as though he were lost in the midst of a bustling multitude of millions of human beings, obliged to recognize the face of a stranger in this crowd who is bringing him a message that may save him, although he knows nothing about this stranger except that he is the bearer of this message that may be his salvation.

He sat down on the edge of the bed: he was shivering and his face was burning hot. He thought: I don't know, I don't know, let Him appear in any way he pleases. Any way at all. If He existed and wanted to save him, He would know how He should appear so as not to pass unnoticed. This last thought calmed him for a moment and he lay down on the bed. But he immediately became agitated again, and soon his state became unbearable. He began to pace up and down the room once again, and then suddenly he found himself out in the street, wandering about aimlessly, as the shipwreck victim, drained of all his strength and huddling in the bottom of his lifeboat, allows it to be swept along by the tempestuous waves and the furious gales.

They have been marching for fifteen hours now in the direction of Jujuy. The general is ill, and has not slept for the last three days; silent and dejected, he sits his horse and lets it take him on, as he waits for the news that his aide-de-camp Lacasa will be bringing him.

The news that Lacasa is bringing! Pedernera and Danel and Arta-yeta and Mansilla and Echagüe and Billinghurst and Ramos Mejía think. The poor general! We must watch over his sleep, we must keep him from waking up completely.

And here comes Lacasa, driving his mounts to exhaustion to bring news that all of them already know.

So they keep their distance; they do not want the general to notice that none of them is surprised by Lacasa's report. And from afar, standing apart in silence, with affectionate irony, with gloomy fatalism, they follow that absurd dialogue, that grim report: all the Unitarists have fled to Bolivia.

Domingo Arenas, the military officer in command in Jujuy, has gone over to the Federalists and is waiting for Lavalle in order to finish him off. "Tell them to escape to Bolivia by whatever shortcut they can find," Dr. Bedoya advised before leaving the town.

What will Lavalle do? What is it that General Lavalle will never do? They all know; no need even to discuss it: he will never turn his back on danger. And they prepare to follow him as he embarks on this last, this fatal act of madness. And at that point he gives the order to proceed to Jujuy.

But the truth is plain to see: their leader is aging by the hour, he feels that death is at hand, and as though he has found himself obliged to live out his natural span, but at an accelerated pace, there is something in his gaze, in his sagging shoulders, a certain ultimate weariness of this man who is only forty-five that already portends old age and death. His comrades contemplate him from a distance.

Their eyes follow that beloved ruin of a man.

Frías thinks: "Blue-eyed Cid."

Acevedo thinks: "You have fought in a hundred twenty-five battles for the freedom of this continent."

Pedernera thinks: "There, marching toward death, is General Juan Galo de Lavalle, a descendant of Hernán Cortés and Don Pelayo, the man whom San Martín called the First Sword of the Army of Libera-

tion, the man who by putting his hand to the hilt of his saber caused Bolívar to fall silent."

Lacasa thinks: "On his coat of arms is an arm brandishing a sword, a sword that is never surrendered. The Moors did not bring down that upraised arm, nor did the Spaniards. Nor will that sword be surrendered now. That is certain fact."

And Damasita Boedo, the girl who rides at Lavalle's side and anxiously tries to read the face of that man whom she loves but who she feels is in a distant world now, thinks: "General, I would like you to lean on me and find repose, to rest your weary head on my breast, to sleep cradled in my arms. The world could not prevail against you, the world can do nothing to harm a child who sleeps in his mother's lap. I am your mother now, general. Look at me, tell me that you love me, tell me that you need my help."

But General Juan Galo de Lavalle marches on in silence, absorbed in the thoughts of a man who knows that death is approaching. The moment has come to draw up the balance sheet, to make an inventory of misfortunes, to pass in review the faces of the past. This is not the time for games or for looking at the mere outside world. That outside world scarcely exists now; soon it will be a dream that has ended. There now come forward in his mind the true, permanent, lasting faces, those that have remained forever and always in the most secret depths of his soul, guarded by a lock with seven keys. And his heart then confronts that worn face furrowed with deep wrinkles, that face that was once a lovely garden and is now overrun with weeds, nearly bone-dry, without a single flower. Yet he can see it again as that lovely garden, and recognize that summerhouse where they used to meet when they were still scarcely more than children; when disillusionment, unhappiness, and time had not yet wreaked their destruction; when those tender touches of their hands, those looks in their eyes announced the children that would come, as a flower announces fruits to come: "Dolores!" he murmurs, as a smile appears in his dead face like a just barely smoldering ember amid ashes that we poke aside in order to have one last little bit of warmth on a desolate mountainside.

And Damasita Boedo, who looks at him anxiously and intently, who almost hears him murmur that beloved name of long ago, turns her eyes away now and stares straight ahead, feeling the tears well up.

They have arrived at the outskirts of Jujuy now: the dome and the church towers are already in sight. They have reached the quinta *of Los Tapiales de Castañeda. Night has already fallen. Lavalle orders Pedernera to set up camp there. He himself will go into Jujuy with a small escort. He will look for a house in which to spend the night: he is ill, about to collapse from exhaustion and fever.*

His comrades exchange glances: what is there to do? All this is madness and they might as well die in one way as in another.

He wandered about aimlessly, he went into little cafés in the port district that he had once gone the rounds of with Alejandra, and as he got drunker and drunker the world little by little lost its form and its solidity: he was dimly aware of shouts and laughter, piercing beams of light bore through his head, painted women embraced him, and then finally great masses of cottony red lead crushed him, pinning him to the ground. Helping himself along with the aid of his little improvised crutch he made his way across a vast swampy plain, amid filth and corpses, amid excrement and mire that might swallow him up and devour him, trying to step on firm ground, with eyes wide open so as to be able to move in that deep shadow toward that enigmatic, distant face, about a league away, level with the ground, like an infernal moon trying to light that repellent landscape crawling with worms, running with his little crutch toward the place where the face seemed to be waiting for him, and from which that summons was undoubtedly coming, running and stumbling across the plain, until suddenly, on rising to his feet, he saw the face there before him, close by, repulsive and tragic, as though he had been taken in from a distance by some perverse magic, and he screamed and sat up violently in the bed. "Calm down, child," a woman was saying to him, holding him down by the arms. "Calm down now!"

Pedernera, lying on the ground on his saddle, suddenly sits up nervously: he thinks he has heard rifle shots. But perhaps it is only his imagination. He has tried in vain to sleep during this sinister night. Visions of blood and death torment him.

He rises to his feet, threads his way among his sleeping comrades, and goes over to the sentry. Yes, the sentry too has heard shots, far off in the distance, in the direction of the town. Pedernera awakens his comrades, he has a grim presentiment and thinks they ought to saddle up and keep on the alert. As they begin to follow Pedernera's orders, two sharpshooters from Lavalle's escort gallop up, shouting: "They've killed the general!"

He was trying to think, but his head was full of liquid lead and garbage. "It'll go away, child, it'll go away," the woman was saying. His head ached as though it were a boiler full of gases under great pressure. As though through enormous old tangles of thick spider webs, he saw that he was in a strange room: opposite his bed he glimpsed Carlitos Gardel in a swallow-tailed coat and another photo, also in color, of Evita Perón, with a vase of flowers underneath it. He felt the woman's hand on his forehead, as though she were seeing how feverish he was, as his grandmother used to do, countless years ago. He began to hear the sound of a Primus stove. The woman had left his bedside and was turning the pressure up, and the hissing of the stove grew louder and louder. He also heard the constant whimpering of a baby only a few months old, off to one side, but he didn't have the strength to turn his head and look. He was again overcome by drowsiness, and dreamed the same dream a third time. The beggar was coming toward him, muttering unintelligible words; he put a bundle down on the ground, untied it, opened it, and displayed its contents; contents that Martín anxiously tried to make out. The beggar's words were as despairingly indecipherable as those of a letter that one *knows* will have a decisive effect on our fate but that time and dampness have reduced to an illegible blur.

The general's blood-soaked body is lying in the entryway. Damasita Boedo is kneeling at his side, holding him in her arms, weeping. Sergeant Sosa looks on like a child who has lost his mother in an earthquake.

Everyone is running about and shouting. No one has any idea what has happened. Where are the Federalists? Why didn't they kill the others? Why didn't they cut Lavalle's head off?

"They don't know who they killed in the night," Frías says. "They were shooting in the dark." "That's true," Pedernera thinks. They must make their escape before the Federalists realize what has happened. He raps out precise orders, the body is wrapped in the general's

*cape and placed on his dapple gray charger, and they gallop off again
to Los Tapiales de Castañeda, where the rest of the Legion is waiting.*

*Colonel Pedernera says: "Oribe has sworn to display the general's
head on the tip of a lance in the Plaza de la Victoria. That must never
happen, comrades. We can reach the Bolivian border in seven days,
and it is there that the remains of our leader will be laid to rest."*

*He then divides his forces, orders a group of sharpshooters to cover
the retreat of the rear guard, and they then begin the final march into
exile.*

He heard the child whimpering again. "All right, all right," the
mother said, continuing to help Martín drink the tea. Then when
she was finished, she tucked him back in the bed and then went over
to the other side of the room where the whimpering was coming
from. She began to hum softly. Martín made an effort and turned his
head sideways: the woman was leaning over something that he then
saw was a wooden crate. "There, there," she said, and began humming
again. Hanging above the wooden crate serving as a cradle was a
colored chromolithograph: Christ's chest was split open as in a Testut
anatomical chart and he was pointing to his heart with one finger.
Underneath were several other little colored prints of saints. And
nearby, on top of another wooden crate, was the Primus stove, with
a teakettle on it. "There, there," she repeated more and more softly
and hummed in a singsong voice that gradually died away. Then
everything was silent, but she waited a minute more, still bending
over the baby, until she was certain that he was asleep. Then, trying
not to make any noise, she came back over to Martín. "You dropped
off to sleep," she said to him with a smile. And then, leaning over
him just a little and putting her callused hand on his forehead, she
asked him: "Are you feeling better?" Martín nodded. He had slept
three hours. His mind was beginning to be clearer. He looked at
her: suffering and hard work, poverty and misfortune had not been
able to erase the gentle, maternal expression from that woman's face.
"You went to pieces. So I told them to bring you here." Martín's face
turned red and he tried to get up. But she stopped him. "Wait a
minute, what's your hurry?" Smiling sadly, she added: "You talked
about lots of things, my boy." "What things?" Martín asked, abashed.
"Lots of things but it was hard to understand what they were all

about," the woman answered shyly, looking down at her skirt intently and touching it, as though examining an almost invisible tear in it. Her voice had that tone of gentle reproach that some mothers' voices have. On raising her eyes she saw that Martín was looking at her with a pained, ironic expression. Perhaps she understood, for she said: "Me too ... you mustn't think ..." She hesitated a moment. "But at least I have work here and I can keep the baby with me. It's hard work, no question about that. But I have this little room and I can keep the baby. She examined the invisible tear and smoothed her skirt again. And then ..." she said, without raising her eyes, "there are so many nice things in life." She raised her eyes and again saw the ironic expression on Martín's face. And again she spoke in that reproachful tone, mingled with pity and fear. "Without looking any farther, take me for example. Look at all the things I have." Martín looked at the woman, seeing only her poverty and her loneliness in that awful hole. "I have the baby," she went on stubbornly, "I have that old Victrola with some records of Gardel's; don't you think 'Honeysuckle in Flower' is pretty? And 'The Little Path'? There's nothing as beautiful as music, that's for sure," she commented with a dreamy air. She glanced at the tango-singer's portrait in color: from eternity, dazzling in his swallow-tailed coat, Gardel seemed to be smiling down on her too. Then, turning to Martín, she went on with her inventory: "Then there are flowers, birds, dogs, all sorts of things.... It's a shame the cat from the café ate my canary. It was such good company." *She hasn't mentioned her husband,* Martín thought, *she doesn't have a husband, or he's died, or she's had a man who's deserted her.* Almost exuberantly, she said: "It's so beautiful to be alive! Just think, my boy: I'm only twenty-five and yet it already makes me sad to think I'm going to die some day." Martín looked at her: he had taken her to be around forty. He closed his eyes, lost in thought. The woman doubtless assumed that he was feeling bad again because she came over to him and put her hand on his forehead. Martín again felt the touch of that callused hand and realized that once she had reassured herself, that hand was lingering a second more, clumsily but tenderly, in a shy little caress. He opened his eyes and said: "I think the tea has done me good." The woman seemed to feel extraordinarily happy at that. Martín climbed out of the bed and sat down on the edge of it. "I'll be leaving now," he said. He felt very weak and very dizzy. "Do you feel all right?" she asked worriedly. "Perfectly all right. What's your name?" "Hortensia Paz, at your service." "And my name is Martín. Martín del Castillo."

He took off a ring, a present from his grandmother, that he was wearing on his little finger. "I'd like to give you this ring." The young woman blushed and refused to take it. "Didn't you tell me that there are certain happinesses in life?" Martín asked. "If you accept this remembrance of me it will make me feel very happy. The one happiness I've had lately. Don't you want to make me happy?" Hortensia was still hesitant. He put the ring in her hand and ran out of the room.

∞ 6 ∞

DAWN WAS BREAKING when he got back to his room. He opened the window. To the east the Kavanagh was beginning little by little to stand out against an ashen sky.

What was it Bruno had said one time? War might be absurd or wrong, but to the platoon one belongs to it is something absolute.

There was D'Arcángelo, for example. There was Hortensia.

Just one dog is enough.

The night is freezing and the moon casts a bright light on the great valley. The one hundred seventy-five men are bivouacking, listening anxiously for sounds from the south. The Río Grande meanders along, shining like mercury, an indifferent witness to battles, expeditions, massacres. Armies of the Inca, carvans of captives, columns of Spanish conquistadors who had my blood in their veins (Lieutenant Celedonio Olmos thinks) and who four hundred years later will live secretly in Alejandra's blood (Martín thinks). Then cavalry troops of patriots driving the Spaniards back toward the north, then the Spaniards advancing toward the south once again, and the patriots driving them back once more. With lance and carbine, sword and knife, mutilating each other and slitting each other's throats with the fury of brothers. Then nights of mineral silence in which the only sound to be heard is the murmur of the Río Grande, slowly but surely prevailing over the bloody—but ever so transitory!—battles between men. Until the battle cries again become tinged with red and entire towns flee to the lowlands, leveling everything, burning their houses and destroying their ranches, only to return later, once again, to the eternal land where they were born and knew suffering.

A hundred seventy-five men bivouack in the mineral night. And a muffled voice, barely touching the strings of a guitar sings:

> *Palomita blanca*
> *que cruzas el valle,*
> *vé a decir a todos*
> *que ha muerto Lavalle*

And when the new day dawns they continue their march north-ward.

Lieutenant Celedonio Olmos is now riding alongside Sergeant Aparicio Sosa, who gallops along without a word, lost in thought.

The lieutenant looks at him. For days he has been asking himself questions. In these last months his soul has withered like a delicate flower in a planetary cataclysm. But he has begun to understand, as this last retreat has come to be more and more absurd.

A hundred seventy-five men galloping along furiously for seven days on account of a corpse.

"Oribe will never get the head," Sergeant Sosa has said to him. And thus, amid the ruins of those towers of his, the adolescent lieutenant was beginning to glimpse another, resplendent and indestructible. Only one. But one worth living and dying for.

A new day was slowly being born in the city of Buenos Aires, a day like any other of the countless ones that have been born since man has been man.

From his window Martín saw a little boy running about with the morning papers, in order to keep warm perhaps, or perhaps because with a job like that one has to keep on the move. A stray dog, not much different from Bonito, was pawing through a garbage can. A young woman who looked a bit like Hortensia was walking down the street on her way to work.

He also thought about Bucich, in his Mack with the trailer.

So he put his things in the seabag and went down the rickety stairs.

❧ 7 ❧

I T WAS DRIZZLING; the night was cold. In furious gusts, a desolate wind drove before it the papers in the street and the dead leaves that had gradually fallen, leaving the branches of the trees stripped bare.

They were making the final preparations out in front of the shed. "The canvas," Bucich said from behind his dead cigar stump. "It may rain hard, you know." They tied down the rigging, leaning one foot on the truck, pulling hard. Workers passed by, some of them talking together and cracking jokes, others walking along in silence with their heads down. "Pull, kid," Bucich said. Then they went into the bar: men in blue coveralls and leather coats, wearing high boots or ankle-boots, were talking together in loud voices, drinking coffee and gin, eating enormous sandwiches, passing on tips on road conditions, trading news about other truckers: Skinny, the Guy from Entre Rios, Gonzalito. They gave Bucich big hearty slaps on the back of his leather jacket, they addressed him affectionately as "Old Cigar Stump" and "you hairy old bastard," and he smiled but didn't say a word. And then after finishing his sausage and his cup of black coffee, he said to Martín: "Let's go, kid. Time to shove off," and leaving the bar he climbed into the cabin of the Mack and started the engine, turned on the parking lights, and began moving off toward the Avellaneda bridge, beginning the endless journey to the south, crossing first, in the freezing-cold, rainy dawn, those districts of the city that brought back so many memories to Martín; then, after crossing the Riachuelo, the industrial zones on the outskirts of the city, and then little by little heading down the broader highway toward the southeast; and then after the intersection with the highway from La Plata, heading straight south, on that National 3 that runs all the way down to the very tip of the world, there where Martín imagined everything to be white and frozen, that tip that curved toward the Antarctic, swept by the winds of Patagonia, inhospitable but pure and clean. Last Hope Bay, Useless Bay, Port Hunger, Desolation Island, names that he had contemplated all through the years, ever since his childhood there in his room in the attic, during many an endless hour of sadness and loneliness; names that suggested a far-distant, deserted country, but a clean and hard and very pure one, places not yet sullied by men and above all by women.

Martín asked Bucich if he knew Patagonia well and with a kindly, ironic smile the latter replied: "Yep, I sure do."

"I was born in '01, kid. And you might say that I've been running around Patagonia ever since I stopped crawling on all fours. My old man was a sailor, see, and somebody on the ship told him about the south, about the gold mines. And the minute he heard that the old man shipped out on a freighter that was going from Buenos Aires to Puerto Madryn. And there he met an Englishman, Esteve, who had also come down to prospect for gold. So the two of them traveled farther on south together. Whatever way they could find: on horse-back, in a cart, in a canoe. And my father finally ended up in Lago Viema, near Fisroy. That's where I was born."

"And your mother?"

"He met her down there, a Chilean, Albina Rojas."

Martín looked at him, fascinated. Bucich was smiling thoughtfully to himself, keeping his eyes on the road the while, with the usual dead cigar stuck in his mouth. Martín asked him if it was very cold down there.

"Depends. In winter it can get down to thirty below on the Celsius scale, especially out on the open plain between Lago Argentino and Río Gallegos. But in summer the weather's nice."

After a while Bucich talked to him about his childhood, about hunting pumas and guanacos and foxes and wild boar, and going on canoe trips with his father.

"My old man never gave up the idea of finding gold," he added with a laugh. "And even though he became a settler and raised sheep, the minute he got a chance he'd go off prospecting again. In '03 he managed to get as far as Tierra del Fuego with a Dane, Masen, and a German, Oten. They were the first white men ever to cross the Río Grande. Then they went back north to the lakes by way of Last Hope. Looking for gold all the while."

"And did they find any?"

"What do *you* think? The whole thing was just a big fairy tale."

"And what did they live on?"

"On whatever fish and game they could catch. Afterward my old man went to work for Masen on the boundary commission. And one time when he was out near Lago Viema he met one of the first settlers in those parts, an Englishman named Jac Liveli, who said to him: "Listen, Don Bucich, there's a fine future waiting for you here, believe me. Why don't you settle down here instead of wandering all over looking for gold? What's gold around here is sheep-raising, and I know what I'm talking about."

And then Bucich fell silent.

In the stillness of the freezing-cold night the hoofbeats of the retreating cavalry can be heard. Heading ever northward.

"In '21 I was working as a day laborer in Santa Cruz, when the great general strike broke out. It was mass slaughter."

He fell into a pensive mood again, chewing on the dead cigar. From time to time he waved to a trucker going in the opposite direction.

"It looks as though lots of people know you," Martín remarked.

Bucich smiled with prideful modesty.

"I've been hauling on National 3 for more than ten years, kid. I know it better than the palms of my own hands. Three thousand kilometers from Buenos Aires to the straits. That's life, kid."

Gigantic cataclysms threw up the cordilleras of the northwest, and for more than 250,000 years winds blowing toward the border from the regions that lie beyond the western peaks have been carving out marvelous and mysterious cathedrals.

And the Legion (what is left of it) continues its gallop northward, with Oribe's forces in hot pursuit. Wrapped in his cape, rotting and stinking, the general's bloated body rides with them on his dapple gray charger.

The weather was changing. It had stopped drizzling, a strong wind was blowing from inland (Bucich said), and the cold penetrated to one's very bones. But the sky was crystal clear now. As they went farther southwest the pampa became more and more open, the landscape began to be imposing, and the very air seemed more decent to Martín. He felt useful now too: when they had to stop to change a tire, he built the fire and brewed their maté. And so their first night came on.

Thirty-five leagues to go still. Three days' march at full gallop, with the corpse that stinks and distills the liquids of putrefaction, with sharpshooters in the rear guard covering their retreat, comrades who perhaps have little by little been decimated, run through with lances, or had their throats slit. From Jujuy to Huacalera: twenty-four leagues. Only thirty-five leagues to go now, they tell themselves. Only four or five days' march, with God's help.

"I'm the kind that doesn't like eating my meals in roadside inns, kid," Bucich said as he parked the truck in a cleared spot along the side of the highway.

The stars shone brightly in the cruelly cold night.

"It's my way of doing things, kid," he explained proudly, giving the Mack a few affectionate little pats with his huge ham hands, as though it were a beloved horse. "When night falls, I stop. Except in summer, when I keep driving because it's cool then. But that's always dangerous: you get tired, you fall asleep, and wham! That's what happened to big fat Villanueva, last summer near Azul. I don't mind telling you that if I stop it's not so much for my own sake as for the sake of the others on the road. You can imagine what could happen with a rig as big as this one. It could flatten somebody else on the road like a pancake."

Martín started making the fire. As Bucich laid the meat on the grill he remarked:

"A nice little broiled rib steak, you'll see. My trick is to buy when the meat's just been butchered. Nothing from a freezing plant, kid, always remember that: it draws all the blood out. If I were the government I swear by this cross I'm wearing that I'd pass a law against frozen meat. You can take my word for it, that's why there's so much sickness going around nowadays."

"But wouldn't meat spoil in the big cities if it weren't for freezing plants?" Martín asked.

Bucich took his cigar out of his mouth, waggled his finger back and forth in front of his face, and said:

"That's all a bunch of lies. The whole system's a money-making proposition. If they were to sell it straight away, nothing would happen—do you follow me? You have to buy it just as soon as it's butchered. And how's it going to spoil then? Can you tell me that?"

As he shifted the meat over the fire in such a way that the wind wouldn't fan the flames and burn it, he added, as though he had been following the same train of thought:

"Take it from me, kid, people in the old days were healthier. They may not have had as many frills as people do nowadays, I'll grant you, but they were healthier. Do you know how old my dad is?"

No, Martín didn't know. He looked at Bucich in the firelight, smiling, squatting on his heels, with his dead cigar in his mouth, already flushed with pride at what he was about to reveal.

"He's eighty-three. And I'd be lying if I told you he'd ever been to a doctor in his life. How about that?—can you believe it?"

Then they sat down by the fire on a couple of wooden boxes, not saying anything, waiting for the meat to get done. The sky was crystal clear, and the cold intense. Martín sat there staring thoughtfully at the flames.

Pedernera orders a halt and speaks with his comrades: the corpse is becoming more and more bloated and the stench is unbearable. It will be necessary to remove the flesh so as to be able to keep the bones and the head. Oribe will never get the head.

But who is willing to do the deed? And even more important, who is capable of doing it?

Colonel Alejandro Danel will do it.

They then take the body down off the horse and lay it on the bank of the stream; the general's garments have been stretched so taut by the swelling flesh that it is necessary to cut them off with a knife. Then Danel kneels down and unsheathes his hunting knife. For a few moments he contemplates the grossly deformed dead body of his leader. The men who have formed a silent circle round about him also contemplate it. And then Danel sinks his knife into the flesh that has already begun to rot. The Huacalera carries several pieces of flesh downstream, as the bones gradually pile up on the cape.

Lavalle's soul sees Danel's tears and reflects thusly: "You are grieving for me, but you must feel grief for yourself and for the comrades who are still alive. I do not matter now. What was rotting within me you are now cutting away and the waters of this river will carry it far away; soon it will help a plant to grow, and perhaps with time it will turn into a flower, a fragrance. So you see, this should not make you sad. And what is more, in this way all that will remain of me is my bones, the only thing in us that is like unto stone and eternity. And I am comforted by the thought that you are keeping the heart. It has been such a faithful companion to me in adversity! And yes, the head too. That head that the learned doctors said was worthless. Perhaps they said that because it repelled me to ally myself with foreigners or because this long retreat seemed absurd and pointless to them, because I could not make up my mind to attack Buenos Aires when we were so close that we could see its domes; those intellectuals who did not know that in the days when I saw once again the countryside where I had ordered Dorrego executed by a firing squad the memory of him tormented me, and it torments me even more now that I have seen that country folk were with him and not with us, when they sang:

*Cielito y cielo nublado
por la muerte de Dorrego . . .**

Yes, comrades, it was those same men of learning who made me commit a crime, because I was very young then and really believed that I was doing my country a service, and even though it hurt me terribly, because I loved Manuel, because I had always been fond of him, I signed that death sentence that has caused so much bloodshed in these eleven years. And that death was a cancer that devoured me, in exile and then after that all during this senseless campaign. You, Danel, who were with me at that moment, know very well what heartache it cost me to do what I did, how much I admired Manuel's courage and intelligence. And Acevedo knows it too, and many other comrades who are now gazing on my mortal remains here. And you also know that it was they, the men with brains, the thinkers, who persuaded me to do it, with insidious letters, letters that they wanted me to destroy immediately. They were the ones. Not you, Danel, not

---

* Sky overhead, firmament veiled in clouds
by Dorrego's death . . .

you, Acevedo, not Lamadrid nor any of those of us who have nothing but an arm to take up a saber and a heart to confront death."

(The bones have now been wrapped in the cape which was once sky blue but which today, like the spirit of these men, is little more than a filthy rag. One would be hard put to say what it represents; it is but one of those symbols of the feelings and the passions of men —sky blue, red—that in the end turn back into the immortal color of earth, that color that is both more and less than the color of dirt, for it is the color of our old age and the ultimate fate of all men, whatever their ideas. The general's heart has already been put in a little flagon filled with brandy. And these men have put away in one or another of the pockets of their ragged garments some little memento of that body: a tiny bone, a lock of hair.)

"And you, Aparicio Sosa, who never sought to understand anything, because you were content merely to be loyal to me, to believe in what I said or did without any need for explanations, you who took care of me from the days when I was an impudent, arrogant young cadet; you, quiet Sergeant Aparicio Sosa, Sosa the black, Sosa the pock-marked, the one who saved me in Cancha Rayada, the one who possesses nothing save his love for this poor defeated general, nothing save this cruel and hapless country: I would like them to think of you.

"What I mean to say is . . ."

(The fugitives have now placed the bundle containing the bones in the general's leather trunk and tied the trunk on the dapple gray charger. But they hesitate as to what to do with the flagon with the heart inside it, until finally Danel gives it to Aparicio Sosa, the one whom the death of their leader has left feeling most helpless and abandoned.)

"Yes, comrades, to Sergeant Sosa. Because that is like giving it to this land, this cruel land, soaked with the blood of so many Argentines. This valley through which Belgrano came north twenty-five years ago with his little improvised band of irregulars, a little improvised general himself, as frail as a young girl, his one strength his courage and his fervor as he confronted the seasoned Spanish forces, for a country that as yet we had no clear idea of, a country that even today we still have no really clear idea of—what it is exactly, how far it extends, who it really belongs to; whether to Rosas, to us, to all of *us together, or to nobody. Yes, Sergeant Sosa: you are this land, this age-old valley, this American loneliness, this nameless despair that torments us amid this chaos, in this fight between brothers."*

(Pedernera gives the order to mount their horses. Shots, dangerously close now, can already be heard coming from the rear guard; too much time has been lost. And he says to his companions: "If luck is with us, we'll be crossing the border four days from now." That is to say, a distance of thirty-five leagues that can be covered in four days march at a desperate gallop. "If God is with us," he adds.

And the fugitives disappear in a cloud of dust, as the sun beats down on the valley, while to their rear other comrades die for them.)

They ate in silence, sitting on the wooden boxes. When they were through, Bucich made maté again. And as they drank it he gazed up at the starry sky until finally he worked up his courage to make a confession he had been wanting to make for some time.

"I don't mind telling you straight out, kid: I would have liked to be an astronomer. Why does that surprise you?"

A question he added simply because he was afraid Martín might laugh at him, since there was nothing in Martín's face that indicated the least surprise.

Martín said no, that didn't surprise him—why should it?

"Every night when I'm on the road, I look at the stars and say to myself: I wonder who lives in those worlds? Mainsa the German claims there are millions of people living on them, that every one of them is like the earth."

He lit a cigar, took a deep puff on it, and sat there lost in thought. Then he went on:

"Mainsa was the one who told me that the Russians have invented some terrible things you wouldn't believe. Here we are, quietly eating our broiled steak, and they send out some sort of ray all of a sudden, and it's curtains for us. A death ray."

Martín handed him his maté gourd and asked who Mainsa was.

"My brother-in-law. My sister Violeta's husband."

And how did he know all those things?

Bucich sipped his maté calmly, and then explained with great pride:

"He's been a telegraph operator in Bahía Blanca for fifteen years.

So he knows everything there is to know about weapons and death rays. He's German, and that tells you everything."

They said no more then, until finally Bucich rose to his feet and announced: "Okay, kid, it's time to turn in," hunted up the gin jug, took a swig, looked up at the sky, and added:

"It's a good thing it hasn't been raining down here. We're going to have to do thirty kilometers over a dirt road tomorrow. What am I saying?: sixty really. Thirty up plus thirty back."

Martín looked at him: a dirt road?

"Yes, we're going to have to go a little bit out of our way, because I have to see a friend in Estación de la Garma. I've got a godchild there who's sick, really sick. I'm taking him a little toy car."

He searched around in the cabin of the truck, brought out a box, opened it, and showed Martín the present with a proud smile. He wound the little car up and tried to make it go on the ground.

"It doesn't run very well on the ground, of course. But on a wooden floor or on cement it goes like a champ."

He put it away again very carefully, as Martín looked at him dumb-founded.

They are galloping furiously toward the border, because Colonel Pedernera has said: "We must reach Bolivian soil this very night." They can hear the shots from the rear guard behind them. And the men are wondering how many comrades and which ones of those who have been covering this seven-day headlong flight of theirs have been overtaken by Oribe's men.

Then they cross the border in the middle of the night and they can at last tumble wearily out of the saddle and finally rest and sleep in peace. Yet it is a peace as desolate as the peace that reigns in a dead world, in a territory laid waste by catastrophe, over which there hover silent, sinister, famished vultures.

And the next morning when Pedernera gives the order to mount their horses and ride on to Potosí, the men climb into the saddle but sit there for a long time looking toward the south. All of them (Colonel Pedernera among them)—one hundred seventy-five faces, brooding, silent men, and one woman as well, looking toward the south, toward the land known as the United (United!) Provinces of the

South, toward the part of the world where these men have been born, where they have left behind them their children, their wives, their mothers. Forever?

All of them look toward the south. Sergeant Aparicio Sosa too, with his little flagon containing his leader's heart clasped tightly to his breast.

As does Lieutenant Celedonio Olmos, who joined the Legion at the age of seventeen, along with his father and his brother, who now lie dead in Quebracho Herrado, to fight for ideas that one writes with a capital letter; words that little by little become blurred, words whose capital letters, age-old shining towers, have been gradually reduced to ruins by the ravages of time and men.

Then finally Colonel Pedernera realizes that they have looked long enough and gives the order to march. All of them pull on the reins of their mounts and turn them northward.

They ride off now in a cloud of dust, in the mineral loneliness, in that desolate region of the planet. And soon the eye can no longer make them out; they are mere dust amid dust.

Nothing remains in the valley now of that Legion, of those wretched remains of the Legion: the echo of the pounding hoofs of their mounts has died away; the clods of earth that they kicked up in their furious gallop have returned to the earth's bosom, slowly but inexorably; Lavalle's flesh has been borne southward by the waters of a river (to be turned into a tree, a plant, a fragrance?). All that will remain is the dim memory, growing dimmer with each passing day, of that phantom Legion. On moonlit nights—an old Indian recounts—I too have seen them. First you hear the jingle of spurs and the neighing of a horse. Then the horse appears, a very spirited one, with the general astride it, a charger as white as snow (that is how the Indian sees the general's horse). The general is wearing a great cavalry saber and a high-crested helmet, a grenadier's helmet. (Poor Indian, if you only knew the general was only a man in rags and tatters, with a dirty straw hat and a cape that had already forgotten the symbolic color it once was. If you only knew that that hapless mortal had neither the uniform of a grenadier nor a high-crested helmet, nor anything else! If you only knew he was simply a miserable wretch among countless other miserable wretches!)

But it is like a dream: one moment more and he suddenly disappears in the darkness of the night, crossing the river and heading for the hills to the west...

Bucich showed him where they were going to sleep in the trailer, laid out the mattresses, and wound the alarm clock, saying: "We'll have to set it for five o'clock," and then walked a few steps away to piss. Martín thought it his duty to piss alongside his friend.

The sky was as hard and transparent as a black diamond. Beneath the starlight the vast plain stretched out to the limitless immensity of the unknown. The warm, acrid smell of urine mingled with the smells of the open fields. Bucich said:

"How great our country is, kid ..."

And then Martín, contemplating the truck driver's gigantic silhouette outlined against the starry sky as the two of them pissed together, felt a perfect peace enter his tormented soul for the first time.

Eyeing the horizon as he buttoned up his pants, Bucich added:

"All right, let's get some shuteye, kid. We'll be off at five. We're going to be crossing the Colorado tomorrow."

ERNESTO SABATO was born in Buenos Aires in 1911. After completing his Ph.D. in physics in 1938, he worked at the Curie Laboratory in Paris, where he first came in contact with André Breton and other Surrealists. He soon abandoned science and dedicated himself wholly to writing. His first novel, *El Túnel* (*The Outsider*), published in 1948, was enthusiastically praised by Thomas Mann, Albert Camus, and Graham Greene. *Sobre Héroes y Tumbas* (*On Heroes and Tombs*) followed in 1961. A third novel, *Abaddon el Exterminador* (1974) won him the French *Prix du Meilleur Livre Etranger*, awarded to such writers as Solzhenitsyn, Böll, Grass, Musil, Singer, and Márquez. Sábato's works have been translated into twenty-one languages.

Involved actively in Communism in his youth, his opposition to Stalin led Sábato to reject the movement. Since then, he has fought all forms of oppression, from the left as well as the right, supporting his principle of 'social justice and liberty.' During the worst years of Argentine dictatorship, he refused to emigrate, even under the threat of death, and continued to denounce both terrorism and repression. He currently lives in a suburb of Buenos Aires, where, reluctant to participate in societies and congresses of writers, he holds his characteristic position of 'sniper'.

ON HEROES AND TOMBS
has been set in Linotype Granjon, designed by George W. Jones
and modelled after the graceful faces of the French Renaissance,
particularly upon the designs of Claude Garamond, the prolific and
superb sixteenth century punchcutter and letter designer. Granjon is
distinguished by its close fit and its exceptional
clarity and legibility.

The book was set by Lamb's Printing Company, Clinton,
Massachusetts, and printed and bound by the
Book Press, Brattleboro, Vermont.
The paper is Sebago Antique,
an acid-free sheet.